FLIGHT *of a* MAORI GODDESS

ALSO BY SARAH LARK

In the Land of the Long White Cloud Saga

In the Land of the Long White Cloud
Song of the Spirits
Call of the Kiwi

The Caribbean Islands Saga

Island of a Thousand Springs
Island of the Red Mangroves

The Sea of Freedom Trilogy

Toward the Sea of Freedom
Beneath the Kauri Tree

Other Titles

A Hope at the End of the World

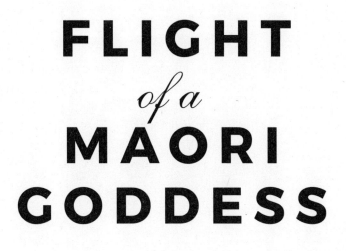

FLIGHT *of a* MAORI GODDESS

SARAH LARK

TRANSLATED BY D.W. LOVETT

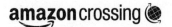

amazon crossing

Previously published as *Die Tränen der Maori-Göttin* by Bastei Lübbe in Germany in 2012. Translated from German by Dustin Lovett. First published in English by AmazonCrossing in 2018.

Published by AmazonCrossing, Seattle

www.apub.com

ISBN-13: 9781503904231
ISBN-10: 1503904237

Cover design by Shasti O'Leary Soudant

Printed in the United States of America

Family Relationships

Peter Burton • • Kathleen O'Donnell — Michael Drury • • Lizzy Owens — Kahu Heke

Ian Coltrane • •

Colin 1848
Heather 1849

Sean 1847

Kevin 1867
Patrick 1869

Kupe • • Matariki 1864 — Colin Coltrane

Atamarie 1883

Matt Edmunds • • Claire Campbell • • James Dunloe

Chloe 1849 • • Terrence Boulder

• • Colin Coltrane

— Heather Coltrane

Ellen Seekers • • Jim Paisley

Fred 1863

Sean Drury Coltrane • • Violet 1865 • • Eric Fence

Rosie 1874

Joe 1881
Roberta 1882

• • marriage
— non-marital relationship

Prologue

Parihaka, New Zealand 1894

Twilight spread slowly over the mountains and the sea. The low winter sun slid toward the water, and its last rays bathed majestic Mount Taranaki in red-golden light. The snow-covered peak offered an impressive backdrop for the village of Parihaka.

It's like a guardian, Atamarie's mother liked to say. *We enjoy its beauty and feel safe in its shadow.*

Atamarie found that a little strange. After all, Mount Taranaki was a volcano, and theoretically it could erupt. But her mother always dismissed the possibility. *Of course not, Atamarie; the gods will keep the peace. The time of wars is past,* she'd say. And then she would tell Atamarie and the other children the legend about the god of Mount Taranaki who battled another mountain god for the love of Pihanga, a forest goddess. When Pihanga ultimately chose his rival, Taranaki retreated angrily to the coast. And that was how war entered the world. However, there was hope. At some point, Taranaki would relent, and if the gods got along again, mankind could count on lasting peace.

Most children listened to these stories wide-eyed, but Atamarie was more interested in the mountain's volcanic activity. Her favorite subjects at school were mathematics, physics, and geography.

This evening, too, Atamarie had little interest in the stories the old people of Parihaka were telling about the constellation that would soon show itself: Matariki, viewed as either the eyes of the god Tawhirimatea or a mother with six daughters on their way to help the exhausted sun to rise anew after the winter.

For Atamarie, the constellation was not magic, but simply the Pleiades, which came into view in late May or early June. It was useful for determining when the winter solstice would occur and also for navigating the ocean between Hawaiki, the original Maori homeland, and Aotearoa, the country in which they now dwelled and which the whites called New Zealand. Naturally, the constellation's stars were pretty to look at, but Atamarie only ever half listened to the fairy tales that surrounded them.

What did interest her were the *hangi*, the earthen ovens that glowed with the heat of Taranaki's volcanic activity. She peered into the holes the men had dug earlier as part of the New Year's festival. Meat and vegetables were wrapped in leaves, piled in baskets, and placed in the hot ground. Then they were covered with wet cloth, and the holes were sealed with dirt. The buried food would cook slowly and be ready in time for Matariki—the Pleiades—to appear in the sky.

Atamarie had come from Dunedin to the North Island expressly for the festival. It was not certain that the Pleiades would show themselves during her short winter vacation, but Matariki and Kupe, Atamarie's mother and stepfather, had taken their chances.

"You have to experience the New Year's festival in Parihaka," Matariki, who was named after the constellation, had insisted. Many Maori names were inspired by nature—Atamarie was named for the sunrise. "It has a particular magic here."

Atamarie had rolled her eyes a bit. For her parents, everything about Parihaka had a particular magic. Long before Atamarie's birth, they had lived in the famous village, back when the prophet Te Whiti had preached peace between the Maori and the whites, the *pakeha*, there. Kupe had been imprisoned after the whites stormed the village and relocated the residents. And Matariki had run away with the man who was Atamarie's father.

Much later, Te Whiti had returned to Parihaka, and many of his loyal followers with him. They had rebuilt the village and were in the process of making it once more into a spiritual center for New Zealand's first settlers. This time, though, they were supported by treaties and not just dreams. Kupe and Matariki had bought a piece of land, though they still did not think it right to give the whites money for their own tribal land. Kupe, now a lawyer, had brought several suits. It was likely that Te Whiti and his followers would receive compensation and, in time, get their land back.

People were coming to Parihaka again, and once more there were children for Matariki to teach. For the time being, however, there was no high school, so Atamarie attended boarding school in Dunedin and spent her weekends either with her grandparents or her friend Roberta's family.

Atamarie could visit Parihaka only during vacations, and that was fine by her. She looked forward to time with her parents and to an escape from the strict rules and routines of school; however, a few weeks of weaving flax, dancing, playing traditional instruments, fishing, and working in the fields were plenty. Although she agreed with Parihaka's motto, "We want to make the world a better place," Atamarie's interpretation of it didn't match the town's. Whenever the girl made an effort to improve something, whether a loom or the fishing weirs, the *tohunga*, the experts in traditional arts, rejected her suggestions indignantly. Sometimes they even let slip unkind words about Atamarie's *pakeha* ancestry, which upset Matariki. Atamarie herself couldn't care less about how much of whose blood she had. She just didn't want to spend any more time weaving than was strictly necessary, and she didn't want to lose fish because the weir didn't close properly.

By the end of vacation, she was always happy to return to Dunedin. Otago Girls' High School was an exceedingly modern establishment, and the teachers supported their students' inventiveness.

Tonight in Parihaka, however, Atamarie scanned the skies for the constellation that would mark the New Year's festival. The old people had sat up watching for three whole nights already.

"It's a time for waiting and remembering," Matariki explained. "The old people take this time to think about yesterday, today, and tomorrow, about the old year and the new."

Atamarie watched as the sun sank into the Tasman Sea. The light over the fields waned until only the mountain's peak still glowed. The sky quickly darkened—and suddenly Atamarie saw them. Bright and clear, the Pleiades climbed up over the sea, led by the greatest of the seven stars, Whanui.

The children began at once to greet the constellation with the traditional song their teacher, Matariki, had taught them:

"Ka puta Matariki ka rere Whanui
Ko te tena o te tau e!"
Matariki is back! Whanui begins its flight.
The sign of a new year.

"And a good sign." Atamarie's mother happily took her husband and daughter in her arms.

Kupe had traveled back from Wellington, where he often had business. Among other things, he was campaigning for one of the Maori seats in Parliament. Now, he kissed Matariki and Atamarie, and listened as his wife interpreted the sign.

"When the stars appear so brightly in the sky, that means a short winter, and we can plant seeds as early as September," she instructed her family and students. "When they look dim and huddled together for warmth, then winter will be hard, and planting can't begin until October."

Atamarie furrowed her brow. If they had not been able to see the stars clearly, her teachers in Dunedin would probably have just attributed the poor visibility to clouds.

"Mom, why are the old people crying?" she inquired. "It's good that the stars appeared, isn't it? It's a new year."

Matariki nodded and pushed back her long, black hair. "Yes, but the elders are still thinking of the past year. They name the people who have died since the stars' last appearance, and pray for them. They mourn the dead for the last time before the new year begins."

The old people had now also begun opening the *hangi*, and Kupe and the other men rushed to help. Steam rose from the earthen ovens into the sky.

"The aroma is rising to the stars," Matariki explained, "giving them strength after their long journey."

Atamarie's mouth watered, but before they could eat, there were various greeting ceremonies for the stars. Young and old sang and danced the traditional *haka*. The adults passed around beer and wine jugs and bottles of whiskey, and Matariki and Kupe grew wistful, as always, reminiscing about the old days in Parihaka. If they were to be believed, life back then was one long festival. The village had been full of young people from every corner of Aotearoa, and every night brought music, laughter, and dancing.

Atamarie and the other children fell asleep at some point, but they went right back to celebrating in the morning. On New Year's Day, there were dancing, singing, games, and, most importantly, kites. Making kites was one of Aotearoa's traditions kept alive in Parihaka. The Maori word for kites was *manu*.

A few kite-making *tohunga* had been teaching in the village the last few weeks, but by the time Atamarie arrived from Dunedin, the men and boys had already finished their work. Now she stood empty-handed while the others waited for the big moment when they would send their *manu* into the sky as mediators between the stars, the gods, and mankind. Atamarie could hardly wait. It wasn't the colorful decorations of feathers and mussel shells or the painted-on faces that she cared about. No, Atamarie yearned to understand how these heavy contraptions of wood and leaves could soar into the air.

She approached one of the boys, who was readying a particularly large kite, lovingly decorated with diamond shapes and tribal symbols.

"It doesn't have a tail."

The boy frowned at her. "Why would a *manu* have a tail?"

"*Pakeha* kites have them," Atamarie said. "I've seen it in pictures."

The boy shrugged. "The *tohunga* didn't say anything about that. Just that you need a frame and string—or two if you want to steer it. He said steering was too hard for kids, but I added two strings anyway."

"But first of all, the thing needs to fly," Atamarie said. "How does that work?"

"By the breath of the gods," the boy answered. "The *manu* dances with their life force."

Atamarie furrowed her brow. "So, the wind, then. But what if there's no wind?"

"If the gods withhold their blessing, it won't fly," the boy answered. "Unless you let it glide down, like off a cliff. But it can't take any messages to the gods that way. And besides, then you'd lose it."

Atamarie helped him stand the contraption on its end.

"It's almost as big as I am," she said. "Do you think someone could maybe ride it?"

The boy laughed. "Supposedly, at least one person has! Nukupewapewa, a chieftain of the Ngati Kahungunu, wanted to conquer the Pa Maungaraki, but his warriors couldn't breach the walls. So, he built a giant *manu* of raupo leaves in the shape of a bird. He tied a man tight to it and let the kite glide down from a rock above the fortress. It landed inside, and the man opened the gates for the conquerors."

Atamarie listened with shining eyes. "Yours is also a *manu raupo*," she said with a smile. "You must have gone out of your way. I don't even know where raupo grows around here."

The boy smiled impishly. "Yeaaah, it wasn't easy to find. But maybe it'll be worth it."

"Rawiri! What are you doing? Don't you want to fly your kite?"

The boy spun around at the sound of the *tohunga*'s voice. They'd missed the start. Most of the boys had already tossed their kites to the wind and were now watching with fascination as they flew. The priests of Parihaka prayed and sang in accompaniment. The kites were to take their wishes and their blessings up to the stars. Atamarie lost herself for a few heartbeats in the gorgeous sight of the colorful *manu* against the clear winter sky. The master, too, had sent his massive *manu aute* into the air now, steering it skillfully between his students' smaller kites.

Rawiri, however, was struggling with his two cords and with managing the very large kite by himself.

"Want me to hold it up?" Atamarie asked.

The boy nodded. She reached for the kite and was almost bowled over as the wind snatched it out of her hands. The kite climbed sharply into the sky, but when Rawiri made his first attempt to steer, it dove just as sharply downward.

Atamarie and Rawiri raced to the fallen kite.

"At least nothing important is broken," said Atamarie. "Just a little bit of decoration."

Rawiri frowned as he attempted to fix the damage. "The *tohunga* says it's really important. The shells are the kite's eyes, and the paint is our message to the gods."

"Well, the gods must be smart enough to figure out what you meant," Atamarie said. "Let's try it again."

She peered into the sky and concentrated on the kite of the *tohunga* who was eyeing Rawiri's crashed bird with sadness mixed with satisfaction, thinking he'd been proven right about steering. But now, Atamarie's ambition was roused.

"You need to attach the lines closer to the outside," she suggested, "and deeper in the frame. And it would be even better if we had four lines."

Rawiri's pride seemed hurt, but after a second unsuccessful attempt to get his kite in the air, he followed Atamarie's direction.

The kite once again flew up quickly, but this time it hovered much more surely in the air, and when Rawiri made a cautious attempt at steering, it obeyed his tug on the cord.

"It works! It flies! It's going where I want it to," Rawiri cheered. His birdlike kite took its place proudly beside the master's triangle.

"Do you want to try?" he offered.

Atamarie took the strings without hesitation. She was the only girl holding the lines of a *manu* here, but that didn't bother her. In great curves, she guided the huge kite through the sky.

"I bet it's true, that legend about the Ngati Kahungunu," said Rawiri. "The kite just needs to be big enough and the gods on your side."

Atamarie nodded. Of course you could ride a kite. The wind had just now almost pulled her into the air.

"But I want to make one that works without wind," she declared.

Gifts of the Gods

Dunedin, Christchurch,
Lawrence, Parihaka,
New Zealand
1899–1900

Chapter 1

Roberta's education class was located in an outbuilding of the University of Otago, and Atamarie found the structure simply hideous. Fortunately, she wouldn't be studying here. The college that had just accepted her was a great deal bigger and more imposing. Canterbury College was all Gothic style, her aunt Heather had said, but imitation, designed long after the Gothic period. New Zealand hadn't yet been settled by whites back when they were building real Gothic cathedrals in Europe.

Atamarie climbed the steps and sat down on the top stair. She was in high spirits, if also a little tired after the long train ride. Still, the route was good. It was no longer an ordeal to travel back and forth between Christchurch and Dunedin.

She hummed to herself as she waited to tell her friend that their paths would now diverge for the first time in nine years. The girls had gotten to know each other when their mothers both lived in Wellington on the North Island, working for one of the organizations fighting for women's suffrage. After that battle was won, both women had married. Matariki and Kupe had moved to Parihaka, whereas Roberta's mother, Violet, and her husband, Sean, had taken Roberta to Sean's hometown of Dunedin. The two friends had graduated from Otago Girls' High School a few weeks before, and they were now looking forward to enjoying the most recent achievement of activists like their mothers: the universities on the South Island had been forced to open their doors to women.

Atamarie heard a buzzing inside the school building, and the students began pouring out. They were almost entirely young women, conservatively dressed in dark skirts and muted blouses peeking out from under prim jackets. A few wore unadorned, sacklike dresses, which were just as boring and spinsterish as the seemingly ubiquitous cloche hats. Though there were alternatives. Neither Atamarie nor Roberta wore corsets, but their fashionable, tailored clothes came from the city's famous Gold Mine Boutique. Both girls called Kathleen Burton, one of the boutique's proprietors, "Grandma." Atamarie's biological father, Colin, was Kathleen's son, as was Roberta's stepfather, Sean.

That day, Atamarie wore a sun-yellow, reform-style dress printed with colorful flowers, and a dark-green mantilla and cute straw hat atop her blonde hair. She noticed the lingering glances from the few male students and the women eyeing her unkindly. No doubt it was unusual, perhaps even forbidden, to sit on the steps.

Roberta finally appeared, wearing her plainest dress and a short black coat. Atamarie leaped up to hug her.

"You look like an owl," she teased. "Do you have to dress like that?"

Roberta blushed, drawing the attention of the male students. No matter how she dressed, Roberta Fence was a beauty. Her long, wavy hair—now forced into a prim bun—was a deep chestnut. Her face was heart shaped and, despite its classical beauty, always looked soft and gentle. She had full lips and blue eyes—not quite the spectacular turquoise of her mother's, but as deep blue and clear as the highland lakes.

"We're supposed to look serious," she replied, "but aren't all students?" She raised a disapproving eyebrow at Atamarie's outfit.

Atamarie shrugged. "I stand out no matter what I wear. And don't tell me that owls are symbols of wisdom. If you ask me, parrots are much cleverer."

Roberta laughed and linked arms with Atamarie. She had missed her friend in the two days she had been gone.

"So, how was Christchurch? Did they accept you into the program?" she inquired as they strolled toward a café.

Atamarie nodded. "Of course. They didn't have a choice, you know. I had the best marks of anybody. But it was funny. Professor Dobbins thought I was a mirage at first."

She scrunched up her nose as if wearing a pince-nez, then imitated the professor's booming voice: "'Mr. Turei—I mean, uh, Miss?' The man was baffled. And here he had been so excited about having his first Maori student. He was probably expecting a giant warrior with tattoos."

Roberta giggled. "And then you turned up."

Far from a broad-shouldered warrior, Atamarie was willowy, and no one would have taken her for Maori at first glance. Her skin was darker than most whites' and her eyes were a little different, but otherwise, she took after her grandmother Kathleen—high cheekbones, a straight nose, and finely carved lips.

"But hadn't the professor seen your name?"

Atamarie shrugged. "The man's an engineer, not a linguist. He just stood there, gaping like a fish. But I introduced myself, gave him my transcripts—"

"And then it was okay?"

Atamarie laughed. "As long as he didn't have to look at me, everything went fine. Whenever he looked up from the papers, he seemed shocked all over again. And then he asked me if I really knew what was expected of me there and listed the required courses: fundamentals of sub- and superstructure construction, surveying, technical drafting, practical geometry, theory and practice of the construction of steam machines, et cetera—" Atamarie grinned with anticipation.

"And what did you say?" Roberta already feared the worst.

"What do you think? I told him I'm interested in aircraft. Then I talked a bit about Cayley and Lilienthal, so he wouldn't think I just have my head, well, in the clouds."

Roberta opened the door to the café. "It's a wonder they didn't send you packing."

Atamarie laughed again. "Then your father would have sued the college. But Professor Dobbins actually smiled. He said he liked it when students aimed high. Then the interview was over, and the only thing left was a tour. The student who was supposed to show the freshmen around nearly fainted when he saw me."

The Canterbury College of Engineering had existed for twelve years and was still quite small. Atamarie would be its first female student.

"And how'd you like Christchurch?" asked Roberta. "What did you and Heather get up to?"

"First we had to find a room for me to rent. But that was simple. Heather and Chloe's friends live together in a big house with spare rooms right near the university, and they own a bookshop. I can get my textbooks there. My room's really big—I just need to inform them of any gentlemen callers."

She giggled. Usually it was forbidden for female students to have men in their rooms. Heather and Chloe, however, were open-minded and modern—and apparently, their friends were too.

"Two days there and you're already looking for a boyfriend?"

"Robbie, I'm the only feminine being in the whole engineering school. I'll have to make friends with the boys. That doesn't necessarily mean I'll be sharing my bed with them!"

Roberta turned red at once. She'd also spent vacations in Parihaka and had been exposed to the Maori culture's more relaxed views on love relations. Nevertheless, she hadn't had any experience with such things, whereas Atamarie had already kissed some handsome Maori boys. Roberta's nature was more romantic—and private.

"Aside from that, we went to the racetrack in Addington. Rosie had her heart set on it. Unfortunately, there wasn't a harness race just then. But it was still fun. Lord Barrington invited us to the owner's box. We drank champagne—and they let us bet on horses."

"Atamie!"

Roberta had grown up around racetracks and hated them. Her mother had taught her that whiskey and gambling could ruin a family; Roberta's birth father had fallen to both.

"Oh, don't be like that. Lord Barrington insisted. And Heather lost, but I won. Twice! It was easy. I just bet on the horse with the longest legs and most aerodynamic body. It's simple physics. Well, the third time, it didn't work. The horse didn't find its gate. I think it was just lazy. But I've got enough money left to treat you to coffee—and cake!

"We also went to a gallery, but I forget the artist's name. Heather was really excited about it. Are you coming tonight, by the way? Or is it not enough to look like an owl? To be a teacher, do you have to go to bed with the chickens?"

Roberta looked at her friend chidingly. "Owls are nocturnal. And of course I'm coming. It's an art opening, after all, not a nightclub. What's the artist's name again?"

Atamarie shrugged. Though plenty of people in Dunedin could afford art, few could summon true enthusiasm for it. Still, the previews at Heather and Chloe Coltrane's gallery were among the most important social events in the city, and invitations were hotly sought after. Chloe was an exceptionally talented hostess, and Heather's artwork had made her famous well beyond New Zealand. The two women had lived together for years, and many assumed they were sisters. That was not true, however. Chloe owed her last name to an unhappy marriage to Heather's brother.

The coffee and cake arrived. Roberta poured sugar into her cup while Atamarie dreamily watched the steam rise. She was already thinking about what she would wear that evening; no doubt Kathleen would have something new for both granddaughters. She always claimed the girls were doing her a favor by accepting the expensive dresses. After all, they were advertising the boutique.

Roberta swallowed hard and forced herself to ask the question that had been eating at her for days.

"Do you know by chance if, if your, um, uncle is coming too?"

Atamarie grinned. "Which uncle?" she asked coyly.

"Oh, um, Kevin?"

She tried to sound casual, but they both knew better. For months, Roberta had been pining after Kevin, named for the same Irish saint as his grandfather. While she was in high school, it was folly even to hope that the young doctor would notice his niece's friend, let alone make advances. But now she was a college student. Plus, Roberta's parents belonged to Dunedin high society. The young woman would surely be invited to concerts and balls, art shows and plays. And Kevin Drury, with his curly black hair and bright blue eyes, was a fixture at such events. On top of being a successful doctor and terribly handsome, he was a keen rider who never missed a steeplechase. Men and women alike thronged to him.

Kevin's younger brother, Patrick, was much less flashy. He had studied agriculture and planned to take over his parents' farm someday. For the time being, he worked as an adviser for the Ministry of Agriculture. Otago was slowly shifting back from gold mining to agriculture, and the new landowners knew far less about sheep breeding and pasture management than they did about panning for gold.

"Kevin's coming for sure," said Atamarie. "Heather says he's got a new girlfriend already. She's supposed to be stunning. Heather might ask her to sit for a portrait."

Women were among Heather's favorite subjects for portraits, and she'd had great success with them. Heather knew how to capture a woman's essence, her character, and her life experience on canvas.

Roberta sighed. "Kevin is very handsome, I suppose."

Atamarie laughed, laid her hand on her friend's arm, and made as if to shake Roberta. "He may be the prince, Robbie, but you're a queen. If you fix yourself up a bit and don't stare at the floor or completely choke on your words when you see him, you'll outshine them all."

Roberta stirred her coffee mournfully. "He'd have to look at me first."

"If he won't look, try fainting!" Atamarie joked. "You let yourself fall, and I scream, 'We need a doctor.' Then he won't have a choice."

"You're not taking me seriously."

Atamarie groaned. "Maybe you're taking Kevin too seriously. And that's not good. I mean, you don't just want a kiss or two, right? You're looking for a man who'll really love you. And for that, Kevin's the wrong guy. He's nice, and he's funny—I do like him, Robbie. But he's not looking for a wife, at least not now. He even said so when Grandma Lizzie talked to him about it recently. As a family doctor, he'll have to get married someday. But for now, Grandma Lizzie says he's like Grandpa Michael. He had 'to sew his wild oats' before he got serious about her. Not sure what that means, but one thing's certain: Kevin doesn't want what you want. He's looking for adventure."

Chapter 2

Heather Coltrane hadn't been exaggerating about Kevin Drury's new girlfriend. Juliet, as Kevin introduced her, not bothering to give a last name, was an extraordinary beauty. She certainly wasn't white, but she lacked the hallmarks of Maori ancestry. Juliet had black hair that tumbled over her shoulders, delicate golden-brown skin, and full lips, as well as astoundingly blue eyes beneath heavy eyelids.

"She looks rather Creole," Heather said to Roberta's mother, Violet. "Where would he have met her?"

On arriving at the gallery, Atamarie had marched straight over to Kevin and his new friend, dragging a mortified Roberta behind her. Roberta hardly managed a word during the introductions, but Juliet didn't look like she intended to remember anyone's name anyway. She spoke distractedly to a few gentlemen who swarmed around her, falling over themselves to ply her with champagne and hors d'oeuvres.

"Because it's the birthplace of champagne, the lady favors France," Chloe observed, and kissed Violet's cheek in greeting. "That's her third glass of the most expensive bottle we have. If she keeps this up, she'll be dancing on the tables by the end of the night."

"Our own little demimonde, then?" Violet remarked.

Her husband, Sean, smiled.

As a young girl, Violet had received a dictionary and, over the years, had read it again and again. Even as an adult, she relished opportunities to try out new words. Of course, those were few and far between in Dunedin.

Heather laughed. "Hardly a good candidate for sheep farming, anyway. Lizzie and Michael will not be enthused."

Kevin and Patrick's parents ran a sheep farm in Otago, and they hoped their sons would marry women who could help them tend the flocks. Kevin, however, was uninterested in farm work and even less interested in rich livestock breeders' daughters.

***

The mysterious Juliet dominated the evening's conversation—the somewhat gloomy paintings on display that day dimmed considerably in her presence. While the women busied themselves trying to guess Juliet's ancestry, the men seemed content just to admire her: Juliet's figure was as fascinating as her foreign-seeming face. Kevin flaunted the young woman like a trophy but was careful not to neglect his many admirers. With Juliet in tow, he wandered from each of Dunedin's ladies to the next, making charming small talk while Juliet smiled coolly and resisted any attempt to draw her out.

"Corsets just make dresses look better," Roberta sighed as Juliet floated by.

In fact, she looked quite charming herself. Roberta wore an aquamarine dress, elegantly tailored to emphasize her figure. A corset would have added emphasis, but without that fishbone armor, Roberta could breathe easily and move with natural grace. On the other hand, Juliet, who, on top of everything, wore a very tight, modern skirt, could only tiptoe forward. Which, Roberta noted, made her look touchingly helpless.

"Corsets also make you more likely to faint," Atamarie teased. "Of course, you could still try that. Check out this painting over here, Robbie. You can't help feeling dizzy just looking at it. Stop in front of it and then swoon. I'll call for the doctor."

Roberta glared at her friend, then went back to watching Kevin and his conquest. Finally, Atamarie pulled her away.

"Come on, smile, Roberta! Look, there's Patrick."

Patrick Drury was an open, friendly man. His profession, after all, forced him to make polite conversation with the most varied people. On the farms, he encountered everyone from British nobility to cloddish gold miners. Roberta was often assigned as his partner at society dinners, and Atamarie had gotten the feeling he liked to be around her. Recently, his eyes had even begun to light up when she walked into the room, recognizing that the sweet young girl had grown into a beautiful woman.

This evening, though, everything was off. Although Patrick dutifully fetched them champagne and chatted amiably enough, he was deeply distracted. Atamarie realized that Patrick shared Roberta's fixation: he couldn't take his eyes off Kevin and Juliet. The young farmer was captivated by the black-haired beauty, but surely, he had no chance.

Patrick wasn't nearly as handsome as Kevin. Instead of his father Michael's full, black hair, he had inherited his mother Lizzie's dark-blonde locks and soft blue eyes. He was also shorter and less imposing than Kevin—not the sort a woman like Juliet would notice.

Atamarie eventually gave up trying to prompt conversation between Roberta and Patrick, and she steered Roberta onward while looking for a waiter. Perhaps Roberta's mood would improve with another glass of champagne. Patrick resumed following his brother and Juliet around like a little dog.

In the middle of the gallery, Roberta and Atamarie spotted Rosie, who was Roberta's aunt as well as Heather and Chloe's maid. The towheaded woman stood stock-still, limply holding a tray of champagne glasses. She looked so bored, it was as if she were trying to imitate a table.

Atamarie took two glasses of champagne and smiled at her.

"How's the foal, Rosie?" she inquired, and Rosie's face opened like the sun bursting through the clouds.

Rosie was a tolerable maid, but only truly happy and exceedingly skillful when it came to racehorses. Chloe had taught her all about them back when she ran a stud farm in the fjord lands with her former husband. Of all the race-horses, only the mare Dancing Rose remained, now relegated to pulling Chloe and Heather's chaise. Last year, however, Chloe had allowed Dancing Rose to be bred, and now a mare foal whinnied in the stables. To Rosie's delight, Chloe was even considering letting the young horse race. After all, she had not seen her former husband in years. Colin Coltrane's name no longer rang out on the racetracks of the South Island. So, why shouldn't little Trotting Diamond be given the chance to shine?

After listening to Rosie raving about the foal, Roberta led Atamarie over to Kathleen Burton and her husband, Peter. Reverend Burton, as always, had a soothing effect on Roberta. She would never forget how safe she had felt in his and Kathleen's house after her mother finally escaped her violent husband. Moreover, she noticed that the reverend was among the few men present who did not deem Kevin and Juliet worth a second glance. Instead, he asked Roberta and then Atamarie about their studies. He was delighted that Atamarie intended to pursue engineering, and he entreated Roberta to teach in his parish after graduation.

"We're building a school, you know. The newcomers are finally settling down and having children."

For years, the reverend had concerned himself with the spiritual and also the very practical problems of new immigrants and those returning frustrated from the goldfields. By then, the gold rush in Otago had abated. European adventurers were now drawn to the gold and diamond mines of South Africa. The unsuccessful miners stranded in Dunedin were forced to find other work, often with the pastor's help. Now, they were building their houses around his church, his parish was growing, and he looked forward to the typical work of Sunday school, baptisms, and weddings.

Heather and Chloe joined the group, their hosting duties now fulfilled. All their guests had been plied with drinks, small talk had been made all around, and Chloe had given a speech about the artist and her work.

"Sales are off to a slow start," Heather observed regretfully. "Even though they're little treasures." She studied one of the meticulous paintings admiringly.

"Maybe you should pitch them to morticians," Atamarie remarked. "I could imagine them in a mortician's parlor, or the mortuary receiving room."

The others laughed.

"You don't know anything about art," Heather chided her niece.

"Cubic modifications of carbon, on the other hand—" Atamarie retorted. "How many of these strange paintings would you have to sell to buy a ring like that?"

She pointed to Heather's finger, which featured a fine gold ring with glittering diamonds.

Kathleen smiled at her daughter. "What a gorgeous ring! And you look splendid in your new outfit. It's just a shame it's not from my collection."

Heather's cheeks burned at the flattery. She was no great beauty with her limp, ash-blonde hair. In Europe, she'd worn it short, but here that was too scandalous, even for artists. People whispered enough about her predilection for wide, Oriental-style trousers, and the bold jackets and blouses that went with them. Heather's features had been delicate and Madonna-like, but now they seemed almost harsh, and her once-gentle brown eyes had grown sharp.

"I think the ring looks much nicer on Chloe," she demurred. "Come on, Chloe, show them yours."

The dark-haired Chloe looked more feminine than her friend. That day, she wore a red empire-style dress from Kathleen's collection, the color reflecting off the diamond of her ring.

"Matching diamond rings," laughed the pastor. "Very fine, indeed! I see I'm not twisting the screws hard enough when I collect for my soup kitchen."

"Heather sold a few paintings," Chloe explained, a bit self-conscious. "And so, she thought, well, the gallery's been around for ten years. We should celebrate."

"Has it really been that long?" asked Kathleen, playing along with the pretext that Heather and Chloe were celebrating their business rather than their love. "In any case, the rings are beautiful. And diamonds are so affordable now that they've found so many in—where was it again, Peter? South Africa?"

Peter Burton nodded. "The Cape of Good Hope. I fear we'll be hearing about South Africa more often. There's talk of war."

"War?" Atamarie's eyes widened. She knew war only from history class and from her parents' recollections of the last skirmishes between the Maori and *pakeha*. It was hard for her to imagine that they had really gone after each other with guns, let alone spears. In Atamarie's experience, wars were fought with words—newspaper diatribes and petitions to try to sway Parliament. "Who's going to war?"

But Roberta had little interest in politics. All of her attention was focused on Kevin, who had just joined them, Patrick on his heels. Juliet leaned in to squint at Heather's and Chloe's rings, but she seemed unimpressed. Her own jewelry was far more eye-catching, though the local ladies were already alleging that it was mere rhinestones. A faux pas. Here, in Calvinistic Dunedin society, people wore very little jewelry, but when they did, it was real.

"The English and the Boers," Kevin told Atamarie. "The latter are really Dutch, but since they settled in South Africa, they've called themselves Boers, or Afrikaners. They lay claim to a few regions there, even though England technically conquered the country a few centuries ago."

The reverend nodded. "And nobody gave a hoot about their claim until all those diamond and gold mines turned up. But no, it's only the noblest of motivations, of course. Suddenly, England can't possibly accept that they treat the natives worse than cattle. Or that migrants in the gold-mining areas don't have voting rights."

Kathleen furrowed her brow. "Since when do miners care about politics? Most of them can hardly read and write, and they don't have any interest in government."

"It's more the other way around." Kevin smirked. "Politics has an interest in gold."

Roberta watched as his shining blue eyes flashed mockingly and dimples softened his otherwise square face. She forced herself to return the smile, recalling Atamarie's encouragement. She had to get Kevin's attention somehow. By saying something, for example. Preferably something smart. Roberta racked her brain.

"But New Zealand has nothing to do with whether England goes to war in South Africa, does it?" she finally asked—then blushed when everyone looked at her.

"That depends entirely on our premier," Heather observed drily. "And Mr. Seddon is known for his strange ideas. And switching sides."

Seddon had made life difficult during the fight for women's right to vote.

"Not to mention that every thinking person has something to do with it when wars are fought for diamonds and gold," the pastor said, and Roberta reddened again. So, her remark had not been so smart after all.

"Do you think they might send New Zealanders to Africa to fight?" Atamarie asked.

"Why not?" mused Kevin, playing casually with Juliet's fingers. The young woman had lasciviously laid her hand on his left arm, and he put his right hand over it. This had been happening all evening—Kevin and Juliet couldn't keep their hands off each other. "They won't force us, of course, but volunteers . . ."

Fear suddenly seized Roberta.

"But you, you—all of you." She scrambled to include the other men. "None of you would go, would you?"

She sighed with relief when the men laughed, but then Juliet spoke up.

"Not without my permission," she declared, leering and pulling Kevin closer. "There are sweeter battlefields than the cape to prove yourself a hero."

Chapter 3

"What do you think this Juliet woman is going to do to your reputation?"

Lizzie Drury stormed into Kevin's office, her husband, Michael, a few steps behind. She had come intending to speak calmly with her son, but after just now seeing the lady in question saunter out of his private apartment upstairs, she could no longer hold her tongue.

"Where'd you even dig her up? And how could you think to bring a woman like that to the Dunloes' reception?"

Kevin jumped up from his desk. "Mother, don't take that tone with me. And please lower your voice." His eyes went to the ceiling.

"Worried she'll hear? Don't worry, the young 'lady' took her leave. She has enough shame to steal away before the maid comes, at least."

A light flush spread over Kevin's face when he realized his parents had witnessed Juliet's departure. He knew what his mother thought about his various female acquaintances.

"Juliet had, well, she had forgotten something in, in my apartment—"

"Best not ask what she forgot," his father quipped.

Kevin tried not to let himself be cowed. "Juliet is an honorable woman who knows how to behave in society. And Mr. Dunloe was quite impressed, you know."

"Which speaks to the woman's talents," Lizzie replied. "Mr. Dunloe may have been 'impressed,' as you say, but Mrs. Dunloe was terrifically embarrassed."

This was a slight exaggeration. Though Claire Dunloe had cast some indignant glances at Juliet's indiscreet dress and sham jewelry, the reception had passed uneventfully enough. Juliet's table manners were perfect, she knew how to chatter meaninglessly, and this time she had reined in her champagne consumption.

"Regardless, everyone is talking about her," Lizzie continued. "So loud that it's reached all the way to Tuapeka." Tuapeka, the town nearest Lizzie and Michael's farm, lay nearly sixty miles from Dunedin. It had officially been called Lawrence since 1866, but Lizzie and Michael could never get used to the change. They seldom came to Dunedin but hadn't wanted to turn down an invitation from Jimmy Dunloe, the bank director. "I hear she broke out in song at Heather and Chloe's gallery!"

Kevin rubbed his forehead. No doubt, Juliet had overdone it. The art opening had been rather boring, the paintings gloomy, the people dull, but there'd been plenty of champagne, which Juliet did love. After a few too many, she had crossed to the trio of musicians and asked them to strike up a popular American hit. The reaction of Dunedin society had not been hostile, but they had certainly looked surprised. Graceful Chloc had saved the situation by speaking briefly with the impromptu soloist and then formally introducing her, thereby solving the riddle of her last name and her history: Juliet LaBree was American by birth and belonged to a vaudeville ensemble playing in Wellington. Or rather, she had until a few weeks ago.

"How does a decent young lady even get here from Wellington? What is she doing here?" asked Michael, though he sounded more curious than disapproving. Juliet had made a strong impression on nearly every man in town. And no matter how ardently they agreed with their wives that she was gaudy and disreputable, they all envied Kevin a bit.

"Juliet, uh, seems to have had enough of her troupe. And she likes it in New Zealand. She's decided to seek a new engagement here."

"Oh really?" said Lizzie. "Then she should be looking in Auckland or Wellington. Not in Dunedin, of all places, city of the Church of Scotland, city with the most closed-minded citizenry of the whole South Island. What does she plan to sing here? Hymns?"

"With her voice, she can sing anything," Kevin insisted. "Besides, you may not have noticed, Mother, but Dunedin has changed. There was a gold rush here."

Lizzie laughed. "I remember. The ruins of the brothel still stand in Tuapeka."

"And you planted the flag of virtue there, did you?" Kevin retorted.

Lizzie glared at her son. "In Tuapeka, I never—"

She stopped, ashamed. She had never told her sons about her past in London and Kaikoura, but Kevin was clever and could no doubt put some things together. By the time Lizzie followed Michael to the goldfields, though, she had long since become respectable—in so far as selling bootleg whiskey could be called respectable.

Michael stepped in to defend his wife. "Kevin, your mother and I weren't angels either, but that's exactly why we're concerned about Miss LaBree. She's running away from something. Believe me, I know the look. Probably this ensemble threw her out, and for good reason. So, she gradually made her way to Otago. The goldfields near Queenstown. A series of pubs, a series of men."

Kevin had had enough. "Fine, that may be, but you can't deny that she's captivating. No matter her past, that's all I care about. After all, I haven't proposed marriage. And I'll remind you that I am not a child. I shall decide what I want."

He cast a pointed glance at the heavy grandfather clock. He knew Lizzie wouldn't want to be late for the fashion show at the Gold Mine Boutique.

"Fine, we'll go," she said. "But if I'm right about Miss LaBree, it doesn't much matter what you want. The only question is what she wants."

***

Juliet LaBree wanted a place to call her own, though she found that hard to admit, even to herself. After all, she had loved her wild life. For years, she had been able to imagine nothing more perfect than to drift from city to city, theater to theater, man to man. This had been the life she'd dreamed of even as a girl. Juliet had never been enthusiastic about books, riding, or little parties and picnics. More than just her exotic appearance differentiated her from the dutiful plantation daughters of Terrebonne Parish, Louisiana. From an early age, Juliet's lust for life had driven her to the big city of New Orleans for concerts and theater and excitement.

Juliet's parents were themselves no prigs. Her mother was a Creole who'd made her way from Jamaica, and Juliet had no illusions about how she'd done it. Yet Juliet's father had fallen for her at once, taken her to his plantation, and had loved and spoiled her as much as any woman might wish.

When Juliet was born, she was the apple of his eye. Nothing was good enough for his beautiful daughter. Juliet had all the best teachers, and learned French and ballroom dancing, though she only really took an interest in the music lessons. When she turned seventeen, she was to be wed to the perfect husband. Her father found him two plantations away, from an old family that had somehow survived the Civil War with its unfathomable wealth intact. But the young man was so bloodless that, during every visit to his plantation, Juliet looked around nervously for vampires. He could give her a grand manor house, but to Juliet it seemed a tomb.

Just before the wedding, she had fled to New Orleans and from there straight to Tennessee. At first, the money she had brought with her sufficed, and after that, she had ample clothing and jewelry to pawn. When she sang in clubs then, it was for pleasure; in Memphis, she soon became a minor star. Then, however, there were difficulties with a certain Mafia boss, and Juliet had to leave the city very quickly, this time without a cent. She was not proud of what she did next to make it to New York. Some time later, she was offered a job singing on a luxury liner bound for Europe. She spent three years playing small clubs across the Continent—and she enjoyed every minute of it. Juliet fell in love rarely, but she kissed men often. Her life was a singular rush.

And then came the engagement that led her to Australia and New Zealand. It was a talented troupe, but not very professional. Juliet was good to the manager, but in the end, he found another girl—a long story. Juliet had fled to the South Island, only to find that the cities there were even more backward than those in the North. There were practically no variety shows, and the venues that hired women to sing and dance were usually just a better sort of brothel.

Juliet had been over the moon when she met Kevin Drury, and she was surprised to find that he still did not bore her after a few weeks. She enjoyed the security Kevin offered, plus the fact that he was extraordinarily good-looking and experienced—Kevin knew how to satisfy Juliet. He seemed enthralled by her skills at pleasing men. What was more, he did not ask questions about her past, and he was generous. Whenever she expressed a wish, it was as good as fulfilled, at least within Kevin's means.

Juliet quickly found that the young doctor was successful, well off—but not exactly rich. She was astonished by how her standards had fallen. She no longer required her beau to rent out a whole club just to be allowed to dance with her, and she did not demand showy jewelry she would only pawn later. The events Kevin took her to were less sophisticated than what she was used to: an art show in Dunedin, a choral concert in Christchurch. On the other hand, she had never caused such a stir as in this nest of provincials. In Memphis, New

York, Paris, and Berlin, she was one beauty among many. Here, though, the men fell at her feet.

Juliet began to dream of settling down, of belonging to Dunedin society—and reigning over it. When she gave her first party here, the whole South Island would talk about it. The salon of the young Mrs. Drury would draw artists and musicians. The newspapers would report on what dresses she wore to which event. Naturally, they would require a suitable house, especially once they had children. Just think of the domestics they would need. Juliet realized that the planning in and of itself was a joy. Perhaps she should write to her parents and tell them about her court at the end of the world.

The dark clouds in this beautiful dream came from Kevin having not yet made a move to ask for her hand. Juliet had learned from asking around that he was considered something of a womanizer. He did not seem to be interested in settling down, which brought Juliet to a crossroads. If she wanted to move Kevin toward marriage, she would have to get pregnant—but really, she did not want a child so soon. Juliet could easily imagine dancing alongside Kevin through the humble Dunedin nightlife for a year or two, wrapping the city's men around her finger, reaping the jealous looks of the women. A child would limit that, at the least delaying her debut as a glamorous hostess and pillar of society.

But if there was no other way . . .

Juliet had been nervous since running into Kevin's mother in the stairwell. Elizabeth Drury had not said anything, but the look she had given Juliet could not be misconstrued. Juliet was willing to bet that this well-dressed matron didn't have a spotless past either. Her husband may have made his fortune as a gold miner, but had his wife merely handed him the shovel, or might she have supported the family some other way?

Regardless, Lizzie had a knowing look—and she'd likely stop at nothing to break off Kevin's affair. Juliet thought she already recognized the first successes in that campaign. Kevin had not taken her to the fashion show, the most discussed event of the season among the women of Dunedin. And recently, he preferred to take her out alone instead of escorting her to society events. Juliet sensed the beginning of the end, and she was bound and determined not to let that happen.

When Kevin left her waiting one evening while finishing up with a patient, she closed the door to his apartment behind her and went through his night table. As a doctor, Kevin did not rely on women to avoid unwanted offspring, which, at first, Juliet had appreciated. Of course, she knew how to perform the usual methods, too, calculating the fertile days and performing a rinse in case of doubt. Kevin, however, relied on sheaths. Juliet had previously known men who put on such sleeves before making love, but those had mostly been made of sheep's guts or other animal matter. Kevin preferred the modern, rubber models. They were thick and cumbersome, but very reliable. Surely no fluid could make it through, as long as they remained undamaged.

Juliet found a whole box of them in Kevin's drawer. And behind it another—apparently, her lover bought protection in bulk. Juliet contemplated whether to tamper with both boxes, but decided one would do. Her period was two weeks past, so her fertile days were near at hand. Two or three nights should suffice.

Juliet reached for a hat pin. In two months at the latest, Kevin would be walking her down the aisle.

Chapter 4

Atamarie never dreamed she would envy Roberta's college experience. It was not as if she were considering teaching children instead of building flying machines, but after two months alone in Christchurch, she was bored to death. Every day after classes, she sat in her room or wandered alone through the city, while Roberta was out with fellow students. Although she wasn't nearly as outgoing as Atamarie, she had quickly made friends and seemed quite happy—except for her hopeless infatuation with Kevin Drury.

Atamarie, on the other hand, had no friends. Not even her landladies' liberal attitude toward visitors could help her. The other engineering students stayed far away. At first, they'd eyed her with suspicion, then soon turned to slander. Favoritism was the only explanation they could imagine for her grades—Atamarie was the best in the class by a mile, and her professors were dazzled by her intellect and avidity. On top of that, the universities remained fundamentally Victorian: boys and girls were not allowed to fraternize without a chaperone. In fields with more girls, they made their own fun away from the boys, but as the College of Engineering was housed in its own building, Atamarie never even encountered other female students.

As a consequence, she remained cut off from all the fun to be had in lively Christchurch. Boat rides on the Avon, rowing regattas, and outings to the Canterbury Plains took place without her. Atamarie lived for her occasional weekends in Dunedin or visits to relatives and friends. Heather and Chloe sometimes came to Addington, a suburb of Christchurch, for horse races, and Roberta's stepfather, Sean, was regularly in the city. Otherwise, Atamarie focused all her attention on her studies—which pushed her grades even higher and made her classmates even more resentful.

Atamarie filled her long, solitary evenings with reading, devouring engineering texts and Lilienthal's and Mouillard's work on the theory and construction of flying devices. She also read novels and newspapers, where she once again came across the country Reverend Burton had spoken of: South Africa, the republic—or colony?—at the Cape of Good Hope.

Atamarie learned that the Dutch had originally settled the area. The Dutch East India Company wanted an outpost for supplying its ships on the way to Java. Later, however, the settlers pushed farther into the country—and at some point, the East India Company went bankrupt, and the British took over the region largely with no fighting. This did not sit well with the Dutch settlers, who now called themselves Boers, but thus far they'd been allowed to oversee their own regions, Transvaal and Orange, and hadn't caused much trouble. Atamarie thought it outrageous that the English allowed the Boers to go on treating the black natives like slaves. But then diamonds and gold were found.

New Zealanders knew the consequences of such a discovery from their own experience: thousands of impoverished Europeans set out for the goldfields, the population exploded, and the gold-mining towns became dens of iniquity. The Boers, mostly farmers and strictly religious, were furious. Soon, the new settlers began complaining of reprisals—and the British Crown seized willingly on the pretext, insisting on its right to rule the whole country. New Zealand's premier, Richard Seddon, had taken up the subject with enthusiasm. Once war seemed inevitable, he gave a gripping speech before Parliament in which he proposed sending the empire a contingent of cavalry.

"New Zealand will fight for one flag, one queen, one language, and one country: Britain," intoned Seddon.

Atamarie didn't understand. England was the motherland, of course, but Atamarie viewed her country as almost entirely independent. Why should New Zealand get involved? Yet somehow, the public seemed thrilled at the prospect of defending the rights of an empire they hardly knew in a faraway country of which they had only just heard. Parliament pledged support with only five votes opposed, and the recruitment offices could hardly handle the deluge of volunteers. A few of Atamarie's classmates flocked to the flag as well, but they were not accepted.

"Even the army knows better than to take those idiots," Atamarie remarked to Reverend Burton during a visit to Dunedin.

It was spring, and the reverend was throwing his annual parish festival. He'd resisted calls from several parishioners to donate the proceeds to the war effort instead of the hungry.

"Seddon ought to go ahead and finance that adventure himself," he replied. "New Zealand won't see a single diamond in the end. Not that I'd want that blood money. But everyone's gone crazy."

He narrowed his eye at a few parishioners who were waving Union Jacks at the festival.

"New Zealanders are just happy that someone else is getting the gold miners," Sean laughed. "But I refuse to accept generalities, Reverend. Not everyone is for it. You know Kupe voted against it in Parliament."

Atamarie swelled with pride for her stepfather.

"And the women's organizations are split," Violet added. Roberta's mother was head of the Dunedin chapter of the Women's Christian Temperance Union, which had fought for women's suffrage. "Many condemn the senseless shedding of blood. I, for one, would not send my son to die in some strange country. Of course, some are on fire to volunteer themselves and show women can prove ourselves in dangerous situations too."

Reverend Burton arched his eyebrows. "As nurses, you mean? No one's about to put a gun in their hands."

"No, I don't imagine so," Violet laughed. She was petite and very feminine. No one could imagine her carrying a gun. "And as for England, the women there don't even have the right to vote. Most universities are closed to them. We should be fighting for them, not for diamonds and gold!"

Atamarie applauded, but Roberta missed her mother's fiery words. Once again, she had her eyes fixed on Kevin Drury. The doctor had just arrived with Juliet LaBree. The young woman wore a tantalizingly tight, dark-blue summer dress in the latest fashion. Apparently, she had become a customer of the Gold Mine Boutique.

"I'm afraid he's going to marry her," Roberta confided to Atamarie a few minutes later. "I go to pretty much every event with my parents and always try to say something to him. Really, I do. But he has eyes only for her."

"Really?" Atamarie was less convinced. Juliet no longer followed at Kevin's heels, fondling his arm. She flitted from one man to another and conversed excitedly—most of all with bachelors and widowers. Patrick alone did not draw her notice, though he still stumbled after her with love written on his face. Kevin no longer exerted himself to keep Juliet away from other men. In fact, he seemed quite open to new acquaintances. His banter with a female parishioner about the price of an ugly tea cozy handmade by one of the pillars of the community looked almost like flirting.

"Well, it seems to me to be petering out," Atamarie said, steering Roberta toward Kevin.

"A tea cozy, dear uncle?" Atamarie teased. "Thinking of starting a household?"

Kevin turned to his niece, giving her as well as Roberta his irresistible smile.

"Just supporting the community," he replied. "I have to buy something. If you two are collecting your trousseaux, I'd be happy to donate it."

"No chance, Uncle Kevin, at least not yet. We're studying, you know."

Kevin nodded and let his gaze wander over the two friends. They were not girls anymore, and they had made themselves up properly tonight. His niece was cute, but Roberta was a true beauty.

"Right, you're our future teacher," he said to his niece's companion. Didn't you want to be a doctor once?"

Roberta turned red. She'd been infatuated with Kevin for years now, and early on, she had dreamed of becoming a doctor like him.

"I can't stand the sight of blood," she admitted. "I'm trying to get better. Last week, it was my first attempt to lead a class alone, and a little girl got a bloody nose. I managed, but it was awful."

"Well," Kevin said, "if you really do take over the school in Caversham, my practice is only a few minutes away. Just send the little patients over to me." He smiled at Roberta conspiratorially. "Or bring them yourself. Then at least I'll have something pretty to look at as I work."

Roberta looked as if she might faint for real. At the same moment, Juliet seemed to sense something amiss. Feigning calm, she strolled over.

"Come, Kevin, they're starting the raffle. You have to draw a ticket for me. I don't have any luck with such things."

Kevin let himself be led in the direction of the raffle—and Atamarie pulled the almost-frozen Roberta over as well.

"Do you need a lucky charm too?" Kevin asked. "Excellent, then I'll offer the three most beautiful ladies here three tickets each. With that, I'll have done my part to contribute to parish upkeep. But I'm warning you: if you win that hideous tea cozy, no one will marry you."

"Lord preserve us." Atamarie laughed and unfolded her three losing tickets.

Juliet acted as if she were having trouble unfolding hers. Kevin helped her and hooted when her third turned out to be a winner.

"A tea cozy. Probably the one I was just looking at. Enjoy it, Juliet."

Juliet just huffed, glaring at him.

Roberta was still holding her tickets, as if savoring the fact that Kevin had touched them.

"Come on, already," said Atamarie. "Even if you win the tea cozy, you can just give it away."

Roberta opened two losers, but then she had a winner—a tiny stuffed horse.

"A horse!" Kevin cheered. "Those are always useful. Though I prefer the living kind."

"But I can't take a live one with me to school," Roberta said—and chided herself at once. She didn't want Kevin to know she'd decided to carry the horse with her from now on. After all, it was almost like a present from him. She squeezed it between her fingers.

"Aw, I bet they'd do great in school. Horses are smart," Kevin said, leaning toward her warmly.

Roberta glowed.

"See, progress," Atamarie said after Kevin left the festival with his Juliet—or rather Juliet with her Kevin. The woman had looked indignant after her boyfriend spent so much time with the girls, and then immediately pushed to leave. "Things are cooling off with Juliet, for sure. She's terribly boring anyway. What is he supposed to talk with her about?"

***

Juliet would never have believed it could be so difficult to get pregnant. More than four months had passed. It was February; summer was waning and so was Kevin's interest in her. Before, he had taken her to lavish receptions; now, at most, he took her to foolish events like that parish festival where, moreover, he spent his time flirting with other women or talking with men about the distant war.

For her part, Juliet was also beginning to look around for alternatives. There were few suitable bachelors in Dunedin, but she'd identified two or three acceptable widowers. No one came close to Kevin in looks—not even his brother, Patrick, who scurried annoyingly after her.

She'd made up her mind to stay in Dunedin. She'd grown used to the city's amenities—the wide streets, the upscale shopping, not least of all the Gold Mine Boutique—and it was time to settle down. A child was still the best path there.

Lasciviously, she peeled away the gold evening dress in which she had accompanied her lover to a concert that evening. A decent social event for a change. The Dunloes had been there and the Coltranes—with their pretty little daughter whom Kevin had eyed like a lovelorn lamb. Kevin didn't realize it himself, yet, but that could change. Little Roberta would no doubt be the dream daughter-in-law for Kevin's gruff mother. Juliet forced herself to smile and swing her hips. She had to watch out. She had been getting plump.

Kevin, who had already been lying on the bed, got up to help her out of her corset. He loved to free her from it, caressing her swelling flesh.

"Unbelievable," he murmured as he opened her brassiere. "They seem to have gotten bigger."

He kissed her breasts and sucked lightly on them, a tenderness she had always enjoyed before. But today it almost hurt. Her breasts were taut and seemed harder than usual.

Kevin's mouth wandered over her body, kissing her stomach and hips. Finally, he picked her up and carried her to the bed. Then he felt in his night-table drawer for a sheath.

"Do we even need it today?" he murmured.

They both knew that two or three days before and after menstruation were likely to be safe.

Juliet calculated with lightning speed. He was right. Surely, they did not need one tonight—in truth, her bleeding should already have started. She shook her head with a smile.

Kevin continued caressing Juliet. Usually, that was always enough to make her wet, but today something was off. Kevin, a patient, imaginative lover, began to occupy himself again with her breasts, drawing circles on her stomach—

Kevin stopped suddenly. He turned the gas lamp up higher. His face lost its soft, dreamy expression. In its place came the probing look of the doctor.

"Juliet, are you—are you pregnant?"

Chapter 5

"No, under no circumstances. I won't marry her."

Kevin had hoped his mother would be pleased, but Lizzie merely sat there with her face puckered, gripping her wineglass. Michael had opened a bottle of her beloved Bordeaux to help calm everyone down. Kevin was exceedingly agitated, so much so that, the day after his discovery, he had left the practice in his partner's hands and ridden up to Lawrence. His parents had listened stoically to his revelation until Michael finally asked about marriage plans.

"She planned it!" Kevin yelled. "I don't know how, but somehow she duped me. Even though she said she didn't want a baby."

"People don't always get to choose." Michael tried to soothe him.

Lizzie looked at her son in a cold rage. "Of course she planned it. I feared this from the beginning. But now she has you, Kevin. Obviously, you're going to marry her."

"What?" Kevin and Michael yelled at the same time.

"No, I'm not," howled Kevin. "I won't have that done to me."

"No one can force him, Lizzie." Michael shook his head.

"Oh no? So, he abandons her. And then what will she do? Alone with his baby?"

"I could pay for it," mumbled Kevin.

"Arrangements can be made," Michael said. "Think about Matariki."

Matariki had been impregnated by Colin Coltrane at eighteen, but she had raised Atamarie alone. It hadn't been easy, and she'd sometimes had to pretend to be a widow. But her parents had stood by her, and Lizzie and Michael had helped financially.

"Exactly! Matariki didn't have to get married," Kevin crowed. "What, you let your daughter do what she wants, but not your son?"

Lizzie rubbed her forehead and took a big gulp of wine. "That was different."

"Oh yeah?" yelled Kevin. "Because she's part Maori and they don't care as much about those things? And what about you and her father?"

"You're risking a slap, Kevin. I don't care how old you are. And no, for your information, I did not want to marry Riki's father. And what happened with her had nothing to do with being Maori. The difference is simply that Colin got Matariki pregnant, not the other way around."

Kevin almost had to laugh. "That would have been a miracle."

"And a catastrophe," Lizzie said. "I'm sorry if I'm not being clear. But tell me, Michael, would you have trusted Colin Coltrane with our grandchild? We were so relieved when Matariki and Atamarie got away from him. And now, this Juliet has our Kevin's baby in her womb."

Michael sighed. "We could just line her pockets."

Lizzie shook her head firmly. "How do you see that working? Are you going to buy her a house in Dunedin and make her financially secure but an outcast in society? Is my grandchild supposed to grow up a bastard?"

The blood shot to Michael's face. Back when he was deported from Ireland, he'd left Kathleen in that very situation, and the money hadn't saved her. In the end, she'd parlayed that money into a marriage: Kathleen financed Ian Coltrane's emigration to New Zealand. In exchange, Ian gave Michael and Kathleen's son Sean his last name. And then spent years letting poor Kathleen know that he thought her a whore.

"She could move to another city," mused Kevin. "Say she was a widow."

Lizzie nodded. "So, we'd lose track of her and your child. That'd suit you, wouldn't it, Kevin? We buy your way out, and the poor little one has to make its own way. Heaven knows what Juliet would do with it."

Michael poured her more wine. "Now, now, Lizzie," he said. "The woman's not a monster. Maybe she really didn't want a baby, but once she has one—"

Lizzie breathed in sharply. In her mind's eye, she could see a shack in London, a filthy hovel she'd shared with another prostitute, Hannah, a mother of two children.

"Oh yeah? She'll make it somehow, right? And all women automatically sacrifice everything for their children? The things you men can convince yourselves of. It makes me sick."

Lizzie hadn't thought about Toby and Laura in a long time, but suddenly she remembered their little bodies next to her when they crawled into her cot at night, afraid and half-frozen. While Hannah giggled with her beau in her own bed. What was his name? Laurence? Lucius? Or had there been a Laurence and then a Lucius? Hannah had always talked of love. Just not when it came to Toby and Laura.

We're hungry, Lizzie. Can you get us something to eat? Lizzie heard the children's voices again, their crying. What had become of them after Lizzie was sent to Australia? When she had stolen bread, it was to feed the children, and Hannah had not even defended her. On the contrary, she had feigned a cozy family life with Lucius and the children.

"Maternal instinct cannot be denied," Kevin lectured in his doctor's voice.

"Maybe among horses," Lizzie snarled, "or cats, most of them, but that Juliet you chose might not care a fig for her baby. She'd take the money, but what would she do with it? There's no question, Kevin. You have to marry her."

"And if we give her money to leave the baby with us?" Michael asked reluctantly.

Lizzie shrugged. "She's out for a husband, Michael. If we don't give her one, she might simply end the pregnancy."

Her son gasped.

"Don't give me that look, Kevin. And don't think her naive. If you leave her, she'll probably do it. Another reason to marry her if you really think it such a sin."

Kevin pressed his hands to his temples. "But I don't want to. I don't even want to get married at all. And now, a woman like her. It was supposed to be just for fun. If I have to marry Juliet, my life is over!"

Lizzie and Michael exchanged a look. They'd both lived lives so much harder than their spoiled son could imagine. Sure, Kevin might have to soldier on with a woman at his side who did not suit him perfectly, but he'd made his bed. Besides, Juliet was clearly not without her appeal. And Kevin's social standing would remain intact. People would whisper a bit, but there were plenty of folks in Dunedin society with a darker past than Juliet LaBree's.

"You just need to rein her in," Michael said. "The woman is already in a position to ruin you. Don't deny it, Kevin. Jimmy Dunloe told me you're running up debts."

"According to Claire and Kathleen, she's spent a fortune in the Gold Mine alone," Lizzie added. "You'll need to curb that, Kevin, even if it's difficult. Make it clear to her that a doctor isn't a plantation owner."

Word of Juliet's family in Louisiana had finally gotten around. Actually, Kevin had been relieved to learn about it. At least she came from society of some sort.

"I'll have to buy a house," Kevin sighed. It was the first thing Juliet had asked for after she got over the shock of Kevin's diagnosis.

"It's already begun," sighed Lizzie. "But fine, maybe we could help with that. As long as it's modest. Don't even think of a palace on upper Stuart. A cozy cottage would be more appropriate—in Caversham, for example."

***

Kevin left his parents' house and rode back to Dunedin in the pouring rain. He hunched over his horse, jacket pulled tight around him. He should have been making plans, but instead he sulked. He did not want to marry Juliet. The longer he thought about it, the more terrible such a union seemed. But why? He had never worried much about love. Whenever he'd imagined his marriage, it had been a pleasant relationship with a suitable woman. Society had firm expectations for a doctor's wife: social engagements, perhaps help with her husband's practice, or at least proper concern for his patients. Cultural interests were desirable, and Kevin did not want an idiot at his side. Mostly, he wanted his wife to be honest and warm—a modern young woman, perhaps educated. Really, he had always imagined he'd settle down with a girl like Atamarie or her friend.

Juliet LaBree only partially fit the bill, although he had to admit she was capable of conforming to it. Yet he doubted that was what she wanted. In the last few weeks, there had been fights about whether this or that event really required a new dress, whether his new carriage was extravagant enough for weekend outings, and so on. And now he was supposed to inform her that his parents might help with a cottage in Caversham, but they were not prepared to buy the town house where he rented space for his office and apartment. It was for sale at the moment, and Juliet had immediately brought it up when she learned of her pregnancy.

Kevin thought with dread of the fights that lay before him. They would be about the house, the furniture, servants . . . Kevin employed only a part-time cleaning woman, but Juliet would hardly want to cook and care for their baby herself. There had already been tears and screaming, Juliet accusing him of destroying her life by getting her pregnant. Based on this accusation, he knew, she would make more and more demands. There'd be no end. Then there was her flirtatious nature. Recently, he had begun to doubt her faithfulness. Would it be like that the rest of his life?

In many respects, Kevin took after his father. Both were charming, sometimes too easygoing, and both shied away from difficult choices. That did not mean that they were inconstant—on the contrary. Michael had carried a torch for his first love for decades, and Kevin had pursued his profession doggedly. Despite any other failings, he was an excellent doctor. Yet Michael had always needed Lizzie to confront his problems for him, and Kevin had had everything in life handed to him. If he married Juliet, he realized, he'd have to fight his own battles.

As Kevin passed through Caversham, his spirits lifted a little. It was a homey area, and he could easily imagine a practice here—plus, cute little Roberta would be that much closer when one of her students got a bloody nose. Kevin was about to smile, but then he tried to picture Juliet in one of these modest cottages, cooking or caring for a child. No, it was impossible.

An absurd thought shot through Kevin's head when he passed a sad building decorated with the bright flags of Britain and New Zealand—Recruitment Office Dunedin. Despite the rain, three young men were waiting out front. Kevin called to them.

"Volunteering for the cape?"

The boys, whose simple clothing and plaid caps designated them as workers' sons, grinned at him and saluted.

"Yes, sir!"

"If they'll take us."

Kevin considered the latest developments in the Boer War. New Zealand's ships had arrived in Cape Town on November 23. The troops had acquitted themselves bravely despite heavy fighting. In the next few days, a troop transport was to weigh anchor from Lyttelton with a regiment assembled and financed by wealthy citizens of Christchurch. Dunedin, not wanting to be outshone, was recruiting its own volunteers.

Maybe it was a crazy idea to dodge domestic battles by fleeing to real war, but, at this moment, Kevin saw no other way. Juliet could pretend that she'd discovered the pregnancy only after he was already gone, so that Kevin would not count as a scoundrel for leaving her. And Juliet—well, society would doubtlessly forgive a soldier's betrothed. What was more, then he could see whether she would wait for him or if perhaps she would ensnare another father.

Determined, he rode toward the recruitment office.

Chapter 6

Kevin's enlistment in the Otago Mounted Rifles proved astoundingly easy. As soon as he gave his profession, the officer's eyes lit up.

"We need doctors. I don't suppose you can shoot too?"

Kevin arched his eyebrows. "I grew up on a sheep farm, sir. Everyone learns to shoot rabbits."

"And ride?" the sergeant asked hopefully.

Kevin smiled and gestured to his long-legged gray hitched out front. "My horse is also here to enlist."

There was nothing more to do but sign the papers.

***

The Mounted Rifles assembled in a camp near Waikouaiti and were given uniforms. In khaki for the first time, Kevin grinned to himself. At least his father couldn't accuse him of becoming one of the redcoats they'd so hated in Ireland. They received some cursory basic training, at the end of which they elected their own officers—a common practice in volunteer regiments. Kevin, as a doctor, advanced at once to captain.

Things continued to move quickly—not even three weeks passed between Kevin's enlistment and his ship's departure. Still, it was enough time to make him feel as if he were walking on tenterhooks. He only once returned to his apartment briefly to gather a few personal items and to speak with his business partner, Christian Folks. Kevin had made Christian an offer. Christian could keep the whole practice, and when Kevin returned, he would start anew. In return, he'd asked for his friend's silence.

"I'm going to write my family as soon as I'm at sea. But for now, I'd rather not discuss it. I just need some time to myself."

Christian laughed. "Do you really need to run to the ends of the earth to get away from Juliet? Man, and here I envied you because of her."

Christian himself had married a childhood friend right after medical school.

"She has her charms," Kevin said. "But, well, I don't want to try to explain. Just keep quiet for three weeks, could you? No matter who asks. Just say I—for all I care, you can say I'm off wandering with the Maori."

Christian made a face. "They migrate in summer, Kevin; it's autumn now. And you know the tribes in this area don't have to move around to find food."

"Then make something up. I don't care. As long as everyone leaves me in peace."

Kevin had hugged his friend quickly and then left the practice with his spirits high. Adventure was calling.

***

When Lizzie and Michael Drury heard nothing from Kevin for weeks, they told themselves not to worry.

"He just needs to come to terms with it," Michael told his wife.

"First and foremost, he needs to make clear to that woman that a child does not entitle her to a Dunedin town house," Lizzie said.

An agitated Roberta reported Kevin's disappearance to Atamarie by letter. She did not dare approach Christian Folks to ask about it, and Patrick was off in the mountains, inspecting sheep brought back from the highlands. His job was to advise breeders and mediate sales.

I'm going mad with worry, Roberta complained. *Something terrible must have happened.*

But Atamarie couldn't imagine what terrible thing could have befallen her uncle on the South Island of New Zealand. At least not anything that would explain disappearing without a trace. If he'd been injured or killed, they would have heard of it in Dunedin.

In any case, he's not traveling with Miss LaBree, Roberta's letter continued. *I recently saw her, but she looked unwell.*

And, here, Atamarie recognized the answer to the riddle. Kevin had left Juliet. The question was why he'd had to disappear to do so. Kevin, she wrote to assure Roberta, would reappear again. And if Roberta was lucky, Juliet would be the one who'd disappeared by then.

Juliet herself was furious at Kevin's absence, but she couldn't imagine her boyfriend actually abandoning his apartment and practice. After all, he had neither taken his things nor closed his account, and the bank still gave Juliet credit in his name. He probably just needed a little time to wrap his head around the new situation. Juliet merely hoped that he would not drag it out too long. She did not want to walk down the aisle with a big stomach.

When Kevin's letter finally arrived, the young woman was dumbstruck. Blind with rage, she threw a few things into a suitcase, then made her way to the small house in Caversham that Patrick was renting. It lay a bit in the country and included extensive stables. Patrick owned a total of three horses—none as hot-blooded as Kevin's, but two reliable horses that bore him securely on his long rides, and a young mare. This last one was whinnying in the stables when she arrived. Patrick was traveling with the others.

Juliet spotted the boy who took care of the horses during Patrick's absences, a redheaded Irish lad. He fell for her right away.

Still, he was skeptical when she presented her request. "Aye, I know you're a friend of Mr. Drury's. You're the, uh—"

"His brother's fiancée," Juliet said firmly. "But Mr. Kevin Drury is absent at the moment, and I need to speak urgently with his parents. I'd ask Patrick to take me, but now it seems he's traveling too. So, please, harness this horse so you can transport me in the coach. I—well, the Drurys—will pay you for it."

The boy bit his lip. "The journey's pretty long. I'll have to tell my mother I'm going. And the horse is still very young. I don't know whether Mr. Drury would approve."

"Patrick will be delighted to have been a help to me," Juliet said majestically. "We can drive past your parents' home. My goodness, don't make such a to-do about it. You're driving a horse from one of the Drurys' stables to the other, and no one's going to kidnap you or the nag on the way. Let's get on with it."

The boy, Randy, finally gave in, but the journey to Elizabeth Station proved torturously slow. Randy was exceedingly worried about overtaxing the mare, and so he had her walk for hours, even though the road was well paved and they could have gone at a good pace despite its raining again. Juliet's nerves were shot. Did it ever stop raining in this country?

"They're the tears of a Maori god," Randy remarked when she complained about it. "The Maori say heaven and earth were originally a couple. The sky god was called Rangi and the earth goddess Papa. But then they had to part, and now Rangi cries about it almost every day."

Juliet raised her eyes to the sky. "Get ahold of yourself, Rangi," she murmured. "You're not the only one to have a lover run out."

The rain continued to beat on the insufficient covering of Patrick's chaise. Juliet's elegant but thin coat was already soaked through, and she cursed herself for not forcing the boy to use a larger carriage. He'd objected that the big carriage was for a team of two horses, but Juliet did not care.

She skimmed for the thousandth time the curt lines in which Kevin explained his disappearance. He did not even address the matter of their marriage. Instead, he spoke of patriotic duty. Complete nonsense. Never before had he shown particular sympathies for the English motherland. And besides, this country here . . . Juliet looked out unhappily into the rain-drenched landscape. They were just then passing the old goldfields.

"Gabriel's Gully," Randy said, pointing to a wasteland topped with meager grass, interrupted here and there by the sad remains of a settlement of wooden shacks. "For years, it was just mud. The gold miners dug around so much, they killed every root."

"Did they at least get rich?" Juliet asked.

Of course, she already knew the answer. It was the same in all the goldfields on earth: for the few winners, there were thousands of ruined lives.

"Mr. Drury's parents made enough for a farm, anyway," said Randy. "We should be there soon now. Mr. Drury says they live just a few miles from Lawrence. We can ask in town."

The few who had stayed after the gold rush lived in Lawrence. Now it was a regular rural town, a supply station for the surrounding farms. It did not have more to offer than a pub, a general goods store, and a café, and every resident knew where the Drurys' farm lay. The few passersby stared curiously at the woman in the chaise. The exotic beauty would surely be the talk of the town the next day.

Randy asked the way and directed the young mare into the mountains on a road that was considerably steeper and curvier. The mare was now getting noticeably tired and moved at a painful crawl. Juliet was beginning to feel queasy. How was she supposed to get back to the city if the little horse could not manage?

The landscape here was enchantingly beautiful, with a light southern beech forest dotted with streams, little ponds, and cliffs. Despite the rain, the mountains were visible in the distance, their snow-capped peaks craggy and imposing. But Juliet was unimpressed. Shivering in this damp, gray hinterland, she suddenly yearned for the lights of Paris, New York . . . Perhaps getting pregnant had not been her finest idea.

"Here it is, the waterfall, like they said," Randy finally called after what to Juliet had seemed an endless journey up snaking paths. "The house must be just up there."

Indeed, the house quickly came into view above the waterfall and the small pond into which it emptied. A robust, homey-looking log cabin—but a disappointment for Juliet. She had expected something closer to the plantation manors of her homeland. The Drurys were considered wealthy, after all. Well, maybe this was just how people built here. Juliet was determined not to be disheartened. These people had to help her find a solution for herself and this accursed child.

Randy stopped the horse in front of the house, but made no move to help Juliet out of the chaise. Instead, he knocked on the door.

Those within had already noticed them. Michael Drury appeared in worn denim pants and a lumberjack's shirt—cutting a far less distinguished figure than at the Dunloes'.

"Who's this, then? Patrick?" Michael's eyes fell on the little mare, which he recognized at once. "Goodness, it's Lady. Wasn't the way up here awfully far for you?"

Lizzie, who appeared behind him, saw the boy first, and turned pale.

"Has something happened to Patrick? What are you doing here?"

Randy smiled. "Nothing has happened to your son, Mrs. Drury. He's still traveling. But the lady said it was urgent . . ."

Juliet clambered awkwardly out of the coach. Her fashionable dress allowed only short strides.

Lizzie approached her, seeming not at all ashamed of her wide, old-fashioned housedress. She, too, had seemed more imposing in Dunedin. It was hard for Juliet to imagine that this short, pudgy person with her hair carelessly tied up was a valued customer of the Gold Mine Boutique.

"Miss LaBree," she now greeted her visitor. "Dear heavens, where's Kevin? How could he send you here alone, and in this weather? But come in first. And you too. Randy, isn't it?"

Randy said he'd go to the stables first. He had seemed a little ashamed when Michael noted that the trip was too much for the young mare. Hopefully, he would not be in any serious trouble with Patrick.

Michael took charge of the boy and the horse while Lizzie led Juliet inside. The interior of the house was no more impressive than the exterior. True, there were a few handsome pieces of imported furniture, but most of it was simple, rustic. Lizzie reached for Juliet's coat, but the young woman pulled away.

"So, you seem not to know where Kevin is. Is this supposed to have escaped you?" Juliet threw Kevin's letter on the table and unwrapped herself from the coat.

Lizzie picked it up and skimmed the few lines. Again, she grew pale, and struggled against a wave of panic that rose within her. War. Kevin was going to war. People would be shooting at him. Lizzie sank down into a chair.

Juliet noted none of her horror. "Was this your idea?" she demanded.

Lizzie could almost have laughed. "If you could summon just a spark of maternal instinct, Miss LaBree, you'd know that no loving mother would send her son to war. Enlisting to escape a marriage! That stupid boy. What if he's shot?"

Lizzie buried her head in her hands, further mussing her hair.

Juliet narrowed her eyes. How could this pathetic woman let herself go like that? "He's a medical officer," she scoffed. "No one will be shooting at him. Don't worry about Kevin."

Fury rose within Lizzie, but before she could reply, Michael entered.

"Miss LaBree." Michael kissed the lovely lady's hand. "What brings you to us?"

"This," Lizzie said, holding Kevin's letter out to him. "I assume a similar letter is waiting for us at the post office. We clearly underestimated Kevin's state of mind. I thought it was mainly panic at having to grow up. But now we know better: he'd rather be shot dead than marry this woman."

Michael looked somber as he read the letter, but he collected himself considerably faster than his wife. "Not exactly flattering for you, Miss LaBree." He smiled. "But don't get excited, Lizzie. He's a doctor. He'll be working in a hospital. Far behind the line, with any luck. It's just a question of what to do with his, er, 'legacy.'"

Juliet put her hands on her stomach. "So, you know that much, at least."

Michael nodded. "Kevin informed us he's going to be a father. And we advised him to marry you. But now, he seems to have chosen a different path, at least to push the question off. What do you have in mind to do now, Miss LaBree?"

Juliet shrugged. "I'm completely without means," she declared. "I was trusting that Kevin—"

"Kevin will be receiving a salary, I expect," Michael said. "Surely, he'll make the money available to you and your babe, and you could live a modest life. Then, when he comes back—"

Juliet gaped at him. "I'm supposed to—you want me to raise the baby in Dunedin? Without a father?"

"Well, you could claim Kevin would of course have married you if he had known. He really contrived a fine mess this time, Lizzie. You have to give him that."

Michael winked at his wife, whose panic was slowly fading. She realized that Michael was right—and so was that impertinent Juliet. Being a doctor, Kevin was not in much danger, especially in this war, as England was sending a hundred thousand soldiers to deal with a handful of obstreperous farmers. So, it really ought not to turn into a bloodbath—at least not on the British side.

"Enough, Michael," she said. "I understand why Miss Juliet isn't eager to run such a social gauntlet. Another offer, Miss LaBree: you can stay here on Elizabeth Station and have the baby. The war can't last that long—it might even be over before Kevin arrives. With the overwhelming force of the English—"

Michael frowned. "They had that on us Irish too," he said proudly, "and still we resisted them for centuries, we—"

Lizzie dismissed this. "They didn't send troops from half the empire after the Irish," she said curtly, "and forgive me, love, but the British could ignore a few bootleggers in the Irish mountains more easily than a country full of diamonds in the hands of religious fanatics. They say even the Church of Scotland is liberal compared to these Boers. They're threatening to close the mines because God doesn't like folks getting rich without breaking their backs in the fields. England won't let it come to that."

"So, what do you think, Miss LaBree?" Lizzie finally came back to her visitor. "Will you stay?"

Juliet played with the border of her jacket, desperate for another way. "Here? But you can't have a baby here, without doctors or anything."

"All three of mine were born here. There's a Maori village a few miles away. The midwife is excellent, much better than any *pakeha*."

Juliet looked up at her, horrified. Months of isolation with Lizzie and Michael had sounded bad enough. But now natives too?

"And when Kevin returns, I bet he'll be so taken with the baby that he'll forget all his misgivings," Lizzie continued.

Though she wasn't sure she believed it. Perhaps there were other possibilities. Matariki and Kupe, for example. Maybe they'd be willing to raise their niece or nephew in Parihaka. Lizzie looked over at the young woman struggling against her desperation. A few days here and she'd get cabin fever for sure.

They all heard the front door open and then the roar of the rain outside. It must be Randy come at last from the stables.

"Well, you can think about it," Lizzie said. "Come back if you want to."

She thought it quite possible that Juliet would still seek a forbidden but nevertheless effective solution to the problem. Lizzie did not view abortions as negatively as her son or Michael, who was raised a strict Catholic. In her former profession, they had been an unpleasant but necessary part of reality. And it would have been better for some children—Lizzie thought of Toby and Laura again—to have been spared painful lives with parents who didn't want them.

Michael seemed to be nursing the same thoughts, but he reached a different conclusion.

"Nonsense, Lizzie. Juliet—may I call you Juliet now? Of course you'll stay here for now. We're not going to let you set out again in this weather. No, no, it's out of the question." He managed a lukewarm smile. "Chin up, young lady. You'll have your baby, and when Kevin comes back, we'll make sure he does what's right."

A tall man in breeches stepped into the room, taking his dripping hat from his head.

Patrick Drury had been passing quite near Lawrence on his way from Otago to Dunedin and, with an eye to the weather, had decided to spend the night at his parents'. Now he stood in his parents' living room, looking from one to the other. Rain was still dripping from his coat, and he nervously smoothed his damp hair.

"There's no need for that," Patrick said calmly. "Kevin can get and stay lost. I'll marry Miss LaBree."

Chapter 7

Land surveying was not exactly one of Atamarie's favorite subjects. It was, however, an important component of the engineering degree, as large portions of New Zealand had yet to be surveyed. Many graduates of the program would contentedly spend their entire careers mapping the country. Atamarie, on the other hand, was striving for something literally higher. She attended to land-surveying calculations listlessly but successfully, easily surpassing the other students, just as she did in every subject. And in the fall of 1900, Professor Dobbins had a surprise in store for his best students.

"Just imagine," he announced to the first-year class, "this very year, a new national park is going to be established. It'll be on the North Island, around Mount Egmont."

Atamarie's ears pricked up. The name "Mount Egmont" was an invention of Captain James Cook, who had of course not bothered asking its Maori name: Taranaki, the very volcano that stood watch over Parihaka.

"There's still some surveying work to do," the professor explained. "And naturally, the government does not want to spend a lot of money on it. Hence, they've appealed to the universities, with a preference, of course, for ours." The students clapped appreciatively. Dobbins laughed. "I gladly accepted the call of duty, as it allows me to take my most gifted students into the field. We'll organize a multiweek expedition for land surveying in unexplored regions. Up there, the landscape is, after all—" He flipped through his notes.

Atamarie raised her hand.

"Miss Turei?"

"Not much grows on the mountain. It's mostly just snow. Surveying will most likely be hindered by the rocky terrain. You have to be able to climb. Around Taranaki, there's rain forest. It rains there constantly, one of the wettest parts of the country." She smiled. "The Maori say Rangi weeps over the gods' fighting."

Dobbins furrowed his brow. "Gods, fighting? You seem to know quite a bit. Have you been there already?"

Atamarie reported that she had even climbed the mountain once, together with a *tohunga* who was telling the children of Parihaka the story of the volcano's unhappy love and performing rituals to restore peace between the gods.

"And around the rain forest is farmland," she went on. "It's very fertile because it's volcanic soil. But there's a dispute over it. The *pakeha* farmers might make trouble about the survey. They won't give up their land, in any case."

Dobbins smiled. "That was very enlightening, Miss Turei, thank you. I had already decided to allow your participation—should you desire and your parents permit. Otherwise, only upperclassmen will be invited. In your case, there were—" The professor stopped himself from an ill-advised digression on women's rights and the university's reluctance to send a girl on an expedition with male students. In the end, Dobbins had concluded that only Atamarie's education was his responsibility, not the preservation of her virtue. "But now that you prove to know the area as well—"

"I'll gladly come along. But if you're really looking for people who know Mount Taranaki, you should ask in Parihaka. Maori have lived in the area for centuries."

"And they'll probably shoot you in the back if you stick a leveling rod in their holy mountain," one of the students sneered.

Atamarie gave him a wrathful look, but she told herself he was probably just jealous that she got to go.

"The Maori support the establishment of the national parks," Dobbins said, coming to her aid. "Miss Turei is right. If there's resistance, it'll most likely come from white farmers. But their land isn't at issue, anyway. It's really going to be a nearly circular surface around Mount Egmont. A good opportunity to review the surveying of circular surfaces. Mr. Potter, why don't you tell us what you know on the subject?"

***

Atamarie knew that the fall was not an ideal time of year to visit, let alone climb Mount Taranaki. In the upper regions, it might already be snowing, and the mountain usually lay under a thick cloud cover. Atamarie anticipated three very wet weeks. She had no concerns about her parents consenting, however. Grandma Lizzie only worried whether Atamarie's tent would be waterproof and her sleeping bag warm, whereas Matariki simply invited the whole expeditionary corps to use Parihaka as a base.

Indeed, autumn's adversities did afflict Dobbins and his students. The ferry crossing to the North Island proved even choppier than usual. Not without some satisfaction, Atamarie noted that almost all of her fellow students hung over the railings with green faces. Only one young man bore himself as bravely as she did, perhaps because the steamship's technology interested him more than his stomach.

"It must be possible to balance out the lurching," he speculated to the moderately interested but violently seasick Professor Dobbins, "by means of stabilizers. For example, one could attach some sort of fin to the side of the ship."

Atamarie joined them. "It would be a help if at least the passenger cabins weren't so affected. You could place them on pivots, so they always remained in the horizontal position."

"That's already been tried," the young man informed her. "Henry Bessemer in 1875. It just didn't work."

Atamarie offered a disappointed pout, which she knew men found irresistible. Normally, she wouldn't bother, but this one was brighter than most. Unfortunately, he had only ships in mind—he peered over the railing as if already looking for places to attach his "fins."

"For such stabilizers, there's already a patent, Pearse," Dobbins said, holding his hand over his mouth. "Oh God, the more you talk about it, the worse I feel. But look it up in Christchurch. I believe it was two years ago now."

The student sighed. "I won't have a chance to. I won't have a library card any longer, you know."

He took a few steps across the deck as if he wanted to end the conversation. Dobbins was bent too far over the railing to notice.

Atamarie followed this Pearse and looked at him more closely. He had short brown hair, a round face, and seemed only a little older than she was herself.

"Are you already done with your studies, then?" she asked. "You look so young. Did you start early?"

The young man shook his head. "No, I never properly studied, just attended a few lectures. Mostly for sophomores. Professor Dobbins was so good as to allow me, even though I was only a lab assistant. But at least I got a few months in Christchurch. And now the expedition—it's all very kind of Professor Dobbins. The school pays a little too. But soon I have to return to Temuka. When I turned twenty-one, I received a hundred acres of land. So, I'm going to be a farmer." The young man looked stricken.

"I'm sorry," Atamarie said, "about your studies. A hundred acres in Canterbury is surely very, um—"

Pearse gave her a sly smile. "So, that wouldn't tempt you either. That's quite a change. The eyes of the girls in the Canterbury Plains start to shine when I mention the acreage. But forgive me, I haven't even introduced myself. Pearse, Richard Pearse."

"Atamarie Parekura Turei."

Pearse nodded. "I know. Everyone at school knows, seeing as you're the only girl and the top of your class. How would you do the pivoting of the cabins?"

Atamarie looked at the water, concentrating. "Forget it. It's too complicated. But I could also imagine tanks. You'd take them below deck and fill them with water, as a sort of counterweight."

"On the sides," Pearse added enthusiastically, "in a U-shape. The water could flow from one side to the other and would even out the rolling of the waves."

Atamarie smiled. "Register a patent. When all the world's steamships are equipped with a tank, you'll make loads of money and can continue your studies."

"Nonsense, it was your idea," Pearse replied, "and someone else probably had it before us. That's how it's been with all of my attempts to invent something. I don't have any luck."

"It'll happen," Atamarie encouraged him, pointing north where the coastline was finally coming into view. "Look, there's Wellington. In half an hour, our seasick comrades will be saved. Do you know if we're continuing the journey today?"

"I think it rather unlikely, considering everyone's condition. And besides, there's a university here."

Atamarie laughed. "We could go and ask if they're giving out scholarships. I'll ask first, and then they'll be relieved when I say it's for you."

***

The group stayed overnight in Wellington, and the students were housed with the families of local university students. Atamarie spent an enervating evening with a female medical student of Dutch heritage. Neither Petronella nor her parents had ever met a Maori, and they'd expected a square-framed, dark-haired form instead of a petite blonde.

"You're not even tattooed," noted Mrs. van Bommel, half-relieved, half-disappointed. "I thought you'd at least have it around the eyes."

"I'm only a quarter Maori," Atamarie explained. "And my tribe doesn't practice *moko* often anymore. Besides, women have the area around their mouths tattooed at most. As a sign that the god of women, not men, gave the breath of life."

Mrs. van Bommel and her daughter were captivated and pressed Atamarie to tell more about her people. She had hoped to go back out for dinner with Dobbins and the other students—one in particular. The van Bommels, however, had no intention of letting their guest out alone into the Wellington night, despite her protests that she'd lived there for years with her mother during the fight for women's suffrage. She even knew the inside of the Parliament Building. That was another story the van Bommel family begged to hear. In the end, they marveled wholeheartedly at Atamarie, despite her disappointing appearance.

"Such a strange course of study for a young woman—and alone among all the young men! Don't they make advances? I, for one, would be afraid."

Petronella van Bommel shivered, and Atamarie rolled her eyes once again.

"As a matter of fact, none of them even talk to me," she informed her hostess, but was happy to remember that, as of today, this was no longer the case.

The thought of Richard Pearse's friendly smile and his engineer's mind made her heart beat faster. She was slowly beginning to feel enthusiasm for the expedition. She had considered it an honor before, but at this time of year, also a chore.

***

The next day, they traveled onward, taking the new and still incomplete North Island Main Trunk railway line. Atamarie sat with Professor Dobbins and Richard Pearse—a seat for which no one fought her. Surely, there would be more talk about her being a teacher's pet. Yet nothing was further from her mind than flattering the professor. Atamarie was focused on his assistant.

"I missed you last night, Miss Turei," Richard said. "I thought you'd come eat with us."

Atamarie covered her delight at this by making a face and launching into a comical description of the van Bommel family. "I would have had to bring Petronella," she concluded. "But, no, her parents wouldn't have allowed that either. Two women and twelve men aren't much better than one woman and twelve men."

Richard considered this. Apparently, it was only now occurring to him how unusual it was for a woman to be traveling with male students. "And your own parents don't object? I mean, uh, not that you're in danger here."

"Maori don't really have a concept of chaperones. And my mother was also raised *pakeha*, but she trusts me. Besides, I'm at the university every day surrounded by men. It would be much simpler to meet secretly with one of them there than here where we're all stuck together all the time."

That was true, of course, but it would not really have assuaged a concerned *pakeha* mother in the van Bommel mold.

Before Richard could say anything more, the professor turned toward them. Dobbins praised the North Island's train line as a wonder of engineering. At first, it led alongside the banks of the Rangitikei River, and the professor did not tire of pointing out various challenges of track construction in the craggy landscape to his students.

Dobbins expounded on the difference between superstructure and substructure in the laying of tracks and the fineness of the bridge construction, especially here in the mountains, but most of his students showed little interest. They were struggling with nausea again as the line passed over narrow bridges. Only Richard and Atamarie discussed with hushed seriousness the advantages and disadvantages of suspension, arch, and truss bridges.

Both were sad when the line ended in Palmerston. They would have to ride the rest of the way. Richard looked unhappily at his loan horse.

"How long's the ride from here?" he asked, swinging himself skillfully into the saddle.

"About three days," Atamarie said. "Well, if you move fast. But with this group . . ." She let her gaze wander over other students, some of whom were approaching the animals with a respect bordering on fear.

Indeed, some of the students proved to be highly unskilled riders, and the wagon in which Dobbins had loaded every possible surveying instrument also held them back. Plus, the balky loan horses did not exactly wow Atamarie, an opinion Richard shared.

"You're from a sheep farm?" Atamarie asked him during a delay.

Professor Dobbins had gotten the wagon stuck in a mud hole. Their instructor was a brilliant engineer, land surveyor, and draftsman—but when it came to chariots, he was no Ben-Hur.

Richard smiled. "Well, I'm from the country, but we have more cropland than sheep. My father has no talent for animal husbandry. I still don't know why he was so set on being a farmer, anyway. I suppose it's tradition in our family—and in Temuka, he could buy a lot of land for a little money. We'd never had much before, back in Cornwall. And we're a big family to feed. Nine children in all."

"Nine! That's almost a rugby team."

"More like an orchestra." Richard smiled. "Every one of us had to learn an instrument. I play the cello myself."

Atamarie was impressed. Aside from a few brief attempts at Maori wind instruments, she had no musical education.

"Are you good?"

Richard shook his head. "I'm only really good," he admitted, "at mathematics and physics. And machine building. I'd love to be an inventor." This last statement came out very quietly, almost as if he were ashamed.

"And you can be one," Atamarie assured him. "You don't need a university degree to register a patent. And you can start where you're at. Farming machines, for example—there's surely room for improvement there, or hauling technology."

Smiling, she pointed at Dobbins and one of his third-year students. They were in the process of thoroughly elucidating the problem of the stuck wagon from a theoretical standpoint.

"This mess is screaming for a lever. Come on, let's make ourselves useful."

With Dobbins's permission, Atamarie took the situation in hand, harnessing two more horses to the covered wagon with makeshift tackle while Richard directed students to apply levers in precisely determined places. The vehicle sprang from the morass, and Richard effortlessly changed a damaged wheel himself. Atamarie realized that he had not only a mastery of theory but also exceedingly skillful hands. Big, powerful hands, which she liked as much as his open, friendly face with its nut-brown eyes and thick, curly hair.

In the end, Atamarie and Richard were smeared with mud, but they reaped the praise of Professor Dobbins. Unfortunately, the other students eyed them with renewed mistrust. Richard, it seemed, was an outsider too. He treated everyone politely, but he appeared to be on his own. And, Atamarie noted, he did not wear a wedding ring.

Atamarie rode her horse contentedly alongside Richard's while he dissertated on vehicle technology. He did have ideas for improving farming machines and seemed invigorated by her faith that he could do so. For Atamarie, the day flew by despite the delays and continual rain. They should already have been able to see the mountain, but Taranaki was veiled by low-hanging clouds.

"Why even bother putting a national park here?" grumbled one of the students. "It doesn't look that different from the plains."

In truth, they were still riding through hilly grassland. Occasionally, they passed harvested fields, but most of the land belonged to sheep breeders. The animals could often be seen as well, large groups standing stoically in the rain. The water ran easily off their thick wool.

"They've got it good," Richard said, gesturing to their own sodden clothes. "If we have to sleep in tents tonight, we'll never warm up."

That night, however, the travelers were in luck. Dobbins found a farm whose owner gladly opened up a shearing shed for the frozen scientists. Though the city-born students wrinkled their noses at the smell of manure and lanolin, everyone was relieved and grateful. The farmer's wife even cooked for them, the farmer let them light a fire, and the family came by in the evening to chat.

"So, you're here to help with the park up there around Taranaki?" the farmer asked amicably. "That used to be Maori land, right? Then the government confiscated it, but not much seems to grow there. Although, that model farming village of the Maori's—what was it called again?—they did a real nice job with it."

"Parihaka," Atamarie answered. "But Maori didn't cultivate the rain forest. It's the land around it that's fertile. And now *pakeha* farmers have almost all of it."

Indeed, not much was left of the hundreds of acres the people of Parihaka had once farmed to feed their many residents and hundreds of visitors. The government had recruited *pakeha* settlers and sold them Maori land out from under them. Now only a fraction of their former fields belonged to the Maori, who made the most of them, using the latest agricultural methods.

"That's right," said their host. "I hear the Maori don't have anything against the national park, unlike the white settlers. Apparently, there were protests." He uncorked a bottle of whiskey and offered it to Dobbins. "Sorry to say, you'd better get used to sleeping in tents, Professor. It's not likely someone there'll offer you a place to stay. Who even had the idea to do this surveying in the fall?"

Two of the students had likewise pulled bottles from their bags and were passing them around with general enthusiasm. It almost reminded Atamarie of festivals in Parihaka or gatherings around the Ngai Tahu's fires. But the atmosphere here was tense. The juniors and seniors formed their own little groups and competed for the professor's approval. For his part, Dobbins conversed politely with the farmer, with whom he had little in common. But Atamarie got along brilliantly with their host, scoring even more points with her professor. She talked about Parihaka and her grandfather's sheep farm, which, to her surprise, the farmer knew.

"Michael Drury? Goodness, child, the world is small. I've got a descendent of his best ram." He poured Atamarie some whiskey, too, and could hardly be kept from dragging her out to the fields to show her the wonder ram. "The national champion—Heribert. As you know, I'm sure."

Atamarie certainly did. A portrait of that ram, eternalized by her aunt Heather in oil paint, hung in the Drurys' living room.

Ultimately, the subject came around to wool production, and Dobbins and Richard began theorizing about the possible employment of electricity in the development of sheep-shearing machines. While Atamarie found that quite interesting herself, the whiskey was starting to make her braver. She liked Richard Pearse better and better, and really, it was about time he recognized her as a woman. She shivered dramatically and leaned casually on her new friend.

After a few moments, Pearse noticed and turned to smile. Atamarie hoped he would put his arm around her, but their host thwarted her plans.

"Well, this really was a pleasant evening," he said, "but I've to get up early tomorrow. And you lot have a long day ahead of you too. Just make yourselves comfortable in the straw. It's far enough from the fire, and that'll go out soon anyhow. Oh yeah, and Miss—what was your name again? Marie? My wife's expecting you in the house. She's made up the guest room."

Atamarie tried to decline, but the farmer wouldn't hear of it. Under no circumstances could the young woman spend the night with twelve men in a shearing shed. So, she accepted—not that she was particularly unhappy about it. She wouldn't have been able to share a sleeping bag with Pearse anyway. After all, this wasn't a Maori village, where a girl and boy who withdrew together had at most to reckon with a little teasing. She would fall into disrepute if she made a pass at Richard, and he wouldn't be receptive, in any case. No doubt he was a gentleman.

Atamarie comforted herself with the cozy bed, which was far more comfortable than straw. There was even warm water, and Atamarie took a great deal of time liberating herself from the mud and grime. She would look particularly cute the next morning. Perhaps she would finally see the light she longed for in Richard's eyes.

***

The next day, it didn't rain nearly as hard. Now and again it even cleared up, and the Pouakai mountain chain, dominated by snow-covered Mount Taranaki, came into view. The sight was breathtaking. Most of the expedition members lost themselves completely in contemplating the majestic peak before the deep-blue sky. A crystal-clear river danced down from the mountains, leaping over rocks and crossing the green foothills through which Dobbins led them.

"This area is extraordinarily lovely," Richard said to Atamarie. "And the mountain is fascinating. It's a volcano, right? Perhaps we should have seismographs set up to monitor it."

Atamarie sighed. She had expected a somewhat more romantic reaction. After all, Taranaki moved other men to spout verse, and Atamarie could imagine a young man comparing his beloved to the goddess Pihanga.

Atamarie knew her skin was rosy after the ride through the rain and the restful sleep that had followed. It had almost made her sorry to braid her freshly washed hair, but she had to be practical for the long ride. Her riding dress was still damp and dirty, so she'd decided to put on her new outfit. It wasn't really a dress, but rather an elegant top and wide-legged pants. Kathleen Burton had designed them for her granddaughter, who refused to ride sidesaddle.

The outfit was dark blue and tailored to flatter Atamarie's figure. The farmworkers she passed reacted at once with whistles, and she spotted a prurient glimmer in the other students' eyes. Even Dobbins managed a genial, "You look lovely, Miss Turei."

Only Richard Pearse remained unmoved. Finally, he commented on the cut of the pants: "Very practical and elegant, if I may say so. It's really skillful the way the cut uses the drape. Are you familiar with sewing machines, by the way? I was allowed to attend a demonstration last year—extremely interesting."

Over the next hours, he regaled Atamarie with stories about the mechanical needle threaders he had invented for his mother as a boy, and they laughed about how they'd both loved to experiment even as children. Richard had built his sisters a zoetrope, and the thought of moving images gripped him as well as Atamarie. It was exceedingly entertaining to travel with him.

Still, Atamarie wished for more than long conversations. It could have been so romantic to ride together through the landscape, which more and more resembled a magic land. It seemed completely untouched, empty even of sheep. The green hills, out of which gray and white rocks jutted, seemed freshly grown, and the little copses that brightened the grassland spoiled the eye with countless shades of green. Atamarie told her astounded friend that, for the Maori, each tree had a personality, and asked him to touch one and try to feel its soul. But Richard looked at her with friendly irritation and changed the subject to motorized saws.

Otherwise, he was a perfect gentleman. He had first-class manners, plied her with bread and tea, and expounded on materials that could surely be used to keep drinks warm. Atamarie found the topic intriguing, but she did wonder whether she herself was this boring.

***

At the end of the day, no farm was willing to take them in, but Atamarie was hopeful that another campfire might let her get closer to Richard. First, though, she was able to help him set up his tent. The brilliant inventor simply could not manage to fit the tent poles together.

"You can't overthink things like this. You just have to do what you're supposed to do," Atamarie laughed, connecting the poles at lightning speed.

"But structurally speaking, it's a poor design," Pearse objected. "Aside from how heavy the poles are, I could imagine a much different construction—round, perhaps. And the poles should be flexible, maybe a soft wood."

He further developed this idea over dinner—and seemed to find it thoroughly pleasant when Atamarie leaned on him while he chatted with Dobbins about seismographs. He even gave her an occasional smile and did not withdraw his hand when she carefully brushed his finger while filling his teacup. Yet he never interrupted his conversation with Dobbins or made a gesture of his own.

Atamarie wondered if perhaps Richard was just shy. And neither were her own advances particularly skillful. Atamarie was still a virgin, despite her summers in Parihaka and her little romantic dalliances there. Her grandma Lizzie had advised her: *Only do it when you really want to. Not because a boy wants it or puts pressure on you. Look at your partner as a gift, and only when you think the gods have truly blessed you by leading you to this man in particular, then give yourself to him.*

Atamarie preferred to think of it like a raffle: she wanted to sleep with a man only if she really felt he was the grand prize. She had encountered only consolation prizes—until now. Richard Pearse, she felt, was a soul mate. Finally, here was someone she could talk to, someone who shared her interests—and someone who did not seem to care one bit that she was a girl.

Atamarie sighed and curled up alone in her clammy sleeping bag. It was such a waste—a few yards away, her very own gift from the gods was probably freezing just like her. Perhaps she should have made sacrifices to the ancestors more often or at least danced a *haka* for them.

Chapter 8

The next evening, an unpleasant surprise awaited the group. After a long ride, they reached the farmhouse on the east side of Taranaki that had been planned as their first staging point for surveying the park. However, the farmer had changed his mind. Dobbins and his students were able to glean from his harangue that the government was planning an access road that would cut through the man's land. The farmer, Mr. Peabody, was enraged, and now Dobbins and his students had to pay.

"And don't you so much as set up your tents here. Go get lost in the woods. And rest assured, I'll be keeping a close eye on all of your 'calculations.' The government's not getting an inch of my land!"

"That same government did him the favor of stealing that land from the Maori to give to him," Atamarie commented. "It would serve him right if the government took it back."

"No politicking, Miss Turei," replied Dobbins, clearly despondent at the prospect of another night in a wet tent. "Let's ride into the rain forest. We'll get to know some interesting insects tonight—a treat for the naturalists among you."

The students responded with groans. Atamarie frowned.

"Professor Dobbins, we should just ride to Parihaka. My mother invited us. She's looking forward to it. Everyone there is."

The students perked up immediately, but Dobbins looked skeptical. "I don't know, Miss Turei. Your mother would certainly be happy to see you. But thirteen strangers and fourteen horses?"

"Arriving in the middle of the night?" Richard added.

He'd unfolded a map and eyed the way to Parihaka. There was no way they could make it before midnight, as they'd still have to ride halfway around the mountain.

Atamarie shook her head. "It's Parihaka, Professor. They used to get two thousand visitors at every full moon. And Maori tribes always come to visit, everyone together, men, women, and children. Thirteen guests, that's nothing in Parihaka. And the sooner we set out, the sooner we'll be there."

After a little more persuasion, Professor Dobbins consented, sensing his students' desire for a roof over their heads. For a few of the young men from Dunedin, this was the first camping trip of their lives, and they'd already had enough after the first rainy night in their tents.

So, the group rode through the night, led by Richard with his map and Atamarie, who showed her fellow students how to orient themselves by the stars. Fortunately, the sky had cleared, and the moon bathed the paths in soft light. Really, they just needed to ride in the direction of the water. Parihaka lay between the volcano and the Tasman Sea.

"Which Maori tribe lives there, anyway?" Richard asked.

The other students listened with interest as well. A few of them had never had contact with Maori before, while others, like Richard, had seen the tribes that lived nearest their families' farms. Their parents might have hired Maori shepherds or servants.

"It's not one tribe; it's Parihaka," Atamarie explained, amazed that none of them knew the story. "It was founded by Te Whiti, an old chieftain and prophet, after the land wars, really to take in refugees. It developed into a sort of model village, but it was also almost like a sacred place. On the one hand, they wanted to show the *pakeha* that the Maori could manage themselves without interference. Parihaka had schools, a hospital, a bank, a post office, everything on the *pakeha* model. On the other hand, they honored the old customs of music and art and religion. And Te Whiti preached. He advocated for Maori rights, and against land confiscation without reimbursement or against the will of the rightful owners. But he also wanted peace. He wanted Maori and *pakeha* to learn from each other. For a few years, thousands of visitors would come to Parihaka every full moon to hear him. And most of the tribes on the island built their own *marae* in Parihaka."

"*Marae* are houses?" Dobbins asked.

"More like community spaces. Gathering places, living quarters, storehouses. In Parihaka, there was a *marae* for every tribe. Just to have a presence, or, as my mother says, to breathe in the spirit of Parihaka and then take it with you to every corner of the island. I wasn't born yet, but my parents say it was wonderful. Lots of work, but also dancing and music. My mother claims every night was a festival."

"But then came the land surveyors," Dobbins recalled. "It was in all the papers."

Atamarie nodded. "The government wanted to settle *pakeha* farmers in the area and sold them the land of the Maori tribes who had lived there for centuries without a second thought. Te Whiti and his people protested—peacefully and sometimes creatively."

Dobbins smiled. "I remember them plowing grassland, right? To make it unusable for grazing sheep?"

"And they tried to fence in the tribal lands to protect them," Atamarie added. "But in the end, that only made the government angry, and Parihaka was stormed and destroyed. Te Whiti and his followers spent time in prison. A few people even died. But later, when Te Whiti was free again, he returned to Parihaka, and many of the former residents came back as well. My parents bought land, so they can't be driven out again. And now Parihaka is becoming, well, you could call it a 'spiritual center.' They teach traditional crafts, celebrate the old festivals, all that. It's wonderful to visit, but I wouldn't want to live there. The loom's already been invented, but in Parihaka, I still have to use techniques from the Stone Age."

Professor Dobbins laughed as Atamarie told him of her attempts to improve the weaving frames and weirs.

"My inventors. Mr. Pearse and Miss Turei, I'm excited to see what technologies you two revolutionize."

***

It did not rain any more that night—Matariki would probably have credited friendly spirits who wanted to do Parihaka proud. As the riders came down from the hills, they saw the village lying before them. Above it rose the majestic volcano, and the Tasman Sea glittered in the moon- and starlight. Parihaka was an impressive sight—many of its residents had fallen in love with the place at once. Dobbins and his students, however, were distracted by the streetlights on the village's thoroughfares.

"Well, I'll be," Dobbins marveled. "This place is more advanced than half the South Island. And it looks like someone's still awake."

Atamarie opened the light wooden gate and ushered her guests inside. A fire was still burning in the first *marae*, and a few night owls were sitting around it. They greeted the guests without surprise and promptly offered whiskey.

"Have a seat, everyone. I'll see if we can rustle up something to eat," a young woman said happily in fluent English. "The bakers are probably at work already, and I'm sure they still have some bread from today."

Swaying a bit, she dashed off while her friends made space for the new arrivals around the fire.

A short time later, a more sober but no-less-enthusiastic welcome committee appeared, including Atamarie's mother. Matariki Parekura Turei was a petite woman with long, wavy black hair, which she wore down in Maori fashion. She had large light-brown eyes that shimmered with almost-golden light, as did her light-brown skin.

"Oh, it's so nice to have you home again, Atamie." Matariki pulled Atamarie into a *pakeha*-style hug before exchanging the *hongi* with her, putting her nose and forehead to Atamarie's. "Kupe is off in Wellington again, and I'm lonely. We'll take your friends to the new guest lodge, and then you'll come home with me."

The new Parihaka consisted of plain, quickly constructed huts but also of rebuilt meetinghouses adorned with artistic carvings. For guests, there were modern apartments with dormitories and even running water.

"They leave a little wanting in terms of spirit," Matariki explained regretfully as she showed them inside. "We really would prefer to house our guests in common lodges in the old style. But most favor comfort over tradition, and a lot of them are *pakeha*. We wouldn't want them to think we can't handle modern conveniences."

Professor Dobbins and his students assured Matariki they had not rested as comfortably during their whole journey.

"Please, stay as long as you like," Matariki said. "You can survey the land starting from here. It doesn't matter, after all, whether you start from the east or the west. The best thing would be to decide based on the weather: when it looks good, stay a few days in the forest, and if it looks bad, just sleep here. In any case, tomorrow night we'd like to invite you to a traditional *hangi* festival. We use the volcano's heat for our ovens. That might interest you engineers."

Atamarie imagined that Richard, at least, would have a dozen suggestions for improvement, but that night, everyone was too tired to think of anything but sleep. Atamarie curled up contentedly on her mat in her parents' house. Although Matariki and Kupe were enthusiastic about Maori traditions, both had enjoyed modern upbringings, and communal sleeping in the meetinghouse did not appeal. Preferring privacy, they dwelled in their own small cabin near the school, decorated with beautiful carvings.

"Has everything gone well so far?" Matariki asked before sending her daughter to bed. "Are you getting along with the young men?"

Atamarie smiled happily at her mother. "Swimmingly," she sighed. "It's the loveliest excursion I've ever been on." She yawned.

Matariki returned the smile indulgently, but she wondered a bit. All this rain and yet her daughter was dreamy-eyed? She'd have to take a closer look at those students in the morning. Clearly, one among them was brightening Atamarie's days.

***

The people of Parihaka happily offered guides to Dobbins and his students for the area of the future national park.

"You don't need to worry about our farmers flying into a rage if you include a square foot or two of their pastures either," Matariki explained. "All the land between the volcano and Parihaka belongs to us. The government—under even Seddon—granted us that much. True, it's far less fertile than the land between the village and the sea. But much of that now belongs to white farmers. We used to work it, but things are different now."

Dobbins assured Matariki that Parihaka was still quite remarkable. He was thoroughly impressed by the bank, the bakery, the stores. His students were already buying mementos for their families. Atamarie was happy when her mother announced there'd be a traditional *powhiri*, a greeting ceremony, that evening.

"Could I join in the dancing?" she asked Matariki before swinging up onto her horse.

She looked the perfect adventurer: equipped with spyglass, maps, and surveying rods, and back in her old riding dress, with a wide-brimmed leather hat in case of rain.

Matariki began to wonder again. Her daughter had learned to dance a *haka* and, as a little girl, had enthusiastically jumped around with the others. In recent years, however, she had not rushed to don the short *piu-piu* skirt with its tight hemp top and flitting *poi-poi* balls. Another sign that something was up. Yet, so far, Matariki had not caught any of the students following her daughter with shining eyes. At breakfast, Atamarie had eaten with the professor and a slender young man with thick brown locks, but she had not flirted with him.

"Of course you can," Matariki said, her spirits high. "I'll see if I can find a dancing dress for you. But not if you're going to complain again about how you're freezing in it."

***

The weather was clear that day, and the students explored the rain forest in wonder. The vegetation zones at the foot of the volcano changed with astounding speed—one moment they found themselves in a bright landscape of fields and the occasional copse of conifers that looked entirely European, and the next they were stepping into a fairy-tale-like half-light dominated by ferns as tall as trees, climbing plants, and lichen.

"It wouldn't surprise me if a snake was lurking around here," one of the students joked as he looked up at one of the massive kamahi trees, its hanging roots forming bizarre patterns. "Or monkeys, like in *The Jungle Book*."

Their guide smiled indulgently. "Mr. Kipling described the jungle in India. Here, the vegetation is completely different. Many plants in Aotearoa are endemic. Like the rimu, for example. It desperately needs protection. The *pakeha* chopped down many trees for their houses and furniture. Once there were whole forests of it, and the individual trees could grow to be hundreds of years old." He pointed at one of the tall trees with its wide needles. "And you don't need to worry about monkeys. There's nothing but birds and insects here. And just one type of snake." He slapped a mosquito.

Professor Dobbins told them that the peak of Taranaki was one of the most symmetrical in the world and how they could make use of this very special landmark for surveying. The students clambered up hills, sketched landmarks, and entered them into maps. Unfortunately, this kept Atamarie away from Richard, whose job required him to stay back with the professor. Instead, Atamarie found herself working with a rather conceited junior. Porter McDougal didn't even deign to acknowledge the girl at his side until Atamarie pointed out a major mistake he'd made. As the day progressed, he gladly left to her all the difficult tasks, watching as she climbed bluffs and clambered through thick brush. He'd probably never been out of Christchurch before.

"Tomorrow we'll climb higher. The vegetation isn't so thick there," Atamarie said as they finally rode back to Parihaka, the girl filthy, with rips in her dress and scratched fingers, the young man spick-and-span. "More bushes and grass. But the slopes are sometimes steeper."

"And I'll expect you to make a bit more of an effort, Mr. McDougal," remarked the professor, looking him over. "You'd do well to take an example from the young lady."

Atamarie enjoyed the praise and was euphoric when they arrived back in Parihaka. The residents were already opening the first earthen ovens, and the village was filled with enticing aromas. She hurried to her parents' home.

Matariki was waiting for her daughter with the traditional *haka* dress in hand. She observed contentedly how the young woman let down her hair, pushed it back with a wide headband in Parihaka's colors, and slipped into the revealing outfit.

"So, which of those gentlemen are you looking to impress?" she asked, trying to sound casual.

Atamarie turned red, then confessed everything. She had never kept secrets from Matariki, and for her half-Maori mother, it was natural that her daughter should be interested in boys.

"I love talking with him. He has all the same dreams and professional aspirations I do. He's an inventor, Mom. We could work together."

Matariki laughed. "Your gift from the gods! So, what's the problem?"

Atamarie sighed. "He hasn't even tried to kiss me. I'm afraid he's not interested."

Matariki smiled. "Dear, you're on a scientific expedition. You're not supposed to be holding hands. It's quite proper for the young man to show restraint. Maybe he's just waiting until you're back in Christchurch."

"Fine," Atamarie conceded. "I thought about that too. It's just, well, he—somehow, he doesn't look at me the right way."

Matariki furrowed her brow. She really would have to take a closer look at the young man that evening.

***

A typical *powhiri* could last hours. But, while both sides normally danced and prayed, this evening, only the people of Parihaka performed.

"*Powhiri* serves to greet, but also to frighten," Matariki explained to the professor and Richard. She had taken a seat between the two men. "Our visitors usually do not come individually but as a whole tribe. We show them what we have to offer in the ways of fighting techniques and spirit."

She pointed at the young men who were presenting a martial *haka*. They stamped their spears in the ground, feigned attacks, and grimaced at their opponents.

"I recognize it from rugby," one of the Dunedin students exclaimed, and Matariki laughed.

"Yes, that's a good example, evidence for Te Whiti's theory that Maori and *pakeha* have something to offer each other: we learned rugby from the English, and from us they learned the *haka* to frighten the opposing team."

The oldest priestess followed this display by sealing the spiritual bond between heaven and earth, hosts and guests, with a full-throated cry, the *karanga*.

"From here on out, it's peaceful," Matariki said.

Now the young girls performed, dancing the *haka powhiri*. Matariki kept an eye on her daughter who, despite her exhausting excursion, kept up admirably. The wings of love. Matariki smiled, then turned her attention to Richard, quickly discovering what Atamarie had meant.

Richard Pearse was watching the dance with great interest and enjoyment. But his eyes did not light up when they fell on Atamarie. Matariki saw none of the lust that was in the eyes of a few other students, nor love.

But it could still happen. It had taken a long time for Matariki's friendly feelings for Kupe to become love. And, since her first catastrophic love for Colin

Coltrane, she put great stock in basing matters of love not just on attraction but also on shared interests and sensibilities. Matariki smiled when Atamarie, still flushed from dancing, sat down next to Richard. She had not changed clothes and would, without a doubt, soon be miserably cold. But before Matariki could fetch her a blanket, Richard stepped in.

"You danced wonderfully, Miss Turei," he exclaimed. "And really looked like a Maori. Usually, your blonde hair makes you resemble the *pakeha* side of your family."

Atamarie nodded happily. At least he had noticed that she was blonde! Progress. But a moment later, she shook her head at herself. She was being as ridiculous as Roberta around Kevin.

"You must be freezing. Allow me to fetch you a blanket."

Richard stood up solicitously, and Atamarie told herself that this really was progress. She let the blanket slide lasciviously down her shoulders as she partook in the *hangi* that had been prepared in the ovens of the same name.

"It always tastes wonderful," she said, and licked her lips.

In the novels Roberta read, this gesture was always supposed to be enticing. But Richard didn't seem to notice, focusing instead on the ovens.

"Yes, it's delicious. But it must be such hard work to have to dig these holes every time. Theoretically, it must be possible to bring the earth's heat to the surface. You'd need some kind of pump."

Atamarie gave up trying to impress him and devoted herself to the food. After the long day, she was as hungry as a wolf.

In the meantime, the other Maori boys and girls began to bring traditional instruments over to play around the fire.

Richard observed the various flutes and finally reached for a *tumutumu*, a sort of percussion instrument, from which he drew a few rather respectable sounds. Atamarie took up an *nguru* and played a melody to accompany him.

"That's rather nice." Richard smiled. "You're really supposed to play that flute with your nose?"

Atamarie nodded. "And I've always found you look like an unbelievable fool doing so," she declared.

"You could never look like a fool, Miss Turei. I believe you're one of the cleverest people I've ever met. But have you ever considered whether the timbre of the flute could be preserved but the playing made a bit simpler if you moved the stops a little farther from one another?"

Matariki, who had just returned to the group, noticed that Richard Pearse's eyes were finally shining. In his gaze were the long-looked-for stars as he watched Atamarie playing the *nguru* and then the complicated *putorino* as well.

"Strange," she remarked to a friend whom she had been telling about Atamarie's unrequited feelings. "And here I always thought a person looked ludicrous blowing into that thing."

Chapter 9

Though Richard Pearse showed more enthusiasm for Atamarie that evening, he nevertheless remained a gentleman. He went no further than light touches on her fingers and shoulders, and Atamarie was unsure whether they electrified him as they did her. Other students were less restrained. After the dance, some disappeared with Atamarie's local friends into the fields and hills.

In the morning, this drew a sharp rebuke from the professor. "It is unacceptable for you to abuse these people's hospitality in this manner. Moreover, we're not here for pleasure. It's nine o'clock, gentlemen. I had hoped to be halfway up Mount Taranaki by now."

Atamarie giggled. She was in high spirits after spending all of breakfast sitting with the girls, gossiping in Maori. Now she knew her classmates' most intimate secrets better than their own mothers, and as she climbed onto her horse, she considered how she might use this against stuck-up Porter. For now, though, she had to concentrate on the path. Today they rode up through the rain-forest belt and over bush-spotted plains that gave way to alpine vegetation. Horses rarely had to climb here, and Atamarie was grateful that her mother had lent her her own horse, a powerful little cob mare.

Porter complained about his mare, which was not in particularly good shape, but nevertheless tried to spur her up every hill. Atamarie opted to climb the hills on her own feet, so as to spare the horse and take measurements.

"Who knows what's hiding in the brush here," Porter huffed when she suggested he do the same.

Atamarie giggled. "You weren't afraid of the brush you were in last night with Pai. And that was much more dangerous. Most of the animals here are nocturnal, you know."

As the landscape grew even harsher higher up, Porter finally saw that he had no other choice but to climb. Atamarie marveled at the rock and lava formations that her map called things like Humphries Castle and Warwick Castle.

"The gods favor us," Atamarie joked as she brought her initial results to Richard and the professor. "Such clear weather for this time of year."

"But it's cold," whined Porter.

The professor sighed. "We're on a mountain, Mr. McDougal," he replied. "You should undertake a thorough review of climate ecology. I'll be returning to it in your final examination. For now, continue your work. The slopes are rather steep, and our guide warned me of chasms. Take him with you, just to be safe—or, no, he's already gone with another group. Well, be careful."

Richard Pearse smiled encouragingly at Atamarie. "You won't slip, Miss Turei," he said. "You're far too graceful."

Atamarie beamed, but Dobbins furrowed his brow. He seemed about to reprove the flirtation but apparently changed his mind.

"Really, you could also climb a bit yourself, Richard. I'd come along, but I'm afraid mountain climbing is too strenuous for my old legs. Perhaps you'd like to accompany Miss Turei."

Richard blushed slightly. "I'm sure it would be a pleasure for anyone to accompany Miss Turei—anywhere. I'm only afraid Porter and I will fight over the privilege of offering her a hand."

Porter McDougal rolled his eyes but dutifully followed the two up the next hill, Lion Rock, which offered captivating views of all the landmarks and also the picturesque bay.

Atamarie thought wistfully how this would be the ideal background for a first kiss, but Richard only made a note on one of the maps and began comparing his sketches to Atamarie's. Still, she was delighted that he repeatedly asked her the Maori names of the mountains and rivers, writing them down conscientiously. Even with his short time in the village, he had grasped that, for the Maori, this was about safeguarding their heritage.

Then, however, Atamarie saw something that made her blood run cold. On one of the crags across from Lion Rock, a large birdlike being arose. It seemed static and flat, but a sort of face flashed from it before it started to twist and turn. It almost looked as if it were bowing to heaven or dancing a *haka*. And yet, Atamarie almost thought she caught scraps of words or songs carried on the wind. Richard, too, raised his head to listen—just in time to see the thing move toward the edge in an apparent suicide attempt.

"Richard!"

Atamarie gripped his arm in horror—but then, when the figure sprang over the rock and was at once seized by the wind, she knew at once what was happening: It was a kite, a massive *manu*. The face depicted was sort of a hybrid man and bird, a well-loved image for a traditional Maori kite. This one, however, was not attached to guide strings. There was no one flying it.

"A glider," Richard said, aghast. "But it's going to fall. The wingspan isn't sufficient."

"I sure hope you're wrong," Porter said, having grabbed his spyglass. "There's a man attached to it."

Atamarie saw him now too. A gust of wind caught the kite and really did make it soar. The man hung on like someone crucified—could he have bound himself to it?

"It's lifting off," Atamarie yelled, fascinated despite herself. "It is working; it's taking off. He—can he steer it?"

Richard shook his head. "He can't even really glide. The wings are too short, and the shape isn't quite there. It's good for children's kites, but it won't bear the weight of the man. What's more, whenever he moves, the thing immediately starts to spin. Not to mention the speed—"

But Atamarie was already running down the hill. The kite had gotten a good launch off the hillside, perhaps thanks to a lucky gust of wind, but there was no way it could stay up. Now the contraption was spinning. With a lot of luck, the man might survive the fall into the sea.

Atamarie glanced back up at Richard and Porter, both staring at the falling flier as if hypnotized.

"Come on!" she shouted. "We have to save him."

Richard snapped out of his stupor and began to hurry down.

Porter followed at his own pace. "Guy's dead anyway as soon as he comes down," he muttered.

Atamarie's mind spun. Since the kite had managed to clear the rocky hills, the danger now was the crash into the water—and the waves in the bay. She raced down the slope at breakneck speed. If the flier really was bound to the kite, he might drown before he could free himself. And once he got free, the waves could fling him against the cliffs. At least he had taken off in the direction of the protected bay instead of the churning open sea. Maybe they could throw him a rope.

Atamarie was halfway down the hill when the birdman hit the water. She rushed across the rocky shore, watching helplessly as he fought for his life. The impact had freed his left arm, and now he was trying desperately to loosen the ropes that held him to the kite. At least the kite was floating. The material must have been light, but the surf played mercilessly with it, tossing the bulky thing back and forth as the man slipped under the water and then bobbed back into view. Atamarie could no longer tell whether he was moving.

Richard scrambled to a stop behind her and slipped out of his jacket. "I'm a good swimmer," he panted. "I'll bring him here, but then you'll have to help us."

With that, he leaped from one of the boulders. Atamarie understood. Getting into the water was easy enough, but getting out without injury was almost impossible. A rescue swimmer pulling someone else did not stand a chance. As Richard neared the accident victim with powerful strokes, Porter arrived and watched with interest.

"We need rope," Atamarie shouted. "The emergency pack. Now."

Grabbing the bag from Porter, Atamarie pulled ropes and spikes out of the bag.

Richard had reached the kite just in time. The flier appeared unconscious.

"Pearse has to cut him loose," Porter observed. "I hope he has a knife."

Atamarie looked up for a moment, then remembered Richard was a country boy. He would hardly have gone camping without a pocketknife. She squinted at the water and saw with relief that Richard had succeeded in cutting the man free and now was pulling him in the direction of the shore.

Meanwhile, Atamarie had decided on a plan. She pointed to a spot on the shore, a tiny inlet.

"We can't have them swimming into a rock," she told Porter. "We'll need to stretch a rope they can use to climb up onto shore. Here, hammer a spike between these two rocks, and there. Get going, Porter; they'll be here in a minute. If I do it alone, it'll take forever."

Porter looked skeptical, but Atamarie pressed the hammer into his hand. Fortunately, despite his phlegmatic nature, the young man proved exceptionally strong. He affixed the first spike with two swings.

Atamarie roared at him when he wanted to debate the placement of the second. "Don't quibble; hammer. And if you stand on that promontory, you won't fall into the water."

He thoughtfully placed one foot on the promontory.

"Dear Lord, Porter, the man is going to drown," she cried, "and Richard might break all his bones if he's dashed against these rocks. Just hammer the damned spike into the rock, and then stretch the rope."

While Porter worked, grumbling, Atamarie slung a second rope around her hips. It would have been better to have someone as strong as Porter in this role as well, but she didn't trust him. So, she tied one end of the rope to the first, which was now securely stretched between the rocks. It would hold her upright in the sea a few yards from the rocky shore. Finally, Atamarie secured another loop for Richard before sliding into the water. The waves tore at her skirt, ready to fling her against the rocks, but the rope held her in securely.

Richard understood at once. He held the unconscious man firmly with one arm, adroitly grasping for the sling with the other and clambering into it. Atamarie reached for the wounded man with both arms. He was a Maori youth with long, black hair. She held him firmly against her, keeping him safe until the others could fish them out. Fortunately, Porter was climbing on the rope and helping Richard up.

Richard collapsed onto the rock a moment, but did not grant himself a break. Instead, he looped the rope around himself as well and slid right back into the water next to Atamarie. Porter stood above them, arguing that they should just pull the girl and the wounded man up at the same time.

"Impossible," wheezed Richard. "Porter, buoyancy, man. Archimedes's principle. Atamarie can hold him in the water, but if you pull them up together, he'll be too heavy for her. Not to mention, wet as he is, he'll slip right out of her hands. I'll take him now, and you help her. Then you'll both pull us up."

A few arduous minutes later, Richard and the kite flier lay on a rock, Richard coughing and spitting water, the boy motionless.

"I told you he's dead," asserted Porter.

Atamarie was ready to slap the dolt. Instead, she turned the Maori youth onto his stomach and tried to pump the water out of his lungs. And, despite her rather unskilled movements, he began to retch and spit up water.

"Maori are a seafaring people," Atamarie said. "You can't kill us that easily."

"Well, it wouldn't have taken much more," said Richard. "Let's see if we can get him to come to. He might have hit his head."

In fact, the boy was just then opening his eyes. He looked confusedly into Atamarie's face, which was red from her efforts, but she was beaming with pride.

"Ha–Hawaiki?" he asked weakly.

Atamarie hooted. "It's not that simple, you know. If I understood my mother correctly, you'd have to go to Cape Reinga first and then tie a rope securely on a pohutukawa tree, climb down and—or do you just try another *manu*? As a ghost, maybe you could. After all, you wouldn't weigh anything."

The young man could process neither the teasing nor the blasphemy.

"He wanted to fly to Hawaii?" Porter asked. "It's thousands of miles away! Lilienthal was proud when he made it a hundred feet."

"Lilienthal flew almost a thousand feet," Richard corrected him. "And on a glider a lot like this. But with arched wings. That way, the lift is—"

"Not Hawaii, Hawaiki," Atamarie interrupted. "For the Maori, it's something like heaven. But it's quite an ordeal for the souls of the departed to slog their way there. They have to wander all the way to the north first, then climb down a cliff. What he meant was, he thought he was dead."

"Rawiri," the boy now said, pointing to himself. "And you are?"

Atamarie broke into a grin, memories of the festival day rushing back. She could clearly recall Rawiri's childhood face. Even then, he had been slender and tall for a Maori. His big dark eyes still shone as they once had and were still shaded by long lashes. Rawiri had a gentle expression. One could hardly imagine him dancing war *haka* or playing rugby. He was not tattooed; full, soft lips dominated his face, not martial *moko*.

"You wanted to fly even back then!" she replied in Maori. "I did too. Do you remember? It's me, Atamarie. So, was this your first attempt?"

Rawiri tried to get up. "Forgive me," he said in English. "You all saved me. Thank you. But where's the *manu*?"

"The kite," Atamarie translated.

Richard pointed out to sea. "I couldn't save it too. Wouldn't have been worth it, anyway. With that frame, it won't carry you. You need to model them more on birds than on statues of gods." Richard had recognized the birdman's form from Parihaka's *marae*. "And nowadays, double-deckers are preferred, for gliders, anyway."

"But the gods," sighed Rawiri. "The *manu* was consecrated to the gods of the air. It shouldn't sink into the sea. It—"

"Well, the gods of the air should have kept a better eye on it," Atamarie noted disrespectfully. "What did you stretch across it, anyway?"

"Sailcloth," Rawiri said, and looked even sadder than before. "It was expensive."

"And heavy," Richard said. "Completely unsuitable, especially in rain. Lilienthal used shirting. It's a waxed cotton material, which—"

"Perhaps the thing will wash up," Atamarie considered, with an eye to the bay. "I'd say it's likely, if the direction of the wind doesn't change."

"I should have used aute bark or raupo leaves. They stroke the face of the sky god. These *pakeha* materials—they probably don't like singing for it."

"Singing?" Richard asked.

"The gods direct the *manu* with *karakia*, songs and prayers," Rawiri informed him.

Atamarie sighed. "I'd say the gods don't have anything fundamentally against sailcloth; otherwise, all the *pakeha* ships would have landed elsewhere."

While Rawiri collected himself, Richard took down the rope system and stowed the materials neatly in Porter's backpack.

"Damn, it's cold," Porter said with a shudder. "Aren't you freezing in that?"

Only then did Atamarie realize that her clothes were completely soaked through. In the rush of Rawiri's rescue, she had completely forgotten the cold.

"Good point. We'd better get to camp as quickly as possible. Maybe Professor Dobbins even has dry clothes in the wagon. At least for you all." She gave the men an envious look.

She turned to Rawiri. "Can you stand?"

He nodded. He had really gotten off easy. Aside from a few cuts and bruises, he was unscathed. Plus, he was almost dry. Despite the cold, he had dressed only in the traditional Maori kilt of hardened flax strands for his flight. His upper body was naked, and Atamarie registered the impressive musculature. Richard's, however, impressed her even more. He had taken off his wet shirt, revealing tan broad shoulders and defined pectorals. He must have spent the summer working on his parents' farm.

He turned toward her now, and Atamarie, embarrassed, looked at the ground, hoping she hadn't been caught staring.

"You must be freezing, Atamarie. Here, take my jacket. It's still dry."

Atamarie looked at the goose bumps he himself had on his arms and wondered if she should refuse.

"Oh, sorry," Richard said. "I didn't mean to use your first name."

Atamarie smiled. "I've done that to you too. Let's keep it like that. Come on."

She held her hand out for him to help her up, then wrapped herself contentedly in his jacket.

***

A few hours later, they were sitting by the fire in Parihaka, enjoying fish and sweet potatoes. There was hot tea to go with it this time. Rawiri and his rescuers simply could not get warm. The trip back had dragged on endlessly. Dobbins had made a campfire on Taranaki, but it hadn't been enough to dry the men's pants, much less Atamarie's clothes. In the end, they had decided on a speedy ride back so they could change. When they reached the village at last, Porter McDougal pulled his weight for the first time, producing a bottle of the best whiskey from his bag and pouring it generously into his fellow students' teacups.

In return, Richard and Atamarie kept quiet when he passed himself off to the other students and the Maori girls as the hero of the day. To hear him tell it, he had rescued Rawiri almost singlehandedly.

Rawiri was now wearing warm *pakeha* clothing and sitting beside Atamarie and Richard. He listened to their conversation with fascination while Matariki ascertained with amusement that her daughter seemed to be getting closer to her goal. That evening, the light her daughter had been seeking was at last in Richard Pearse's eyes. Atamarie was beaming with happiness, and the two even held hands and wandered off together.

"What a funny pair," Matariki's friend Emere said. "When I passed by, they were talking about the systematics of flight technology, whatever that is. Didn't sound much like butterflies in the stomach to me."

Matariki laughed. "Atamarie's primarily interested in butterflies for their wing shape. It seems the young man really is a soul mate."

***

Atamarie and Richard wandered happily over the moonlit hills around Parihaka, talking excitedly about whether, in running down these elevations, someone could attain a sufficient angle of approach for a glider, whether Lilienthal's crash at Gollenberg could have been prevented by more skillful steering out of the thermal displacement, and whether one really could fly farther by means of a raised angle of approach and thereby more limited speed.

When Richard dropped the young woman off in front of her parents' house, he gave her a shy kiss on the cheek.

"You're the most wonderful girl I've ever met," he whispered. "I never imagined I might find someone who understood me this way, Atamarie."

Atamarie rose up on her tiptoes and bravely kissed his lips.

"One day," she whispered, "we'll fly together."

When they finally parted, she practically danced her way into her parents' house.

"He loves me," she sang, embracing her mother. "Oh, Mommy, he loves me. We're meant for each other."

***

Rawiri no longer thought of the defeat he had suffered that day. Fine, the gods had withheld their blessing. Probably he had not sung the right notes to conjure the wind as the god Tawhaki, who brought knowledge to humankind with the help of a *manu aute*, had once done. And maybe his rescuers were right—that *pakeha* with the curly hair and the strange girl who was at once Maori and not. It was quite possible that the gods disliked the form of his kite. He would have to try something else.

And perhaps there was still more to it. Perhaps *karakia* was not enough. Perhaps he needed more of that knowledge Tawhaki had bestowed on humankind. The *pakeha* sometimes seemed to make better use of Tawhaki's gift; Rawiri's head still spun when he thought of Richard's lecture on thermal displacement. He had not dared to ask further questions, at least not of this *pakeha* to whom he owed his life. But maybe he would ask the girl. That beautiful girl who had appeared to him like a greeting from heaven in the moment he'd returned from among the dead. Atamarie, sunrise.

The gods may have denied him flight that day, but they had sent him a girl he could love. A girl who shared his dreams. Rawiri turned his face to the stars and thanked the gods for Atamarie.

Someday they would fly together.

Strong Women

East London, Wepener,
Africa
Dunedin, Lawrence,
New Zealand
1900–1901

Chapter 1

While his brother planned a wedding with Juliet LaBree in New Zealand, Kevin Drury shipped out, first to Albany in Western Australia. The town was located along the Great Australian Bight and had once housed an infamous penal colony. Kevin thought of his parents, sent from Europe to Australia as convicts. Lizzie and Michael, however, had been taken to Van Diemen's Land, an island off the coast. Whereas Michael had found the prison conditions exceedingly harsh, Lizzie had actually been quite content—so grateful was she to have escaped her abusive employer.

Kevin was surprised by Albany's inviting coast, its beaches, and forested slopes. It was hard for him to imagine a terrible prison in this bright sunshine. Various troop transports already lay at anchor in the well-tended natural harbor. The Australians, too, were sending more troops to South Africa.

The unit tarried in Albany just long enough to take on more provisions and make small repairs to the ship. But Kevin and his new friend, Vincent Taylor, a veterinarian, managed a quick expedition to town to restock their whiskey and do a short nature hike. The fauna of Australia fascinated Vincent, but Kevin had little appreciation for snakes, spiders, and stinging bugs. He was relieved to make it back from the bush alive.

"Africa's not lacking in the like," Vincent teased. "Lions, rhinos, cheetahs . . ."

Kevin laughed. "I'm fairly certain they won't be coming into my hospital tent. Which you can't say about the critters here. That black snake—what's it called again?—is almost everywhere, you know, and monstrously poisonous. By the way, can you take another look at my horse later? Its gait seemed a little unsteady. That might be my fault. I've inherited the fear of stepping on snakes."

***

For the crossing to Africa, Vincent secured Kevin's horse a space on deck alongside his own.

"Maybe they're more likely to spook there, and it'll be uncomfortable in strong winds. But the stalls belowdecks are intolerable. I've already made complaints. It's far too stuffy, especially in the heat we're expecting. But of course, command says what's good enough for the men is good enough for the animals. They do pack the men in like sardines. Only, the horses didn't volunteer."

Vincent himself didn't seem all that enthusiastic to be there either. He'd been driven to sign up by financial troubles and, as he confessed to Kevin on their third night crossing the Indian Ocean, an unhappy marriage.

"I didn't marry her for her money, certainly not, though I didn't say no when her father wanted to finance my practice. I probably should have been more skeptical about his generosity." Vincent took another mouthful of whiskey. "In any case, she gave me cuckold's horns that would have made any ram jealous. At first, I didn't even notice. I worshipped her. She was a beautiful girl, a sheep baroness. But in the end, half the city was talking about it. Mary Ann just couldn't turn any man away, from her father's shepherds to the merchant around the corner. I suppose it was pathological. With mares, you call that sort of thing 'continual heat.'" Vincent downed his whiskey in one gulp.

"With people, it's called nymphomania," Kevin said.

Vincent, a tall, blond man, shrugged his shoulders. "She never got pregnant, anyway. Thank goodness. That made the divorce a great deal easier. Unfortunately, her father was not pleased when his promiscuous princess came back to him. I was ruined, so enlisting seemed my best option. It does fill the coffers a bit. And believe you me, lions, cheetahs, and rhinos don't scare me. Not even snakes. Compared to Mary Ann, vipers are cute."

***

As officers, Kevin and Vincent were comfortably lodged, bunking together in a first-class cabin. Vincent focused all his attention on the horses. He went from one to the other, scratching them and talking to them.

Kevin observed this with concern. He'd heard that the Boers did not treat their animals well and especially hated the large English horses. Their own horses, though they apparently acquitted themselves brilliantly, were small, and were outmatched in combat by the English cavalry's Thoroughbreds. For that reason, the Boers applied themselves expressly to injuring and killing their opponents' mounts. Vincent might soon have more patients than Kevin, and it would not be easy for him to watch his cherished friends die in a hail of bullets.

Kevin himself used the voyage to educate himself about the equipment of the field hospitals. Beyond that, he was obliged to provide the men with first-aid courses.

"In the veld, the South African plains, you will have to rely on one another," Kevin said, repeating what he had been told during training. "Enemy raiding parties like to retreat there, and you won't have a field hospital at hand every time you pursue them. So, pay attention. This course might save your or your comrades' lives."

Kevin had everyone splint limbs and apply tourniquets. He found this training sensible—much more so than the rudimentary shooting exercises in training camp. The farm boys had learned nothing new, and the workers from the city had learned far too little to survive a battle. Kevin observed that four of those who'd been hopeless with guns handled themselves ably in the first-aid course. He was determined to request them as medical assistants as soon as the field hospital was manned. All of his superior officers had proved to be reasonable men, at least so far.

"But you all realize that, when we get there, we'll have to deal with English career officers, right?" one sergeant pointed out at a gathering. "And some of them aren't all there. This Buller, for example, the commander, you hear the craziest things about him. Apparently, he travels with a whole hotel kitchen, requisitions wine by the gallon from the local vineyards, and leads herds of animals with him for slaughter, just so no one goes hungry. But then he'll go and use a few thousand soldiers as cannon fodder just to take some meaningless hill that no one cares about the next day. We'll have to watch out for our men."

Mostly, though, the news was encouraging. After the Boers' early successes in seizing several towns, the British offensive was picking up speed. Most of the occupied towns had been liberated, and the English were advancing into the Boer republics. The New Zealand contingent, too, was celebrating its first victories. After suffering heavy casualties at Jasfontein, the men had pulled themselves together and fought like lions. On January 15, they had valiantly beaten back a

Boer attack. The hill on which the fighting took place received the name New Zealand Hill in commemoration.

"The country can't be all that well settled if they still have to name the hills," remarked Vincent as the officers on the ship gleefully toasted this victory. "If you think about it, back home, each one's already got two names."

"The first settlers there surely have their own place names too," said Kevin. "It's just the Boers can't be bothered to care. They don't even know what the tribes call themselves. Or do you really think they dubbed themselves Hottentots and Kaffirs?"

"What I'd like to know is which side the tribes are on." Vincent arched his brows.

"They're trying to stay out of it," explained a sergeant. Sergeant Willis was one of the few career soldiers in their unit, but he'd never seen action and was hopeful that, with this deployment, bullets would finally be whizzing past his ears. "What's more, the English want them to stay out of it. That's why we're not sending any Maori regiments, even though their boys are beating down the recruitment office doors. It seems the Crown doesn't want to make things any more complicated than they already are."

***

After five weeks at sea, Kevin's unit reached the small town of East London. Originally, they were supposed to land in Bera, like the contingent before them, but while they were still at sea, a radiogram arrived for Major Jowsey, the troop commander, explaining riders were needed in the Orange Free State, one of the rebellious Boer republics. There had been unrest in the south and east and, most importantly, attacks on the train lines.

East London itself seemed peaceful—and much more manageable than its great namesake. It lay along an exceptionally beautiful coast where sandy beaches alternated with hills and reddish rocks. The city consisted of a fort and a collection of well-kept, whitewashed buildings and farms. The climate was subtropical, the streets sewn with palms and colorful flowers. The Buffalo River flowed to the sea here, making it the only river port in South Africa.

Kevin joined Vincent, who was overseeing the unloading of the horses. The young veterinarian was highly pleased with the condition of his charges, especially his own mare, Colleen. Kevin led his gray, Silver, from the ship himself.

"I thought they spoke Dutch here," Kevin said to one of the officers receiving the new troops, "but these people's English is perfect. And I imagined the natives with darker skin."

Colonel Ribbons laughed. "East London is an English settlement," he explained to the young doctor. "Originally a military base against the Xhosa—a formidable native people. Then, German settlers came after the Crimean War. They already knew how to speak English, too, from serving in the British German Legion. Boers don't like to live on the coast anyway. 'Boer' means farmer, and you can take that literally. They live off the land, don't like strangers, and they only go to school long enough to learn to read the Bible. There've been lots of settlers in East London."

"And the natives don't have any objections? About all the immigrants, the change of ownership?" Kevin was still looking at the light-skinned workers.

"Depends on the tribe. Around Cape Town, where I'm from, they're supposed to have always been very cooperative—although they were almost exterminated by the Dutch there. The workers you're staring at are actually from India, auxiliaries for the army. They also work as medical assistants. We'll assign you some. Very willing, efficient, and handy."

Kevin furrowed his brow. "You mean there aren't any native blacks anymore? But aren't we partly here to liberate them?"

"You could say that. And, of course, there are still natives. But the Xhosa here and the Zulu around Durban don't make good laborers. If we recruited them, they could massacre the Boers in a heartbeat. Command is probably afraid that, once that was done, they'd make short work of us too. Farm work, on the other hand, like cutting sugarcane on the plantations around Durban? They'll only do it if someone forces them, which is still common. As you said, it's . . . among the reasons for our presence." Colonel Ribbons smirked ironically. "That and what's hiding in the ground, right? Around here, in any case, we don't force anyone under the whip. We let the people do what they want. Most of them live inland and do their own farming and husbandry."

They were joined by Vincent and Sergeant Willis.

"When do we move out?" Kevin asked.

"Not for a few days," Willis reported happily. "It seems they learned from the disaster with the first contingent, practically sending them straight from the ship to the battlefield. That means we have time to prepare. I'd like to arrange a training exercise on horseback for tomorrow."

But Vincent shook his head firmly. "Sorry, sir, but I must insist the animals get a little time to adjust too. If we want them to serve us well in battle, it's better if they slowly regain their land legs without riders. I'm told there are large paddocks around the barracks where they can rest."

"Here, they're called 'kraals,'" Colonel Ribbons explained. "As are the natives' villages."

"That gives us a good idea of what they think of the blacks in this country," Vincent replied. "Imagine what our Maori would say if we went around calling our animal pens *marae*."

Ribbons shrugged. "It's true, we don't live very peacefully together. As a rule, everyone fights with everyone, at least in the aggregate. On a purely personal level, close relationships sometimes form between black and white families. Most of the Boer regiments have black trackers—and they're both outstanding and completely loyal. Just like those on the English side. Granted, officially there are no black auxiliaries, but some officers can't take a step without their 'boys.' A few even serve in the officers' mess. Why don't I take you there now? We'll toast to your safe crossing—and if you want, tomorrow or the day after, when your horses are fit again, I'd be happy to take you out into the veld for some sightseeing."

***

Over the next two days, Kevin and two other doctors assembled their field hospital, while Vincent tended the horses. At the time, he was the only veterinarian in all of East London, so the neighboring farmers rushed to consult him, and he proudly reported birthing calves and saving horses from colic.

"I heard about some Boers with an injured pony, but they didn't want my help," he said sadly as he rode with Colonel Ribbons and Kevin into the bush on the third day of their stay.

"The Boers?" asked Kevin. "I didn't think there were any here."

Ribbons nodded. "Hardly any. They coexist pretty peacefully with the English, like the Cape Boers where I come from. On rare occasions, there's even intermarriage."

Kevin had to laugh. "Rare occasions?"

Ribbons, however, was deadly serious. "A Boer girl who marries into an English family is an abomination for these people, almost as bad as if she'd taken a black lover. Not that the fathers have to lock their daughters inside. They look at us English like we're the devil himself. It's more common for a rebellious young man to lose his head over an English girl. The parents handle that better, but it can be difficult as well. My brother-in-law is a Boer, a vintner, so I know firsthand. We don't have anything against Pieter, but since Joan married him, we hardly see her. I'd bet his family gives him hell whenever he visits his in-laws. They tolerate Joan in his village as long as she doesn't speak a word of English. And they snub Pieter in church. Now, these folks are the most moderate. They're not even taking sides in the war. The others—"

"At any rate, they did not let me treat their pony," Vincent said regretfully. "Their English neighbor wanted to take me there. He has to see the poor thing every day with its swollen leg. A puncture wound—it needs to be wrapped in a cast with carbolic acid. The Boer treats it by peeing on it. That's not entirely wrong, but it still needs to be put in a cast, and the wound needs to be examined. If it's really deep, then none of the, uh, fluid is getting to it."

Kevin and Ribbons laughed.

"The Boers do have their home remedies," said Ribbons. "And hardly any real doctors. It's not just the horses that die of treatable diseases. Can you imagine, they take their wives with them to war? I'm serious: the wives drive their oxcarts behind the troops and doctor their husbands—even doing amputations. They're a tough people, the women too. And religious. When in doubt, they pray."

Kevin was fascinated. He could hardly wait to meet these strange Boers in person. For the time being, he got to know some of the country's four-legged residents. What they called the "veld" was primarily overgrown grasslands. There were also clusters of trees, some of them in bizarre shapes, and low shrubs. Kevin was completely taken aback when he saw a small brown antelope emerge from a thicket—followed by a whole herd.

"Impalas," Ribbons whispered. "The Boers call them *rooibok*."

A few minutes later, Kevin's horse, Silver, almost panicked when a giraffe appeared between two trees, its mouth full of leaves.

"Unbelievable," Vincent said. "Are there lions here too?"

"Rhinos," Ribbons replied. "But for them we'll have to ride farther inland. They're very fast, you know. Don't ever get too close, lest they attack."

Kevin preferred to spare his horse more encounters with strange animals. He knew that the giraffe posed no threat, but it was still uncanny to ride right past wild animals without the protection of fences. Kevin felt for his weapon whenever something stirred in the bush while Vincent excitedly identified various kinds of antelope.

Finally, they also passed a real kraal, a native village. It seemed less developed than the Maori villages in New Zealand, but it was much warmer here, of course, and there was less need of extensive buildings. The village, consisting of circular huts, was surrounded by a perimeter wall of thornbushes to keep the wild animals at bay.

"It was also a decent defense against spears," Ribbons said, "but not much good against firearms. Once, there were army camps, too, much larger than these little villages. But now the blacks are just happy when we leave them in peace."

That seemed to be true enough in this case. Though the people in the kraal eyed the riders skeptically, they made no move to welcome or frighten them off.

"This country," Vincent raved that evening, "it's paradise."

Kevin kept quiet. South Africa was no doubt beautiful, but he did not feel at ease. Perhaps the British would get things sorted once and for all, improving conditions for the native people and getting control of the mines. But did they really know what they were doing?

Chapter 2

"Tomorrow, we move out. We're going to help liberate Wepener," Major Jowsey told his officers the next day. "And, in case one of you still hasn't heard of that backwater"—the men laughed—"it's a small settlement three hundred miles north on the Jammerdrif, which is a tributary of the mighty Caledon." More laughter. Apparently, no one was much interested in South African geography. But Major Jowsey, a short, agile man with a big mustache, would not be deterred. "It's a central point for the local agriculture," he explained, unfolding a map and pointing to the tiny town on the border of Basutoland.

"I hear that's all Boer country," Kevin offered. "Farms, fields, cattle, and it's where the enemy settlements are. So, don't ride to the nearest farm if you're wounded. The local colonel I've been talking to says the women are as good a shot as the men."

The men laughed again, but the major nodded. "Listen to the doctor. He's entirely right. Wepener lies on the edge of the Orange Free State, and it's a nest of rebels. For a week now, it's been held by a British garrison of two thousand men. We're among the troops meant to relieve the garrison. The people there are waiting for us. So, we ride tomorrow at daybreak, and we ride fast."

That included Kevin, who was directed to leave behind the field hospital carts.

"Load two horses with whatever's most critical," Jowsey instructed him. "We're assuming the other regiments nearby have doctors, bandages, and medicine. For us, speed comes first and foremost. The town needs to be liberated."

The ride took the New Zealanders through the veld, and Silver soon acclimated to the omnipresent antelope herds. Later, they passed over demanding, rugged terrain. In the evening, the men pitched their tents on mountains and hills, some of which offered distant views of the plains. There were probably natives in the area, but they did not show themselves.

"From here on, it gets dangerous," the major warned on the sixth day when they left the mountains behind. In front of them lay fertile plains—farmland, Boer land.

"The Orange Free State," announced Ribbons, who had been assigned to accompany them as a guide. "Founded by the Boers after the British annexed the colony at the cape—and outlawed slavery. That didn't suit the Boers, so they flocked inland. It must have been a terrible slog in oxcarts. They still speak today of the Great Trek. This area was by no means uninhabited either. There were Zulu here, Basotho, and Batswana, and none of them wanted to give up their land. There was bloody fighting. Other colonizers would have given up. But not the Boers. They pushed through—and, in the end, England agreed to recognize their state."

"Until they found gold," Kevin said.

Ribbons frowned, then winked. "The official explanation is that we could no longer tolerate how they treated foreigners and natives. And there were provocations, not to mention—"

"Diamonds," Vincent noted drily. "Without a doubt, we're here as liberators."

The Boers certainly had an eye for valuable pasture and farmland. Here, there was little wild free space left for antelopes and gnus, and probably no one had laid eyes on a rhinoceros in a long time. Instead, well-tended fields stood in rows, one after another. Some were ready for harvest, and once or twice the riders even saw people working them—primarily black and occasionally white women, girls, and little boys. None of them acknowledged the garrison riding by. The black workers did not even raise their heads. At most, the whites gave the uniformed men hateful looks.

"My goodness, that little boy looks like he's ready to start shooting at us," Vincent remarked as they passed a wheat field in which five tall black men were being supervised by a white boy of no more than ten. The child glared at the riders with unconcealed rage.

"His mother probably took the gun from him because she was afraid of precisely that," Ribbons replied. "And because she'd like to hold on to her little boy awhile longer. The gun too. Really, the people were supposed to surrender them. These areas have long been in English hands, and we collected their weapons. But they're all still armed to the teeth. And as for the blacks—as I said, they're loyal.

Perhaps because they have nothing else left. Their tribes have been decimated. Their lands belong to the whites. If they don't want to go hungry, they stay put and obey the *baas*, as they call the white masters here. And their children."

Now the first farms were coming into view, and they reminded Kevin of modest country estates at home. These were simple wooden houses, the verandas larger than in New Zealand because people spent more time outside. Only the round huts a distance from the main houses were unfamiliar. That was where the black workers lived.

"The houses in East London are a lot prettier," Vincent said.

"The ones at the cape are prettiest," Ribbons boasted. "They're often wineries, and the owners won't be outdone. You also expect a bit of joie de vivre from a vintner. Here, on the other hand, the people don't touch a drop of alcohol. Their leader, that Ohm Krüger, even asked for milk at the German kaiser's table. They pray and work and are convinced God led them into this land like the Jews into Israel. And they cling to it tooth and nail. This war's getting tough."

***

Kevin was soon to get a taste of that. After four days of hard riding, they finally reached Wepener. The commander of the English forces gathered his army in an open field with a view of a ridge where the Boers had apparently dug in.

The relief army consisted of Scottish and Australian units as well, and their respective leaders had to overcome their differences before they were truly ready to attack. For the moment, they had their men set up camp and wait.

Kevin did not catch much of the battle preparations. He was immediately assigned to the commanding staff doctor, a Dr. Barrister. Barrister wore the rank insignia of a major but did not seem terribly concerned with hierarchy. He greeted Kevin amicably and was delighted to see the supplies he'd brought.

"It's always good when people use their heads," he declared. "We'll need all the bandages we can get our hands on. The soldiers were all sent here so quickly that the supply wagons can hardly keep up. The field kitchen, however, is fully furnished. Our esteemed commander in chief saw to that. No matter what else you can say about him, Buller believes no one should die with an empty stomach."

"If we don't even have tents," he asked, "where are we supposed to operate?"

"We have one tent," Barrister replied. "I managed to swipe it from the kitchen crew. It's not enough, of course. We need to get our hands on a farm. Right away."

"What, sir? Get our hands—?" sputtered Dr. Tracy, an Australian.

Barrister laughed. "New to war, son? Fine, then, I'll explain this once. The requisition of defeated opponents' possessions is a common practice during hostile encounters between nations. You waltz in and take what you need. In this case, you don't have to feel too bad. The people will probably get their farm back once things are through. So, we'll be on our way to look for the nearest property. I take it you all know how to shoot?"

The fourth doctor, a burly Scotsman named McAllister, looked insulted.

"Do you really think we'll need to shoot anyone, sir?" Tracy asked indignantly.

Barrister waved a hand dismissively. "In this war, you should prepare yourself for anything. Really that's true in any war, but these Boers are something else. So, always keep your wits about you. We'll go ahead and take the whole staff with us. The soldiers on staff should arm themselves, and as for the Indian orderlies, well, try and look armed, would you?"

The four Indian orderlies responded with friendly laughter. They'd served under Barrister for some time, it seemed.

Kevin immediately felt more comfortable. "Well, then, off we go."

***

The nearest farm was just behind the second nearest hill, a well-tended and beautiful estate situated along a river. It reminded Kevin a bit of his parents' home. However, here they raised crops, not sheep. There were barns and silos instead of shearing sheds, and just behind the vegetable garden, the fields began. So far, only a few had been harvested. Yet they were in dire need of it. At the moment, there was no one to be seen. The owners had likely barricaded themselves inside out of fear of the approaching army.

"Maybe they fled. That'd be the best thing," observed Barrister—but energetically held back the young doctors when they attempted to ride into the yard. "Dismount. Leave the horses outside," he ordered. "And helmets on, weapons ready, prepare for battle. Approach slowly, always under cover from your comrades."

"You'd think we were storming a fort," Kevin joked to the redheaded Scot as the two took cover behind a tree. "I'll feel like an idiot if the house is unoccupied."

The Scotsman snorted. "Your predecessor said the same thing," he replied. "And then they fired from every window in the house. The medical company lost three men."

For the first time since he'd arrived in South Africa, Kevin was genuinely afraid. He sprinted for cover behind a barn next. The other soldiers and doctors worked their way closer to the house like this until they were finally close enough to see two gun barrels aimed in the windows on either side of the entrance.

"Not a step closer." The woman sounded young but determined. Her English was clear, but her accent was strong. "Anyone comes closer, we shoot."

Barrister raised his voice. "Please be reasonable, miss. My name is Barrister, Major Barrister, commander of the Fifth Medical Unit. We are going to establish a hospital on your farm. However, we have no desire to displace you. All you need to do is open your barns to us, and perhaps a room or two in the house for the doctors."

"You will do no such thing." The girl emphasized her defiance with a gunshot. The bullets lashed the red sand at Barrister's feet.

"You can't stop us, miss. It's our right."

"Right?" The woman now shot even closer to her target. Barrister rushed back behind a tree. "You do not have any right here. Not to this farm, not to this land. Get out now."

Barrister raised his hand, and the first orderlies opened fire.

Kevin shuddered at the noise. He had no desire to get into a firefight with a young woman. He stared at the house, trying to picture its layout. There was no veranda in the front, but the farm had to have one, probably in the back, overlooking the river. Which meant there'd be a back door.

"Come on," Kevin called to the Scot. "Let's try the rear."

"How do you know that no one's waiting there with a gun?" asked McAllister, but he followed his colleague.

"I don't. But as long as Barrister is talking to the girl in front, no one will expect us in back—I hope."

The two doctors slipped around the back of the barn and then took cover behind a hedge. Behind the house lay a garden enclosed with thorny bushes—and a large veranda with a wide, double-winged door leading into the house.

"Well then!" Kevin gathered his courage. "Come on, we'll split up and slink in on the left and right. We'll open both doors at once for the element of surprise, and then take cover in case anyone inside starts shooting."

"But we'll be coming from bright light into dark," McAllister warned. "By the time our eyes have adjusted, they could have us. Let's look through the windows first."

Kevin nodded appreciatively, and the two made their way over.

"A kitchen," McAllister whispered from his side of the veranda. "And no one inside."

"And a sort of dining room on this side," Kevin responded from his. "Also empty. Shall we take our positions?"

The Scotsman nodded. "All right, on three: one, two—"

The men swung the doors open carefully, letting bright sunlight into the room. It was furnished with a large roughhewn table and nine simple chairs. The dining room bordered on an equally large kitchen. In a glass cabinet stood blue-patterned ceramic dishes.

"Very good. Now, stick to cover, and we'll make our way to the front," McAllister said. "If we run into anyone, don't let them scream. It'll blow our cover."

Kevin swallowed the question of how he was supposed to stop them.

The doctors held their weapons out in front of them as they pressed through the door that led out of the dining room.

"No shoot!" A strained-sounding woman's voice, but not determined like the woman in the front, and completely terrified. "Please, no shoot, *baas*."

Kevin squinted down the dark corridor—and nearly did pull the trigger when he saw a hunting rifle pointed at him. In her panic, she seemed to have forgotten about it. This was no flinty Boer, but a frightened black woman with curly hair and giant round eyes.

"No make Nandi dead. Please, no. Please."

Kevin lowered his gun. "We're not going to harm you," he said very quietly. "But you need to lower your gun. Like this, see?" He pointed his in the direction of the ground.

The young woman immediately did the same.

"Heavens, girl," Kevin said, the fear still in his limbs. "I nearly shot you. You—"

"You have to tell us who else is in the house." McAllister seized the young woman roughly by the arm, pulled her back into the dining room, and pushed her into a chair. "Who told you to watch the back?"

"Mejuffrouw Doortje, the *baas*, but I—"

"That's the bitch shooting at our men?" McAllister demanded.

"Uh?" The woman's English seemed overtaxed.

"Doortje. She is the woman with the gun?" Kevin asked more gently.

"His three woman," Nandi replied. "De *baas* Doortje and Bentje and Johanna. And de little *baas* Thies and Mees."

"Thies and Mees are little boys?" Kevin clarified.

Nandi nodded.

"How many guns?" asked McAllister, pointing to his. "How many of these?"

The girl held up two fingers. "And—" She pointed to her own gun.

Kevin nodded. So, they would only have to overpower two women with guns—or perhaps a woman and a child. But he did not want to think about that.

"Listen," he said to the girl, who was visibly shaking. "We won't hurt you, but you must keep quiet. Stay here and don't move an inch."

"And if you attack us from behind, you're dead," McAllister hissed, shouldering the girl's gun.

"Sorry, Drury," he whispered when the men again slipped into the corridor. "I know she seems harmless. But I've seen children turn into hyenas. The girl won't die of a few threats. If it comes to a shoot-out, though—"

They could hear Barrister's voice again, interrupted repeatedly by shots from the house. This meant Kevin and McAllister only needed to follow the shots to know where the women were barricaded. They made their way up to a door that probably led to the entryway. They heard Barrister's voice, though they could not make out the words, and Mejuffrouw Doortje's answer, another shot. She did not seem to suffer from a lack of ammunition.

"Get ready," whispered McAllister while the sound of the shot still reverberated. "As soon as I open the door, you take shooter one; I'll take shooter two. And don't threaten. Attack and disarm. They're far more prepared than you to take a bullet."

Kevin was stunned but readied himself as best he could. As the door swung open, Kevin took in the people in the room. Staring out the window was the young woman with the gun: slender, dressed in a dark housedress with bright lace, her hair covered by a bonnet. The other gun lay in the hands of a ten-year-old boy likewise aiming at the attackers. Behind them, in a corner of the room, an older woman held three children.

"Nobody move," roared the Scotsman, the order immediately drowned out by the children's screams.

Both shooters turned around—but Kevin had already reached the young woman and knocked the weapon out of her hand. Unimpressed by the gun barrel pointing directly at her chest, the young woman hammered at Kevin with her fists, and he reflexively let go of his gun to defend himself with both hands. One of the other children—a girl, perhaps thirteen years old—immediately tried to pick it up, but Kevin deterred her with a kick. He succeeded in wrenching one arm of one woman behind her back, thus taking her out of action. The boy McAllister had disarmed cried in rage. Meanwhile, the Scot held the others in check with his gun.

"All clear, Major Barrister," he called. "You can come in."

At once, the room filled with staff doctors and soldiers. The young woman whom Kevin held fast howled with anger and began to kick at him and bite.

"Well done. McAllister and Drury, was it? Very well done. But perhaps someone should take this little fury off your hands."

Kevin smiled. The little fury was remarkably strong, and somehow intriguing in spite of her violence. Kevin had imagined slave owners differently. He was curious to see her face, but for now saw only the back of her white bonnet. The young woman smelled entrancing. Not of perfume like Juliet and the other girls in Dunedin and not earthy and fresh like Maori girls. Mejuffrouw Doortje smelled like fresh-baked bread—underneath the sweat and gun smoke.

"Perhaps she's ready to behave a little more civilly," said Kevin. "Then I could let her go. Come on, Miss Doortje. Give me your word. We won't harm you."

"How do you know my name?"

The young woman broke free the moment Kevin eased his grip, turned around, and glared at him. Her face was broad but not coarse. Her light complexion burned red with rage and exertion, and her eyes were deep blue. Kevin recalled the Dutch porcelain in his parents' dining room.

Before he could answer, a figure cautiously slipped through the open door.

"Baas?" Nandi asked.

The Boer woman leaped forward and roared at the girl, then shrieked something that sounded like a wild curse. Nandi hung her head and chewed fearfully on her lips.

"What did she say?" Kevin asked his comrades.

"Something like 'filthy traitor,'" Tracy translated. "I'll spare you the rest. The young lady's language is quite, uh, unladylike."

"You speak Afrikaans?" Barrister asked, taken aback.

He was pleasantly surprised by the reinforcements. First, Kevin's initiative with McAllister, and now unexpected linguistic abilities from this rather priggish-seeming Australian.

"Dutch, sir. I studied for a year in Leiden."

Mejuffrouw Doortje now flung a few curses in his direction.

Barrister sighed. "Hold your tongue a moment, miss. We won't get anywhere this way. Now, about the house—is this your mother?"

He looked at the older woman still holding the children in her arms, and wondered whether she was protecting the three or holding them back. The girl looked just as fierce as her sister. The woman, in contrast, had very pale eyes that stared into nothing.

"My mother does not speak English," Doortje said. "And she is blind. If you touch her—"

But Tracy had already addressed the lady of the house in Dutch. She answered reluctantly.

"This is Mevrouw Bentje van Stout," he announced. "Along with her daughters, Doortje"—he pointed to Kevin's prisoner—"and Johanna." Tracy, ever the gentleman, bowed slightly to the younger girl. "And her sons, Thies and Mees. She would not say where her husband is. He's likely in the veld. There are two black families that belong to the estate, but with the exception of this young lady"—Nandi looked startled when he bowed to her as well—"they all apparently hid themselves when the army approached. Perhaps they'll return. We could use the help."

"What does she say about our field hospital?" Barrister asked.

The woman spat out a few furious words.

A light red spread over Tracy's narrow face. "I don't know if—"

"You go to hell," screamed the woman.

Barrister rubbed his forehead. "Good, so the lady does speak some English. No matter, we'll nonetheless be dealing primarily with you, Miss D—"

"No," the girl said. "Do not expect any help. Neither I nor my siblings will accommodate. We—"

"We know, we know," Barrister replied. "You expressed yourself quite clearly before. Nevertheless, please show me the farm. As I already told you, we do not wish to disturb you more than necessary. We're interested in your barns—straw for provisional sickbeds, perhaps some fresh victuals if you can spare anything. Is the oven out back? It smells so wonderfully of fresh bread."

"Choke on it," Doortje spat.

Barrister tugged on his earlobe but remained polite. "I take it you no longer have any livestock?"

"You people stole the animals."

"Lies," McAllister noted to Kevin as they followed their reluctant guide outside. "The relief force didn't requisition any ponies, guaranteed. The cavalry has its own horses, and the kitchen and supply wagons were hitched long ago. Mijnheer van Stout probably took the animals. The blokes simply take their horses and join up with a commando. It's all frightfully undisciplined. Everyone comes and goes as he pleases. But they're fearless—and they surprise you over and over. That's why they had their successes at first. But we'll win in the end."

Kevin nodded, but he wondered how long it would take before the last of these commandos surrendered. It wasn't so much one country at war with another but more like a great army against thousands of little groups. And what could the Crown do with a colony in which even such small children opposed it so vehemently?

Chapter 3

Over the next few days, a few of Doortje van Stout's claims would prove false. For example, a few of the orderlies caught Nandi with a pail of fresh milk. Apparently, the family's black workers had not fled, and they were tending the hidden dairy cows somewhere in the hilly veld.

Kevin, whom the men informed of their discovery, did not, however, denounce the Boers to Barrister. He could understand why the people wanted to keep their property—and, after all, the English were not exactly suffering from starvation. On the contrary, a kitchen wagon was immediately made available when it became clear the van Stout women truly refused to extend the slightest courtesy to the doctors. Barrister tried a peace offering. He invited the van Stout family to dine with his officers. Doortje, however, took umbrage when he briefly requisitioned the van Stouts' kitchen.

"Please, miss, let our cook work his magic. General Buller counts him among his best. But a genius can't prove himself in a wagon."

Doortje, Johanna, and their mother listened silently, cleared out with sour faces, and withdrew to the river to wash.

But the little boys went straight for the kitchen, sniffing the air hungrily. On the van Stout farm, no one went hungry, but there had no doubt been no meat for a long time. True, the women might have hidden some hogs and oxen, but with the British Army around the corner, they would hardly risk a slaughter.

The scent of the lamb roast was irresistible, but none of the van Stouts appeared at the festively set table that had been moved to the veranda.

"I tried," sighed Barrister, and uncorked a bottle of wine. "But I should have known better. This Doortje is a tough cookie, and her mother and sister no less so."

"What's more, the sister's a tattletale," added Tracy. "She has eyes in the back of her head, and if the little boys or one of the blacks show us even an inkling of cooperation, she runs to tell Doortje. Then she rains fire and brimstone on them. Poor Nandi's afraid the angel with the flaming sword is lurking behind every hill."

"That poor, sweet girl," said Kevin.

In the meantime, Nandi's brother had returned to the farm, and the two siblings worked in the fields from dawn to dusk. Doortje drove them mercilessly, but she worked herself and her family hard as well. Johanna mostly assisted her blind mother in the kitchen, but the little boys had to help with the harvest. Nandi seemed completely exhausted when she returned from the fields in the evening, but she was still expected to serve meals, haul water, and perform extensive household chores. It was often late at night before she was able to prepare herself something meager to eat. The van Stouts, Kevin noticed, never shared their own food with the black workers.

"Well, well," McAllister laughed, wagging his finger at Kevin. "Someone's not falling in love with the curly-haired black, is he? Well, I'll warn you—they say these Zulu women aren't very passionate."

The doctors had learned that Nandi was a pure-blooded Zulu. And her name was not a malapropism of Nancy, as Kevin had first supposed. In fact, she had confided that she was named after the mother of the legendary king Shaka Zulu.

Kevin raised his brows in astonishment. "Nandi? Please, she's still a child."

Dr. Tracy, who abstained from bawdy remarks but had proven himself a sharp observer, smiled. "Of course," he said. "Dr. Drury's comportment is above all reproach." Tracy took a long sip from his wineglass before continuing. "But he does have eyes for Miss van Stout."

Kevin almost choked on his lamb. He coughed violently and hoped the other men would think that the cause of his blushing.

"Doortje?" scoffed McAllister. "That'd be like making love to a razor blade."

"Colonel! Is that any way to speak of a young lady?" Major Barrister chided.

The men fell silent, and Kevin was relieved not to have to say more. He could not have explained his attraction to Doortje van Stout. Her face was pretty, sure, as was her flaxen hair. But he'd known women of greater beauty. What was it, then, that drew him to her? Her unbridled energy? Her passion? Or was it her obstinacy, her deep convictions, which, though Kevin did not share them, fascinated him nonetheless? He had known himself to be rather superficial, and had sought out complementary companions—Juliet, for one, was a butterfly that flitted from flower to flower. Doortje, however, was unwavering, true, and serious.

Kevin shook his head at himself. When had those ever been attributes he valued in women?

"The young lady is doubtlessly a challenge," remarked Tracy.

He was about to say something else, but was interrupted by the sound of hooves. A man on horseback paused in front of the house, spoke with one of the orderlies, then rode around to the rear veranda where Barrister and his officers were dining.

The rider, a young Australian, blurted out his message without dismounting.

"Major! The first encounters with the enemy occurred outside of Wepener with two wounded. You're to please man the first-aid tent and get the field hospital operational. The battle will begin tomorrow."

Major Barrister disbanded the table at once and gave assignments. He would head to the front himself to provide first aid.

"Dr. Tracy will assist me for the first ten hours, then Drs. McAllister and Drury will relieve us. I'd like every new doctor to first work alongside doctors with front experience. Later, the assignments don't matter. Perhaps even one doctor will suffice then, and the others can operate here. We'll see how bloody it gets."

"What's this supposed to be, a crash course in surgery?" Kevin asked McAllister as Barrister and Tracy rode away. The two of them were to prepare the beds and once more look over the operating rooms in the makeshift hospital. They would not be getting much sleep the next day. "I'll admit it's not my specialty, but what can you really teach me in ten hours?"

McAllister smiled bitterly. "You learn quickly here—the hard way, especially for the patient. I'm convinced I killed my first ten amputees. But it's not what this is about. It's more about you learning to see blood, Dr. Drury, more blood than you ever dreamed of in your little city practice. What's your first name, again? I'm Angus, but call me Gus."

***

Kevin was lying in his bed of straw in the barn, still thinking about McAllister's words, when he heard crashing and the splintering of wood. Alarmed, he leaped up—it sounded as if someone were plundering the house. Had some marauding Boers fallen upon the field hospital? He reached for his rifle.

Angus McAllister, however, was already coming toward him. The Scotsman had likewise jumped out of bed, but he was now grinning from ear to ear.

"It's not the war, Kevin, just your future sweetheart. Miss van Stout is smashing the family porcelain. And the chairs in the dining room. Tainted by British fingers and arses. Unthinkable that a van Stout should eat from the one, let alone sit on the other ever again." He laughed. "And now you've seen a Scotsman in his underwear. I hope she calms down before she claws her own eyes out."

Kevin slapped his forehead. Yet he could not stop himself from picturing Doortje as he fell asleep. A blonde angel of vengeance smashing dishes and furniture—and then kissing him with the same passion.

***

The next morning, they awoke to the sound of fighting. Previously, shots had sometimes rung out, but sporadically. They had sounded more like practice than a battle. Now, however, grenade explosions followed weapon salvos. The sound was loud even on the van Stout farm. It must have been infernal at the front.

Dr. Barrister's representative, Dr. Willcox, arrived at the field hospital. He had been in the first-aid tent at the front, treating minor injuries. Yesterday, things had gotten serious, but both wounded men had survived the night. One was only lightly wounded. Willcox had immediately operated on the other—he had already finished when Barrister and Tracy arrived. Now he was escorting the two invalids to the hospital.

"The next transport will likely follow in an hour at most," Willcox declared. "The battle's been raging since dawn. The first casualties were arriving as I rode off. Get ready."

Fortunately, the first two patients were in good condition and properly bandaged, resting comfortably in one of the three transport wagons. The orderlies needed only to transfer them to the straw beds in the barn.

Then, however, the second transport arrived, and Kevin got a glimpse of how things must be at the front. It was unimaginable that just two doctors and a few orderlies had provided first aid to this many wounded, but the quality of the treatment testified to it. Wounds had been provisionally covered, and limbs in need of amputation had been tied off, but that was all. The men lay packed together in the too-small wagons. Some screamed, moaned, or wept.

"These two first," Dr. Willcox directed, pointing to a man with a bloody stump for a leg and another with a shredded arm. The first was unconscious, the second whimpering. "Ever taken someone's leg off, Drury? I see the answer's no. But you do know how to use a saw, right? Don't turn green, man. Grab the surgical instruments and assist me."

Kevin fought down his disgust. He had never had reason to amputate in his private practice, and he had operated little during his residency in a Dunedin hospital. Kevin liked interacting with people and had preferred general medicine to surgery. Nevertheless, he was a skillful and determined medical professional. Once he had gotten used to being soaked in blood, he worked quickly and efficiently.

Willcox seemed satisfied. "Just don't let the screams get to you when the opiates wear off," he said. "We're actually well supplied, but in the heat of battle, it's hard to gauge the right dose, and you have to work quickly."

And work quickly they did. On Willcox and Kevin's operating table, one patient followed another and another. The orderlies changed them so quickly, the doctors didn't have a moment to catch their breath. On the second table, McAllister was working with an Indian orderly. The two of them took care of the lighter cases—and did a sort of screening. By his fifteenth patient or so, Kevin wondered aloud how he and Willcox had so far managed to save everyone.

"The worst cases don't make it to us," Willcox explained, gesturing toward McAllister with his chin.

Kevin's eyes widened. "But that's monstrous. We should treat them first."

Willcox shook his head. "Young man, if we try to save one like him"—he pointed to a boy shot through the lung—"we'd be at the table at least two hours, and three others would die in the meantime. For maybe a fifteen percent chance of success. It doesn't work that way in war. It makes me sad too."

The man who'd taken the bullet to his lung looked so young that he must have lied about his age in order to enlist. Willcox looked him over regretfully.

"They should have just let him die at the front. But Barrister sometimes has a soft heart."

For Kevin, the first ten hours flew by. He was still operating when the last transport arrived at nightfall, accompanied by Dr. Tracy, who would not be dissuaded from immediately assuming Kevin's place at the table.

"You're to ride for the front at once, Drury. Barrister could use help. McAllister will follow you in two hours. By then, things should have calmed down."

"But you should rest," Kevin said.

Dr. Tracy still held himself like a gentleman, but he looked horrible. His uniform, spick-and-span the night before, with perfectly ironed pleats, was filthy and drenched in blood. His face looked gaunt. His eyes lay sunken in his skull, and his gaze had changed. Dr. Tracy seemed to have looked into the abyss.

"We all need rest," Tracy said curtly, and Kevin wondered whether he looked as bad as his colleague. He still felt quite alert, however—probably he wouldn't truly feel his exhaustion until the work was done.

"Besides, I'd like to save someone for once," Tracy added. "If I—if I see any more dead men, then—" He squared himself and swallowed what he obviously wanted to say. "Then—then I might lose my composure."

He reached for the scalpel. Kevin bowed his head and handed it off.

***

Before heading to the stables, Kevin quickly checked the condition of his patients. The orderlies—the Indians as well as the recently trained New Zealanders—were acquitting themselves well. The wounded lay on clean straw beds, and the orderlies went from one to the next, encouraging them and giving them water and soup. One of the new orderlies sat next to the boy shot in the lung, speaking to him and praying. Kevin thanked him and wondered whether there was a pastor who should be doing this.

He asked another of the orderlies about the van Stouts. Perhaps all the suffering that day had touched even this family's heart, and they would finally treat at least the doctors and orderlies more amicably. The orderly shook his head. The van Stouts had not shown themselves all day.

"They're not in the field either," another reported.

The cook, whose assistant had just hauled a large pot of stew into the barn, snorted.

"They're praying," he declared, filling a bowl for Kevin, who only then realized how hungry he was. "For hours now. I don't understand their gibberish, but if you ask me, it's for the Boers' victory. Can't we put a lid on that, Doctor? It drives me crazy."

Kevin smiled tiredly between rushed spoonfuls of stew. "That is probably their aim. Better just to ignore it. You'll have to put your faith in God. He doesn't listen to everyone, you know. By the way, this is delicious—where did you say your restaurant was? Melbourne?"

Kevin conversed a bit more with the cook, then reluctantly went to leave—and, to his amazement, caught sight of Nandi's brother stealthily placing a bucket of water at the entrance of the barn. His masters seemed not to know that he was helping.

"He's been bringing us water all day," an orderly said. "An enormous help. We all had our hands full here. And the Zulu woman brought half a bucket of milk earlier. I think they're on our side, the blacks. They don't like the Boers either."

Kevin thought to himself that the native people did not have much reason to like the British either. After all, the Crown didn't have to recognize the Boer republics and their slave holding in the first place. They should have fought for the blacks when they first took over the country, not just after gold turned up. Then, however, he thought of Doortje. As he rode past the house, he heard her resonant voice. She was speaking in Dutch, or Afrikaans rather, and she seemed to be reading from a prayer book. In the light of the gas lamp, he saw her slender silhouette and that neat bonnet. She seemed never to take it off. He would have to ask someone if there was a reason. Kevin imagined loosening the bands and watching her hair fall in soft waves down her back. Like gold but without the metallic shimmer. Doortje's hair was like the soft gold of grain.

Kevin thought it might be worth fighting for that gold.

***

Quiet prevailed in the British Army camp when Kevin arrived, deathly tired. It was just as he'd supposed: the exhaustion had come as soon as he stopped moving. A few orderlies sat smoking in front of the first-aid tent. Next to them lay innumerable long bundles wrapped in canvas. Kevin averted his eyes.

"Dr. Barrister?"

One of them gestured to the tent. "Still operating. A few serious cases who've held out so far. Go on in."

Barrister was just as dirty and bloody as Tracy. He looked exhausted but not as devastated as his younger colleague.

"Come on, Drury, lend me a hand. Stomach wound, no great chance of survival. But he hasn't died yet, so we'll try. Were you able to help the boy shot in the lung?"

Kevin shook his head. "Dr. Willcox—"

"Will give it a go tonight if the boy's still alive. But we should get at least two hours of sleep. It'll be the same tomorrow. The Boers in Wepener aren't about to surrender. They'll fight to the last bullet. And their position is excellent. It could be two or three days till we take back the town."

Kevin grabbed a scalpel. "But we'll win in the end?"

Barrister nodded. "There's no question. The Boers really should give up. But they won't. And besides, they're to our rear as well. Most of the young men here"—he gestured around the tent—"weren't hit while attacking the town, but rather by marauding commandos that came out of nowhere. There are now whole sections of the army assigned to securing the surrounding hills. Many of your countrymen, as it happens. It's said they ride as madly as the Boers. I don't know if that's supposed to be a compliment, but they're already calling them the Rough Riders. And they seem to be successful. I've had hardly any of them on my table."

In spite of their efforts, the three difficult cases they had put off died on Kevin and Barrister that night—and Kevin began to understand the haunted look he'd seen in Tracy's eyes. If the whole day had passed that way . . . well, he would see the next morning. Kevin's ten official hours of service at the front would begin at sunrise. Two hours before that, he collapsed on a straw bed next to his last patients.

Chapter 4

Lizzie and Michael wanted to hold Patrick and Juliet's wedding at Elizabeth Station, and Patrick was all for it. He loved the farm—after all, he would inherit it one day—and he was also close to the Maori tribe living nearby. This additional "family" could take part in the wedding, and lodging could be found in Lawrence for friends and family from Dunedin.

Juliet, however, vehemently rejected a wedding "in the middle of nowhere." Instead, she wanted a ceremony in Saint Paul's Cathedral and a celebration in a grand Dunedin hotel. She did not get the former. Patrick insisted on Reverend Burton officiating. Juliet pulled out all the stops, including crying and claiming that she felt ashamed in front of the pastor and his wife. After all, the two of them had known her as Kevin's girlfriend and might guess about the baby. Patrick merely shook his head.

"Dear, they'll learn about it one way or another. The Burtons and the Drurys are very close. Sean is Kathleen's son and my half brother. And no doubt you intend to have your bridal gown made at the Gold Mine? What were you going to tell Kathleen? No, dear, we're getting married in Caversham, and Reverend Burton will do the honors."

Regarding the hotel, however, Patrick let himself be convinced, and even defended Juliet's position to his parents. "She's the bride. She has a right to celebrate in Dunedin with her friends."

"I keep hearing about these friends," Lizzie said. "Well, a year ago no one here even knew Juliet LaBree, and I still haven't seen these supposed well-wishers and bridesmaids."

"Mother, come. It's supposed to be the loveliest day of her life. She's earned it."

"Earned it?" Lizzie asked more heatedly. "How? By letting herself get pregnant without asking if your careless brother even loved her? Possibly doing it just to get her claws in him? Really, she's earned a beating. She should be grateful that you're giving the child your name at all."

"I understand why you don't like her," Patrick said with resignation.

Lizzie sighed. "I wanted a nicer girl for you, Patrick, someone sincere and loving. But I'll get used to her. And she'll get used to me. If the world is supposed to believe the baby's yours, she'll have to spend the next few months with us in Tuapeka. She does understand that, doesn't she?"

Patrick nodded. "And precisely for that reason—"

"We ought to grant her a reception in Dunedin," Michael finished. "Come on, Lizzie, have a heart. We'll celebrate with the Maori a few days later. But let Miss LaBree be the belle of the ball one last time. Especially since—"

He stopped himself with a quick side-glance at Patrick. His son nodded eagerly, not noticing that Michael hadn't finished his thought. But Lizzie understood. Michael had held his tongue out of consideration for Patrick. For Juliet, this wedding was a terrible disappointment. She was not getting anything she'd wanted. Only a husband she didn't like and a baby no one knew if she would love.

***

And so, the Drurys rented the ballroom of the Leviathan Hotel in Queen's Gardens. Patrick engaged musicians according to Juliet's wishes—"Your mother would probably have hired a chamber music group and your father a fiddler from an Irish pub"—and Kathleen designed the snow-white wedding dress, as well as pastel-green creations for the bridesmaids, Roberta and Atamarie.

"We won't need to advertise this year's bridal fashion," Claire said contentedly when she saw Juliet in her gown for the first time. "Every single girl in Dunedin will dream of looking so beautiful walking down the aisle."

"A little slimmer around the stomach would be ideal," Kathleen observed drily. "No one'll notice, though. She corsets herself mercilessly. The poor baby'll probably be gasping for breath."

"Baby?" squealed Claire. "You think she's pregnant?"

Kathleen nodded. "And a ways along too. I don't mean to gossip, but do you think it has something to do with Kevin's sudden rush to the imperial banner?"

Claire giggled. "You don't mean to gossip. Right. Of course not, Kate. That really wouldn't suit a pastor's wife. Come on, whom should we tell?"

***

Naturally, Kathleen and Claire did not tell anyone, and aside from the perceptive seamstress, only a few wedding guests noticed that Juliet looked plumper than before. Her dress hid it brilliantly. It was a truly glamorous creation: the headdress, skirt, and sleeves were modeled on the feathery form of rata blossoms, while the top was tight, emphasizing Juliet's lifted breasts. Kathleen took her inspiration more and more from the country's rich flora. Last year, her white camellia wedding dress had caused a sensation. The delicate flower shape had emphasized the bride's sensuality—and moreover, the white camellia was a symbol of women's suffrage.

"I want one like that when I get married," Atamarie had declared.

Now there were cheers as Patrick led Juliet in her rata-blossom dress up the middle of the little church in Caversham. The reverend gave the congregants a reproving look. He was well aware that the small church's pews were packed in part because the women of Dunedin wanted a preview of his wife's designs before the fall fashion shows.

"Doesn't rata first grow as a parasite?" Lizzie asked her husband under her breath.

But Patrick was beaming from ear to ear. He wore a light-gray suit, which made him look dapper.

"Not quite as dashing as Kevin," Claire whispered to her husband. "I hope Mrs. Drury isn't disappointed."

Jimmy Dunloe repressed a smirk.

Both bridesmaids looked unreservedly enthusiastic about their role. Atamarie could guess why Roberta was beaming so. Kevin's enlistment had hit her hard, even with Atamarie's reassurance. *Look,* she had said, *he's guaranteed not to see a woman there for months. Then, when he comes back, he'll see you with new eyes*. This wedding, at least, gave Roberta hope again. No matter what happened, she wouldn't have to follow Kevin and Juliet down the aisle.

Atamarie, for her part, had not yet had a moment to tell Roberta about the romantic developments in her own life. She had just come from Taranaki, arriving in the nick of time to dress and do her hair. The friends would have to exchange stories later.

Now they listened attentively as Juliet and Patrick said their vows, he in an emotional but firm voice, she almost uninterested.

"It's amazing she can even speak," Violet whispered to her husband, "as tight as that corset is. I wonder—"

Sean Coltrane smiled. "Perhaps Kevin's following in a certain family tradition," he replied. Everyone knew that Michael had left a pregnant Kathleen years before, though for very different reasons. "At least Patrick's getting what he wants. I hope she makes him happy."

***

That day, at any rate, Patrick was the happiest man in the world. He enjoyed the party at the Leviathan and swung Juliet first to waltzes, then to more-modern music. The bride, however, soon became dizzy, which was no wonder. Juliet's corset was so tight that she could hardly partake of the excellent food.

"And hardly any champagne," Chloe whispered to her beloved. "I guess she's not going to sing tonight."

"It's a shame, really," replied Heather. "She does it very well. If all she sings in the future are lullabies, it'll be a waste of her talent."

Chloe raised her eyebrows. "Do you really think she'll have children soon? If you ask me, a woman like her knows precisely how to prevent that. After all, it ruins the figure."

Heather furrowed her brow and observed Juliet with the probing eye of a painter. "If she doesn't want any children—why then is she giving up her art and marrying Patrick? Besides, am I mistaken, or is she already a bit swollen?"

***

Atamarie and Roberta took no notice of the bride's figure. They let themselves be asked to dance a few times, but in truth, they wanted to be alone to talk. Finally, Atamarie snagged a bottle of champagne, and the girls withdrew to the balcony. It was cold out there, but no one bothered them. Only the cheerful music—the band was now playing Sousa marches—drifted out and colored their conversation.

"And then he just left?" asked Roberta.

Atamarie had been telling her about Rawiri's rescue and the magical evening when she strolled the hills with Richard Pearse and told him of her dream of flying.

"He thinks just like I do. He feels what I do. And then, he kissed me."

"But he left the next day?" Roberta repeated.

"Well, it wasn't his choice," Atamarie said, frowning. "Professor Dobbins thought we couldn't finish. We weren't progressing as quickly as planned—no wonder, with those clueless snobs like Porter. Anyway, Dobbins split us into two groups. My group continued surveying from Parihaka, but the other group had to go to the other side of Taranaki. Under Richard's guidance." She made a face.

"And it absolutely had to be Richard?" Roberta asked. "Couldn't someone else do it? I mean, this Richard of yours isn't even a proper student, right? Could it be that Professor Dobbins—that he wanted to separate you?"

Atamarie shook her head. "Nah, I don't think so. Actually, I got the impression he thought we were cute together."

"Cute?" Roberta echoed. She could not imagine a university professor using that word.

"Well, not 'cute' maybe, but, um, well suited. Whatever, I got the feeling he was supportive. He was less pleased about Porter and the others disappearing into the bushes with the local girls. And about me and Richard, he did notice that my mother saw, so—"

"Your mother saw?" squealed Roberta. "You, with Richard, in the bushes—"

"I wasn't in the bushes with him," Atamarie said with a regretful sigh. "He's too much of a gentleman. We just went for a walk. In the hills, like I said. Because of the updraft. And the angle of approach. I thought it would work for a flight attempt, but Richard said you wouldn't reach the necessary speed for a pure glider flight. At most with a double-decker. Lilienthal—"

"Atamie. I don't want an engineering seminar. Tell me more about Richard. Did he at least hold your hand?"

"He did. And we kissed." She neglected to mention that she was the one who'd kissed him.

"And then he left the very next day," repeated Roberta. "Couldn't you go along to the other side of the mountain?"

"No, the professor wouldn't allow it. I was the youngest in the group, after all, and the only girl."

"But he asked?" inquired Roberta. "Richard, I mean."

"Yeaaah." In truth, Atamarie had asked. Richard seemed not to have even thought of it. He was much too excited about his appointment as the leader of the expedition. It was an honor, of course, especially since he had hardly taken more classes than Atamarie. "But, anyway, he had to go," Atamarie insisted. "The professor knows he has a great future ahead of him."

Roberta frowned. She looked charming that evening. She had been thrilled when Kathleen helped her into the green bridesmaid's dress. She knew she'd been dressing too morosely of late. But without Atamarie around, she fell under the influence of the teaching academy. The girls there dressed dourly, already prepared for their future positions. None of them planned to marry any time soon, as a teacher who did so was still pressured to retire. In fact, many of them already seemed like spinsters. They took part in the harmless student gatherings, but they never flirted with the male students. Granted, those men held no attraction for Roberta either. Of the three in her year, one was already married, one seemed unmanly, and the third was all skin and bones, and as awkward as if he had just turned fifteen. Besides, if Roberta dressed too nicely, the whole school stared. And Roberta hated drawing attention.

"And when did you see him again? You did ride back to Dunedin, didn't you?"

Atamarie tugged at a strand of her gold-blonde hair. "Well, yes, we rode back together, of course. It was so nice. We talked the entire time."

"Talked?" asked Roberta. "Nothing else? After he'd already kissed you?"

"Well, not with everyone there." Atamarie turned away in embarrassment.

Roberta raised her eyebrows in alarm. That didn't sound like Atamarie. Shyness was alien to her, and she always found a way to get things she truly wanted. Sneaking off for a little time alone with Richard Pearse could hardly have been beyond her.

"But he did kiss me good-bye," Atamarie said defiantly. "In Christchurch, before we parted. He was so sweet, a little shy, but completely, totally captivating. He told me how much he enjoyed spending time with me. And that we absolutely must see each other again."

In truth, Richard Pearse had mostly spoken of his farm in Temuka where he now had to return. He had hated the mere thought of it, and Atamarie had comforted him. *I could come visit you,* she'd said hopefully. *We could build a kite.*

Richard had then shown her his gentle, shy, now almost desperate smile. *You are always welcome, Atamarie,* he'd said. And then kissed her very tenderly. On the cheek.

This time, in front of the uptight university, with no *hangi* and no whiskey, Atamarie had not dared to repeat her advances. She just stood there, unsatisfied.

"We'll write each other," she insisted.

Roberta pursed her lips. She lacked experience, true, but this didn't sound like passion.

***

Patrick and Juliet spent that night in the bridal suite of the Leviathan Hotel, and as Juliet had half hoped and half feared, Patrick was very considerate. Juliet had nothing against her new husband; on the contrary, Patrick's devotion flattered her, and his helpless compliance almost made her feel tenderness for him. Passion or even love, so far, she could not summon, but she tried to remain optimistic. This man was Kevin's brother. It could hardly be that he was so incapable of his brother's wildness and imagination. Juliet was hoping to be surprised. True, she found it strange that Patrick did not touch her before their wedding night, but maybe he was saving his energy.

Tonight, however, it was exactly as she had expected. Patrick lifted her up, laughing, and carried her in his strong arms to their room. He laid her on the bed where he had even thought to have rose petals scattered. Then he began to kiss her tenderly and to undo the fasteners on her dress.

"You're not too tired, dearest?" he asked kindly when she at first made no move to help him.

"Nonsense," murmured Juliet. "If only you could free me from this corset—I just can't move."

"Why do you need to wear your corsets so tight, anyway?" Patrick struggled with the silk-covered buttons. "You know I would just have gladly married you in one of the reform-style dresses."

"Why not a circus tent?" Juliet shot back, and tugged at one of the buttons herself. What was all this caution for? She was not going to wear this dress again. Kevin would long since have ripped it from her body.

Patrick laughed nervously, then applied himself to undoing the corset's bands. Juliet let out a great sigh when he finally succeeded. She lay relaxed and naked before him while the sight seemed to take Patrick's breath away. Juliet almost giggled hysterically at the thought. One of the two was always out of breath.

"You're so beautiful," Patrick whispered. "I just don't know. I don't know—"

Juliet closed her eyes. It couldn't be. She had married a virgin.

But then Patrick did take the initiative. He began to kiss her body and to caress her, moving his fingers in circles. It was thoroughly pleasant. Juliet gave herself to his caresses—and her own fatigue after the stressful day. But then she pulled herself together. She could not, under any circumstances, fall asleep. So, she returned his touches, intensified them, trying to drive Patrick to wilder kisses, to harder, stronger advances. But it was in vain. Patrick was a slow, considerate lover. A shy virgin would have enjoyed this consummation, but Juliet was experienced and spoiled. She liked to play, to switch roles; she wanted to laugh, scream, and arch her back. Patrick's tenderness did not excite her. When the time came, she feigned climax. She had done it for many men. But how sad to do it on her wedding night.

"That was quite lovely," whispered Patrick. "You make me very happy, my beautiful beloved. We shall have a wonderful life together."

Juliet did not answer, quarreling instead with her fate and hopes. She had wished for security, and here it was. Security, but also boredom.

Not passion.

Chapter 5

Kevin was awakened by the first grenade blasts of the day. He had slept through the early-morning gunfire, and he wouldn't have believed there'd been fighting if not for the two Scottish soldiers waiting to have wounds from grazing shots bandaged.

"We weren't supposed to wake you, Doctor," one of them said. "We're hardly dying."

"Not like the bastards who attacked us," the other declared. "Pure luck that McDuff has such a weak bladder. Otherwise, they would have taken the guards by surprise. But he went out the back of the tent."

"And my gun was at hand. It's not the first time we've fought the blokes, you know." The Scottish regiment seemed to have participated in the war from the beginning. "I shot one of them right off his horse, and then everyone was awake."

In spite of all the guards and patrols, two Boer commandos had attacked the British camp around three in the morning. The Australians, however, had fought them off just as successfully as the Scots. On the British side, there were no casualties to mourn, but three Boers had been left for dead or dying.

Kevin heard Dr. Willcox, who had just arrived, dressing down two orderlies. They had woken neither Kevin nor Barrister when the badly wounded foe was brought in. Now he was dead—and Kevin saw for the first time one of the dreaded Boer fighters. He did not look very impressive—he wore neither uniform nor boots, just a bloodstained jacket, corduroy pants, and thick, soft leather shoes. He had blond hair, a broad face, and a stocky build.

"We couldn't have done much for him, probably, but this is unacceptable," Willcox shouted at the orderlies. "Even when it's the enemy, we treat him. It's our humanitarian duty. Now, take the man out and see if he has any papers on him—maybe you'll find out his name. It should be recorded, so the family can be informed after the war. We fight hard, boys, but we're not animals. It's bad enough that the other side has no respect for the rules."

Willcox greeted Kevin, and the doctors had just enough time to look over the serious cases they had stayed up operating on the previous night. One man had died, but Barrister and Kevin had at least saved two. Willcox had them sent off to the field hospital on the van Stout farm.

"Tell the driver to go slowly, so they don't get shaken too much," he instructed the orderlies. "For now, it should be fine. If dozens need to be transported again—"

The sounds of battle from the direction of Wepener did not bode well. Kevin and Willcox were already deep in surgery before the cook had brought them breakfast. They gulped down bread and coffee between two patients. The wounded followed one another much faster here than in the field hospital. The doctors on the front mostly handled first aid—and screening. Kevin was horrified when Willcox classified two cases as hopeless and had them laid on straw to die.

"But we could still try," he said. "A bullet grazed the lung, seems like. This one does have a chance."

Willcox looked at him sympathetically. "He would have a chance if we had more time and more doctors. But like this, he's taking someone else's place. I'm sorry, Drury. If he lasts until tonight, I'll try it then."

Kevin now saw the military chaplains. They were much needed here, comforting the wounded and giving others last rites. He wondered how they could even hear themselves think. The groans and screaming in the first-aid tent were infernal. Kevin and Willcox could not keep up with the administration of opiates. Add to that the incessant noise of battle, and after only a few hours, Kevin was completely demoralized. His uniform clung to his body, soaked through with sweat and blood.

"Are we at least making progress?" he asked a lightly wounded soldier, having pointed the man toward a hospital transport wagon.

"I think so, sir. The howitzer bombardment is having an effect, and they're running out of ammunition in the fort. Plus, we seem to have the commandos outside under control. They seem to realize they can't defeat a whole army. But are we going to enter the town today?"

***

Kevin was almost surprised when the day at last reached its end. With the dwindling light, the shooting ebbed, and in the last hours, fewer wounded had come to them. He and Willcox were finally able to turn to the difficult cases. Kevin did what he could, but it was cold comfort. He had seen too much blood that day and been unable to help too many men.

Late that night, Tracy arrived to relieve him. In the field hospital, things had also calmed down. He had been able to change his clothes and looked crisp once more. Not to mention more optimistic. It had done him good to be able to undertake successful operations.

"It ought to be over tomorrow," reported Willcox, having spoken with a high-ranking officer. "Their defenses are holding, and they'll fight to the last bullet, if not to the last drop of blood. But in truth, they're already beaten. We'll be marching into Wepener no later than the afternoon."

"So, all for nothing," Tracy said.

Kevin was already saddling his horse to ride back to the van Stout farm. Tracy followed him outside and lit a cigarette.

"The Boers had the town, then we had the town, then the Boers again, now us again. For each of these exchanges, a hundred men have died. And in the end, we'll give it back to the Boers. We can't keep it garrisoned forever, you know. It's mad. This whole war is mad." He took deep, rapid drags.

Kevin was about to ask why Tracy had volunteered for war with that mentality, when Sergeant Willis appeared.

"Doctor? Good, you're still here. I can't find Willcox. But there's something you should see. We've taken a few prisoners."

"Wounded?" asked Tracy.

Kevin moved to rehitch his horse.

"Yes and no. We captured a sort of Boer field hospital. Three wounded and two women."

Willis led the doctors to a heavily guarded covered wagon. The canvas was pulled back, and three English soldiers pointed their guns at the people inside. Two middle-aged women, their neat clothing smeared with blood, and a brown-haired, bearded man with his arm in a sling. His clothing was like that of the dead man Kevin had seen that morning: once-white corduroys combined with a vest and a sort of frock jacket along with a hat with a wide, floppy brim. His bright eyes stared wrathfully at Kevin. The women were caring for two other men lying on straw beds.

"The two men are heavily wounded," said Willis. "One of the women started cutting already, took a bullet from that one's shoulder, I think. The other's bleeding like mad, and they can't get it under control."

Kevin climbed into the wagon. The bearded man put himself immediately in the way and spat a few words of Afrikaans at him.

"Remove him," Willis ordered.

The guards did not need to be told twice. However, they really had to wrestle the man away. Simply threatening him with a weapon had no effect. He seemed ready to let himself be shot. The women likewise resisted when Kevin now turned to the wounded men, but at least they did not become violent. They did not respond when Kevin warmly introduced himself as a doctor and there to help.

"Do they not speak English?" he asked.

Willis snorted. "Earlier, they understood it quite well."

Tracy had joined them and tried translating, but could not wring a reply from the women either.

Kevin gave the men a cursory examination. "The one needs rest more than anything," he declared. "The operation to remove the bullet could have been done more precisely, and the poultice the ladies made doesn't exactly inspire confidence. But fine, home remedies sometimes work. The ladies seem to have experience. I'm fairly certain we can save him. But the second one needs an operation as soon as possible. Before that, his leg must be bound better or he'll bleed out. I suggest we do that at once, and then take the whole group to the field hospital. We can operate there, and the women can look after their patients afterward." Kevin turned to the older of the two women. "Is he a relative of yours?"

She glared at him. "You my son not touch. I care my son."

Kevin shook his head. "If we don't operate, your son will die. Dr. Tracy, could you translate? I don't think she understands me."

Tracy repeated Kevin's words in Dutch, but the woman's expression did not change.

"My son not touch!" she repeated, then launched into a sermon in Afrikaans.

Tracy raised his hands helplessly. "Oh, she understands you," he said. "But she won't, under any circumstances, allow an Englishman to operate on her flesh and blood. What's more, she's convinced she can save the boy. With God's help."

"Can't anyone convince her that God sent us to help?" asked Kevin, flinching as the woman let loose a cannonade of curses.

Tracy rubbed his forehead. "I don't need to translate that, do I?"

Kevin shook his head. "Can we move her a little ways off?" he asked Willis. "So she can still see him, but—"

Willis nodded and turned to the remaining guard. "Private, keep these women at a distance while the doctor does his work. Actually, wait a moment. I'll get reinforcements so they don't scratch your eyes out."

In fact, it did take two soldiers to tear the women away from the wagon. They then watched, cursing and lamenting, as Kevin and Tracy applied a professional tourniquet and a compression bandage. The patient was quite young, twenty at most. Kevin was touched by his pale face and his blond, patchy beard. The boy reminded him of Doortje.

"That'll hold until the hospital." He finally turned to the soldiers. "Please have these people sent to the van Stout farm immediately. On this wagon, so the patients aren't moved. I'll be right behind. We'll have to perform the operation tonight. If we tie it off too long, the boy will lose his leg. Oh yes, and watch out when you let the women back in. Don't let them tear the bandage off."

Kevin thought he saw a happy flash in the woman's eyes when he mentioned the farm. The soldier let her go, and she rushed to her son's side.

Tracy held out a pack of cigarettes to Kevin and lit one for him. Kevin caught himself sucking in the smoke as fiercely as Tracy had before.

"What is wrong with these people?" he asked. "The woman would rather let her son die than have an Englishman save him. Maybe I should have explained I'm really a New Zealander."

Tracy shook his head. "We're all the same to them," he said. "I tried explaining I'm from Australia, but it got me nowhere."

"So, you had Boer patients yesterday too?" Kevin asked.

"No, but I—" Tracy fell silent a moment and took another deep drag. "For me, all this here is terra incognita. I haven't done an amputation since school. I've been an ophthalmologist for five years. And, well, we didn't have anything to do on that farm for three days. So, I offered to fix Mrs. van Stout's eyes."

Kevin looked at him in disbelief. "And she refused?"

Tracy nodded. "She's got cataracts, easily operable. She'd regain her full power of sight." He mused. "But yes, she refused. God had decreed that she be blind, and she was not about to let some filthy Englishman change that."

Kevin rubbed his tired eyes. "That—that's incomprehensible to me. What did her daughter say?"

"The charming Mejuffrouw Doortje?" Tracy mocked. "She delivered a few scathing Bible verses. Old Testament, of course. They seem to see it as something of a weakness that Christ didn't ascertain the nationality of the sick before healing them. No chance, in any case. And you'll certainly have fun with that lot, Drury." He gestured to the covered wagon just then rolling out of the camp. "Honestly, I'm glad I don't have to deal with them."

***

When Kevin's horse arrived at the van Stout farm, the covered wagon stood at the main entrance, but he saw no sign of either the inmates or the guards. Kevin hoped to find both in the barn, but he saw only the guards, in a heated discussion with Drs. Barrister and McAllister.

Kevin greeted his superior and his colleague. "So, you've already heard," he said. "A tear of the femoral artery. We need to operate immediately to save the leg. Now, where the hell is he?" Kevin looked around.

"It really wasn't our fault," the soldier who had driven the covered wagon said. "I thought, you know, the women seemed to know each other, and no one would have anything against it if they took care of the men themselves."

"Which women?"

"The ones from the wagon and the van Stouts," McAllister explained. "If I understand these men here properly, our hostesses took in the new arrivals. It was apparently a warm greeting. The private thinks they're related. At any rate, they had their servants carry the men into the house—and now they've barricaded themselves in one of the children's rooms. Knives between their teeth and ready for anything."

"What?" Kevin asked, horrified. "And you let them go?"

The private shrugged.

"We made a mistake, sir," the higher ranking of the two admitted. "But like he said, it seemed they were family. And the women on the farm, they did allow a hospital here and—"

"After everything I just did trying to save him, how could you—" Kevin took a deep breath. "How do we get them out?"

"We don't," McAllister said. "They don't have guns anymore, sure, but they've got kitchen knives. And they're threatening to gut themselves before they let us touch their men again. Is it worth it?"

"It's about the principle," Kevin declared. "We're the British Army, damn it! Couldn't we take them by surprise?"

McAllister shook his head. "No. They won't fall for that again. And they chose that room strategically. The only way would be to storm it. And then we'd have to explain to high command why we had to shoot a bunch of women."

Kevin groaned. "But there has to be a way."

"It is about the principle, Dr. Drury. You're absolutely right," said Barrister. His long fingers raked nervously through his mustache. "But perhaps not military principles. We're doctors. People come to us when they want to be healed. When they don't want to be healed, they stay away. In civilian life, we don't force anyone. But now you want to drag patients onto the operating table by force? That won't do, Drury. As much as it pains me not to help. The staff corporal here tells me the boy's practically still a child. But he's under his mother's guardianship, and she gets to decide. Our hands are tied."

Kevin wanted to argue, but he saw that his superior was right. As was Angus. It would be unfair to endanger soldiers' lives by forcing them to overpower these desperate women. Still, that boy's face . . .

"I would agree, Dr. Barrister, if it were really the patient's decision," he said carefully. "But no one asked him. Does he really want to die?"

"So, ask him if you get a chance, Drury. Or convince the van Stouts. It's not up to us."

Chapter 6

"And so, they built the camp. They tied the heads of the horses and oxen together, and arranged the covered wagons in circles to provide cover. Everyone gathered wood and thornbushes and filled in the gaps that way. The men anchored the wagons in the ground and readied their muskets. The women and children would reload them after the men fired. Oh yes, Thies, they had weapons, our grandfathers. They knew, you see, that they would need to fight for their land, but they also knew that God was with them. And so, they said prayers once more before the Kaffirs came. Even as the savages rushed the wagon fort, our brave forefathers called on God, for he had led them here. No, Mees, the Kaffirs did not have guns. God did not allow it. They had only knives and spears. But what spears! Long and sharp as razor blades, and giant shields stretched with skins. And how they looked! Hundreds and hundreds of giant warriors, dressed only in loincloths and feathers, their shameful bodies damnably painted."

Doortje van Stout tied on a fresh white bonnet, listening with half an ear as her mother told her little brothers of the Great Trek. Of wagon forts and battles, of many dead, and ultimately, of victory. Of the land God had promised the Boers, and which they had paid for in blood.

Doortje could also have told these stories, and someday, when she had her own children, she would. Knowledge of how the land was taken must be kept alive. Doortje's mother, Bentje, had not been present on the Trek. And her grandparents must still have been children when the English had conquered Cape Town and tried to take everything from the Boers: their language, their laws, their church—and most of all, their slaves. God had not wanted it so. And so, the pioneers had set out over the mountains, their households loaded in oxcarts, their livestock driven alongside them by slaves. At night, they had circled the wagons to protect themselves from wild animals. And from the heathen blacks who would not accept that God had sent the Boers. He punished them gruesomely for that: in the Battle of Blood River alone, three thousand Zulu warriors had fallen. But the right arm of the Lord shielded the Boers. Not a single dead and only three wounded.

Doortje recalled having once asked why God could not have simply destroyed the English from the start. Or never have made the Zulu Kaffirs. They weren't good for anything, anyway. Only a few were suited for work on the farms, and even they were fools. She was still furious with Nandi for her failure to defend them. Bentje had possessed an answer for that, but Doortje could no longer recall it. Surely, it had been a silly, improper question. Like asking why the English were winning again now. For they were; Aunt Jacoba and Cousin Antina said so. The English had annihilated Uncle Jonas and Cousin Cornelis's command, and now Aunt Jacoba's husband was missing; Antina's husband, Willem, was gravely wounded; and Cornelis lay dying. If that English doctor was to be believed. Aunt Jacoba and Cousin Antina insisted he was already better. The bleeding had stopped, at least. And they would all pray for him together again in a moment.

Doortje felt the lace around her bonnet and checked that her hair was modestly hidden beneath it. She must look proper, especially for prayers. Before her mother lost her sight, she had sent the girl back to her room regularly to change an imperfectly ironed bonnet or a smudged apron. It had been difficult for Doortje to learn these things. She much preferred to work in the fields than in the house, and most of all, loved sticking her nose in books. But that was sinful, of course—if also occasionally useful. Doortje's father had made his children learn English. It was easier to defeat an enemy you knew, he preached, and that made sense to Doortje. However, it was not simple to learn a language and hate it at the same time. None of the other children had gotten very good at it, but Doortje had worked hard to please her father. Alas, she still saw the disappointment every time he looked at her.

Adrianus van Stout had wanted a son, but after Doortje, Bentje had not become pregnant again for many years. Doortje had been forced to hear her parents pray every day to be blessed with male offspring. Only when Doortje was already eight years old was Johanna born. Another girl. Adrianus had resigned himself to bestowing the painstaking, puritanical education he had wanted for his son on Doortje. She learned the history of her country. She learned who her enemies were and how to fight them. She learned how she was to be a proper Boer woman, hard on herself and others. No one had ever seen Doortje van Stout cry since her sister was born.

But then God had relented and sent his servant Adrianus two sons. Since then, Mees and Thies had been at the center of the family. Mother and sisters coddled them, and their father was utterly devoted. Until he had gone to war a few months before, he had instructed the boys every day—both could already shoot and speak a little English.

As for Doortje's education, Adrianus considered it complete. She could write and read the Bible, not to mention shoot and manage a household. Nothing more was proper for a Boer girl. But Doortje could not get enough. After evening prayers, she would sneak to the bookshelf where, next to the family Bible, stood two English books. By the miserable light of a candle, she would struggle through the strange language of William Shakespeare, developing an ever-greater vocabulary. Cousin Cornelis, however, had laughed when he heard her speak English for the first time.

"Doortje, that's not how the English talk anymore! Those books were written hundreds of years ago."

After that, he had secretly lent her more-modern books, like Dickens and Kipling. Cornelis's family, the Pienaars, lived in Transvaal and had taken part in the Great Trek. Another branch of his family, however, had stayed behind at the cape and now made wine there. This was a deadly sin in the eyes of Adrianus van Stout.

"Father says God will punish them for it one day," Doortje had once told Cornelis anxiously. She hoped his family would not be smitten right away. She liked Cornelis very much, even if he sometimes thought forbidden things and even did them.

"Well, so far, he's just made the grapes grow abundantly," Cornelis had replied irreverently. The young man had visited his relatives many times. "The Cape Boers are richer than us, you know."

Cornelis's parents, too, thought it important for him to learn English, but for more practical reasons. And Cornelis did not learn from a dusty lesson book. He was supposed to get to know the Englishmen. Cornelis now spoke fluent English, and he was happy to pass on his knowledge to Doortje. However, she worried about his exposure to corrupting influences.

Doortje tore herself from her thoughts and tied on a lily-white apron. Bentje was still out in the living room, telling the children how Andries Pretorius had set after the fleeing Zulu warriors.

"He took with him one hundred fifty riders on ponies. Yes, one hundred fifty against the many thousands of Kaffirs. And with them, he drove the hordes into the river. God guided their bullets. They shot at the heathens as at rabbits, and the river ran red with their blood."

Doortje wondered whether it had not simply been the sight of the stampeding ponies that had driven back the Kaffirs. In one of Cornelis's books, there had been talk of the ancient Greeks, who did not ride their horses, instead only hitching them to wagons. When they saw the first riders, they took them for centaurs. Perhaps the Zulu had been similarly misled. But of course, they deserved it, because they were dirty heathens.

Doortje was untroubled by Cornelis's argument that the Zulu had simply never heard of God the Father or God the Son before the whites came. After all, her mother said that was proof of their lesser value. God had not bothered to reveal himself to them.

Content with her appearance, Doortje entered the front room.

"Shall we hold devotion now?"

Bentje van Stout raised her head, and Doortje looked into her eyes, startled as always by their empty gaze. Her mother had once moved through the world like a hawk, from which no detail escaped. But then God had punished her with blindness. Doortje tried not to think about the Englishman who said he could heal it. Her mother was no doubt right to submit to God's will and reject the enemy's offer.

"Yes, yes, of course, child," Bentje answered. "I've almost finished my story. I only wanted to tell of the land our forefathers took possession of. Johanna, go get Aunt Jacoba and Cousin Antina. Maybe one of them can come to devotion."

Doortje reached for the family Bible. "I'll go into the sickroom later and read a few verses to Willem and Cornelis too."

She had wanted to hold devotion there, but Thies and Mees's room was simply too small. It was quite dark too. But easily defensible with only one way in. She would not make that grave mistake again. Doortje cringed to think how ashamed her father would be that she'd allowed the farm to be taken.

Bentje finished her story while Doortje sought a suitable Bible passage for devotion. Suddenly, a knocking came from the door, then the window. Doortje recognized the angular face and dark hair of the English doctor. No, not English, supposedly. Where did he come from? New Zealand, wherever that was. He gesticulated wildly when he saw Doortje had noticed him.

"Miss, that is, Mejuffrouw van Stout." Doortje almost had to laugh at his mangled pronunciation. "Please, may I have a brief word?"

Doortje reluctantly got up. They had agreed to ignore the men, but if she did not act now, the bothersome fellow might disturb their devotion. And Jacoba and Antina desperately needed comfort.

"Yes?"

Doortje opened the door and looked coldly at the doctor. For the first time, she really looked him in the eye, exerting herself not to notice how handsome he was, with his fine features, blue eyes, and full lips. Yet he also looked exhausted. His eyes had dark circles beneath them, and wrinkles formed around his mouth.

"Mejuffrouw van Stout, you're a clever woman," Kevin began somewhat desperately. "You must recognize the condition that young man we brought here is in."

"My cousin Cornelis," Doortje replied. "His life lies in God's hands."

"Your cousin," Kevin repeated, his voice betraying relief. "Miss van Stout, you have to let us operate on your cousin. If we don't, he'll die of blood loss."

"My cousin is recovering," Doortje said. "My aunt Jacoba says he has not lost a drop of blood in hours."

Kevin sighed. "Of course not, or he'd be dead already. Miss van Stout, Dr. Tracy and I tied off his leg. At the moment, no blood is flowing at all. That means, in a few hours, the only option will be to amputate it."

"He can live with one leg," Doortje responded, but it was hard for her to feign confidence.

Cornelis was more bookworm than farmer. But he had not wanted to become a pastor, nor even a clerk like Martinus. He loved riding out into the veld and observing animals; once, he had admitted to her that he would like to be a veterinarian. His parents would never let him study, though. Nevertheless, he had lovingly cared for the ponies and helped the cattle calve. That would be hard with one leg.

"He'll die in that case, too, Miss van Stout, if we don't operate," Kevin pressed. "The leg won't simply fall off. It'll rot slowly. It's much worse than bleeding to death. He must already be in terrible pain. Is he conscious?"

Doortje bit her lip. She had avoided approaching Cornelis's bed. It was too painful to see her friend and cousin so pale and sick.

"I do not think so," she replied, speaking for the first time in a normal voice. "I believe he is still sleeping."

Kevin nodded. "Thank goodness. But he won't stay like that, Miss van Stout. He'll wake up, and he'll die in horrific pain. Let me operate on him, Miss van Stout, please."

Doortje eyed the doctor. He really seemed to be serious. But how could a subject of the English Crown care so much about a Boer? Doortje hardened herself anew as she had been taught to do.

"I do not make decisions for my cousin, Doctor. His mother is with him. Speak with her."

Kevin would have liked to shake the girl. She was so smart, and yet she was condemning her cousin to death from sheer stubbornness, blind patriotism, and adherence to a merciless faith.

Desperately, he pointed to the Bible in Doortje's hand. "Ever read that?" he asked. "I mean not just the 'eye for an eye, tooth for a tooth' passages, but really read it? Some of it's about charity. About love for your neighbor. About help for the helpless. Do you really believe your cousin wants to die? Will you play executioner when God has sent someone who can help?"

Kevin turned away before Doortje could reply. But now, her mother was calling from inside. The young woman followed the call, although she felt quite dizzy. Oil lamps lit the room, but Doortje fumbled with her Bible as if she were blind. She opened to a random passage. The first book of Samuel: "So the Lord saved Israel that day."

That seemed suitable. It was something about the war between the Israelites and the Philistines, and Israel seemed to be at a disadvantage. Just like the Boers at the moment. Doortje began to read. "'And the men of Israel were distressed that day: for Saul had adjured the people, saying, "Cursed *be* the man that eateth any food until evening, that I may be avenged on mine enemies." So none of the people tasted any food. And all they of the land came to a wood; and there was honey upon the ground. And when the people were come into the wood, behold, the honey dropped; but no man put his hand to his mouth: for the people feared the oath. But Jonathan heard not when his father charged the people with the oath: wherefore he put forth the end of the rod that was in his hand, and dipped it in a honeycomb, and put his hand to his mouth; and his eyes were enlightened.'"

Doortje stopped, distressed. His eyes were enlightened? God healed a blind man by having him break an oath? Her hands cramped around the Bible.

"'Then answered one of the people, and said, "Thy father straitly charged the people with an oath, saying, 'Cursed be the man that eateth *any* food this day.'" And the people were faint. Then said Jonathan, 'My father hath troubled the land.'"

Doortje's voice died off. This could not be. She lowered the Bible, then lifted it hastily again and opened to a different passage.

"'Trust in the Lord with all thine heart; and lean not unto thine own understanding. In all thy ways acknowledge him, and he shall direct thy paths. Be not wise in thine own eyes: fear the Lord, and depart from evil. It shall be health to thy navel, and marrow to thy bones. Honor the Lord. Amen.'"

The verse had not reached its end, but Doortje thought that was enough. Her listeners seemed happy and comforted, despite the strange passage. The second had been right. She must not think she was wiser than God. She must trust in him.

Doortje van Stout breathed in deeply. "Shall we say a few prayers? Mother?"

Bentje van Stout began to intone a prayer. Then, however, she was interrupted by a cry from the sickroom. It was Antina, who had stayed with Cornelis.

"Aunt Jacoba, your son is waking up," Antina said.

Jacoba turned her eyes to heaven. "Thank the Lord," she whispered.

Bentje and the others repeated the phrase. "Thank the Lord."

Only Doortje stayed quiet.

***

Doortje spent almost the whole following night in a desperate search for that first Bible verse. But she couldn't find it no matter how she turned the pages by the feeble light of the oil lamp. It might have been that she was so distracted. Again and again, she heard the groaning and the screams from the sickroom. She exchanged a few words with Jacoba or Antina when she went to the kitchen to make tea or prepare a poultice.

"It eases his pain," averred Jacoba, looking more and more desperate as the night wore on.

Doortje thought about what the doctor had said. Usually herbs would ease the pain, but not in this case, not if his leg was already dying. She took her brother in her arms when he came into the room, unable to sleep.

"Cornelis won't stop moaning, Doortje. Can't God make his leg stop hurting?"

Doortje bit her tongue. But then, sometime after midnight, she could not take it any longer.

"I can watch him awhile, Aunt Jacoba," she offered as she entered the sickroom. "You should lie down. You look exhausted."

"But I—I can't just leave him."

Jacoba looked as if she were about to shatter into a thousand shards. Her day on the battlefield had been long. She had followed the commando and had seen it annihilated. Seen her husband die. Jonas Pienaar had been the leader.

Doortje still remembered how he had called the men together. Her own father and her fiancé had already set out. They had leaped onto their horses the moment war was declared. But the Pienaars had waited. Until things looked bad for the Boers. Until luck sided with the British. Was it luck? Or God? Or simply the fact that a hundred thousand soldiers from all parts of the British Empire had landed on the coast? Cornelis had thought the latter.

Doortje stepped close to his bed. "You don't mind if I stay awhile with you, do you, Cornelis? Your mother needs to rest."

The wounded man nodded. Doortje was horrified by his appearance. His face was deathly pale, sharp, and sunken, but his eyes seemed to burn. Surely, he had a fever.

"Go, Aunt Jacoba," Doortje encouraged his mother again. "Rest."

Antina had already given in to her exhaustion. She lay snoring on a mat next to her husband.

Doortje sat on Cornelis's bed once Jacoba had reluctantly withdrawn. He groaned.

"Is it very bad?" she asked.

Cornelis nodded again. He seemed unable or unwilling to speak. Maybe he was afraid he would scream. Doortje went to hold his hand—and found shreds of the sheet in his fingers. He tore at it, desperately, in his pain.

"I'm dying," he managed. "For nothing."

Doortje stroked his hair, which was soaked with sweat. She remembered how angry Jonas Pienaar had been at his eldest when it was time for their commando to depart. Cornelis had arrived last and tried to change the men's minds.

"We can't hold Wepener. There are too many of them; you all saw for yourselves how many troops they're massing. We—"

"We'll attack them from behind," his father had proclaimed. "We'll be like hornets that fall upon them."

"But a few hornet stings are not going to drive them away," Cornelis had insisted.

He had looked like the other Boers in his corduroy pants, his thick jacket over his vest, and with the Boer hat on his head, while his father had donned some sort of general's costume. Doortje had wondered where he could have gotten it—or the bowler hat he wore on his head. She wasn't sure whether the effect was imposing or laughable.

"We can kill a few, sure," Cornelis conceded, "but to what end?"

"To what end?" Jonas had drawn his old-fashioned saber—naturally, he'd be fighting with a rifle, but he seemed to think the sword indispensable if he wanted to look like an officer. Now he waved it in his son's face. "You ask why we should kill this race of snakes? Quite simple: So they don't kill us! And so they don't produce any more children to kill our children. Death to the English! With God's help, we shall wipe them from the face of this, our promised land!"

The men of the unit, barely a hundred in number, cheered. They had elected Jonas Pienaar by an overwhelming majority and now felt confirmed in their choice.

"So, will you join us, Cornelis Pienaar, or are you going to hide on your farm like a cowardly Kaffir while we liberate our country?" asked Willem DeWees, the husband of Antina, Cornelis's cousin.

Doortje had looked in Cornelis's tortured face and wondered at his hesitation. She would have left with the men at once. When her father had left, she had once again regretted that she'd been born a girl. Yet, on the other hand, she had never thought Cornelis a coward.

"He won't have a farm anymore if he proves to be a chicken now," Jonas Pienaar declared. "In fact, he won't even be my son. Right, Jacoba?"

Jacoba glared at her son. "You'll never set foot in our home again."

Cornelis had lowered his head and simply added his pony to the column of others. That was how he had gone to war. And now he lay here.

Doortje made a decision.

"You're not going to die," she said quietly. "Wait—and don't make a sound. Don't wake Antina. And for heaven's sake, not your mother."

***

Kevin started awake when someone shook him. Despite his concern for the dying boy, he had slept deeply, bone tired after the endless day. Now he thought he was hallucinating when he saw the face of the girl hovering over him. Not composed, cool, or mocking as usual, but excited and afraid. Doortje's strict coiffure beneath her bonnet had loosened. The braids were hanging down, and her hair was freeing itself from the braids. How beautiful it would look falling loose around her face.

"Doortje," whispered Kevin. "For-forgive me, Meju—"

"Do not talk," Doortje said coolly. "Just save my cousin."

Chapter 7

While Kevin roused the other doctors, Doortje led a few strong orderlies into the house. Though she had hoped to sneak Cornelis out unnoticed, her cousin Antina slept too lightly for that. She awoke and wailed, which woke Cornelis's mother, as well as Bentje and Johanna van Stout. But the sleep-dazed women were easy to overpower. Two orderlies held them fast. The others carried the wounded man. Kevin heard the cries of protest and curses—and felt sorry for Doortje and the hell she'd have to pay. Kevin chided himself for not having kept her in the barn. Then she could have claimed the dastardly English had taken her by surprise as well. Soon, however, he forgot the women in the house and devoted himself entirely to saving his patient. The more experienced surgeons, Barrister and McAllister, took over the operation itself. Kevin was responsible for the anesthesia, but it was hard to correctly dose the ether so that the man, weak from blood loss, did not die from it. In the end, though, Barrister was able to save his life, and even the leg.

"Looks like we're done, at least for now," he declared. "We'll have to see how things develop. If we have bad luck, we'll have to give it another go tomorrow."

In the barn, Cornelis lay recovering on a straw bed. Morning light was already spreading, and Kevin knew that he really ought to lie down if he wanted to get a little rest before the arrival of the first wounded soldiers. But then he saw a muted light in the front room and so crossed once more to the house. Doortje would want to know how the operation had gone.

And indeed, Kevin could see her through the window, sitting at the table and studying the Bible by the light of a candle stub. Kevin opened the door slowly and as quietly as possible—he did not want to startle her nor, heaven forbid, alert anyone else to his presence.

"You'll ruin your eyes," he whispered, pointing to her book, "reading in such bad light."

Doortje did not look surprised. Perhaps she had expected him.

"If God wishes to punish me with blindness, then—" She broke off. "How is Cornelis?"

"He's alive, and we hope he'll be able to keep his leg. But please don't come at us with knives if we do have to amputate. His leg went a long time without blood. Now, at least, you have a real reason to pray."

Kevin would have liked to sit next to the young woman, but he did not know how she would react to that, and so remained standing. Doortje looked up at him. She looked wan, exhausted.

"That is what I was doing this whole time," she said. "We, we are not like you. For us, God is not a last chance. He is with us always."

Kevin shrugged. "He'll be leaving your people in Wepener today. They're still fighting, against all reason, but it'll be over today. Soon you'll get your farm back. And hopefully won't think too badly of us when we're gone. We did save your cousin, after all. Maybe your God sent us."

Kevin bit his lip. But the expected outburst did not come. Doortje was silent.

***

The morning once again brought an onrush of wounded men, but only a few very serious cases. The besieged seemed to have run out of ammunition. They were now trying to beat back the attackers with sabers, knives, and clubs. Around midday, the transports from the front stopped completely. The last of the lightly wounded who'd come to be bandaged reported a victorious entry into town.

"But there wasn't much to conquer," one New Zealander explained. "The men in the garrison were half-starved. They had broken off pieces of the mill to strengthen their barricades. The houses are shot up. Really, you'd need to rebuild the whole town—the Boers can do that after the war."

"The Boers really are getting it all back?" Kevin marveled. "The whole town?"

Barrister rolled his eyes. "Of course they'll get it back, Drury. What does the Crown want with this backward hill town? And we don't intend to drive out the Boers either. They just need to submit to British law, recognize a governor—maybe even learn English. It'll be the official language, anyway. Until they accept that, we'll man and hold fortifications like Wepener. As soon as there's peace, we'll withdraw. Spare us your musings about it all. Here, at least, there's a town at stake. A few weeks ago, our men and just as many Boers died for a hill, a stupid little hill no one needs. That's war, Drury. It's a matter, as you said yesterday, of principle. Anyway, you can go see your favorite patient now. He's awake. And maybe you can even entice your favorite shrew to come in and visit her cousin. Miss van Stout's been slinking around the barn like a ghost."

Kevin wasn't sure whom he should go to first. His heart pulled him toward Doortje, who was surely going through a hard time. The women in the house would now spurn her, yet she was, without a doubt, determined to continue hating the British. Kevin decided he'd best leave her be. Her family would surely hold any contact with him against her. So, he went to Cornelis. The young man looked markedly better that morning and provided a surprise when Kevin introduced himself: he smiled.

"I owe you my life. You and Doortje. I really thought it was the end. Thank you. Truly, thank you."

Kevin returned his smile. "I had rather expected curses," he confessed. "After all, we weren't sure if we were acting against your will."

Cornelis Pienaar looked him straight in the eye, and Kevin recognized deep pain in his watery blue eyes.

"I'm nineteen years old," said the boy. "I'd like to go to college. I'd like to be a teacher or doctor, or most of all, a veterinarian. But if I have to, I'll till my family's land. As for dying, I don't want to do that for many years. But I know I'm a coward. I'm a disgrace to my people. That's how they'll see it. They're all volunteers, you see. You are too, aren't you? The English are all volunteers."

Kevin shrugged. "The New Zealanders and Australians are all volunteers," he said. "Though, if you ask me, we're all just running away from something. So, we could argue about who the coward is here. Your cousin, in any case, isn't one. Thank her—and if it comforts your mother, tell her that the ladies scared the hell out of our people. The whole British Army hadn't the guts to pull you out of that house against their will."

Cornelis nodded. The sadness in his eyes seemed still to grow. "I understand," he murmured. "I know my mother."

***

Doortje did not dare visit Cornelis that day, and she did not exchange a word with Kevin either. In the end, he asked Nandi to inform her that her cousin was out of the woods. The black girl reported that, in contrast, the condition of the other wounded Boer, *baas* Willem, had dramatically worsened.

At that, Kevin made his way to the house once more and tried to talk to the women. Little Johanna van Stout sent him packing with wild curses in rather bad English.

"There's nothing you can do," said Barrister. "This time it is the clear will of the affected, alas. And your Doortje won't dare another affront, if only because the man is hardly as close to her heart as her cousin. Did you think to ask if he might be her intended?"

Kevin felt the question like a needle to the heart. Until then, he had not considered whether Doortje van Stout might already be promised to a man. He had better get away from here before he could fall deeper in love with the steely woman. The hospital would be disassembled as soon as the serious cases were ready for transport. Willcox and Tracy were already preparing rooms in Wepener where the men could receive further treatment.

The worsening of Willem DeWees's condition meant, at least, that the women in the house didn't have time to be furious with Doortje. By evening, she was even allowed to lead the Bible reading again.

And when Cornelis came around that evening, Kevin couldn't stop himself from asking gingerly about his relationship to Doortje.

"Adrianus van Stout would never dream of me as a son-in-law." He shook his head, smiling. "Even if Doortje and I loved each other. But, no, we've been like brother and sister since childhood. A van Stout girl could never marry a cowardly bookworm like me. I don't have an office in the church either, and our farm isn't particularly big. Martinus, on the other hand, is already a land owner. He'll be called to the council of elders as soon as he's started a family. His farm borders this one and—"

"Martinus?"

The wounded man nodded and tried to find a comfortable position. Kevin helped him and was grateful that Cornelis couldn't see his face while he continued his story. "Doortje's intended. Old Voortrekker nobility. His great-grandfather trekked with Doortje's great-grandfather. They're distantly related, somehow. In any case, it's always been certain that Doortje and Martinus would marry. It was planned for this year. Of course, Martinus and Adrianus were the first to go to war. Doortje would have followed them—as my mother and Antina did—but it would not have been proper for a girl so young to go alone, and Aunt Bentje needed help at home because of her blindness. Now, they're waiting for Adrianus and Martinus to come back."

Kevin sighed. "Martinus is probably also a daring rider and excellent shot."

Cornelis smiled. "You sound jealous, Doctor."

Kevin did not answer at first. Then, however, he thought he might as well ask the question, since everyone saw his feeling anyway.

"Mijnheer Pienaar, your cousin Doortje, well—Martinus, does she love him?"

***

The field hospital on the van Stout farm remained operational for almost another week. It took that long before the last seriously wounded men were ready for transport or had died. Besides, the units and staff doctors were waiting for new orders.

Doortje van Stout avoided Kevin studiously. Nor did she seek out Cornelis any more than his own mother did. Kevin worried what would come of the boy when they left.

Cornelis answered all of Kevin's questions about South Africa and its people. He described the Boers from a completely different point of view than Ribbons and the English at the cape, such that Kevin even came to enjoy the long-winded stories about the Voortrekkers.

"They were uncommonly brave—the way they moved off into the unknown with their oxcarts and families. No one had ever been on the other side of the mountains, you see. Nature was treacherous: the plateaus, the deserts. You had to get past those first. And then there were the natives."

"Who didn't want their land stolen for, oh, inconceivable reasons," Kevin said.

Cornelis nodded. "That's how you see it. But those people, the Voortrekkers, they saw themselves as successors of the Israelites, entering God's promised land. They were completely surprised by the Zulu attacks—insulted, really. And they felt themselves pursued on all sides: the English at the cape, the blacks inland. So, they built a wagon fortress and lashed out on all sides."

"With great success, I've heard," Kevin objected. "Three thousand dead black warriors in a single day."

"Before that came a few hundred dead Boers caught in an ambush. Neither side was squeamish. You shouldn't think of the Zulu as a naive people living in tiny villages. It was a kingdom with a well-functioning commonwealth and an exceedingly powerful army. Just as brave in the face of death as the trekkers. Their downfall was that the Boers had guns, and they didn't. I bet it wasn't any different in New Zealand. You have darkies, too, don't you?"

Kevin waved this away. "Our Maori are Polynesian. And peaceful, for the most part. They didn't have anything against the white settlers. At least not at first. Later, there were some conflicts, of course."

Cornelis grinned. "That's a nice word."

"A true word," Kevin said defensively. "There was shooting, there were dead on both sides, but never on this scale. They were local skirmishes. Wrong was without a doubt often done to the Maori, but now they're seeking recompense legally. I don't mean to say everything is perfect. Still, the Maori sit in our Parliament, they have the right to vote, they own land. Marriages between Maori and *pakeha* are not exactly common, but nor are they so rare."

"Marriages?" Cornelis asked in amazement. "Between black and white?"

Kevin nodded. "What's more, there was never slavery. The way you treat your black servants here—"

Cornelis raised an eyebrow. "Maybe your Maori are more civilized. Our blacks are like children. They need guidance. And they are truly subservient to us. Forty Kaffirs fought with our commando alone."

Kevin blinked rapidly in disbelief. "Children? And yet they had a kingdom, a country, cities, an army. Is a person an adult only when he holds a gun?"

***

Cornelis was considerably more enlightened than the other Boers Kevin had met. But when it came to the treatment of the native population, he could be no more reasoned with than Doortje or her family. All logical contradictions aside, he was utterly convinced of the inferiority of dark-skinned people and did not trust them. Kevin pointed out to Cornelis repeatedly that this was a contradiction in itself, since he never grew tired of emphasizing the servility of black workers. After a few conversations with Pienaar, Kevin became convinced that the Boers actually feared them.

"It's not courage that drives them on, but a sort of fear that causes them to lash out," he explained to his friend Vincent.

The veterinarian had arrived at the field hospital with three wounded horses, asking Kevin for help.

"They've got bullets stuck in their large muscles, Kevin. They need to be cut out, but I can't manage it alone. They won't hold still either. Please, could you help?"

At first, Kevin wanted to refuse this "interdepartmental cooperation," but the haggard face of the young veterinarian made him change his mind. Vincent looked as if he had aged years in the three days in the field. His friendly, trusting face had crumbled into a mask of grief and incomprehension.

"It was horrible," Vincent told him as Kevin first opened a bottle of whiskey. "They—they—until now, I always thought men waged war, well, against men. Yes, a horse will get hit now and again, but you shoot at the rider. And these Boers, you'd think they loved horses. They all ride beautifully. So, to see how they aim for our horses, massacre them. Five of our unit's horses are dead, Kevin. And so many others. Totally senseless. These people are—they're—"

Kevin forewent informing him of the equally senseless loss of human life. Vincent would presumably have argued that the soldiers had volunteered to fight. Instead, he'd opted to share his observations about the Boers.

"They're afraid of the blacks and what they've inflicted on them, so they lash out, like frightened dogs."

Vincent smiled weakly. "That may well be. But does it change anything?"

Kevin shook his head. He thought of Doortje, whom he preferred to understand as misguided and fearful rather than greedy, evil, and belligerent. But he could not possibly tell his friend that.

"It doesn't change anything," he said. "But it frightens me. For these people, the war will never end. But come, let's see about those horses. I wonder what Barrister will have to say about this."

***

Two of the three horses survived the surgery. Vincent seemed a little happier when he returned two days later to check on the animals. He also took the opportunity to relay the New Zealand contingent's new marching orders.

"We won't stay together. The New Zealanders are being placed under Major Robin, some of the Australians as well. The new regiment now has an official name: the Rough Riders. The English seem impressed by our cavalry."

"Cavalry" was one name for the thrown-together band of mounted New Zealanders. Mostly, they were young men from the plains who grew up in the saddle. They did not have much aptitude for rank-and-file exercises, and did not particularly like following orders. Yet the British leadership saw that as an opportunity, not a deficiency. In essence, the generals decided, the cloddish Kiwis were not so different from the Boers. It was a great deal easier for these sheep farmers to comprehend the locals' way of thinking than it was for professional British soldiers. As a consequence, the Rough Riders were not assigned to a relieving or attacking force but to the guarding of trains in the Transvaal province. Their assignment was fighting against marauding Boer commandos, inspecting remote farms that often served as hideouts, and the general pacification of the area.

"Keep our rear safe," was the order from Field Marshal Lord Roberts, who had now overtaken supreme command along with General Kitchener.

Vincent was assigned to the Rough Riders as their veterinarian, Kevin Drury and Preston Tracy as their doctors. They would transport their improvised hospital with them on two packhorses. Both were loath to part from Barrister, Willcox, and McAllister, who were riding with the troops in the direction of Bloemfontein.

Barrister thanked the men for their work. "You've both proved that you can handle the sight of blood. You'll get along fine on your own."

"And maybe we'll see each other again," McAllister said. "The war's supposed to be over soon, but you never know. Besides, maybe you'll be staying here, Kevin. It would be romantic for you to return to your Doortje victorious."

Kevin laughed along with the others, but he wanted to howl when he thought of Doortje. She'd continued to keep her distance, and he was coming to accept that he must mean nothing to her. Cornelis's answer to his question about Doortje's feelings for her fiancé still rang in his ears: *Love has nothing to do with it, Doctor. Doortje and Martinus—they're of one tribe, one blood. Not literally, but in their beliefs, their wishes, their dreams. I wouldn't call it "love," but neither*

Doortje nor Martinus probably thinks about that. They suit each other admirably. They'll have wonderful children.

Cornelis's gaze had taken on a yearning quality, and Kevin had felt sorry for the young man. Cornelis was different, and he stood by his convictions. Nevertheless, he clearly wanted nothing more than to belong.

Kevin went to him one last time before the doctors rode off to unite with their regiment in Wepener.

"Are you sure I should leave you here?" he asked doubtfully. "We can take you along to Wepener for further care."

Cornelis shook his head. "That's very kind of you, but no. Once you're gone, my mother will take me back." He sighed. "She'll claim you operated on me against my will, no matter how I deny it. And Antina, maybe she's softened a little since Willem died."

The older man had passed away after a long struggle with gangrene. Antina DeWees had laid him in his grave with curses against the English and their allies.

"Okay, then. Give my regards to Doortje," Kevin said. "I thought we might be able to talk once more, but she—"

"She can't," Cornelis told him. "The others would never forgive her. But I'm sure she thinks of you as a friend."

Kevin smiled sadly.

A short while later, as he mounted his horse, he saw Doortje standing at the well with Johanna and Nandi. Nandi smiled shyly at the men riding away, Johanna acted as if she didn't see anything, and Doortje only raised her eyes once, briefly. Kevin's heart beat faster when he saw no hate therein, but something more like regret.

"Good-bye, Nandi," Kevin said, then took a provocatively long pause. "And Johanna and Mejuffrouw van Stout, I hope we didn't inconvenience you overmuch."

Doortje looked as if she were struggling against herself. Then, her face broke into a smile.

"Don't get your tongue twisted. Just call me Doortje. Anyway, we have to take what God gives us."

Kevin almost thought he saw her wink. He returned the smile.

"Everything happens according to God's will," he replied in a preacher's voice. "And I hope you won't hold it against him if one day we meet again."

With that, Kevin let his horse go, but when he looked back once more, he saw Doortje watching him. Even though Johanna was speaking to her angrily. And something in her gaze gave him hope. What did Cornelis know, what did the oh-so-perfect Martinus know of Doortje van Stout's innermost wishes and dreams?

Kevin caught himself whistling. In invoking God, he was thinking less of the Old Testament than of aggrieved Taranaki and Rangi, the divinity who still wept for Papa.

Chapter 8

Lizzie Drury was generally a peaceable person and deeply patient. She had learned early on to make the best of life's adversities. But life had not prepared her for having Juliet as a daughter-in-law.

"She could at least do something," Lizzie moaned to Michael a few weeks after Juliet moved in.

It was winter, and the sheep wandered around the yard. They needed to be taken care of, so she and Michael had their hands full. Added to that, many ewes had been bred early, and their lambs were already being born, providing extra excitement. Lizzie was constantly carrying a rejected or orphaned lamb around until it was strong enough to follow her everywhere, bleating. Most female visitors melted at the sight of the fuzzy creatures. During their visits to the farm, Matariki and Atamarie had doted on them. Yet Juliet seemed to find the baby animals disgusting, and neither could she tolerate the dogs, well-trained and very friendly border collies.

"Now, no one's asking her to help with the lambing," Lizzie replied angrily when Michael reminded her not everyone liked to share their homes with animals. "She doesn't need to bottle-feed the lambs or train the puppies, but she could cook dinner sometime when we're outside all day. Or at least clean the house—I'd be happy if she just swept. Instead, she sits around and complains she's bored."

Juliet had reluctantly accepted the fact that her child could only pass as Patrick's if she pushed back the official birthdate a couple months. If not, she would be exposed to gossip; worse to Lizzie's mind, the child might be bullied when it got older. Since it was impossible for Patrick to leave his work and take

Juliet abroad as the young woman hoped, the only solution was for her to spend months on Elizabeth Station, even after the baby came. A newborn could be recognized as such, Patrick had told her reluctantly, and they'd have to wait a while before they could fudge things and get away with the lie that the baby was younger than it was.

When Juliet had mockingly asked him how he knew so much about babies, his serious and confident reply was "sheep breeding." Patrick and his family spoke so openly about sheep pregnancies and births that it made Juliet blush. The Southern belle was anything but a prude, yet the birthing process had been left out of her education. And afterward—well, afterward there would be nannies, of course.

The months were long for Juliet, who had little in common with her new family. Music and art interested the Drurys little. They did attend Heather and Chloe's openings if they happened to be in Dunedin, and Lizzie also liked to go to concerts, but she lacked discernment. She found music "nice" in general, no matter what was being played, and could scarcely discuss it seriously with Juliet. Nor could they talk about fashion. Though Lizzie was a loyal customer of the Gold Mine Boutique, she was mostly interested in which patterns were most slimming. What was *en vogue* in Paris last year and what might cause a sensation in London the next did not matter to her. That left literature, and Juliet's first sight of the Drurys' large bookshelf had given her some hope. However, Michael read only books on sheep breeding, and Lizzie liked to read but did so slowly. For a novel that Juliet finished in a week, she needed months. Little in the way of literature filled her shelves. Lizzie mostly hoarded books on viniculture.

"I do find it alarming that Juliet rarely leaves the house," Michael admitted. Deep down, he still found Juliet somewhat charming. He enjoyed it when she occasionally flirted with him. "It can't be good for the baby to have her sitting around unhappily all day."

"Exactly," Lizzie said. "She needs to get out, move around. I thought maybe the grape harvest would do the trick. She likes to drink wine, after all. But no, first she refused to even come look, and when she did finally come out, she was wearing thin little calf-leather gloves and a mantilla, as if she were going to the opera. And it was freezing. I sent her right back inside. Fresh air won't do the baby any good if its mother gets pneumonia."

Michael sighed. "There's just nothing for her here. She doesn't know country life. She—"

"She comes from a big plantation in Louisiana," Lizzie reminded him venomously. "It was very much in the country, and she still remembers quite well how many acres it was. In fact, I recall you being rather hurt when she complained what a garden plot this was compared to Daddy's kingdom. If she never did a day of work, it wasn't for lack of opportunity. But then again, the people there have their black workers toil for them and moan about the loss of slavery."

***

"Lizzie simply doesn't like her," Michael complained.

The Maori were celebrating Matariki once more, the *manu ante* were dancing toward the stars, and Michael lay beside his Maori friend Tane on thick mats in front of a tent, gazing into the sky. With every gulp of whiskey, the starlight grew brighter, and both men had made sure of a plentiful supply. Michael and Tane had known each other for decades. First, they had gone whaling together, then worked on a sheep farm, and finally Tane had taken over Michael's whiskey distillery in Kaikoura. Tane's tribe maintained close relations with the Ngai Tahu who lived near Michael and Lizzie. Once a year, Tane's *iwi* wandered to Otago, and the men enjoyed a jolly, boozy reunion. This time, Tane's people had come to the New Year's festival. The greeting ritual had gone on all day, but now the friends had found an opportunity to talk.

"Yet you'd think the two must have a bit in common," Michael continued. He was used to confiding in Tane, who knew both his and Lizzie's past. "I mean, I don't want to speak ill of Juliet, but she also spent a few years getting by in a, uh, milieu that—"

"She whored about?" asked Tane placidly. "Since when don't you call prostitutes what they are?"

"Well, because I wouldn't exactly call it that. More like, uh, mistressing, or something."

Tane nodded and thought a moment. "Why? Is she like Lizzie, without her own people? Or did she fall in love with the wrong man? Did her father maybe—look at her and touch her as one shouldn't with children?"

Tane still supplied the brothels in his region with whiskey, and he was a friendly bear of a man. In the last few years, more than a few prostitutes must have poured their hearts out to him. He knew why most women sold themselves.

Michael shook his head. "Not that I know of. She's from a rich family. She's more like . . ." He wondered how he could describe an American cotton plantation. "Like a sheep baroness." It came to him. "Spoiled rotten, honestly. But she wanted to be a singer, so she ran away, traveled all over. And she seems to have had quite a time of it."

Tane laughed. "And you wonder why Lizzie doesn't like her! Lizzie hated selling herself. Most girls do. But this Juliet did it willingly. She gave up everything that Lizzie and those other poor girls wished for—a stable home and a family—just to sing in bars and flit from man to man, probably taking the best-paying clients away from hardworking, proper whores. And now she's snapped up Lizzie's sweet Patrick. It's not at all suitable. If anything, I would have pictured her with Kevin."

Michael sighed. "What art are you a *tohunga* in again? Clairvoyance?"

Tane grinned and uncorked another bottle. "Doesn't Lizzie always say, 'In whiskey there's truth'?"

"In wine," Michael corrected him. "But you're right. Truth might be in wine, but it floats on top of whiskey. Fine, I'll tell you. The tribe knows anyway. Just don't tell any *pakeha*."

Tane whistled through his teeth when Michael told him about Juliet's pregnancy by Kevin.

"And this makes Patrick happy?" he marveled. "Where is he, anyway? He always comes to the festival. And where's the girl? I'm getting curious."

Michael took a long pull from the new bottle. The Maori had begun to sing. The constellation stood clearly visible in the night sky. It was cold and dry, and there was a full moon—perfect weather for the festival. Both tribes would dance and play music all night. The aroma of food wafted over to the men. Michael glanced around for Lizzie, but she was off celebrating with the women. She spoke Maori well, and the Ngai Tahu considered her a woman with a lot of *mana*, status and charisma. Michael didn't want her to hear him saying anything bad about Juliet.

"Juliet didn't want to come with us," he finally told his friend. "She doesn't understand our friendship with the tribes. It's understandable because, in her country—"

"In America, they made Africans slaves, and there had to be a war to stop them," Tane said, surprising Michael with his worldliness. "That was more than thirty years ago now. And she's not even in her country. It's no excuse to treat like filth everyone whose skin is a different color."

"She doesn't," Michael protested. "It's just that, for her, it's not—natural to socialize together and—"

"And Patrick?" Tane interrupted his stammering.

"Patrick didn't want to leave her alone," Michael admitted. "He says you can see the stars from the farm, too, and the *manu aute*. When the baby's born, he'll build it one, and they'll come fly it at the festival."

Tane snorted. "You're kidding yourself, Michael. She'll find reasons to keep her white, golden child away from the dirty Ngai Tahu children. Tell me, Michael, so I really get it: Patrick rode all the way here from Dunedin to celebrate with us, but she talked him out of it?"

Michael nodded sheepishly. "I also have a wife with a lot of *mana*. You know how Lizzie can be."

Tane laughed. "So, you're claiming this Juliet has *mana*? With which tribe? The people in Dunedin? If she had *mana*, she wouldn't need to hide her baby and crawl into the bed of a man she doesn't love. If she had *mana*, Kevin wouldn't have left her. God knows that boy needs a wife with *mana*—just like you did, my friend."

He punched his old buddy on the shoulder. They failed to notice that Lizzie's friend Haikina had approached. She laughed and sat down next to the men.

"I'm supposed to tell you to come to the fire and eat. But first you need to dance the *haka*, Tane. Your mother says not to feed you until you've danced. You're getting fat." She slapped Tane's formidable belly.

"Speaking of women with *mana*," moaned Tane.

Haikina smiled. "You were discussing the Juliet problem, I take it?"

"You hate her too," said Michael, almost whining. "Like Lizzie."

"Name one woman who can stand her! We may have *mana*, Michael, but we don't use it to lead men around by the nose. In that art, Juliet is a true *tohunga*—and she makes your Patrick dance like a *manu* on a string."

***

The months leading up to the birth of Juliet's baby passed torturously slowly. Patrick was unhappy because he saw his wife on weekends at most, and even then, he was sometimes advising on farms far away and could not manage to ride to Lawrence.

"Another reason it's good you're here with my parents," he told Juliet when she complained about her loneliness. "In our house, you'd be completely alone, and if the baby came . . ."

There were about four more weeks until the birth, but Juliet already felt like a beached whale. Patrick had been too cautious to sleep with her for a while already, making Juliet even more bad-tempered. Patrick couldn't hold a candle to Kevin in bed, but she still felt deprived.

"Well, the care here isn't exactly the best either," she replied, turning the conversation to one of her favorite subjects, the question of help with the birth.

After endless fighting, they had reached a compromise: Juliet would have neither a Maori midwife nor a doctor from the city. Instead, the midwife in Lawrence would come—as long as she didn't have another delivery just then. Juliet was horrified that her husband and in-laws thought a single midwife could cover a whole region.

Patrick and Lizzie, though, were concerned that a city doctor wouldn't go along with falsifying the baby's birthday—even people in Lawrence were capable of counting the months between a wedding and a birth. Fortunately, no one there knew that Juliet had been with Kevin before, so the gossip would not be all that malicious. Lizzie still would have preferred the Maori woman. She was excellent at her job and worried far less about the paternity of children.

***

In the end, everything turned out well—at least in the eyes of the Drurys. Like most first-time mothers, Juliet was in labor for many hours, giving the midwife plenty of time to get to her. Moreover, the baby chose a Saturday to enter the world—Patrick was already on his way to Lawrence when the contractions began. He arrived at almost the same time as the midwife and found a completely hysterical Juliet. She had been having contractions for hours and was convinced she was going to die.

"I keep telling her that human births take longer than sheep or horses," Lizzie informed her son, who seemed about to get worked up himself. "She just won't believe me. I have no idea what world she was living in before now. At any rate, I did what I could. She has a neat room, a clean bed—I made her tea and even opened a bottle of wine, in the hopes it would calm her. And now Sharon's here, so she's in good hands."

A scream came from Juliet's room, and Patrick went pale. "Is there anything I can do for her?"

Sharon Freezer, the midwife, stepped into the room.

"Of course," she answered. "Go in. Maybe you can comfort your wife. Everything's going well. The baby's in the right position, and the birth canal is opening slowly. It might take another five, six hours. A prospect that seems to have, um, dismayed your wife. She's a little overwrought. But maybe if you soothe her a little? Could I get some tea, Lizzie?"

Lizzie and Sharon drank tea while Patrick, with unwavering patience, devoted himself to his spouse. He told Juliet about all the births he had witnessed—from ewes to mares to sheepdogs. Nor did he skip the dramatic details. Juliet felt first bored, then disgusted, then finally frightened to the point of panic. Still, she was not screaming anymore, instead whimpering to herself as the contractions grew stronger. Patrick noted the short gap between the contractions with the cheerful relaxation of the professional livestock breeder. He probably could have handled his own child's birth. Juliet, however, found his presence demeaning—how was she ever supposed to charm and captivate this man again after he had seen her so unshapely, sweaty, and screaming? In the end, she shouted urgently for the midwife, and Sharon threw Patrick out at once when she saw that things were progressing.

"Have you two decided on a name?" asked Michael to distract his son.

Patrick shrugged. "Anything but Kevin," he joked. "I like Joseph. Joe's easy to say. Or Harold, Harry. But Juliet wants something French—Baptiste or Laurent."

"What?" asked Lizzie, but was interrupted by a shrill scream from Juliet's room.

"That sounded terrible, but also relieved," she observed. "Heads up, it's almost over."

Indeed, the scream was not repeated. After just a few minutes, the door opened. Sharon stepped out, beaming, a bundle in her arms.

"Here's your daughter, Mr. Drury. Isn't she the most charming baby you've ever seen?"

Patrick looked stunned but accepted her happily. He grinned as he gazed into the tiny face.

"A girl?"

Sharon nodded. "And look how cute she is."

Lizzie had to stand on her tiptoes to get a look at her granddaughter. "She really has a lot of hair, doesn't she? And a bit of a darker complexion? I haven't seen such a handsome baby since my Matariki."

Michael looked somewhat skeptically at the baby. He adored all his children but had never been able to comprehend how people could discern family resemblance in the red, wrinkly creatures, let alone future beauty.

"What should we call her?" he asked.

***

Nothing short of warfare broke out over the naming. Patrick did not care much. He was simply delirious over the baby and relieved that everything had gone well. He was also ready to fulfill Juliet's every desire. Lizzie, however, fought bitterly against her daughter-in-law's suggestions.

"Celine, Laetitia, Monique! To think of giving such names to a baby!"

"A bit exotic, sure," said Patrick, "but just because we haven't heard them."

"It speaks well of you, Son, that you've never heard them," remarked Michael, who shared Lizzie's position in this matter. "But the names aren't that unusual really. They're—"

"Your father means to say that he knows at least half a dozen whores who chose such noms de guerre," Lizzie said. "In New Orleans, such names may be normal, but here, you can't inflict that on your own daughter."

Patrick bit his lip. It was true; he did not know any prostitutes. In Dunedin, the Church of Scotland kept them well in the shadows.

"Why not a good Irish name?" asked Michael. "Why not—"

"Anything but Kathleen," Lizzie warned him, and lifted up the baby, who was beginning to whine. Beyond the ardent search for a name, Juliet hardly took care of her baby and also declined to breastfeed her.

"I know she doesn't exactly look Irish," Michael continued, "but Mary or Bridget might be good. The main thing is that her name doesn't embarrass her and isn't too hard to say."

***

The conflict was finally resolved when Juliet consented to Michael's choice, but she insisted on a French spelling. As Lizzie predicted, the registrar in Dunedin misspelled "Marie Brigitte" twice when entering it.

Reverend Burton entered it in the family Bible without a problem, but he furrowed his brow.

"What do you plan to call her?" he asked the parents, who had come to arrange a baptism.

Juliet and Patrick spoke at the same time: "Marie," she answered. "Bridey," he said, earning a glare from his wife.

Kathleen, who was just then bending over the baby, saw a dark, smooth little face in the light of the summer sun.

"Either way, she's beautiful," she declared. "In Ireland, we say, 'lovely as a day in May.' Come, little May. Let me hold you a bit. My, but she's big for her age!"

And the nickname stuck, despite Juliet's best efforts. For now, little May was passed from one enthusiastic Dunedin matron's arms to the next. Everyone was charmed by the baby, and Juliet lapped up the attention. May's baptism would be held in Dunedin, and Juliet felt as if she had finally returned to the world after a year in prison. Patrick and Juliet Drury proudly presented their daughter to the city, and no one questioned the ostensible birth date—not out loud, at least. Juliet finally moved into Patrick's house on the edge of the city, which made Patrick boundlessly happy. But Juliet's relief was dampened by Lizzie's presence. Her mother-in-law insisted on staying with them until the baptism at least.

"You need help while you get used to motherhood," Lizzie insisted. "And get to know the little one. You've still hardly ever changed her yourself, or fed her. I understand you don't want to breastfeed, but—"

In truth, Lizzie did not understand that, but she knew that Juliet's milk had dried up by now anyway. Since the birth, the young woman had adopted a strict diet. She was hell-bent on getting her old figure back before she presented herself to Dunedin. She had nearly succeeded, too, and the society women, Kathleen and Claire first and foremost, noticed.

"But it wasn't necessary to castigate yourself like that," Claire said when Juliet returned to the boutique, looking for a dress for the baptism. "These days, you can wear looser reform dresses, especially so soon after giving birth. It can't be healthy to wear such tight corsets either."

Juliet twisted her lips disdainfully. "I'm not going to run around like a fat cow," she said, with a sidelong glance at Lizzie, who fortunately did not hear her.

Claire and Kathleen, both slender, did often wear corsets. Lizzie, however, had given them up. She preferred reform dresses, which suited her. Lizzie was rather short and, now that she was getting older, slightly stocky. The loose dresses elongated her figure, and they were comfortable. Lizzie felt good in them and radiated that. Besides, the reform dresses in Kathleen's collection were, of course, works of art. Lizzie did not look at all dowdy in them, at least not to anyone but Juliet.

"Still, this looks amazing on you." Claire praised the shining blue silk dress Juliet had picked out. "Do you already have a baptismal dress for the baby? If not, perhaps our apprentice could make one. There's still some material left, and the girl has artistic ambitions."

Juliet accepted, flattered—and beamed when Marie Brigitte Drury was the first baby in Dunedin to be held over the baptismal font in a Gold Mine creation. The dress was stunning, and the young tailor raked in praise. Juliet was highly satisfied—until Patrick received the bill two days later.

"Juliet, I don't understand. So much money for a dress? I could have bought a horse for this."

Lizzie, who was ready to be home but could not bring herself to leave her granddaughter, laughed. "That's what nice dresses cost, Patrick. The Gold Mine Boutique is especially exclusive. But don't worry, it doesn't have to become a habit. A baptism is a special event, and this is an error, anyway. Juliet's and May's dresses belong on my tab. You'll let me treat you, won't you, dear? As a little peace offering for having to put up with us this past year?"

Lizzie smiled at her daughter-in-law, ready to make amends.

Patrick smiled gratefully. "That's very kind, Mother. Thank you. But we'll have to rein in our costs pretty dramatically. I've paid off the wedding, but not the christening party. I don't make very much, Juliet. We can't afford the Gold Mine Boutique."

Juliet fixed her husband with a look of confusion but also rising anger.

"But where else . . . ?"

"Dear, there are a half-dozen department stores in town. And you'd look lovely in every single dress they sell."

"But I—but—Kevin—"

Lizzie gasped. This harlot really dared to mention Kevin?

Patrick looked like he'd been struck, and his eyes flashed angrily. Then, however, he dropped his chin to his chest.

"Kevin—" he began.

But Lizzie interrupted him. "Kevin would not have been able to afford it for long either. And now, stop harping on it, Juliet. You just got a new dress. You look gorgeous in it, and Kathleen's dresses are timeless. You'll be able to wear it for years. And you won't have much use for it for a while, anyway. You have a baby, Juliet. You can't come and go as you please anymore, especially not late at night. The season's art openings and concerts will take place without you. It's time you got used to it."

She placed May, whom she had been rocking, in Juliet's arms. The baby woke up and began to scream indignantly.

"We could, of course, live on the farm," Patrick said, "and help out with the sheep. We could expand, make more money. The farm is doing well."

In truth, the Drurys made good money with their livestock breeding, but a portion of their income came from the gold in the river. It was far from exhausted because both the Drurys and the Maori drew from it sparingly. Over the past year, there had been a tacit agreement that no one would pan for the gold—the risk of Juliet discovering the secret seemed too great to both Lizzie and the tribe. Lizzie hoped her son would likewise keep it from the woman. If Juliet found out and ran her mouth, it could set off another gold rush—and with it, the destruction of the Drurys' pastures and the Ngai Tahu's village.

Juliet shook her head in horror while Lizzie suppressed a smile. Patrick was so guileless that he'd made the suggestion in earnest. Fortunately, with that, the brakes were applied to Juliet's spending for now. She would accept anything in order not to have to live in the country again. How that would work out in time—after all, Patrick was supposed to inherit the farm—Lizzie did not want to contemplate for the moment.

***

Patrick had hoped living with Juliet would be paradise. He had dreamed of seeing her every evening, talking with her, holding her in his arms at night, and making her happy. He had also looked forward to the baby and was excited do his part in caring for the little one. He enjoyed giving May her bottle, and her little smiles made his heart sing.

Now, however, he had to admit that nothing was as he'd hoped. Juliet was neither willing nor able to do housework. The first evening he came home, he was greeted by the inviting smell of food and a clean house—but also by Mrs. O'Grady, the mother of his stableboy, Randy. The resolute Irish woman held a happy and full May in her arms, and eyed Patrick with an expression between apology and indignation.

"I'm sorry, Mr. Drury. Your mother told me not to come anymore."

Mrs. O'Grady had been Patrick's occasional housekeeper. Sometimes, she also surprised him with a stew on the stove when he came home late, a mixture of working relations and good neighborliness. Now that he had a family to support, Patrick needed to save the money he paid Mrs. O'Grady, and he'd let her go. Mrs. O'Grady understood. Interfering with the new wife's household was far from her intention.

"But Randy said he heard the baby crying all the time, and I stopped by to see if I could help."

Juliet had then immediately rehired the woman, this time with much more far-reaching duties. Mrs. O'Grady had cooked, changed and fed the baby, cleaned the house, and set the table. Meanwhile, Juliet had perused a book of music she had ordered by mail.

When Patrick came into the living room, she smiled at him.

"Dear, we absolutely need a piano. I can read scores, but it would be so much lovelier to play them. I could hold concerts for you in the evening." Her eyes flashed seductively.

And Patrick's anger flew away. He could not stay mad at Juliet. On the other hand, though, she had to be made to understand.

That evening, Patrick explained his financial situation to Juliet in the most minute detail, and he did it again the next night, after Mrs. O'Grady had opened the door for him again with the baby in her arms. The resolute Irish woman proved considerably less friendly than the evening before and made it clear that she was happy to see to his household but not without pay.

"Tell your wife that she needs to take care of her baby," she'd snapped at him. "If you don't care that your house goes to ruin, that's not my business, but I can't listen to this little one wail."

"Don't all babies cry now and again?" Patrick replied helplessly, whereat Mrs. O'Grady glared at him angrily.

"Surely, but not for five hours at a go. And when I picked her up, the diaper was soaked, and she was hungry too."

***

"I need a nanny, at least," Juliet said when Patrick confronted her. "And a pram. I need to get out of here sometimes. I go crazy when I'm always alone; you know that."

Patrick once again explained his finances to her, yet bought the pram the very next day. That assuaged Mrs. O'Grady at least; she no longer heard May crying all day, because Juliet took her out.

The young woman strolled the city streets, and as soon as May began to cry, she would pay someone a visit. This functioned marvelously, at least at first. Kathleen and Claire, Heather and Chloe, Violet and Laura—everyone loved May. They were happy when Juliet allowed them to change or feed the little one, or they asked their servants to care for the child.

"We seem to have stayed too long in town," Juliet would excuse herself as she stood at the door with the screaming baby. Then she made conversation until it was time to go home. Nothing got cooked for dinner, of course, but at least the house wasn't a terrible mess. Juliet had put her foot down that Mrs. O'Grady must come at least twice a week to clean.

No one was really happy with this arrangement. Juliet was bored. After all, she had already established that she had little in common with the ladies of Dunedin. She most liked to visit Claire Dunloe, who owned a piano and had nothing against Juliet playing it, and also knew and liked to talk about music and art. Claire had grown up as a doctor's daughter in Liverpool and had enjoyed a commensurate education. However, she was soon trying to diplomatically convey to Juliet that she was keeping her hostess from her work. Claire and Kathleen managed the Gold Mine together; Claire was responsible for sales, while Kathleen designed the clothing and oversaw the seamstresses in the back room. When Claire received a visitor, Kathleen had to mind the shop. Neither Claire nor Kathleen liked such interruptions to their usual routine to happen too often.

"I get the impression she's using us as nannies," Kathleen observed one afternoon when Juliet had finally gone. "She just can't wait for Paika to take the baby."

Paika was Claire's maid. The young Maori woman loved children.

"Not just you two," said Heather, modeling a new canary-yellow dress in front of the mirror. "She drops in on us at least once a week. Not that I mind, exactly. May is adorable, and at the moment, she mostly sleeps after someone has changed her. But before you know it, she'll be walking. Then she'll have her hands all over the clothes here and will be knocking over my easels. Not to mention, Rosie isn't as keen about caring for her as Paika. Rosie likes horses; she only takes care of children when she has to. And well, I don't know about you, but we don't find Juliet such stimulating company that we want to open a kindergarten."

Soon, Juliet found the women of Dunedin closing their doors to her. She sat at home again for hours and took out her bad moods on Patrick when he came home. Yet he tried with all his heart to make her happy. On one of the few weekends Juliet and Patrick spent in Lawrence, Michael caught his son panning for gold.

"It doesn't bother you, does it?" Patrick asked with a crooked smile.

Michael sighed. "Yes, Patrick," he finally replied, "it does. Since you asked, I'll answer honestly. You're unhappy, and you're living beyond your means. And you're putting us all at risk. Where do you mean to sell the gold, Patrick? Dunloe Private Bank? A gold trader? Either one will ask questions. I mostly sell it in small amounts in far-off towns I pass through selling or exhibiting sheep. Then you can get away with nonsense like, 'Oh, we were panning a bit for fun, and last week we got lucky. Where? Oh, somewhere by Lake This-or-That. I didn't think to mark the place.' And the tribe sends different people out. No gold trader remembers a random Maori selling tiny amounts. But the farmers and bankers know you. After all, you advise them on advances and loans. If you suddenly appear with gold, and then do it repeatedly—"

"It's just this once. I, well, Juliet wants a piano."

Patrick lowered the pan and sat in the grass beside the stream. For a few moments, he found peace gazing at the waterfall, the hills overgrown with green, the forest, the pastures.

Michael rubbed his forehead and sat down next to his son. "We'll give her one," he offered. "We can manage the expense. But I'm afraid that then she'll just move on to her next demand. You have to set boundaries, Patrick, no matter how much you love her."

Michael took the pan from his son's hand and threw its contents into the stream. The black sand on the streambed flashed with gold.

Patrick bit his lip. "But I feel sorry for her," he admitted. "She hasn't made any real friends in Dunedin, and she's lonely. It's all too much for her."

Michael raised his hands. "Son, she knew what she was getting into when she married you. Now, she has to accept it. And if she's bored and refuses to do any housework, then she should earn some money herself."

Patrick leaped to his feet and gave his father an outraged look. "But she can't—"

"She's gotten along just fine until now," Michael said. "She's educated, has manners. Maybe a hotel needs a reception lady. I could even picture her as a saleswoman at the Gold Mine Boutique. Maybe Kathleen and Claire could use somebody. And with a piano, she'll be able to give lessons as well. Don't act as if she has only one talent, Patrick. It's degrading to her."

Patrick reddened. "I'm not going to ask you to elucidate what that 'one talent' is, Father," he said icily, and walked away.

***

Michael, whose education had begun and ended with Sunday school, could not have defined the word "elucidate." However, his son's situation was beginning to worry him.

"How will this end happily?" he asked Lizzie, Haikina, and her husband, Hemi, who had come down to Elizabeth Station for dinner.

The two were good friends of Patrick's and had been eager to see him—he had, after all, not made an appearance in the Maori village since his wedding. He had really been looking forward to their visit. However, Juliet hardly allowed him any time with his friends. Although all of them worked admirably to include her in the conversation, she gave only short, sullen answers. She wrapped herself in a shawl, even though the evening air on the veranda was warm, sipped at her wine, and took desultory bites of the lamb cutlet Michael had grilled. Before long, she retired with the excuse that she had a headache. Patrick looked concerned and quickly followed.

"It will all shake out," Haikina assured Michael. "He's just infatuated. Everyone knows how young couples can't stand to be apart."

"Can't stand to be apart?" Hemi asked. "She said she had a headache. Isn't that *pakeha* for 'You're definitely not getting it tonight'?"

Haikina and Michael laughed. But Lizzie stared with an expression between sorrow and rage across the valley in front of her house.

"Oh, it'll end soon," she said finally. "You can read it in her face. She has that shifty look in her eyes. It'll end very soon. And it'll break my poor Patrick's heart."

Chapter 9

Juliet was delighted by her piano, but it didn't hold her attention long. She was not the kind of artist for whom working through a composition or perfecting a performance could be an end unto itself. Juliet lived for the audience. She needed someone she could flatter, stir, and bewitch with her voice. Patrick alone wasn't enough, and he was too uncritical. He seemed equally enthusiastic about May hammering on the keyboard and Juliet presenting a polished piece. Mrs. O'Grady proved a true philistine. She found the music annoying. Randy, at least, whistled along out of tune as he tended the horses.

Heather and Chloe took pity after Patrick begged them for help. They were holding another opening and asked Juliet to provide musical accompaniment.

"It works too," Chloe remarked to her mother, Claire. "We're going out on a limb with this exhibition. *Beauty and Love—Female Nudes*. If Juliet messes around a bit at the piano, it can hardly make a difference. What do you think? Should I invite the usual folks, or would a smaller circle be better?"

The exhibition certainly did cause a sensation—half of Dunedin was fascinated, the other shocked, and the press coverage was immense. Newspapers from all over the South Island sent correspondents. Most were regional freelancers, but one paper from Queenstown sent the chief editor of the culture page, who happened to be in Dunedin for family reasons. He was impressed by the exhibition—and even more so, for Juliet did not "mess around" at the piano, instead playing New Orleans blues impeccably. She wore one of her older dresses, which she had to starve herself to fit into, but the sight of her in the red tight piece with its deep, elegant neckline was grand.

After her performance, Pit Frazer, the journalist, did not leave her side, which was not hard since Juliet was keeping her distance from Patrick, who had May squirming in his arms. The little one did not fall asleep, observing everything with wide-open, attentive eyes. Apparently, she liked music and charming one guest after another. At the moment, little May was flirting with Roberta Fence.

Juliet gave the young woman a brief, appraising once-over. The girl had been head over heels for Kevin before. Might she now make a move on Patrick? There did not seem any danger of that, however. Roberta always dressed like a spinster, and she could hardly bring herself to look at the nudes gracing the walls. The baby was, thus, a welcome distraction. Roberta seemed delighted about holding and rocking her. Patrick watched indulgently but also with some anxiety. He did not like to hand May over.

Juliet turned her attention back to the journalist from Queenstown. She lit up when he spoke knowledgeably about the music of the American South. In his opinion, Australia and New Zealand had so far achieved little more than "Waltzing Matilda." Juliet and Pit luxuriated in mocking the musical backwaters of New Zealand and Australia—completely ignoring the whole Maori culture, their ingenious instruments, and deep musical tradition.

"There are hardly any performance opportunities here for real artists, you know," Juliet lamented to him as he placed his hand, as if by accident, on her arm before letting his fingers wander up to her shoulder. "The occasional traveling ensemble or the one or two theaters that only play the classics and are still looked at askance by the strange Christian sects. With the Church of Scotland, you're damned if you so much as wear a red dress."

Pit leered. "A damnation I would gladly share with you."

Heather, who was passing by, gave him a disbelieving look. "You'd like a red dress, Mr. Frazer?" she asked. "I think I have one. It's reform style, a loose cut. Maybe it'd fit you?"

Juliet giggled, but Heather wasn't laughing. "Maybe you'd play us another song?" she asked amicably but with a subtle tone of command.

Heather had noticed Frazer's hand on Juliet's shoulder, and she wanted to prevent a scene.

"I was thinking more of the place of damnation," Frazer corrected himself once Heather had moved on. "I'd gladly share hell with you."

Juliet purred like a cat. "It'd be too warm there for dresses anyway," she said breathily, toying with the straps on hers.

She did, however, sit down at the piano. It wouldn't do to spoil things with Heather.

Frazer was waiting with a glass of champagne when she finished. "Your voice is unbelievable. Crystal clear and yet secretive, promising."

Juliet bathed in his admiring looks but hardly listened to his flattery—until his next remark.

"You absolutely must perform. You can't bury yourself away in a suburb of Dunedin. Listen, we have something very interesting in Queenstown—Daphne's Hotel. Originally, it was a pub like any other. It's also a bit, well, very libertine. But recently, the proprietress had a stage built. There's singing and, uh, dancing. Now, gentlemen bring their ladies with them."

"It's a nightclub?" Juliet asked.

Frazer thought a moment. Then he nodded. "It's on its way, anyhow. Queenstown is becoming civilized, you know. It's not just adventurers and gold miners. Now there are more big-time livestock breeders, and the gold comes from mines whose owners aren't poor or uneducated. And they're trying to make the city more attractive for visitors. It really is beautiful—the mountains, the lakes."

Juliet was not interested in mountains and lakes. "And the proprietor of this club engages artists?"

"Yes. But it's actually a proprietress. Daphne O'Hara. Irish, apparently, although she doesn't sound it."

Juliet pouted. Really, she'd had enough of the Irish. Still . . . "Perhaps we should talk more about it tomorrow." When she casually interlaced her fingers in his, only Chloe Coltrane noticed and immediately moved in her direction. "I think I have to sing some more. But let's meet for coffee tomorrow. Did you say you were staying at the Leviathan?"

***

Pit Frazer surprised Juliet with the good news as soon as she entered the hotel: he'd telegraphed Queenstown already, and Daphne O'Hara was quite interested in a singer from New Orleans. Juliet was not pushing May around with her that day. Mrs. O'Grady had come to clean, and Juliet had managed to foist the child on her. The resolute Irish woman was still head over heels for the little girl. She would feed, rock, and then sing her to sleep with her execrable voice. May loved Mrs. O'Grady and did not seem at all bothered by the false notes. In truth, she only screamed when she was in Rosie's or Juliet's care. Neither paid her the attention she needed.

"How marvelous," Juliet cooed. Her hand brushed Frazer's as she reached for the telegram on the table. "It seems I've finally had some luck."

Frazer smiled and opened a bottle of champagne. "It so happens I'm a good-luck charm."

***

Juliet wore a demure outfit when she visited Claire Dunloe two days later. Not much was going on in the shop, and Claire could not find a plausible excuse not to invite her visitor to tea. Kathleen could have joined them but feigned urgent alteration work. Juliet bored Kathleen—and her flirting with the journalist had irked her. Even after so many years, Kathleen felt loyal to Michael's family. There was not just her old love for Michael, but also the brief affair between Matariki and Kathleen's son Colin, out of which Atamarie was born. Kathleen and Lizzie would never be true friends, but when it came to Juliet LaBree-Drury, they were of the same opinion. A long time before, Kathleen, too, had married a man she did not love to give her baby a name. She knew it must be hard for Juliet, but she had done well with Patrick. The man practically did not let her feet touch the ground, whereas Kathleen had been bound to a husband who exploited and abused her. She thought Juliet an ungrateful brat. In any case, she wasn't willing just then to make conversation. If there was any news, Claire would fill her in later.

***

Claire's housemaid, Paika, took little May at once and, giggling, disappeared into the kitchen with her. Claire hoped she'd still remember to make the tea. Otherwise, this visit would drag on for hours. But, to her surprise, Juliet also seemed to be in a hurry that day. When tea was served, she quickly downed the contents of her cup.

"Mrs. Dunloe, I, um, I wanted to ask if I couldn't leave my daughter with you a short while," she said. "I still have a few errands to run, and your girl—"

"Paika would be happy to watch May, I'm sure."

Claire answered kindly, but her gaze narrowed a bit. On what sort of errands might the baby not be welcome? There was also the matter of her unusual outfit. Elegant, closed-necked—a traveling outfit? Claire's curiosity became suspicion.

"What do you have to do?" she asked casually. "Do you need to go to the gallery? Another performance? We all very much liked your singing, Mrs. Drury. You have a gorgeous voice and a style all your own. I think Heather and Chloe were very pleased."

Claire recognized a flash in Juliet's eyes at the word "performance."

"It made me really happy," Juliet replied.

When Juliet provided no answer to Claire's question, suspicion became certainty.

"Mrs. Drury," she said quietly, "please, don't do this to him."

Juliet could not hide her alarm. She wanted to react angrily but then changed her mind. Claire had seen through her, and it was too late to find someone else who could watch May. The coach to Queenstown would leave in a half hour. Nervously, she raised her hands to her hair, which was perfectly put up under a delicate little hat.

"I can't sacrifice my career for Patrick's happiness," she declared histrionically. "I'm sorry, but that's asking too much."

Claire looked at her mockingly. The banker's wife was one of the few women not intimidated by Juliet's beauty and arrogance.

"What exactly is your career, Mrs. Drury?" she inquired. "A dingy nightclub? A new man?" She paused. "But that's not my business. And I truly don't want to meddle. It's just that Patrick—"

"You want me to stay with him? Change the baby's diapers? Maybe have another one?" Juliet's shrill voice edged toward hysteria. "Just so Saint Patrick gets what he paid for? With a signature?"

"With a name," Claire said. "It might not mean much to you, but being named Drury and not LaBree will open doors for your child. But your marriage doesn't interest me, Juliet. Do what you want. But don't ruin Patrick's life."

Juliet laughed nervously and cast a glance at the grandfather clock. "He won't die of a little heartache."

Claire sighed. "You're not understanding me. It's not about whether you leave Patrick. In fact, nothing better could happen to him. But don't just run out like this. Talk to him. Arrange the divorce."

Juliet frowned. "What would that change?"

Claire rubbed her forehead wearily, but then she became angry. "Apparently, nothing for you. You'll transform instantly back into the beautiful, free-spirited Miss LaBree. No one will know you; no one will know about your marriage or your child. But Patrick, he'll stay here. Everyone knows him."

Juliet made a face. "Gossip fades, Mrs. Dunloe. Of course, people will talk, and maybe they'll even make fun of him. But it'll pass."

"People won't make fun," Claire corrected her. "They'll pity him. But it will never be over if you don't end things properly. Heavens, Juliet, don't you realize that Patrick will never be able to marry again. Or only after a complicated process. Believe me, I had to go through it myself. My husband disappeared from one moment to the next. To China, supposedly. Before that, he sold our house out from under me. That was far worse than gossip and lovesickness. But the worst was that I wasn't free. I was neither a wife nor a widow—and in the circles of my current husband, people can't just live together like that." Claire's gaze softened as she looked around her grand living room. "We finally effected a divorce, thanks in part to Jimmy's connections, but it was difficult—and expensive. We printed advertisements in all the country's newspapers, looking for my former husband. After a long time, a judge finally released me. I wouldn't wish that on anyone, Juliet." Claire's voice turned pleading. "So please, put your cards on the table. Give Patrick back his name."

Juliet looked at the august lady in her dignified cashmere skirt and her carefully ironed white blouse. Boring. Just as boring as her request.

"My coach leaves in twenty minutes," Juliet announced, trying to put some regret in her voice. "It's too late now. As for Patrick, what you propose would only cause him pain. But it's good we talked, Mrs. Dunloe. I'll keep your words in mind. Maybe I'll write."

Juliet stood up. She took her leave politely before she went. But she went.

Claire was too agitated to go back to the shop. She was afraid she'd blurt everything out, and that would not be right if there were customers there. So, she took another sip of tea, went into the kitchen, and took the baby from Paika.

"I'm so sorry, darling," she murmured. "But forget about that. You're better off without her." She kissed the baby, then turned to the young maid. "I need to go out, Paika. Please tell Mr. Dunloe that I went to Reverend Burton and then to Mr. Patrick Drury—I won't be home till late."

For the Sake of Love

Transvaal, Karenstad,
Africa
Dunedin, Christchurch, Temuka,
New Zealand
1900–1902

Chapter 1

The siege of Wepener was to be Kevin Drury's only major combat experience in the Boer War. After New Zealand's Rough Riders left the van Stout farm, their war took the shape of a prolonged camping excursion through Transvaal, punctuated by skirmishes with small Boer commando units. The Riders moved mostly via the train lines, which were quiet for now, as the Boers would have been dismantling their own supply and escape routes by striking the tracks. For that reason, the Rough Riders would leave the tracks to patrol the veld—and Kevin sometimes felt himself in a dreamworld more than a war.

The landscape around Waterval Boven was different from anything he knew in New Zealand. Vincent reveled in observing elephants and zebras, whereas Kevin was less delighted when he nearly got too close to a crocodile. And although their native guide, Mzuli, assured them that the creature's meat was especially tasty, the soldiers opted to withdraw carefully. In general, the wild animals frightened Kevin more than the Boers. Nevertheless, he asked himself whether the Rough Riders were more hunters or hunted. On the rare occasions when the Afrikaners took refuge on an isolated farm and were careless enough to put their ponies to pasture in a visible yard, the New Zealanders would take ten or fifteen prisoners. More often, though, Boer commandos attacked the Rough Riders. The first time, Kevin's unit lost one man, but thereafter, the New Zealanders were cautious, sleeping lightly and setting watches.

They also learned quickly to differentiate the noises of wild animals from the hoofbeats of Boer ponies. As soon as the watchman sounded the alarm, the defense quickly began, but in general, the adversaries only shot into the air. Night in the veld was pitch black, and there was ample cover. It was pure chance when someone was hit. Kevin, Preston, and Tracy thus had little to do, and Vincent nothing. The endless, peaceful rides suited the horses, as did the dry grass they stuffed themselves on at night. When the men came upon a farm, they requisitioned oats and restocked their own provisions. These encounters with belligerent farmers were the most dangerous moments of the mission.

The doctors spent the long nights at the campfire, telling each other their life stories and drinking whiskey. And then, suddenly, the war was over—or supposed to be. Bloemfontein and Pretoria had fallen. The Boer president, Ohm Krüger, had fled to Europe. On September 1, Transvaal was officially annexed as a British colony. Queen Victoria made Lord Roberts an earl, while Lord Kitchener stayed behind to organize the withdrawal of the British troops. But Kevin and Tracy's regiment didn't get the news until a few days later. They were two days' ride from Pretoria.

"We're at peace?" Kevin asked. "So, what was that yesterday, then?"

He'd been in the middle of changing a wounded man's bandage when a messenger arrived to proclaim the official end of hostilities. The evening before, a Boer unit had attacked their camp at twilight. The New Zealanders had killed two men and taken four prisoners. Vincent was treating one horse grazed by a bullet.

"I suppose the Boers didn't know about the peace agreement either," Preston replied. "Probably we still need to watch out until we reach Pretoria—the commandos aren't just going to drop their weapons and ride home."

That evening, the whiskey flowed in streams, and during their last rounds through their improvised hospital, Kevin and Preston brought a bottle to the wounded Boer prisoners.

"There's peace, men," Kevin announced, already tipsy and quite content. "We're friends again." He held out the bottle, but they glared at him uncomprehendingly. Kevin sighed. "Now you can learn English instead of shooting," he declared.

In the end, he entrusted himself to the uniting power of whiskey, pouring some for each of them—and stepped back in shock when the first of the prisoners threw the booze back in his face.

"Preston?" Kevin called. "We need an interpreter here."

Preston, ever the gentleman, had moderated his drinking, and thus was alert enough to dodge the tin cup one of the prisoners threw at him while spitting hateful words.

Kevin looked irritated. “Does he not get it? The war’s over.”

“Not for him,” Preston translated. “Or at least not for his people. Personally, he doesn’t have much hope for himself because he’s a prisoner.”

“But he’ll be released soon.” Kevin still felt the Boers should share his elation. “Man alive, boys, they’ll hold you for a few weeks, but then they’ll let you return to your farms. You’ll be a little nicer to your workers and—”

The prisoners unleashed a torrent of curses on the doctor.

Preston pulled him back. “Come along, Kevin. Your excitement is wasted on them. Not to mention the whiskey. These blokes knew quite well that the war was over. Hence the foolhardy attack last night. They thought we wouldn’t shoot back and half of us would be dead before we realized they hadn’t come to celebrate with us.”

“They knew?” Kevin seemed sobered.

Preston nodded. “They admitted it. They don’t see themselves as bound by any peace treaty. Ohm Krüger might have surrendered, they say, but not General de Wet, not by a mile. For the commandos, the war is just starting.” Tracy took a long swig from the whiskey bottle. “We should still set guards,” he said. “The wounded prisoners are fit enough to get up to trouble. All the watch posts need to be manned tonight and tomorrow. All the way to Pretoria. I’m excited to see what the situation there is.”

***

But their contingent never even got to set out for the capital of Transvaal. Instead, another unit of New Zealanders arrived the next morning, battle-hardened men who had come to South Africa on the first ships. A major by the name of Colin Coltrane led the unit of forty as if they were approaching a proper cavalry regiment instead of a mishmash of swashbuckling riders in uniform.

“And as of now, I’m taking over command here,” Coltrane declared to Kevin’s startled captain. “What sort of a slipshod unit is this? You’re the commanding officer? Why doesn’t anyone salute you?”

Captain Jones, a carpenter in civilian life, turned red at once. He had been chosen leader by his men and led the unit more like an expeditionary corps than a military regiment.

"This isn't a fishing trip, soldier. This here is the British Army, and we're going to act like it from now on. You're still not standing straight, Captain. Did no one show you how?"

Captain Jones and his men spent the next half hour on bearing drills and the following hours doing exercises on foot and horse.

"Who the hell is this guy?" Vincent asked when he sat down next to Kevin and Preston at the fire that night. "And what is he doing here? I thought the war was over." The veterinarian had just come back from the horse paddocks and had stumbled on a new guard who barked at him to give his name and rank. "My lands, if the second guard hadn't recognized me, I might have been shot. By a kid ready to piss his pants for fear of his major."

Vincent looked around for the whiskey bottle.

Kevin fished it out from under a woodpile. "Here, but hide it again when you're done. They might start rationing."

Vincent looked incredulous.

"The war is by no means over, as it turns out," Preston explained. He'd been treating blisters the Rough Riders had gotten from the drills, and heard all the gossip. "Only the cities are liberated. In fact, now the Boer commandos are making good on their threats. In the last three nights, there were attacks on the train lines between Johannesburg and Cape Town. In each attack, several hundred yards of track were blown up at distances of about fifty miles. Lord Kitchener is in a rage. He's reinforcing all units and forming new patrols. There's no more talk of withdrawal."

"And that's why we have to do drills and ration our whiskey?" Vincent asked. "Under the command of blokes like Coltrane?"

Preston shrugged. "He's apparently a New Zealander. That's what the Aussies say, anyway. The Kiwis claim he's Irish. But no doubt, he's a professional officer with a diploma from Sandhurst. Something must have happened along the way, because he left the service and is now back as a volunteer."

"The way he looks, he must already have a few battles under his belt," Vincent remarked, helping himself to the whiskey.

Indeed, the major's face was covered in scars, several teeth were missing, and his crooked nose and chin had been broken more than once. His blond hair had a metallic sheen.

Kevin shook his head. "If I'm not mistaken, he didn't get those wounds in war but in fistfights with lowlifes and bookies. I could be wrong—Coltrane's a common name, and I was pretty young back then. But man, if he doesn't remind me of the lout who got my big sister in the family way and then abandoned her when my parents wouldn't hand over a massive dowry. Instead, he married a rich heiress and made her miserable. She financed a racetrack for him, which he ran into the ground. There was also supposed to be something about bet fixing. But before all that, he did attend a certain renowned military academy. The Sandhurst diploma's real."

Vincent and Preston gaped at him.

"It's a small world," Preston remarked.

Vincent and Kevin laughed. "New Zealand is a village," Vincent told the Australian. "The South Island, anyway. But what are we going to do about this guy?"

"What can we do?" Preston replied. "Dowry hunting is far from gentlemanly, but nor is it illegal. And rumors of bet fixing aren't going to interest high command either. At least not if he's a good officer. So, let's see how he does—and hope he doesn't recognize Kevin."

The very next day, Major Coltrane inspected the medical station.

"You're the staff doctors? Not assigned to any proper unit? Then you now belong to this one. We'll be receiving further reinforcements as well. The Boers are expanding their commando units."

"Expanding?" Preston asked. "How? They don't have any conscription, and since the war is officially over anyway—"

"Smaller groups are banding together," Coltrane said. "And because of the peace agreement, all those Boers we'd beaten in the towns have been freed. Somehow, command didn't think it necessary to declare them prisoners of war."

Coltrane fell silent a moment, seeming to contemplate the severity of this mistake. "So, be ready to work. We'll be fighting the devils without any mercy now."

***

For the Rough Riders, that meant, first of all, living up to their name. Under Colin Coltrane, the New Zealanders were now definitively to become the hunters, and for that, they needed to control a bigger area and move around more quickly in it. Over the next few weeks, the men spent up to twelve hours a day in the saddle. Coltrane forbade the firing of weapons so as not to give away their position, which meant they couldn't hunt. As a consequence, meals consisted of hardtack and dried meat, mostly choked down quickly in the saddle. After a few days, Vincent complained the horses were losing weight.

"Sir, the grass here isn't particularly nutrient rich," he explained. "If the horses are supposed to live on it, they need more time to graze."

Coltrane made a face but accepted the argument. His solution, however, took a different shape than Vincent had hoped.

"I'm looking for volunteers for a task force," he thundered when they broke camp the next morning. The Rough Riders now rode dutifully in rows four wide, trailed by the kitchen wagon and the doctors. "The task force will break off from the train lines and ride to targeted Boer farms. There, it will requisition oats for the horses—and potentially quarter there for the night. Sergeant Beavers will have command."

"Him?" Vincent said with a grimace. "That's the nasty kid who almost shot me the first night because I didn't know the password."

"Well, you wouldn't choose a kindly fellow to dispossess Boer women of their oats," Kevin replied. "Do you want to ride with them, Preston? They might need a translator."

Preston Tracy nodded, trotted up to Coltrane, and reported for duty. Coltrane looked him over, then nodded.

"Having a doctor on hand is always good. As for making ourselves understood, though, I'll rely on Beavers. He'll make it clear to the womenfolk what we want."

***

The task force split from the main unit, which had its first success that day. They caught a very young Boer boy, a scout, who led them to his unit's hideout.

That surprised Kevin, who had been instructed to set up the hospital tent and wait near the train tracks for possible casualties.

"They're normally so stubborn," he said to Vincent. Coltrane had not wanted him in the attack party either, although Vincent normally liked to stay close to the front. After all, one could not load an injured horse onto a cart as easily as an injured soldier. "But now, Coltrane says a few words to the kid, and he betrays his unit?"

Vincent bit his lower lip. "Did you see the boy when they rode out? I didn't get too close, but it looked as if he could hardly stay in his saddle. Let's just say Coltrane didn't limit himself to words."

The Boer camp was near enough that the doctors could hear the sounds of fighting. A short time later, a few lightly wounded men arrived.

"We caught the blokes with their pants down," a corporal reported. "That Coltrane's a tyrant, but he knows how to fight a war. Planned the attack precisely. Probably nothing would have happened to any of us if that little scout hadn't taken off. At the last moment before we charged, he put the spurs to his nag and rushed right into the middle of the kraal where they were holed up. Coltrane shot him from his horse, but he'd already given us away."

Vincent gave Kevin a horrified look.

"Were there any, uh, further deaths?" asked Kevin.

The man nodded. "Dozens. The major said shooting them was better than taking prisoners. Where are we supposed to put the blokes? In any case, it was a great victory."

"The task force was also successful," announced another man, whose hand Vincent was bandaging. "They smoked out a farm and made quarters for the night. That's where you're supposed to set up your field hospital, Dr. Drury. Dr. Tracy is already there."

As Kevin rode toward the farm, he saw smoke was still rising from the rubble of the main house.

"There was no other way," Beavers was telling Coltrane. "The womenfolk had barricaded themselves inside."

The major had just arrived at the farm with his regiment and, despite the massacre, fifty prisoners.

Kevin and Vincent did not listen further. They had spotted Preston Tracy at the entrance to the barn and were anxious to hear his version. Both were shocked at the appearance of the young doctor. Preston's face was pale and twisted with disgust and horror. He looked considerably worse than after the battle for Wepener.

"Do you know how to treat burns?" he asked Kevin before offering a word of greeting. "I've never dealt with any, and the two children here—"

A frightful scene awaited Kevin and Vincent in the barn. The little boy wept bitterly with pain; a girl toddler was unconscious. An old woman, maybe their grandmother, rocked her in her arms. Kevin did not know much about burns either, but he saw at once that the little girl couldn't be saved. Vincent confirmed that. The veterinarian actually had the most experience with burns. He had treated multiple horses after a fire in a stable in Blenheim.

"I only hope she doesn't regain consciousness," he whispered with a look at the horrifically burned child. "Do we have morphine for the boy?"

Kevin hurried to unload the mules, but the old woman, whose hands and arms also showed burn blisters, refused any help. She became hysterical when Vincent tried to touch the dying child. The veterinarian did not ask Tracy to translate. The woman's recriminations were clear.

"What in heaven's name happened here?" Kevin asked.

Preston, Vincent, and Kevin worked a few hours, treating the two New Zealanders who'd been seriously wounded. Amazingly, there were no wounded Boer commandos. They could not get another word out of Preston. He seemed to lose even more color when Kevin and Vincent treated the burned boy, though there was little they could do but excise the destroyed skin and apply clean bandages. The old woman still would not let anyone approach, and the tiny girl died without ever regaining consciousness.

Now, the little boy slept under the influence of morphine, and the grandmother sat beside him and stared into nothingness. The doctors withdrew, exhausted, with a bottle of whiskey. So far, the rationing had not affected them—Preston Tracy was discerning when it came to whiskey, and instead of drawing from the communal stores, they had always drunk from bottles they had hoarded themselves. Now, Preston drank in powerful gulps, clearly seeking oblivion in the alcohol.

"It was horrible," he told them in a quiet, flat voice. "There were three women, three generations. One was still quite young. And three children, probably two, five, and nine." He paused, looking back toward the barn where the younger ones lay. "They were all armed—well, the women and the older child—and firing, of course. The women had barricaded themselves inside the house, and we wanted oats more than anything, so we could have just checked the barn. But Coltrane's men, they set the house on fire. And shot at anyone who ran out. They shot the younger woman, but the children fled back inside. Then the oldest child came out, his clothing on fire, and they shot him again. In the chest. You can check; he's lying behind the barn. But they—they shot an eight-year-old in the chest. Then the house collapsed, and the old woman crawled out with the little boy. I found two men who looked as horrified as I was, and we searched for survivors. We managed to pull the baby girl out." Preston shivered. "Not that it did her any good."

"Dear God," Vincent moaned. "I shouldn't have said the horses needed to eat."

Kevin filled his colleagues' cups. "Then he would have found another excuse," he told Vincent. "Beavers is a bastard. And Coltrane too. He knew what he was doing, giving Beavers command. But there'll be consequences. We'll report it."

"That," said Preston, draining his cup in one swallow, "will not bring these children back to life."

Chapter 2

The regiment stayed two days at the burned-out farm, the name of which the New Zealanders never learned. Then the prisoners were transported to prison camps, the old woman and the surviving child as well. Neither was doing well. The woman had a fever after consistently declining both treatment and food. The child's wounds seemed to be healing, but it would be a long time before he was completely healthy.

"He still needs a lot of morphine," noted Preston as he gave the boy another dose for the road. "Do they have enough in the camps?"

Colin Coltrane looked at him indignantly. "The treatment in English camps is exemplary," he declared stiffly. "Probably these primitive people have never been as well housed, not to mention the food and medical care. So, don't fuss, Doctor. Nothing'll happen to the brat."

Preston did not answer, and the three doctors tried not to think about their little patient when the Rough Riders finally continued onward. They were still hoping for an opportunity to report Beavers and Coltrane to senior officers, but soon it became a moot point, as Kitchener's new orders justified the massacre after the fact. Now the British were by no means withdrawing. Instead, they deployed more and more soldiers to patrol the train lines and attack the Boer commandos. And yet, for every commando unit destroyed, a new one seemed to form. The damage they inflicted was immense, and the empire's troops largely powerless. This country was simply too large to control.

"And they can hide anywhere," Kevin observed as they camped overlooking a valley. A deep-blue lake lay in the shadows of rugged rock formations, and forested slopes protected the cropland on its shores.

"They'll never go hungry either." Vincent cast an envious look at the fields. The Rough Riders had been living off emergency rations for days. "They're taken in on every farm."

Lord Kitchener also came to this realization and drew horrendous conclusions from it. With the next yearned-for delivery of provisions came new orders. From now on, the soldiers were to lay waste to the Boers' farms and fields.

"They can fight," Kitchener explained, "but they won't have anything to eat."

"And where are we supposed to get our supplies from?" asked Kevin, disgusted as he saw the second farm that day go up in flames. The women and children had been captured alive, at least, and were now awaiting transportation to a prison camp.

"They won't let us starve," Preston replied. "But what about these camps? In the past week, we alone have taken fifty women and children prisoner. If you add up all the units in the field, that must make thousands. And here we're burning the harvest that should really be feeding them."

Kevin thought nervously about the van Stout farm. Had they destroyed Doortje's home too? What had happened to her father and her fiancé? Based on what Cornelis had told him, it seemed unlikely that either man had laid his weapons down.

And now, the destruction of their farms seemed only to enrage the Boers more. The few times that Coltrane's regiment caught a commando, the men fought with courage born of desperation. Often, no prisoners were taken at all. The Boers fought to the death.

Kitchener then adopted further measures that revealed his desperation and, moreover, cost the empire a fortune. Blockhouses were erected along all the train tracks in Transvaal, round huts of sheet iron each manned with seven soldiers. Between the huts, the British stretched barbed wire and, beyond that, built barriers—traps into which one could drive the Boer commandos.

To Vincent's dismay, the trapped Boers rode their ponies furiously into the fences. Most of them shied back, but some of the animals tried to jump them. If they did not succeed, Vincent would have to patch them up—or shoot them.

"They drive cattle herds into the fences too," reported Preston, who had scrounged up a newspaper somewhere. The men were camping at Witbank, near Pretoria. "The bulls trample the barbed wire, and General de Wet and his men are promptly back on their way."

"And afterward, the injured bulls die hideously in the veld," grumbled Vincent. "I know the Boers fight with uncommon bravery, but I can't stand them."

The other medical officers laughed.

"And I can't stand Coltrane," Preston declared. Nightfall, and it was raining, a rare event here, and the doctors had set up their medical station in one of the blockhouses. So far, only a few soldiers had come by, seeking advice about little booboos. That could change in a heartbeat, though. This blockhouse was equipped with a telephone, and the report had just come in that Coltrane and his men were pursuing a Boer commando.

"The bloke's like a viper, ice-cold. Those women and children on the farms . . . The last woman whose house he burned down was a widow—she didn't even have men fighting. And the house was hardly more than a hut. All this destruction only stokes the hatred."

Kevin sighed. "It's what Kitchener ordered," he said sadly.

Preston raised an eyebrow. "So, we should just go along with a war against women and children? Incidentally, it's making us unpopular with the rest of the world. The international newspapers give rather unflattering reports. Some of them side quite clearly with the Boers."

Vincent raised his hand. "Be quiet," he said softly. "There's something outside."

Indeed, the horses out front were shifting nervously from one hoof to the other, and Kevin heard Silver whinnying.

"The jades don't like this rain," Kevin said. "When Silver gets back to New Zealand, he'll have to reacclimate to our weepy sky god."

But then the whinnying repeated, full of longing. Kevin jumped up. That particular call could only mean the animal had caught the scent of unfamiliar mares. Vincent recognized it too. He reached for his gun.

"Let's go check it out."

Kevin followed, as did three of the soldiers manning the post. Outside the blockhouse, it was pitch black, and Kevin felt for his lamp. The soldier next to him, however, shook his head. The soldiers strained to peer into the night—but Kevin only needed to watch Silver to know where to look. The horse pricked its ears to the west, where the tracks curved and ran toward another blockhouse. Kevin followed its gaze and managed to just make out the silhouette of a pony. There was a low clicking noise.

"Just one?" whispered Vincent.

"The first one cuts through the barbed wire at the curve," the soldier, a corporal, explained. "When he's done, the others come with the dynamite." He pressed himself deeper into the cover of the blockhouse's shadow.

"Shouldn't we take him prisoner?" asked Vincent.

The corporal shook his head. "No. We stay here and wait until they're all inside. Why catch one when we can get five or six? Or more. I'm certain that's the commando unit Major Coltrane is after."

Kevin and Vincent exchanged a look. If these men could be captured before Coltrane arrived, perhaps they wouldn't have to die.

Spellbound, their weapons at the ready, the men observed how the first Boer struggled through the barbed wire with pliers and then gave a hand signal, at which more of his countrymen began to creep through the hole in the fence—eight in total. The corporal had, in the meantime, put out word, and the crew in the next blockhouse behind the bend in the tracks was ready. As soon as the Boers set to work on the tracks, they would attack.

"They've got two guards. We'll have to take them out," whispered the corporal. He gestured to the doctors' guns. "Know how to use those?"

Kevin and Vincent nodded.

"Good, follow me."

The men stalked noiselessly forward. The Boers were so focused on their work, they didn't notice anything. Only the two guards kept watch.

"Drop your weapons!" called a soldier from the next blockhouse. "Surrender."

Flashlights lit up, blinding the Boer gunmen. They fired in the direction of the English, who returned fire at once, taking them down. The corporal next to Kevin took out another man who was reaching for a gun. A fourth attempted to detonate one of the mines, but a muzzle flashed from the second blockhouse and the man collapsed over the dynamite. Three attempted to flee—one by trying to climb the barbed wire on the other side of the tracks, two by running along the tracks. The soldiers stopped them from running farther by shooting the ground in front of them. British soldiers ran forward to cut off their path. They had no chance. Reluctantly, they stayed where they were, apparently ready to surrender. Only one, a lanky young man, had immediately thrown down his tools and raised his arms—he clearly did not intend to sacrifice himself to the "Boers' holy matter."

Kevin approached and shone his flashlight in the man's face.

"Cornelis!" he cried.

"Greetings, Dr. Drury." Cornelis sounded almost cheerful.

The young Boer began to limp toward Kevin. And then all hell broke loose. Shots whipped through the night. Their noise mixed with the hoofbeats of galloping horses. Kevin pulled Cornelis down to the ground with him and covered his head as a panicked Boer pony leaped over the two prone men.

"Into the barrel! Drive them into the wire!"

Kevin ventured a quick look up and caught sight of more ponies stumbling over the tracks with their riders. Behind them followed the Rough Riders, firing from the saddle. And not just at the fleeing Boers. Horrified, Kevin saw the men who had already surrendered fall. The crews of the blockhouses screamed—they were afraid, and not without reason, to be taken for Boers and likewise cut down. Kevin remained prone and held a dazed Cornelis down. The screams and shots were now moving farther away, but the combat did not abate. Kevin could imagine what was happening. One of the traps had been prepared a few hundred yards beyond the blockhouse—the Boers would find an apparent escape route, but it would be sealed off. They could then surrender or stand and fight. He dropped his face to the ground.

"Kevin! Is everything all right?" The veterinarian pointed his flashlight at his friend. "Did that horse trample you?"

Kevin stood up. "No, it leaped clean over us. The Brits should requisition it. That pony has potential in a steeplechase. But I thought I'd better stick to cover. Besides—"

He pointed to Cornelis, who now struggled to his feet.

Vincent shone the light on him. "The patient from the van Stout farm? What are you doing here? Your leg has hardly healed."

The young man looked at him with a mix of defiance and shame. "I'm a Boer," he said wearily. "A Boer laughs at a lame leg. At least, it doesn't stop one from riding when God and country call him to arms." Cornelis smiled wryly.

"Then this is Adrianus van Stout's unit?" Kevin asked. "This far north of Wepener?"

Cornelis shook his head. "This was Martinus DeGroot's unit. Adrianus van Stout died two months ago. Martinus took over command—and recruited me. Just a month after you patched me back together." He rubbed the dirt from his face.

Slowly, the alarm of battle fell silent. The Boers had either escaped or, more likely, been killed or captured by Coltrane's regiment.

"But weren't you a prisoner of war?" Vincent asked. "Let's go to the blockhouse and set up the hospital tent, Kevin. Patients will quite certainly be arriving any minute—if again only British ones."

Kevin looked to the corporal with whom they'd stopped the saboteurs. He was now inspecting the men who had surrendered and then been mown down. He shook his head in Kevin's direction. No need for the doctor to examine them.

"My mother and aunt smuggled me out," Cornelis explained. "Right after you moved out."

"With the operation still fresh?" Kevin asked. "With the artery that could have torn open again at any time?"

Cornelis shrugged. But then he looked more closely at the fallen Boers, and a raspy, shocked sound came from his throat. It was the man who had attempted to escape through the barbed wire. The tall blond had died from a bullet to the back.

"Martinus," Cornelis whispered incredulously.

Kevin stared at him. "Martinus?"

Cornelis nodded.

Kevin and Vincent helped him to extricate the body of Doortje van Stout's fiancé from the wire barricade.

Chapter 3

One month later, Kevin Drury stood before Major Robin, to whom all the regiments from New Zealand had answered since the beginning of the war. Two other soldiers acting as accessors had heard Kevin's complaint against Colin Coltrane and now listened to the major's response.

"Major Coltrane is unaware of any blame," Robin declared. "I understand he was approaching at a full gallop. Furthermore, it was night. The riders could not tell whether the saboteurs on the tracks had surrendered."

"They had their arms raised," insisted Kevin.

"If that was the case, Major Coltrane and his men missed it. The man they shot in the back was attempting to flee, was he not?" Robin moved papers around in front of him.

"The man was stuck in barbed wire. He was no longer capable of fighting, nor was there any chance of escape. It was completely unnecessary to shoot him. And it was just as unnecessary to shoot fleeing riders."

"That lot offered a firefight," one of the accessors, a lieutenant, noted. "Major Coltrane had no other choice than to fire back. After he had demanded they surrender, of course."

"And the fact that they were all dead?" asked Kevin. "Not a single treatable injury? My colleague and I looked at the corpses. Some of the bullets seemed to have been fired point-blank."

Robin raised his arms. "Dr. Drury, you've been here for months—you know the Boers. They fight to the death, and more than one of our soldiers has paid with his life for bending down to help an injured Boer. You keep your gun ready, if you have any experience. And fire it too. Point-blank. To imply that the men purposely finished off prisoners . . ."

"Besides, you weren't there," the other lieutenant added.

Kevin rubbed his forehead. "And all the other assaults, burnings—"

"Everything within the bounds of high command's orders," Robin remarked. "Lord Kitchener's strategy may not please us—I'm sure Major Coltrane does not like waging war against women and children. But he's conducted himself completely correctly. Your incriminations are without merit, Dr. Drury; accept that."

Kevin swallowed and clicked his heels. "As you say, sir. However, I cannot accept it, and if you must, punish me, but I cannot reconcile my conscience further to serving under Major Coltrane."

"Colonel Coltrane," one of the men said. "He was just promoted."

"Ah, that's right," said Robin. "Thank you, Lieutenant."

Kevin took a deep breath. "I refuse to serve further under Colonel Coltrane. Reassign me or lock me up."

The British officers inhaled sharply, but Major Robin remained calm. Kevin's behavior might have been inconceivable for the British Army, but Robin thought it a waste to arrest often brave and, particularly in this guerilla war, valuable insubordinates just for disciplinary reasons.

"As luck would have it, I've already thought of a new post for you." He smiled. "Perfect for someone who still has friendly feelings toward the foe, in a manner of speaking."

Kevin stiffened. "I don't have any intention of fraternizing—"

Robin, a powerful man with graying hair, shook his head. "We don't mean to insinuate that either. On the contrary, we appreciate your sympathy for the Boer women and children. For that reason, I would like to offer you a post where you could truly offer help. Medical Officer Drury, from now on, you will oversee one of the refugee camps in Transvaal."

***

"Refugee camp?" Dr. Barrister laughed. "Dear Lord. You should hear Emily Hobhouse on the subject. She calls them 'concentration camps,' sometimes 'death camps.'"

"I hear the lady exaggerates," Kevin responded.

He had heard in Robin's command post that his former superior officer was running a military hospital in Pretoria and had sought him out. Dr. Barrister had been delighted by the reunion and invited him at once to the officers' club to eat. Kevin enjoyed an excellent if somewhat exotic dinner, at which lion steak was served.

"Personally, I find her quite levelheaded," Dr. Barrister declared, taking a drink of wine. "An agitator, sure, but I've spoken with her myself; I know the family. And the numbers can't be denied: almost eight hundred dead, just in the past month. The conditions are supposed to be execrable. And 'refugee camp' is surely not the right word. The women aren't going of their own volition. On the contrary, they're dragged in and held under armed guard. It doesn't much matter what you call the camps. According to Miss Hobhouse, inhuman conditions prevail there, which is unsurprising—they lie at the bottom of the priority list, so to speak. They only receive the food and medicine that the troops, offices, hospitals, and city populations don't need. And those supplies are bad to begin with. To think we've burned the grain fields of an entire country."

Kevin looked stricken. "You mean to say I ought to decline the post?"

"Certainly not. Then you'll risk disciplinary measures. Although the camps have newly been placed under civilian administration, so strictly speaking, you won't be going as a medical officer. Nevertheless, after your complaint against that Coltrane fellow, you won't have a leg to stand on with the army. And in principle, Major Robin's right. Someone has to do the job. So, better they send someone who still has fellow feeling, in general or personal. Have you heard any news of our cantankerous Mejuffrouw van Stout?"

Kevin shook his head. "We didn't exactly exchange addresses," he said with a wry smile.

Barrister sighed. "I'm afraid it wouldn't have mattered. Miss van Stout won't have an address anymore. You said it yourself: her father and fiancé were commandos."

"They're dead," Kevin told him.

Barrister nodded. "But that doesn't change the fact that the family came to the army's attention. If things went the way they always do, her farm must have been burned."

Kevin leaned forward. "You mean Doortje is in one of the camps?"

Barrister shrugged. "If she didn't die when they cleared out the farm. You know her, Drury. Not much for surrender."

Kevin bristled. "Then my decision is clear. I'll accept management of the camp—yes, I know, there are many, and Doortje is probably somewhere else entirely. But if she survives the war, I'll still be able to look her in the eye. No one's going to die in my camp."

***

"For my part, I'm happy to assign the man to you."

Lord Alfred Milner, the new civilian manager of the concentration camps in Transvaal, proved amenable to Kevin's request to appoint Cornelis Pienaar as his translator and prisoner liaison. No one wanted to take on management of the camps, so Milner was grateful for every qualified man, and Kevin was even allowed to choose where he wanted to work. Three of the new sites lacked overseers.

"It's cheaper than sending him to Saint Helena," Milner continued. Most of the male prisoners of war were now being deported to camps outside of Africa. "But are you sure you're doing him a favor?"

Kevin furrowed his brow. "I should think so, sir. Mr. Pienaar and I always got along. He's one of the few reasonable people on the Boer side. I'm sure he'd be happy to come and will do good work."

Milner shrugged. He had received Kevin in his well-appointed Pretoria office and generously offered whiskey and sandwiches. Kevin eyed the expensive furniture with dismay. If the lack of supplies was really so great in the camps, luxury should not be flaunted here.

"I don't doubt that the young man is willing," the lord replied. "But you're not thinking of the mood in the camps. These Boer women, yes, yes, according to the papers, they're dying like flies and can hardly stay on their feet, but in reality, they have plenty of energy to spit venom. Whenever they get hold of a reporter, they give statements encouraging their menfolk to fight on. They resist anything and everything: medical care, schooling for their children, and when one deviates and concedes even a little to camp management, she becomes a target." Milner took a sip of whiskey. "A few weeks ago, we tried to lodge a few male prisoners of war in Chrissiesmeer. It proved impossible. The women cursed the men as cowards for surrendering instead of letting themselves be shot. In the end, we had to remove the men before those harridans could rip them apart. Think hard about whether you want to subject Mijnheer Pienaar to that."

Kevin nodded. "With his liberal mentality, Mijnheer Pienaar would probably stand out in the men's camps as well. But I do appreciate your concern. It might help if he were with people from his own region. Could you tell me where the Boers from Wepener were sent? And whether that camp might happen to need an overseer?"

***

Karenstad reminded Kevin more of his homeland than the savannahs he had crossed with the Rough Riders. The town lay in the foothills. It was not nearly as hot as in the plains, and the air seemed wonderfully fresh, the mountains jagged, and the luscious pastures inviting. Surely there were fish in these streams. Kevin and Vincent felt they were on a fishing excursion again when they bivouacked alongside one such stream. Coincidence—and Kevin's choice of the camp—had brought the friends back together. Vincent, just like Kevin and Preston, had testified against Coltrane, and Major Robin had them both reassigned. Preston ended up in Barrister's hospital in Pretoria, while Vincent was sent to Karenstad as its veterinarian. So, the men rode together, while Cornelis Pienaar was brought on a prisoner transport.

"It's absolutely impossible for him to ride with you," Milner had declared when Kevin suggested taking his future liaison with him. "The women would assume that he's entirely on your side. If he comes on a normal transport, at least he has a chance."

"It really is pretty here," Kevin said as they approached Karenstad, looking with regret on the ruins of a burned-out farmhouse. It had been log-cabin style, similar to his parents' home, but now nothing more could be discerned. "I like it better than the veld."

Vincent laughed. "You're just assuming there are fewer lions and rhinos here," he teased his friend. "But look, it's not lacking in antelopes."

A herd of animals was just then moving across what had once been a cornfield. Nature was already reclaiming the farmland.

"Then I wonder why they don't have any meat in the camps," said Kevin. "They could certainly go hunting here."

But the closer the men came to town, the fewer wild animals they saw. No wonder—Karenstad was surrounded by train tracks, which were moreover secured with barbed wire. Undoubtedly that frightened off the antelope.

And the men, too, were leery of their new offices. Karenstad was hardly more than a collection of tin huts. The original town had been a railroad hub and camp for military deliveries. There had been hard fighting for the area, and most of the farms were destroyed at the beginning of the hostilities. Thus, Karenstad had filled with refugees, but the British military didn't relish hundreds of Boers camping out near a British munitions depot. So, they'd requisitioned the village houses for the supply camp garrison, and a concentration camp was created. At first, they penned in the local families, then also the displaced from elsewhere. The town itself bustled with the English. Several cavalry brigades were stationed here, and additional units passed through, provisioning themselves for deployments. As a consequence, a constant coming and going prevailed around the town, with soldiers galloping heedlessly over the unpaved ground.

"My lands, they do kick up dust," Vincent remarked, coughing. A cloud of it lay over the town like fog. "It's terrible for the horses."

Kevin squinted. "And no better for the people. And the camp's downwind. The people there must be suffocating. I'll have to see to it that they institute a rule about riding at a walk."

Vincent laughed. "Good luck with that."

Kevin looked annoyed. "You could support me. It certainly affects your charges too. What do you bet the officers' quarters are better shielded than the stables?"

The camp itself lay among truly beautiful surroundings. The tents were pitched to the right and left of a river, which, unfortunately, tended to overflow its banks. Kevin, who approached from the north, was horrified at the mud and water people had to channel out of their tents in improvised ditches.

"The northern portion of the camp urgently needs to be relocated," he declared, having only just met the Scotsman he was to replace as camp commander.

Lieutenant Lindsey resided in one of the stone buildings that also housed the administration. The prisoners' tents looked provisional, but Lindsey's domicile was quite comfortable. It was appointed with carved furniture that reminded Kevin of the van Stout farm. The pieces must have been confiscated from a nearby home.

"You go right ahead and give it a try," Lindsey scoffed, and placed a bottle of whiskey and two glasses on the table. "But first, have a drink. It's always worth having a drink before going out there. Protects against contagion, or so they say."

"Contagion?" Kevin furrowed his brow.

"I wanted to relocate the north camp myself when the river overflowed the first time, but the people didn't want to and still don't. They cling to the place as if it were their childhood home, even though they've lived there only a few months. And don't start cursing me when you see the hospital. Yes, it's half-empty even though the people are sick. If anyone comes, it's women with their dying children. But then they're already in the final stages, and there's nothing more our doctors can do. Which only confirms their belief that our medicine is the devil's work."

"The final stages of what?"

Lindsey threw his hands up. "Typhus?"

Kevin rubbed his forehead. "Very well," he said. "I'll take a look at the hospital first, then the tents. How many inmates do you have here?"

To Kevin's amazement, Lindsey shrugged again. "Don't know," he replied. "It changes constantly."

"You don't keep records?"

Lindsey rolled his eyes. "What am I supposed to do? There are hardly any assistants, and everything falls to me. What can I do about it when they only send us one doctor? Did I determine the rations? Someone's always complaining that the meat is stringy and bony or that there are no vegetables. Am I supposed to plant carrots?"

Kevin looked at the lieutenant. "Why not? A completely sensible activity. Maybe the women could be moved to do it?"

Lindsey laughed. "I can only repeat: live and learn. But for now, let's get you over to see the hospital. I'm determined to be on the next train to Bloemfontein. Back to my old regiment to hunt a few Boers. I'll thank heaven when I'm sitting back on a horse. It won't complain all the time about the oat rations."

***

The hospital was one of the few solid buildings in the camp, pieced together out of sheet metal. It must have been unbearably hot in summer, and even now, the stink was eye-watering and flies swarmed around the patients. Typhus seemed to run rampant, and the care was completely insufficient. Family members sat beside some of the sick and seemed to take it on themselves to clean them. But the older patients, many of them women but also an old man here and there, lay in their own filth. It was very embarrassing for the only doctor, Dr. Greenway.

"I do what I can, Dr. Drury," he defended himself. "At the moment, I have twenty-seven patients and no nurses."

"Can't you get any of the women to help?" Kevin asked.

The doctor and Lindsey snorted in unison.

"They won't do anything," Greenway said bitterly. "Nothing that might remotely help us. They opened a sort of competing clinic in one of the tents. They treat them there with home remedies. Yesterday, a woman wanted to kill me because I couldn't provide her a dead goat. In all seriousness. She was convinced the only way she could heal her child's lung infection was by wrapping it in the skin of a freshly slaughtered goat. She declined real medicine, likewise a bed in the hospital. The child died this morning. It plays out like a tragedy, Dr. Drury, a singular tragedy."

"Do you only have these two rooms?" Kevin asked.

Though he was used to large sickrooms, he was pained by the thought that people had to die in these stinking communal lodgings. In the hospital in Dunedin where he had done his residency, there had at least been folding screens on hand to preserve a modicum of privacy.

Dr. Greenway shook his head. "No, there are also four smaller areas. If you'd care to see them."

He led Kevin down a sort of hallway and pulled a curtain aside, opening a view of an improvised two-bedded room. It had surely not been cleaned in a long time, but Kevin held his tongue. It could hardly be expected that the lone doctor also reached for the broom and mop.

"These small rooms are unoccupied?" he inquired.

Dr. Greenway grimaced. "Oh, two are occupied. But the woman in one has already died. I just don't want to separate the children from her right away. We're sending her to the cemetery as soon as we've found someone to take in the orphans. And the other, it's one of those dramas that almost makes these people's attitude toward us understandable." The doctor closed his eyes.

"I don't understand," Kevin pressed.

"He's trying to let you know tactfully that our own men are responsible for the girls' condition," Lieutenant Lindsey explained. "A mess without equal. The matter should absolutely have been investigated. But the women won't say anything, you see—and the fellows who transported them didn't answer to me.

Otherwise, they'd all be rotting in jail until the women gave their statements. You can count on that."

The lieutenant was working himself into a rage, which amazed Kevin, considering how little sympathy the man had shown until now.

"What the hell happened?" Kevin asked. "I'd like to see the women, if you'd allow me."

"If it were up to me, of course," said Greenway. "You're a doctor, after all. But the women won't let anyone near them. One is completely deranged; the other scratches and bites when you try to examine her. Yet she'd do well to allow it. She still has hemorrhaging."

Kevin stared at him. "You mean to say they were raped? Here? In camp?"

Lindsey shook his head. "In transport. The men who brought them here insist it wasn't them. They blame a cavalry regiment that escorted their unit part of the way. That's sometimes done when we suspect Boer guerillas in an area. Then the transport units ask for protection."

"Protection?" asked Kevin bitterly.

Lindsey looked away. "I can only tell you that this sort of thing rarely happens. Or we don't hear of it, at least. You can't necessarily tell a woman's been raped. But in this case, the girls were beaten. Probably they resisted. Anyway, we had to hospitalize them. We couldn't put them in a tent in that state. Even if they might be happier among their own."

Kevin bristled. "I'd like to see them. Maybe they can be convinced to give a statement. Do they speak any English? If not, my interpreter should arrive tomorrow."

"They don't speak at all," said Greenway, and led them to the next room. "One is catatonic, and the other won't even look at you."

The doctor pulled the curtain aside and let Kevin enter.

"Ladies, I regret to disturb you again so soon." Greenway chose his words with deliberate politeness and care. Kevin's reservations about him disappeared. The man surely did what he could to create humane conditions in this horrific hospital. Kevin looked over the primitive cots on which the women were resting—wrinkly, grayish-white bedding, lumpy pillows. The girl on the closer bed lay on her back. Her light-blue eyes stared at the ceiling, one of them swollen shut. Her right cheek was lacerated, her lips askew. Although she was so disfigured, the girl seemed familiar to Kevin. "But we have a new camp commander,"

Greenway continued. "Dr. Kevin Drury will care for you along with me in future. He—"

Kevin looked at the second bed. The woman in it had her face to the wall. Only her small frame could be seen underneath a blanket and bonnet, out of which light-blonde hair spilled. Had she started when Greenway mentioned his name?

The camp doctor posted himself next to the first bed like a resident during rounds. "Johanna van Stout, fourteen years old, multiple contusions and injuries from violent contact."

Kevin froze. At that moment, the woman in the other bed turned toward him. Kevin looked at deep-blue eyes filled with hate, a swollen face, and broken lips. But he still found her beautiful.

"Doortje," he cried. "Me-Mejuffrouw van Stout."

A nasty smile spread across Doortje's battered face. She could hardly move, but her eyes burned with rage.

"You do not need to twist your tongue, Doctor," she said. "I am a maid no more."

Chapter 4

"And what do you intend to do now?" Atamarie asked.

Really, it was an idle question. Roberta would do exactly what her studies had prepared her to do. The newly minted young teacher would look for a suitable position, and that would be that. Atamarie sipped her champagne in frustration. Violet Coltrane rarely allowed alcohol at her table, but Roberta's graduation had to be celebrated. It was a beautiful evening, and Atamarie was on vacation. She didn't know why she was in such a bad mood.

Roberta already had pink cheeks and shining eyes after her first sips. She looked happy and adorable in her new dress of dark-blue silk, but also agitated—Atamarie hadn't seen her so keyed up in a long time. During the two years of her studies, after all, she had tried her best to fit the image of a spinster grammar-school teacher.

"Well, I think that's been established for years," Reverend Burton said with a smile before Roberta could answer. "Our school is waiting for you, Roberta. We're all looking forward to it."

Roberta blushed even more deeply, and Atamarie recognized the look Roberta got when she had big news. Her curiosity was piqued. It was one thing for Roberta to hide something from her parents, but since when did her friend keep secrets from her?

The ever-perceptive Kathleen Burton gave her husband a disapproving look. "Now, don't push her, Peter," she chided. "Who knows, maybe she has other plans. Perhaps she wants to marry."

Patrick Drury winced with pain. He had never heard another word from Juliet. No one else was the slightest bit worried about the brazen singer, but

Patrick spent hours at a time worrying about her. Atamarie smiled at him and his daughter. Little May sat on Patrick's lap, captivated by the bubbles in his champagne and babbling happily to herself.

Atamarie choked back a comment that the toddler apparently shared her mother's tastes. Heather, who sat across from Atamarie, seemed to have the same thought—Atamarie caught a stifled smile on her face, and she whispered something to Chloe that made them both laugh.

Roberta shook her head decisively. "No, certainly not. I didn't study so hard just to turn around and get married. But I, well, I thought." Roberta took a deep breath. "I signed a contract yesterday," she announced. "I'm going to South Africa, for one to two years."

"South Africa?" Patrick Drury spun to look at her. "Do you want to shoot Boers?"

Roberta laughed nervously. "No, just the opposite. I—have you all heard of Emily Hobhouse?"

Her mother looked probingly around the room. Of course, Kathleen and Peter Burton knew of Miss Hobhouse's protests. They viewed the war just as critically as Sean and Violet did. Nor did anything having to do with women's rights escape Heather and Chloe. Only Patrick and Atamarie were clueless.

"Miss Hobhouse is campaigning for the dissolution of the concentration camps," Violet explained. "Camps in which Boer women and children are penned in together to demoralize their menfolk and move them to surrender."

"It's about time they did surrender!" declared Patrick. "This guerilla war—"

"That's a different question," Sean said. "But Miss Hobhouse argues quite rightly that it's beneath the British Empire's dignity to wage war against women and children."

"Are they really that bad, these camps?" Atamarie asked, taking another sip of champagne. She needed time to ruminate on Roberta's decision. Her friend had never before expressed special concern about refugees. "I've heard they have to live in tents, but—"

"It's not a camping trip, Atamarie, even if the army likes to portray it that way," Reverend Burton said sternly. "These women and children starve, die of infections, and Miss Hobhouse is right. The camps are a disgrace to England."

"But now things are supposed to change, you see." Roberta seized the word with unusual decisiveness. Normally, she would not have dared to interrupt the reverend. "Miss Hobhouse has collected money. Her Relief Fund for South

African Women and Children is sending nurses and teachers to the camp. Along with groceries and medicine and all that, of course. I leave next week on the *Beauty of the Sea*."

"I hope that's not a troop transport?" Heather asked, taking another appetizer.

Roberta shook her head. "No, it's a completely normal passenger ship. There aren't many of us, you see. Just two nurses and myself. A few are coming from the North Island, but most of them from England, no doubt."

Violet nodded, visibly torn between pride in her daughter and disappointment at only now being let in on her plans.

"But why haven't you said anything, Roberta?" she asked sternly. "Don't misunderstand me. I have nothing against it in theory. On the contrary! But we—"

"We could have collected donations," Reverend Burton said. "Money and goods. People are always more generous when someone gets involved personally in a matter."

Roberta lowered her eyes. "I, uh, decided rather late."

Atamarie knew Roberta was lying. She'd probably been plotting ways to get to South Africa for months. Miss Hobhouse's initiative had hardly been the catalyst.

***

Atamarie pounced as soon as the guests had dispersed throughout Sean and Violet's large apartment with coffee cups or liqueur glasses. She dragged Roberta into her room.

"Admit it," she began. "This is about Kevin. You just didn't say anything so that I couldn't talk you out of it."

During dessert, Roberta had relaxed again and even chatted quite calmly about her planned assignment on the cape. Now, however, the blood shot to her face anew.

"That's not true! It's just—the conditions there are so terrible. I'd like to help and, um, see a bit of the world."

She lowered her gaze, in which not a trace of wanderlust was to be seen.

Atamarie rolled her eyes. "I'm sure. You're completely crazy for lions and rhinos. You always wanted to ride an elephant! Spare me, Robbie. How can you still be in love with him?"

Roberta glared at her. "You're still in love too! With that Richard of yours, even though you haven't seen him in months."

"That's completely different," her friend insisted. "Richard is, well, he moves slowly. But Kevin—Robbie, he's a womanizer, and he never noticed you. Besides, South Africa is a huge country. How are you going to find him?"

Roberta bit her lip again. Without a doubt, this was her plan's weak point.

"I don't have to find him," she said quietly. "I just want to be near him. And who knows—"

Atamarie threw her arms up. "Now I'm going to hear about the gods' gift again."

Roberta's gaze was level. "You believe in it too," she replied. "So, why don't we help them out?"

***

In the week that followed, Reverend Burton's parish donated enough powdered milk and medicine to fill a huge crate. Violet held a fiery speech in front of the local Women's Christian Temperance Union, after which they collected clothing, diapers, and toys. Sean spoke to his clients and Kathleen to the Dunloes who, after all, knew everyone in town with money to give away. The attitude of most people in Dunedin was ambivalent. New Zealand was still supporting England's war with all its heart, and critical voices were not suffered gladly. At the same time, it was easier to support women and children—especially when a nice, young Dunedin lady personally requested it. So, Roberta had to go along to donation drives and charity dinners. She was completely exhausted when Atamarie finally accompanied her to the ship. The *Beauty of the Sea* gleamed white and inviting in the deep-blue water of Dunedin's natural harbor. Atamarie would have loved to come along.

"I'm simply no good at giving speeches and all that," Roberta complained. The night before, Heather and Chloe had held a reception and auctioned two paintings, with proceeds going to help the camps. "That was more stressful than teaching for six hours."

Atamarie laughed. "Teacher college spoiled you for the wider world. Everyone there went around like they were at a funeral, and you were probably only allowed to speak when you raised your hand. Now you have to be loud again."

Roberta blushed. For her appearance at the gallery, she had promptly slipped back into her teaching uniform, and she'd hardly managed a word at the podium.

Atamarie squinted at her friend's traveling outfit. "Even if you do find Kevin, he's never going to notice you in clothes like that," she teased, and confidently waved the three porters carrying donations to the pier.

Roberta looked at her friend enviously. Atamarie would have raised her voice before an audience of hundreds uninhibited, but the man she loved did not pay attention to her either. Roberta was ashamed to find this last thought comforting.

"Plus, you're traveling to Africa," Atamarie continued. "How much do you want to bet the Africans aren't as stiff as the Church of Scotland? I picture them being more like the Maori. I'm sure they like colorful clothing and laughing and dancing."

Atamarie let the wind play with her blonde hair. During vacation, she saw no reason to force it into austere buns. In her red-and-green summer dress, she looked like a colorful flower.

Roberta shook her head. "Atamie, the Church of Scotland is a nightclub compared to what I've heard about these Boers. And I won't have anything at all to do with the black population. Miss Hobhouse reports only on white camps."

The young women reached the ship's gangway and watched the baggage being taken aboard. Sean and Violet were collecting some final donations, but had assured Roberta they would be there in time to say good-bye.

Atamarie did not know much about the Boer War, but at the mention of "Africa," she pictured wild animals and black people. What about them?

"So, if Miss Hobhouse is just concerned with the whites, where are all the blacks?" she finally asked. "The Boers have slaves, right? Isn't that part of what this war is about? They surely also lived on the farms that were burned down. Did they run away?"

Roberta looked caught out. She shrugged desperately. "I just want to help whomever I can."

"Well, you'll write me and explain the situation once you're there. But no empty letters, please. Tell me everything. And, of course, I'll keep my fingers crossed you find Kevin. As long as you face the fact that—"

Roberta raised her hand. "Maybe you should worry about your own great romance for once," she said sternly. "There might be some facts you're not facing either. Atamarie, Kevin may not want me, but, well, he's already far away, and it's been so long, and Juliet—" Roberta fell silent, and Atamarie sighed theatrically.

Roberta swallowed and reached into her bag to touch the stuffed horse she had carried since Kevin won it for her. "But Richard," she pressed on, "he doesn't even live a hundred miles from Christchurch. And he did notice you. You talked for hours and even held hands and kissed. If he doesn't visit you now, then—"

Atamarie started to protest, but their conversation was interrupted by Violet and Sean's arrival.

While Sean unloaded another sea chest full of donations, Roberta said her tearful farewell to her mother. Afterward, she embraced her stepfather and, finally, Atamarie.

"I'll write for sure, Atamie. Every day. And don't be mad about what I said."

Atamarie laughed and pressed her friend close. "Every day might be a bit much," she said. "Once a week is fine. And, of course, I'm not mad. You're right: something has to happen in this business between Richard and me."

***

Atamarie was already planning her journey to Timaru as she watched Roberta waving from the departing ship.

She was at least as brave as her friend. If Roberta could follow Kevin to South Africa, Atamarie would spit on convention and go visit Richard on his family's farm. She needed to get him alone and find out for certain whether he still loved her.

Chapter 5

"Miss van Stout, I can only tell you again how sorry I am and how much I repudiate the actions of—" Kevin rubbed his forehead. For days, he had been trying to appeal to Doortje van Stout, but she declined to even look at him. "Regardless, I deeply regret what was done to you and your sister. We would like to file a report, but for that, you would need to make a statement, describing the men, giving any names and ranks if you can. Please speak to us, Miss van Stout."

Kevin swallowed. "Doortje, talk to me."

But Doortje van Stout did not look at Kevin. Dr. Greenway had approved her release from the camp hospital. Johanna, too, could go. The young girl moved like a sleepwalker.

"I think it's best the two of them go to their family now that they're better," the doctor had said. "Perhaps you could assign them to a single tent."

Greenway knew as well as Kevin the state of the camp's occupancy: Karenstad was hopelessly overfull.

Indeed, it took Kevin hours just to find out where the blind Mevrouw van Stout and her young sons had been lodged. No one knew precisely how many Boers lived in Karenstad, nor where individual families could be found. Only the number of dead was registered, and that was shockingly high. In general, everything having to do with death in this camp was exceptionally well organized. They had a gravedigger, a carpenter who cobbled together primitive coffins, and a photographer who made portraits of the dead children for their fathers. Lord Kitchener had to be heartless or simply stupid if he thought this would force the men to capitulate. On the contrary, the conditions in the camps stoked their anger.

Now, Kevin led the silent van Stout sisters over the muddy paths between the long rows of once-white tents. Each was laid out for fifteen people, but meant for soldiers, who only slept there. They had not been designed for families who would have to spend their days there. Furthermore, the overcrowding meant lodging several families together. At least two, more often three, mothers and their children or the elderly they cared for shared a tent—mostly with stoic equanimity, at first. Over the course of the months, tensions almost always developed, which sometimes exploded in fierce fighting.

"We wanted to offer communal food supplies," Kevin told Doortje as they passed provisional kitchens built alongside the tents. "But the people wouldn't eat it. Someone started the rumor the English were mixing broken glass into the porridge to kill their children."

Doortje gave him a disgusted look. "You are killing them already," she said angrily, pointing to a howling mother whose dead child was just then being carried out of one of the fly-swarmed tents.

These were the first words Doortje had spoken since their reunion, but Kevin could not be happy about them. The child had died of typhus after his mother had refused to bring him to the hospital. And so, here was another tent where the disease would take hold—and from which the flies would transmit it. The swarming insects were another problem Kevin could not get under control. They were attracted by unwashed dishes and dirty bodies, which could be prevented only by placing enough water at the women's disposal. Drinking water, however, was in short supply, and though washing water could be fetched from the river, the way was far and the women often too weak. There was hardly any soap, a fact about which Lindsey had already complained repeatedly, but command simply did not send more. The women could not keep themselves or their children clean. Their clothes also became tattered quickly when worn day and night. Kevin heard that no one in Karenstad disrobed to sleep.

"The people sleep on the ground," Cornelis had explained. "Most don't even have covers. It's too cold to take your clothes off—not to mention, there are strangers in the tent."

Kevin had nodded and put in a request for more blankets, as well as canvas to partition the tents for privacy. Vincent helped out with a few horse blankets and advised Kevin not to wash them.

"They say fleas don't like horse sweat," he'd said. "So, maybe a small help against all the pests?"

Kevin did not share this hope. He had discovered that new admissions to the camp brought fleas and lice. Whether the vermin were lodged in the crannies of the transport carts, or perhaps in the blankets with which they were upholstered, he did not know. Maybe the Boers caught the pests in the veld. Regardless, Kevin ordered the wagons thoroughly cleaned, but the mischief had, of course, long since been done; all of Karenstad was crawling with vermin.

"We do have flea powder, as it happens," Kevin had told Cornelis, "in large quantities. It's just no one seems to know how to use it. Dr. Greenway has kept it under lock and key after two women shook it into their children's food. I don't understand your people. They live in the same world as we do, they can read and write, but they—"

"They reject this world," Cornelis said curtly. The young man was even more shocked at the conditions than Kevin and was naturally more affected. His patriotic attitude had so far remained bounded, but now he, too, was developing anger toward the British. "Boers learn to read only so they can read the Bible, and the men work the land of their forefathers. Their women keep the house clean and the children healthy with remedies handed down from their foremothers. If one dies, then it's God's will. But this—"

"This here is surely not God's will. On that, we agree. But maybe you can explain to the women how to use the flea powder. Try using a Bible verse."

Cornelis grinned. "'And I will sever in that day the land of Goshen, in which my people dwell, that no swarms of flies shall be there; to that end thou mayest know that I am the Lord in the midst of the earth.' Book of Exodus."

Kevin nodded. "Wonderful. I thought we might need divine intervention. Please, do all you can."

Cornelis had disappeared in the direction of the hospital while Kevin exhaled. It had been a clever decision to bring Cornelis Pienaar. He had not needed any explanations of the danger he ran in the camp. To ward off accusations of cowardice, he exaggerated his limp and acted as if his right arm were almost entirely unusable, rendering him no use at the front. Since he claimed to have fallen into the clutches of the British wounded and unconscious, the women grudgingly forgave him for surviving his last battle. Indeed, Cornelis even received some mothering—at least until Kevin had tracked down Bentje van Stout. Doortje's mother was suspicious of the second injury. She suspected Cornelis of fraternizing with the enemy. Even Doortje herself refused to see her cousin. Kevin took it that she was ashamed—and his anger at Doortje and Johanna's attackers grew.

"It's just up ahead," he said now, turning to the young van Stouts. "Your mother is in a tent by the river, but you won't be there long term. We're going to relocate that settlement. The Karenspruit overflows its banks with every rain, and then—"

"We shall stay right here until our men come and liberate us," Doortje said calmly. The sight of the conditions in the camp seemed to stir her spirit of resistance. Her mention of the men, however, cut Kevin to the quick. Apparently, she knew nothing about the death of her father or Martinus DeGroot. "Now, where is my mother?"

Kevin found Bentje van Stout sitting in front of her tent, telling a group of children about the Great Trek.

"And don't you believe the children hid under their blankets. No, they moved bravely around the camp, bringing their fathers water and food to replenish their strength for the fight, and when the Kaffirs attacked, they stood behind them and reloaded their weapons."

Bentje's blind eyes beamed with patriotic ardor. The eyes of many of the children, on the other hand, shone feverishly. Even Bentje's youngest son, who snuggled in her lap, did not look healthy.

"Mother!"

Kevin turned away as Doortje embraced her mother. However, he did not miss that Johanna stared past Bentje just as she had past the doctors. Something inside the girl had been broken. Kevin ached to fix it.

"Doortje," he said softly before he took his leave. Where should he begin? He felt the deepest shame, but also desperate love for the young woman who still held her head high despite everything. "Doortje, if Johanna doesn't—come back, please bring her to the hospital. Perhaps she needs further examinations or different medicines."

Kevin did not really know what could be done, but Johanna needed constant supervision at the least. She did nothing of her own accord. In her first days in the hospital, someone had even had to feed her. Now she spooned her food herself again when someone pressed a bowl and a spoon into her hands. If it was simply put on the table, she left it there.

"She has everything she needs," Doortje informed him. "Isn't that what they say about these camps? That we are better off than on our farms? That the care is exceptional and we are comfortable?"

Kevin turned to go without another word.

***

In the next few days, Kevin struggled against the urge to check in on Doortje. Not that he lacked for things to do. Everything he tried to do to change conditions in the camp ran up against the British supply posts or regulations—or the prisoners, who were not prepared to cooperate even in the smallest matters. Kevin complained about the food rations, which were wholly insufficient. The stringy meat could have been used to make stew, but they lacked any vegetables. Meager quantities of rice or potatoes were sometimes delivered, but often it was only flour, which the women used to make flatbread. With drinking water, at least, Kevin had some success. Above the military camp, there were wells as well as clear streams, in contrast to the mostly muddy water in the river. Horse-drawn wagons carried it to town, but Vincent diverted a few of them to the women's camp every day. However, the families had to retrieve it, and that was not possible if a mother lay sick in her tent. Cornelis hauled buckets to needy families half the day, but the camp held almost fifteen hundred people. It was hopeless to think the limping young man could provide for them all.

Cornelis also became increasingly skilled at convincing women to entrust themselves or their children to Dr. Greenway's care. However, the lone doctor was dangerously overextended. Ultimately, Kevin convinced the garrison doctor from town to loan them a few orderlies: three experienced and eager Indian men. Unfortunately, the Boer women reacted hysterically when men—moreover, men of a different color—tried to touch them.

"Where exactly are the blacks?" asked Kevin one evening. He had invited Dr. Greenway over to his lodgings. Both doctors sank, exhausted and dispirited, into the armchairs in Lindsey's former living room, which had once been elegant but now looked unkempt. The whiskey stores, at least, seemed inexhaustible. Kevin had already transitioned into using the stuff medicinally. He remembered his mother's stories about the passage from London to Australia—the ship's doctor had ordered feverish men to be rubbed with gin. "All of these people's servants, slaves, whatever."

Greenway took a deep drink and contemplated his glass. "Did no one tell you? The blacks have their own camp, just about a mile upriver. You oversee that too."

"What?" Kevin asked, the blood draining from his face. "And you're only telling me this now?"

Greenway raised his hands apologetically. "I thought Lindsey would have told you, or operations command."

"Didn't you wonder why I never went there?" Kevin emptied his glass in one gulp and poured himself more whiskey.

Greenway shrugged. "I think Lindsey only ever visited once. And I—heavens, you know what I have to do here."

Kevin tried to remain calm. "What are conditions like?"

"In some ways better, in some worse. It's, well, different."

"Different how?"

"Food isn't distributed to the blacks. They have to work for it. When the family has a provider, when the women grow vegetables, then they do fine. There are also more men there—many came willingly. They weren't forced like the Boers. Some of them cooperate. The Boer guerillas don't have a chance near the blacks. That's why command likes to settle them along the train lines. But it's bad for the families that only consist of women and children, especially in camps where the people come from different tribes. The families starve—I hear the death rate is even higher than in the white camps."

"And I don't have to ask if there's medical care," Kevin remarked. "I'll ride upriver tomorrow. I need to have a look."

"Dr. Drury." Kevin and Greenway both spun around at the sound of Cornelis's voice. "Forgive my intrusion. I called from the front door, but you didn't hear."

Kevin nodded. "What's the matter?"

Cornelis lowered his head. "I need to ask for a few flashlights so we can search the camp. A girl has disappeared."

Kevin leaped up, but Greenway only rubbed his tired eyes. "If she's in the camp, young man, we'll find her in the morning. I know the women don't want to believe it, but there are, among these very, uh, Christian women, a few who sell themselves for food or soap."

Cornelis looked up, his gaze hard. "That may be, sir. But not in this case. It's Johanna van Stout."

Kevin felt dizzy. Damn it, he should have held the girl in the hospital.

Resigned, he reached for his jacket. "I'll come," he said. "And alert the guards, would you, Greenway? They should form search teams. I'll telephone town as well." Kevin knew Vincent was always on call for emergencies. "Dr. Taylor can surely organize more men. But I don't think we'll get far searching in camp. Let's go to the river."

***

Johanna van Stout's body washed up the next day, downriver. A soldier on patrol discovered it. The body showed no new traces of assault, which did not prevent Bentje van Stout from accusing the guards of murder.

"One of you pushed her. Somebody pushed her. We are Christians. My daughter would never do such a thing." Bentje sobbed and screamed.

"But that's out of the question, Mevrouw van Stout. The banks are gentle everywhere here. No one could be pushed in," Kevin told the woman helplessly. Finally, he turned to Doortje. "Miss van Stout, can't you explain this to your mother? It's a tragedy, it is, but Johanna wasn't killed; she—"

Doortje turned her snow-white but tearless face to him. "Johanna was too weak to live with the shame. God may forgive her that. But if he forgives the man who killed her, not last night, Dr. Drury, but that night in the veld. If he forgives that man, then—" The young woman balled her fists.

Kevin clenched his as well, wishing for nothing more than to take Doortje van Stout in his arms.

"He's not likely to stand trial soon before his God," he said as calmly as he could. "Unless you're finally prepared to give a statement. Then, he'll hang."

Doortje bit her lip. And remained silent.

Chapter 6

Deep down, Atamarie was convinced that Richard Pearse must love her, but she had to admit that the proof left something to be desired. Since Richard had left the university after the excursion in the fall of the previous year, she had seen him only once. He had needed to take care of something in Christchurch and had taken the opportunity to visit Professor Dobbins. Atamarie had been overjoyed when Dobbins relayed that Richard was in town, and that he'd gone to the patent office to register a lightweight bicycle with a bamboo frame, gearshift, and back-pedal brake.

"Did he not write you to say he was coming?" the professor asked. "You do exchange letters with him, don't you? Did I misunderstand?"

Atamarie hastened to assure Dobbins that Richard wrote regularly. The truth was, after the excursion, they had exchanged only two letters. Furthermore, Richard's had been short and vacuous. Of course, it had been harvesttime, and he'd surely been busy. Still, Atamarie began to fear he had forgotten her. But then she received a rather euphoric letter, in which Richard raved about the new workshop he had set up in his barn. He could now concentrate again on new technologies. Atamarie answered amiably, and, from then on, could not complain about a lack of mail. Richard vividly depicted his plans for the light-frame bike and reported assiduously on every attempt, every bit of progress, every setback. Atamarie commented knowledgeably and provided suggestions for improvements. The integrated air pump for the wheels was one of her innovations.

"I expect he wanted to surprise me," she said.

Atamarie squirmed under Dobbins's penetrating gaze. The professor rubbed his cheek, a gesture that always betrayed his uncertainty. Was there something he wanted to say?

"Is he going to come back here today?"

Atamarie knew this question gave her away, but if Richard was in Christchurch, she wanted to see him. It was bad enough he had not announced himself to her.

Dobbins nodded reluctantly. "Of course, Miss Turei. I told him—er, he wants—he's going to pick you up after class. To celebrate."

Atamarie beamed, and in fact, Richard was waiting for her at the college gates. Though he only greeted her with a kiss on the cheek, that was surely most proper in public anyway. He was visibly pleased by her solicitousness, invited her to dinner, and after two bottles of wine, held her hand as he walked her home. The patent for the bicycle, however, was not much on his mind. He spoke the whole evening about his newest project: an aeroplane.

"And not a glider, Atamarie, a propeller aeroplane. It must—"

"It must work even without wind," she laughed. "I've always said so. Simple wings or a double-decker?"

They discussed the advantages and disadvantages as they strolled along the Avon. Atamarie was perfectly happy—or almost. Other couples they passed did more than just hold hands, after all. The boys would put their arms around the girls, and the girls snuggled against them. Atamarie pressed closer to Richard, who understood at once. He pulled her closer while he talked of operating power and propeller size.

"Twenty-five horsepower, I'm thinking. Do you suppose that's enough? Or am I overdoing it? I don't want the machine to get out of control." Somewhat at a loss, Richard stopped in front of Atamarie's house.

Atamarie wrapped her arms around his neck. "A little loss of control isn't always bad," she said, looking at him and parting her lips.

Richard Pearse hesitated briefly but then kissed her. Afterward, Atamarie danced up the stairs. He loved her. Of course, he loved her. And it was very thoughtful not to take her to his hotel. It would have been too embarrassing if they'd caught her sneaking in.

Although—no, it was better not to think about it. Atamarie reined in her inventive spirit. She would not admit to herself that Richard might have other reasons for not asking her to spend the night.

***

But now that the university had closed for the summer, Atamarie was determined to visit her friend. Richard's farm was about fourteen miles from the nearest train station. Surely, she could find a ride. Of course, Richard could have picked her up—Atamarie thought about writing. But then he might find excuses, such as the lack of a chaperone. It sounded as though Richard was alone on the farm. Atamarie would compromise herself by visiting him, especially overnight. She did not care about that herself—she saw herself as Maori and only held to the mores of the *pakeha* in order not to scandalize. On this isolated farm, she would do what she wanted. Atamarie was looking forward to it—and she was convinced that Richard would feel the same, once he overcame his inhibitions. This time, no one would bother them when they finally consummated their love.

So, Atamarie climbed aboard the train bound for Timaru. From there, she would be able to continue straight on to her grandparents'. It was an unusually clear day, and the snow-covered southern mountain peaks floated over the vastness of the Canterbury Plains. The knee-high tussock grass waved in the wind like a green-brown sea.

The train pulled into Timaru late that afternoon. The sun was shining, and the small town looked familiar and homey, like so many towns on the South Island. Atamarie strolled along the harbor and through town a bit. Finally, she decided to ask in a general store about how to get to Temuka, where Richard's farm lay. The proprietress, a plump, friendly lady, gave her rucksack an odd look, but then smiled.

"Well, you're in luck, girl. See that wagon outside? That's one of Pearse's neighbors. His name's Toby Peterson—just wait here, and we'll ask him as soon as he comes in to pay."

Toby Peterson, a tall, scrawny man in worn farmer clothes, was loading feed sacks into the bed of his hay wagon. Atamarie hoped he would let her ride along on the box. She was wearing a stylish travel outfit and didn't want to sit on the dusty sacks in it. For the moment, however, she had to answer to the merchant. The woman was curious about this beautiful girl who was visiting Richard all alone and carrying such unconventional luggage.

"You're not family, though," the woman began. "There are a lot of Pearse children, but they don't have a blonde one like you."

Atamarie briefly considered identifying herself as a cousin, but to what end? Even cousins were considered compromised if they spent a night alone. Simpler just to be honest.

"I study engineering, you see, like Richard."

To Atamarie's surprise, no commentary on her unusual field of study followed. Instead, the woman began to talk about Richard.

"Oh aye, he's always had crazy ideas, Dicky Pearse. We know the family well. Sarah Pearse used to work here, you know. And Digory with his farm, a massive property in the Waitohi Plains. So, he came shopping here, and"—she giggled—"now they've got nine children. Life's funny like that."

Atamarie nodded, confused. Richard had made it seem like the farm he had inherited was by no means a large estate. If half the Waitohi Plains really belonged to his family, they surely could have afforded Richard's studies.

"And now Richard's taken over the farm?" Atamarie asked. She had never quite understood why the gifted engineer absolutely had to become a farmer.

The merchant laughed. "No, no, dearie, the Pearses aren't that old yet! They gave him a farm of his own. Very generous, about a hundred acres, and a house already on it. Now he just needs to take a wife and lead a God-fearing life."

The woman looked at Atamarie as if determining whether she might be in the running for this position. Atamarie looked back innocently.

"I think Richard would rather be an engineer," she said. "An inventor."

Renewed giggling. "Aye, as I said, just crazy notions. His parents were almost driven to despair. Even in school, he'd dream all through class and was always building little machines no one understood. His brother, Tom, he's the total opposite. Determined, clever—studies medicine in Christchurch, you know. He's going to be a doctor one day!"

So, it wasn't education itself that Richard's parents didn't support but rather his choice of subject. Still, a hundred acres of land—if he sold it, he could pay for school himself.

Toby Peterson now entered the store, interrupting the merchant's happy gossip. Atamarie stole a glance and decided he seemed trustworthy.

"Tobbs, this little lady wants to go to Dicky's. She's another of them engineers. Can you take her?"

The man considered Atamarie with a wide grin. "If she doesn't fly away from me," he joked, "or blow up my wagon. We've had our share of inventing around here, missy. Don't you frighten my dog."

The collie leaped up to greet Atamarie, who laughed as the dog tried to lick her face.

"I promise not to blow anything up," she declared, raising her hand to swear. "I can't fly either, or I wouldn't need a ride."

Mr. Peterson nodded. "Then climb up right onto the box! I'll settle accounts here, and then we're off. It's about fourteen miles to Richard's. We'll make it before dark, no problem."

***

The roads to Temuka were dusty after a few days without rain, but they were well traveled, and the wagon made good time. Mr. Peterson proved a pleasant traveling companion. He told Atamarie everything about Waitohi, where—once again contradicting Richard's reports—people primarily raised sheep.

"Sure, we work a few fields, too, and that's mostly what the Pearses do. They don't care much for sheep. Still, all that land sure would lend itself to it. I've told Cranky near a hundred times."

"Cranky?" Atamarie asked.

Peterson tugged on his hat brim. "Oh, sorry, no offense. That's what we call Dick. Others call him Mad Pearse, but that's not fair. He knows his stuff, you see. Last year, my plow was busted, and he got an idea for an improvement. His fix held until I was able to sell a few sheep and could afford a new one. I gave Dick the old one. He collects old machines, tries to make something grand out of them—with motors and the like. Farm's full of scrap. But he's a good fellow, really. What business do you have with him? Is it serious?"

Atamarie had to laugh. The farmer's openness was refreshing.

"I don't know yet," she admitted. "We haven't talked about it."

Peterson chuckled. "I believe that. He never talks about anything normal. When he does talk, it's all technical nonsense. Boy's got his head in the clouds."

"He does want to fly someday," Atamarie replied. "So, that's not a bad thing."

Peterson shook his head. "But not especially good for the body. Mark my words, one of these days he's going to get himself killed with his crazy machines. If God wanted men to fly, he would have given them wings."

Atamarie shook her head so heartily that Peterson looked over at her with concern. He could not know, of course, that now they were addressing her own dream.

"One day, people will fly, Mr. Peterson," she said earnestly. "They already do. Think of Lilienthal gliding, of hot-air balloons, of Maori *manu aute*. The legend says people already flew hundreds of years ago. We just need to figure out how to do it without wind. And all signs point to combustion engines, like in cars."

Peterson waved this off. "Sure, those contraptions," he said. An automobile had been driven on the South Island for the first time the previous year and been duly admired. "But are they going to catch on?"

Atamarie smiled. "I'd bet on it. In fact—"

She broke off abruptly when something big and unwieldy came rolling down a hill in front of them. The thing was pulled by four horses, which looked frightened to death.

Peterson roared, "Whoa," and steered his own team off the road with lightning speed. The wagon shook threateningly, and the collie hid its head in Atamarie's skirt. She clung to her seat as she watched the three-wheeled monstrosity trundle toward them. The horses had now freed themselves. Atamarie took it that a mechanism in the machine released their reins as soon as it had gathered enough speed. The animals fled heedlessly into the field while the rattling, kitelike machine made a sort of hop. Then, however, it veered sideways and crashed into a broom hedge.

Toby Peterson stopped his team. "Like I said, one of these days . . ."

Atamarie leaped from the box and ran to the flying machine.

One of the canvas-covered wings had ripped off, but Atamarie saw with a glance that they had only been attached by wire to the carriage. That could easily be repaired. The sight of Richard caused her considerably greater concern. The inventor was hanging forward in his seat, blood streaming over his face.

"Richard! Richard, can you hear me? Is it bad? Mr. Peterson, come help."

Richard, however, was already stirring. The main problem seemed to lie in getting out of his precarious position.

"Just a scratch," he demurred as Peterson sauntered over.

"Stay calm, little lady. The hedge broke Cranky's fall," Peterson said while the young woman tried to help the flier out of his seat. "This isn't the first time, you know."

"What?" Atamarie asked, supporting her wobbly friend. "You've done this before? Are you crazy?"

Richard wiped the blood off his face with the sleeve of his coveralls. He looked frightful, but the only serious injury seemed to be to his foot. He could hardly stand.

"I need to get the hang of the climbing speed and a better grip on the motor," he muttered. "It stalls, which—"

Peterson slapped his forehead.

"Cranky!" the farmer said. "That's not how you greet a lady. The right way would have been: 'Miss Turei, what a lovely surprise! Forgive my somewhat inappropriate dress, but I'm so terribly pleased you've found your way here.' That's how you act when a lady comes to visit."

Richard turned toward Atamarie. "Atamie, you, oh! I hadn't, well, I didn't realize it was—but I'm happy you're here, of course. It's quite grand, you—"

"Wait, why does it stall?" She eyed the motor critically. "Something to do with the combustion?"

Peterson rolled his eyes. "Now I see the attraction. And I'd love to leave you to your flirting, Dick, but I'm afraid your mother would kill me. That foot is probably broken. So, where do you want to go? To the doctor or to your mom?"

Richard balked at this, and Atamarie was likewise unenthused. She would have preferred to doctor Richard quickly herself in order to more quickly transition to the romantic portion of the visit—not that she would have objected to taking the motor apart first. It was obviously his own construction, and Atamarie was dying to analyze the problem.

"Can you move your foot?" she asked.

Richard did so, then nodded.

"Good, then to your mom," Peterson decided. "Climb up, miss. I'll help Dicky up. Or wait, we should catch the horses first and get 'em back to the farm."

***

Atamarie was startled when she laid eyes on Richard's farm. The barns and stables looked dilapidated. A few pigs and chickens made their way between rusted plows and harrows, bicycle parts, and creative conglomerations of canvas and aluminum. One barn had clearly been transformed into an aeroplane hangar. In one corner, new cylinders and crankshafts were meticulously arranged alongside old cigarette packs and cast-iron drainpipes. Atamarie tried to divine the constructions to which Richard had screwed them.

Peterson, unimpressed, drove the pigs and chickens into the hay barn with his dog. Two goats followed, bleating.

"It's the only structure around here that shuts properly," the farmer explained. "Now, if we can just find some feed . . . Dicky's critters sometimes get the desire to wander, y'see. And my wife's vegetable garden is just half a mile off. These goats paid a couple visits recently. You can't even mention Dick's name to her anymore."

Atamarie was surprised. Richard had kept such scrupulous order when they were surveying. Yet, here, he seemed in over his head. Although it threw her plans into disarray, she was now curious to meet his family. Were they also such hopeless farmers?

When Peterson had secured all the animals, he and Atamarie returned to the wagon. Richard, who'd been resting there, whined that his foot was already better, but Peterson said they were going to his mother's whether he liked it or not.

"Your inventing is all well and good, Dicky, but you can't run a farm like this. Have you even hired harvest workers yet? Most will be spoken for by now. And I can't keep on helping you forever. I have my own harvest to bring in."

Richard did not answer, merely staring despondently ahead at his parents' house. It was not showy, just a nicely painted farmhouse in good condition. Alongside it were a tidy windmill, barns, and reaping and threshing machines, likely already prepared for the harvest. As they approached, dogs began barking, and Digory Pearse stepped out the door at once. Richard's father was taller and squarer than his son, his face harder and more angular. Richard must have gotten his hair and soft features from his mother. And perhaps also his rather dreamy, patient manner. Digory exchanged only a few words with Peterson before exploding.

"You did what? Again? I don't understand it, Dick. You put all your money into nonsense, and in the end, it's going to get you killed. I'm going to have a chat with your friend Cecil Woods, too, next week. He supports you in your madness, I know."

"Cecil Woods?" Atamarie asked. "Didn't he build the first combustion engine in New Zealand? You're friends with him?"

Richard started to reply, but his father spun toward the young woman.

"And who are you? No doubt the Maori girl who planted even more ideas in this dunce's head? Not that you much look it."

"This is Atamarie Parekura Turei," Richard announced. "We know each other from the expedition to Taranaki."

"And she's the only girl Richard ever talked about," exclaimed a far friendlier voice. Sarah Pearse came out of the house behind her husband and considered all present with a winning smile. She did indeed have the same brown locks and soft eyes as her son. "A pleasure to meet you. Now, Digory, don't frighten the young woman. Ask her inside. Oh heavens, Dicky, what happened this time? Another attempt to take to the air in that infernal machine? Come in, we'll wrap your foot right away. And, wait, Mr. Peterson, I'll give you something to take to Joan as a little apology for the business with the goats. We made marmalade today. Jenny, go grab a jar."

This last comment was directed at a lanky twelve- or thirteen-year-old who had watched the scene from the entrance to the farmhouse. Along with at least five other children. Atamarie smiled at them.

Sarah Pearse seemed to be one of those uncommonly capable women who could do everything at once. She swept Peterson and Richard into the house and put each child to work attending to their guests. Within short order, she had Peterson and her husband installed on the porch with homemade blackberry soda, and now she turned to Richard.

"Come along," she said to Atamarie while she forced her son into a chair, eyeing the wounds on his face. "We'll clean those first. Miss, you can hold the water bowl."

Atamarie dutifully did as she was told. If this was a test of her squeamishness, she had nothing to fear. It did not bother her that the water in the bowl slowly turned red while Sarah Pearse cleaned out her son's cuts with gauze. Richard flinched when she rubbed a salve onto it. Atamarie likewise made a face. Her grandfather used the same stuff on his horses and sheep—it burned like fire.

Sarah Pearse then pulled off her son's shoe and sock in order to bandage the foot, which had swelled up. During all of this, she spoke to him incessantly.

"You need to stop this nonsense, Dicky. The whole neighborhood's already talking, you know, and it hurts me to hear them call you 'crazy.' You have a nice farm. You could make something of it—and what a cute girl you've won over." Richard's mother gave Atamarie a warm smile. "You'll absolutely have to tell me more about yourself, Atamarie. May I call you that? I imagined you quite differently. I thought you were Maori. But that'd've been fine by me, you know. So long as my Richard finds a girl. I think a woman would ground him, so to speak."

Richard shot Atamarie a pleading look, but she was too busy digesting the news that Richard had been talking about her to worry about Mrs. Pearse thinking her halfway to being a housewife on Richard's dilapidated farm. Atamarie was most certainly not going to ground anyone.

"You'll stay for dinner, of course, Atamarie. I want to get to know you. We'll find a bed for you too. There's no way of getting back to Timaru tonight. Dicky, we're going to keep you here too. Joe'll have to ride over and feed your animals."

Atamarie swallowed. Mrs. Pearse might want to play matchmaker, but surely in the *pakeha* fashion. If things continued like this, there would not be any lovemaking—nor investigation of the stalled-out motor. But, for now, Atamarie smiled kindly at Mrs. Pearse, thanked her for the invitation, and then helped set the table. Unsurprisingly, Sarah Pearse was an exceptional cook and was not to be thrown off by surprise guests. Only then did Atamarie realize how hungry she was. Mrs. Pearse watched happily as she filled her plate with mashed potatoes, beans, and roast, and then cleaned it.

Richard, in contrast, picked at his food and barely said a word the whole meal. The unsuccessful flying attempt seemed to have discouraged him—that or the lively conversation, which at first focused again on his "crazy ideas" before shifting to subjects like harvests and reseeding. Mr. Pearse held forth about Richard's failings while his wife tried to learn more about Atamarie's family. What she heard seemed to please her, though Atamarie's grandparents' farm interested her considerably more than Matariki's position as school director or Kupe being a member of Parliament.

"How nice that you practically grew up on a farm," Sarah Pearse said, "but you won't inherit the land, will you?"

Atamarie almost choked on her food, shocked at the question's indiscreetness. She was tempted to claim they would have to sell the farm to finance her engineering studies, but then bit her tongue. There was nothing to be gained by being insolent to the Pearses.

"My uncle Kevin doesn't have any interest in sheep," she emphasized with a glance at Richard. "But his brother Patrick studied agriculture and is going to take over the farm one day. Kevin is a doctor."

With this, she unintentionally brought the conversation around to Richard's brother Tom, about whom Sarah and Digory both gushed. This gave Richard some respite from his father's recriminations. Atamarie wondered why the young engineer struggled so. Digory Pearse was speaking of hiring harvest workers and directing maintenance—simple organizational tasks that she thought herself plenty capable of. Yet Richard did not seem to have much of a knack for either farm management or getting along with his neighbors. Atamarie gleaned from the conversation that Peterson was the most sympathetic. The others complained about the noise his machines made, the weeds that spread from his fields, and the animals that got loose.

"Fred Hansley told me recently he's not going to lend you his hay tedder again." Digory Pearse now grew heated again—the conversation had switched back from Tom's achievements to Richard's failures. "And that the 'improvements' you made last year—"

"He wouldn't let me explain them," Richard complained. "It was quite simple and much more effective. The whole thing rotated better. You just had to—"

"You'd better see where you can scrounge up another tedder, or you'll have to turn the hay by hand," his father warned.

Richard hung his head and pushed his food around his plate. In the end, everyone sighed with relief when Sarah Pearse cleared the table. She, at least, seemed content. Atamarie Turei was clearly in the running as a wife for her son. Surely, the young woman would trade her strange studies for a farmhouse and some nice children.

For her part, Atamarie was happy when she could at last take refuge in a small but well-kept bedroom—probably once belonging to the wonderful Tom. On the wall hung various pennants from agriculture exhibitions. Plaques and trophies proclaimed sporting victories. Atamarie wondered whether they had allowed Richard to display his little inventions in his room. She felt increasingly sorry for her friend. It was good for him that she, at least, had passed his mother's examination. She congratulated herself on her diplomacy: she had not mentioned her dream of flight.

Chapter 7

The next morning, there was a hearty breakfast with more depressing conversation. Finally, Mr. Pearse drove his son and Atamarie back to Richard's farm, then launched right into another tirade when his horses shied in front of the flying machine, which was still stuck in the hedge. He continued while he steered his team into the yard. "This place looks like a junkyard. It's past time to throw this trash away. And see to it you get the harvest organized! Shall I take you straight to the train station, Miss Turei?"

Atamarie was startled. Digory Pearse had scarcely said a word to her.

"No, thank you. I'll stay here a bit. Richard, well, we haven't gotten a chance to talk. He still hasn't properly shown me his aeroplane."

Digory snorted. "Fine. But the train leaves at twelve. If you want to pull that contraption out of the hedge, you might miss it." He fixed the young woman with a look between questioning and disapproving.

Atamarie squared herself and withstood his gaze. "Then I'll leave first thing in the morning," she said. "There is still quite a bit to do here, anyway."

Without waiting for Digory's reply, she grabbed her rucksack and hopped down, walking toward the house. Richard followed, sighing with relief. After he fished the house key out from under the soiled welcome mat and opened the door for Atamarie, however, he looked uneasy again.

"My parents will think—"

Atamarie glanced into the house, which was as shabby as the yard. But then she looked back to Richard, who seemed anxious and beaten, and seeing him like that touched her heart. Atamarie looked up at him mischievously and wrapped her arms around his neck.

"Let them," she said.

***

Atamarie kissed Richard in his run-down kitchen and was thrilled when he returned the kiss. Then, she set about cleaning a bit while he harnessed two horses to remove the aeroplane's wreck from the hedge. It was not particularly difficult. The heaviest thing about it was the motor.

"It needs to be lighter," Atamarie observed when what was left of the flying machine finally stood in the hangar. Richard had chased the animals back out in short order. "Or the wings need to be bigger. The wheels are a good idea, but pulling it with horses—"

"It's been done with gliders before," Richard said. "And see, you need to bridge the time until the motor kicks in."

"But the motor could just drive the aeroplane from the start, like an automobile," Atamarie offered. "And only then lift off. You'd have to be able to steer it too."

The two of them discussed the problem extensively until the door opened and Mr. Peterson drove in Richard's pigs and goats.

"Damn it, Dick, lock up your animals! They were in my garden again. Joan is beside herself. This can't go on."

Richard nodded, agreed, and thanked his neighbor. Then he returned immediately to the subject of highly charged magnetic ignition.

"I'm simply not satisfied with the contact breaker point connection as Woods built it. The construction of the spark plug—"

Atamarie raised her eyebrows. "Richard? I think we need to focus on building a hogpen first."

By the evening of their first day together on the farm, Atamarie and Richard had built secure sheds for the animals. Put more precisely, she hammered together the pens while Richard developed a groundbreaking new locking technique based on a system of ratchet levers and braces. The clever goats would surely not be able to open these locks as they could the usual simple latches.

Brilliant," Atamarie observed. "Make a few more tomorrow and give them to Peterson as an apology. He can secure his garden gate with them."

While Richard fed the animals, she combed through his weed-infested garden for something edible, ultimately finding a few carrots and potatoes, as well as plenty of beans, and making a soup. It was nothing special, but Richard hardly seemed to notice what he ate. In fact, he did not stop talking about the advantages of the simple kite system over the double-decker until Atamarie finally stood up, loosing her hair with light, natural movements and moving to open her blouse.

Richard looked at her with big eyes. "Atamie, you—I—are you sure you really want to?"

Atamarie smiled. "What does it look like?"

Richard turned away. "Atamarie, you don't know me," he said quietly.

Atamarie furrowed her brow. "Of course I do. You're like me."

He shook his head. "I'm not, Atamarie, believe me. I'll disappoint you."

Atamarie snuggled against his back. "Because you've disappointed everyone else?" she asked gently. I'm not like your parents. I don't want a farm. I don't even want to get married. Just you, Richard, I just want you."

Richard turned around to face her. "You don't know what you're getting into," he said.

Atamarie smiled. "You mean this mess here? We'll put that in order quickly. So, you're not a born farmer. But, with a little help—"

"I'm no good for you, Atamie. I'm no good for anybody." Richard's voice sounded throaty, resigned.

Atamarie shook her head. "Oh, you're good for me," she whispered. "You're my gift from the gods."

Richard smiled now, too, weakly but hopefully. "If you really think so," he murmured, and pulled her into his arms.

Atamarie did think so, and she thought of the wisdom the god Tawhaki gave humans and the beauty of the earth they owed to the god Tane. She did not think of Pandora's box.

***

Richard Pearse proved to be an exceptionally tender, slow, and thoughtful lover. Atamarie had feared she would have to encourage him again in bed and then wouldn't know what she was doing herself. Richard, however, led Atamarie to fulfillment with all the patience, solicitousness, and care she had hoped for.

Atamarie briefly wondered where he had gotten his obvious experience. In Christchurch during his brief studies? The country girls of the Waitohi Plains surely did not go to bed with their neighbors' sons. At least not without a promise of marriage. Whence arose the question of why Richard still did not have a wife, or at least a fiancée. Did the girls not want to marry him, or had he refused them? Had his reputation and gloomy misgivings scared them off? Atamarie decided that he had simply waited for his soul mate—her. That night, she fell asleep happily in his arms, dreaming of more lovemaking in the morning. Richard, however, was up before the cock crowed, brimming with energy.

"I need to look at the carburetor again," he declared. "That stalling, it might have to do with the valve. The air-to-fuel mixture isn't constant."

Atamarie frowned. "Did you think of that while—"

"While we were making love? No, of course not, Atamie. Only, um, later. I, uh, don't need much sleep. But don't you think that could be it? The fact is, a thicker mixture . . ."

Atamarie sighed and climbed out of bed. She did find carburetors exciting, but so early in the morning—and after that night? But Richard no longer had eyes for her. By the time she had dressed and come into the kitchen, he had already made coffee but was in no mood to breakfast cozily with her. He quickly downed a cup of the strong, black brew and rushed to his workshop. Atamarie was shaking after the first sip. She needed bread and butter. There had to be flour somewhere, and the chickens must lay eggs.

On her way to the coop, she realized Richard had forgotten to feed the animals. She would have to put some things here in order.

***

Over the next few days, Atamarie put Richard's farm to rights. In addition to cleaning the house and caring for the animals, she visited Joan Peterson, his neighbor, apologized for the escaped animals, and haggled with her for vegetables, butter, and milk.

"Long term, you'll have to get your own garden working. Well, if you plan to stick around," the bustling farmer's wife said, offering seeds and starter plants.

Atamarie remained coy with regard to her and Richard's undeveloped future plans. She accepted the plants with thanks but did not bother planting them. Richard would not maintain the garden afterward, and she did not plan to stay long. As intimate as her relationship with Richard was growing, she was determined to finish her studies before she even thought of starting a family. And then, she most definitely did not want to live on a farm. But that would work itself out later. First, Richard's harvest needed to be brought in and his chaotic housekeeping brought under control.

So, Atamarie inquired about harvest workers. However, Peterson had been right: there really weren't any left. The other farmers were already cutting their grain and flapping their gums about the failings of Cranky Dick. Luckily, there was a Maori tribe settled nearby, and Atamarie went over to hire some men to work for Richard. The women gladly helped her out with sweet potatoes and other vegetables—in exchange for Joan Peterson's seeds and starter plants. With reference to the farm work, however, some consultation with the elders was necessary—and, to her surprise, the Ngai Tahu proved astoundingly well informed about Richard Pearse, his dreams, and also his problems. Waimarama, one of the old women, knew him as Birdman.

"He was here once," she declared. "After Matariki this year. He had seen the kites. Then, he came from deep darkness. But through the *manu*, he found his way to the light again. He seeks to touch the gods. But he does not know what he's doing."

Atamarie smiled indulgently. "But he does, *tupuna*. When it comes to technology, he's a *tohunga*."

Waimarama nodded amicably. "He is that, no doubt, child. But Rangi will decide for himself to whom he opens his heart."

Atamarie smiled. "The sky god should be happy when any of his children come to visit! Then he would not have to cry all the time." After the beautiful weather the day before, that day she had been forced to ride through long threads of summer rain to reach the Maori village. "We'd also bring Rangi greetings from Papa."

Waimarama looked slightly disapproving at Atamarie's blasphemous expression, but then held up her wise hand as if in blessing.

"Perhaps Rangi is also crying for your friend. For the darkness all around him," she said patiently. "You don't sense it, but it threatens him. That is why he strives for Rangi's light."

***

Atamarie did not understand the *tohunga*'s remarks, but she sighed with relief when the elders assented to her request. The very next day, three stocky, young Maori men appeared on Richard's farm. Though they spoke only broken English, they were glad for the work. Richard welcomed them, then disappeared promptly into the barn. Fortunately, reaping and threshing machines were nothing new for Hamene, Koraka, and Kuri. They set about harnessing the horses at once.

Naturally, Richard's neighbors began to gossip about the new arrivals. Maori men sometimes did things differently than *pakeha*, and the other farmers worked themselves up about that. Richard, however, ignored their criticism and did not tell his workers how to do their job. He worked dutifully alongside them and toiled just as hard as any other farmer. Still, his thoughts were not with wheat and corn but with the spark plugs and carburetors he would return to as soon as the day's farming was done. Richard lived for his inventions, a fact the Maori man observed with equanimity and reverence.

"Dick *tohunga*," one of the workers explained to a flabbergasted Toby Peterson. "Build machines. Must speak to many spirits."

Atamarie did not care about Richard's ineptitude as a farmer, but his behavior did sometimes puzzle her. They made love every night, often for hours. Richard seemed not to be able to get enough of her, and Atamarie shared his passion. Beneath Richard's caresses, she forgot her exhaustion. After making love, she snuggled in his arms, happy and content as a child, and would have slept like one if Richard had not tossed and turned all night. After another sleepless night, he always got up in the early hours, disappearing into the barn with his motors.

The first few nights, this annoyed her a bit—for one, she did not like sleeping alone, and for two, she would have liked having a part in the development of the motors. Then, however, she began to worry about the fact that he never seemed to sleep. It was getting eerie. Atamarie told herself he must nap in the fields during the day. The Maori workers couldn't confirm that, but then again, they did not constantly have eyes on their employer.

Reluctantly, Atamarie took on the duties of a farmer's wife, and Richard accepted her unskillful attempts at homemaking without complaint. At the same time, neither did he show any enthusiasm when something did turn out well, such as the chicken pies she prepared out of necessity when he absentmindedly ran over a chicken with a crop wagon. Richard shoveled the food down and then returned wordlessly to his work. Atamarie could only hope that things would get better when the harvest was over and they could devote themselves together to his flying machine. She already had lots of ideas about wings and, most of all, the propeller. People always assumed it had to sit to the rear of the machine, but one could just as easily attach it to the front. Atamarie would have loved to present this idea to Richard at once, but she was afraid he might drop everything and disappear into the barn for days or weeks. He had done that once after Atamarie had asked a question regarding the air-to-fuel mixture in the carburetor, which had given him an explosive idea—in the truest sense of the word.

Atamarie comforted herself with the fact that their love life, at least, was in no way lacking. Richard's enthusiasm did not abate; he made love to her ever more ecstatically. When he kissed her, whispered tender words, and they climaxed together, she felt happy and convinced herself that feeling applied to her whole life with Richard.

Only when she found the time one afternoon to write a letter to Roberta and wanted, after all her swooning over Richard, to tell her about daily life, did Atamarie realize how lonely she was. People came and went all day. Particularly now, during harvesttime, the farmers had a lot of contact, lending one another machines and stepping in to help a neighbor make hay when rain clouds appeared. They were pleasant to Atamarie, but did not seem to see her as more than a sort of cog in a machine. They did not even seem too worried about her "living in sin" with Richard. Occasionally she caught comments like "But it suits him," or "Not half as crazy as before," and "A nice girl, otherwise." Everyone seemed to be relieved that Richard Pearse finally "functioned." The local matrons felt confirmed in their opinion: only a woman had been needed to put the strange young man back on the right path. Even if it was a somewhat exotic woman who did not fit their image of a proper wife.

That it was actually Atamarie who was "functioning" while Richard only appeared to do so did not interest anyone. This was normal for *pakeha* society, but as a Maori woman, Atamarie expected her contributions to be recognized, and these people were denying her *mana*.

Atamarie observed her surroundings with growing distrust, but for the moment, she made no protest. After all, every day of drudgery brought the end of the harvest closer, and then she would work together again with Richard, instead of just enabling him. Atamarie daydreamed about the aeroplane's design while she cooked and cleaned. Making the wings moveable, she realized with excitement, would make it possible to steer the thing better. Once it actually flew.

And then, the last fields were finally harvested. Richard paid his workers generously, and even his father found a few words of praise as he inspected the full barns and grain lofts.

"There's a celebration tonight," Richard's brother Warne said happily. "Starting at seven in the Hansleys' depot. And you won't believe it—I'm going with Martha Klein."

Atamarie grinned at the boy. Warne was one of the few people in Temuka with whom she could laugh and joke around. He was clever, like all of the Pearse children, and still too young to look askance at Atamarie and her relationship with Richard.

"I'm sure wedding bells will be ringing soon," she teased. "As long as you don't step on her feet too often while dancing."

Warne giggled, then declared that he needed to go pick flowers. Maybe he would make a crown for Martha.

Atamarie loved the idea of weaving flowers into her hair. She picked a few daisies from the side of the road and hoped they would stay fresh until evening. Their bright purple complemented the brightly colored flower-print dress from the Gold Mine Boutique that she'd packed for special occasions. She hoped for undiluted admiration when Richard saw her in it. She had washed her hair and now wore it down, not braided or up as usual. The golden-blonde locks reached almost to her hips, and the crown of flowers made her look like a fairy. Atamarie was very pleased with herself, but her good mood evaporated when she saw Richard shamble into the kitchen in his work clothes.

"Is there nothing to eat today, Atamie?" he asked in surprise. Atamarie always had something prepared when he came in from the fields, no matter how long she had worked herself. "I'm happy to make something myself, but I know you—" Richard looked up. "Why're you dressed like that?"

Atamarie shook her head. "Did you forget? Tonight's the harvest festival. Your brother says they'll be grilling food. But you need to get dressed quickly. And bathe."

Richard frowned. "You honestly want to go? I wouldn't have thought that you—"

"Take an interest in something other than motors and updrafts?" Atamarie shot back. He could at least have said something about her dress. "I do, Richard, if you can imagine it. I love dancing. I like to dress up sometimes, and I like to take my man out in public. As long as he's clean and properly dressed."

"I, uh, just thought we'd go to the barn later and work on the motor," Richard replied.

"You want to tinker alone while everyone is celebrating? Then you can't wonder why they call you Cranky Dick. Richard, that engine's not going to run away, but they're only playing music tonight. Tonight, we can eat, dance, and chat with the neighbors a bit. Sometimes you just have to. And it's not so terrible, anyway. We'll have fun. So, come on, hurry. I can harness the horses while you change. Hopefully, I won't get my dress too dirty in the process."

***

In fact, Atamarie did manage to hitch the horses without reeking of stables afterward, and Richard, too, made a good impression when he came out of the house in his one good suit—Atamarie recognized it from Taranaki.

"Well then!" Atamarie laughed and snuggled against him on the hay wagon's box. "And now smile, would you? It's a beautiful evening, Richard. Look at the stars—that's Sirius. Will we fly there, too, someday, Richard? Up to the stars?" She laid her head on his shoulder.

"I'd be happy to make it over the next hill," Richard said. "Where's the festival? I didn't pay attention to whose turn it was to host."

This year, the Hansley family had moved its wagons and harvesters outside, and the local wives had been busy sweeping out the depot and decorating it festively. It stung Atamarie a little that she had not been invited to help, but Richard had been one of the last to finish harvesting, and the women might have assumed she was needed on the farm. So, Atamarie shook off the slight and immediately approached the women to assure them of how beautiful and inviting the space looked.

That was when she realized she'd made a grave sartorial error. All the women, Richard's mother and sisters included, wore Sunday dresses, but they were dark, demure affairs. Everyone but Atamarie was corseted, and they all wore their hair modestly pinned up. Some of the older women even hid it under bonnets. She only spied flowers in the hair of very young girls—like Warne's friend Martha, who must have been twelve or thirteen at most.

Atamarie's reception thus proved rather frosty. The matrons looked disapprovingly over her free-flowing hair and wide dress, the younger women turned away contemptuously, and the girls openly gaped. Atamarie pretended not to notice. She chatted with Joan Peterson and Richard's mother. Both were noticeably curt.

"I'll see where Richard's at," Atamarie mumbled, then immediately realized she was making another misstep.

At least until the official beginning of the dance, the men stood with the men and the women with the women. Richard was trying to excite Peterson and Hansley about the unasked-for improvements he had made to Hansley's hay tedder the previous year.

"Before long, everything's going to change in agriculture," he was saying when Atamarie arrived. There was only fruit punch for the women, but the men were drinking beer, and it seemed to have gone straight to Richard's head. "Much more work will be done by machines. Even draft animals have nearly outlived their usefulness. In a few decades, you won't see horses or mules in the fields. Automobiles will pull the plows, or there'll simply be motorized plows as well as harvesters and threshing machines."

Richard's eyes shone as he thought of it. The other farmers, on the other hand, bellowed with laughter.

"The animals won't shy from flying machines, then," Peterson mocked. "Which'll be important, because we're probably all going to have one, right? Dream on, Cranky."

"Actually, it's entirely possible that every household will have a flying device someday." Atamarie came to her friend's aid against her better judgment. "Particularly here, in the countryside. In cities, the automobile is more likely to dominate."

The men laughed even louder.

"And girls will fly them!" Hansley laughed. "I can just picture my Laura fluttering off to the store."

"Like a hummingbird," Peterson added drunkenly, and slapped his thigh. "You're already wearing a colorful enough little dress for it, Miss Turei. It's just a question of how long the nectar will be flowing for you on the Pearses' farm!"

The men roared with laughter, but Atamarie did not understand what was so funny. Richard seemed angry and embarrassed.

"We shouldn't have come. We don't belong here," he observed as he followed her to the buffet.

The long table was lined with cakes and bowls of salad. From outside wafted the scent of grilled meat. Atamarie filled her friend's plate. Richard needed to put something in his stomach before the beer inspired him to reveal more of his dreams.

"These people are simply narrow-minded," she said. "In Christchurch and Dunedin, people discuss such subjects much more seriously. Soon, automobiles are going to change the cities completely, if not the whole world. And after them will come the flying machines, whether stupid farmers accept it or not."

Richard grimaced. "Those 'stupid farmers' will still be my neighbors," he said, then busied himself with devouring massive amounts of food. After the hard work in the fields, he must have been starving, but Atamarie knew that if he were alone, he'd have gone straight to work on his motor without bothering to eat. She was suddenly seized by the overwhelming desire to take Richard away. He would never be happy in Temuka.

Then, however, the improvised band struck up a tune, and Atamarie abandoned her gloomy thoughts as well as her weariness. Richard only swung her around the dance floor once, somewhat reluctantly. Afterward, he went to see his father. "I have to make an appearance. Otherwise, my dad will accuse me of sticking to the dirt farmers again," he said apologetically.

Digory Pearse sat with the area's other prominent landowners. Atamarie had already gathered that the Pearses were considered somewhat apart here. The term "gentleman farmer" had been used more than once. Pearse certainly could afford more harvest workers and better machines than the others, and even Richard's property was considerably bigger than Hansley's or Peterson's lands. Sarah Pearse wore a much lovelier dress than the other women, and her children's new clothes stood out among all the worn hand-me-downs. All of this bolstered Atamarie's opinion that this family could easily have afforded Richard's education. Forcing him to farm must be a sort of punishment. They didn't want a black sheep who dreamed of flying machines and horseless plows.

Now, Richard sat somewhat unhappily beside his father, silently nursing a beer. Soon, however, he couldn't sit still. Atamarie watched with concern how he ensnared the pastor and local schoolteacher in conversation, gesturing grandly. Probably he was already stepping in it again, but Atamarie determined not to let Richard's troubles spoil her mood. She tapped her foot to the music, and when one of the other young men asked her to dance, she accepted. The next followed right after—Atamarie flew all evening from one arm to the next.

"Our hummingbird," she heard Peterson say when one of the farmers' sons swung her past him.

Atamarie did not worry about whether that was meant snidely or as flattery. She allowed one of the boys to sneak her a beer when the village matrons were looking the other way, and then enjoyed herself even more. The only thing that bothered her was that the boys she danced with often held her too aggressively. Dunedin dances had not accustomed her to partners who felt up her back and whose hands sometimes wandered to her rear. The boys' breathing would get faster, and they whispered flattery that bordered on the obscene. Atamarie disliked it but was afraid to make a scene. She wondered if the people out here were a bit bawdier than the children of Dunedin society—or the young Maori in Parihaka. Granted, Maori men and women did not dance together, except perhaps in a *haka*. Neither girls nor boys needed the excuse of a dance to touch one another, as these village youths apparently did. And certainly, no Maori man became importunate when a woman did not clearly signal agreement.

Here, though, that wasn't the case. The more the evening wore on, the more energetically Atamarie had to fend off her dance partners. She wanted to go home, but Richard was conversing excitedly with two younger farmers and even making drawings, likely depicting a new invention. Besides, she was a little cross that he showed not a trace of jealousy. It was good, of course, that he trusted her, but she would have liked a little more interest on his part.

Atamarie slipped outside for some fresh air. She had become fond of Richard's workhorses and had snuck a piece of bread for them. They whinnied at her approach. But then someone grabbed her arm and spun her around.

"It's nice you wanted to come out here with me, sweetheart, but you have to give a bloke a heads-up. I had to come looking for you."

Atamarie found herself staring into the face of her last dance partner. She shook her head and tried to free herself from his grip.

"I didn't want 'to come out here with you,'" she said. "Please leave me alone."

The young man laughed. "Come on, little mouse, are you trying to pretend you aren't waiting here for Jed Hansley, or Jamie Frizzer?"

Atamarie pulled away energetically, still hoping to clear up the misunderstanding. "I—"

"Both?" The boy cackled. "Come on, then, you can do me quick too. What do you bet I'm better than Cranky Dick?"

The young man pulled Atamarie closer and tried to kiss her. His hot breath, heavy with beer, rolled over her face. She tried to free her arms and fend him off, but it was hopeless, as was her attempt to bite his wet, disgusting lips. Rage welled up within her. Atamarie raised her knee and struck with her full weight between the legs of the would-be rapist. He roared and let go.

"You—you—you piece of shit. Maori slut! First you lead a fellow on, and then—" He doubled over in pain.

Atamarie felt triumphant at first as she ran back to the depot, but was shaking by the time she found Richard.

She felt insulted and sullied. After the attack, she saw the advances of her previous dance partners in a new light. Did these men believe she would give anyone what she gave Richard? And then there was that insult. *Maori slut.* Atamarie shivered. She had long since noticed that the farmers in Temuka wanted little to do with their Maori neighbors. None of the harvest workers had been invited to the party, even though several farmers had hired Ngai Tahu men after they proved their worth to Richard. Atamarie disliked Richard's neighbors more and more. Narrow-minded racists. Her brilliant Richard absolutely had to get out of this place.

Atamarie nudged him when he did not notice her at first.

"I'd like to go," she said curtly. "We shouldn't have come."

Richard nodded distractedly—the reason for Atamarie's change of heart did not seem to interest him. When they reached his farm, he murmured something incomprehensible and wandered to the barn. Atamarie unharnessed the horses and collapsed into bed, hoping Richard would come soon and comfort her. But this time, she waited in vain. Richard Pearse made up for the time lost at the party and worked the rest of the night on his precious engine.

Chapter 8

Roberta hadn't expected to enjoy the voyage to South Africa much, but all her worries fell away as soon as the steamer left Dunedin. During the passage to Australia, she shared her cabin with the two nurses, who were friends from Christchurch. Tall, blonde Jennifer was a devotee of Wilhelmina Sheriff Bain, who had demonstrated against the war from the beginning. She wanted to go to Transvaal for purely altruistic reasons like her idol, Emily Hobhouse. Daisy, a shorter, pudgier girl with black hair and shining blue eyes, had joined her out of pure love of adventure. Sure, she wanted to help, but also to see lions and rhinoceroses, and touch an elephant if at all possible.

"I desperately wanted to get out of Christchurch," she explained. "I would have applied right when they sent the first contingent of soldiers, but I was still in nursing school, and my parents wouldn't let me, anyway. But now I'm done—and I'm not headed to war, just to refugee camps. My parents couldn't say no! Especially with Jenny coming too." Daisy beamed gratefully at her friend.

Jenny and Daisy were younger than Roberta but considerably more open-minded than the students from teaching college. That surprised Roberta. From everything she had heard, nursing schools were run like cloisters. Daisy giggled, though, when Roberta asked about it.

"Every cloister has its secret exits," she said with mock saintliness, adjusting an imaginary veil. She folded her hands and raised her eyes to heaven.

Roberta laughed.

"There was a tree outside our window," Jenny explained. "A nice southern beech. Saturday nights, we would climb down and go dancing."

"Dancing?" Roberta would not even have known where to go dancing in religious Dunedin, but then, Christchurch was far more open. "Did you meet any men?"

"Of course!" Daisy squealed. "Half our patients were men."

"They didn't let us near the young ones," Jenny said. "Which was better, anyway. I mean, who wants to go dancing with a girl who has, um—"

"Washed his rear end." Daisy laughed and lolled in her berth. "Go on and say it." She turned to Roberta. "Didn't you have any men in your classes?"

Roberta described the three hopeless male students. Only a few days later, she felt close enough to her new friends to tell them of her love for Kevin Drury.

She expected mockery similar to Atamarie's and kneaded her stuffed horse nervously, but Jenny and Daisy found her mission romantic.

"Oh, you could write a book about that," Daisy sighed. "A girl who goes to war to find her lost love again. And then he's definitely wounded or the like, and only you can save him, and then—we'll need to teach you a bit of first aid, just in case."

Jenny made a face. "He's a doctor, Daisy! And if he happens to sprain his wrist while operating, there must be twenty other doctors around. But seriously, Robbie, why do you think you won't be able to find him? All you need to do is ask army command. There's a Major Robin responsible for all the New Zealanders. We've been sending him tons of protest letters about the camps, so I know his address in Pretoria by heart. When he tells you where your Dr. Drury is stationed, you can write him."

Roberta blushed. "I could have written him a long time ago. It's just, I don't know if—"

Daisy rolled her eyes. "You travel halfway around the world, and then you won't even write to him?"

Jenny was more sympathetic. "You can pretend it was a coincidence. You followed Miss Hobhouse's tracks to the cape, and then it occurred to you that he's—or no, his mother said you needed urgently to contact him. Mothers are always good for that sort of thing. Do you know his mother?"

***

Miss Hobhouse's organization also gathered its forces in Australia—not in the military port of Albany, but in Sydney. Roberta thought she'd have to join the dour-looking teachers, but Jenny and Daisy wouldn't hear of it, and she went with them to see the natural harbor and the old prison buildings from when Australia had been a penal colony.

"Botany Bay, Van Diemen's Land," Daisy announced gravely. "Girls, back then, this place was crawling with handsome men who back home stole a sheep one day. We could have presented ourselves as jewel thieves and—"

"This one listens to too many Irish folk songs," Jenny remarked with a long-suffering flutter of her eyelids. "But, Daisy, if you're hot for blokes you can shear sheep with, why are you going to South Africa? You come from Canterbury. The plains are full of young men who reek of wool."

***

On the passage from Sydney to Durban, Roberta shared her cabin with the six other teachers and did not have half as much fun. Since they'd be assigned to different camps, none of them wanted to bother making friends. The young women engaged in a politely distant manner—half of them were seasick anyway. Roberta spent as much time as she could on deck with the nurses. There were more than fifty on board, and very few of them were dour. The young women flirted with the sailors and made bets about who could get the officers' attention first. The bravest even snuck off to dance in the evenings. One sailor played the accordion, another the fiddle, and Daisy improvised a drum. Roberta envied the fun they were having, but did not dare to join them. The other nurses covered for their colleagues, but if the older nurses caught a young one at such "shameless" pleasures, they would no doubt report her. Roberta was under no illusions: the ladies' committee around Miss Hobhouse clung to virtue just like the Women's Christian Temperance Union. Roberta and Atamarie knew how their mothers had been forced to hide any drop of champagne while they worked for those disputatious women in Wellington. Matariki in particular had hated that.

"Wouldn't it be a shame if we had to part now?" said Daisy on the last night of the voyage. The young women had slipped onto deck with the excuse of wanting to see the lights of approaching Durban. "What do you think? Who do we need to convince to assign us to the same camp?" She slipped a flask to Roberta.

Roberta took a sip, then coughed at once: watered-down whiskey. "This tastes terrible!" she laughed. "And I can't imagine they'll ask us our opinion on assignments."

"But you're going to speak with that Major Robin anyway," Jenny mused, and took an appreciative pull from the flask. "While you're at it, you could also bring the conversation around to whether we—"

Roberta felt herself blush. She would die of embarrassment if an opportunity actually arose to approach the major with her requests. On the other hand, if she did not venture it, she would lose face in front of her friends. She took another sip of the whiskey. After all, they did say the stuff gave a person courage.

***

In the end, the business proved laughably simple. The representatives of a local charity committee welcomed the young women, but they did not distribute any posts. When the women were asked if they wanted to be sent to the camp in Orange or in Transvaal, Daisy elbowed Roberta.

"Transvaal's where Pretoria is. Jenny and I will choose it, too, so you won't be alone."

Jenny and Daisy did not much care where they worked. Daisy would probably have preferred Transvaal anyway because it lay farther inland. She wanted to see as much of Africa as possible and was already spellbound by the many different skin colors of the people they encountered in Durban. Unfortunately, however, she did not have any real contact with the tall, deep-black Zulu people who fascinated her most.

"It's funny. I thought we were fighting here to give them more rights," she observed, "but the English treat them horribly. Mrs. Mason's girl did not even dare speak to me."

Jenny and Daisy had been lodged with a Mrs. Mason until they left for Pretoria. Roberta and her colleagues were taken in at a girls' boarding school. They did not see any black students or teachers there either. Native help was employed only in the kitchen.

"Though there are a lot of Indians," Roberta replied. "It seems the English get along with them better."

"Well, the Indians speak English," Jenny pointed out. "And at most, the blacks speak—what's it called? Afrikaans? We should probably try to learn some if we want to work with the Boer women."

Since Afrikaans wasn't recognized as its own language, Roberta bought an English-Dutch dictionary and hoped it would do the trick. She planned to study it on the train ride to Pretoria, but the landscape through which they rode captivated her as much as it did Jenny and Daisy. The train line led straight across the country, and Roberta's colleagues were a little on edge, since there were still Boer guerillas who might want to blow up the tracks.

"Surely not in broad daylight," Daisy scoffed. "Besides, they would have scared away the gnus over there. And the zebras! Look, zebras! They really do look like striped ponies. I thought they'd be bigger. Oh my goodness, a giraffe! A real giraffe!"

After some time, Daisy's enthusiasm grew tiring. Even the twentieth giraffe elicited screams of excitement. But then the flatland gave way to the foothills of the Drakensberg. There was always something new to discover, and Roberta's dictionary couldn't compete. Once night fell, the girls fell asleep, and the next morning, they woke to find themselves already in Transvaal. They rode past burned-out farms and wasted fields, but most chilling were the endless miles of barbed wire. Every few hundred yards, there was a tightly secured blockhouse.

The young women fell silent when one of the camps for the black population came into view: Simple round huts, skinny children sitting in dirt, and exhausted women toiling in fields under the scorching sun. Barbed wire surrounded the camp, too, and soldiers who looked almost as unhappy as the prisoners watched the gates.

"How terrible," Daisy said after they had left the camp behind and slowly found their voices again. "I expect it's better in the camps for the whites where we're going."

Jenny shook her head. "Not according to Miss Hobhouse. Haven't you read the reports?"

The black children would not leave Roberta's head. For a short time, she forgot Kevin Drury and the reason she had gotten into this adventure. She was not here to chase a dream. She was here to help.

"If it's better in the white camps," she declared, "then we need to go to the black ones."

***

Pretoria, where the train arrived in the late afternoon, was a lively city, which surely had something to do with the many British Army units stationed there.

The English seemed determined and optimistic, the normal residents anxious. They walked the streets with lowered heads.

"Boer women, I'm sure of it!" hissed Daisy, again unable to hide her fascination. "No one in New Zealand or Australia still dresses like that. Look at those bonnets!"

They saw few Boer men. They were likely either prisoners or still fighting the occupation. Among the men in the street, military uniforms dominated. Roberta started when one of the Boer women spat at a lieutenant passing by.

"They don't like us," Jenny said, "but can you blame them?"

They also saw few black Africans. Indian "boys" served the officers in their clubs.

A young Indian man opened the door to the office of Lord Milner, the gentleman in charge of the concentration camps in Transvaal. Milner received the roughly thirty female nurses and teachers in a meeting room.

"Welcome, ladies. We're exceedingly grateful to you and naturally to our, hmm, esteemed Miss Hobhouse for your engagement," he remarked. The military's contempt for the peace activist was no secret. "You are needed in the refugee camps for the care of the inmates as well as their schooling. You will discover that many of these women lack any basic knowledge of civilized housekeeping." Roberta screwed up her face in confusion. That made no sense. Plus, the women in Pretoria looked quite kempt. "They are also uncooperative and unwilling to learn. Difficult tasks lie before you, my valued ladies. If there is anything I can do to ease them, do not hesitate to address the camp command. Now, if there are no further questions—"

Lord Milner clearly intended to end the audience as quickly as possible. Roberta's breath caught when Daisy raised her hand.

"Three of us are friends who would like to work in the same camp, sir," she declared. "Do you think that could be done?"

Lord Milner smiled amicably at the buxom, black-haired girl. "Unfortunately, we cannot assign three nurses to one camp. We have too few for that, but—"

"We're two nurses and a teacher," Daisy interrupted him.

Milner looked stern for a moment, then nodded indulgently. "That should be doable. Sergeant Pinter," he addressed an adjutant sorting papers behind him, "please select a suitable workplace for these young ladies. And if others have particular requests regarding their assignment, we'll be happy to address them, as long as it lies within our power. We do want you to feel comfortable here. Which likewise goes for our, hmm, Boer, hmm, charges. If there are occasional grievances in the camps, then they are, hmm, by no means intentional, and besides, well—thank you once again, ladies, for your selfless action. I turn it over to you, Pinter."

The lord left the room while his secretary reached for his pen.

"If you would please step forward, ladies, one after the other."

Daisy cheekily placed herself first in line. Jenny and Roberta followed a little self-consciously.

"So, you're the troika. Let's see, two nurses and a teacher. Well, you could go to Barberton or Klerksdorp or Middelburg. Springfontein is in a very lovely area. Oh yes, and Dr. Drury asked for two nurses in Karenstad."

"Dr. Kevin Drury?" Roberta stammered.

Daisy grinned from ear to ear. "Many, many thanks, Sergeant Pinter. We'll go to Karenstad."

Chapter 9

Johanna van Stout's death led to unrest at Karenstad. The rumor that the girl had been murdered by the guards spread like wildfire. Bentje van Stout was highly respected, her husband's unit famous. When she made accusations, the other women took them seriously.

"What sort of riot is she going to cause when she hears of her husband's death?" sighed Kevin.

He had just finished another tour of the camp, assuring the women that the guards had not even had access to the camp the night of Johanna's death. The women could only laugh at this. Greenway was right. Not every Boer woman shared the strict moral principles of Doortje van Stout. A few saw no sense in letting their children starve, so they'd formed a sort of camp brothel. The guards paid in bread or marmalade, tins of fish or sweets. And the children did not starve, but they were subject to mockery and disdain. Kevin did not want to imagine what would happen once the camp was dissolved and no one was there to stop the women from tarring and feathering the "Tommy whores." In any case, everyone knew the guards did not respect the ban on entering the camp at night.

"As a widow, she'll really be a heroine."

Cornelis nodded. "I should tell her. And tell Doortje about Martinus. But then I won't have a leg to stand on here."

So far, the two men had stuck to Cornelis's story about his unit being ambushed. Supposedly, two men had been shot, Cornelis wounded and taken prisoner when his pony was shot out from under him. The rest had ostensibly escaped, including Adrianus van Stout and Martinus DeGroot.

"I don't dare to think about how Doortje would react," Kevin said sadly.

Cornelis looked at him sympathetically. "I know you're in love with her, Doctor, but it's hopeless. She's—" Cornelis searched for words.

"She's a Boer, but she's a woman too," Kevin said. "She could laugh, love, and enjoy things. If she would only let herself."

Cornelis shook his head. "She'll never be who you want," he insisted. "She can't be broken in—"

"Heavens, I don't want to break her in," groaned Kevin. "I just want—I want to love her, to be good to her, to spoil her."

"For that, you'd need to upend her faith, along with her patriotism. And then, who knows what would be left, Dr. Drury. Or if you'd even still want her."

Kevin looked him in the eye. "I will always want her, no matter what," he insisted. "If only she'd give me a chance." He looked away when Cornelis did not respond. "Shall we ride upriver tomorrow? I still really need to see the blacks' camp."

Cornelis nodded distantly. "As you wish."

Kevin sighed again. Cornelis might have been unusual for a Boer, but he had no appreciably different attitude toward black people than his cousin. Cornelis, too, thought the natives robust but inferior. He would have ignored the black camp like Lindsey had, and moreover, he held it against them that some had cooperated with the British. Sure, he did so himself, but only to help his countrymen. Many black workers betrayed their former white masters, and Cornelis could not see past that, let alone understand it.

***

"We were always good to them," Cornelis insisted the next day as he rode Vincent's black mare alongside Silver. "Before my people came here, they were primitive savages. They didn't know the Bible."

"Primitive? The Zulu had a powerful empire with a well-organized military. As for the Bible, Cornelis, don't you realize every land has its own gods? I'm no theologian; I don't know how it all coheres. But I do know it's no excuse to enslave other people."

"But we didn't," Cornelis persisted. "They came of their own free will. There are still Kaffirs with the guerillas."

Kevin made a face that spoke volumes. "I'm sure free will has long since been beaten out of them. And what about the Voortrekkers your aunt tells such vivid stories about? The ones who slaughter three thousand Zulu in one day? Only to take their land and generously let them live there as slaves?"

Kevin was working himself up, but his words soon caught in his throat. The blacks' camp suggested that the English thought as little of the native population as the Boers did. The refugees were housed in conditions that almost made the whites' camp seem luxurious.

"What kind of hovels are those?" Kevin asked a soldier. The gate he guarded was pro forma, as the black inmates were not forbidden from leaving. Many men worked outside, and whoever had money could go shop in town at any time. "Were no tents delivered here?"

"No, sir, the people were supposed to build for themselves. Some have."

Alongside a few handsome round huts were rows of provisional shelters constructed from oil drums. Many women and children apparently slept outside on the muddy ground or in tiny tentlike shelters made out of sheets.

"No wood," one of the refugees explained in broken English.

"That is to say, nothing to build with." Kevin turned sternly to the guard.

"These people can work, sir. They're supposed to earn the materials for their houses and then build them."

Kevin scowled. "Something needs to change here and quickly. Cornelis, we need a translator. What about the van Stouts' servants? Nandi and her brother spoke good Afrikaans and a little English too. Maybe they're here."

The guard confirmed there were no records in this chaos, so Kevin set off in search of them, followed by a reluctant and repulsed Cornelis. Here, there were no latrines, the insect infestation was unbearable, and the "hospital" was just an emergency shelter without any sort of doctor. It was overflowing with the sick and starving. Many of the women were no longer able to feed their babies, and Kevin discovered several corpses among the living. Unlike in the other camp, no functionaries here removed them, let alone gave them funeral rites. If family members were well enough, they would bury the body themselves.

When Kevin was about to give up, he found Nandi. The young woman lay weakly in one of the huts pieced together with oil drums. Two young men seemed to be guarding her, but they let the camp director and his assistant in. They eyed Cornelis suspiciously.

"Miss Nandi." Kevin tried to hide his shock at her emaciated face.

"Mijnheer Doctor, you back? What with *baas* Bentje? And Doortje? And children?"

Kevin took a deep breath. "Johanna has died," he reported honestly. "But the others are all in the other camp here. Miss Nandi, I—"

"Brother also dead," she said—with a fearful glance at her guards.

One of them was just then negotiating with a man who wanted to enter. Cornelis seemed to catch a few words. He looked disgusted. Nandi looked away in shame.

"What happened? Was he sick?"

Nandi shook her head, tears welling up in her eyes.

"I would bet those two had something to do with it," Cornelis remarked, nodding to the men at the entrance. "Take a look around, Doctor. This isn't anyone's living quarters. This is where the blokes put their goods on display. No doubt, her brother was not willing to let them sell the girl."

Nandi made a choked noise. And Kevin saw what Cornelis meant. There was no place to cook or any bedding other than the straw where Nandi lay on a filthy blanket. In broad daylight, although the hut itself was dark and stuffy, stinking of paraffin oil, and crawling with flies. Nandi looked awful, but not so weak she could not leave the bed.

Kevin stood up.

"Nandi, we're going to take you with us to the white camp," he declared. "And I'm going to see to this whole camp, beginning with a sort of census. We need to find out how many people live here. Furthermore, we're going to offer work—not just to the men, but first of all to the women. After all, we're short-handed on everything, and since the Boer women don't want to help . . . Nandi, if you like, I can offer you work cleaning my house. And we'll take ten other women right away to help Dr. Greenway in the hospital and clean the guard posts. Nandi, are there more, uh, girls like you?"

Nandi lowered her eyes. She was clearly scared to death, but Kevin had gotten to know her bravery and pride at the van Stouts'. When Kevin helped her up, she pointed the way to two more huts like hers. One of the girls was burning up with fever and no longer responsive. The other, no more than seventeen, could stand only with great effort. Kevin sent Cornelis to retrieve a few guards to escort the women to the gate.

"We'll have these women picked up with the workers," he informed the guards. "I'll send the military police for the two rats who imprisoned them."

"But, sir," complained the corporal who had let them in, "the womenfolk can't just go back and forth between the camps every day."

"They won't need to. We're going to house these women and their children in the whites' camp."

The watchmen and Cornelis gasped.

"That's out of the question, Doctor," Cornelis sputtered. "You can't keep the Kaffirs together with the white families. You—you just can't."

"You won't believe what all I can do," Kevin informed his assistant fiercely. "Anyway, blacks and whites lived next door on your Boer farms. We'll give the black women their own tents, of course."

***

By that afternoon, two hay wagons had carried more than thirty volunteer workers and their children to the whites' camp, as well as a few seriously ill people Kevin thought stood a chance with treatment. But Dr. Greenway shook his head decidedly when Kevin explained he wanted to requisition two of the whites' tents for them.

"Drury, the Boers would revolt. You won't get any support from the military command either. There are reasons they keep the camps separate."

"But you're—" Kevin looked at his colleague in disbelief. "And aren't you happy to finally have help?"

Greenway pursed his lips. "If you insist, let's bring the sick into the hospital first, in the smaller rooms, please, even if it gets crowded. But for the love of God, think of somewhere else to house the black workers, Dr. Drury. Otherwise, more lives could be lost."

Sobered, Kevin helped the women from the wagon, enduring threats and jeers from the camp's white inmates. He gave up the idea that the white women might make some room for their former servants, and asked the volunteers to wait in his own quarters until he found a solution.

Next, Kevin telephoned Vincent.

"Stable tents?" the veterinarian echoed. "I need to ask, but I assume the larger cavalry units have some. Do you need them now? I'm in the middle of something."

"Vincent, I have thirty women and children here."

"I'll need a few hours. For now, the best you can do is hope—and pray, if that's something you do—while I take care of this horse. It belongs to the commander of the supply station, and it's his favorite."

"Vincent," whined Kevin.

"What I mean is, he'll be grateful to me if I save his horse. So grateful, in fact, that he'd surely be happy to do me a favor. And if anyone has tents, it's him."

A few hours later, an extremely relieved Major McInnes personally delivered a spacious stable tent to the camp, as well as a shipment of victuals.

"These are donations," he explained, "from New Zealand. More should be arriving soon, along with clothing and toys. And three nurses."

"Three nurses?"

"Well, one is a teacher, I think," McInnes corrected himself. "Which—well, maybe she can make herself useful, nonetheless."

Kevin could hardly believe his luck.

What's more, the Boer women did not protest when the cavalrymen pitched the stable tent in a far corner of the camp, even though its ventilation was considerably better than in their own soldier tents. They were merely content with the knowledge that the blacks were sleeping in a place meant for animals, befitting their lower status. An extra share of provisions further soothed tensions—and in the morning, a clean and tidy office awaited Kevin. Nandi must have gotten up in the dead of night to sweep and make him breakfast. Still, she seemed weak and febrile.

"Nandi, you can take your time with the work," he assured her. "You need to get better first—the best thing would be for you to come with me to the hospital now, and we'll give you a proper examination. Maybe you'd also like to see Doortje and her family. Though, first, we need to do something about getting you clean clothes and a bath."

"Afraid going to river," she explained with embarrassment. "White women—"

"You can wash in the river outside of camp," Kevin said. "You're workers, not prisoners. If you want to go, go."

Nandi did not need to be told twice—and wept with happiness when Kevin gave her a precious bar of soap. Kevin had wanted to give Doortje a bar, but the Boer woman declined any preferential treatment.

Nandi had no such compunctions. She was back again in a flash, in soaking wet clothing but smelling like lilacs.

"All better," she announced, but Kevin nonetheless insisted on taking her with him to the hospital.

The next surprise awaited him there. The hospital had already been rid of dust and the sickrooms scoured to a shine. The sick black women and children lay in cleanly made beds.

"It looks good," Kevin praised Dr. Greenway who sat in his office, sorting patient files. "Like a proper hospital."

The doctor snorted. "Only without any patients."

Dumbfounded, Kevin realized Greenway was right. Aside from the handful of black women and children he'd brought over, the hospital was cavernously empty. The Boer women must have carried their family members back to the tents—for the most part, women and children with highly contagious diseases.

"But what—?"

"I told you," Greenway said. "The Boers won't mix. They don't want to be tended by them either, since they see the black women as traitors. You can have a hospital here for whites or one for blacks. Not for both at once."

Kevin was distraught and disappointed—but now anger was rising within him. There was plenty of space in this hospital. And what was more, there were now willing nurses. If the Boers would rather see their children die . . .

"We won't give ground," he decided quickly. "This hospital is open to everyone. If the women won't come, I can't help them. But our next job is to inspect the camp, Greenway. And we won't shy away from compulsory admittance when an extreme danger of contagion exists."

***

The inspection took a toll on Kevin and Dr. Greenway, as well as on the watchmen, who had to drag contagious children out of their tents, and Cornelis, who had to explain it all to the women. All were cursed and spat on—and in the end, only thirty children lay in the hospital again, crying with fear, their mothers no longer allowed to visit.

"We can't keep this up," Dr. Greenway said wearily.

The volunteer workers had performed exemplarily. Everything was clean, and a tasty stew awaited the hospital occupants. However, the Boer children would not eat any of it, no matter how hungry they were. The older children repeated the refrains about broken glass in the soup, and the younger ones did not dare to cross them.

"There's no forcing these people. The best thing would be to send the blacks back to work in their own hospital."

"As doctors?" Kevin scoffed. "Greenway, these women are extremely capable, but they aren't medical professionals. No, you and I will be riding to the blacks' camp every day from now on. We'll have more time since the women are assisting us."

"And since no patients will come here anymore," Greenways retorted just as biliously. "I don't know of any solution either, Drury, just that we can't tie children to the beds and force-feed them."

Chapter 10

The Boer women were obstinate, but then Kevin remembered his thick Irish skull. He kept the hospital open, continued to carry out compulsory admittances—and achieved the minor success of at least getting the sick children to eat. It was pure coincidence that one of the black assistants had worked for little Matthes Pretorius's family all his life. Ten-year-old Matthes greeted her cheerfully and ravenously ate up all his porridge when she brought it to him. When he did not die—and moreover, to the doctors' relief, quickly recovered from his pneumonia—the other children also dug in.

For the doctors, however, the work remained all-consuming. Kevin was ashamed that he hadn't yet managed to return for a full inspection of the black camp. Until, on the fourth night since the black women had been employed, when the pitter-patter of naked feet in the hall awakened him. Instinctively, he reached for his gun, but it no longer lay next to his bed as it had in his months with the Rough Riders. Kevin cursed and readied himself to fend off an attack with his fists. Then, however, he heard a shy voice.

"Mijnheer Doctor, sir?"

"Nandi?"

Kevin felt for the matches and lit the gas lamp next to his bed. The young woman entered nervously, wearing a high-necked, lace-trimmed nightgown. It was new, having come from a donation of secondhand clothing that had arrived the day before. The black women had sorted through the items for distribution to the Boer prisoners, and Nandi had been unable to contain her excitement about the dream in lace. Surely, Kevin decided, he was acting in the spirit of the donors when he told her to keep it. Nandi was, after all, no less needy than the

Boer women. Now, however, the business made him nervous. Did Nandi think she was now required to "thank" him for the gift?

"Is everything okay?" he asked carefully. "Why aren't you in the tent with the other women?"

Nandi shook her head. "I hear, *baas* doctor, sir." The young woman imitated moaning to illustrate. "At door."

"Door? What door? Where exactly were you when you heard this, Nandi?"

Nandi looked sheepish. "Here. Kitchen."

"You were sleeping in my kitchen?"

Nandi nodded. "Not be angry, not punish, sir. But such pretty dress, like white *baas*. Want to keep clean."

Kevin winced. There was no way he could allow Nandi to sleep in his house. He dared not imagine the rumors that would result from that. On the other hand, the kitchen was an outdoor annex, hardly more than a space for grilling.

"We'll talk about that later. Now, go on. You heard a moaning at my door? And now it's gone?"

Nandi shook her head. "No, not gone. Want to run away when see me, but child too heavy. Now to hospital."

"A woman with a child?" Kevin climbed out of bed, his bedsheet wrapped around his waist. "I just need to get dressed. You can tell the woman—"

"*Baas* Doortje not speaking to Nandi."

Doortje was the patient? Something must be terribly wrong if she was stealing away to him in the middle of the night.

Kevin threw on his breeches, leaped into his boots, and ran out, shirt in hand. Nandi, who had been waiting in the hall, followed close behind.

"Go to bed with the others, Nandi," he said as they rushed past the stable tent. "I'll head to the hospital on my own."

"I help?" she asked.

Kevin wrestled with himself. He really could need some help, and being alone with Doortje could compromise him just as much as the business with Nandi.

"Send the two women who help Dr. Greenway," he decided. The doctor had chosen two especially bright women to help with the daily care of the sick. He hoped soon to be able to send them as "nurses" to the black camp.

***

Doortje's dingy bonnet sat crooked on her blonde hair. The ties hung loose. Nothing could be seen of the young woman's face. She was pressing it into the damp, sweaty locks of her youngest brother's hair. With the child in her arms, she was crouching in front of the hospital entrance.

"Doortje—Miss van Stout. For heaven's sake, did you carry him all the way here?" Kevin rushed to the young woman and took Mees's limp body from her. He was burning up with fever. Doortje looked at Kevin—with a cool look between hope and disdain. "And why didn't you knock if you wanted my attention?"

As he spoke, Kevin carried Mees into the tent and straight to the treatment area. Doortje watched him rapidly light the lamps.

"I did not want to bother you," she said stiffly. "Since you were not alone." She spat out the last words.

Kevin saw all of his fears confirmed. Not just with reference to the business with Nandi, but also to the suffering of the child on the couch. Mees's upper body showed characteristic reddening. Typhus.

"Of course I was alone. What nonsense is this?"

He looked for a stethoscope. He had to at least act as if he could help. But the boy's chances at this stage in the illness were poor.

Doortje snorted contemptuously. Then she changed the subject. "Is there anything you can do?" she asked, and stroked Mees's sweat-damp hair. "He's been sick for two weeks."

Kevin nodded. "You needed to bring him earlier."

Doortje looked up at him, and for the first time her gaze became soft. "My mother, Dr. Drury, you know my mother. She prayed and washed him in the river to cool him and—"

"Typhus is caused by bacteria, which likely swim in that same river where he was bathed. And no doubt he drank from it before." Kevin went to take Mees's temperature. He already knew the number would be dizzyingly high.

Doortje nodded. "The river is so close. Water is water. Mother filtered it too."

Kevin groaned. "Cornelis would have gladly brought you drinking water every day if you weren't constantly calling him a coward and traitor. He no longer dares get close."

"His place is with his unit," Doortje insisted. "He should not be here."

Kevin undressed the boy and began to wash him. Cold vinegar water could bring some relief. He could also try compresses, and above all, the boy needed liquid.

"Cornelis isn't here of his own volition. He was taken prisoner," Kevin began, and cast an eye at the thermometer. One hundred four.

Doortje threw her head back. The soft expression had disappeared. She was again the truculent Boer.

"Then he failed. My father was not taken prisoner. Martinus DeGroot was not taken prisoner."

"No," Kevin blurted out. He loved Doortje, but her stubbornness tested his patience—and now exhausted it. "Your father and your fiancé were killed. I'm sorry you're learning about it here and now, but I was present when Martinus died. Regarding your father, you'll have to ask Cornelis the circumstances. But Martinus did not die in battle. He had surrendered, but a commander had his men fire anyway. I protested against it. That's why I'm here now. I quit the service. Under protest. Not that you're likely to believe me. Now, you'll probably hate me and the British even more, and I even understand that. But you shouldn't hate your cousin. It was pure chance Cornelis survived. Now, help me and hold the lamp. I'm going to lay your brother in a sickbed and give him fluids artificially, since he probably can't drink anymore."

"Not for two days," Doortje whispered. All the color had drained from her face. "My father is dead, and Martinus—"

"Was taken prisoner and shot during an attempt to blow up railroad tracks," Kevin repeated. He was beginning to feel guilty for his rash confession. "I'm truly sorry, Doortje. But please don't refuse to let your brother be treated in this hospital. He might lie in a bed next to a black child, but skin color isn't contagious. Typhus, on the other hand, is. Your other brother and your mother could get sick, too, if they haven't already."

Doortje's silence provided the answer he feared.

Kevin picked up the little boy. "I'm going to take him to a sickroom now. You can stay with him, give him cooling poultices, and clean him if he has more diarrhea. Or you can leave that to Sophia." He indicated one of the black assistants entering just then, dressed in a clean nurse's apron in spite of the hour. "Honestly, it'd be better for you to go back to your tent and bring your other brother and your mother, too, if possible. Maybe we can still save them, at least." Kevin squeezed shut his eyes. That, too, had been a mistake. He should not have said how bad Mees's condition was. On the other hand, he did not want to lie to Doortje anymore. Kevin looked her directly in the eye. "I'm going to do everything I can to keep him alive. But I can't promise. You should pray for him."

"Pray?" Doortje asked, her voice thick. "What about the 'wonders of modern medicine'?"

"Prayer and modern medicine complement each other nicely," he replied. "How does it go? Help yourself, and God will help you. Really, that ought to be in line with your philosophy. So, will you go? Or don't you trust Sophia and me?"

Doortje swallowed. Then she left without a word.

***

Kevin himself prayed that night more fervently than ever before in his life, but for naught. Little Mees visibly worsened. Sophia did the best she could for him, and in the morning, Nandi also came to help.

"He know me. With me calmer," Nandi claimed, and Kevin allowed her to help, although Mees was far too sick to recognize anyone anymore.

To Kevin's horror, Thies was hardly doing better. Doortje brought him with the help of two other Boer women. She could not have carried him alone. Dr. Greenway, more experienced with typhus than Kevin, shook his head.

"It would take a miracle for him to pull through. It's a crying shame. Finally, one of the women brings herself to let us help, but it's too late."

Kevin refused to believe that. He fought desperately for the life of the van Stout brothers while Greenway cared for a little girl one of the other women had brought along. This was the day's single glimmer of light. Little Wilhelmina was undernourished and had a nasty cough, but she could certainly recover. Greenway lodged her and her mother in one of the smaller sickbays, separated from the black patients.

"Those white nurses are supposed to come soon, aren't they?" he asked Kevin around noon.

Kevin was in the middle of changing the infusion bag at Mees's bed. Doortje was making a vinegar poultice following his instructions. She had not spoken to him since that morning. Her stoic face filled Kevin with reluctant admiration. Her stubbornness drove him crazy, but the dignity with which she bore her fate was impressive.

"Dear heavens, the nurses! They're arriving today. Someone needs to fetch them from the train. But I can't possibly go now. Couldn't you?"

Greenway looked down skeptically. His smock was filthy, and he was drenched in sweat from toiling in the stuffy tent.

"I'd have to spiff myself up first, or I'll scare them for sure," he remarked. "Besides, Sophia just told me we have three new patients. The Boer women are finally giving in and bringing their children."

Doortje spun on her heel. "We are not 'giving in,' Doctor," she said sharply. "We are simply bending to force. In our row of tents alone, twelve people have died in the last few days. I hope it makes you happy to have broken our pride."

Kevin began a reply, but then gave it up. He was tired of repeating himself. And right now, he had another problem.

"I'll call Vincent," he said, getting up. "He'll complain again about having to help us so much that he hardly gets to his own work, but I imagine he'll enjoy picking up a few girls instead of just giving horses enemas all the time."

***

Kevin tried desperately for another two hours to save Mees van Stout. He tried to bring the fever down and gave cardiotonic and other treatments against diarrhea. Dr. Greenway shook his head at the waste. The camp hospital was perpetually short on medicine, and he had long made it a habit not to squander the supply on the obviously dying. When a patient arrived in the last stage of typhus, he kept them warm and clean but limited treatment to the infusion of liquid. He viewed Kevin's struggle as senseless, and was right, of course. Mees died that afternoon in Nandi's arms. Doortje was caring for Thies, who still recognized her sometimes. His illness, however, was on a very rapid course. Greenway assumed he would follow his brother that same day.

"Has anyone seen to the mother?" the doctor asked as he accompanied Kevin from Mees's deathbed to Thies's sickbed. "One of the neighbors said she was also doing very poorly. And she's cursing her daughter for not being with her."

Doortje had heard these last words. She stroked Thies's hair once more and stood.

"I will go to her now. But it was her decision. I—how is Mees doing?" She did not collapse when Kevin gave her the news, nor did she cry. Only trembling hands betrayed her pain. "Then I will go," she whispered.

Kevin wrestled again with his desire to pull her close. "Doortje, I did what I could. I—I even prayed."

He thought he saw a trace of warmth in her eyes.

"I know," she said softly. "Thank you."

Chapter 11

The long train ride to Karenstad was beginning to wear on Roberta, although the view out the window remained impressive, and Daisy and Jenny were charming company. But Roberta could hardly believe that her voyage was coming to an end—and that only a short time separated her from a reunion with Kevin Drury. The whole thing seemed a marvel. So far, everything had been far too simple. And now she would be working with him. Kevin would no doubt notice Roberta, talk to her, get to know her—and maybe even fall in love with her.

Roberta's heart beat fast at the thought of it. But she also felt a bit queasy. She had not seen Kevin in so long—what if her feelings had changed? Maybe she would not feel this burning in her chest anymore when she saw him, maybe the sound of his voice would no longer give her goose bumps, and she would not feel electrified when her hand accidentally brushed his. Again and again, she felt for the stuffed horse in her bag and was holding it tight when the train pulled into Karenstad. It was an ugly little town, but Lord Milner's secretary had already told them that. In fact, he had urgently advised against this camp—there were others in much lovelier regions, in which conditions were supposed to be less chaotic. Emily Hobhouse's protests had already had some effect, particularly in the larger, more centrally located camps. Roberta, however, had been set on Karenstad, and Daisy and Jenny came along enthusiastically. Daisy was hoping for romance, and Jenny had never intended to make things easy for herself. She was also happy about the news that Karenstad had a black camp as well.

"One of us will work with the whites and the other with the blacks," she declared. "What about you, Roberta? Are you going to open a mixed school?"

Roberta did not answer. She had not even thought about it, too distracted by dreams of Kevin. And now, the train was stopping and—Roberta hoped deep down that he would be there to welcome them himself and thank them for the donations. The crates should already have arrived. But now, at the last moment, she was seized by fear. What if he wasn't happy that she was there? What if he found her presumptuous? Roberta dawdled with her luggage while Daisy and Jenny rushed to the exit and peered out curiously.

"Hey, is that Kevin?" asked Daisy, pointing to the platform. "He looks pretty good in his uniform, dashing even. Although, aren't the camps under civilian management now?"

Roberta, too, was now in a hurry to get off the train. It would not be right for him to speak with Daisy and Jenny first. She could not be shy. She must—

Roberta tugged a bit on her elegant, dark-blue traveling outfit and then stepped determinedly onto the platform. Kevin Drury was not waiting for her, though. Instead of his angular, adventurous face, she was looking at a good-natured countenance with friendly gray eyes framed by short, wavy blond hair and full eyebrows. Attractive and manly in his khaki uniform, this kind, wiry man was, nevertheless, unequivocally not Kevin Drury.

Roberta tried not to be disappointed. It was completely appropriate for Kevin to send a colleague. The insignia on the man's lapel did, however, identify him as a medical officer. Yet, a *V* stood out beside it.

The man came over to them and gallantly helped Jenny from the train. "Ladies, I'm Dr. Vincent Taylor, and it's my pleasure to welcome you to Karenstad. You're urgently awaited. There's a great deal to do here. Dr. Drury, the camp director, begs your forgiveness. He's taking care of two deathly ill children."

"But you were able to make it?" Daisy began flirting at once.

The doctor smiled. "My patients are easier to please. They're generally in better condition than the inmates, and in serious cases, I have plenty of orderlies at hand."

"So, you work here in town?" asked Jenny. "You treat the British soldiers?"

Roberta was busy dragging her suitcases out of the train. One of them still contained donations from New Zealand that had been forgotten during the earlier transport. Now, Dr. Taylor took them from her. He seemed to forget Jenny's question when he saw Roberta's face. Roberta was startled by the expression in his eyes. Surprise? Amazement? Joy? She lowered her gaze. Had she stared at him? Had he stared at her?

"For-forgive me," he whispered. "You are—"

Roberta blushed, but then forbid herself to be self-conscious.

"I'm Roberta Fence," she said firmly. "The teacher."

"My name's Vincent Taylor," the young doctor repeated—and then seemed to find his way back to reality. "Forgive me." He now turned to Jenny. "What was—what did you want to know? Oh yes, the British soldiers." He smiled. "I wouldn't call them that. They didn't choose to serve. But they do work for the army. I'm the veterinarian here, Miss—?"

"Harris," Jenny said with a laugh. "So, you treat dogs and cats?"

"Horses! The dog-and-cat department in the British Army is rather small. But now, come, I've borrowed a halfway-comfortable vehicle. And two of my recovered patients." He pointed to a hay wagon, which offered two rows of seating, pulled by two bays. "If you'd be so kind."

Roberta wanted to lift up her suitcases, but Vincent took them from her, brushing her fingers as he did. Both pulled their hands back quickly. Roberta smiled shyly and was again unsettled by Vincent's gaze. He looked at her like Kevin had looked at Juliet. But that could not be.

"Forgive me," he said again.

Roberta left the suitcases to him. She took a seat beside Jenny in the second row while Daisy swung up next to Vincent on the box.

"I'll see more from here," she declared cheerfully. "I'm absolutely fascinated by this country. Is it far to the camp? Will we go through the wilderness?"

For a while, the wagon rumbled down well-traveled paths between the train station and the town. Aside from cheerless army buildings and tents, there was not much to see. Daisy, however, quickly drew the young veterinarian into an animated conversation about Transvaal's flora and fauna. Robert felt admiration and something like jealousy. She could not chat so easily with strangers herself.

"And you, Miss Fence?"

Roberta was startled from her thoughts. "What?"

"Do you like it too?" Vincent repeated his question. "South Africa?"

Roberta winced. She had not thought much about it so far. He was going to think she was stupid and maybe tell Kevin so.

"I, yes, I do. It's very pretty," she murmured. "But also, very difficult. Well, they say the people are difficult, and the war . . ."

Vincent Taylor nodded seriously. "Yes. The disconnect is sometimes frightful. The beauty all around and the, well, stubbornness of the people. You'd be tempted to think this vast country, this wonderful nature, would fill one with humility."

But Roberta wasn't having it. She had grown up as the stepdaughter of an attorney who worked on Maori land rights.

"Some men see nature; others see resources," she replied. "Or farmland. It's always like that. One person sees a kauri tree and thinks of the stories of Tane Mahuta; the next thinks of lumber and the price of wood."

Vincent turned around to Roberta. "Very true, Miss Fence. You've put it wonderfully."

"Some see a person," Jenny added, "while others just see labor."

They were then passing a supply depot, in front of which a few black workers were loading sacks into a wagon. The men looked undernourished and despondent.

"And yet, really, it's their land," Roberta observed.

She wondered how the black population had lived here before the Boers invaded.

"The situation with the blacks really is a big problem here," Vincent said, and told them all about Kevin's attempts to reform the camps.

At Jenny's cheerful offer to work in the blacks' camp, he reacted happily but not as euphorically as he had at Roberta's commentary. This did not go unnoticed by Daisy.

"Well, you've won someone over," she whispered to Roberta as Vincent exchanged a few words with some approaching riders. "The veterinarian's already eating out of your hand. Now, you just need to impress Kevin."

Roberta blushed. She liked Vincent Taylor very much, but he did not have anything approaching Kevin's effect on her. Vincent now drove the wagon over unpaved paths, and Jenny complained about the dust clouds.

"It's even worse in the camp," Vincent said. "Intolerable, really. But, honestly, everything there is."

"Well, now that we're here," declared Daisy, "we'll take care of that."

***

A half hour later, they drove through the camp gates. The watchmen looked bored. They eyed the female newcomers hungrily but kept bawdy remarks to themselves. And then Roberta and the nurses spied the first Boer women and children. Haggard forms in threadbare dresses that hung loose from their scrawny bodies. Most of them were barefoot or wore oft-patched shoes, but almost all clung to the tradition of wearing a bonnet, no matter how dirty.

"The children aren't even playing," Roberta noted as they drove between the rows of tents—round tents colored reddish by the ever-present dust, with primitive cooking stations in front. "And the women, didn't they have proper houses before?"

Vincent nodded. "They did, and they were exceedingly tidy. Army command likes to depict the Boers as primitive, and they don't really shine in education, but neither do the rural populations in England and New Zealand, right? Regardless, it's a barefaced lie to claim they're better off here than on their own farms. Especially considering the outbreaks. With all the cholera and typhus, consumption, gangrene of the lungs, our doctors are powerless. Look, we're coming up on the main buildings. There's the hospital—primitive construction, I know, but it does the job. The guards and doctors sleep in the few solid buildings. That flat one in front there is the office and also Dr. Drury's residence. Let's see if he's in."

The women followed the veterinarian somewhat shyly across the bleak square between the houses and the hospital. Vincent opened the door to Kevin's house without knocking. It led into a vestibule and then directly into the office. All the rooms were unoccupied.

"Do they not lock up here?" Daisy asked, surprised.

"Doesn't seem like it," Vincent observed. "Probably there's nothing to steal. And the women aren't thieves either. As I said, these are extremely proper people, even if their culture and beliefs are different from ours." Vincent knocked on the door to Kevin's apartment, but no one was there either.

"He must be at the hospital. Hopefully that child didn't die on him. He was giving it his all." Vincent was half talking to himself as he led the women back outside, closing the door behind him. "Never leave doors ajar. Otherwise, the dust and flies will get in," he advised the women. "And you'll be tempted—the air doesn't get in through closed doors either. Especially in the tents, the heat quickly becomes unbearable when there's no air circulating."

Vincent walked toward the hospital, and Roberta felt her heart hammering. Soon, soon, she would see Kevin again soon.

The veterinarian led them to the hospital entrance but allowed a young Boer woman the right of way. She kept her head down, but Vincent seemed to recognize her at once.

"Good day to you, Miss van Stout," he said. "I heard about your brother. It was wise of you to bring him here."

The woman looked up, and Roberta saw her pale, careworn face, which was nevertheless of a rough beauty. The young woman's eyes were a fascinating blue, like fine porcelain. And as thin and embittered as she now was, her features were still charming somehow.

"He died earlier," she said tonelessly. "And my mother . . ."

Vincent held the door open for her. "I'm very sorry, Miss van Stout," he said softly. "I'm sure Dr. Drury did all he could."

The woman made no reply, just moved determinedly toward the rear section of the hospital while Vincent first showed Roberta and the nurses the larger rooms and the treatment area. Here, too, they saw neither hide nor hair of Kevin, but they did receive a first impression of the conditions. The Boer women may have given up their resistance to the treatment of black patients in this hospital, but they still enforced a clear hierarchy: in one section of the room, white women and children lay in their beds; in the other, the blacks, especially black children. The whites' beds were furnished with blankets and pillows; the black children had only piles of rags on which to rest their heads. Their covers looked more threadbare than the whites'. The black nurses seemed complicit in this. Jenny looked like she might cry.

"There are smaller rooms for the most seriously ill," Vincent explained, leading the women through the sickbays toward the back. "Drury and Greenway will be there." A moment later, he pulled aside the curtain that separated one of the four smaller sickbays.

Roberta would never forget the image that presented itself to her here. Kevin Drury, somewhat thinner but still elegant and handsome with his tangled black hair and his angular face, was just standing up from the child's bed. He turned to the woman Vincent had addressed as Miss van Stout. His face took on an expression of helplessness, despair, and—love.

"Doortje, Doortje, I, your, Thies—"

He could not get it out, but the woman saw that the child had died. She faltered. And that was when Kevin took her into his arms.

Roberta felt something break within her. She had traveled halfway around the world to see Kevin Drury again. But she found him just as she had last seen him—in the arms of another woman.

Yet, Doortje van Stout did not willingly snuggle into his arms as Juliet LaBree once had. In fact, the woman only submitted to the embrace for a few heartbeats, just long enough for Roberta to recognize her surrender. Then she freed herself abruptly, casting a hateful look at him and another woman whom Roberta only now noticed. A beautiful young woman with deep-black skin. She had been sitting in the shadows, holding the child's hand.

"How dare you. How could you, after—"

Doortje had raised her hand as if to strike Kevin, but now she let it drop.

"Doortje, I didn't mean to offend you. I just wanted—I'm so sorry."

Roberta could sympathize with Kevin's despair, even though she knew nothing about his connection to the bereaved woman. But over the whole scene hovered her bitterness and sorrow at her lost dream.

Chapter 12

"But she doesn't even care about him," Daisy declared.

The three young women had moved into their own tent, feeling a bit guilty when they realized the Boer women were fifteen to a tent. Of course, Daisy brought the conversation immediately around to Kevin, who had made an excellent impression on the two nurses. He had needed some time to recover from the business with Doortje. Vincent, as good an observer as Roberta and without a doubt better informed, had hustled the threesome out of the room.

"Dr. Drury is still busy," he said calmly. "I'll introduce you to Dr. Greenway first."

Greenway had greeted them amicably and at once had undertaken yet another tour of the hospital. Roberta would have preferred to join Vincent, who had quickly and discreetly taken his leave and disappeared into the room where the child had died. Heated voices emanated outward, but Roberta could not understand. After a few minutes, the black woman ran out, and then Vincent led the Boer woman out of the room. Kevin only joined his colleague and his new assistants somewhat later, composed and in a clean smock.

"I must apologize for my inattentiveness. I should have been the one to greet you and give you the tour." Kevin smiled at the young women in his usual charming way and seemed honestly delighted to see Roberta again. The light in his eyes would have made her happy—were it not for that embrace, which had sent all of her illusions up in smoke.

"Roberta! Or, I ought I to say, 'Miss Fence'? After all, now you're all grown up and a teacher—although, really, you're too cute for the job. How will the children ever be afraid of you?" He gave her a mischievous look. "But in all seriousness, Roberta, we need to sit down together as soon as possible and plan out your work here. Though some might think the children need better food first and only then instruction, one should never underestimate intellectual sustenance. The children simply must learn English."

Kevin had invited the women into his office, and the same black woman had served coffee and tea. She looked tearful and timid even though Kevin treated her warmly. He thanked the women for the donations, told them a bit about the camp, and, finally, showed them to their tent.

"Tomorrow, you'll go straight to the hospital to report for duty, Nurse Towls and Nurse Harris, and we'll talk about the school, Roberta. When I find a moment, I'll also show you the black camp."

***

"You got exactly what you wanted!" Later, in the tent, Daisy analyzed the conversation with Kevin. "He was nice to you, he noticed you—he even called you cute! And tomorrow you have a meeting with him. Alone."

"But Roberta's right about that Boer woman," Jenny said. She, too, had been watching closely. "He's pretty clearly in love with her."

Roberta was crestfallen. She would have preferred to pull the covers over her head and cry instead of discussing the matter with her friends.

"She doesn't care at all about him," Daisy insisted anew. "Sure, he hugged her, but she was about to give him a slap. I'd be more worried about that Nandi. She really is beautiful. I mean, if you like black women. And she works for him."

"But he doesn't look at her like that," Jenny objected. "No, no, the Boer's your rival. And you'll come out ahead. Maybe he's tired of her. Sure, she's pretty, but given time . . . Dress up nicely tomorrow, smile a little, and above all, don't fly the white flag so soon."

Roberta nodded because she knew it was expected of her. But she knew that if she did not bury her hopes now, she would never forget that look, the one Kevin Drury had given so many women—just not her.

***

The next day, the newcomers experienced a burial. Kevin had not mentioned it, perhaps had not thought of it, but as Dr. Greenway explained, they could expect a funeral every three days.

"This time, we have an especially large number of fatalities—because of the Boer women's disastrous boycott of the hospital. You met Doortje van Stout yesterday. She's one of the bereaved, as you know."

"Is there anything particularly special about Miss van Stout?" Daisy probed. "I mean, because Dr. Drury—"

Greenway waved her off. "Dr. Drury knows the family. Their house was once requisitioned for a hospital. And here in camp, the family has influence because Adrianus van Stout is an infamous commando—or was. His wife led classes of a sort here." Roberta's ears pricked up. Was Doortje also a teacher? "Which we did not take kindly to. She only told stories to incite the children against the British. But now she's passed too."

"Doortje van Stout passed away?" Jenny asked.

The doctor shook his head. "Her mother. A real tragedy for Doortje—yesterday, both brothers, tonight her mother. Normally, Miss van Stout gives Bible readings at the burials. She leads devotions, too, and she does it quite nicely. Fortunately, she sticks to religion—at least when we're present. These people like to mix religion and politics. In the Boers' view, the Bible is a sort of instruction manual for the subjugation of South Africa. Anyway, Miss van Stout will hardly be capable of leading her own family's burial. So, it falls to us. Probably to Dr. Drury."

When Kevin arrived, he apologized briefly to Roberta and Jenny, as both the school discussion as well as the ride to the black camp had to be postponed. He then stepped very calmly in front of the women waiting in the cemetery behind the hospital. The gathering overflowed the little square—it looked as if everyone who could haul herself out of her tent had come to Bentje van Stout's funeral. Doortje van Stout stood stone-faced in front of the two small coffins and her mother's quickly cobbled-together coffin. The camp carpenter could hardly keep up, but he always put his best efforts into giving the children a dignified burial.

Doortje had foregone the services of the photographer. There was no one left in her family to whom she could have shown the pictures. Still, she did tolerate Cornelis at her side—it looked as if he were the last living relative to whom she was, or had been, halfway close. Now, he crossed to Kevin.

"Dr. Drury, it would be better if I took over," he said seriously. "My aunt Bentje, it's true she didn't much like me either, but, well, a British soldier speaking at her graveside—there could be a riot. And Doortje's at the end of her rope. It'll be better for her if I lead the funeral."

Suddenly, a choir of children's voices began singing a hymn that seemed vaguely familiar to Kevin—probably it existed in English too. Who could have organized this? Dumbstruck, he spotted Roberta among the children. And one of the nurses was handing wildflowers to the little ones.

"And now, prayer," the other nurse prompted in terrible Dutch.

"Our Father . . . ," said Roberta.

It sounded as if the women had only just learned the foreign words, but the Boer women joined in, and one of them quickly took the lead. When they were finished, Roberta determinedly opened the Dutch Bible and began to read.

"'I am the resurrection and the life . . .'"

The words passed her lips haltingly, but after a few lines, she put the book in the hands of a young girl who timidly read a few sentences and then passed it to the next.

Kevin supposed the Boers would have chosen a passage from the Old Testament. And yet, Roberta's tender, improvised funeral nonetheless placed the women under its spell. No one protested when, finally, Cornelis said a few words, depicting his aunt as a stern but loving woman, obedient wife, and selfless mother. When the coffins were lowered into the graves, many people cried, and the children followed Roberta peacefully to the graves and threw in their flowers just as Roberta, Daisy, and Jenny modeled for them.

Doortje let Cornelis put an arm around her. She accepted Kevin's expressions of sympathy wordlessly. Her eyes remained dry.

"You did wonderfully," Vincent Taylor declared as the crowd dispersed. "Truly, Miss Fence, exceptionally moving."

"Above all, you've prevented a riot," Kevin said. "Well done, ladies. I already see what an advantage you'll be for our work here. I wouldn't have thought it possible, but you've already established trust with the women. I can't thank you enough. But what brought you back so soon, Vincent? Aren't there any sick horses?"

Vincent turned red at once. "There, hmm, another aid shipment has arrived addressed to Miss Fence, and I thought I'd—" He smiled shyly at Roberta. "I thought it would be all right with you if we—"

Daisy nudged Roberta. Kevin also seemed to recognize the look in his friend's eyes.

"Oh yes, hmm, well," he hemmed and hawed. "Then, uh, do go on and help her unpack it. If you have nothing else to do."

***

Kevin disappeared into the hospital while Vincent helped Roberta pry open the crate and sort through the clothing and toy donations. There was also a small blackboard, which reminded Roberta of her actual task.

"But where can I even set up the school?" she asked. "There aren't any available rooms, and—"

"Just do it outside," Vincent suggested. "Ask the carpenter to make a few benches. It'd be a welcome change of pace from the endless coffins. Hang the board on a tree, and see if the children come. It probably won't be easy at first, even with your coup today. The mothers surely don't want their children learning English. But in time? No one here has anything else to do."

"I'll lure them in." Roberta smiled. "They're all hungry, after all, and we have food donations. For a few weeks, at least, that'll be enough for a school lunch."

Daisy soon instigated something similar in the hospital. "No wonder you're not getting volunteer helpers! You need to offer them something," she explained to the astonished Dr. Greenway. "Extra rations for those who help cook and clean and care for the sick. That also does away with the problem of the Boers rejecting the black assistants. Speaking of, Jenny and I have thought of something: we'll send the black women back to their own camp, and they can build up the hospital there with Jenny's help. And I'll train the whites here. That'll take more pressure off you doctors, and you can ride to the black camp every day. What do you think? And when do we get to see that camp? Jenny's quite impatient."

***

Roberta and Jenny accompanied Kevin the very next morning to the black refugees' camp and were just as horrified by the conditions as he had been a few days before. Jenny moved herself and all the black nursing assistants over the very next morning—together with the large stable tent, which, to the Boer women's horror, Jenny intended to share with Sophia and the other workers. Into Roberta and Daisy's tent—to the even greater horror of the Boer women—moved Nandi.

"I not go back and leave *baas* Dr. Drury," Nandi declared with great seriousness. "And beautiful house. Someone must clean."

Nandi's English improved every day. The young woman was intelligent and willing to learn, but she was scared to death of being sent back to the black camp after what had happened to her there. Kevin was very relieved when Daisy and Roberta offered to share their lodgings with her.

"Otherwise, the whole thing would have caused me a lot of trouble, you see," Kevin confessed to Roberta. The two of them rode together almost every day to the black camp now, Kevin to do rounds and Roberta to teach school. Whereas the Boers only hesitantly took her up on her offer of instructing the children, the black children were wild about learning to read, write, and speak English. Especially when that was connected to bread and jam or other delicacies at lunchtime. "The women in camp already talk about me and Nandi, which is total nonsense, of course."

"Oh?" Roberta plucked up her courage. "I mean, Miss, um, LaBree was also rather dark skinned."

Kevin turned red at once. He had heard about Patrick's marriage to Juliet but only now learned of the further developments from Roberta. The subject was exceedingly unpleasant for him. Still, he really had no reason to feel guilty regarding Nandi.

"Roberta, please, the girl must be eighteen years old. She's still practically a child and completely uneducated."

Roberta's heart beat faster. If Kevin put such value on education, things between him and that Doortje would not go far. Although she could still read and write and likely knew half the Bible by heart.

"But she's very pretty," Roberta said.

"That's why people are quick to impute something to me. Regardless, I'm happy she's staying with you two. Otherwise, I guarantee she would have set herself up in my kitchen again, and Doortje—" He bit his lip and changed the subject. "So, what's all this about riding lessons, Roberta? It really does slow us down to have to drive the wagon back and forth every day."

Now it was Roberta's turn to blush. For days, Vincent Taylor had been offering to teach her the fundamentals of riding on a well-behaved horse, perhaps a Boer pony. But Roberta had resisted. Horses still reminded her of her childhood at the racetrack: her abusive father, her mother's constant fear of his losses, and the fight between Chloe and Colin Coltrane. What was more, she was nervous about spending time with Vincent Taylor, who so obviously wished to be near her. Under no circumstances did she want to get his hopes up, especially if there might ever be any chance for her with Kevin.

All this made Roberta feel stupid and dishonest. And Kevin's encouragement to take Vincent up on his offer additionally pained her, no matter how much she told herself he wasn't playing matchmaker but merely wished to ride more easily from one camp to the other. The path to Karenstad II, as they had started calling the black camp at Jenny's suggestion, was in terrible condition. They advanced slowly and were always risking a broken axle. A rider, by contrast, could make it there in under half an hour.

"Well, we would have needed the wagon today, anyway," Roberta said, pointing to the bed.

It was filled with crates stuffed with clothing and food donations, more and more of which had been arriving. The bleak reports of Miss Hobhouse's nurses and teachers had begun to reach England and the colonies.

"Did you apportion them equitably?" Kevin asked with a smirk.

The apportionment of the donations was a constant theme among the women in the camp. While the nurses and Roberta wanted to distribute everything equally, the Boers would not accept that black children should receive toys and school supplies too. As for the rare medicines, there was a proper brawl over them after the first white women began to learn the fundaments of modern medical care. Daisy's approach of paying them with extra rations had been astoundingly successful, and they fast proved themselves highly competent. The Boer women and girls were not stupid, only shockingly uneducated. Some, like Doortje and Cornelis, had been taught by their fathers, but other families thought instruction unimportant. Moreover, reading material other than the Bible was rejected as unchristian. The Voortrekkers' church desired members who were plain and devout. Alert, critical thinkers like Cornelis were not wanted.

Roberta raised her chin proudly. "I saw to it the food was equally split. As for the goods, they're mostly books, so none of our white ladies were keen on them. The only one who reads is Miss van Stout. And even she doesn't want to be seen with my books. I caught her at the river reading secretly."

***

To general surprise, Doortje had counted among the first women to report for duty at the hospital. Roberta had at first suspected she was trying to get close to Kevin, but in fact, the Boer went out of her way to avoid him. Jenny suggested that she wanted to distract herself from her enormous loss.

But Daisy made an interesting observation. "She's in it for the extra food," she declared. "I saw her yesterday, wolfing it down like she was starving. The others always give the families some of it, but Miss van Stout doesn't have anyone anymore."

"She's put on a little weight too," Jenny agreed, thinking of the skeletal women in the black camp. "She looks astoundingly good when you consider the circumstances."

Indeed, in spite of all her grief, Doortje seemed to recover. Kevin could hardly take his eyes off her whenever she—now once more in clean clothing and with a starched bonnet—passed through the hospital. Thanks to the new donations, the hospital laundry was at last furnished with plenty of soap and starch.

Kevin did not comment on what the nurses said about the young Boer woman. He never spoke with them about Doortje van Stout, even though Daisy was always trying to get information out of him about his time in Wepener. She was somewhat more successful with Cornelis. She had immediately wrapped him around her little finger, even though Roberta thought a calm, learned type like Cornelis suited Jenny better. He viewed Jenny's focus on the blacks' camp with suspicion, however, and so would never have tried to get close to her.

Now, though, Kevin had an idea. "Maybe you could make more use of Miss van Stout in the school," he told Roberta. "Surely she knows better than we do how to talk to the women and children."

***

With an aching heart, Roberta took his advice. She did not like Doortje, and not just because of jealousy. Doortje's abrasive self-confidence, her apparent lack of feelings, and her stubbornness put Roberta off. She could easily understand why sweet Nandi was afraid of her and still spoke to her reverently as *baas* even after the *mejuffrouw* had forbidden her from doing so.

As for the school, Doortje did, nevertheless, help her make rapid progress.

"Teach the girls something useful. Then the mothers will send them," she said. So far, hardly any Boer children had come to Roberta's outdoor schoolroom.

When any did, it was only boys, and they usually proved themselves quite defiant.

"What could be more useful than reading and writing?" Roberta asked.

Doortje laughed mockingly. "Sewing, spinning, and weaving, to start."

Roberta suppressed a sharp response and accepted the advice. She could not spin thread herself, and the carpenter would first have to make looms. She had a good mastery of sewing, though. As a young girl, her mother had worked a short time at the Gold Mine Boutique. She had sewn Roberta's childhood dresses herself and raised her daughter to mend or alter her clothes as necessary. So, the young teacher took a few dolls out of the toy donations and cut up an old dress for cloth. She let it be known that she would teach the girls to make little dresses for the dolls—and they did so with verve. The words "sew," "doll," and "dress" stood on the board, and the children learned to pronounce them as they worked.

In short order, Roberta took her little students' hearts by storm. The boys, too, slowly fell in love with the openhearted young teacher. Roberta told funny and romantic stories in which princesses and adventurers appeared—no slaughtered Zulu warriors and rivers red with blood. While she was teaching, there was even occasional laughter in the camp. And the death rate sank, not only due to the nourishing school lunches. Roberta noticed immediately when one of her charges was ailing, and marched the student to the hospital at once. Not every mother appreciated that. Roberta occasionally lost a student because of it, but at least the child remained alive.

For her part, Jenny made incredible strides at the blacks' camp. She oversaw the hospital, now staffed with the trained assistants and visited regularly by doctors, conducted school when Roberta could not make it over, and spurred the guards to action until the criminals and pimps could not conduct business. That put her life in danger. After Jenny was threatened several times, she agreed to live in the whites' camp and was accompanied there by two guards every evening. In the morning, she would ride back together with Roberta—on captured Boer ponies. When had Jenny expressly asked Vincent for riding lessons, Roberta could no longer put it off herself.

"It can't really be that you don't like horses," remarked Vincent. "I've seen that little stuffed horsey of yours."

He was surprised when Roberta turned beet red.

"It's, um, lucky," she stammered, "a, um, present."

Vincent did not press further, instead introducing her to a gentle little gray mare.

"Here, see, the animal's quite tame, and you can even give her a name."

He did not mention that the Boer commando to which the pony had belonged had been annihilated a few days before. The British strategy was slowly showing successes. As stubborn as the Boers were, being constantly on the run demoralized them, as did the knowledge of their wives' and children's internment. They had also begun to run low on weapons and ammunition—the British had brought in more troops, who patrolled the veld and crippled lines of communication. More and more Boer guerillas were shot down or simply gave up. High command was already talking about dissolving the concentration camps soon. The remaining men would then have to return to their farms—after all, they could not leave their wives and children alone in the smoldering ruins of their lands.

Roberta stroked the pony hesitantly. She smiled when it rubbed its soft nostrils on her hand.

"I, of all people, shouldn't be afraid of horses. I'm even named for one," she admitted, and told Vincent and Jenny of the miracle mare Lucille who had brought her father high returns on his bets, forcing her mother to move to Woolston and give birth on the road—Lucille was Roberta's middle name.

"Well then, go on and name this little gray Lucie," Jenny suggested.

Jenny let Vincent show her how to saddle her gelding and christened him George, after an uncle he apparently resembled.

Vincent meticulously instructed Roberta in handling the saddle and reins, and cherished every smile she gave him. And, in the end, Roberta let herself enjoy both spending time with Vincent and riding. Lucie was exceedingly gentle and never shied. Roberta was radiant when she returned from her first ride in the veld, having seen zebras and gnus. Vincent beamed like the happiest man in the world when she thanked him from the bottom of her heart.

***

Kevin was also making progress in his courting of Doortje van Stout. Roberta's comment about her covert interest in books had given him an idea. He began leaving books lying around in the hospital, watched Doortje, and then approached her after she'd had some time to read a bit of one of them. He lent her the books and later tried to talk about them with her, noting that her English got even better with each one. When the rainy season set in and it became impossible for her to withdraw to the river to read, he offered her his office.

"No one goes in there except Nandi. And she won't bother you or tell anyone."

Doortje resisted at first, but the chance to escape the mud and clamor for a short time proved too enticing. New families had moved into Doortje's tent, and it pained her to see the strangers lying on her brothers' and mother's mats. Doortje also found the noise in the tent unbearable—the two new women had loud, shrill voices and were constantly bossing their children around. She knew it was weakness, but lately, every little thing got under her skin.

Doortje longed for quiet and suffered from a constant, aching hunger, despite devouring all her extra rations herself instead of sharing them with the children in the tent as her mother would doubtlessly have done. Nor did she always live up to her duties. She felt too tired to sing and pray with her fellow sufferers. Fortunately, there were many fewer funerals of late. Kevin's attempts to get close to her sometimes made her blood boil, only to touch her strangely the next day. Doortje had the definite feeling that something was wrong with her. Perhaps, she reasoned, she would feel better if she escaped camp life for a few hours now and again. What was more, Kevin's books took her to a strange world. She devoured novels like *Pride and Prejudice* and *Jane Eyre*. Later, though, she chided herself for her enthusiasm over these superficial love stories, especially so soon after the deaths of her family members. What was the heartache of an English governess to the sorrows of the Voortrekker? To soothe her guilt, she switched to scientific and historical books. Kevin smiled one evening when he found her in a recliner in his office, her blonde head bent over a picture book about New Zealand.

"Do you like my country, Doortje?" he asked gently. "The fauna is not as varied as here, nor nearly as impressive. But in turn, the creatures are harmless."

Doortje turned to him. It grew harder and harder for her to hate him, but finding a British doctor attractive was even worse than amusing oneself with English novels.

"Is that why you came looking for war in our country?" she asked. "Because it's too peaceful in your country?"

Kevin pulled over an armchair and sank into it. "No, though I admit I was running away from something. From a woman, to be specific, before you start imagining crimes. As for the war, I'm a doctor. I came here to help. I've only saved people, not killed them."

Doortje arched her eyebrows. "What about my brothers and my mother? All the deaths here? You're responsible for them, regardless of what you say."

"The leadership of the British Army is responsible," he insisted. "And the obstinacy of your guerillas, who want to drag on a war they know they can't win. Nonetheless, you should not have been interned and your farms burned. I completely agree with you about that. I can't change it alone, however. No more than open-minded Boers like Cornelis could stop the guerillas. Couldn't you and I, at least, make peace, Doortje? You know I don't mean you any harm."

He held out his hand to her helplessly. Doortje did not take it. But she blushed.

"Peace is not possible," she declared. "This is our land. You are not supposed to be here. You—"

Kevin buried his face in his hands dramatically. "Not this again, Doortje. Not this exasperating business of who should be where. Let's just talk about the two of us."

Doortje exhaled sharply. "Trying to seduce a second member of my household? Is Nandi not enough for you anymore? Even with your wild ideas of equality, white skin is more attractive to you, isn't it, Doctor?"

Kevin clenched his jaw in frustration.

"I don't mean to seduce anyone," he replied heatedly. "Nor do I need to. I have never needed to convince women to go to bed with me. There are plenty of volunteers." He bit his lip when Doortje stared at him in revulsion. Of course, her people did not speak openly of sexual love. Added to that came her horrific violation, which Kevin imagined she might never come to terms with. "Forgive me," he said softly. "I did not mean to speak so bawdily. But you needn't always provoke me. It hurts me when you don't believe me. It insults me when you—"

"When I'm not excited about your dalliance with my maid?" she asked. "When it insults me that a white man fornicates with a she-Kaffir?"

Kevin sighed. But he would not let himself be provoked again. Especially because he suspected this was less about race and more about jealousy.

Kevin had an idea of how to vex the young woman a bit himself. "With respect, Doortje, I've explained to you repeatedly that there is nothing between me and Nandi," he said at ease. "I did so because it's the truth. If I really loved Nandi, there'd be nothing to clarify. As a matter of fact, it would be none of your concern." He noted with contentment that she was staring at him, stunned. "I'm not tied down, and neither is she. So, we wouldn't need to make any secret of it if we wished to be married."

"Married?" Doortje squeaked.

Kevin nodded. "Is that not the proper way? If I loved Nandi, naturally I'd ask her to marry me."

"But she's black."

Kevin laughed. "I couldn't care less whether my wife is black or white. As long as she's smart, eloquent, and passionate." He moved to the edge of his seat and leaned closer. "Nandi's a dear girl, Doortje. And she's survived great hardship, just as you have. She was also abused; her family is also dead. If it made her feel better to sleep in my kitchen a few nights, who can blame her for that? I didn't even know about it until she woke me up when you came. I'm telling you this for the last time, so believe me or don't. Regardless, I must beg you to be kinder to her. You two have no one else left."

Kevin looked Doortje in the eye and watched her vacillate between anger and the desire finally to admit to the feelings with which she had so long struggled. Did he dare kiss her? Or at least touch her hand?

"Kevin?"

Violent knocking came from the front door, and they heard Vincent Taylor's excited shout. Doortje jumped as if someone had caught her out. Or perhaps just in fright at a strange man's voice.

"It's all right, it's only Dr. Taylor." Kevin stroked her hand, which was white knuckled around the chair's arm. "Did you hear that, Nandi?" he called. "Open the door."

Vincent did not wait for Nandi to lead him in. Instead, he threw off the waxed jacket that had protected him from the rain.

"Kevin, good news! Oh, Miss van Stout, good evening. How nice to see you here. Then you shall hear it too. Kitchener is dissolving more camps. And this time, Karenstad's included! The area around Wepener has been pacified. The men are returning home to their farms, and the women and children are to be repatriated. Pretoria is sending a cavalry unit to escort them."

Doortje, who had smiled at first, stiffened. "Escort us?"

Kevin shook his head. "Oh, Doortje, no. I won't allow any further assaults. I shall petition to accompany you myself. It will take some time to organize things, anyway. And if my petition hasn't been approved by then, I'll come without permission."

He smiled at her encouragingly. That smile died, however, when he wondered what he was supposed to take her back to. The farm no longer existed; the van Stout family no longer existed. What were Doortje and Nandi supposed to do alone on a few acres of burned-up ground?

"We—we'll talk more about it later," he said helplessly.

Doortje, who had similar thoughts going through her head, was silent.

"I must leave now," she said. "I thank you, Dr. Taylor, Dr. Drury."

Kevin leaped to his feet and wrapped Vincent's coat around the woman before she stepped out into the rain. "Or you'll be soaked to the bone before you get to your tent, Doortje." Doortje did not say anything but accepted the coat. Kevin looked at Vincent apologetically once she had gone. "Sorry. I'll lend you mine for the way back."

Vincent grinned and went to the cupboard where Kevin kept his whiskey. "Doortje? Not 'Miss van Stout'? Did I miss something?"

Kevin gladly accepted a glass of whiskey. "Let's say I'm making progress," he replied. "Or I was. But now, now it's all over."

Vincent looked just as somber. "Yes," he said. "We'll all be heading home soon. The nurses too."

Kevin grinned at him. "You mean the teacher."

Vincent sighed. "Yes, I'm afraid you can tell by looking at me. In any case, I don't think Miss Fence will be traveling back in a troop transport. Besides, they'll still need teachers, I imagine. The children are supposed to learn English. Miss Fence might be sent far away, and I'll be out of sight, out of mind."

Kevin emptied his glass. "Doortje won't forget me. But she'll hate me again. I wonder which is worse."

Chapter 13

Atamarie did not tell Richard anything about the attack at the dance, and she tried not to hold the lonely night afterward against him. However, she was now bound and determined to dissuade him from haphazardly running a farm alongside his inventing work. And she would no longer support him on this false path by playing the martyred housewife.

The very next morning, she followed Richard into his barn. Luckily, Hamene, one of the Maori men, had shown up again to help and took over the feeding of the animals.

"And what about the fields, Atamarie?" the young man inquired. "They need to be plowed. And the new planting?"

"You'll need to check with Richard about that," she replied, "but I think he'll happily pay you to take it off his hands."

Richard was fervently occupied in taking apart his motor for probably the hundredth time and had not the slightest interest in replanting the fields. When Hamene offered to do it, he agreed but was distracted and impatient.

"Thank you so much, Hamene," Atamarie told the willing worker, who was clearly insulted by Richard's behavior. She would have to work to counter that—it did not bear thinking about the young man not coming back and leaving everything dependent on Richard again. "You know which fields are Richard's. Go ahead and plow them, and sow whatever you see fit."

To be honest, Atamarie was just as uninterested as Richard. Next year, by the time the grain or whatever Hamene planted was ripe, she wanted to be long settled back in Christchurch—with Richard.

***

And then, Atamarie was finally rewarded for her efforts. Richard welcomed her into his inventor's barn, showing her everything and discussing his results with her. Over the following days, she took apart his aeroplane's motor a few more times and refined the tension of the canvas on the wings. They discussed takeoff speed and displacement, whereby Richard put his practical experiences ahead of theory, preferring to try things rather than engage in long calculations. He couldn't seem to sit still. It made Atamarie uneasy when he ran hectically around the workshop, moving items from here to there compulsively. His decisions were often made too hastily and then were hard to reverse. And many of the cheap fixes he thought up to solve problems seemed downright dangerous. During the excursion to Taranaki, Atamarie had gotten to know Richard as a very even-tempered and considerate man, but now, he seemed possessed.

"Nothing serious will come of it like this, Richard," she ventured after a few days. "If you really want to make the thing fly, you need to invest some money. You need a proper engine, not this piecemeal thing, which is also far too heavy. You need an automobile engine. And high-quality canvas. You do have money from the harvest."

Richard snorted, and Atamarie knew it had been a misstep. While Richard always listened to her suggestions, he reacted fiercely to direct critiques.

"Money from the harvest, if only!" he ranted. "With that, I have to buy a tedder. You heard my father. My parents gave me the farm, sure, but not the equipment. Some of the other machines aren't even paid off."

He leaped to his feet again to pace.

Atamarie summoned her courage. "Okay, then. Sell the farm. Take the money and build a flying machine that, well, really flies. Build a proper runway. The best thing would be for you to come with me to Christchurch and look for a suitable piece of land outside of town. You can keep studying and work on your machine on the side."

Richard cackled and fidgeted with his improvised motor parts. "And what will I live on?"

Atamarie raised her hands imploringly. "Well, at first, you'd have the money from the farm. And then, Richard, if you're the first person to put a motorized aeroplane in the air, then, then you've won, Richard. Then the world will be your oyster. You'll be supported from all sides."

Richard looked at her as if she were out of her mind. "My father would kill me."

"Your father would disapprove," she corrected him. "As he disapproves of everything you do. This way you can get it out of the way all at once. But it's one thing or the other. You're not a good farmer, and you can't be a good aeroplane builder simply because you lack the means. Make a decision, Richard. Do what you really want to."

Richard shook his head and finally seemed to come to a rest, at least for a moment. "I can't," he said sadly. "It's not just my father. It's also my mother and my siblings. If I break away from them, I'll be all alone."

Atamarie felt the words like a blow to the stomach. She wanted to scream, to accuse him of not loving her. But the desperation on his face kept her from that. Maybe she had it wrong. Maybe he believed she did not truly love him—or only loved him when he "functioned," as was apparently the case with his family.

Atamarie suddenly needed to get away. She put her hand on Richard's shoulder before she left.

"You would never be alone," she said softly, "but even if you were, wouldn't it be worth it? Richard, if you don't leap, you're never going to fly."

***

Atamarie left the barn behind and ran out into the plains, at first somewhat aimlessly, but then she directed her steps toward the Maori village. Out here, the hills around Temuka transitioned into flatlands. Atamarie was soothed by the sight of the vast green plains, behind which the southern mountains rose so close, you could almost touch them. She asked herself for the first time whether she might somehow be able to live in this area—because now it looked as if her soul mate might never leave.

Until then, she had assumed that Richard's life as a farmer was just an episode. After all, the man was a gifted engineer. He belonged in a city, at a university. And it was the same for Atamarie. Life on the farm was like life in Parihaka for her: it was nice for a while, but she did not want to grow old among chicken coops and tedders or hand looms and *haka*. Atamarie wanted to build machines, or, at least, survey land. She wanted a proper workshop and to exchange ideas with like-minded people. She wanted to finish her studies and take part in all the exciting innovations the new century had to offer. Atamarie did not just want to be with Richard. She wanted to fly with him.

By the time the young woman had finally reached the *marae* of the local Ngai Tahu tribe, she had calmed down somewhat. She greeted the old people who were keeping an eye on the children while their sons and daughters were working in the fields, and then ran into a few women her age who were in the process of digging out *kumara* from a garden. Atamarie gladly helped with the harvest of the tasty sweet potatoes and was soon drawn into a conversation. The women wanted to know everything about the *pakeha* with whom Atamarie lived. And as always, with the tribes, no one minced words.

"Aren't you supposed to marry *pakeha* if you want to share a bed with them?" one of them asked.

"I don't want to marry yet," Atamarie replied. "Nor does Richard. But I, I would like to go away from here with him."

The girls nodded.

"He's a *tohunga*," one of the oldest mused. "He needs to wander to learn. But I don't know if he will. The *pakeha* here, they don't wander."

Atamarie sighed. No one could have said it better. Richard needed to go. In Temuka, people worked the fields; they did not conquer the sky.

***

On the way back to the farm, she set about making plans. They had foreseen trying the motor again the next morning—Atamarie had insisted on testing it in the workshop first and incorporating it back into the aeroplane only later. If it ran well, however, then nothing stood in the way of a flight attempt. Maybe they would even manage it before her vacation ended—though that would mean giving up on visiting her grandparents in Lawrence. Even if they achieved only minor successes, once they showed Dobbins the schematics for a finished flying machine, the professor would truly advocate for Richard. No doubt there was a position at the university, perhaps a research grant.

Atamarie got lost in her dreams of a fellowship for Richard and a final departure from the farm—until the stillness of the countryside was interrupted by an infernal racket. Then followed the clip-clop of hooves, and Atamarie only just managed to fling herself to the side as a mule team dashed past her. The animals dragged a plow behind them, to which a cursing Digory Pearse clung fast, trying desperately to control the animals.

Atamarie feared the worst. She began to run and spotted the trigger for the animals' panic just around the next bend. On a low hill above Richard's farm, the engine roared—and Atamarie saw to her shock and anger that Richard had reinstalled it in the aeroplane. The wings had only been provisionally repaired, and Atamarie's improvements had not yet been incorporated. Richard must have summoned monstrous energy to install the engine and pull the aeroplane up the hill in the few hours she was gone.

Atamarie wondered what this was all about. Did he want to prove something to her—or to himself or to his parents? It was plainly crazy to try taking off in the same contraption he had crashed a few weeks before. And, of course, he had harnessed the horses again. Atamarie screamed and waved for him to stop, but the horses were beside themselves with fear of the screaming motor. They pranced miserably in place while Richard climbed into his machine, then rushed in panic down the slope the moment Richard released their reins. Behind them, the flying machine trundled down the bumpy runway—which upset the air-to-fuel mixture, as Atamarie had learned. Attempts at flight in such machines had to happen on smooth roads, at least until carburetor technology improved.

Richard's attempt had no hope of success, but nevertheless, Atamarie followed the machine's acceleration with bated breath. It actually was now making a sort of hop, but Atamarie attributed that more to a bump on the path than true liftoff. The poor horses ran heedlessly, steering the machine in the direction of that same broom hedge before their lines disconnected and they could flee. The massive hedge then arrested the three-wheeled vehicle's motion once again, but this time, Richard crashed with much greater force. The deafening sound of the motor died, and the sudden stillness seemed almost unreal. Nothing stirred beneath the wings.

Atamarie felt fear rising within her. She sprinted to the site of the accident and found Richard slumped forward in his seat. He was bleeding from lacerations on his forehead.

"Richard!"

Atamarie's heart raced. She hastily undid the belt that held him in his seat, but he still did not budge. Atamarie dragged him out but could not stop him tumbling from her arms.

"Don't die, Richard. Please, don't die."

Atamarie cried as she opened his shirt, unsure what to do. Richard's heart seemed to be beating, but she had to get him to a hospital.

"What's wrong with him? Is it bad?" Atamarie shook with relief when she heard Peterson's voice behind her. "Dear Lord, girl, is he dead?" The farmer bent over his neighbor. "Not yet, anyway. He does have an awfully hard head. Now, come on, Dick, wake up."

He shook the injured man, which frightened Atamarie even more. Richard did not react. Atamarie insisted on laying him down flat on the ground.

"He needs a doctor, a hospital. Is there a hospital here?"

Atamarie looked around as if one could somehow be hiding in the next barn.

"In Temuka," Peterson said. "Wait here. I'll pull up the wagon if the nags are brave enough. They've started getting used to Cranky's machines. A few more crashes, and they'll pass by like it's nothing."

Atamarie cradled Richard's head in her arms while Peter brought his hay wagon. The farmer laid the wounded man on a few old sacks. Atamarie rode with Richard, holding him tight as the wagon rumbled over the uneven pastures before they reached the relatively even paths and then the roads. Sitting in back spared Atamarie from having to answer Peterson's commentary on Richard's renewed attempt at flying.

"He can't leave it alone. I thought as much when I heard the engine. And then the jades running through the brush as if chased by the furies. Hope somebody catches them before they break a leg. Anyway, I came straight. Got lucky, old Dick did, that I was only three fields off. But his dad must have been somewhere nearby too."

Atamarie could have confirmed that, but, for the moment, she was not worried about Digory and his riled-up mules. The miles to Temuka stretched on endlessly, and Peterson did not drive very fast. He laughed when Atamarie implored him to speed up.

"If we break an axle, that won't get us to town any quicker," he noted with equanimity. "And Dick, he'll wake up. It's the luck of the Irish, girl. Probably, the kid'll outlive us all."

Still, Atamarie thanked the gods when they finally reached the little hospital and two orderlies loaded Richard onto a stretcher. The doctor's eyes grew wide as Atamarie breathlessly told him the story.

"He flew? So, he fell?"

Atamarie shook her head. "Not exactly, but it doesn't matter. Please do something. He might have cracked his skull."

The doctor disappeared into his treatment room with Richard but soon returned with a question.

"Are you his wife? Or a relation?"

Peterson stepped in. "No, she's just a Maori girl who lives with him."

Atamarie looked at the man in shock. She was what? That made it sound like she was some kind of girl of easy virtue with whom Richard was enjoying himself a bit before entering a serious relationship.

"An employee?" the doctor clarified.

Peterson shook his head and grinned. "Nah," he said again, and made a hand gesture so obscene that the blood shot to Atamarie's face.

"I'm—" she started.

At that moment, the door opened, and Richard's mother rushed inside, followed by her husband, who looked badly scraped up himself. His wild ride on the plow must have ended in a hedge too.

"How is he? How's Dick? Is he—? He's not—?"

Sarah Pearse was pale as death, whereas Digory Pearse simply seemed angry. He seemed to share Peterson's belief that a family never lost its black sheep.

"A bad concussion and a broken arm, but he'll recover, not to worry. But, again, how did this happen? The young woman seemed a little confused. Or is it the language? She's Maori? Doesn't look like it."

He eyed Atamarie with a probing, almost lecherous gaze. Atamarie felt rage welling up within her. Once again, people were treating her as if she were not even present, or at most, an object. She glared at the doctor.

"I'm a fellow student of Mr. Pearse," she explained as calmly as she could, "a student of engineering at Canterbury College in Christchurch. And yes, this happened in an attempt to get a flying machine to take off. We—"

"Don't listen to her. The girl's as mad as my son," Digory Pearse interrupted her, turning to his wife. "I told you from the start we shouldn't tolerate their living in sin. But no, you said it was better that people talk about him whoring around than being crazy. And now it's both! Soon, we won't be able to show our faces in public. But I'm taking a different tack now. For starters, get gone, young lady. You weren't very helpful, you know."

"I wasn't what?" Atamarie asked, too astounded to argue.

Sarah Pearse turned a pale, haggard face to her. She did not seem hateful like her husband, only resigned.

"I thought you'd prevent things like this," she said to Atamarie. "I thought—dear Lord, I wouldn't even have had anything against you two getting married. Whether you're Maori or not. You don't look it, anyway. If only he—if only he'd finally be normal. But my husband's right. You've only made everything worse. Go, Miss Turei. And stay away. It's better if he never sees you again."

***

Atamarie let herself be turned out of the hospital without resistance. She knew she should have put up a fight, but after the last few hours, she lacked the strength. That the people here rejected her, she could have lived with that—if only they were not so underhanded. Atamarie recalled their feigned friendliness, but also what she had felt since the beginning: they had only accepted her because she seemed useful. And Richard's parents would never be able to accept him as he was. Yet, this fact, which before had filled her with pity, now made her angry. Richard, too, had betrayed her. His senseless, doomed-to-failure flight attempt had been meant to show her that he could do it without her. That he did not need her, that her ideas regarding his life did not affect him any more than her suggestions for improving his aeroplane. He did not love her. Clearly, he did not love her.

Blinded by tears, Atamarie ran down the street. She would have preferred to jump on the next train, but she had to return once more to Richard's farm for her things and her money. So, she walked for hours, hiding at the edge of the road when a wagon rolled by. She refused to see that cad Peterson again. She still felt sick, thinking about his obscene gesture.

It was night before she reached Richard's farm. The horses had returned and were waiting at the stable doors. They did not seem very hungry. As Atamarie unharnessed and locked them up, she vengefully hoped they had eaten their fill in Joan Peterson's garden.

After she'd packed up her things, Atamarie took a last look at the flying machine, which hung in the hedge like a broken bird. Should she take the plans she had sketched and show them to Dobbins? She decided against it. Richard would have to fight his battles himself. With regret, she cast an eye over the workshop. She had been so happy there.

The Blessing of the Gods

Karenstad,
Africa
Dunedin, Parihaka,
Christchurch, Temuka,
New Zealand
1902–1903

Chapter 1

"Well, at least he's not a dowry hunter."

Heather Coltrane's remark surprised Atamarie. She'd needed to talk to someone at home about Richard, and Roberta was in South Africa. Aunt Heather and Chloe were more worldly than most. They might even have an explanation for Richard's bizarre behavior. She had expected every possible reaction except for Richard practically finding grace in Heather's eyes.

"But why would he? I don't—" She stopped. Her aunt was right: from a financial standpoint, Richard could not have done any better than asking for Atamarie's hand. Atamarie had never given much thought to money, but of course, her family was well off. Kupe made good money as an attorney and member of Parliament, and Matariki was paid for running the school in Parihaka. Neither ever spent much, so they had significant savings. Atamarie could count on a proper dowry—and support for her research besides. Though Kupe and Matariki lived a life focused on the traditions of their people, they were not narrow-minded like the Pearses. "Damn it, you're right. I could have helped him!"

Chloe groaned, surely thinking of Colin Coltrane, who'd abandoned Matariki to marry Chloe for her money.

"It's a good thing you didn't think of it," she said drily. "I don't want to imagine what would have happened if you'd financed him too. Now at least you know where you stand. Richard doesn't care about you. So, forget him and find someone else. Or build your own aeroplane if you know how! Why waste all your talent building a man's for him?"

"But I need him. I'd never be able to do it without him," Atamarie said plaintively.

Heather laughed. "I believed that once, Atamie," she said. "My Richard was named Svetlana. And in a certain sense, she was good for me. She helped me find out who I am and what I can do. But people like that—just think of them as engines. They help us get going. But if we get too close, they run us over. Besides, this Richard strikes me as weird—a man who never sleeps, who everyone else believes is crazy, who is calm for months and then can't get a grip on himself? Chloe's right. Forget him. Are you hoping to go to Parihaka too? Isn't your vacation over in a few weeks?"

Atamarie nodded, lost in thought. Maybe her relationship with Richard would have developed differently and could still develop if he only left Temuka. Maybe he needed to be out of sight of his farm in order to realize he was better off without his family.

"Three weeks is tight, for sure, particularly with all the time it takes to get there," she finally managed. "But I'm going to go anyway. I need a little of the 'spirit of Parihaka' after the small-town fug."

Chloe laughed. "Sounds like your Parihaka spirit frightened the small town. You could at least have rented a hotel room pro forma, you know. Or pretended to stay with the Maori or something."

Heather shrugged. "Eh, subterfuge would just have incited the villagers more. Stop brooding, Atamarie. Go to Parihaka. And not just for the spirit's sake. The village is full of good-looking young Maori men. One of them will help you forget Richard."

***

The very next day, Atamarie was back on the train without having visited anyone else in Dunedin—she needed to get to Parihaka. Her heart was pounding when they stopped at the station in Timaru. She wanted so badly to know how Richard was doing. But getting out and asking in the hospital was unthinkable. And his injuries had not been life threatening, after all. He could write to her himself if he wanted to be in contact. If not—Atamarie felt like crying, but she controlled herself. Her next steps had to lead away from Richard.

***

"People treat flying like a joke," Atamarie complained to her mother. Together they watched as colorful kites climbed above Parihaka. "But these are such fabulous *manu*. Is it my imagination, or do they stay in the air much better than they used to? And isn't kite flying just for New Year's, anyway? I thought it was *tapu* the rest of the time."

Matariki laughed. She was thrilled to see her daughter, although she could tell something was wrong. She hoped Atamarie would talk to her about it later.

"Nonsense," she answered her now. "You can fly *manu* anytime, as long as you sing the right *karakia* for it. And aside from conversing with the gods, people used to do it regularly, to send messages between the tribes. After the death of the founder of the Ngati Porou, the people in Whangara are supposed to have sent a *manu* into the sky that people saw all the way on the South Island. That way, Porourangi's brother, Tahu, the patriarch of the Ngai Tahu, would know to mourn him."

Atamarie looked somewhat skeptical. She had heard of such giant *manu*, which supposedly required thirty men to control. But were they just legends?

"Anyway, today's kite festival is just because Rawiri happens to be here," Matariki explained. "He's back from his wanderings in the north, where he studied with just about every *tohunga* famous for the construction of *manu*. Now he's considered a *tohunga* himself, and is instructing the village children this week—adults, too, if they're interested. You're surely welcome to participate."

Atamarie nodded. Rawiri seemed to be serious about flying. Or was it more about messages to the gods for him? Atamarie could no longer quite recall what he had told her back when she and Richard had pulled him out of the water, but at least some of it had sounded like spiritual nonsense to her. On the other hand, Rawiri was like her: he wanted to fly. Surely it would be interesting to hear what he had learned about kites. Maybe it would give her some insight into Richard's flying machine.

***

Rawiri's eyes shone when Atamarie reported as a student that evening. But she had eyes for only the kites, which the children were sending up to the stars with their messages to the gods. Atamarie made a face when the young *tohunga* instructed her with great seriousness in the singing of the proper *karakia*.

"As if that would change the laws of nature," she remarked to her mother later. "If the thing has the right aerodynamic form, it flies. If not, then it doesn't."

Matariki laughed. "Rawiri knows that as well as you. But look at it this way: the *karakia* serve to remind us of the laws of nature, to thank nature for giving us solid footing, but also for setting rules."

"But the rules are exactly what we're trying to overcome," grumbled Atamarie.

Matariki shook her head. "You were just saying that's not possible. And it's not. You can't conquer nature. But you can understand it better and make use of its laws. The dialogue with the gods helps with that—regardless of whether we send *manu* into the sky or say prayers while we harvest medicinal plants. All of it is right, Atamarie. Rawiri knows what he's doing. Trust him."

***

Rawiri was less sure of himself than Matariki. That night he asked the gods for their blessing, not for his kite but rather for him and Atamarie. He did not know if he should greet it as a coincidence or a gift from the gods that she had come back to learn the art of *manu* construction, but he knew he loved her. At the first sight of her beautiful, clever face, that warm, happy feeling he'd experienced after his failed glider flight welled up within him again. Since then, he had carried her image in his heart, and to his own dream of flying was added the dream of making her happy. Everything Rawiri had done since that day was in the name of this. It was not enough to experiment with kites he had made himself. He had to learn from the best. He had to become a *tohunga* just like Atamarie. For that was what she was going to be. Atamarie was learning the wisdom of the *pakeha*—and Rawiri would now offer her the wisdom of the Maori.

Rawiri could hardly wait for Atamarie's visit to his workshop now. Already before dawn, he was preparing aute bark and raupo leaves, as well as manuka and kareao wood for the frame. At first, only a few children appeared. Rawiri was bent over their work and so failed to notice Atamarie approaching. He started when he heard her voice.

"A hawk, a pinion, and a canoe," Atamarie said, listing the forms of the children's kites. "So, which flies best?" She lifted a *manu pakau* and eyed it critically. "The area of the sails on a flat kite is completely different from, for example—"

"The wind lends its power to every *manu*," Rawiri declared gently. Atamarie seemed particularly beautiful to him that morning. She wore her hair down over a traditional woven top, which she had paired with a wide green skirt. "But the *manu* does not steal the wind's strength. It merely channels it over his wings. The *manu* dances on the wind, or the wind pulls it upward."

"It rests on the airflow or uses the lift across its sail area," Atamarie translated into the language of science. "I want to know more about the latter. We also need that for the development of aeroplanes. And this box-shaped construction is interesting. The kites consist of several squares, right? To give them stability." Rawiri looked a bit uncertain, and Atamarie smiled apologetically. "It doesn't matter how one expresses it, of course," she said. "Just show me how it works."

She listened attentively to Rawiri's explanations, although he did not tell her much she did not know. In truth, she could have easily reconstructed the kite if someone had placed a prototype at her disposal. But she liked to listen to Rawiri's voice—melodic and soft, it reminded her a bit of Richard's. True, Richard had mostly spoken in frantic, staccato sentences, whereas Rawiri sounded almost like he was singing, but still. Atamarie let herself be charmed by the young man's passion for flight and almost felt as if she were back in Richard's barn.

***

Atamarie's kite was already finished by evening, a fact that Richard or Professor Dobbins would surely have admired, but which seemed to disappoint Rawiri. Though she had followed his technical advice, she had done her level best to ignore the spiritual side of kite building. The young *tohunga* transmitted the songs, invocations, or meditations traditionally bound up with each stage of work. The spirits of the winds and clouds wanted to be conjured. Now and again, one called on the power of the bird god and pleaded for his blessing.

Atamarie still wasn't having it. "The raupo leaves will grow back whether or not I earn the grace of the spirits of the bush."

"But it's about the principle," Matariki argued, and quietly sang to the *turu manu*:

> 'Fly on from me, my bird,
> dance restlessly on high,
> swoop down like the hawk upon his prey."

"It's beautiful, Atamie, really."

"It's a question of the oncoming airflow against the kite's sail," Atamarie replied. "And the thing's not supposed to dance at all. It would spin out too quickly. Help me a second, Rawiri. Should I have made the wings wider? For more stability?"

Atamarie had decided on the form of the birdman partly out of sentimentality, since it was Richard's name among the Maori, but also because it was the most similar to the *pakeha* gliders and so to Richard's future aeroplane.

Matariki rolled her eyes but was pleased to see that Rawiri was not discouraged by Atamarie's lack of spirituality. He continued his prayers, but also listened with interest to her scientific expositions.

"There, you see," Rawiri said as they both finally left their kites to test the previously discussed point of balance. "If the *manu* stands proudly upright and speaks with man, then you need more strength to hold it, though it will not truly climb. Like a man, who shows off his *mana* but does not possess the blessing of the gods. When the *manu* gives itself to the wind and bows to the spirits, then it will climb quickly."

Atamarie laughed. "That's what I said: the higher the kite's point of balance, the stronger the drag! When it lies flat, lift increases."

Matariki, who sat with her friend Omaka, laughed. "Everyone says prayers in their own language."

Omaka nodded. "But these two," she said, "are undoubtedly praying to the same god."

***

Atamarie had enjoyed her day with Rawiri and did not withdraw when, later at the fire, he began to court her. He chatted with her, fetched her food and drink—and with every sip of whiskey, Rawiri's poetic compliments touched her more deeply. After all, the young *tohunga* not only knew how to steer kites and flatter the gods with beautiful words but also how to describe his delight at Atamarie's gold-blonde hair, her eyes, which he compared to dark amber, and her hands with their long, skillful fingers.

"You must fly my kite. Your fingers will speak with it; they'll lead it and send it up into the realm of the gods. And it will convey to them my wish that one day you will also want to touch and lead and raise me to the peaks of love."

Under other circumstances, Atamarie might have let herself soften, lean on her admirer, accompany him on a walk in the hills, grant him a kiss. She might even have made love to him. She was, after all, no longer a virgin, and Richard's embraces had made Atamarie desire more. After her experiences in Temuka, though, she had grown suspicious. She knew that Rawiri would not condemn her if she offered him her body for a few nights. Maori women did not wait for their wedding nights to experiment with love, and before they had decided on a man, unequivocally and in front of the entire tribe, no one demanded monogamy of them. But the behavior of the villagers in the Waitohi Plains had shamed and hurt Atamarie. She did not want anyone to believe that she'd give herself to someone she did not truly love. And she was not in love with Rawiri.

***

The two did get closer over the next few days. They developed new kite designs together and researched the behavior of the various *manu* forms while gliding, but whenever Rawiri went to touch Atamarie, she pulled away.

"I'm sorry," she finally said on the last night of her stay, "but I was with a *pakeha* man, and I can't simply forget Richard so easily. He, I, we had so much in common. We wanted—I simply can't start anything new yet."

Rawiri nodded. "You two wanted to fly," he said understandingly. "You wanted to fly with him. Conquer the sky. Whereas I don't even speak your language. But I'll learn it, Atamarie." He indicated the copy of *Scientific American* Atamarie had loaned him, and which he had been studying ever since. "I'll learn to make *manu* according to your fashion and ask the gods to invite me to share the sky with them." He smiled mischievously. "I'll compete with your *pakeha*, Atamarie. And we'll see whose 'aeronautical devices'"—he pronounced the words from the magazine very slowly and precisely—"find grace in the eyes of the spirits."

***

Atamarie did not completely understand what Rawiri meant, but she still had his smiling face, framed by his long, dancing black hair, in her mind when she boarded the train a day later.

Chapter 2

The news of the concentration camps' dissolution spread like wildfire in Karenstad. It unleashed joy but also new anxieties about the future. Like Doortje, many women would find neither home nor husband nor father when they returned to their land. Cornelis moreover feared ostracism or worse, especially as his leg had fully healed. There was no urgent reason for Cornelis to return to his village, anyway; though he would inherit his father's land, he had never felt called to be a farmer. Still, he wavered between his desires and his sense of duty: his mother had survived and saw it as a given that he would rebuild the farm, look for a wife, and possibly take other older relatives into the household.

This idea was frightful to Cornelis. He would prefer to apply for a post, maybe as an interpreter, to earn a little money for a college degree. Perhaps even the veterinary studies he so yearned for. Daisy supported him in that dream—even if she would have preferred to see him become a doctor. To general amazement, she requited his affection. No one would have expected the lively woman to fall in love with the serious man. But it seemed to please Daisy to have the reins, and she directed Cornelis softly but decisively.

"I could consider staying here," she declared one day. "It's a lovely country. But I wouldn't want to live in the middle of the veld. It would have to be one of the cities. You can decide, Cornelis: to Cape Town, Johannesburg, or Pretoria with me—or with your mother on a farm."

Daisy flirtatiously brushed back a strand of her black hair, which had fallen loose from her demure nurse's bonnet. No one doubted what Cornelis would choose. No one except Doortje van Stout.

***

Doortje viewed Cornelis's courting of the young nurse with suspicion, but she could not really imagine that it was anything serious. She had begun to make her own marriage plans. For all the hesitant feeling Doortje nursed for Kevin Drury, when she looked at her future realistically, really only a marriage to Cornelis was possible. It presented obvious advantages to her and to him: Doortje would be taken care of, and Cornelis could decide whether he wanted to rebuild his or her farm. The van Stout farm was closer to Wepener, which would surely become an agrarian center again once the English withdrew. No one there knew Cornelis well, so they would not accuse him of cowardice. He could live esteemed in the parish and no doubt even deck himself in church offices.

Doortje would surely forget Kevin Drury in the shortest of times and be a good wife to her cousin. She could live with her aunt Jacoba as a mother-in-law. Martinus's mother had also been very demanding, and Doortje had been prepared to marry into his household. For Boer girls, this was expected. Several generations lived together on the farms without complaining. No women lived alone in Boer society—Cornelis had obligations to his cousin on this point as well. If he and his family did not take her in, Doortje stood before the void.

But then came the news that Cornelis wanted again to betray his people. Doortje was in the hospital cleaning syringes when Daisy gleefully reported her engagement. The young woman did not even notice the awkward silence of the Boer nursing assistant—she merely glowed at Dr. Greenway's friendly well-wishes.

"And I'll talk him out of veterinary medicine," Daisy declared, beaming. "He can become a proper doctor, you see, and then we can open a practice together or work in a hospital."

Daisy herself had absolutely no intention of giving up her profession. On the contrary, if Cornelis was going to start his studies, she needed to be the one making money for the first few years.

For a Boer woman, such an arrangement was unthinkable. Doortje grew dizzy as she considered the consequences of Daisy's cheerful revelation. Pale as a ghost, she dropped the tray with the syringes. Everyone looked at her as the glass broke on the ground.

"But that's not possible," stammered Doortje. "He has to know that I—he is, after all—"

Doortje wanted to speak of the obligations of her only living male relative, but she stumbled and fell to the ground, grateful for the merciful oblivion.

However, her awakening was to prove even more frightful.

***

"Nurse Daisy, if I'm interpreting correctly what Miss van Stout wanted to say, I must ask, as much as it pains me: Is your affianced the father of her baby?"

Doortje heard Dr. Greenway's voice as if from far off as she slowly came back to consciousness. A baby? This English hussy was already pregnant? Doortje groaned. If Daisy was pregnant, there was no way out. Cornelis really would go away with her, and—

Daisy, however, protested indignantly.

"Most certainly not. If there had been something between her and Cornelis, I would have noticed. And she still seems cross with him."

Doortje was confused. About whom were they speaking?

"Perhaps for reasons of a failed, uh, relationship?" Dr. Greenway speculated.

"Nonsense."

Doortje felt Daisy arranging something in her bed. Was she giving her an injection? Was she ill? Would she die too?

"Anyway, Doctor, you said yourself she was six months or so along. Has Cornelis even been here that long? And why did she keep it a secret?"

Doortje summoned all her strength and opened her eyes. She tried to sit up, but Dr. Greenway pressed her gently back into the bed.

"Lie back, Miss van Stout. Rest. You need to think of the baby."

Doortje shot up. "The what?"

***

"I can't believe we didn't notice." Kevin paced restlessly. "Fifth or sixth month?"

Greenway uncorked the whiskey bottle. "Calm yourself, Drury. The young woman didn't even know herself. I was there; her surprise was genuine. And it certainly is possible. The women hardly ever undress in their cramped tents. Not to mention, bloated stomachs are common with malnutrition. That wouldn't have stood out to us. The period can fail to occur for the same reason, but you know that. We don't have anything to blame ourselves for. That is, as long as neither of us is the father."

Kevin let out a pained grunt. "Not this time," he remarked, and took a gulp of whiskey. "But the paternity is obvious, Greenway, when you consider how Doortje and Johanna arrived here. We know they were raped."

Greenway slapped his forehead. "Of course. And idiot that I am, I suspected Cornelis." He poured more whiskey. "Heavens, that only makes it worse. Any child out of wedlock would complicate Miss van Stout's life monstrously. But the fruit of such violence—"

Kevin rubbed his temples. "Is there at least someone with her now? To ensure she doesn't do herself harm like her poor sister?"

Greenway nodded. "Miss Fence. We had her sent for. Nurse Daisy was available, but the two women have a somewhat, hmm, unsettled relationship. Apparently, Miss van Stout wanted to marry Cornelis herself."

"She wanted to do what?" Kevin shouted. "Doortje van Stout wanted to marry Cornelis Pienaar? Who told you that?"

Greenway shrugged. "Mrs. Vooren, the nursing assistant. You know, the little Boer girl who's not even twenty years old and already has three kids? A very bright young woman and not as bullheaded as the others. Miss van Stout passed out from a circulatory disruption while Nurse Daisy was announcing her engagement, and I wondered if there was a connection. Mrs. Vooren confirmed it. That's why I assumed—but it seems to have been more a question of familial duty than of love."

Kevin set his glass on the table. "I'll go to her," he said. "She must be in complete despair. Perhaps I can help."

He acted as if he did not see Greenway's inquisitive looks as he rushed to the door, but then turned around at the last moment and grabbed the book about New Zealand.

"It might distract her a bit."

Greenway smiled. "Well, good luck, then, Drury."

***

It was already dark when Kevin walked over to the hospital, but the main rooms were lit by oil lamps. One of them was also burning in the screened-off room where Doortje lay. Roberta sat beside the bed, reading a book.

"Don't ruin your lovely eyes reading in such miserable light, Roberta," Kevin remarked amiably.

Roberta looked up when she heard his voice, and he was charmed anew by how cute and earnest she really was. When he saw Doortje's narrow face on her pillow, framed by the luxuriance of her unbound hair, however, he forgot Roberta. He beheld Doortje without a bonnet for the first time, bewitched by how much younger the long, blonde strands made her look. Doortje had her eyes shut, but her face was tense.

"Is she sleeping?" Kevin asked.

Roberta shook her head. "No. She doesn't want to talk. She doesn't want to believe it, either. But—can you really not realize you're pregnant?"

Kevin thought he saw a twitch in Doortje's facial muscles. He pulled himself together.

"Yes, Roberta, it can happen. In certain circumstances. And I, well, I'll stay here with her. If you'd be good enough to leave us."

Roberta felt the old pain again. When she had been told of Doortje's pregnancy, she had felt something almost like triumph, although she was ashamed of it. Doortje was pregnant by someone else. Perhaps she would push Kevin away. And he would forget her or seek comfort elsewhere. Roberta felt guilty about Vincent. He'd recently begun to win her over a bit, but if Kevin did turn to her now—but Roberta did not want to begin dreaming anew. She had been trying so hard to let her feelings for Kevin die.

She stood up. "Of course," she said stiffly. "I can come back later."

Roberta left the room but stopped outside the curtain. Her heart was pounding, and she was ashamed of eavesdropping. But she had to know.

***

Doortje opened her eyes when she was alone with Kevin.

"You believe me?" she asked weakly.

Kevin nodded. "I told you that you could trust me and that I wanted to trust you. So, I believe that you didn't know anything about this pregnancy. But what's all this nonsense about Cornelis Pienaar?"

Kevin pulled the chair he had taken from Roberta closer to Doortje's bed. He had to stop himself from brushing the hair out of her face. How badly he wanted to touch her, to comfort her.

"Cornelis isn't the father," Doortje said tensely. "Tell your little nurse. There's no reason for her to doubt him."

Kevin shook his head. "Of course not. Doortje, you and I know how this baby came to be. And I'm so very, very sorry. But now you need to make a decision. What do you want to do? How will your future look now that you have the baby?"

"I don't want the baby." Doortje sat up. "I don't want to have it." She bit her lip hard and balled her fists. Any other woman in Doortje's situation would have broken out in tears, but instead, Doortje looked angry and wildly determined. "I won't give birth to it. I—" She broke off.

Kevin laid his hand on hers, very carefully.

"The baby won't ask if you want to give birth to it," he said softly. "It's there. You can't change that. If we had noticed it earlier, then perhaps we could have, hmm, encouraged a miscarriage. But now, it has been growing inside you for nearly six months. It should already be moving. Does it not, Doortje?"

Doortje nodded reluctantly. Until then she had thought the rumbling was a bellyache from the months of strange food and bad water.

"There, you see. In three months, it will come into the world. And it will be just as beautiful as you, Doortje."

"Its father is a monster," Doortje blurted out.

"But its mother is an angel," Kevin said. "You will love it, Doortje."

"I'll hate it. I'll take it to the veld and leave it to the vultures."

"Your God forbids it," he said.

Doortje laughed angrily. "You dare hold that against me? In this camp? In this war?"

Kevin shrugged. "The baby can't do anything about the war. And we two, didn't we agree not to be enemies?"

"It will starve anyway," Doortje declared. "No family will take it in, and no one will take me in either. I can try to sell the farm—or what's left of it. But the money won't last forever."

"Won't your church help you out?"

Kevin knew the answer already. No puritan parish would support a fallen woman, whether or not the woman was at fault for her misery.

Likewise, Doortje didn't dignify the question. "Dr. Drury," she said, "for me, there are exactly two possibilities. I can walk into the river like Johanna, or I can make my living like the whore the British have made me." Deep red spread across her pale face.

Kevin could no longer stand it. "You could also come with me to New Zealand," he said hoarsely. "As my wife. I love you, Doortje van Stout." He smiled, perhaps to give himself courage. "Really, you must already know. There's nothing I would like more than to marry you."

Doortje looked at him uncomprehendingly. "With this baby?" she asked, choked up.

Kevin nodded. "Of course. It would grow up as our child." He thought guiltily of Juliet and Patrick. "If we married here, no one would have to know anything. I would recognize the child, and I would love it."

"Love?" Doortje spat the word out. "This? This devil's spawn?"

Kevin took her hand between both of his and pressed it firmly. It felt cold and delicate despite the calluses from lifelong work in the kitchen and stables. There was no comparison to Juliet's beautiful hands with their long, manicured fingers.

"The child is blameless, Doortje. For me, this baby will be the most beautiful on earth just because your smile will fall on it when you hold it in your arms."

"It won't have anything in common with me," Doortje cried. "It will be English and grow up English like its father." Hate blazed again in her eyes.

Kevin sighed. "New Zealander," he corrected her. "And if you like . . ." He had to swallow his pride, but he would have done anything for Doortje. "If you like, we could live on a farm. My parents have one, and it's very beautiful there. I'm no farmer, but I could open a practice in town. Then the child could grow up in the country like you did."

Doortje shook her head fiercely. "It won't be a Boer," she moaned. "It can't be a Boer."

Kevin took a deep breath. "That's true, it can't," he replied. Not fiercely, but too quickly. He could not hide from her that he did not regret this fact. Kevin had fallen in love with Doortje, but he still lacked sympathy for her people.

At this, Doortje fell silent. She went to pull her hand out from under his. Kevin pulled it to his lips before he let it go.

"Think about it, Doortje," he said quietly, laying the book on New Zealand next to her on the sheets. "I'm not a Boer, and our son won't be one. His country won't be in Africa, and no one will tell him he's God's chosen or whatever. But New Zealand is also a beautiful country, and his grandmother knows a lot of stories about it. She'll tell him about Papa and Rangi and their true love and about Maui who caught massive fish and tried to outsmart death. And when the Pleiades appear, we'll fly kites. It could be beautiful, Doortje. Think about it."

Doortje did not answer, but she did not turn away. Slowly, she put her hand on the book.

***

Outside, in front of the curtain, Roberta rubbed the tears from her cheeks. No matter whether Doortje said yes or no, Kevin would never be hers.

Chapter 3

Atamarie thought back on Rawiri's friendly face often in the following months—when she despaired at Richard's silence. No letter came from Temuka, and sometimes it was all she could do to keep from writing herself. Atamarie could not come to terms with it simply being over. They had so much in common. She could not imagine Richard throwing all of that away.

And then, almost half a year after her forced departure from Richard's farm, there was a letter waiting one day when she got home from the university. Atamarie ripped it open with trembling hands and felt her heart beat faster when she saw his large, boldly rounded letters. From Richard, a few words filled an entire page; this time, he needed four just to apologize for his behavior.

> *I don't know what got into me. I didn't want to shut you out. But I just had to try to get the flying machine in gear. In truth, I wanted to surprise you, Atamarie, fly to you. And now, I've only disappointed you. I understand if you don't want to see me anymore, but perhaps we could, at least, start writing letters again. Yours always meant a lot to me.*

Atamarie was surprised Richard did not write anything about his family, but perhaps they had not told him what happened after his crash. He probably thought she had simply walked away after hearing about his stupidity. It offended her that he could believe she would act so childishly, and she was still hurt by his long silence, which he did not even mention. On the other hand, she was happy he'd resumed contact. Even if his letter did not contain any lover's oaths. She told Heather and Chloe of the letter—and was sobered when they both advised her to throw it away at once.

"Atamie, he didn't write that you mean a lot to him, only that your letters do," observed Heather. "Probably, you mostly quote Professor Dobbins. He should correspond with the professor himself."

"But if you do write him, be sure to tell him everything that happened," Chloe added. "How his family treated you and how his neighbors acted. Maybe that would bring him down from the clouds for once. And don't compromise. If he really wants you, he needs to move to Christchurch or some other big city."

Atamarie nodded. "If he wants to fly too," she said wearily.

***

She did write, though she couldn't bring herself to tell him about how she'd been treated. Furthermore, the subject of flying remained taboo between them. The young man seemed to have given up his dream for the time being. The aeroplane had been badly damaged during his last attempt to take off, and Richard had lost his courage after the serious injuries. In any case, he seemed to have shifted focus to farming machines. He proudly wrote Atamarie about new patents and how even Peterson used his improved hay tedder now. He was currently working on a new type of manure spreader.

Atamarie told him about her studies at Canterbury College. Machine construction was on her schedule, which interested her a great deal more than land surveying. Dobbins and the other instructors were introducing their students to the secrets of the steam engine—and then, near the end of 1902, Dobbins brought a surprise with him into the lecture hall.

"Here," he announced proudly, "gentlemen, and our lady, an Otto engine—or rather a spark-ignition engine. We'll be occupying ourselves for some time studying how something like this works, what applications these motors have in automobile construction, and—"

Atamarie's hand shot up.

"That's a two-stroke engine, sir, isn't it? With twenty PSI?"

Dobbins smiled. "Twenty-four, Miss Turei. But it sounds like you've already had some experience with such motors. Would you like to tell us something about them?"

Atamarie faltered a moment. "Yes—no, later. I really wanted to ask something."

"Go on."

Atamarie stood up so she could better see the compact engine.

"How much does it weigh?" she asked breathlessly.

***

"You want to do what?"

A few days after the beginning of the next summer vacation, Heather and Chloe and Rosie stopped by Atamarie's lodgings. They were on their way to the racetrack in Addington. The little mare Trotting Diamond was going to make her debut, and Rosie could hardly contain her excitement. Heather and Chloe had planned to invite Atamarie to go with them, but they found her already sitting on packed bags, an Otto motor in the middle of her room.

Her agitated landladies had told Heather and Chloe all about it when they rang at the door.

"We've never said anything about the oil stains on Atamarie's clothes, even when they get on our furniture. But this hellish machine! We almost fell out of bed when she started the thing. 'Just to try it out.' Please talk to her. That thing has to go."

As for that, the landladies had nothing to fear. Heather and Chloe were flabbergasted when, by way of greeting, Atamarie at once launched into her plans for the motor.

"It only weighs one hundred twenty pounds," she announced proudly, "and it runs totally smoothly. It lasts too. It's simply ideal for—"

"Start again, Atamarie, without the technical details." Heather sat down on Atamarie's bed. "You want to give this to Richard Pearse for Christmas?"

"Yes! And it was really cheap. Well, I had to ask Mom for money, of course, but I could easily—" She stopped. Not even Heather was allowed to know about the gold source on Elizabeth Station. "Well, I could earn enough if I took some job during vacation," she corrected herself. "Dobbins says the institute is going to get a newer one next year. The things are progressing at a rapid pace. But so far, no one's had the idea of putting one in an aeroplane. Except Richard. Only, he couldn't afford one. But now, now we have a motor! And it's so light. Don't you understand? We're going to fly."

Chloe shook her head. "All I understand is that you want to go back to that backwater where everyone hates you," she replied. "To a man you haven't seen in almost a year, though he could easily have taken the train to apologize properly in person. We already told you, Atamie: if you're so convinced you can fly, then build your own machine. But this Richard—"

"Is a genius," Atamarie insisted. "Chloe, Heather, we could be the first. We could be the first to take off in a motorized aeroplane. We—"

"And then he'll love you?"

Chloe looked at Atamarie. Her face was very serious.

Atamarie lowered her head. "He doesn't have to," she said defiantly.

Heather sighed. "Well then, good luck. I'll help you get this monstrosity shipped to your 'genius.' After all, you cannot simply take it in the train compartment."

Atamarie smiled gratefully.

"Besides, I'm coming with you," Heather continued, at which Atamarie's smile was replaced with dismay. "I want to see the man myself. Chloe can ride with Rosie to Addington before she bursts with excitement. I don't know much about racing, anyway."

***

Atamarie and Heather arrived by train in Timaru. A freight company would deliver the motor. Atamarie had telegraphed Richard and hoped that he would pick up both the women and the motor in town, but Heather rented a hotel room straightaway.

"And you'll do that in the future if you visit him," she advised Atamarie. "Of course, everyone will assume that you're spending the night at Richard's. But you have to keep up appearances."

Atamarie wanted to reply to that, but then she stopped. Richard's horse team was turning down the main street in Timaru. Heather held on tightly to her niece's skirt to keep her from running toward him.

"Keep your composure, child," she ordered. "Let him come to you."

So, Atamarie waited obediently next to her aunt until Richard had climbed down and greeted her. He behaved as if she had been gone for no more than a weekend and kissed her on the cheek like a friend.

"Where is it?" he asked before Atamarie could introduce Heather. "And it really only weighs one hundred twenty pounds? I can hardly believe it, Atamie!"

"The marvel still hasn't arrived," Heather remarked. "So, you can have a cup of coffee with us first while you wait. My name is Heather Coltrane, by the way. I'm Atamarie's aunt."

Judging by Richard's face, Atamarie had either never mentioned her family, or he had simply not been listening when she spoke of things other than technology. Now, however, he caught himself, apologized for his rudeness, and led the ladies to the nearest café, where he politely made conversation. Heather tried to sound him out a bit, but his answers were vague. Why yes, he had inherited a farm, so to speak, and now worked it. Sure, he would have rather been an engineer, but there was not much he could do about it now. He was now resigned to seeing inventing as a pastime.

Heather did not let her feelings show but occasionally looked at Atamarie with concern. Did her niece really not see how little Richard's plans for the future didn't fit with her own? The young man seemed unwilling to part from his soil any time soon. Yet Atamarie sat with beaming eyes next to her friend and appeared overjoyed that he held her hand under the table. Only, Heather had seen that she had felt for his hand, not the other way around. Nor did Heather recognize any signs of his being in love with Atamarie. She attributed Richard's obvious excitement to the business of the motor. He could hardly wait to retrieve it from the local general store.

As they approached, the driver was just then unloading it from the wagon, reverence all over his face. Atamarie and Richard quickly fell into a lively technical discussion. Heather turned away from their obsessing and to the driver of the freight wagon. The tall, square-built man seemed vaguely familiar to her.

"Can I pay you, or is it better to arrange that with your employer in Christchurch?"

The man's grin covered his whole round face. "I'm the employer," he declared proudly. "It's just one of my workers couldn't make it, madam, so I made the delivery myself. If you'd go ahead and sign the papers for me, Mrs.—"

"Miss," Heather said, straining to recall how she knew this man. Interestingly, he seemed to be in a similar predicament. At least, he was paying her signature an unusual amount of attention. Then, however, the decisive epiphany came when she saw the inscription on his delivery wagon.

"Bulldog Delivery—Strong and Quick for Your Freight"

Heather smiled. "Bulldog? Can it be that my stepfather gave you that name when we all traveled together from London to Dunedin?"

The man beamed. "That's right! You're Reverend Burton's daughter! I slept in your church."

Heather laughed. "Well, not in mine. Didn't you plan to look for gold?"

Almost twenty years before, Peter and Kathleen had traveled to England on a matter of inheritance, and Heather had accompanied them. On the return voyage, Violet and her family had also been on the ship—in steerage, while the Burtons traveled first class. Heather had constantly worried about Violet and her little sister, Rosie, until a fifteen-year-old boy had begun to look after the two of them. Reverend Burton had called the boy Bulldog for his square frame—Heather never learned his real name. Now, the easygoing entrepreneur shrugged.

"Nothing came of it," he explained. "Like the reverend said'd happen. And then I remembered what he said. The others kept on going and going, but when I finally found just a little gold once, I used it to buy a mule. I'd ride out to the men who weren't panning in the main spots but somewhere out in the wilderness. I sold 'em whiskey, mostly." Heather nodded. She could picture it as clear as day. "But I'm no salesman. I prefer going across country. Now I've got five wagons, twenty horses."

Heather smiled. "I'm so happy to hear that. What is your real name, by the way?"

Bulldog grinned. "Tom Tibbs." He tugged blithely on his cap. "Could I ask you—"

"Heather?" Atamarie tapped her aunt on the shoulder. "We want to get going. You'll come to the farm, won't you?"

Heather turned her attention away from Bulldog and furrowed her brow. "Gladly, but we're not riding with Richard, Atamarie. We'll rent a chaise. My Lord, girl, people are already guaranteed to be talking." Heather pulled out her purse. "Forgive me, Mr. Tibbs. It was really nice to see you again. But now I need to take care of my niece before we become the talk of the town." She rolled her eyes. "Head over heels." Heather smiled as she counted out the money for Bulldog. "That's how you were for Violet back then, weren't you? She's doing very well. But now I really must—"

Heather said a friendly good-bye and made her way inside to ask the saleswoman about a rental stable. Bulldog was left behind with his questions. Although he did wonder how Violet was doing, he had not been in love with her.

When he thought of the girls back then, he did not picture the little beauty with her mahogany hair and bewitching blue eyes, but rather felt a small, shy hand in his own. Rosie had only touched him once—when a storm had tossed the ship here and there, and a couple of lowlifes had gone after the girls. But he still recalled how sweet she had been, how anxious and delicate. Something precious he had wanted to protect. He had been successful when it came to Rosie—at least on the ship. His own sister, Molly, he had not been able to keep safe.

Bulldog rubbed his forehead. He did not want to think of Molly, and it was better not to think of Rosie either. But he would have liked to know how she was doing.

***

Atamarie climbed obediently into the chaise Heather had rented while Richard drove his engine back to his farm alone. Nevertheless, the news of Atamarie's return had spread rapidly in Timaru—as had word that Cranky Dick was threatening to fire up his flying machine again.

A surprise was waiting for Atamarie when she finally arrived at Richard's farm. She had been worried about Heather's reaction to the place, which had surely gone to seed in her absence. However, a few things had changed since the last harvest. Disassembled farming equipment and engines still lay everywhere, but no animals wandered freely, and everything seemed tidier. The fields, too, which would soon be harvested, looked kempt. The solution to the riddle appeared in the form of young Hamene. Atamarie greeted him happily.

"Do you work here full time now?" she asked. "It was a good idea of Richard's to hire you."

Hamene, who had adapted enough to wear *pakeha* farm clothes and go without his long hair and warrior bun, smiled at her.

"It wasn't Richard's idea; it was Shirley's," he explained, "and the elders didn't have anything against my helping here. The *pakeha* can't do everything. He is a *tohunga*, after all."

Hamene gave his employer, who was about to unload the motor, an admiring look.

But who was Shirley? After brief reflection, the image of a short, stocky blonde woman came to Atamarie, one of the Hansley daughters. Atamarie had seen her a few times, but back then she had never exchanged more than a few words with Richard—let alone with Atamarie. Yet now she was opening the door to Richard's farmhouse as if doing so were completely natural.

Shirley was wearing an old-fashioned-style dress with a white apron. She gave Atamarie and Heather a forced smile.

"And what are you doing here?" Atamarie asked. She knew it was impolite, but she had lived so long on Richard's farm that she almost felt like the lady of the house.

Shirley returned her deprecatory gaze—for a moment, she eyed Atamarie just as disapprovingly as Atamarie had done with her. Then, however, she smiled again and raised her hands apologetically. Her face was round and somewhat childlike.

"Oh, I help out a bit," she replied. "Mr. Pearse and my parents, well, they thought Richard needed some help around the house. And that's certainly the case!" She giggled conspiratorially. "But please, do come in." Shirley stepped back and held the door open for her visitors. Heather gave Atamarie a questioning look. A young housekeeper in a bachelor's household? In Dunedin, that would have been unthinkable. "I've made something to eat, and if you like, you can stay the night."

Again, Atamarie met with a not-very-friendly sidelong glance, which she returned. She had never made a secret of sleeping there for weeks.

Atamarie sensed something like matchmaking afoot—not exactly in typical *pakeha* manner, but tailored precisely for Richard. Atamarie certainly would not put it past Richard's parents to adapt their moral position to serve their goals.

Ultimately, Atamarie decided to go help Richard and Hamene carry the motor into the barn. Richard placed it on a clean sheet and wanted to take it apart at once. But then Shirley appeared.

"Richard, my lands, you don't really mean to play with this thing now, do you?" she asked disapprovingly. "You have guests, Richard. I've made food. Eat with your guests now, and you can bother with that devilish contraption tomorrow."

To Atamarie's amazement, Richard obediently followed the woman into the kitchen.

Atamarie walked alongside him grumpily. "What is she, your nanny?"

Richard looked at her apologetically. "I do sometimes need someone to remind me of manners." He smiled and looked so mischievous that Atamarie was appeased at once. It did not sound as if he were sharing a bed with Shirley, at least. And the looks he exchanged with Atamarie, once the engine was out of sight, did not suggest there was another woman for him.

Besides, the local girl would not find the way to his heart through his stomach, Atamarie thought as she dug into the unimaginative food accompanied by unimaginative conversation. Mashed potatoes and ribs, cooked with too much salt. Shirley might have been a good housekeeper, but she was not a good cook.

"I'll be on my way back to the hotel. Do you want to come with me or stay here?" Heather asked Atamarie outright after the meal.

Atamarie was unsure. Her gaze wandered back and forth between Richard and Shirley.

"You mean to go?" Richard's voice sounded puzzled and disappointed.

Atamarie had to struggle not to blush under Shirley's withering look, but then her joy that Richard had clearly missed her won out.

"No," she said, "of course, I'll stay."

Shirley lowered her gaze, but then pulled herself together and smiled.

"As I said, everything's prepared," she remarked, pointing toward the bedrooms. "I'll be going now."

Shirley took off her apron with short, quick movements. She kept an iron grip on herself, but Heather, an exceptional observer, still saw the burning rage behind her feigned indifference.

***

In Richard's bedroom, Atamarie did indeed find a freshly made bed, and her night with her beloved did not disappoint. Again, Richard made love to her tenderly, taking his time. He finally whispered words of love to her, kissed and caressed her, and brought her as close to flying as was possible without an aeroplane. And once again, he seemed to forget everything as soon as he laid eyes on his engine the next morning.

Fortunately, Hamene was already there to feed the animals. He found nothing unusual about Richard disappearing into the barn with the briefest of greetings.

"He's speaking with the spirits," the tall Maori declared to Atamarie with reverence. "And it's not as with our *tohunga* who call on the gods and only receive their response in their own spirit. The gods answer Mr. Pearse quite loudly. It's true. I've heard it."

Atamarie smiled. She knew that Richard had been experimenting for some time with a phonograph, recording sound on wax discs. The technology was new, but he hoped to impress his mother by improving it enough to record the music of the family orchestra for posterity. Hamene must have been witness to a few of these attempts—and no doubt he had not heard about the invention of the gramophone. Atamarie began explaining the principle to him herself.

"Richard would also like to record the song of a *haka* or a prayer during a *powhiri*."

Hamene, however, only shook his head. "Why?" he asked. "To anger the gods? It won't please them if we no longer sing and dance ourselves but build a machine for it. Mr. Pearse has good reasons, I'm sure. And Waimarama says he needs the blessing of the gods to overcome his darkness. But honestly, I can't see the use of his inventions."

"Then why do you help him?" Atamarie asked. "I thought—"

Hamene shrugged. "Shirley says I should."

Atamarie saw the glint in his eyes. So, Hamene was in love with Shirley. But did he stand a chance? Or was it perhaps not for Richard's sake that Shirley was there? Was she looking for a way to be close to Hamene?

Chapter 4

Heather laughed at Atamarie when, that afternoon, she reported a possible romance between Hamene and Shirley. Beforehand, she had raved about her day in Richard's barn. It did look as if the motor was precisely what he had been lacking to make further innovations in the field of flying. She did not need to tell her aunt how happy he had made her the night before. Heather could see that in her shining eyes. As for Shirley, though, she did not let her niece get her hopes up.

"That girl and a Maori, Atamarie? You don't even believe that yourself. She's the embodiment of country living—a sort of saint—or at least, she might see herself that way. There she is, sacrificing herself for your Richard, only to have him run back to you with open arms. That requires grit. And she has her parents' blessing as well as his. Only Richard doesn't seem to be playing along. This is bizarre, Atamarie. Believe me, I've been all over, and I've known very eccentric people. But he—at first, I thought he might just be cold, but then, he practically panted over that motor."

Atamarie laughed. "He's definitely not cold."

Heather shrugged. "But nor is he some great lover in the romantic sense. The man is not right, Atamarie. Be careful. Plus, right now, the greatest danger comes from Saint Shirley sticking a knife in your back."

***

Atamarie did not take her aunt's concerns seriously but returned with her to Christchurch the next day.

They met Chloe in the White Hart Hotel, where she told them about Rosie. She had left the maid in the care of one Lord Barrington in Addington. Barrington was a British gentleman and a sheep baron who mostly left his farm in the hands of a capable manager while he devoted himself to the promotion of horse racing in New Zealand. He had offered Rosie a position working with his own horses, mostly to do Chloe a favor. Rosie herself would have preferred to get a job at a harness-racing stable with Trotting Diamond, but the lord rejected this.

"Do forgive me, Chloe. I know your, erm, husband was also part of this new, erm, movement, and there are certainly serious stables, but the trainers they have there—well, that awful fellow Brown is still around."

John Brown had organized the first harness races in New Zealand. In England, harness racing was considered a sort of racing for the common man. The rules had been confusing, and the riders, spectators, and referees sometimes came to blows. To people like Lord Barrington, this was abhorrent, and the racing union only very reluctantly opened its track to the harness racers. The movement, however, would not be stopped, and the events had eventually taken a more orderly and serious shape. A few years before, a new track in Addington had been built primarily for harness races, and since the consolidation of the two racing clubs, they had been planning larger, more lucrative events there. However, there were still shady characters to be found among the horse owners and trainers. And in Lord Barrington's view, Addington was full of them.

"And right after, we had a very unedifying encounter," remarked Chloe. "You remember Joseph Fence, Violet's son?"

Atamarie nodded. Her friend Roberta had sometimes talked about her brother. Violet had apprenticed him to a horse trainer when she left Invercargill with Roberta.

"An unpleasant child even then," Chloe continued, "just like his father. I thought I was having a stroke when I saw him on the racetrack. And Rosie went white as a sheet, the poor thing, but she got ahold of herself. I think she's over that unhappy business with Eric Fence."

Heather looked unsure. Rosie had hated and feared Violet's late husband. Neither Heather nor Chloe wanted to hear anything about it, but there was surely something to Joseph's claim that the girl had a hand in Eric's accident on the racetrack.

"Anyway, Joseph has a racing stable in Addington. Barrington thinks it's a den of thieves. And there could be no question of Rosie working with him, of course. I made a few allusions to their history, and, well, now Rosie's Trotting Diamond is stabled alongside Barrington's Thoroughbreds, and our Rosie is living in his servants' quarters. The Barringtons practically have their own town hall, you know."

"I know," Heather said with a laugh. She had contributed significantly to its decoration with oil paintings of noble racing horses.

"And next, little Rosie and her little horse are going to teach Roberta's brother the meaning of fear on the racetrack?" Atamarie asked. "I mean, based on what Roberta says about Joseph, and now Lord Barrington too—shouldn't we be worried?"

Chloe shrugged. "I trust Lord Barrington. He owns half the racetrack, not to mention half of Addington. No one would dare hurt someone under his protection. And it's time for Rosie to grow up. But now, what about you, Atamie? How were things in Temuka?"

Heather let her niece talk, and Atamarie delivered an enthusiastic report. She spoke of Richard's joy at their reunion and his excitement at the motor. Chloe listened silently but occasionally looked questioningly at her girlfriend.

"Do you intend to go back during vacation?" Chloe asked when she was done.

Atamarie played with her hair. "Of course," she replied. "It really was nice. And the motor—"

"No technical lectures, please," Chloe interrupted. "Automobiles are quite lovely—I got to ride in one, Heather! Lord Barrington isn't only crazy about horses. Anyway, I couldn't care less about how they work. I'm more interested in how things are working for you, Atamarie. In all honesty, I expected you to stay there, as crazy as you are for the young man. Is it because of this girl? The 'housekeeper'?"

"I don't know if there's anything between him and Shirley," Atamarie admitted, "but if so, then it's nothing very serious. I—" She spoke quickly before Heather or Chloe could protest. "I at least want to know how things progress with the engine, with the aeroplane. I'd like Richard to fulfill his dream. Then, he'll—"

"Then he'll love you back?"

Atamarie bit her lip. "Then, everything will be different."

***

After her brief visit to Richard's, Atamarie spent the first months of her break in Parihaka. She did not know whether she'd hoped to see Rawiri again or feared it. But to her amazement, the young *tohunga* was no longer there.

"Is he visiting kite makers again so he can sit at their feet and learn more *karakia*?" Atamarie asked Pania, Rawiri's mother. "He's already got the technique down, so no one's going to be able to make better kites than Rawiri, and no one can fly them better either, unless they can cut the strings and steer them with song."

Pania laughed. She was a doctor in Parihaka's hospital and had a similarly skeptical view of her son's excessive spirituality. "No more *tohunga*, Atamarie, which I'm grateful for, as much as I love Parihaka and open myself to its spirit. But really, I'd always pictured Rawiri at the university rather than singing prayers and crafting kites. Yes, I know it's one of our people's great arts, but as a full-time occupation? In any case, I'm thankful to you for pushing him in another direction. Since you visited us last time, Rawiri has subscribed to *Scientific American*, spent two semesters at the engineering school in Wellington, and now he's in the United States."

"He's where?" Astonished, Atamarie dropped the weirs she had been repairing to go fishing that afternoon. "In America?"

Pania nodded. "In a town called Dayton, wherever that is. But there's a factory, the Wright Cycle Company, and he's working there."

"He had to go to America to build bicycles? Couldn't he have done that in Auckland? I mean, America's a world away. First you have to go to China or somewhere over there, and then—"

"He was traveling for three months," Pania confirmed. "And don't ask me what exactly he's doing there. He must have arrived by now, but that's all I know."

Atamarie was amazed. "He always was strange," she remarked, and wondered with concern whether that applied to all the men she found attractive.

The rest of Atamarie's time in Parihaka passed without incident, although there were plenty of other men who courted her. But she did not want any further complications. And after three weeks of fishing, weaving, dancing, and jade carving, she had once again had enough, and decided, before the beginning of classes, that she ought to visit her relatives in Dunedin—Timaru being an easy stop along the way, of course.

***

With Heather's and Chloe's words in her ear, Atamarie rented a hotel room in Timaru and a horse to take her to Temuka, where she was completely surprised by Richard's transformation. He greeted her full of vim and vigor and seemed not to know whether he first wanted to pull his friend and beloved into the barn or into the bedroom. While Atamarie was in Parihaka, he had made himself intimately familiar with the motor and was now developing new plans for his flying machine. He was frenetic again, but, at the same time, somehow more relaxed. Atamarie was overjoyed when he drew her into the construction of the aeroplane. Richard had now decided once and for all against a double-decker, and his drawing almost resembled Rawiri's kites. Atamarie, however, thought the kite designs more elegant. She took a pencil and altered the plans slightly.

"Integrate more crossbeams and bring them in at an angle," she explained. "It's bamboo after all, Richard. The little bit of extra weight won't make a difference, and the aeroplane will gain stability."

Richard happily incorporated her suggestion. He declared euphorically that the flying machine's stability was better now than in any previous model. He had tested it by holding the machine by only one wing and pushing it along, which he then demonstrated. Again, she marveled at the enormous energy he summoned.

"It won't break off, even when I run quickly alongside it and let it run downhill. It'll work, Atamie. This time it won't all end in the broom hedge."

Atamarie giggled to herself, imagining what a sight Richard was presenting his neighbors, walking an aeroplane as one might a dog.

"They call it my 'Beast,'" Richard admitted, laughing when Atamarie made a comment to this effect. "And it simply has to fly this time, or I'll make an irrecoverable fool of myself."

Atamarie was happy that he was able to laugh at himself again. Richard seemed pleased and self-confident, and he was also doing better in everyday matters. Even without Shirley, who had yet to make an appearance. Nevertheless, the house was not even half as squalid as before. Atamarie still had to sweep and change the sheets before she felt halfway comfortable, but perhaps every bachelor's home was like this.

Hamene continued taking charge of the farm work. The young Maori looked crestfallen when she asked about Shirley.

"Richard sent her away," he said. "Or she left on her own. I don't know. Mr. Pearse is wildly angry about it, and Mrs. Pearse—"

Atamarie pricked her ears. "What did she say?"

Hamene raised his hands helplessly. "I don't know English that well. I only understood half of it. But it was about Richard being ungrateful. And that Shirley was there when he needed her, whereas you—"

"Well, sure, they ran me out of town," Atamarie exclaimed. "I would have been happy to stay with him."

Hamene looked at Atamarie seriously. "You wouldn't have liked it."

Atamarie frowned. "What?"

Hamene tugged on his lower lip. "After Richard came out of the hospital. It was, it was as if, as if he were dead. He didn't do anything. Not on the farm, not in the barn. He didn't speak with the gods either. Just sat there. Waimarama said the darkness had enveloped him. She prayed for him."

"He didn't do anything at all?"

Atamarie could hardly believe it. What about Richard's sleeplessness, his enormous energy, the overabundance of ideas he had always had. On the other hand, after getting out of the hospital, he had not written Atamarie for six months.

"Anyway, that's when Shirley came," Hamene continued. "And so, it slowly got better again. But now, she's gone."

"And Richard has me," Atamarie insisted. "He doesn't need her anymore."

Hamene looked at her skeptically but held his tongue.

***

In the months that followed, Atamarie came to Temuka more often, even long after her vacation was over. She happily followed how the work on the flying machine progressed. Richard no longer seemed impatient the way he had the year before, instead submitting his machine to countless tests before he finally tried it once again. Peterson rolled his eyes as he watched Cranky Dick, as he still called him, in his horse pasture. Richard rolled the flying machine down a hill, running after it and handling the control lever with lines firmly attached to it.

"Maybe that thing will pull your plow, at least," he teased. Then he spied Atamarie. "Oh, and our Miss Turei is back again." Atamarie was watching Richard's test run from a hill. "She's what gives you wings, right?"

Atamarie did not respond. She still disdained Peterson and was annoyed at being seen. During her last few visits, she had not caught sight of any of

Richard's family or neighbors, but now all their gums would be flapping again. It could not be helped, and Atamarie did not want to hide anymore. She suggested holding the first test flight closer to town, in front of the school.

"The road there is smooth, and there's a hill to roll down. Plus, there are always people around."

Richard, however, shied away from the attention. "I don't want them to laugh if it goes wrong again. It'd be best to do it secretly."

A few days before the big event, he began to doubt himself again. His father had just taken him to task. The endurance tests and attempts to steer the "Beast" had not escaped Digory Pearse's notice.

Atamarie huffed and gathered the silverware. She had cooked for Richard and eaten dinner with him, happy that he'd taken the time for that. She had been worrying anew of late because he had not been eating or sleeping.

"Secretly? The first flight in a motorized aeroplane? Richard, you're going to make history that day. Your name will be in every paper, and in fifty years, probably in every schoolbook and encyclopedia. But for that, you need witnesses. The best thing would be to find a photographer and invite a few newspaper reporters. This needs to be documented. Maybe we should give the aeroplane a name too."

Richard snorted. "A name? It's a machine, not a dog or horse."

"People name ships," Atamarie objected, "and zeppelins. It would be lovely if there were a name in the newspaper."

She energetically banished the thought flitting about her brain that Richard might name the aeroplane Atamarie, or at least Sunrise. He shook his head, however.

"Childish nonsense," he declared. "And besides, I need to take off before anything appears in the newspaper. Let me fly, and then you can tell the whole world, for all I care."

Atamarie was confident it would work, even if she would have done little things differently in its construction, which he had not addressed. Lately, Richard had been hypersensitive to criticism again. Atamarie never knew exactly where she stood with him. Fortunately, now he would finally be celebrating success and should be correspondingly euphoric. In fact, he brought her from one climax to another on the night before the renewed attempt at flight—he no longer seemed the querulous procrastinator of the last few days.

And then, the day was there. Atamarie and Richard used the morning to make final tests. Around midday, Richard surprised Atamarie by rolling the aeroplane a long way down the road toward town, stopping in front of the school, as she had suggested. Class had just ended, and the pair had a grateful audience in the schoolchildren. However, other spectators quickly assembled, too, when Richard made his first attempt to start the engine. Atamarie was horrified when it did not function right away. Everything had gone so well during their last test. Now the machine roared a few times before dying again.

Atamarie groaned. "What did you put in for fuel? A new mixture? Oh no, please don't say that. We agreed not to do any more experiments. Now we need to clean the spark plugs again. Shall I?"

She looked down at herself somewhat unhappily. For this memorable day, she had worn a simple but still-clean light-green dress. A reform dress, but one of Kathleen's creations, elegant and conservative. There was even a matching hat. Like this, Atamarie would not look too exotic should someone take a photograph, and the neighbors' talk would, she hoped, stay within bounds. Today, the talk should focus on Richard's attempt at flight and not on the woman at his side, which it would if she witnessed Richard's triumph in a shabby, oil-stained dress.

"I've got it," Richard snapped, as if Atamarie's offer insulted him.

She could clean cylinders and change oil just as well as he, but he did not seem to want to reveal that to his neighbors. More and more were assembling, and they did not have to wait for the first jeers. No wonder, since Richard was tinkering with his motor in front of everyone while Atamarie tried to make small talk. It was unbearably embarrassing to chat with Peterson and Hansley about the weather while Richard grew perceptibly more nervous. Atamarie worried about the winds that were picking up as well. It might influence the aeroplane's handling. In the end, what was it but a steerable kite supported by a motor?

Atamarie reflected that it probably would have been better not to start in the direction of the Pearse farm but in precisely the other direction, but she did not want to make any more suggestions to Richard. He was already tense enough. And then, when really no one was expecting it anymore, when the mass of spectators was beginning to disperse, the motor suddenly sprang to life.

Richard leaped into the pilot seat—here, too, he had undertaken improvements; greater mobility in the seat should prevent injuries in a crash—and the machine rolled forward. The spectators ran behind and watched as he lifted into the air. Atamarie could not contain herself. She screamed in quite unladylike excitement as the aeroplane rose, light as a bird, until it hovered some ten feet off the ground. Then, suddenly, she shook her head violently. Richard was fiddling with the elevator. He wanted to go even higher.

"Slowly, Richard," Atamarie roared, though she knew that he couldn't hear her. "Don't take such a steep angle, or it'll become unstable. It—"

It happened even as she was yelling. The machine's nose lifted up, and the aeroplane lost its balance, which was exacerbated by the wind now seizing it from the side. Richard's flying machine fell into a spin and crashed to the earth, landing in yet another broom hedge. The spectators who had just been dumbstruck broke into booming laughter.

"These hedges must have some irresistible magnetic force!" Peterson shouted. "Come on, men, let's go fish him out."

"But he flew this time," cried Atamarie. "You all saw it, didn't you? He flew!"

Hansley laughed. "Sure, sure, he flew. No offense, little lady, but if birds landed like that, they'd've all died out." The others joined in his laughter.

"He's just more kiwi than swallow, our Dicky," another neighbor scoffed—kiwis being flightless birds and blind to boot.

Atamarie had a terrible, sinking feeling. Even this incredible success would not make Richard's community respect him. What was more, he seemed to have injured himself. He held his shoulder as Peterson and Hansley pulled him out of the aeroplane. She decided not to pay any attention to the smirking spectators and threw her arms around Richard.

"You did it," she said, and tried to sound happy although his bowed posture and his empty gaze did not bode well. "You flew, Richard. You're the first. You're the first with a motorized—"

"I didn't fly," said Richard.

He sounded almost uninterested. He did not respond to Atamarie's embrace either. He let Peterson push him toward his wagon with a frozen gaze.

"We'll take you to the hospital instead. Something seems broken."

Atamarie tried again. "But everyone saw, Richard. Everyone can testify. You—"

"I didn't fly," Richard whispered.

Atamarie looked at him in shock as the men led him away.

Chapter 5

"Once again, Miss Turei. And this time slowly and from the beginning, and don't spare the details. Richard Pearse incorporated our old Otto motor into a flying machine, and the thing took off?"

Professor Dobbins steered Atamarie into his office. Really, he had a lecture to give, but the students would have to wait.

Atamarie followed the professor, cheered and relieved. Since Richard's flight, she had slowly begun to question her sanity, or at least her perception. A man had made history, but the witnesses could not think of anything better than to amuse themselves about crash landings in broom hedges. Richard's parents were furious with him for having ended up in the hospital again, this time with a fractured collarbone. And the pioneer himself repeated again and again that the flight had not taken place.

Richard's family had ignored Atamarie at the hospital where she had waited on news of her friend. The doctor informed her curtly that Mr. Pearse did not desire any visitors, but he allowed Shirley, who came with his parents and seemed just as agitated as they.

In the end, Atamarie had not known what to do and had fled to her hotel room in Timaru. The next day, Atamarie decided to return to Christchurch to tell Dobbins everything. The professor did not even mention her absence while school was in session. On the contrary, he was bowled over by Richard's achievement.

"It's really incredible," Dobbins gushed, "and you no doubt had your share in it, Miss Turei. Don't deny it. But why am I only learning about this now? It should have been in the newspapers. Did someone photograph it? You have to document such things, Miss Turei, but you know that already."

Atamarie nodded and decided to confide in her teacher, pouring her heart out to him. She described Richard's concerns before the flight, his inability to savor his triumph—and finally found herself telling the professor about his violent mood swings and family problems.

"Pearse always was—well, he tended toward melancholy," the professor replied. "They say it occurs frequently in geniuses, such episodes of self-doubt and then soaring spirits. And he is a genius, no question. It places demands on his family. And on his fiancée? I don't mean to be indiscreet, but you are a couple, are you not? You must always bring him back to earth, Miss Turei, or in this case, back into the air. He needs to do it again. The flier wasn't damaged too much, you said? And even if it was, then he must repair it and make another go before the eyes of the world—not just in front of a few hicks in the Waitohi Plains. Alert the press, but under no circumstances the *Timaru Herald* or whatever the rag's called there—the press in Christchurch instead, the *Otago Daily Times*, and the newspapers in Wellington and Auckland would be best. You now know the machine works, so there's no risk in having all the reporters come. Make a to-do of it, Atamarie, before someone beats Richard to it. Motorized flight is"—Dobbins laughed excitedly—"up for grabs. Others are working on it too. So, get ahold of your sweetheart, and document that he was first."

Atamarie sighed. She looked into the ecstatic face of her professor, but only thought of Richard's empty eyes. *I didn't fly*.

How was she supposed to pull him in front of the press like that?

***

Atamarie let another weekend pass before she returned to Timaru. She did not know how long it took for a fractured collarbone to heal, but Richard should surely be back on his farm—if his parents had not brought him to theirs to recover. So, Atamarie braced for renewed disappointment. Under no circumstances did she want a confrontation with Richard's family. If it came to it, she would simply turn around and go back on the night train. Just in case, she wanted to get a room in Timaru—and was surprised when that proved not to be so easy.

"I have only a rather cheerless room to offer you, Miss Turei," explained the proprietress of the inn where Atamarie usually stayed. She was friendly and discreet—and had never breathed a word about Atamarie not even spending most of the nights she paid for in her room. "I'm only even offering it because you've become a sort of regular. I hate to turn you away. But this weekend, you really should have booked in advance. It's the annual fair and farming exhibition, you know. They'll be showing off everything from the best stud bulls to the biggest pumpkins. All the region's farmers are here."

Atamarie thanked both the innkeeper and fate. Richard would hardly come to Timaru to present produce. But Joan Peterson would be dying to see the pumpkin competition. Surely the Hansleys—Shirley and her mother, at least—would have some oversized vegetables to present, and with a good deal of luck, so would Richard's parents and siblings. Atamarie would have her friend to herself. She made her way contentedly to the farm on her rental horse, happy on the one hand but also regretting the lost opportunity: the fair in Timaru would have been ideal for showing off Richard's aeroplane to a larger crowd. There were more than enough hills around. But Atamarie knew she had to build Richard back up before they could make another attempt. She was determined to be happy for small favors and sighed with relief when she spied neither Peterson's nor Digory Pearse's wagons in Richard's yard. The "Beast" sat sadly in a nearby field.

At first glance, the farm looked abandoned, but then Atamarie saw Hamene puttering about one of the barns. He was tinkering with a plow, which alarmed Atamarie. Since when did Richard leave the care of his equipment to Hamene? He might hardly have taken care of anything else on the farm, but his equipment was always in good condition.

Atamarie wanted to ask Hamene about it, but then she spied Waimarama. The old Maori was just stepping out of the house.

"I brought her," Hamene said, and gave Atamarie a searching look. "I thought she might be able to help. Richard's—well, he's not doing anything again, you see."

What Atamarie saw was that Hamene had also used the absence of Richard's family to take matters into his own hands. Buy why did Richard need the Maori healer? She bowed reverently to the old woman.

"You're back?" Waimarama asked. "Do you mean to stay now?"

Atamarie frowned. "I'm afraid I won't be asked to. But I want—Waimarama, no matter what he says or how he's doing, he flew!"

"He yearns for the light, but his path leads to darkness," said Waimarama. "Perhaps the gods do not want to share the sky with him."

Atamarie fought down a bad feeling. But it was nonsense, of course.

"Maybe the hedge spirits have an unhealthy relationship with science," she replied. "We should entreat them not to constantly pull him magically to them. He flew, Waimarama. There are no two ways about it. And he should be proud of that instead of moping about. He is moping, or did I misunderstand Hamene?"

Waimarama raised her hands helplessly. "He is too weak right now to fight back the darkness."

"He should try harder," she replied. "Is he in the house? I'll go in and try to cheer him up."

Atamarie moved toward the house as self-assuredly as possible, but her first sight of Richard was shocking. The young man sat at the kitchen table, his head bent over an issue of *Scientific American*, but he wasn't reading. It was more as if he were staring past the lines, as two weeks before he had stared past his flying machine and Atamarie's excited face.

"Atamarie." Richard looked up when she entered, but he made no motion to stand, let alone to embrace her. "Did you want to help with the harvest again? The harvest is over. We need to plow and pay the rent and buy seeds."

Atamarie went determinedly up to him and kissed him, though only on his cheek—Richard smelled as if he had not bathed in ages. And his clothing was wrinkled and filthy. The cleanliness of the house and farm could only be attributed to Hamene and perhaps Shirley.

"The harvest was already over when you flew," Atamarie said energetically. "And you don't need to worry about all this other junk anymore. Dobbins says you're set for life once word of your motorized aeroplane gets around."

Richard smiled meekly. "But I didn't fly, Atamie. At most, I hopped a bit. That's what Peterson says. I hopped a bit. As usual. I—"

Atamarie was not a very patient person. She felt anger rising within her. "Richard, I don't care what Peterson says. You need to do it again. You need to show others. First and foremost, the press. But if you're not comfortable with that, invite Dobbins." How could she not have thought of it before? She should have just brought the professor with her. "And his students too. If half a college in Christchurch sees you fly, no one can deny it."

Not even you, she added in her head. Richard, however, only gave her another vacant smile.

"I didn't fly," he repeated.

Waimarama stepped in. "It's not important for him," she said quietly. "For the moment, it's not important for him. He has to find his path out of the darkness, Atamarie. You want to make him famous. I understand what this is about for you, Atamarie. I'm not stupid." Waimarama pointed to the magazine on the table. "My English isn't good, and I can only read a bit. But I know what it's about, what a big deal it is to *pakeha* to get such a flying machine into the air, that no one's done it before."

Atamarie nodded. "Then, you also understand that he has to pull himself together now, has to show the world that—"

"He must find the path out of the darkness," repeated Waimarama.

The old woman brought out a few herbs. Apparently, she was planning to use magic to free Richard.

Atamarie gave up. She knew Waimarama would repeat her diagnosis again and again, just as mechanically as Richard insisted he had not flown. Atamarie needed some air.

"I'm going to go look at the flying machine," she announced.

She hoped Richard would react to that, but he only lowered his head over his magazine again. Atamarie fled before he could deny that there even was such a machine.

She quickly stepped out into a clear, early-fall day. It was sunny but cool. The sky was blue except for a few herringbone clouds, and the wind was unusually still. Atamarie thought fleetingly about what an ideal day it was for a flight attempt. In weather like this, Richard would have been able to keep the machine under control. Lost in thought, she wandered over and took a look at the aeroplane. It was true: nothing was broken. Only the canvas covering, which had been fastened by wire to the linkage and chassis, had torn loose in one place. Atamarie repaired it with a few quick motions. Then she pulled the aeroplane forward. It was light. She could move it effortlessly.

She again admired its construction, with special affection for the motor and the eight-bladed propeller attached about the seat. Atamarie swung into the seat to take control of the little marvel of engineering. She had helped Richard craft the propeller, and attaching it in front had been her idea. Atamarie felt the aileron and elevator. She knew how to use both. She had seen the plans. And it really was not so different from Rawiri's kites.

Rawiri. She thought of him and how he had entrusted her with his kites, first when they were children, and then when she'd studied with him. In her hand, his *manu* had taken off like a bird, and Atamarie had been able to execute lightning-fast maneuvers with it. It was better, by contrast, to keep Richard's flying contraption horizontal.

"I name you Tawhaki," Atamarie said to the flying machine, "after the god who brought mankind knowledge."

The aeroplane rolled lightly next to her. She did not need any horses to pull it up the hill. Atamarie trembled with excitement. She could repeat Richard's flight and prove to him that he had not failed. With everyone at the fair, no one would see her. And even if someone did, at a distance they would confuse her blue riding dress for Richard's overalls. As for her hair, Richard's cap still lay in the aeroplane. No one would recognize her.

The Otto motor roared to life at once when the young woman started it, and ran smoothly—Richard must have just been nervous when he ignited it before. Atamarie held tight to the seat and pushed off with her foot to start the plane rolling slowly forward. Atamarie held her breath as the machine went faster and faster—and then instinctively seized the right moment. She pulled on the elevator and took off. Slowly, Tawhaki rose into the air, reached a height of about fifteen feet, and held there effortlessly. Atamarie tried to keep the aeroplane balanced, but she found it too risky to continue flying along the street. What if someone came toward her, or the landing was a disaster?

Then, however, the broom hedge came into view, and she seized the decision to break this shrub's spell. She engaged the aileron and was amazed when the machine followed her steering motions. And a little higher. Atamarie pulled Tawhaki three more feet into the air and cheered when the machine flew over the hedge. Richard's horses and goats fled toward the stables as the machine approached. Atamarie lowered it slowly and touched down in the paddock where Richard had practiced steering. The ground was even here, and it ran slightly uphill. Tawhaki rolled softly to a stop. Atamarie beamed with happiness as she climbed out.

Hamene and Waimarama stared at her, speechless.

"What are you looking at? I told you he flew," Atamarie called to them.

Hamene laughed. "Did you take the gods a message?" he teased.

Atamarie pointed to the hedge. "I stuck my tongue out at a few cheeky spirits," she declared.

Waimarama did not smile. She looked sternly at Atamarie's triumphant face.

"Don't tell him," she bade her. "It wouldn't help. You would only push him deeper into the darkness."

***

Atamarie felt she would explode if she didn't tell someone about her flight. However, she could not possibly brag about it to Dobbins, and her family probably would have called her crazy. Not until the next day, when she set out for Christchurch, did she think of someone who would take interest without betraying her.

I know, she wrote to the Maori *tohunga* Rawiri, *I shouldn't have done it, but it was so easy. It seemed almost natural to me.* Atamarie thought she could hear Rawiri's deep, friendly voice: *Of course it was easy—your spirit sang the right song. The gods welcomed you, Atamarie Parekua Turei. You've been chosen.*

Chapter 6

Doortje van Stout did not make any decision at first. She got up the day after her collapse, offering her assistance in the hospital again. Dr. Greenway gave her easy work, and as an expectant mother, she received extra food rations. Doortje accepted the special treatment without a word. Now, in retrospect, some things—the ravenous hunger she had been ashamed of, the constant fatigue and irritation—became clear. If only she had realized it earlier. Though Cornelis would not have married her anyway. He and Daisy had left for Pretoria as soon as the dissolution of the camps and the freeing of the prisoners of war had officially been announced. Since then, the last of the Boer commandos had withdrawn. In May, the final peace treaties were to be signed. Doortje would have been alone then—with or without a baby.

Yet, she still could not imagine leaving her country to follow Kevin into a whole new world. And she didn't want to admit to herself that she would perhaps be glad to do so. It would be a betrayal of her people and her family, of all the values she had been taught, of her church, which would cast her out if her belly got any rounder. Already the women in camp had begun to avoid her. The respectable women talked behind her back; the camp whores openly laughed in her face. Doortje knew that Kevin was waiting on an answer, and time was running out. The commander in charge of closing their camp was expected any day.

He appeared on a weekend when Roberta, Jenny, and Vincent had gone on a multiple-day excursion into the veld, along with several British officers who had been stationed in Karenstad for almost the entire war and did not want to go home without having set eyes on a lion at least once. Vincent had hired a few Zulu refugees as guides.

In the camp hospital that day, the assistant nurses were cooking, and Doortje squatted to peel potatoes in front of the building. The hot, stuffy air inside got to her more and more, and she preferred staying out of the other women's way. Only Antje Vooren still spoke to her. All the others whispered about the suspected Tommy whore. Many had not survived the six months of imprisonment, and the others had seen so much sorrow, sickness, and death that they no longer even recalled what had happened to Johanna and Doortje during their transportation to Karenstad. Also, because Doortje's belly was still hardly rounded, they assumed she had conceived her child in the camp, perhaps while her mother and brothers lay dying. They spat in front of Doortje when she approached. She would not be able to bear it much longer.

She began to dice the potatoes for the vegetable soup, struggling to shoo away the invasive flies forever swarming around her. Then, out of the corner of her eye, she saw a tall black horse stop in front of the camp director's house. A blond man dismounted. She recognized his form at once, even if she could not see his face. She knew the colonel's self-assured gestures, his quick, military-imprinted gait, his way of standing up straight. A cavalryman, an officer—but not a gentleman.

Doortje leaped to her feet, and the potatoes hit the dirt.

***

Kevin was taking care of paperwork in preparation for handing over the camp to the official who'd disband it. Anyone who wanted to know about the history of Karenstad would be able to find notes on it. Complete and unvarnished. Someday, he was sure of it, the incarceration of women and children in this war would be considered a crime.

Kevin looked up when he heard knocking. Nandi would open it. He sighed at the thought. Some solution would have to be found for her too. After having spent her entire life on a Boer farm, could she integrate into a Zulu tribe? Make her way in a city? Now he heard her high, friendly voice.

"Welcome, *baas* colonel. We awaited you. I announce you to doctor, yes?"

The answer was a raw laugh. "Well, isn't this a friendly welcome? Wouldn't have expected it from old Drury. And what a nice little praline, black and delicious. I see the good doctor knew how to sweeten his life here. So, will you be staying with me when I take over for him?"

A shiver ran down Kevin's spine. Nandi's voice now sounded frightened.

"I not understand, *baas* colonel. I announce you."

Kevin opened the door to his office and struggled to smile comfortingly at the young woman.

"That's all right, Nandi. You can go."

Then he looked up at the destroyed face and the startling green-brown eyes of Colin Coltrane.

"You?" he asked.

Colin laughed. "We meet again, Dr. Drury. But don't worry, no hard feelings. Your whining over the dead buggers was quickly forgotten. As soon as we took care of the next two commandos, the big shots in Pretoria loved me again. All in all, a lovely war. No sieges, no cannonballs flying about your ears, just a few idiot farmers you hunt like rabbits when you're not setting their houses alight. A nice country too; I'll be staying here. It'll need a few years of military presence, after all, before the dogs are finally tame." He smirked. "Maybe I'll settle here. Sell the Boers a few proper horses and take a pretty girl. There're plenty enough around."

Kevin looked at Colin Coltrane hatefully. "You're supposed to take over the camp management? The repatriation of the families? Who had that brilliant idea? I'll protest it, Coltrane. The women and children of the men you killed are here."

Coltrane shrugged. "It was war. That's how it is. You won't find a cavalry regiment that hasn't shot Boers."

"You burned these people's farms to the ground. They'll recognize you."

Kevin felt helpless. Everything within him bristled at entrusting his charges to Colin Coltrane for the trek back to their homes.

"Then they'll know what's waiting for them if they don't get a move on, you see," Coltrane observed. "Besides, I'm a gentleman, Dr. Drury. I know how to handle women. Ask your sister, the charming Matariki."

Kevin struggled not to punch him. Colin Coltrane was no doubt the more experienced brawler.

Coltrane acted as if he did not notice Kevin's rage. "So, show me around," he ordered placidly. "We can start with your field hospital—I'm supposed to dissolve that first."

Kevin followed him as if numb. He needed to think of something. He would join the trek, of course, but he could not be everywhere at once. Nor did he know exactly from what he really meant to protect the women and children. Coltrane was a decorated officer. He should be able to keep a grip on his soldiers—if he wanted to.

The men stepped out into the torrid sun. Kevin squinted in the brightness, taking in the peaceful scene that spread out before him. In front of a nearby tent, children were playing. Kevin recognized two of Antje Vooren's children and two older girls. At the hitching post between the house and hospital stood Colin's black horse, and Vincent was just then helping Roberta Fence down from her white pony. The safari participants must have heard of Coltrane's arrival, and Vincent had doubtlessly rushed back to warn Kevin—too late. Not that warning him would have helped much.

From the hospital came Doortje. Though her silence regarding his proposal racked his nerves, the sight of her always made his heart beat faster. Today, however, Doortje moved woodenly. Her face was as pale as a corpse's and completely emotionless. Her body seemed tense—and she was holding something in her clenched fist. Kevin could not tell what it was. Colin Coltrane was now turning with a smirk to Vincent, who instinctively stepped protectively in front of Roberta.

"Another old acquaintance. Who would have thought? Our veterinarian. Our most sensitive men all in one place. We're just missing that Australian, what was his name?"

Kevin saw with astonishment that Doortje was marching straight toward Colin Coltrane, who was facing away from her, and Roberta cried out in horror when she spied the knife. Coltrane stopped short, irritated. At that moment, Kevin recognized Doortje's intention and rushed forward, but it was too late. Doortje van Stout stabbed Colin Coltrane in the back with all the power she possessed. The knife bounced off his shoulder blade, but Doortje still held it in her hand. Coltrane spun around in alarm and reached for the army revolver in his holster.

When Doortje raised the bloody knife again, Kevin sprang into action. He could stop Coltrane or Doortje. But if he took Doortje down, Coltrane would shoot his attacker. Kevin could not risk that. He rushed Coltrane, seizing his arm and pulling it behind his back. He had not intended thereby to offer Doortje Coltrane's unprotected chest.

Doortje thrust without hesitation.

"This is for Johanna, you pig," she yelled, and pulled the knife out of the wound. Coltrane gasped, and Doortje rammed the blade between his ribs anew. "And that's for me. And for my baby. And for—"

Only when Doortje went to thrust the knife into Colin Coltrane's breast a third time did the veterinarian run to her and hold her back.

"Doortje, for heaven's sake, Doortje."

Doortje dropped the knife when she saw that Coltrane's body now hung limp in Kevin's arms. Kevin stared at her in shock.

"He—he was the one," whispered Doortje. "He and his people. They had Johanna and they, they killed—and he had me."

She broke into sobs, pressing her bloody hands to her belly. Kevin let Coltrane drop to the ground, went to Doortje, and took her in his arms.

Vincent kneeled down and felt for a pulse. "He's dead."

Doortje's first attack must have punctured the lung, and the second must have found the heart.

Roberta looked around. The square was abandoned. "What do we do now?" she asked.

Vincent looked at her uncomprehendingly. "There's nothing more we can do. As I said—"

Doortje and Kevin stood there motionless. Neither of them made a move.

Roberta felt a flash of the old pain. For a heartbeat, an ugly thought announced itself: if everything now were to take its proper course, Kevin would never see Doortje van Stout again. Or if he did, it'd be at a murder trial. Roberta's path would be clear again.

She pulled herself together. She could not sacrifice Doortje to her hopeless love. And Kevin—he, too, was in danger. Roberta decided to save the man who had never taken her seriously.

"Vincent," she told him quietly, "if this gets out, she'll be sentenced to death. And Kevin, heavens, he held the man down for her. That's aiding or abetting or whatever. Hopefully no one saw."

"We saw," murmured Vincent. "But you heard her. It was Coltrane who raped her. And set his men on her sister."

Roberta raised her hands as if she wanted to shake him. "But she's not allowed to stick him like a pig. If we don't do something now, they'll hold her responsible."

"Here, take blanket." Nandi's shy voice interrupted Roberta's desperate attempt to pull Vincent out of his lethargy. "Take man in blanket." She pointed to the administrative building.

Roberta nodded, relieved. Nandi had apparently seen the murder, too, but she was still thinking clearly. And they could certainly trust her.

"Come on, Vincent, quickly before somebody comes," Roberta ordered. "Wrap the fellow in the blanket. And, Nandi, you help him. Carry him in—"

"Into shed," Nandi prompted.

Nobody would find the corpse there by accident.

"Yes. And you, Kevin, take Doortje into the house."

Nandi's help invigorated Roberta. Everything had to move very quickly. Now, at the hottest time of day, the women were lying in their tents. But soon this quiet would pass. Dr. Greenway had ridden that morning to do rounds in the black camp. He would be returning any minute.

Vincent now squared himself to act. He wrapped the corpse in the blanket and threw it over his shoulder. The young veterinarian was stronger than Roberta had thought.

Now Nandi saw another issue.

"I clean that away."

She indicated the puddle of blood on the ground. Roberta's head whirred. How did one remove blood from sandy soil?

Roberta nodded. "Thank you, Nandi. See what you can do. And I'll check at the hospital to see if there are any other witnesses. I doubt it, but you never know. If it comes to it, we'll have to explain to them what he did. Then they'd keep their mouths shut."

"Keep their mouths shut?" asked Kevin.

Roberta groaned. "Kevin, get ahold of yourself. There are only two options: either we all stay mum about what happened here, or your sweetheart goes to jail and so do you. Is that what you want? Then take her into the house, now."

Roberta's inspection of the hospital was to her satisfaction. No one was in the front area, and the first sick bay was empty too. Antje Vooren, who was distributing food in the second hall, asked about Doortje.

"She was acting so strangely. She ran in here, said something like, 'I can't,' and ran out again. Is she ill?"

Roberta was about to say no, but then changed her mind.

"Yes, she was sick just now. And then felt very weak. Dr. Drury is seeing to her."

Antje Vooren gave a knowing smile. It had not gone unnoticed how much he exerted himself for her. The women now suspected that he was the father of her baby.

"And I just came to ask if I might be able to lend a hand." Roberta hoped for a no and was relieved when Mevrouw Vooren shook her head.

"No need, we'll be fine." Aside from Antje Vooren, two other Boer nursing assistants were caring for a few patients, but they did not seem to have picked up on anything either. "Nurse Jenny will be coming back soon. She can help us before she goes to her Kaffir."

The thought of her friend gave Roberta another fright. Jenny had been with them on the safari and must be arriving any minute. Every additional person who knew made the business more dangerous.

"I'll be going, then," she told the Boer woman. "I'll go check on Miss van Stout."

She heard giggling behind her and innuendo in Afrikaans. Apparently, the women were of the opinion that Doortje was in good hands with Kevin.

Roberta realized with surprise and delight that the blood in the square was no longer visible. Nandi was spreading sand over the spot.

"No one will see, *baas*—miss." Nandi recalled that neither the nurses nor the young teacher liked to be called *baas*. "I did always on farm when slaughtered pigs."

Roberta thanked her again, then went over to the house. Her hands clenched around the stuffed horse she was carrying as always in her skirt pocket.

***

In the office, Vincent was speaking heatedly to Kevin. Doortje huddled in the armchair in front of the fireplace. Kevin was kneeling in front of her and would not stop stroking her trembling, bloodstained hands. It crossed Roberta's mind that Doortje needed to wash up and change her clothes. And Kevin's shirt was just as bloodstained as Doortje's apron.

"That wasn't self-defense, Kevin. Use your brain." Vincent went to the cupboard where the whiskey was. "She killed him in cold blood. She won't get off scot-free. You won't either if we tell the truth. So, we need to think up something else. A fight, or something like that. Think, Kevin. How could it have happened?"

He took the bottle out and filled glasses. For himself, for Kevin, and for the women. Kevin urged Doortje to accept one.

Roberta took the glass, her mind spinning. A better explanation for Coltrane's death was a good idea. But a fight? Who was supposed to have fought with him? And nothing would explain the wound in the colonel's back.

"But what," she said quietly, "if the fellow simply never arrived?"

***

Vincent drove the camp's hay wagon out of the camp in broad daylight. As expected, the gate was not watched. Since the women were officially free, no one manned the dusty gatehouse anymore. The veterinarian had hitched Roberta's mare, Lucie, to the wagon, and Roberta rode Coltrane's fiery black horse alongside. She was scared to death on the animal, and from close up, no one would have believed the lively gelding was Vincent's well-behaved mare, Colleen. But from a distance, a black horse was a black horse. No one would suspect anything. Coltrane's corpse lay beneath several sacks on the wagon bed, still wrapped in the blanket in order not to leave any bloodstains.

"Why don't we just bury him in our cemetery?" Kevin had asked after Roberta shared her complicated plan. "It is dangerous, you know, for you two to travel miles cross-country."

After a second glass of whiskey, Kevin had been able to take part in the discussion. The shock was slowly fading, and the consequences were becoming clear to him. If Coltrane's corpse was found in the camp, someone would answer for it in court. At first, Kevin thought of taking the fall himself, but then Doortje would again be left on her own with the child. No, the only solution was to make Coltrane's body and his horse disappear—and to staunchly deny that he had ever appeared in the camp.

That was not so simple, however.

"We haven't had any deaths in a week," Roberta had reminded him. "If we dig a fresh grave now, what are you going to tell Greenway? And if Coltrane told someone where he was going, they'll be looking for him here too. Then someone might recall that you two weren't the best of friends and decide to investigate. No, no, he has to be taken away from here, far away."

Kevin sipped his whiskey again. "But where? Some alley in Karenstad? As if it were a bar brawl?"

Roberta chewed on her lip. "That's not bad, but it's risky. If someone sees us—no, no, I was thinking—"

Vincent's eyes lit up. "In the veld," he said. "We'll take him to the—"

"Lions," Roberta finished, giving Vincent a complicit half smile.

It was the first time that she had shared a thought with him.

***

While Roberta and Vincent slipped out of the camp, Kevin and Dr. Greenway tended to the sick in the hospital, and Nandi, hidden in the house, was caring for Doortje, who still seemed as if she were paralyzed. The path, over which the guide had brought Roberta and Vincent back that morning, was easy to find, but the wagon held them back, so it was late in the evening before they reached the place where they had spent the previous night. Only the traces of the campfire and the trampled-down savannah grass testified to human presence.

Roberta trembled as she helped Vincent lift the dead man from the wagon. Beforehand, the veterinarian had lit a fire on the old one's ashes and also improvised torches on the sides of the wagon to illuminate their return trip. The animals in the bush would keep a distance. They feared people, and fire even more so.

"Will they even come?" Roberta asked anxiously. Vincent had deposited the corpse under a tree. Now, he was burning the bloody blanket. "Do lions scavenge corpses?"

Vincent shrugged. "If the lions won't, the hyenas or buzzards will. And they'll come, as soon as the fire's out. By the day after tomorrow, nothing will be left but a few bones. If someone finds them, all the better. As long as there's no corpse with a knife wound in its back. Now, let's go. Or do you want to pray first?"

Roberta shook her head. She just wanted to get away—and lean her head on Vincent's shoulder. She still did not know if she loved him, but she now knew him far better than she had ever known Kevin Drury. He might not have been as excitingly devil-may-care as Kevin, and he was not as good-looking. But he was intelligent and kind. Shivering, she watched him take the bridle off Coltrane's horse and hang it on a bush as if the horse had sloughed it off.

"It would be better to leave it on, but then the animal might get stuck somewhere. Take care, old boy." Vincent slapped the horse amiably on the neck before raising his arms and driving it away. The black horse set off galloping across the veld as if the devil were on its heels.

The campfire only glowed now. Roberta climbed onto the box. She did not resist when Vincent put his arm around her. "What happened to your lucky horsey?" he asked to break the tense silence on their return trip through the darkness. "The stuffed horse. We needed it today."

Roberta shook her head. "No, we didn't. It didn't bring me much luck, you know. At least, not the kind I'd wished for."

Vincent leaned down to her and had to resist kissing her hair.

"Not every granted wish makes us happy," he whispered. "Did you get it from a man? Were you—were you promised to him? And is that why it's so hard for you to find something different, something new? Is that why you can't love me?" The last words broke out almost against his will.

Roberta squeezed her eyes shut. "He never promised me anything," she said quietly. "It was just a sort of dream."

Vincent pulled her closer. "Then you could throw it away, you know."

Roberta nodded. "I could."

Before they reached the camp, she allowed Vincent to kiss her.

But she did not throw the stuffed animal away.

***

Colin Coltrane's horse arrived at the barracks in Karenstad that night, with no trace of its rider. A few people had seen him head out of town, but then his trail went cold. Questions in the prison camp were fruitless, as were the patrols sent out to search the area. Ultimately, they declared Colonel Colin Coltrane missing in action. Since he had not provided a home address, his mother in New Zealand was not informed.

***

Kevin Drury and Doortje van Stout were married one day after the official peace agreement in a church near Pretoria. Doortje had wanted a wedding according to the rites of the Dutch Church, but the ceremony disappointed her. The pastor performed it curtly and impersonally, and his parishioners left the church when they became aware of the groom's nationality, so only Vincent, Roberta, Dr. Greenway, Jenny, Daisy, and Cornelis attended, as well as Dr. Barrister and Dr. Preston Tracy.

"I'll be damned I lived to see it." Dr. Barrister laughed. "You did always say so, Tracy, that our iron lady had a soft spot for Drury—I could only see it the other way. But that something like this should come of it?" He benevolently indicated Doortje's now considerably inflated belly.

"It would have been even lovelier in Dunedin," Kevin noted with regret when he finally led Doortje to a hotel room. The young woman was pale and looked strained. It had been easy to break away early from the small group of celebrants. "But we can always make up for the party."

"Who says it had to be lovely?" asked Doortje with clenched teeth. "And what do you want me to do now?"

Kevin sighed. Though she had definitively said yes to him the day after Coltrane's death, afterward she had kept her distance again. She had even let the wedding ceremony pass over her in stoic calm and had insisted on wearing a black dress. The white bonnet and lace collar had lightened it a bit, but she was far from a cheerful bride.

"You don't have to do anything," Kevin said wearily. "Just sleep. Today was stressful. And tomorrow we leave for Durban. Our ship sets sail in two days."

***

Everyone would be setting out in the next few days. Vincent Taylor was returning home to New Zealand on a troop transport. He would remain in contact with Roberta and was overjoyed when she allowed him to kiss her in parting. Daisy and Cornelis were moving to Durban, where Daisy felt freer than in Pretoria. Dr. Greenway and Jenny would be accompanying the repatriation of the women of Karenstad to the region around Wepener.

Kevin had booked private passage for himself and Doortje to Australia and from there to Dunedin. Roberta was joining them, and she would share a cabin with Nandi, whom Doortje had asked Kevin to bring along.

"She belongs with the family," she said stiffly. "I'm responsible for her."

Kevin took that as a sign that Doortje was slowly dismantling her black-and-white thinking. Roberta, however, sensed her displeasure when Nandi shyly went aboard behind them and a steward carried her meager luggage just like the white passengers'.

"If it were up to Doortje, they would lodge Nandi in the cargo hold," Roberta whispered to Daisy, who was seeing them off. "And the shipping company isn't excited about a black passenger either, even though it's an Australian ship, and they all pretend to be so open. They've already suggested I keep her in the cabin during mealtimes, so as not to hurt the feelings of the Afrikaners traveling with us. But I'll only play along so much. For all I care, we can eat in our cabin, but we won't let ourselves be locked up for the whole voyage. And I'm going to teach Nandi. By the time we get home, she'll be able to read and write and speak English better than Afrikaans."

The latter was not hard. The Boers had always insisted that their servants communicate only in Afrikaans.

"She'll do you proud," Daisy said.

Daisy waved good-bye, then laughed when Roberta immediately began negotiating heatedly with a steward. Roberta Fence was no longer chasing after hopeless love. And she was no longer shy.

***

"I'll sell your land for you," Cornelis said in parting from Doortje. He, too, had accompanied them to the ship. "Then I'll send you the money."

Doortje eyed him coolly.

"Don't bother," she said. "You already sold out your land." Her disdainful gaze wandered from him to Daisy. "Isn't that what they say in English? 'Sold out'?"

Cornelis gave Kevin his hand in parting but stepped back when he wanted to embrace him like a friend. "Good luck," he said with a glance at Doortje, who was now staring stoically up at the Drakensberg. "You'll need it."

Chapter 7

Atamarie was finally ready to give up on Richard Pearse and his aeroplane. It had been too disappointing to see him sit there for hours and hours, saying trivial things, and not receiving any more attention either as a woman or as a friend. Professor Dobbins, however, continued imploring her.

"Don't just think of him, Miss Turei, but also of your country. Flight is being pursued everywhere, but now a man from New Zealand, of all places, has succeeded. You also had your share in it, and thereby also honored the Maori people. You—"

"The Maori view motorized flight as entirely unnecessary," Atamarie replied crossly. She had just received a letter from Pania. Rawiri's mother thanked her for what she had written, promised to forward it to Rawiri, and shared his address with her. Naturally, though, the letter would take months to get there. "They have an interest in conversing with the gods, but they fly kites for that. No one needs to make the effort personally."

Dobbins laughed. "Oh, I don't believe it. Just think of the story with Pa Maungaraki and the glider, by means of which he opened the gate to the conquerors."

"Where'd you hear about that?"

The professor smiled. "From a young Maori who applied to attend here. We would have accepted him, but then he learned about a position with the Wright brothers and thought they might help him reach his goal more quickly."

Atamarie was startled. Was he talking about Rawiri?

"The Wright brothers? As in the bicycle makers?"

It was the first she had heard of Wilbur and Orville Wright's other occupation.

***

At Dobbins's insistence, Atamarie rode once again to Temuka, only to find that the flying machine had disappeared.

"What happened?" she asked Shirley in alarm.

The young woman had not greeted her with a smile this time, but neither had she dared simply to turn her away, especially since Richard was again puttering around the farm and seemed somewhat better kempt and more responsive than during her last visit. He greeted Atamarie placidly and as if in passing. Shirley seemed to note that with satisfaction.

"Oh, Dick is getting better," she informed Atamarie brusquely. "His father gave him a talking to, and now that that infernal machine is gone—"

Atamarie looked at her, horrified. "Mr. Pearse got rid of the aeroplane? He didn't destroy it, did he? Oh, Shirley, Richard, tell me it isn't true."

Shirley made a face. Richard did not even react. Atamarie let her gaze wander in desperation over the yard. Finally, it landed on Hamene. He would at least tell her the truth.

"Hamene," she pleaded in Maori, "where is the aeroplane?"

A weight was lifted from her shoulders when Hamene smiled. "We have the bird," Hamene said, employing the word *aute*, which was also occasionally used for kites, "sitting next to our *marae*. I took it with me after Mr. Peterson started looking at the engine covetously, and Richard's father was talking about how much money he could get for the thing. So, I thought I'd take it somewhere safe. The bird is, you know, something sacred. It flew up and, well, it must've delivered the gods some sort of message."

Hamene winked at Atamarie conspiratorially. Atamarie would have liked to hug him, she was so relieved.

In the meantime, Shirley had regained her composure. "You were asking about the aeroplane!" she finally realized. "You don't even care about Richard."

Atamarie glared at her. "I can see that Richard is alive and well." Richard was off tightening this and that on a farming implement. He did not seem to notice the women or Hamene. "But I couldn't help fearing someone had destroyed his dream. Shirley, it has always been his dream to fly. He's been talking about it as long as I've known him. And he's supposed to give that up? Just because he landed in some idiotic hedge again?"

Shirley raised her chin proudly.

"Man was not meant to fly," she declared. "Richard has to accept that. Maybe God put the hedges in his way."

Atamarie rolled her eyes. "People will fly, Shirley. Soon. And if God put this shrubbery in the way"—she turned to Richard—"then it's only so he can fly over it, not hide behind it."

With that, she swung back onto her rental horse and took off in the direction of the Maori village.

***

A short time later, Atamarie ran her fingers gently over the wings of the flying machine, which Hamene had placed on a hill above the *marae*—in starting position. Atamarie thought this a happy accident. Just as it was exceptionally convenient that she had put her hair up that day, such that it would fit perfectly under Richard's cap. And here, she was far enough from the *pakeha* farms that no one would hear the motor's roar.

Atamarie checked whether there was still enough fuel. Then she turned the motor on, rolled down the hill, and flew.

***

Of course, over the following months, it did not stay hidden from the villagers in the Waitohi Plains that Cranky Dick—or at least someone they thought was him—was flying again. Atamarie was lucky that they never talked to Richard about it. Maybe Peterson and the others were a little ashamed of their malice after the last attempted flight. It had not escaped anyone how much Pearse had subsequently withdrawn; of course, there was talk that he had finally lost it for good. At least he did his farm work and appeared occasionally in town, mostly in the company of the charming Shirley Hansley.

Dick Pearse was known for vacillating between euphoria, total withdrawal, and almost boring normalcy. The last phase did not last long, though, and so it hardly amazed the villagers that he had apparently been drawn into the clouds again. For his neighbors, the only difference was that the flying machine was not crashing into the broom hedge now. In fact, reports were mounting that the machine really flew, and for long stretches. An astonished farmer described almost two thousand yards. Moreover, the Beast could be steered. Three harvest workers all reported that the machine had turned away when the pilot saw them.

Atamarie was still trying to convince Richard to do a public demonstration. She would not admit to herself that she mostly just came to Temuka to fly. Richard's condition changed gradually. It almost seemed as if he were waking from a sort of sleep. Though he continued to deny his success, he did talk to Atamarie again and took an interest in her studies and her reports of life in Christchurch. Atamarie was on track to finish her studies in record time. If everything went smoothly, she would graduate before Christmas.

And then, just before exams, when Atamarie had rented her hotel room for a whole week, Richard slept with her again. He even made the first move and romanced her fervently. Atamarie enjoyed herself immensely.

If she was being honest, though, her attraction to him had waned over the last months. Though he was coming into flower again, Atamarie was reaching the conclusion that this man was too difficult for her and that he could not return her love to the degree she expected. In time, she would have to end the relationship, but first, she wanted to give Richard a present.

Shirley had disappeared anew when she recognized that Richard was turning back to Atamarie, and Richard seemed halfway to high spirits. Atamarie saw no more reason to keep her flying secret from him. Maybe he would become enraged and throw her out for good. But maybe it would put him back on the right path. Maybe he would finally declare himself ready to present his invention to the world. Atamarie also saw it as a sort of last chance for their love: if, after the successful flight, he nonetheless wanted to stay in Temuka and share his farm with the likes of Shirley Hansley, she could not help him.

The next morning, Atamarie enticed her friend to the Maori village.

"There's something I need to show you, Richard. No matter what, even if you're mad at me after. But you have to see it, and you have to believe it, and you have to—"

"It's not that stupid machine again, is it?" Richard asked indignantly.

Atamarie pushed him determinedly past the *marae* and up the hill where she liked to park Tawhaki. She had aimed for the slope during her last landing and then pulled the aeroplane all the way up, so it would already be in the correct starting position.

"Come on, I've changed a few things." Atamarie pulled Richard toward his flying machine. She had curved the wings a bit, as much as the bamboo construction allowed, and brought a few steering elements farther forward, so they were no longer impaired by the air eddy behind the wings. "But just little things," she claimed. Richard should definitely not feel she had gone over his head.

Now, he was mistrustfully eyeing the improvements—the effects of which really were rather great. Atamarie had enthusiastically remarked how much better the flier stayed in the air because of them and how much more precisely it could be steered. However, she did not want to minimize Richard's achievement by praising her own developments. It was his aeroplane; he had been the first.

Richard did not comment on the changes. The sight of the flier seemed to close a door within him.

"I didn't fly," he repeated mechanically once more.

Atamarie struggled for patience. Then she reached for the pilot's cap.

"Well, I did," she said decisively. "Watch."

With practiced motions, she started the motor, swung quickly into the seat, and rolled down the hill. The flying machine took off smoothly, and Atamarie effortlessly kept it about fifteen feet above the ground. She did not make any turns—the day was windless, and she surely could have, but she did not want to show off. So, she kept the aeroplane straight and hovered for about eight hundred yards. Then she landed softly and let the flier roll to a stop.

Richard ran to Atamarie.

"Well?" she asked with triumph and fear hanging in the balance. "You see, the machine flies. And it did when you steered too. You just had bad luck with the wind. Now will you show the world this wonderful thing you've invented?"

Richard stared at her, and then the spell broke.

"It flies, it flies!" Richard pulled Atamarie into his arms and danced her around the aeroplane. "I was right. You were right. The first motorized flight, Atamie. I, you—"

"Well, to be honest, I've done it often," Atamarie admitted. "But anyway. Shall we invite some journalists now? And Professor Dobbins? Will you finally show it to them?"

Richard nodded and made Atamarie the happiest woman on earth that night. Had she really been thinking of breaking up with him the night before?

Atamarie shook her head at herself—and then Richard spoke of marriage for the first time.

"It wouldn't have been possible without you. You're my soul mate, my other half. I'd like to be with you. Forever."

Atamarie snuggled happily into Richard's arms. At least for that day, she had banished darkness from his life. If now all his dreams of flying, of fame, and of unlimited financial means for his research and inventions came true, what reason would he ever have for melancholy?

"What do you think, when should we show it to them?" she asked after they had awoken together and made love once again that morning. "What would be a good date for the first motorized flight in history?"

Richard laughed and sprawled. "I don't know. You tell me. Maybe a date everyone can remember. The first of January?"

Atamarie frowned. "But that's weeks away, Richard. Shouldn't we—"

Richard shook his head. "I, well, I still need a little time. How about the twentieth of December? Or Christmas?"

Atamarie thought feverishly. "I'll still be in Christchurch on the twentieth," she said. "For exams. So, either this week or Christmas, really. Let's just do it now, Richard, please. Before I go back to the city."

Richard pulled her close. "You can't wait, huh, Atamie? But really, all the people you want to invite, they can't come that quickly. But Christmas . . . I can tinker with the machine a bit before then until it well and truly works."

Atamarie sighed. He was still hesitating. On the other hand, he did need to get comfortable with the machine again. After all, he did not simply want to fly a few yards, but take off beautifully and stick a clean landing. She could have done that again the very next day herself. She wrestled a bit with the fact that she'd get none of the glory. But that was egotistical. This was Richard's project. He should get the time he needed.

***

Atamarie and Richard spent a few more dreamy days in Temuka, though they could not carry out more flight attempts. The day after Atamarie's demonstration, the sky had darkened, and it rained continuously. Atamarie suggested flying anyway, but Richard declined.

"Let's not take any more risks," he decided. "What if I make another bad landing, and the supports break? No, we'll wait for it to clear up."

"But I might already be in Christchurch by then," Atamarie objected.

Richard waved that away. "So?" he asked. "Do you think I can't do it without you? Atamie, sweetheart, I built this."

And I learned to fly it, Atamarie thought, but she stayed quiet. And surely her concerns were unnecessary. After all, she had figured out how to handle the aeroplane alone. Richard would show just as much skill. Maybe he even preferred getting comfortable with his Beast alone. One indication of this was that he even declined to fly on a gloomy but rainless day.

"No, no, it might start raining again once I'm in the air. But we should bring the bird home, don't you think? Come on, let's take a walk and roll it from the Maori village into our barn."

Atamarie frowned. "But why? It's safe where it is. The hill is ideal for rolling down, much better than the road here. And—" She bit her lip in order not to mention the hedge.

"But it's much more central here," Richard observed. "You don't really want all that press lining up in front of the *marae*, do you? The Maori wouldn't like that much."

Atamarie thought the Maori probably would not have cared. But she complied. The evening before her departure for Christchurch, the flier stood in its barn again, and Richard studied the changes Atamarie had made.

"I don't know; I'd have preferred to have the steering elements closer to the center of mass," he objected, but nonetheless listened to Atamarie as she explained why she had moved the stabilizer. She hoped he would not change anything back before he took off on his triumphant flight—but if so, there was nothing she could do about it. Really, nothing could go wrong. Richard had already managed a few hundred yards straight ahead last March. She could still convince him later.

During their last night before Atamarie's departure for Christchurch, Richard made her forget all her technical questions and disagreements. They made love into the early morning. All his energy had returned. Atamarie tried not to think about how he had been similarly euphoric before his last attempt as well. This time everything would go smoothly.

***

Atamarie passed her first exam with distinction and was correspondingly carefree when, two days later, she went to the college for her second. The two other students were using their last minutes to cram, but Atamarie preferred looking dreamily out the window. In just a moment, she would surprise Professor Dobbins with her invitation and leave for Temuka the next day. And then there were only five days until the Christmas that would change the world.

"Atamarie, have you heard?" The professor stepped out of his office. He held a newspaper in his hand. "Does Pearse already know?"

"Know what?"

Dobbins looked at her probingly. "So, no, then," he confirmed when he saw her perplexed face. "Come in, please. Take a look for yourself."

The professor pulled a chair over to the little table already prepared for the exam and opened the newspaper in front of her.

> *Kitty Hawk, North Carolina, USA*
> *Two Brothers Make History*
> *On December 17 of this year, Orville and Wilbur Wright accomplished the first motorized flight in history.*
>
> *The brothers, both previously known as brilliant bicycle builders and businessmen—they led their Wright Cycle Company from a small handicraft enterprise into a large business—took off into the air several times in their FLYER 1 from a specially laid track in the sands of North Carolina. While Orville Wright was the first man in the pilot's seat, he was surpassed in terms of distance flown by his brother, Wilbur. In 59 seconds, he covered 284 yards.*

Atamarie dropped the newspaper. "But that's nothing," she whispered. "Richard flew a few hundred yards the first time. And I—" She bit her lip.

Professor Dobbins looked at her sympathetically. "But no one will believe him now," he said. "Oh, damn it all, he was so close. And he had months to publicize it. I'm so sorry, Atamarie. I know how hard you tried. And he—"

Atamarie stood up. She tucked the newspaper distractedly in her bag.

"I have to go. I have to go to him. I'm sorry, Professor Dobbins, I just can't take the exam now. I have to go to Richard. If he hears it from anyone else—"

Dobbins shook his head, chagrined. "He probably already knows. It's in all the papers today."

Atamarie rubbed her forehead. "The newspapers don't reach Temuka so quickly. You don't know the area, Professor. It's the end of the world." She looked at the grandfather clock in the exam room.

"If I hurry, I can still make the early train. I'm really sorry. I—"

Professor Dobbins waved it away. "Oh, forget it. You can't take a final exam today now, anyway. Get going, we'll set a new date. And please, tell Richard how sorry I am, truly. I always believed in him."

Atamarie nodded and pulled herself together. "Wish me luck, Professor," she said quietly.

Chapter 8

Atamarie did not even take the time to change, instead rushing to the train in her exam clothes. She seemed very nervous in her dark skirt, white blouse, and prim, black blazer. Her hair was put up under a pert little black hat. In principle, she thought this outfit too formal for a visit to the country, but considering that her intent was damage control, the clothing did not seem unsuitable at all. After all, someone had to speak to the press, even if at first it was just Timaru's local rag. Richard needed to present himself and his aeroplane to the public immediately. Fine, he would no longer be the first person to have accomplished motorized flight—or at least it would be hard to prove with just a few villagers as witnesses. But still, they could break the Wright brothers' record without breaking a sweat. After all, what were a few hundred yards straight ahead with not-so-soft landings in sand compared to the two thousand yards Richard's machine managed?

And if Richard showed a bit of magnanimity and let Atamarie fly, she could even make an elegant turn and skillfully let the machine roll to a stop in front of the journalists. It wasn't a bad idea, actually. Atamarie's cheeks burned as she thought of being in the newspapers. If she were recognized as the first female pilot of a motorized aeroplane—nobody would be talking about Wilbur and Orville if a woman took to the air at practically the same time. Atamarie could have giggled. Yes, it could work. Of course, she would mention Richard's name in every interview. They would simply share the glory. If only he would agree. If only he had not yet heard about the business with the Wrights from someone else and lost his courage. Atamarie would have liked to spur the train on like a horse. The hours passed torturously. And then she could not ride a horse in her tight skirt, so she had to rent a chaise, which slowed her down further.

She did not turn down the path that led to Richard's farm until late afternoon. She saw no sign of Richard, but she soon spied Hamene—who, to her astonishment, was not busy with farm work, but was instead staring off into space in the direction of Temuka.

"Atamarie." Hamene turned to her with relief as soon as he heard the carriage. "Atamarie, the spirits have sent you. Something is wrong with Richard. His brother came by earlier and brought this newspaper. Richard read it, and then, he was completely beside himself. He tore it up. He—Shirley says he cried."

"Shirley?" Atamarie's frustration discharged as anger. "What is she doing here again?"

Richard's brother had probably brought her along. To comfort him, so to speak, after the Pearse family had found nothing better to do than rub Richard's nose in his failure. Atamarie felt rage welling up within her.

"It doesn't matter," she muttered. "We'll deal with that later. First, I need to—where's Richard, Hamene? How's he doing now? What's he doing?"

Atamarie was afraid she would find her friend in the kitchen again, staring blankly, this time at the newspaper.

Hamene pointed helplessly in the direction of Temuka. "He took the bird," he reported. "I wanted to help, but he hauled it out of the barn alone. It was as if he were out of his mind. And then he went up the hill with it. I was on the lookout for him when you came."

Atamarie swung back into her chaise and took up the reins. "I'm going after him, Hamene. Oh God, I hope he doesn't do anything stupid."

She trotted up the road. Shirley stood in front of the broom hedge, looking in the same direction as Hamene. Atamarie ignored her. She had to stop Richard—he could not be allowed to fly in such an agitated state.

After just a few strides of her horse, however, she realized that it was too late. She heard the motor and saw the machine hovering over the road. Richard held it straight and not too high above the ground. Atamarie's heart slowed. He was flying beautifully. So, he was not dangerously wound up after all, but had struck on the same idea she had. He'd just wanted to test the flier once more before calling the press.

But suddenly, the aeroplane left the road. Instead of simply flying past Richard's farm, it turned precisely, losing altitude.

"No!" Atamarie screamed, but of course, Richard couldn't hear her. And this was no accident either. The machine did not trundle; it didn't fall. The pilot was steering it directly into the broom hedge. The aeroplane's left wing shattered on impact.

Atamarie leaped off her horse and left it to its own devices on the grassy side of the road. She needed—what did she need to do, actually? Something inside her had died, but something else had awakened when she saw Richard fly. Only when she saw him hanging motionless under his flier, apparently unharmed but also unwilling to get up, did it become clear to her what she felt: rage, such wild, burning rage that she had to control herself in order not to tear him from his seat and shake him.

"So? Feeling better now?" she roared at him. "You broke our flier. Before you can do a demonstration flight now, you'll have to repair it. That's going to take even more time. And your stupid neighbors will laugh again—it's not good press, Richard, when they call you Cranky Dick."

Richard looked at her, and she felt her heart definitively go cold.

"I didn't fly," he said.

Atamarie did not feel pity anymore—and even her love, which had been flaring up again, was extinguished in the face of his vacant gaze. The only thing she still felt was rage.

"No," she said cruelly, "you didn't fly. You don't have the spunk to fly, Richard Pearse. You'll stay in your broom hedge and hole up like a blind bird without wings. You'll never conquer the sky, Richard. At least not until you finally trim or tear out or burn this hedge. You'll—"

"I didn't fly," Richard repeated.

"You—" Atamarie sought new words of abuse to fling at him.

"Leave him—" Shirley suddenly stood behind the crashed flier. "Leave him alone."

That only goaded Atamarie on. "I loved you, you coward. I supported you, gave you the motor. But you, I never got anything back from you. You only took and took and took and took. You—"

"Did you want to be paid for your love?" Shirley asked mockingly.

Atamarie glared at her. "No. Just respected. I wish I hadn't listened to Waimarama. I should have flown myself, in front of all the world."

Shirley laughed. "Finally, you admit what you really wanted, Atamarie," she said. "You wanted to fly. You didn't care about Richard."

Atamarie threw her head back. "That's just not true. He wanted to fly. And I, sure, I wanted to, too, but I also wanted him to love me. I—"

"You only loved him when he was doing well," said Shirley. "You left him when he was doing poorly. You only thought of yourself."

Atamarie looked over at Richard, who did not seem to be following the confrontation between the two women. He continued staring into nothingness.

"I didn't fly."

Atamarie rolled her eyes.

"Then you can both stay here and bury each other on this farm," she spat at Shirley. "I just wish you a lot of strength. One thing's for sure: he doesn't have it."

With that, Atamarie climbed into her chaise and rode away with her head held high. She cast a last, sad look at Richard's flier.

"Farewell, Tawhaki," she murmured. "It wasn't your fault."

The wonderful wizard of oz

Dunedin, Lawrence,
Christchurch,
The South Island
1903–1904

Chapter 1

"And how do you see that working?" asked Michael Drury. He was at a livestock auction in the city, and Kevin had met him in a pub. "For your brother, I mean. It was always understood that he would inherit Elizabeth Station. You never wanted it. But suddenly you change your mind because your Boer girl needs country air. So, what, now you want to be a farmer?" Michael took a deep drink from his beer glass.

Kevin shook his head, sighing. The decision to move to Lawrence had been hard enough for him anyway. All that had been missing was for his parents to oppose it. Still, it was a stroke of luck to be able to speak with his father alone. Lizzie might have expressed herself more drastically.

"Of course not, Father. I am and will remain a doctor. I'm sure I can practice in Lawrence. And I'm not disputing Patrick's inheritance. It's just, well, maybe for a few years. Until Doortje has gotten used to life here. And Patrick doesn't even live on Elizabeth Station. He—"

"He resigned his job at the Ministry of Agriculture," Michael revealed, ordering another stout. "It's not working for May to live in Dunedin anymore. She's getting too big. He can't keep leaving her with different nannies. He's going to keep working through the shearing, but then he's moving in with us at Elizabeth Station. He can take care of the sheep, Lizzie can look after the kid, and I'll devote myself to viniculture." He grinned. "Maybe we'll finally get something really drinkable and make it big."

Kevin made a face. Doortje would not appreciate the winemaking on Elizabeth Station. After all, her church forcefully rejected the enjoyment of any alcohol. Yet, even if she made a few comments on it—staying with his parents on the farm could hardly be more of a disaster than their shared life in Dunedin.

While Michael held forth on the chances that the young woman would ever adapt to New Zealand, Kevin thought about the months since his return from South Africa.

The voyage had passed largely without incident—if one excluded the handful of passengers who complained about Nandi's presence on the top deck. There were never problems when she was with Doortje, for whom she acted as a servant. But that headstrong Roberta Fence, driven by the same ironclad convictions as her mother and Matariki, had insisted on strolling the deck, chatting and laughing with the black woman. Kevin did not find anything repellent about it himself, but she could have shown a little consideration. At any rate, Roberta's provocations had exacerbated the tension between Doortje and Kevin.

Doortje's behavior was slowly driving the young doctor mad. He had to sleep next to her—the luxury cabin he had booked offered a shared bed. Doortje, however, showed no signs of embracing him. On the other hand, she left no doubt that she intended to be an "obedient wife." She would have held still if he had taken her, but certainly not participated. And almost immediately after their arrival in Dunedin, she had given birth—bitter and ashamed because Kevin's former partner, Dr. Folks, delivered the baby. Kevin would have been happy to grant her wish of a midwife, but her contractions set in on their second day in Dunedin, a bit earlier than expected. Kevin had nearly had to deliver the baby himself, which would no doubt have agitated her even more. Fortunately, Dr. Folks had been available. After a few torturous hours, in which Doortje never let a tear fall, he laid a son in the young woman's arms.

"He takes after you," he said amiably. "Look, what adorable blond hair he has. What's his name going to be?"

Kevin was exceedingly embarrassed that neither he nor Doortje had thought of names for the baby. He suggested Adrian, after Doortje's father, but she rejected that so forcefully that Christian Folks looked frightened. Kevin then saved himself with Abraham, the first and only name from the Old Testament that occurred to him. People could call the boy Abe, after all. Doortje had no objections this time. She also put the child dutifully to her breast, although she held him like a doll and did not give him a single smile. Subsequently, she cared for him commendably—or at least, supervised Nandi in his care. Kevin had not yet been able to tell whether Doortje loved her son.

For Kevin, the return to Dunedin proceeded without any complications, at first. They could move into an apartment at once, and Dr. Folks welcomed him back into the practice.

"There's more than enough work for two here," he declared cheerfully. "Only the ladies with minor discomforts fell off once you left. Now, you'll no doubt be drawing them back in."

Very soon, invitations were once again raining down on the young doctor. Dunedin society was dying to hear his war stories and, most of all, to meet his foreign wife. Here, however, the difficulties began. Doortje's appearance on the streets of Dunedin provoked a minor scandal. Kevin was horrified when he saw her coming back from her first shopping trip in the new city. Laura Folks, Christian's wife, who had accompanied her out of generosity, seemed mortified.

"I suggested we go straight to buy her some dresses, but she did not want to," she said with a mystified look at Doortje, who, in her old-fashioned blue dress, white apron, and starched bonnet, seemed to come from another world. She had bought this outfit in Pretoria, and Kevin had not said anything at the time. On the ship, there were plenty of Cape Boers to whom this traditional style was familiar. And it had been a maternity dress, so Kevin had assumed he would be able to buy his wife new, modern clothing in Dunedin. Now, everything had moved faster than planned. Doortje had quickly taken the dress in and was out and about in it. She paired it with a black shawl, which would have lessened the strange impression except that Nandi followed her in similar style with little Abe in her arms. On her, the outfit would have passed for a maid's uniform, but her deep-black skin drew attention to them both.

"Doortje, you can't walk around like that here," Kevin declared. "In Dunedin, people don't wear aprons and bonnets unless they work as housemaids. A married woman in better society wears a dress or an outfit like, well, like Mrs. Folks." He indicated Laura's gown.

Doortje looked indignantly at the train of her skirt, the complicated button border of her long jacket, and most of all, her tightly corseted waist.

"You can't work in something like that," she objected. "And—and that hat!"

Laura wore a fashionable creation with a gauze veil cut to look like a turban.

"You don't need to work, you know," Kevin said gently. "You need only look pretty. So, please, Doortje."

"Vanity is a sin," Doortje announced. "My dress is still in very good shape. There's no reason to replace it."

Laura looked at her, astonished. "You only have the one, my dear?"

Kevin sighed. Worlds lay between these two women. There was no helping it; he would have to deliver Doortje to the only boutique in town where, with a little luck, spiritual guidance would be included: the Gold Mine.

"Doortje, we'll go out this evening," he said. "To the Burtons. They're old friends of our family. Kathleen runs a bou—a dress shop. And her husband is a pastor."

***

What was more, Kathleen Burton was the mother of Colin Coltrane, but that had not been mentioned in Dunedin for years. Thus, Kevin felt relatively safe when he brought his wife and her exotic attendant into the parsonage in Caversham. Safe, that was, until Kathleen caught sight of little Abe's face. She turned pale and pulled Kevin aside.

"What's going on here? This baby is the spitting image of Colin. My God, he looked just like that as a baby."

Kevin blanched and looked around for Doortje, but luckily, she was speaking to Reverend Burton already. Though she took a more than critical stance toward Anglicanism, the friendly, obliging pastor had quickly managed to draw her in.

"Unfortunately, I'm not surprised," Kevin whispered to Kathleen. "But for heaven's sake, don't let Doortje hear that. I'll come by tomorrow. We can talk about it then."

Kathleen did not broach the topic again, but she was stiff and occasionally cast scrutinizing looks at the young Boer woman, who acted similarly. Reverend Burton, who had not met Colin until he was more than ten years old, did not notice anything. He knew the Old Testament as well as the New and found plenty of evidence that God had not banned music, good food, or wine. One could infer God felt the same about beautiful clothing, he claimed, and ultimately, Doortje permitted Kathleen to outfit her fashionably.

Kevin would not let himself think of his bank account. In the end, the overly modest Doortje would be just as expensive for him as fashionable Juliet. Which brought his brother back to mind, but that problem had been pushed off for the time being. Patrick was traveling through the sheep farms of Otago, and Kevin had not yet seen his daughter, May.

***

The next day, he sought out Kathleen at the Gold Mine and explained the matter with Colin Coltrane—in a highly understated form. Kathleen was horrified by the report of the rape, but accepted the declaration of "missing in action" with composure. She had not heard anything from Colin for years, and "missing" did not necessarily mean "dead." No doubt he had his reasons for going to ground.

"I truly regret what happened to the young woman," Kathleen said finally. "I'm ashamed of my son. And I have a great deal of respect for you for wanting to raise the child as your own. But do you really want to leave your wife in ignorance? How are you going to explain the child's resemblance to Atamarie? She is Colin's daughter, after all. Or the fact that Heather and Chloe share his family name? Are you going to lie to her?"

"I mean, I don't know. Atamarie is studying in Christchurch, isn't she?"

"Kevin! She often comes to visit, and she'll soon have finished her studies. And then? She should tell Doortje everything. Maybe it will even help Doortje to talk with Matariki and Chloe. Colin did all of them wrong. And if she hates me because I'm his mother, there's nothing I can do about it."

Kevin chewed his lip. If the business with Colin had been the only problem between him and Doortje, he might have taken Kathleen's advice. However, there was incomparably more that was out of joint, and the last thing he wanted now was to unsettle Doortje further. Even months after the birth, the young woman was closed off, monosyllabic, and rejected physical contact. Kevin, of course, accepted that she needed rest and that their relationship needed time to develop. But he yearned for a kiss now and then, for any sign of feelings—feelings Doortje had certainly nursed for him in South Africa.

Now, however, no more of that could be seen. Doortje only peered nervously and tensely into the strange new world he had spirited her away to. Nandi seemed to make her way much better—she was already chatting quite contentedly with other housemaids and serving boys.

"I'll think about it, Mrs. Burton," he said politely, "but please, don't say anything in the meantime. Under no circumstances is she to hate you until you've at least taught her how a person dresses in Dunedin."

***

Kathleen and Claire ultimately sold Doortje several modest reform dresses from last year's collection, which lessened the expense. The wide dresses worn without corsets were going out of style again. The S-bend corset defined the silhouette of the modern woman. The stomach and waist were tied tightly, emphasizing the breast. The skirt was cut in a bell shape and ended in a train. The whole thing was incredibly uncomfortable and would unnecessarily impede Doortje's entrée into city life. Besides, Doortje looked captivating in the wide-cut empire dresses. Kathleen and Claire also advised her to get her hair cut—just braiding it and wrapping it around her head would not do at all—and they picked out three hats for her. Doortje was torn by the image of herself in the mirror. She had to admit she looked beautiful. But she no longer bore any similarities to the women of her homeland.

Further problems became obvious when Claire invited Doortje to tea after shopping. Doortje Drury did not have the slightest idea how to balance a teacup between the thumb and index fingers, to nibble on tea cakes, or to make polite conversation. Now, all of that could be learned. Kathleen, too, had been forced to work hard on herself. Still, she had slowly grown into society life, and what was more, Claire, so self-assuredly stylish, had stood by her side. Not to mention, the Dunedin of her youth had little in common with the lively, modern city of the day—Doortje would hardly have stood out among the puritanical city founders. The Church of Scotland had a great deal in common with the Dutch Church. Now, however, the young woman was being thrown into a life for which nothing had prepared her, and she also lacked any of the enthusiasm that would have eased her acclimation. As a consequence, Doortje made various faux pas at official dinners by mixing up the order of silverware, and, at a reception of the Dunloes', refused champagne and asked for milk instead.

"Like Ohm Krüger at the German kaiser's table," Sean Coltrane joked.

He did not mean anything by it, but the comment soon got around, and the guests no longer saw an exotic beauty, but a possibly hostile-minded Boer.

Disgusted and beet red, Doortje left an exhibition in Heather and Chloe's gallery that featured nude drawings, and she spoke during a chamber concert because she was bored and could not tell the difference between the featured performance and background music at receptions. Ultimately, Kevin no longer dared to take her anywhere, and Doortje covered up her embarrassment with surliness. She preemptively rejected every cultural offering because it was English, dug out her old Boer clothing, and spoke Afrikaans with Abe. She no longer touched English books, which could have helped her orient herself. Kevin wondered what happened to the girl who had once secretly read Shakespeare. Now, Doortje was obdurate and loath to do anything.

***

After a few months of this, Kevin no longer knew what else to do. He had to make good on his promise to Doortje of a life on a farm like the one she knew.

Unfortunately, Michael and Lizzie were proving anything but enthusiastic about the prospect. Moreover, the situation with Patrick was more complicated than Kevin had thought.

"Doortje just needs a bit longer to acclimate," he now asserted to his father. "Life in the city is too much for her. My God, can't you of all people understand? You still moan about how stiff everything is here and how much you hate having to sort your forks at dinner."

Like Kathleen, Michael came from humble circumstances and had slogged through New Zealand as a whaler, distiller, and gold miner until he achieved wealth by means of gold and the sheep farm it financed. To that day, he still felt uncomfortable among Dunedin's dignitaries.

"Exactly," Michael replied, taking a big swig of beer. "I never got used to it. What makes you think she will?"

Chapter 2

At a brisk, even tempo, Dancing Rose's Trotting Diamond rounded the track in Addington near Christchurch. Rosie Paisley sat in the sulky, maintaining light contact with the reins and floating on air. She had missed this feeling in all the years she had worked for Chloe and Heather—and as much as she loved Chloe, her savior and idol since kindergarten, there was simply no comparing flying down the racetrack with housekeeping. Rosie also liked her new job as a stable hand in Lord Barrington's racing stables. Her heart leaped every morning when the horses whinnied in greeting. She loved every single one of the animals entrusted to her.

That day, she had summoned the courage to speak to the stable master and ask for a few hours off. As a little girl, Rosie had gone mute for years after being forced to witness frightful scenes between her sister, Violet, and Violet's husband, Eric Fence, as well as Violet's near death from the complications of her son's birth, and even now, she much preferred horses to people. Besides, Lord Barrington's stable master was really quite strict. Still, he had granted Rosie's request. After all, she was never late and always did an excellent job. Rosie knew that, as the only girl in the stables, it would take a lot for her to be recognized.

Luckily, Rosie could do even the hardest stable work without breaking a sweat. She was powerfully built, not like her willowy sister, Violet, or her niece, Roberta. Nor was she as pretty, though. With her dark-blonde hair, heart-shaped face, and light-blue eyes, she could at most be described as cute. Most men didn't notice her at first, and Rosie had no problem with that. She had witnessed Violet's gruesome marriage from beginning to end. The last thing she wished for was a husband.

Rosie looked at the large clock above the totalizer. She still had a little time, but then she would have to take Diamond back to the stables and go fetch Roberta from the train. Or should she hitch Diamond to a different carriage and surprise Robbie with a ride behind a lively racehorse? No, Robbie had always been rather afraid of horses. Though the animals had never done anything to her. Eric Fence had been dangerous—and Colin Coltrane, too, of course. But never the horses. Horses were good.

Rosie had Diamond speed up on the long sides of the racetrack. That weekend, she would run her first race, and Rosie could hardly wait. It was risky starting Diamond in a race without her ever having trained alongside other horses while pulling a sulky, but Rosie avoided the other trainers. She was wary of raucous old Brown, and as for her nephew, well, the sight of Joe nearly made her break out in hives. He looked so much like his father, she could have sworn Eric had risen from the grave. Regardless, Joe was a far better racer. Never would he be done in by negligence like his father's.

Rosie took a deep breath and flicked the reins. She did not feel guilty about Eric Fence's deadly accident. True, he had ordered her to harness the horse for him, and Rosie had not done it properly. However, a good driver should check the seat of his carriage before the start. Eric Fence had neglected doing so. After all, he'd still been half-drunk from the night before. It was his own fault.

Nevertheless, Rosie avoided her nephew at all costs. Joe had been a witness to her actions and had later accused her of murder. No one had believed him, but whenever he looked at Rosie, she saw the old hate in his watery eyes.

Just then, Joe appeared, steering a gorgeous black stallion that was pulling a sulky onto the racetrack. A tall, strong-looking man with red-blond hair followed. Rosie cursed under her breath. Maybe she could guide Diamond out of the racing grounds before the men made it back around . . .

But when she brought Diamond down to a walk and stopped in front of the exit, which was blocked by a bar, Joe was there, still talking to the reddish-blond man. Just the sound of his voice sent cold shivers down her spine. It, too, was an echo of his father's—with the inflection of Colin Coltrane.

"Of course, he'll win, Mr. Tibbs," he was assuring the man. "He'll have to if he's going to advertise for your delivery service, now won't he?" Laughter. "It's really a good idea, by the way. I always tell people that a gentleman takes a stake in races. But when, as in your case, it also serves business—"

Rosie frowned as he furtively secured an overcheck on the stallion's bit. The checkrein was supposed to ensure the horse stayed at a trot, but it also encumbered it, and Rosie shared Chloe's opinion that a good trotter should not need any assistance, and a good trainer did not reach for measures that caused the horse pain and fear.

But Mr. Tibbs, clearly interested in buying the stallion, did not seem to notice Joe's actions. He had just spied Rosie and was hurrying to open the gate for her.

"It's all right, boy, no need to get down."

He laughed when she gratefully tipped her cap, revealing her chin-length hair.

"Well, I'll be—you're a girl! Beg pardon, miss."

The man doffed his newsboy cap as gallantly as a gentleman would his top hat. His round face reminded her a bit of a bulldog's. A shy smile stole over Rosie's face. But before she could get Diamond moving, Fence called out.

"Well, lookee what we have here, little Rosie. Done, are we? And here I thought I could show my client how his future horse would trot past your pony." He grinned.

Rosie's heart was pounding, but she did not take the bait. Trotting Diamond was not tall, but that had little to do with a trotter's speed. Joe only wanted to provoke her. And the stranger had a funny look on his face. Recognition? Curiosity? Still, the man did not seem lecherous or greedy. On the contrary, he looked quite friendly.

"Would you do us the honor, my lady?" he asked Rosie with a slight bow. "Mr. Fence here would like to sell me a horse, and it'd be nice to see it compared to another. I mean, maybe harness racers are generally well schooled, but I know how it is with my cold-bloodeds and cobs. They're perfectly calm when they have the road to themselves, but as soon as another horse comes a-trotting—"

"That happens with racehorses as well," Rosie confirmed in a husky voice.

Hardly ever to Joe Fence's horses, though. He knew every trick in the book and did not tolerate any nonsense from his horses.

Mr. Tibbs smiled. "Then we're in agreement, Miss Rosie, was it?" His voice grew soft. "My favorite name, that. Will you help me test out my horse?"

Rosie turned a burning red at once, but she steered Diamond into starting position. Meanwhile, Joe Fence climbed into the sulky behind his black stallion with a smirk. "I'll give you a show, Mr. Tibbs," he promised. "But first, I've got to warm up Spirit's Dream. Does that bother you, Rosie?"

Rosie did not manage an answer. In fact, it did bother her. She was going to be late to the train station. Of course, Roberta wouldn't hold it against her. She was probably less excited to see Rosie than the lovely new veterinarian, who would also be meeting the train. Dr. Taylor's eyes had shone when he said he knew Roberta from South Africa—even more than during his examination of Diamond, whom he adored. But really, Dr. Taylor loved all horses—and Roberta. Even for Rosie, that was plain to see. He surely wouldn't mind if she left her niece alone with him for a bit.

But what if Roberta minded? Rosie always considered the possibility that women were afraid of men, and she should stand by Roberta's side, just in case. Her head spinning with all this, she almost failed to realize that Mr. Tibbs was speaking to her. He was observing Joe's stallion as it now moved around the track at a calm, working gait.

"A beautiful horse, fine movements. Of course, begs the question of how fast it is. Do you know it?"

Rosie blushed again. Naturally, the man assumed she knew most of the trotters around the track. And in Invercargill, she had. But here, her work meant she rarely had a chance to watch the training sessions.

Mr. Tibbs waited. Rosie pulled herself together. She thought about it. Spirit's Dream.

"I—no, but I think I knew its father, Spirit. A black Thoroughbred? Tall? Former racehorse?"

Mr. Tibbs pulled a paper out of his bag and studied it slowly. "So he is, miss." He beamed. "You're a real horse expert. So, what do you think of the stallion? Honestly, I mean. Or are you an employee of Mr. Fence's, is that it?"

Rosie shook her head fervently. "No. No, never." The thought alone drained the color from her face. "I—"

Tibbs beamed, putting Rosie in mind of the portraits of soulful-eyed herding dogs Heather used to do before she had made her name as a serious painter. She noticed with confusion that she felt comfortable in this man's presence.

"Then you can speak openly," he encouraged her.

Rosie wrinkled her nose, a gesture that made her look childish. Again, that strange, inquisitive expression appeared on Mr. Tibbs's face.

"Spirit was good," Rosie said. "He was her grandfather." She gestured to Trotting Diamond.

Tibbs now smiled broadly. "Well then, a family reunion. Which reminds me—"

Now, however, Spirit's Dream was nearly back.

"I'd take the overcheck off," Rosie blurted out hastily, before Fence could reach them. "The checkreins."

Tibbs nodded seriously. "I know what it is. That's got to slow the horse down."

Rosie shook her head. "Not necessarily. Not when it's well trained. But—but, it hurts them," she said quietly, and felt like a fool. Most people did not care if they caused a horse pain, as long as it looked good or won races.

"We certainly don't want that," Tibbs agreed. "Besides, it'd interest me to see whether the stallion would remain at a trot if your cute little mare were to overtake it. So, I'll free him from the overcheck, and you'll give us a good race, agreed?"

The man stepped onto the track and waved for Fence to stop. After a short discussion, Tibbs released the snaffle rings that forced the horse to hold its head unnaturally high. Rosie looked on with incredulous admiration. How could he dare order Fence around? This Mr. Tibbs must be an influential man. And somehow, he reminded Rosie of someone.

Joe Fence shot an accusatory look at Rosie. He kept the reins short as the stallion crossed the starting line at a light trot. Rosie maintained her gentle rein connection. Diamond kept calm even with Spirit's Dream trotting alongside her. Rosie kept her in this position as Joe increased his speed. Spirit's Dream was doubtlessly fast—and he held a trot, too, even without the overcheck. Joe grinned triumphantly as he passed the mare.

Rosie rolled her eyes. Trotting Diamond loosely kept pace with Spirit's Dream although the race was really speeding up. She strained at her reins a bit now, but Rosie calmed her. There was nothing to be gained by spending one's strength before the final stretch. Finally, they passed the curved side, and the finish line came into view.

"Now."

Rosie gave Trotting Diamond the reins, and the mare flew, effortlessly placing herself next to Spirit's Dream. The horses jockeyed back and forth—Rosie's heart danced with joy, and she even tossed Joe Fence an animated look. However, he wasn't paying attention. With his face puckered, he was struggling with his stallion, which obviously didn't want to trot. Diamond left the dead-even position and pushed ahead of the stallion. She was trotting faster and faster. Rosie could have cheered. Diamond exceeded all her expectations.

And next to her, Spirit's Dream pulled the reins out of Fence's hands and galloped ahead—shooting triumphantly past Diamond, still dutifully trotting. Rosie's sweetest smile spread across her face. Her Diamond would not let herself be goaded. Joe Fence glared at her apoplectically as his sulky rolled past hers.

"He's fast, to be sure," said Mr. Tibbs with an indulgent smirk as Fence stopped in front of him. "You still need to work on his gait, though."

"I told you, he needs the overcheck!"

Joe Fence launched into a list of excuses, but Rosie was not listening. To her surprise, she saw Dr. Taylor and Roberta climbing down from the stands.

"Rosie, that was wonderful." Roberta smiled radiantly and embraced her aunt as Rosie got out of the sulky. "Vincent picked me up, and we figured we'd find you here. And what a surprise, we got to see our very own race!"

Vincent Taylor was downright giddy. "Rosie, that was unbelievable. I've never seen a horse move so effortlessly, especially against a stallion that fast. He won on the last race day, didn't he, Mr. Fence?"

"There you have it, Mr. Tibbs," insisted Joe. "Allow me to introduce the track's veterinarian. If anyone would know, it's him. Let the horse run with the overcheck."

Tibbs, however, made no reply. He had eyes only for Rosie and Roberta.

"It can't be," he said, visibly moved. "It's completely impossible that you're old enough to be Violet Paisley, but you look just like her."

Roberta laughed. "I'm Roberta Fence, Violet's daughter. But my mother does still look very young." She offered Tibbs her hand. "How do you know my mother? And Rosie?"

The man looked at Rosie with misty eyes. "Tom Tibbs is my name," he said, again comically doffing his cap. "But they called me 'Bulldog' on the ship."

Roberta had never seen Rosie smile so unabashedly. "You looked after us," she said quietly. "I remember you asking my dad to scrub the cabin."

Bulldog boomed with laughter. "Well, I wouldn't say I 'asked,' but it was clean afterward! I can't believe I—pardon me, Miss Paisley, but I can't believe I found you. I never forgot you, you know?"

Rosie smiled again. "I didn't forget you either," she said.

"Quite the reunion here," Joe Fence scoffed. "Hi there, little sis. To what do I owe the honor of your visit? You've never bothered with me before."

"Joe!" Roberta blanched. She had not seen Joe since childhood and was taken aback by his resemblance to their father. "I didn't even know you were here."

Though Chloe had informed Violet of her son's whereabouts, she hadn't yet had an opportunity to tell Roberta. She was busy helping out in the Caversham school but had yet to take a definite position. Roberta knew that if she could return Vincent's love, he would ask for her hand. But if she married, she would no longer be able to work as a teacher. This weekend in Addington was supposed to bring her closer to a decision. And it was harmless. She was not, after all, officially visiting Vincent, but Rosie. If things went well, Roberta could see herself taking a position in Christchurch. That way, she could get to know Vincent in peace. Like Rosie, Roberta had been scarred by Violet's disastrous marriage to Eric Fence. Though she did not shy away from men like her aunt did, she would have preferred to settle down with someone she'd known from childhood. With Kevin, she would have felt secure. Vincent had to prove himself worthy of her trust.

Now, Vincent looked stunned at the revelation. "Seriously, Joe? Roberta's your sister? You two must have loads to tell each other."

It was plain the siblings had nothing to tell each other, but Vincent had at least managed to break the tension.

"And you emigrated from England with Roberta's mother and Rosie, Mr.—?"

"Tibbs," Bulldog repeated. "I still can't believe it."

"I'm sure you'd like to catch up too," Vincent surmised.

Bulldog nodded eagerly, Rosie with a slight blush.

"Shall we all have a cup of tea?" Vincent looked around encouragingly.

"I can't," grumbled Joe. "I have to take the horse back. What do you say, Mr. Tibbs? Will you buy it?"

"I have to take Diamond home," Rosie said shyly.

Bulldog smiled his puppy-dog smile, but this time, he showed his teeth a little, and Roberta saw where his nickname came from. He really did look like a friendly fighting dog, but one you had to take seriously.

"It depends, that, with the stallion," he now mused. "First, the price; I think we need to talk a bit about that. Your horse doesn't hold his trot as well as you claimed, Mr. Fence. And as for the trainer—"

"The horse can remain in my stables, of course," Fence declared. "I'd even insist you have it continue preparing for races with experts. To which I might add, I have the best address in Addington."

Bulldog furrowed his brow, doing his name further justice. "Continue training with you? So that, during the next race, whether Spirit's Dream gets shown up by a pony depends on a piece of leather?" He winked conspiratorially at Rosie. "No, Mr. Fence, whether I buy Spirit's Dream will depend on his future trainer, or traineress. Would you take my horse's training into your charge, Miss Paisley?"

Rosie flushed with happiness. "Yes—no, I have to ask Lord Barrington if—I mean, yes. Yes, well, if his lordship allows it, then yes."

Lord Barrington would likely have nothing against it, and Chloe would be willing to ask him. But right now, Rosie was so excited that she might even dare to address the lord herself.

Bulldog grinned good-naturedly. "Well then, wonderful. I'll work something out with his lordship. I know the man. I have a delivery company, you see, and whenever the Barringtons get furniture or the like from England, I drive it here or out to the plains. Just wait a moment while Mr. Fence and I reach an agreement. Then we'll take the horses home together."

Chapter 3

Vincent Taylor cursed his luck. He'd finally had Roberta all to himself, and then, the sudden reunion made him afraid she might not find time for him. And then there was the stuffed horse. He'd seen it in her handbag when he helped her out of the train. Vincent once again had the feeling of having to fight with a phantom.

Rosie and Bulldog had left the racetrack gleefully, which could not be said of Joe Fence. Tom Tibbs had paid Roberta's brother a good price for his stallion, but the thought of Rosie competing with him as a trainer was not to Joe's liking. Roberta watched with concern as her brother stormed off. She knew that face from her father, and she would not want to trade places with the person Joe was now going to let out his anger on—she just hoped it was not a woman.

But Joe wouldn't ruin this for her. She was here to see Vincent.

"What shall we do now?" she asked him. "Will you show me Addington?"

The question of what a fellow did in Addington with a girl he wanted to marry was one Vincent had asked himself. Aside from the racetrack, the suburb had rather little to offer. Nonetheless, Vincent led his friend dutifully down the rows of the brightly painted workers' houses and then out into the rural surrounds. Vincent talked about how lucky he felt to have found the position at the racetrack. He loved being able to work exclusively with horses. The methods and machinations of some trainers, however, he rejected, and he was happily surprised when Roberta agreed with him. For the first time, she told him in detail about her family and her childhood.

"We even lived near here for a time. Back then, the racing center was Woolston. And my mother loves to talk about how she often took us to

Christchurch, on foot no less, to hear the speeches of the women's rights activists. That's where she got to know Kate Sheppard." Roberta smiled. "And reconnected with Sean Coltrane."

"The lawyer who used to be in Parliament?" asked Vincent. "He's your stepfather, right? Is he really brothers with that ghastly Colin Coltrane? I still don't understand how all of you are related."

Roberta laughed. "Half brothers," she corrected him. "Sean's also a half brother of Kevin Drury. He shares a mother with Colin, a father with Kevin. But Colin and Sean didn't grow up together. When Kathleen left her husband, Colin remained with his father. He's supposed to have been a similar, um, a similarly unbalanced character."

Vincent smiled and put his arm around her carefully. "Roberta, once you're certain you love me, would you say 'bastard' when you mean bastard? It's nice to express oneself decently, but sometimes, one does not find—how should I put it—exactly the right word in high-brow dictionaries like your mother had."

Roberta made a face. "I'm vulgar enough as it is," she complained. "Miss Byerly, my superior in the Caversham school, is constantly chiding me about it. And the stories I tell my students. Africa was not very good for my, um, career."

Vincent pulled her closer. "Perhaps you should consider a different sort of career," he said. "As a veterinarian's wife, you could even curse. Not on Sundays, of course."

"You're trying to get a rise out of me."

"No, I'm trying to bring about your fall," Vincent declared. "You see, I'm taking you to a pub. Don't worry, it's not one of the gin mills by the racetrack. Lord Barrington frequents it when he's here, as do all the local notables. And tonight, they're holding a concert. There'll be other ladies present, and we don't need to tell Miss Byerly. Will you come?"

Roberta thought about it. It was nice to walk with Vincent's arm around her, along a stream with reeds growing along its banks. As for the pub, she trusted him. It would be silly to sit at the inn with Rosie, hearing all about horses instead of going to the concert.

"Singing or instrumental music?" she asked bravely.

Vincent smiled. "A singer will be performing."

***

Juliet LaBree-Drury had long since had enough of New Zealand. The country was simply too small and too provincial for her art. There were no stages on which she could adequately present herself, no audience worldly enough to appreciate her refined songs and piano arrangements.

The establishment in Queenstown that Pit Frazer had swept her off to, for example, had revealed itself to be little more than a cathouse. It was called a hotel, of course, and the proprietress was trying to class it up, but Daphne's didn't begin to compare with the nightclubs where Juliet had performed in New Orleans. Moreover, she and Daphne O'Hara were soon butting heads. Juliet did not like to have either her program or her interactions with the audience dictated—for which Daphne showed little sympathy. When Juliet, for only the second time, was standing with one of the little city's notables at the bar, allowing him to buy her a glass of champagne, the determined red-haired madam with a feline face pulled the singer aside.

"Just so we understand each other, sweetie, you don't work here on your own account. My girls are treated decently, but they have to give me fifty percent of what they make, and that goes for you, too, if you sell yourself here. You understand?"

"Sell myself?" Juliet responded indignantly. "I don't know what you mean. But while we're on the topic of decency—perhaps you could sell some decent champagne. No one can drink this swill."

Daphne rolled her eyes. "You know exactly what I mean. Even if you're selling yourself as higher class or whatever, it's the same in the end. Or do you mean to tell me you're doing baldie over there out of love?" She indicated the man waiting patiently at the bar. "Were you on fire for him all week? Just like the scribbler who brought you here? No, sweetie, don't bother. Either you keep your legs closed, or you give me my share. In exchange, you work in a nice room with fresh sheets every day. Now, now, don't act like you wouldn't settle for less. You've seen worse days, I can tell."

Naturally, Juliet would not stand for this and traveled onward the next day. That man had already provided the necessary seed money. He really was generous—it was insolent to treat him like a client. Juliet would herself have used the word "patron." She headed for the booming West Coast, where swanky hotels were popping up, even if most were still under construction.

Unfortunately, their proprietors proved excessively prudish. They seemed to be concerned with distinguishing themselves from the coal miners' pubs in the city center. Juliet was sent packing twice for intending to end the evening with gentlemen in her room—even if very distinguished ones. At least that was handled discreetly, unlike with Daphne. However, there could be no thought of longer engagements, and while the patron's money did suffice for a halfway glamorous life, it was not even close to enough for first-class passage on a ship to America or even Europe.

Now, there was this backwater Addington, outside of Christchurch—since she had not found an engagement within the city itself. No doubt there were a few rich men living there, but they were apparently more fixated on horses than beautiful women. The bar was not to her taste either. The Addington Swan could at best be described as blandly bourgeois. New Orleans jazz fit here like a lobster with mashed potatoes.

Juliet sat down at the piano and eyed the stodgy audience in the ridiculously overlit room. They were too solemnly dressed for a visit to a club and lacked any refinement. Heavens, compared to Addington, Dunedin had been Paris.

But, wait, the young woman in the last row was an exception. Her dress was simple but emphasized her figure—it was one of these reform dresses, which were fortunately going out of style again. Most women, after all, had looked as if they were wearing a potato sack. But this woman, with her braided, chestnut-brown hair, somehow looked the part of a classical goddess. Really only one tailor could make reform dresses like that: Kathleen Burton at the Gold Mine Boutique.

Juliet stole another look as she began to sing of longing and love. The goddess in the last row whispered something excitedly into the ear of her companion, a slender young man whose honest face bored Juliet. But the girl—Juliet had without a doubt seen her before.

Juliet's voice bewitched and beguiled the audience as she mentally reviewed all the people she knew from Dunedin. Finally, it came to her. Kevin's little admirer. The shy girl he had made happy with a stupid stuffed horsey. Juliet decided it would be better to avoid her after the concert.

But when Juliet had finished and left the stage to rather scattered applause from her uncomprehending audience, the young woman rushed over to her.

"Mrs. Drury! That was beautiful. But I didn't know—Patrick didn't mention. Anyway, are you coming back to Dunedin? May is so adorable."

Juliet struggled to smile. "You're, um, Kevin's little niece, is that right?"

"Not quite. I'm Roberta Fence, Atamarie's friend. Atamarie's Kevin's niece, and, naturally, Patrick's too." Her voice now sounded a little recriminating.

Juliet was annoyed. It had been gauche to simply forget Patrick.

"Yes, yes, of course, forgive me. There were so many things that happened all at once in Dunedin."

She let her gaze wander to Roberta's companion, and smiled seductively. Really, that was the surest way to bring a conversation with another woman to an end.

But the man had no eyes for Juliet. He seemed to worship Roberta alone. And she, well, either she did not care about him or she trusted him completely.

"You can renew your acquaintance with all of us when you come home," Roberta remarked with sugary sweetness.

Juliet registered with certain respect that the young lady seemed to have overcome her shyness.

"Oh yes, Dunedin." Juliet sighed theatrically. "I don't know yet if I'll be passing through. My obligations, you know."

She brushed a strand of hair out of her face lasciviously and smoldered at Vincent once more.

"Allow me to introduce Dr. Vincent Taylor," Roberta said stiffly. "He's the veterinarian for the racetrack here. Vincent and I were together in—"

"South Africa," Vincent completed the thought with a bow.

Juliet's ears pricked up. "Then you know Kevin Drury?" she blurted out. "How's he doing?"

Vincent nodded guilelessly. "Certainly, Kevin and I were in the army together. And Miss Fence was a teacher in the Boer camps, and worked wonders, if I may say so." He beamed.

"Kevin's well," Roberta added. "As are Patrick and May. Oh yes, and Kevin is—"

"You can see for yourself when you get back to Dunedin," Vincent said eagerly. "Roberta says you're married to Patrick Drury?"

Juliet nodded distractedly. So, Kevin was back? Of course, that crazy war overseas was over. Her mind raced feverishly.

"I'll think about it, all that with Dunedin," she said.

Roberta smiled—sardonically, Vincent realized to his astonishment. He had never seen such an expression on her.

"Patrick would surely be extraordinarily happy." Roberta beamed at her former rival. "And Kevin, well, I'm sure he'd love to introduce his wife. She's a Boer woman, an exceptional beauty. And the two of them have the most charming little boy."

Chapter 4

Lizzie changed baby Abe while keeping a watchful eye on May, who was tussling with one of the collies on the kitchen floor. The dog was good-natured, but the girl was two years old now, and if she got too rough, it might protest. Mostly, though, May was gentle and oddly graceful for her age, and Lizzie never got tired of her exotic beauty. Kevin and Doortje's son had a finely carved little face, and his first locks were golden blond. Sometimes Lizzie thought she saw a metallic shimmer like in Atamarie's hair. She had thought that hair color only ran in Kathleen's family.

Lizzie pulled on Abe's little pants and shirt, stroked May's black locks, and thought for the umpteenth time what gorgeous grandchildren had come her way. She would have been perfectly content—if only the children's mothers were a bit easier. Lizzie still thought of Juliet with dread—in her opinion, the singer's flight was the best thing that could have happened to Patrick. Unfortunately, Patrick Drury wasn't over it. Though he took exemplary care of his "daughter," who was actually his niece, he couldn't seem to shake his heartbreak. But he must have known that Juliet did not love him. Lizzie doubted that she had offered even Kevin honest affection, but those two had had something, at least.

Lizzie was slowly starting to worry about her younger son. Patrick had always stood a bit in Kevin's shadow—Kevin, who was his father's son, was without a doubt the more scintillating personality of the two, and even Lizzie could hardly resist her elder son when he galloped up to her door with a radiant expression and curly black hair blowing in the wind. Patrick, on the other hand, took after Lizzie. His exterior was unassuming, but he was warm, loyal, and intensely reliable. Unfortunately, he lacked the thick skin that Lizzie had developed during her youth in London and exile in Tasmania. It had been too easy for Juliet to break his heart. Lizzie could only hope he'd get over it someday.

And now Kevin with his Doortje, this girl he really seemed to love. But was it a happy marriage? The way the two of them acted around each other, Lizzie kept wondering how they had ever produced a child. The young couple had been living for a few days now on Elizabeth Station, but Lizzie simply could not warm up to her new daughter-in-law. Of course, Doortje was the exact opposite of Juliet. She was interested in everything that happened on the farm, and she was never lazy—only her care for Abe left something to be desired. Doortje seemed to think it built character to let the baby scream now and then before she fed it, which caused Lizzie pain in her soul. Doortje, however, informed her that the boy needed to get used to privation.

"But surely not in his first six months," Lizzie objected.

Doortje's conviction, though, was ironclad, as in so many things. And she never lost her composure. Never in her eventful life had Lizzie met a woman who was so self-controlled, although she clearly suffered from constant stress. Someday that volcano would have to erupt, and Lizzie was already dreading it.

"Can I help somehow?"

A friendly, high-pitched voice with a strong accent interrupted Lizzie's reflections. Once again, Nandi had slipped into the house without a sound. The young woman always went barefoot and moved like a lissome cat.

Lizzie smiled at her. Of all the feminine beings to have taken up quarters in her house in the last few years, she liked Nandi best by a mile. Nandi was helpful and willing to learn, her English was constantly improving, and she always seemed happy. With big, astonished eyes, she gazed at the new world, which must have been even more foreign to her than to her mistress. Mistress—Lizzie trembled at the word, but she also refused to translate *baas*, which Nandi still called Doortje, any more generously.

But Lizzie no longer believed that—not after the ugly incident with Haikina and Hemi, who came to visit shortly after Doortje's arrival. Michael had been with the sheep, Lizzie in the vineyard, and Kevin at his new practice. The Maori had only encountered Doortje and Nandi in the garden. They were bringing gifts from the tribe for the young woman, tried to start a conversation, and heard Nandi addressing Doortje as *baas*. When they repeated it, Doortje did not correct them. On the contrary, when Haikina came by a few days later to help harvest grapes, Doortje insisted on the title. Lizzie then had a stern talk with her and was horrified at her reaction. "Your Kaffir can't simply call you by your names," she had replied.

Once again, Doortje would not budge an inch, despite Lizzie explaining the close relationship between the Drurys and the tribe—without mentioning the gold, of course.

"She'll learn," Haikina told Kevin. "Bring her along to our festivals. Maybe she could read a few books or newspapers, too, about the women who fought for the right to vote and the Maori Parliament."

"Haikina would be happy to lend you a few books," Lizzie told her a few days later.

Doortje had been perusing the bookshelf almost as discontentedly as Juliet before her. Only, she found Lizzie's books on viniculture not only boring but morally objectionable, just like the women's journals Lizzie occasionally bought and that Juliet had devoured.

"The black woman can read?" Doortje asked, horrified. "That's against God's will."

Now Lizzie understood why Nandi so carefully hid her small treasury of Kevin and Patrick's old children's books.

"Haikina is a teacher. She taught your husband how to read," Lizzie informed her daughter-in-law, now really angry. "And since it's quite far to the school in Lawrence, she'll also be teaching Abe. Unless you have designs on that yourself. But he's sure not going to learn in Afrikaans or out of that old Bible of yours alone, over my dead body."

Doortje had stared at her wrathfully at that, but had not replied. Thankfully, it was still a long time until Abe's schooling.

Lizzie sighed. The thought of having to contend with this daughter-in-law for years made her sick.

"You can take May out for a bit," she now told Nandi, "before it rains again. If you like, you can take Abe with you too. Are you already done in the garden? Where's Doortje hiding?"

"Tries to milk sheep," Nandi informed her. "I not help. *Baas* said I not have to help if I am afraid." Nandi gave Lizzie a concerned and guilty look.

Lizzie had nothing against Doortje's attempts at cheese making per se. Unfortunately, Michael's prize-winning wool producers were not about to hold still. Normally, they lived free with their flock and really only knew people from shearing time—and the occasional assisted birth. Neither was a positive experience. The animals fled any touch. During Doortje's attempts to tie them down and milk them, they kicked and thrashed about. Nandi had earned painful bruises and was now afraid of them. Doortje, by contrast, would not let it go. Every day she struggled with three independent-minded ewes—and would not accept defeat.

"Every year we have a few orphaned lambs, Doortje. You could simply tame two or three of them and acclimate them to milking," Kevin suggested. "Then, in two years, you'll have ewes who will hardly leave your side, and the cheese will be better too."

Doortje, however, was set on immediate cheese production—she seemed to draw some kind of satisfaction from the daily melee with the animals.

Lizzie could only shake her head at that.

"You only have to do one thing, Nandi," she now said amiably, "and that's to stop calling Michael *baas*. He's not your master. Call him Michael, or Mr. Drury, if you must. But I don't want to hear this 'slaves can't' here. Which brings me to the question of your wage. It's not right for you to work for us for free."

Nandi looked shocked. "But what I do with money?"

Lizzie had a few suggestions. However, hoofbeats and the sound of wagon wheels interrupted them. Lizzie looked out the window—and with a mixture of joy and trepidation, she recognized Lady, Patrick's mare. It was good that Patrick was back, but it would have to bring the confrontation between him and Kevin that Lizzie had long feared. Juliet still stood between them, and now Doortje, who was acting like a farmer's wife, might too. It could not please Patrick to see Kevin and his wife on the farm. Elizabeth Station was his inheritance, whereas Kevin had received his lengthy medical studies and the practice in Dunedin. Lizzie could only hope that her younger son did not take Kevin's move to Otago as an affront.

Yet Patrick did not look unhappy. Lizzie took May in her arms to go meet him, and Patrick danced through the door, stroking the collie on the head when it leaped up on him, then hugging Lizzie and May at the same time. Lizzie had not seen him this happy in ages.

"Mother, May, my sweet. You'll never believe whom I've brought with me."

May gurgled amiably in response—but a bad feeling took root in Lizzie and was quickly confirmed.

"Patrick, surprise or not, you can't just leave me sitting in the wagon. It's raining."

In the door stood Juliet LaBree-Drury. Lizzie looked at her in disbelief. Nandi, in contrast, was visibly interested. The beautiful Creole was the first person of color she had encountered in New Zealand.

Juliet laughed. "Cat got your tongue, Lizzie?" With feigned nonchalance, she went up to Lizzie and greeted her with kisses on the cheek. "Patrick thought you'd be thunderstruck, but well, you did have to reckon on me coming back someday."

Lizzie cleared her throat. "No," she admitted, "honestly, we had not reckoned on that."

Juliet turned to Nandi and eyed her without any compunction.

"Heavens, I don't believe it. A black woman. A cute one at that. But he always did have good taste. Let me look at you, girl. You're Kevin's wife?"

Nandi stared at the ground, embarrassed.

"Forgive me," Patrick said apologetically. "My wife is, um, somewhat impulsive. But I had also, if you'll forgive me, pictured you differently."

Lizzie stepped in. "Nandi, this is Patrick Drury, my younger son, and his, er, wife, Juliet. Juliet, Patrick, this is Nandi. Doortje's lady's maid," she said, choosing the most status-enhancing term she knew.

Juliet made a face. So, Kevin's wife had had a servant at her disposal—a lady's maid, even.

She cast a look at the blond—and certainly white—child in Nandi's arms.

Nandi was approaching Patrick with him. "This Abraham. Your nephew, yes?"

Patrick smiled at her. "Yes, that's right. You're learning English, miss?"

Nandi nodded.

Another woman was now entering the kitchen. Doortje Drury was wearing her usual Boer work clothing: blue dress, apron, bonnet. Everything had been clean and fresh that morning but had not survived the battle with the ewes unscathed. She looked rumpled and dirty, her dress dusted with bits of straw and sheep manure. Added to which, she had run from the sheep barn through the rain. Doortje's eyes nevertheless flashed triumphantly, and no one could deny she was exceptionally beautiful.

"I have milk," Doortje declared, and held up a bucket. "I managed to milk two of them."

Lizzie suppressed a laugh. "Allow me to introduce you. Doortje Drury, Patrick and Juliet Drury. This is my younger son and his wife."

Lizzie's daughters-in-law eyed each other, equally stunned. Juliet stared at Doortje's manure-smeared apron, Doortje at Juliet's mixed-race features.

Patrick relieved the tension a little by offering his sister-in-law his hand. "I look forward to making your acquaintance," he said formally. "That is, both yours and little Abe's." He took the baby from Nandi and rocked him in his arms. "The family resemblance is unmistakable," he remarked guilelessly. "He looks like Atamarie, doesn't he?"

Chapter 5

Lord Barrington had generously allowed Rosie to lodge Bulldog's black stallion in his racing stables and to train on his grounds. To which end, he acquired a trainer's license for her, which was not exactly simple: the racing association might look past female harness racers as long as no one shouted it from the rooftops, but licensing a female trainer?

His lordship proved rather inventive here. He accompanied Rosie to the Canterbury Trotting Club and supported her request for a license.

"Ross Paisley," he introduced Rosie, who had hidden her short hair under a newsboy cap and her figure under a shapeless shirt. She wore dungarees to match. "Very gifted, a real asset for the club."

The secretary of the Canterbury Trotting Club looked up reluctantly from his work. "So, what's the man's proper name?" he inquired. "I need the full name for the papers. It's Ross, isn't it, or is that short for something?"

His lordship bent down to him. "Certainly," he whispered. "But would you like to have the name 'Rosamond Paisley' emblazoned on your documents?"

The secretary chortled. "His name is Rosamond?" he boomed.

Rosie blushed. Really her name was Rosemary, but she had thought it impudent to show up as a boy with that name.

The secretary could hardly contain his laughter. "Well, some parents deserve a thrashing. Although, the boy looks a little ladylike, don't he?"

Rosie held her breath, but the man was already reaching for his pen. A few minutes later, she held a trainer's license with the name "Ross Paisley" in her hands.

Joe Fence and the two other trainers in Addington tried to create an uproar. Rosie's sex was, after all, universally known on the racetrack. The racing club, however, would not be moved. Lord Barrington had major influence in Addington, and Tom Tibbs might be an up-and-coming name among the horse owners. After all, he had money and a knack for horses. No one in the racing leadership would force a new trainer under the protection of both to pull down their pants in public. Besides, the horse Paisley trained acquitted itself excellently.

***

Vincent Taylor, however, was not so enthusiastic when Rosie Paisley called him to examine her mare, Trotting Diamond, for the third time in two weeks.

"Rosie, there's nothing wrong with her," he insisted. "There wasn't on Monday, and there isn't today either. Maybe she's a little excited. Her pulse is a bit quicker than it should be, but—"

"She trembled," Rosie insisted, "and she's sweating differently than usual. Something's not right, Dr. Taylor. I notice these things."

Vincent shook his head. "I can't find anything, anyway. Is she racing well as always?"

Rosie nodded. "She qualified for the Auckland Trotting Cup," she declared proudly. "I just don't know how I'll get her to the North Island—it's so far."

"Fence also sends horses there," Vincent said. "But of course, you won't want to transport her with them. What about Mr. Tibbs?"

"Oh, Mr. Tibbs is very satisfied," she reported eagerly. "The stallion is doing well, you know. He won second place on the last race day. But Auckland? Maybe next year."

"I meant he could sponsor your trip," Vincent said. "He doesn't lack for money."

Though Bulldog's freight company might have seemed small, the enterprise was actually spread across the whole South Island. Tibbs maintained branches in Blenheim, Queenstown, and on the West Coast. He was already thinking of motorizing and buying shares in the railroad.

"Oh no, I wouldn't want to do that," Rosie murmured. "He already spends so much on Dream."

"He pays you an entirely normal training rate," Vincent replied, "nothing more or less. And in return, you do very good work. You don't need to be embarrassed about it."

"But I'm happy to do it," Rosie insisted, "for, um, Mr. Tibbs."

Vincent now smiled conspiratorially at her. "Haven't you ever considered that Mr. Tibbs might be happy to do something for you too?"

The light in Rosie's and Tibbs's eyes could not be missed. However, the relationship did not quite seem to advance. Of course, Vincent wasn't doing much better with Roberta. He sighed as he patted Trotting Diamond in goodbye. Everything had looked so promising, but after their encounter with that slick, unscrupulous singer, Roberta seemed to withdraw back into herself. It must have something to do with Kevin. And according to Roberta's last letter, this Juliet character was now back in Dunedin, or Otago. There seemed to have been something of a clash between Kevin and his brother. This last piece of information he had from his friend's own mouth. Kevin had accompanied his father to a meeting of the livestock breeders' association in Christchurch, and he came to Addington to see Vincent. He was none too eager to hobnob with the livestock barons.

"It's really more your brother's job, isn't it?" Vincent asked during their first round of whiskey.

Kevin looked into his glass. "Patrick won't budge from Juliet's side these days, and he insisted that she move to Otago with him, to our parents' farm. So they'd have more time together and could reconnect."

He gave Vincent the rough outlines of Patrick's marriage so far. The veterinarian listened attentively. And pursed his lips when he put two and two together.

"This Juliet wouldn't happen to be the girl who drove you to war, would she?"

Kevin grimaced. "How'd you figure it out?"

"Roberta's reaction to her hinted as much. She's usually so polite, but she really crossed swords with this Juliet person. And now you're all living on the farm? You with Doortje and Patrick with Juliet? Your poor parents."

"No, no. Juliet and Doortje can't stand each other. Although, I don't know what Juliet has against Doortje."

Vincent almost choked on his whiskey. "Might I offer a few conjectures?"

Kevin looked at him punitively. "Laugh it up," he said melodramatically. "Unfortunately, what Doortje has against Juliet is clear. Juliet is Creole—oh, right, you've seen her. A rare beauty, don't you think?"

Vincent tilted his head. "Beauty isn't everything. She doesn't hold a candle to Roberta. She's got something hounded about her, if you ask me. But you do like the difficult cases. Doortje—"

"Could hardly be dragged to a table with Juliet," sighed Kevin. "Nor was Juliet particularly congenial. She treated Doortje like a bumpkin, and Doortje didn't have a quick counter to that. Still, she marveled aloud that a 'colored girl' could speak in complete sentences."

Vincent groaned. "Something's going to have to give, Kevin. She's still so, so—"

Kevin buried his head in his hands. "We're still not living a marriage," he admitted. "She doesn't resist, and I have to confess I—I've taken her twice. And she did not object. On the contrary, she said she'd wondered, but she lay there, stiff as a board. It's not right, Vincent. Nothing's right. And now, I'm living with her in the old log cabin."

"Where?"

"It's a gold miner's hut my parents built for themselves long before they had the farm. It's old, but sturdy, and closer to Lawrence, which is certainly a pro for me. My parents suggested it after Patrick—well, he's made himself quite clear. He doesn't want me or Doortje anywhere near Juliet."

"Somehow, I can understand that."

"I'm so glad you're amused," Kevin retorted bitterly. "At least, Doortje was immediately in favor. She spoke of a farm of our own, which upset Patrick again. The gold miner's hut sits on Elizabeth Station land. But at any rate, he had nothing against us living there for the time being. And now Doortje acts as if she's completely satisfied. She has a few sheep, a cow, and she's planting a garden, or is at least supervising Nandi while she plants a garden. The poor thing is breaking her back, but for Doortje, the division of labor is clear: the coarser work is for the Kaffir; the more sophisticated is for the *baas*. She bakes the bread herself, makes the cheese. It would almost be nice if she—well, if we were a loving couple. You know what I mean?"

"Of course."

For a moment, Vincent lost himself in dreams of building a home far out in the country, but then shook it off. Roberta was a city girl, and Addington might already have been too provincial for her. Was that the reason she had cooled off toward him? But no, he did not believe that. Roberta's withdrawing had to do with Juliet. And—though he hated to admit it—Kevin.

"But out in that wilderness, she must be bored to death," Kevin complained. "That's how it is for me, anyway, when I come back from the practice. Doortje puts dinner on the table, I try to start a conversation, she tells me a bit about her day—but then that's it. There's nothing to say."

"And Nandi?" asked Vincent.

"She sleeps in the toolshed. Which I hate. Doortje treats her like a dog. The whole thing's a mess. I wish I could move back to Dunedin."

Kevin ordered another whiskey. He seemed determined to get drunk. Vincent took another sip too.

"You should, then," he advised. "'I will follow where you lead' and all that. It's pure Old Testament. Besides, you're not doing her any favors by allowing her to set up a little Africa in Otago. Not to mention, you can't let your son grow up on the Dutch Bible and bloody Voortrekker legends. Take Doortje to Dunedin and force her to assimilate. She'll manage. She's intelligent, and I bet—I bet Roberta would help." He swallowed. "And while we're on the topic of Roberta . . ." He pressed ahead in a feigned lighthearted tone. He had to know. "Have you—have you ever been attracted to her?"

Kevin looked up, startled. "Your Roberta? Oh, come now, don't tell me she's still pining for me. She had a crush when she was little, but now she's grown. I thought she was nearly engaged to you?"

"So, you don't find her attractive, then?" Vincent asked seriously.

Kevin laughed. "No, Vincent, I really don't. She's cute, no doubt. But she's—listen, my niece and Roberta grew up together. My lands, I even gave the sweet girl a stuffed horsey a few years ago. Roberta Fence is like family. I have no interest in her that way."

Vincent Taylor's heart felt a bit lighter. If Kevin posed no real threat, a few dreams and a stuffed horse were all he would have to contend with.

***

Around the same time, Doortje's establishment of a personal little Africa was going off the rails—independently of Kevin and Vincent's schemes.

Patrick Drury had honestly wanted to improve relations with his new sister-in-law when he stopped by during a ride through the sheep pastures. It had not escaped him how much Doortje and Juliet disliked each other—he already had his misgivings about why Juliet rejected the Boer, but he could not comprehend the deep antipathy from the other side. Patrick did not know anything about South Africa, and this sort of overt racism was foreign to him. As a result, he did not grasp why Doortje seemed personally offended by Patrick's marriage to Juliet. He regretted the conflict with his brother and wanted, on the one hand, to set it aside, but, on the other, to keep as much space between Kevin and Juliet as possible. All of that was very difficult, and Doortje's hostility did not make it easier. Here, however, Patrick told himself things could be remedied. If he drank coffee now and then with his new sister-in-law—without Juliet contributing spiteful comments—he could surely win her over.

So, on that radiant spring day, he hitched his horse in front of the cabin and knocked. No one answered, so Patrick decided to walk around back. His mother had said Doortje was planting a garden, and the sheep had to be housed somewhere too.

He heard someone singing a foreign tune as the garden and stables came into view. And then he saw Nandi.

She wore a summer dress—really just a colorful band of cloth, which she had ably wound around her body, ending above the knee. Despite her light garment, Nandi was sweating, which was no wonder. She was striking a spade over and over into the dry ground with all her might to clear a bed.

"Nandi," he called, "what are you up to there? That's much too hard for you."

Nandi turned around. When she saw Patrick, joy spread across her narrow, aristocratic face. "*Baas* Patrick," she said cheerfully. "Good day." She curtsied and giggled.

"A lovely day to you as well," he greeted her, and bowed just as formally.

She giggled again. "Always funny, *baas* Patrick."

"Well, I don't see anything funny about it," he said. "I'm here to visit Mrs. Drury. Is she here?"

Nandi shook her head. "She went up to Mrs. Lizzie Drury, bringing fresh cheese."

Patrick nodded. All their differences aside, Lizzie and Doortje sedulously exchanged agricultural products. At first, Lizzie had wondered at that. She had expected Doortje would be happy finally to be rid of her, but Boer women seemed to do things like the wives of the farmers Patrick advised. You shared with your neighbors whether you liked them or not, and moreover, if they belonged to your family, you did your best to minimize conflicts.

Patrick took the spade from Nandi's hands. "Let me do this while I'm waiting for Doortje. She won't stay up there long, I'm sure. And this work's too much for you."

"Oh no, *baas*, um, Mr. Patrick." She looked at him, seeking approval, although Patrick had not reproved the title before. In truth, he had no idea what it meant. "I, we always did. It's our work on farm."

"What do you mean 'we'?" asked Patrick. "I mean, the little fellow can't contribute much just yet." Smiling, he indicated Abe, who was sleeping peacefully in a basket in the shadow of a rata bush. Next to him lay an open book, *Alice in Wonderland* by Lewis Carroll. "Or does he read to you while you dig?" He winked.

Nandi laughed again. "No, he can't read yet. He is still baby, Mr. Patrick. 'We' is father and mother and brother and Nandi. We always worked in fields of *baas* van Stout."

At the thought of her family, Nandi's eyes clouded over.

"That sounds like at least two men, Nandi. But here—" He let his gaze wander over three beds that had already been planted. "Did you do all that alone?"

Nandi nodded. "Mr. Drury says to help when has time. When he has time," she corrected herself. "But much work in hospital. Doctor is hard work. But good. Good to help people." Nandi picked up the baby, who had woken and begun squirming.

"But you need help here too," Patrick observed. Then he cast an eye on the book, which Nandi was tucking into Abe's basket. "By the way, that was my book once."

Nandi's eyes widened. Patrick found her captivating. He had never before encountered a person with such an expressive, candid face.

"Oh, forgive me. I not know. Give back, of course. Please forgive."

Patrick waved it away. "You don't need to apologize. I'm sure my mother gave it to you, didn't she? Consider it a present from me."

"Really, Mr. Patrick? My own book? Then I have three now. Two from Miss Fence and now this one. This prettier than others. Others about children, poor and sad. Poor little Oliver and poor little David. But here funny animals. Rabbit talks. And girl."

Patrick laughed. "Kevin always picked on me for that—for reading girls' books. And I have to admit, these belonged to Matariki first, my half sister. Books like this are passed down, Miss Nandi. You can give it to my daughter in ten years. By then, you'll probably be reading Bulwer-Lytton."

Nandi smiled. "Little May very cute," she said. "But now I keep working, *baas* Doortje otherwise angry. And must also cut grass and feed sheep and milk cow before she comes back."

Patrick had paused his digging. Now, he struck the spade into the ground with all his might.

"What does my brother pay you for all this, anyway?" he asked. Nandi seemed afraid of Doortje. The haste with which she dug, her attempt to hide the book. "You play nanny, dig, feed the livestock. You're doing the work of a whole crew—you do see that?"

Nandi looked away. "I not getting money. Not God's will. *Baas* gives work and food; Kaffir works. God's will." Her voice was flat.

Patrick lowered the spade again. "You're toiling here unpaid? Because it's God's will that whites supervise and blacks work? For food and lodging? Well, I'd like to hear what Miss Morison of the Tailoresses' Union has to say about that. She'd take Doortje to task. And Kevin too. How dare he?"

"Mr. Drury says he wants to give me. Calls 'pocket money.' Pocket money is maybe God's will?" Nandi looked doubtful.

"Nandi, God has very little to do with wage laws in this country. It's the unions that occupy themselves with that. And here, at least, the constitution forbids slavery. You don't have to dig this garden for Mrs. Drury for free."

Nandi looked at him nervously. But an idea was taking root in Patrick's head.

"Listen, Nandi, my wife's wanted an abigail for a long time now."

"Abi—?"

"A lady's maid, a woman who helps a lady dress and do her hair," he explained. "You'd keep Juliet's clothes clean, and we'd also need you to watch May sometimes. But it's not manual labor. I can manage a pound a week to start and, later, maybe two."

"A week?" Nandi asked. "Then I'll be rich soon."

Patrick smiled. "If you're good about saving it," he teased her. "So, what do you say? Can I win you away?"

Desire and duty battled each other on Nandi's face. She had found Mrs. Juliet intriguing—a *baas* of color was unthinkable in South Africa, and maybe she would be kinder than a white *baas*. And Mrs. Juliet lived in the house of Mrs. Lizzie Drury. It would be a dream to return there. Mrs. Drury was so nice, and Nandi would not have to sleep in a shed but would get her own room with a bed and clean sheets. But—

"I can't, Mr. Patrick. I belong to *baas* Doortje Drury; our family work for her family. Always. Is God's will. And Mr. Drury also paid ship. I have to work that off, says *baas* Doortje."

Fury rose within Patrick. So, Kevin knew very well that he was doing wrong by Nandi—which meant he would not dare protest. And honestly, Patrick no longer cared what "*baas*" Doortje might say on the matter.

"Listen, Nandi, I'd like for you to come with me now. We'll take Abe with us. Kevin and Doortje can pick him up later, and then I'll explain to them why you're now working for Juliet and me. This is a free country. You can go where you want and work for whom you please. And don't worry about the ship—you've long since worked that off. It's your decision: slave for Mrs. Drury or lady's maid and nanny for Juliet and me?"

Nandi took a breath. Then she grinned slyly at Patrick.

"I would like to work for Mr. Patrick, and Mrs. Juliet very pretty. Miss May very sweet."

Patrick smiled. "Don't start calling my daughter 'Miss.' She's spoiled enough as it is. Now, let's see if my horse can carry us both." He glanced at Nandi's bare legs. "Or, no, that wouldn't be proper. You'll ride, and I'll lead the horse. A little exercise would do me good. My brother, too, for that matter. He should dig his own garden."

Chapter 6

Kevin Drury stopped by his practice in Lawrence before riding up to the cabin. No one was waiting in front of it, so no one was likely to have missed him while he'd been at the hospital in Christchurch. Kevin had overestimated the villagers' need for medical help when he had offered to take over old Dr. Winter's practice. Of course, Lawrence was very small, and almost no former gold miners ran to the doctor with every little booboo. Their wives preferred the midwife, and there was also a Maori healer in the area. No, Kevin would not be leaving anyone in the lurch if he moved back to the city. He entered the treatment room to look for his bottle of whiskey. Kevin was ashamed that he drank secretly, but Doortje would not tolerate alcohol in the home. That was something else he should talk to her about. Vincent was right—his happiness mattered too.

"I thought you'd come." A dark, sensual voice.

Kevin almost dropped the matches with which he meant to light the gas lamp.

"Juliet."

She smiled and waggled the whiskey bottle. "I prefer champagne, but I suppose that's not strong enough to drink your little Boer away. Isn't that what you're doing? You don't need to drink to make her look good. She's beautiful. But cold, isn't she, Kevin? Cold as a—is it cold in that strange country she comes from?"

Kevin shook his head. Juliet was sitting in his chair. Between them stood his capacious desk. The chair he offered to patients remained for Kevin to sit in, but he stayed standing indecisively.

"Nothing's cold in her country," he answered. "It's hot and dry."

Juliet giggled. "A country where the gods don't cry. A happy country?"

"No, not a happy country. What are you doing here, Juliet? You shouldn't be here. People will think—"

"No one saw me come in," she said. "And if someone sees me when I go, so be it. I'm your sister-in-law, Kevin. Or did you forget?"

She left the chair and lolled lasciviously on the desk. She wore a skin-tight, dark-red dress.

"Precisely," said Kevin with a husky voice. "That's precisely why we should not get too close. Patrick has done enough for me, for us."

"Now, don't act as if Patrick acted selflessly," she purred. "And if it assuages you, I've rewarded him generously. All for a little name for the child."

"She's very lovely," Kevin said, trying desperately to bring the conversation back to a neutral footing, but it was hopeless. Juliet had him back under her spell. Kevin desired his wife more than he ever had Juliet, but what good was that when Doortje's heart was shut to him? When she hid her golden hair under a severe bonnet? Juliet's thick, black locks were spilling over her shoulders. Her fine, slender hands, which usually danced over piano keys, grasped his fountain pen and brushed it across the tops of her breasts as if she were writing a love poem. Kevin thought of Doortje's honest, callused hands, her cheese making, the dough she kneaded. He tried to recall her scent, fresh and earthy and warm as bread, but Juliet's heady perfume pushed it aside. Tomorrow, Kevin would recall why he had fallen in love with Doortje van Stout. But now, she was gone. "He's my brother, Juliet," he pleaded. "We can't—"

Juliet waved this away. "He won't know, and I'll compensate him, not to worry." She smiled wickedly as she now saw jealousy in Kevin's eyes. She would make him forget his Boer woman soon. As for his brother, perhaps they would come to hate each other. It was no concern of hers. "But now and again," she whispered, "I need a real man. You know what I mean, don't you, Kevin? You know Patrick. He is"—she laughed—"far too good. And sometimes you need a real woman. Or isn't she good, your cold beauty from a hot country? Does she kiss you like this, Kevin?" Juliet's lips moved toward his. "Does she love you like this?"

Juliet swung herself around on the desk and wrapped her legs around Kevin's hips. Kevin Drury gave up. He pulled Juliet into his arms.

Chapter 7

Doortje was beside herself when Kevin got home.

"Nandi's gone," she cried. "Look."

Doortje held out a piece of paper, on which Patrick had explained the circumstances in brief words.

Kevin shut his eyes. "I can't do anything about that." Under no circumstances was he going to fight with Patrick now. Kevin was ashamed of what he'd just done, and he was desperate to make up for it. Instead, however, he was going to further destroy his wife's world. "Nandi doesn't belong to us, Doortje. If she would rather work for Patrick, that's not our business. I told you we should pay her. This is a free country."

"But she's ungrateful," Doortje erupted. "Her family lived on our land for generations. We gave them food, tended to them when they were sick—"

"Before you came, it was probably their land, Doortje. They weren't waiting for you and your home remedies. You're not in Transvaal anymore. And you don't even need Nandi. Sure, you'll have to take care of Abe yourself. And we can talk about hiring a housekeeper who also takes him off your hands sometimes."

"Housekeeper?" Doortje scowled. "What are you talking about? Where are you going to get a housekeeper here? And what about the garden and the livestock and—"

"We're going back to Dunedin," Kevin announced calmly, but his heart was in his throat. He hated this, but Vincent was right. She would never assimilate out here. "And we can't take the livestock with us. I'm sorry, Doortje. This isn't South

Africa, and you're not a *baas* or a farmer anymore. You're the wife of Dunedin's Dr. Kevin Drury. And you'll act like it from now on."

"But you—you promised." Doortje looked at Kevin, stunned. "We would live on a farm."

"I can't take it anymore, Doortje. And I certainly didn't promise you a farm in the veld with a kraal for the blacks and vespers in Dutch. At most, I promised a New Zealand farm, but you didn't like it on Elizabeth Station either. I really do want you to be happy. Think about the vow you took, 'Wherever you go, there, too, will I go.' And you—you do love me a bit. In Africa, you loved me a bit."

Doortje's gaze vacillated between despair and hate. If she had ever loved and wanted Kevin, those feelings were now buried deep.

"I never wanted this," she said tonelessly. "This with you. It simply happened. But it's not pleasing to God. Even if it looked so simple. Because a name for the child pardoned everything. But the child is cursed anyway. And so am I."

***

"You can't lock your wife up on Elizabeth Station." Michael Drury felt it necessary to lay down the law with Patrick. Any sympathy he'd had for Juliet had long since evaporated. And the tiresome woman was desperately unhappy in the country. "If you overdo it, she's just going to run away again." Michael tried the only argument he thought might have the slightest chance of success.

"At least no one will seduce her out here," Patrick insisted. "And she didn't leave of her own accord. It was that scribbler, that—"

"Patrick! The man didn't throw her over his horse and gallop away. Juliet packed her bags, abandoned the baby with Claire, and quite willingly climbed into a stagecoach."

"But he promised her an engagement," Patrick repeated the explanation Juliet had given him, "that she couldn't resist."

"And next time, she'll book one herself. Patrick, she can't take it much longer. Nor can we. And don't give me that business about the piano again. We're most certainly not going to set one up here. The house isn't big enough."

"The house doesn't seem big enough for mother and Juliet, anyway," Patrick shot back.

"I can't deny it, Patrick. Your mother and Juliet don't get along. In the long run, we'll have to think of something. But right now, you need to offer Juliet a change of scenery. She's going to go crazy here and your mother with her. Take her to Dunedin, at least for a few days. Go to a few social events, a few concerts—make her happy, Patrick. Try to make her a little bit happy."

***

One expected obedience from a Boer woman—joyful obedience. Doortje knew this from her mother and grandmother: a Boer woman willingly followed her husband over the mountains, into the wilderness, and into battle. She learned to load and fire guns. When she had to, she waded through blood. She was ready to kill and to be killed for her husband's sake, and she stood unyielding behind him—against exterior foes, but if necessary, also against the rest of her family and even her children. Doortje van Stout had been taught all of this from the earliest moments of her life, and now she did her best to fulfill her duty in her new country. Without another word, she left the cabin in Otago, her livestock, and her freshly planted garden. Kevin took them back to the apartment over his old practice, but he offered to look for a somewhat more rural home.

"Perhaps in Caversham, at the edge of the city," he proposed. "There are very cute little cottages with gardens. And Kathleen and Reverend Burton live there. You like them. You could work in the church, caring for the children and the poor."

But Doortje had only looked at him with big eyes. Caring for total strangers was unknown in her society. Families were big and stuck together; strangers rarely came to the villages or the farms. Besides, the Dutch Church shared the view of the Church of Scotland: as a rule, whoever was suffering deserved it, and everyone's fate was predetermined anyway. The past year had made Doortje question these fundaments of the faith, but her doubt did not yet go so far that she would volunteer at an Anglican soup kitchen.

At first, though, Doortje had to get her bearings—not halfheartedly this time, but as part of her husband's firm charge to assimilate. So, she put away her beloved apron and wore the reform dresses Kevin had bought her during their first stay in Dunedin. Now the more comfortable clothing was completely out of fashion. But corsets were out of the question, and Doortje looked captivating in the wide dresses. Dunedin society fought over the picturesque doctor's family. Kevin insisted on accepting every invitation, and Doortje tried in vain to make witty conversation at art shows, struggled through multiple-course dinners, and was so occupied with learning the proper way to hold silverware from watching Kevin and Roberta that she often missed other guests' attempts to communicate with her.

Roberta was an inestimable help. The young teacher seemed to like being with her and Kevin, and her friendly manner almost made Doortje forget her unacceptable fraternizing with Nandi on the ship. Roberta also inducted her into the mysteries of dance steps so that Doortje survived her first ball without any major faux pas.

Doortje attended concerts and let other society women invite her to tea, but she did it all reluctantly. When she did enjoy something—Heather's exhibition of female portraits had deeply touched her, the music of a violin plucked at her heart, and she had almost liked the feeling of Kevin's hand on her hip when they waltzed—she would not admit it to herself. Doortje's smiles were always forced, and even if others didn't notice, it tore at Kevin's heart.

***

Patrick Drury took Juliet on excursions to the city as his father had advised. They attended theater performances and art shows—and the couple began to receive invitations from Dunedin society again. Of course, they'd have to run into Kevin and Doortje at some point. It happened at a soiree at the Dunloes'. Doortje, who entered the salon on Kevin's arm, suddenly felt his tension. She followed his gaze and was horrified—if for completely different reasons than he.

"They let coloreds in here?" she asked incredulously.

"She's my brother's wife!" Kevin snapped. He had gone pale and saw in Doortje's eyes that she'd noticed. "Now, do me a favor and stop talking about her skin color. Juliet is Creole, but if I understood her correctly, her father's plantation is roughly twice the size of all Transvaal. You don't have to be her friend, Doortje, but please be polite."

Doortje tried to be an obedient wife once again, but Juliet did not make it easy. The young Boer was not socially sophisticated, but she recognized a mocking look when it was directed at her, and she saw the glint in Juliet's eyes at the sight of Doortje's husband. Patrick Drury followed his wife reluctantly as she approached Kevin and Doortje. He reminded Doortje of Cornelis. A coward.

"How nice to see you, Kevin, and, Dorothy, isn't it? Like the little girl from Kansas whom the tornado rips from her home. How does it feel to be a tornado, Kevin Drury?"

Juliet smiled. Conspiratorially? Seductively? Doortje felt like a fool for not understanding Juliet's allusion.

"Doortje," she said, "or Dorothea, if you can't pronounce it."

"Oh, I think I'll manage. If I put my mind to it. But you should think about 'Dorothy.' It really is a cute name. And she wears wide little dresses like that too."

Juliet's own dress was floor length and tight. Kevin saw it was the same dress in which she had seduced him in Lawrence. He struggled not to flush.

"Juliet, please," Patrick interjected, "you're embarrassing your sister-in-law. Doortje, forgive us. You look absolutely charming."

Juliet nodded and screwed up her pretty face—Doortje realized with astonishment that she wore makeup.

"Yes, forgive us. I always become unbearable when my throat is dry. Kevin, do fetch us some champagne? Or do you still drink milk, Doortje?" She now pronounced the name quite correctly.

Doortje bit her lip. She had never drunk alcohol before. But she was not about to let this hussy score any points.

"I would gladly have a glass," she said quietly.

When Kevin returned with the champagne, Doortje looked unhappily at the bubbly liquid in the crystal flute. She carefully took a sip—and was pleasantly surprised. She had always imagined alcohol burning the tongue, but this pricked softly and tasted slightly acidic, a bit like watered-down blackberry juice. Maybe it did not fall under the sinful, intoxicating drinks about which her pastor had always warned. Doortje triumphantly downed it just as quickly as Juliet.

Meanwhile, Kevin and Patrick struggled to converse politely.

"Are you going to work for the Ministry of Agriculture again?" Kevin asked his brother. "I mean, is that what brings you here?"

"No, no, I'm staying in Otago. We're just here for a few days. After a while, you get cabin fever on a farm, you know." He smiled sadly. Everyone knew Patrick Drury adored Elizabeth Station. "And the practice? No problems with Folks? I mean, first to South Africa and back, then Otago and back again."

"Oh, Christian is flexible. And I more or less have my own patients." He laughed nervously. "Christian mostly gets the young families, and I get the hysterics. And it can't be denied that the hysterics pay better. So, it means more income—for him as well."

"Mr. Drury?" Nandi approached nervously, little May in her arms. "Mr. Patrick, you said, I tell—" Patrick furrowed his brow a little. "I mean, you told me I should tell if May cries," she corrected herself. "And she was. So, I thought—"

"Beautifully said." Patrick took the little girl from her arms.

May seemed to have already calmed down. She babbled happily at those around her—she loved social affairs.

"*Ba*—Mr.—Dr. Drury."

Freed of the child, Nandi curtsied to her former employer. He looked around for Doortje, but she had disappeared with Juliet. This startled Kevin, but at least she was approaching other people without him.

"You look lovely, Nandi," Kevin said, smiling at her neat maid's dress with apron and bonnet. Almost the uniform Doortje had worn on the farm. "And you speak English so well."

"I thank you, Dr. Drury. You are not mad at me?"

Kevin thanked heaven Doortje was elsewhere. "For taking a better job? We regretted it, to be sure, but it was your choice, of course. Do you like working for Juliet?"

"I like it very much," she said, "with little Miss May—and Mrs. Drury."

The second name came a bit late, for Juliet was the drop of wormwood in Nandi's happiness. Nandi was used to being chastised, but she'd always known what to expect from the van Stout family, whereas Juliet Drury's moods changed from one moment to the next. Sometimes she gave Nandi lovely hand-me-down dresses and hats. Sometimes she cursed her for the smallest mistake. For Nandi, that was just as irritating as New Zealand's fickle fall weather, where sunshine quickly followed pouring rain, and the reverse.

"Please, not 'Miss May,' Nandi," Patrick said. He was glowing at the child, but Kevin noticed that he also kept an eye on Nandi—with a similarly loving expression. "It's bad enough Juliet bedecks her like a princess."

Kevin looked at the child closely for the first time. May looked like Juliet, but also like him and Michael. She took less after Patrick and Lizzie. Kevin decided to withdraw before other guests noticed. And Patrick was busy with May and Nandi, anyway. He was bouncing the little girl in his arms and conversing happily with her nanny. Kevin excused himself, saying he wanted to look for his wife.

Before he found Doortje, however, he ran into Reverend Burton.

Peter Burton was standing around, looking bored. He attended events like this for Kathleen's sake. He preferred quiet gatherings with a few close friends to making shallow conversation at parties like this. Now, he smiled at Kevin.

"Do you have a moment, Reverend?" Kevin asked. He had been meaning to speak with him for a long time. "Though, maybe it'd be better if I visited you in your church."

"Whatever you have on your mind, it usually gets said better over a glass of whiskey than by candlelight. Of course, my church has had electric lighting for some time now."

"But still no whiskey shelf, I take it," Kevin teased. "Just wait; I'll fetch us a couple glasses."

"The terrace recommends itself," said Burton, "since it's not raining at the moment."

Kevin came back with the whiskey, and the two men stepped outside and took a few sips in silence. As they did, they looked out over the dark, still garden, which offered a soothing contrast to the brightly lit house.

"So, what's going on, Kevin?" the pastor asked. "Troubles with your brother? I'm told things have been tense."

"Just misunderstandings. That's not what this is about. I wanted to ask, what do you know about Calvinism?"

The reverend smiled. "A theological lecture? Now, that I was not prepared for. Let's see: Calvin was a sixteenth-century Swiss theologian, quite influential. The Presbyterians refer to his teachings, the Church of Scotland—and, of course, your wife's Dutch church. The Five Solas form its fundament—"

"The simplified version, please. I'm just trying to understand what they think about damnation and being chosen."

"Yes, I see. Well, the *sola gratia*, it claims that man is saved by the grace of God alone, and not, as we preach in my church, because of good and bad deeds in life or through forgiveness and atonement. Calvin taught that mankind was divided from the beginning into the chosen and the damned. Which group you belong to was determined long before your birth."

"But that's madness," Kevin argued. "Why would someone behave well if it didn't matter either way?"

The pastor arched his brow. "I hope the Commandments have value to you on their own, and you don't just follow them because you're afraid of hell."

Kevin laughed. "Well, heaven does have a certain charm. But if you could behave however you wanted—"

"Life would certainly be easier sometimes," Reverend Burton admitted, and emptied his glass. "It was smart of you to bring the whiskey bottle. Even if it means neither of us are chosen. But about Calvinists' behavior—it's kept firmly in check. The community can impose punishments on anyone who steps over the line. More importantly, in their eyes, a God-fearing, ascetic life proves one is chosen. It's a sort of reverse conclusion: we assume that we're saved if we sin as little as possible. The Calvinists assume that salvation shows itself in sinning as little as possible."

"So, it comes down to the same thing?" Kevin's head was beginning to spin.

"Well, there are a few differences. For example, the way the chosen treat the unchosen. One sees a certain, hmm, cruelty in it."

Kevin groaned. "Let me guess: Zulu, Maori, mulattoes, Indians, they're all assumed to be unchosen."

"Exactly," replied Burton. "And they believe that being chosen also reveals itself in economic success. So, one doesn't care for the poor because they must be damned. Not to mention the slaves our Calvinist fellow Christians work to death on their plantations. Slavery and murder, but the sugarcane sells well, so it must be pleasing to God?" He smiled weakly. "I'm sorry, Kevin, you can tell I don't approve. Surely most Calvinists are good, upright people who never harm anyone but themselves. Some deny themselves even the smallest luxuries, any leisure, any joy in life. It must be terrible to be allowed to feel contentment only in self-righteousness."

Kevin pondered and refilled his glass. "And if one of them had always believed he was chosen, and then something happened that made him think he was damned after all?"

"That's a good question. In truth, I don't know anyone from that community. At least no strict adherents. There are surely those in Dunedin who profess to be of the Church of Scotland, but they nonetheless drink champagne and have their clothes tailored by Kathleen. The person you describe, well, I'd say he—or she—must feel like their world has collapsed. Kevin, are we talking about your wife?"

Kevin set his glass on the terrace table. "I need to go back inside, Reverend. Thank you. Things are clearer now, I think."

"You'll need lots of patience. And Doortje will need a new faith. But when you consider that her people crossed oceans and mountains and fought wars—"

"In big groups supporting one another," Kevin retorted, "and believing they were all chosen, of course. While Doortje—" His voice softened. "Doortje is all alone."

Chapter 8

Doortje Drury was having a grand time. She had now drunk her second glass of champagne and escaped from her wretched sister-in-law. Sean Coltrane and his wife, Violet, were charming, despite their terrible last name, but "Coltrane" seemed as common here as "Hövel" was in South Africa. Sean even explained that business about Dorothy.

"Dorothy and her dog Toto are the main characters in an American children's book called *The Wonderful Wizard of Oz*. It's rather new, and Roberta is quite taken with it. I'm sure she'd lend you her copy. In any case, Dorothy lives in the American countryside. But then, a tornado takes her away to a magical land where four witches and a wizard rule. There she has adventures with a lion without courage, a scarecrow without a brain, and a tin man without a heart."

Doortje giggled. The champagne was going to her head, and she had never felt so light and relaxed.

"A cowardly lion?"

"Yes, but as the story goes on, it turns out that the lion can be brave when he sees his friends in danger, and the tin man has great sympathy, and the scarecrow is clever. They only believed they were damned."

Doortje blanched.

Violet looked at her with concern. "Are you all right, dear? Everything here must still be rather stressful and foreign. And Juliet was wrong to make fun of you, even if the comparison to Dorothy from *The Wonderful Wizard of Oz* isn't insulting. She's a wonderful girl."

"Wait here," added Sean. "I'll fetch you another glass of champagne. That'll revive your spirits. And you, too, Violet. I don't see anyone from the abolitionists' coalition. You can let your hair down a bit." He winked and turned in the direction of the bar.

"Abo—what?" Doortje asked.

She could not remember ever asking so many questions or chatting so fluently. At least, not since her old life in Transvaal. Of course, at prayer meetings and communal handicraft evenings, the Boer women had not gossiped about children's books or dresses.

"Abolitionists," Violet explained. She regaled Doortje with a history of the women's movement in New Zealand, which had begun with the uprising of matriarchs against their husbands' alcohol abuse and had led to the women's right to vote.

"And, just imagine, the world didn't end!" she concluded cheerfully. "You just watch, one day we'll have a female premier."

"Sure, when South Africa has a black president," teased Jimmy Dunloe, who was approaching with Sean. "Enough with the speeches, Violet. It's a party."

He pressed champagne flutes into the women's hands, then disappeared with a wave back in the direction of the bar.

"Our host insisted on bringing you champagne himself," Sean remarked. "Sorry, Violet, I'm sure he didn't mean it like that. Naturally, I'd welcome both a female premier and a black governor at the cape. But the people there aren't ready for—"

"A Kaffir as governor?" Doortje asked. "But they—they don't have any brains."

Violet almost dropped her glass, but Sean jumped in before she could make a scene. "That's what they said about the scarecrow in the land of Oz too!" he quipped. "But in the end, the wizard names him as his successor. Read the book to your son when he's bigger, Doortje. We can all learn something from it."

***

When Kevin finally spotted Doortje, she was standing with Heather and Chloe Coltrane—and she was laughing wholeheartedly. He could hardly believe it. And, as he approached, Doortje's countenance didn't even harden. She smiled at him.

"Heather was in the Netherlands!" she announced to Kevin. "In Amster-dam!"

Heather smiled indulgently. "I think it's about time you took your wife home," she whispered to him. "She's more than a bit tipsy. But also charming. I never would have thought she could be so funny."

"Just think, you can meet people there like Mijnheer Rembrandt," Doortje gushed. "He paints like Heather. Heather would like to paint me too. Do you think that's allowed?"

Kevin smiled and linked arms with her. "That's an outstanding idea, and of course it's allowed," he said. "Mijnheer Rembrandt is already dead, though. He was a great artist and very diligent. Maybe you could pay Heather a visit sometime. I'm sure she has copies."

Chloe nodded. "She copied Rembrandt's pictures herself," she declared. "But whoever sees them understands why we don't hang them up." Heather pretended she wanted to throw her glass at her girlfriend. Chloe giggled. "But now, of course, she's long since surpassed him." She offered Doortje her hand. "It was so nice getting to know you better, Mrs. Drury."

Heather and Chloe said their good-byes warmly, but with emphatic looks at Kevin. Doortje's tipsiness was still cute, but if she and Kevin stayed any longer, things could go south.

"May I escort you home, my love?" he asked hopefully. "You know I need to get up early tomorrow."

"But I don't," declared Doortje triumphantly. "I can sleep in. But that's a sin, of course."

Swaying slightly, she allowed Kevin to guide her in the direction of the exit. On the way, they encountered Juliet and Patrick. Nandi was likely putting May to bed.

"Leaving already?" asked Juliet with a smug smile. "You used to last longer, Kevin." She cast a glance at Doortje and recognized her state at once. "Was the champagne to your liking, Dorothy? Well, let me warn you. When you come back from fairy-tale land, you'll have a monstrous headache." Juliet's gaze wandered over to Kevin and turned mocking. She pressed closer. "A fleeting fairy tale for you," she whispered in his ear. "Watch out, she'll fall asleep before you get started."

Doortje pulled her husband away.

"I'm not in a fairy-tale land," she declared. "No lions here and no scarecrows. Just a she-Kaffir without a heart."

***

Kevin took his wife for a stroll through town. They could have taken a cab, but the apartment was not very far from the Dunloes', and the fresh air would do Doortje good. The rain, too, which had set in again.

"It's always raining in this country," Doortje complained.

Kevin thought for a moment; then he told her the story of Papa and Rangi. Doortje listened with unaccustomed alertness. Usually, she shut down at talk of Maori legends.

"It doesn't rain so often at home," she said finally. "One doesn't cry so quickly there."

"But look, Doortje," he offered. "If the gods don't cry, the earth dries out. Now and again, a person can show a little emotion."

They had reached the practice, and he pulled her inside the doorway and took her in his arms. Doortje was close to coming back to herself, but decided to stay hidden behind the bubbly wall of champagne between her critical faculties and her feelings of guilt. It was nice to be kissed. She vaguely recalled Martinus's kisses. She had returned those too. And Martinus had almost reprovingly said she was wild. But Kevin did not seem to have anything against it. She let him pick her up and carry her up the stairs to their apartment.

"What about Abe?" she asked as he tiptoed down the hall with her.

"He's been asleep for a while now," Kevin whispered, and quietly opened the nursery door.

Abe was not in his crib, but next to it in the rocking chair in which slept Paika, Claire's child-loving maid whom they'd hired to babysit. Abe slumbered peacefully in her arms, his little head nestled in her breasts, his little body stretched out on her belly.

"But she shouldn't—"

Renewed resistance stirred in Doortje. She had strictly forbidden Paika from rocking the baby to sleep in her arms. Abe should learn from early on to sleep on his own. But Kevin shut the door as quickly and silently as he had opened it.

"Let them sleep tonight. Tonight, we'll forget everything. Education, the gods, England, South Africa. Tonight, there's only us."

Doortje did not resist as he undid her dress and began to cover her neck in kisses. As he pressed into her, she thought fleetingly about being damned. But really, it wasn't so bad in hell.

Chapter 9

The next day, however, Doortje's view of hell had changed. She awoke with the most atrocious headache she'd ever known, and when Kevin pushed tea on her, she threw up at once.

"I'm sick," she gasped. "Everything hurts. What is this?"

"It's the aftereffects of too much champagne," Kevin assured her. "Don't worry, it'll soon pass."

"You mean, I was drunk?" Doortje asked in horror. She remembered now how she had shamelessly fraternized with the English.

"Only a bit tipsy. You're just not used to alcohol. But it wasn't bad, dear. On the contrary, you were quite enchanting." He sat down next to her on the bed and tried to kiss her. Doortje sprang away in disgust.

"You can't! Not when I'm sick."

"You just have a hangover," he repeated. "Not that you have to kiss me either way. I just thought, yesterday you did like it."

Doortje looked at him indignantly. "I didn't like anything," she lied. "Maybe I gave in to temptation. Can it be that she hexed me? The she-Kaffir? She forced the champagne on me. She—"

Kevin did not want to talk about Juliet—whenever her name came up, he feared Doortje would see the deceit in his eyes.

"You asked for a glass," he reminded her. "And she did not stir in any poison. I don't mean to dispute that there's something witchlike about Juliet, but you can't hold her responsible for your feeling tipsy."

"She looked at you," Doortje observed pensively.

Kevin shifted uncomfortably. "That's what you do when you converse with someone. Forget Juliet for now, even if sooner or later you'll have to apologize. What you said to her, well, she's been called heartless often enough in Dunedin, but calling her a she-Kaffir is inexcusable. But for now, I'm going to fetch you some powder from the practice that will help your headache, Doortje. You can sleep a bit more."

"That's—" Doortje shot up and then immediately reached for her smarting temples.

"You're sick. You just said so yourself. So, lie down. I'll take Abe to the office with me. No, don't worry. He won't catch any contagious diseases."

Doortje stretched out and tried to think, despite her throbbing skull. Of course, her intoxication and the resulting complications were Juliet's fault. The woman had intended to make her behave badly. And she looked at Kevin as no decent woman should at her husband's brother—nor even at her own husband, really. Certainly not in public. Doortje thought of Jezebel, of Potiphar's wife, of Solomon's warning to his son: "[T]he lips of the foreign woman are sweet as honey, and her throat is smoother than oil, but afterward, she is as bitter as wormwood and sharp as a double-edged sword."

That was Juliet exactly: a honeypot, a trap. And Kevin was likely on his way to falling into it. Doortje made a decision. She did not yet know how to go about it, but it was doubtlessly the duty of every good wife to prevent her husband from taking such a false step.

That very afternoon, Doortje made her way to the Gold Mine Boutique.

***

"I'm sorry, but Kate went home." The beautiful, elegant Claire Dunloe, who still intimidated Doortje, shook her head regretfully. "Reverend Burton's women's group is collecting clothing for next Saturday's bazaar, and they insist on having Kathleen present when they go through the donated items. They all know how to redo stitching and iron blouses, but if Kate does it with them, it adds prestige. Maybe I can help you?"

Doortje shook her head. No, she did not want to lay out her worries to Claire Dunloe. That would have been just too embarrassing. On the other hand, she did not want to wait until the following Monday.

"Can I, well, do you think Mrs. Burton would find it untoward if I called on her at home?" Doortje rubbed her temples, which were hurting a bit again.

"Certainly not, Mrs. Drury! As I said, the women's group is there. They would be happy to see you. They gab about you not coming to church as it is. If you don't show your face soon, people will think you worship some Zulu god or another."

Doortje resisted growing indignant. She was slowly learning to tell from the tone of someone's voice whether they were joking—another thing she found strange. Where she was from, people were straightforward and called a spade a spade.

"Then I'll be going. Thank you."

Claire waved amicably after her.

Doortje sighed as she pushed the unwieldy perambulator back onto the street. She had not known of this in South Africa either. There, they had simply carried their babies around in a basket or, like the black mothers, tied to their backs with cloth.

That day, though, it was lucky she did not have to carry Abe. She had been to Caversham only once before, and though she thought she remembered the way, she did not recall how long it had taken. Kevin had harnessed Silver to his chaise, and the two miles had flown by. Now, however, they stretched out before Doortje. Her fine footwear, which had replaced the sturdy leather shoes she had worn in Transvaal, was not meant for miles of marching. At least Abe slept sweetly, and the fresh air drove out the last of Doortje's malaise. She felt like herself again when she lifted the doorknocker on the pastor's cottage. However, no one opened. Disappointed and unsure, she turned to the garden gate—and recognized Violet Coltrane approaching with a large bag.

"Mrs. Drury, how nice. Are you coming to the women's group too? I'm sure you can sew." Violet paused when Doortje did not answer. "Or no, of course not, how silly I am, forgive me. You probably only wanted to pay Kathleen a visit. But I'm afraid she's with the other ladies in the community room. I'd be happy to bring you along, even if you're not an Anglican. It's always good to help the poor, and we are all Christians." Violet chattered on amiably as she led Doortje around the cottage to the church. The community room, where Peter led Bible circles and held Sunday school, was located next door. "I've picked out a few really nice things," Violet declared, pointing to her bag. "We'll make the people so happy—God, how happy I was when I received a dress from Heather as a girl. But you know the feeling. Weren't you in one of those horrible camps? It's a crime what the British did there."

Doortje would never have thought that a rich lawyer's wife like Violet Coltrane had ever depended on hand-me-down clothing—let alone that she'd admit it. Even in the camp, her people had been ashamed to accept the donations. And then Violet had criticized the British without a second thought. Doortje would have liked to have more time to think about this. But Violet was opening the door to the community room, in which some fifteen women sorted clothing, laughing and chatting. Violet helped Doortje push the perambulator inside.

"We could put on a fashion show like you do in the Gold Mine Boutique," one of the women suggested, holding up a dress. "That would be fun. Is it true, Mrs. Burton, that you're going to have a real, live black woman show off your clothes?"

Doortje froze while Kathleen answered with a laugh. "We've asked Nandi, the Drurys' serving girl, to do it. But she's shy, despite being so beautiful—she hardly even needs a corset."

Doortje could hardly comprehend how these women found Nandi beautiful—and "asked" before giving her a job to do. But now Kathleen had seen her.

"Someone else on whom our clothes look marvelous." She smiled. "Come in, Doortje. Help us sort. Oh, and you've brought little Abe along!" Kathleen turned with shining eyes to the baby, who had just woken up. "May I pick him up?"

Doortje nodded uncertainly. She was used to women thinking Abe adorable. But he seemed to be the apple of Kathleen Burton's eye. And Abe liked her just as much. He began to make cheerful humming sounds as Kathleen rocked him.

"You two look good together." One of the parish women laughed. "You know what? He looks a little bit like you."

Doortje registered that this startled Kathleen. She almost dropped the baby.

"Oh, nonsense, of course not, how, how could he, now?" She quickly laid Abe back in his perambulator. "What, um, what would you like to do, Doortje? Do you prefer ironing or mending?" She pointed to two long tables where the women were working. "Violet, you must sew. Ladies, Mrs. Coltrane is almost as good as I am at it. She worked in our store as a girl. But quick as you can, Violet; we most certainly did notice your tardiness. And don't tell me about some petition for the Tailoresses' Union. Grab a needle and thread, and learn why they're petitioning."

The other women laughed, but Violet did not seem to take offense. She laughed along with them, reached for a little girl's dress, and got to work. A moment later, Doortje found herself next to her, mending a blouse. The work was nothing for her—finally, something she could do just as well as the other women in Dunedin. The women pulled her straight into conversation, talking about their children and grandchildren and personal experiences with hand-me-downs. Many of them had come to New Zealand with their husbands in the wake of the gold rush and gotten to know Reverend Burton's soup kitchen as recipients. They did not seem particularly interested in what country Doortje came from; here, she was an immigrant like everyone else.

Only one of the women mentioned offhandedly that there was supposed to be gold in Doortje's country. "My Herbert took notice as soon as the news broke. Dear Lord, if he was twenty years younger, I probably couldn't've held him back!"

"Was it as higgledy-piggledy over there as it was here?" a longtime Dunedin citizen asked Doortje. "I tell you, we woke up one morning, and the hills were white with tents. Half of England and Ireland turned up!"

Doortje looked up reluctantly from her work. "Our people did not work in the mines," she said stiffly. "We considered wealth without work immoral."

She was hurt when the women laughed again.

"Dear heart, you sure as Sunday have never seen a goldfield," declared the wife of the fanatical Herbert. "Believe you me, there's no wealth without work there. Lord in heaven, how we broke our backs. Morning to night like animals. And sometimes we didn't even get enough for dinner. There were a few lucky ducks, of course. But that gold just ran through their fingers. No, no, the carpentry business is ten times easier. What's more, we've the reverend to thank for finding Herbert work." She gave Peter Burton an adoring look. "What's that saying: 'A trade in hand finds gold in every land.'"

Doortje's head was spinning when she left two hours later. She had mended a large pile of clothing for the bazaar while everyone had taken turns with Abe. A few of the younger girls draped the better articles excitedly on the mannequins Kathleen had brought along from the Gold Mine.

"I think I'll buy one," said the same woman who had proposed a fashion show. "One of Kathleen Burton's—I could never afford one otherwise."

Kathleen smiled. "Do, Mary. Everything's going to the soup-kitchen fund."

"So, you're selling the clothes?" Doortje asked as she finally followed Kathleen and Reverend Burton to their house, little Abe in the doting reverend's arms.

Kathleen had invited her as if it were the most natural thing in the world. She seemed to sense that Doortje had something weighing on her heart and had not come only to sew.

The pastor nodded. "Yes, though most at very low prices. The children's clothes only cost a few pence. But people simply feel better when they pay for things. No one is eager to accept charity, and happily, there are always a few pieces from my wife's collection, for which people pay a fair heap of money. So, the truly needy women find themselves lined up with parishioners who want to treat themselves to a little luxury. That way, no one feels humiliated. Not to mention, Kathleen and Claire are both on hand to advise the women on their selections—even the poor. You wouldn't believe how much good it does them when the owners of the Gold Mine Boutique pick out a dress just for them."

Doortje could not think what to say. For her, all these considerations were so foreign that she sometimes thought the pastor and the others were speaking a different language. No one at home would have cared how a pauper felt.

"So, what brought you here, Doortje?" asked Kathleen as she brewed tea. "Surely you didn't just want to darn a few socks?"

Doortje hemmed and hawed a bit, but then it burst out of her like a torrent.

"That nasty Juliet is looking lewdly as my husband," she explained. "And she treats me like a stupid child who doesn't know anything. And what's worse is she's right. For her, everything here's a game. She knows how it all works."

Kathleen nodded seriously. "True, she is constantly leering at men, not just at your husband. And yes, she seems to have had an excellent social education. If you don't want her to outshine you, Doortje, you'll have to catch up. But, some good news: it's really not that hard. Here, look."

She took a book from the cupboard: *How to Behave*.

Amazed, Doortje thumbed through the already rather worn book of manners.

"All of that's in here?" she marveled. "Eating and talking and dancing and all that?"

"The basics, at least. Dunedin society's really not so highbred, anyway. Most of the wealthy are more or less the nouveaux riches. The book might not be enough for an introduction to the queen, but you'd make up for that with your personal charm."

"Oh," Reverend Burton added, "and you should subscribe to at least one of the fashion journals. You'll learn sentences like"—here, he put on a high-pitched, honeyed voice—"'This straight-cut skirt looks rather flattering on you, love, but don't people prefer bell shapes this season?'"

Abe giggled from his place on the man's knee.

"That was teasing?" Doortje asked cautiously.

Reverend Burton nodded cheerfully. "Yes, my dear. You're learning."

Chapter 10

When Kevin said good-bye to his last patient, Juliet Drury was sitting in the waiting room.

"What are you doing here?" he asked reluctantly.

He wanted to close up and get home to Doortje.

Juliet pursed her lips. "Well, what else?" she asked in a silky voice. "I'm a patient. You can hardly deny me an examination."

"You don't look sick."

"As opposed to your little Boer, I wager. She was quite full of champagne last night. Did it at least make her cuddlier, Kevin? Or was she still feeling feisty? 'She-Kaffir!' Well, when she does open her mouth, your Dorothy's got a sharp tongue."

"Her name is Doortje. And she's just not used to champagne. Besides, I seem to recall nights where you overdid it yourself. Anyway, let's keep this brief. What complaints do you have?"

He held the door open for Juliet. Whatever she wanted, it was better to discuss in his office. The waiting room was not soundproofed to the corridor.

Juliet took off her light jacket and began to undo her dress without any further preamble.

"Maybe you could feel my breasts. They're a little tight. Could I be pregnant? And my heart, it's been racing lately."

Juliet's dress displayed a row of buttons in the front—chosen with refinement for moments like this. While Kevin desperately tried to concentrate on his stethoscope and her heartbeat, she unbuttoned even farther and loosened the ties to her corset.

"But really it only races whenever I see you," she warbled sweetly.

Kevin raised his stethoscope. "I can't detect anything that would arouse concern," he said stiffly. "And as for a pregnancy, when was your last period?"

Juliet stretched out on his examination recliner. "Just a week ago, Kevin. So, there's no danger. Even if you don't have one of these little guys handy." She produced a condom out of nowhere.

Kevin clenched his jaw. He could not deny that her body aroused him.

"A pregnancy cannot be established at this stage," he informed her. "So—"

"Kevin." Juliet bared her breasts and licked her lips. "Fine, maybe you're not finding anything now, but believe me, I'm melancholic. I'm pining away for you. And I have to watch a stupid little thing yank you around and not even look particularly happy about it. What's this about with the Boer girl, Kevin? Why did you marry her?"

"Perhaps for the same reason you married my brother. I love her. And he loves you. If he doesn't make you happy, I'm sorry. But I—"

"You left me in the lurch," Juliet yelled, "with your bastard in my belly. What was I supposed to do, Kevin Drury? Wait for you? I could have put you in some hot water." A cruel smile flashed over her face. "And your little Doortje too. After all, what would she have said if a little daughter had been waiting for you here? And a bride left at the altar?"

"You were never my bride, Juliet."

Juliet let her dress fall to the ground and undid her stockings.

"But I could be. Come now, dearest, everything can be reversed. And you don't even have to get your hands dirty. I'll just tell your little Boer about May and Patrick."

Kevin struggled not to look at Juliet's heaving bosom.

"Maybe she wouldn't be as shocked by it as you think," he said brusquely.

"Oh? Might there be other revelations awaiting us? Is the little one not such a touch-me-not after all? Now that I think about it, little Abe doesn't look like you at all."

"Abraham takes after Doortje," he explained stiffly.

"Well," she cooed, "May takes after you." She slowly undid her garters.

Kevin told himself that he was only playing along with Juliet in order to keep her quiet. But he was lost the moment he touched her. Juliet began her game with him on the examination recliner, but at some point, they were again on the carpet under Kevin's desk. Laughing, she tied him up with bandages, found the brandy he kept ready for patients who threatened to pass out, poured drops of it onto his chest and his nether regions, and licked them off.

"We could play nurse," Juliet said breathily. "Isn't there a little bonnet around here somewhere? Maybe that's what turns you on about her, that absurd bonnet. Nandi told me that every woman at the van Stouts' table had to wear one. If one of them didn't have one, their father put a handkerchief on her head. Should I put a handkerchief on my head, Kevin?"

Juliet undid her hair and caressed Kevin with the strands, and finally he agreed to play doctor with her. He listened to her heartbeat as he pressed into her, and he claimed to be testing her reflexes when her back arched under him.

"We shouldn't do things like that," he said as they lay beside each other to catch their breath. "Patrick—it would break Patrick's heart."

Juliet laughed. "Oh, nonsense. You're a doctor, Kevin. Have you ever seen a broken heart? And even if. We're made for each other, Kevin. I've never had this much fun with anyone. And you haven't either, I know it. So, couldn't we say that this here is God's will?"

Kevin got up. "More like damnation. Juliet, this won't happen again. It can't."

Sure of victory, Juliet smiled. "Don't worry. Not tomorrow or the day after. We probably won't come back to Dunedin for a few weeks. But then, I'll be lying in wait somewhere."

***

Kevin would surely be happy to hear about her visit to Kathleen—she only hoped he would not be upset about the two new dresses and the corset she had acquired. Kathleen had driven her and Abe back to town in her chaise—she was horrified that Doortje had pushed a pram the whole way out—and had taken the opportunity to guide her into a lingerie store and then to the Gold Mine.

"Unfortunately, whoever wants to be beautiful this season has to suffer," Kathleen had explained. "I regret that the reform style did not win out, but if you insist on it against the prevailing fashion, Juliet will keep teasing you. In this dress, though"—Kathleen and Claire stood admiringly in front of Doortje, who was trying on a shimmering deep-blue satin dress with a row of aquamarine buttons and appliqué—"in this dress, all eyes will be on you."

But Kevin's eyes that evening were unsteady at best. He acknowledged Doortje's purchases only curtly, which exacerbated her guilt. The bill really had been exorbitant. He only picked at his food and afterward withdrew immediately back into his practice.

"I have a few more things to work on, Doortje. Don't be mad."

Doortje remained behind, confused. He had been so attentive just that morning. And she really did want to speak with him. About Violet, maybe, and the women in the parish. Frustrated and a little sad, Doortje went to bed early and took the book of manners with her. Over the next few days, she studied it assiduously. Juliet would not show her up again.

***

Doortje's next encounter with Juliet was a triumph—Kathleen and Claire had not exaggerated the dress's effect. Two weeks later, Patrick and Juliet had come once again to Dunedin for a weekend, and at a Saturday evening dinner at Heather and Chloe's, Doortje outshone everyone. Roberta Fence was another big surprise. She, too, was unexpectedly wearing a corset, and her chocolate-brown dress with cream-colored lace was genuinely breathtaking. Kevin paid Roberta compliments, which seemed to make her glow. But then she saw Doortje in her new finery. The woman was so beautiful, and Kevin's eyes shone so undeniably when he looked at her—Roberta had to accept yet again that there was no chance of claiming her old love. Doortje was assimilating.

Roberta sighed, but she was determined not to hold it against Doortje. So, she chatted especially warmly with her, asking about life on Elizabeth Station and in Dunedin, and wondering at the glint in her eyes whenever she mentioned Juliet.

"Patrick lived on the farm with his wife. There wasn't space for us," Doortje said regretfully. "We then tried the old cabin, but Kevin wanted to come back to Dunedin after all."

Roberta attributed her animosity toward Juliet to this displacement. Then, however, Patrick and Juliet entered the room—and perceptive Roberta was immediately alarmed.

Both Drurys stiffened when Juliet rushed in, wearing her dark-red gown—technically on Patrick's arm, but as if dragging her husband behind her. Roberta saw a flash of fear in Doortje's eyes, but also anger and resolve, while Kevin . . .

Roberta could not interpret his expression. He seemed annoyed, yet he couldn't look away—like most of the men. The low-cut dress was unquestionably not from the Gold Mine Boutique. Kathleen's designs emphasized women's beauty, but they were not obscene.

"Don't gawk," Chloe Coltrane teased Heather discreetly. "It's enough that she's walking all over the men."

Heather giggled. "I know the type, dearest. She'd gobble up our sort as an appetizer and a few blokes afterward. But a little jealousy looks good on you, Chloe Coltrane."

During dinner, the hostesses made friendly conversation with their respective dinner partners. Chloe had mixed the group colorfully. Patrick sat next to Roberta, while she had assigned Juliet an older merchant. Though Donald MacEnroe was a moderate adherent of the Church of Scotland, flirting with seductive young women was apparently not outside his comfort zone.

Chloe had not thought Doortje ready for a stranger as a dinner partner. She sat next to Kevin and seemed to feel halfway comfortable. For the first time, she had no trouble with the order of forks, knives, and spoons beside her plate. Kevin, however, was distracted. He did try to entertain his wife, but Roberta noticed that his gaze kept sliding over to Juliet.

For her part, Heather caught Roberta staring at Kevin. When the ladies strolled into the salon after dinner to drink coffee and liqueur while the gentlemen huddled for whiskey and cigars, she spoke to the young teacher bluntly.

"So, what's that vet of yours up to, Roberta? An engagement's just about due. You've already been back more than a year."

Roberta was evasive. "Vincent's gone to Auckland with the racehorses. He invited me to come, but that wouldn't work, of course."

"Come now, Robbie. Of course that would have worked, if you'd wanted it to."

"The young man is really quite charming," Chloe added.

"So, why aren't you two in Auckland?" Roberta asked to change the subject. She was sick of hearing what a nice fellow Vincent was. "Shouldn't you be cheering on Rosie and your horse?"

Chloe sighed theatrically. "Heather won't let me. We have our contemporary women's art festival coming up. It's got a fantastic title: *L'art au féminin*. Heather came up with it." She looked lovingly at her friend.

"But it was Chloe's idea to make it such a grand event," Heather added cheerfully. "We've even rented spaces outside the gallery. Aside from the art shows, there'll be presentations by Violet and other women who fought for the right to vote. We'll also have music: an all-female chamber group, a pianist, and Matariki will even be coming from Parihaka with a *haka* group and two female Maori artists. The Maori will have their own exhibition: jade carving and textile art. It's quite an undertaking. No one's done anything like it here. And then, a month before, Chloe comes to me about the Auckland Cup! I'm supposed to organize everything myself while she holds her mare's little hoof?"

Chloe sighed. "I couldn't have known Trotting Diamond would qualify. Otherwise, I would have scheduled the festival a month later."

"Then it would just have conflicted with this new race in Christchurch. The New Zealand Trotting Cup, founded by a couple businesspeople from Christchurch, among whom I suspect a certain Bulldog. We'll be going to that one. As will you, Roberta, no ifs, ands, or buts. We're also dragging Sean and Violet. Violet has to see Rosie's triumph. Perhaps Kevin and Doortje would also like to come, and—" Heather hesitated.

Chloe spotted Doortje standing alone on the other side of the room. "Please excuse me. I'm going to go rescue our foreign friend."

Roberta seized the opportunity to broach the subject that really lay on her heart.

"I don't like the way Kevin looks at his sister-in-law," she said quietly to Heather.

"No one does," she agreed, "at least, no one who notices. Most men seem blind and deaf on that score, but it doesn't escape the women. Tomorrow, half of Dunedin will be gossiping again. Juliet's aimed every weapon in her arsenal on Kevin. And Patrick watches like a wounded animal. I think he's just hoping Nandi appears to ask for help with May—the little pipsqueak always makes a scene when she isn't included in parties. Patrick makes his rounds, and then he flees to put May to bed, and Juliet has the field to herself. If she were my wife, I'd divorce her so fast, her head would spin. As for Kevin, he clearly loves Doortje, but he's just a man—and not a terribly reliable one, alas."

"Kevin is very reliable," Roberta declared indignantly. "What he did in the camp was—"

"Robbie, sweetie, you still haven't given up on him, have you? Heavens, child, wasn't it enough to chase him all the way to South Africa?"

Roberta cringed. She had told herself no one knew about her secret love.

"Robbie," Heather said as gently as she could, "you're beautiful and clever and would be a wonderful partner for anyone. But Kevin, he's only interested in difficult women. He used to fall for the artists we featured at the gallery, one after another. He liked them even better if they weren't interested in male companionship. He did everything he could to turn them. It was embarrassing. Once he caused a real scene when he did get one of them into bed, and her girlfriend—I thought they were going to duel!" Heather checked for Doortje, but she was still chatting politely with Chloe. "At any rate, our Dr. Drury needs witches like Juliet or tough nuts like Doortje. He would never make you happy, Robbie. You're grown now, and he's married. It's time to accept that."

Roberta hung her head in shame.

She watched as Claire Dunloe now approached Juliet, separating her with gentle force from the men's side of the salon and herding her toward the women. Doortje had been performing beautifully, but as Juliet made a beeline, she became visibly nervous.

"Dorothy. How nice to see you again. And dressed like a grown-up this time. But doesn't the corset squeeze your little heart, my dear?"

"We Boers," Doortje shot back, "are rather tough. We've survived more than a few laces and gibes. Most of all, Juliet, we never give up." She paused a moment to let her words take effect. "And besides, Dorothy's house strikes dead the Witch of the East, and later she destroys the Witch of the West. So, take heed, Juliet. And remind me, which direction is New Orleans from here?"

Doortje arched an eyebrow at her sister-in-law, spun on her heel, and crossed to Claire Dunloe and Kathleen Burton. Juliet was left with her jaw hanging open.

Heather, Chloe, and Roberta looked at each other, astounded.

"To think I never believed Kevin when he said Doortje had threatened him with a gun," Heather said. "Juliet really should take heed. She's a good shot."

Awakening

Parihaka, Auckland,
North Island
Dunedin, Christchurch,
Temuka,
South Island
1904

Chapter 1

The full moon once again hung over Parihaka, making the sea shimmer and bathing Mount Taranaki in a ghostly light. A priest carried out a full-moon ceremony and pleaded for the goddess Hine-te-iwaiwa to bless the pregnant women in the village.

Matariki would have liked to sit with the children and tell them about the phases of the moon—the scientific explanation, yes, but also the Maori myths and the moon's importance to the Polynesians for seafaring. That night, however, she could not give herself over to the dreamy and festive atmosphere. She was determined to put her foot down with Atamarie.

"It can have something to do with the moon?" Atamarie was asking the healers she sat with. "I never noticed anything."

"There's a reason that madmen are called 'lunatics' in English," said Makutu. "I often can't sleep during the full moon."

"I don't know. Sometimes he slept like the dead, and sometimes . . ." Atamarie frowned.

Matariki sighed. Over the past weeks, Atamarie had been desperately trying to interpret her experiences with Richard. It was normal—her daughter, previously spoiled by life, had been disappointed for the first time. But Atamarie seemed to view the unhappy affair as a personal failure, and Matariki felt enough was enough.

"You're repeating yourself," she said sternly after sitting down next to her daughter. "At this point, we all know Richard Pearse's peculiarities. But no one can explain them."

"Well, Omaka had a very coherent theory before, something about a *taku* and *toku*—well, when you take that out of its *pepeha* context—"

"Atamarie!" her mother exclaimed. "You can't analyze your people's spirituality like an engineering problem. You keep trying to isolate the broken cog so you can repair it and make everything turn out differently. But it won't, Atamarie. Stop already. You can't hide yourself away in Parihaka and obsess about a lost love."

"But that's not at all what I'm doing," she said with a pout. But she knew her mother was right.

Atamarie had always demanded clear answers and had usually found them. Professor Dobbins had actually been the very first person she had told about Richard's last flight—and her confrontation with him and Shirley.

After leaving Temuka, she had taken the train back to Christchurch. She had been angry and desperate, disappointed and hurt. She did not shut her eyes that night, and showed up for class the next day looking wrecked. Generally, Dobbins kept a studied distance from students' personal problems, but he invited Atamarie to his office after asking an assistant to reschedule the exams he had meant to administer. Atamarie thought fleetingly that the exam takers would hate her for that, but then, in her exhaustion, she poured out the whole tale.

"I'm so angry with myself, Professor. It was egotistical of me. If we had done our demonstration a few days earlier, if I hadn't insisted on taking my exams first—"

Dobbins shook his head and set a steaming cup in front of Atamarie. "Have some coffee, Miss Turei. You look as if you need it. And for heaven's sake, don't blame yourself for Pearse's failure. This isn't even the first time."

"Not the first time? I mean, sure, he went through a phase after the first flight ended in the hedge. But in between—"

"In between, he's always stable, easygoing—and then one day, he falls back into melancholy. Richard is undoubtedly a genius, but also, very, hmm, unstable. I always thought you did him good, Atamarie."

"His family thought the opposite," muttered Atamarie.

Dobbins shrugged. "Maybe they're right. I'm an engineer. If you give me a stuttering motor, I can take it apart and find out what's wrong. But a melancholic person? That was, by the way, the reason he lost his position as a research assistant here. I don't know how he explained it to you, but money was never the issue. A talent like that, we would have made it work somehow. But he retreated to Temuka and did not come back for a long time. Later, he reappeared, making excuses about family problems and, and, and. Well, I took him along to Mount Taranaki. Then he told me about the farm he had received."

"He could have sold it," Atamarie exclaimed.

The professor raised his hand. "He could have done many things. But he didn't. And that most certainly is not your fault, Atamarie. Don't drive yourself crazy over a few days' delay. Richard flew a year before the Wright brothers. He had plenty of time to announce it, and to patent his aeroplane. But he didn't. You are in no way to blame.

"First things first, let's get your last exam out of the way the day after tomorrow. And after that, think about what you want to do. You have money, yes? Why not go to Europe? There's a lot of research being done there on aeroplane construction. Or the United States. Seek out the Wrights." Dobbins laughed. "Maybe you'll fall in love with one of them. They also seem to be difficult men."

"I can't exactly marry them both," she noted drily. "As for Europe, women aren't even allowed to study there. And certainly not engineering. The men wouldn't take me seriously."

Dobbins made a face. "Do you know what a man would have done in your position? Or, at least half of your fellow students here?"

Atamarie looked at him inquisitively.

"They would have claimed all the glory for themselves. If you had flown, Atamarie, it would have been sensational. Not only would you have made your friend's invention public, but you would have brought your sex forward by leaps and bounds."

"But I would have betrayed Richard. He would have been named in all the announcements, of course, but he would have stood in the second row."

"Instead, he betrayed you. And now he's not even in the announcements. But nothing can be done about it now. I'll see you the day after tomorrow, my dear Miss Turei. Be sure to get some rest before your exam."

***

Atamarie had passed her last exam with distinction—despite spending the intervening two days in the library reading everything she could find on the subject of melancholy. Some symptoms applied to Richard. Others did not. Regardless, she did not find any medical explanations for the malady or insights into relieving it.

And so, the day after the exam, Atamarie set out for Parihaka to seek spiritual explanations. She spoke to Maori healers, but they could only tell her that this state of sadness was called *kainatu*, and one should leave those affected in peace. There were theories, of course. One renowned healer explained that people affected by *kainatu* could not bear the sight of *nga wa o mua*—the future that emerged from the past. The principle of *taku* and *toku* was highly complicated, and Atamarie had only a limited grasp of it. The *tohunga* recommended first finding out everything about the affected's ancestors, conjuring the canoe with which they came to Aotearoa, and seeking the root of the evil outside of time, so to speak. Atamarie would have dismissed that as nonsense just a few months before, but now, she pondered it endlessly. Until Matariki put her foot down.

"You're starting to seem affected by *kainatu* yourself," Matariki scolded. "Whatever the reason this young man is strange, let that Shirley person worry about it. You're coming with me to Dunedin to see Roberta and to get to know Kevin's wife. The reports from Kathleen and Violet are wildly contradictory. Besides, we're going to take part in Heather's exhibition of female artists. I told you about it, remember?"

"But I'm not an artist," grumbled Atamarie.

"Even as a little girl you wanted to reinvent the weaving frame," Matariki said. "We know you don't lack creative imagination. Why don't you make a *manu*?"

"A kite? That's really more Rawiri's thing."

"But he's still not here," noted Matariki.

She had nursed the suspicion for a while that this, too, was holding her daughter in Parihaka. Atamarie was waiting for Rawiri—whether recalling his dogged courtship or just wanting firsthand information on the Wright brothers, Matariki did not know. Rawiri had written her about the historic flight, describing everything precisely. Of course, he could not know he was salting her wounds. Matariki had not asked Atamarie about the contents of the letter, but she had spoken with Rawiri's mother, who had also received mail from her son.

"He was not particularly euphoric," Pania had said. "From a purely technical standpoint, he understands why their aeroplane rises into the air, but it does not open itself up to him spiritually. The Wrights lack humility before the spirits, in his opinion. Perhaps it was not entirely wrong of you to send your Atamarie away to school in Dunedin. Rawiri appears to have internalized the spirit of Parihaka a bit too much."

"Come on, Atamarie, you're excellent at building kites," Matariki now continued. "You won't be taking anything away from Rawiri. So, up, child. Get to work. It would be delightful if we could fly a few of our Parihaka kites in stodgy Dunedin."

***

So, Atamarie acquired manuka and kareao wood. If she was going to build kites the traditional way, she would also need raupo leaves. She sought out a *tohunga* who told her where to find them and with how much reverence she was to pluck the leaves and thank the plant. Atamarie planned to abbreviate the whole spiritual to-do, but on the very first day of work, she suddenly found herself surrounded by a horde of children who also wanted to make kites.

"Rawiri made *manu* with us every year for Matariki," one little boy explained with grave concern. "But now he's gone again. We're going to forget the whole *tikanga*!"

Atamarie had to laugh. She could hardly imagine that an art such as this could be lost in Parihaka, but fine, she would do her part for cultural preservation.

She asked the older children to practice the songs, prayers, and calls that had to be sung and spoken during the construction process. Then she urged the little ones to retain the traditional kite forms, but also to try out new ones. They built double-deckers and parachute-like constructions, and experimented to find out which ones flew best.

"But it's not really that important how the *manu* fly," declared a girl. "What's important is the message to the gods!"

Atamarie laughed. "But to reach the gods, the kites first have to get into the air. Now, draw a smiling face on yours, Wai, so Rangi will be in a good mood and not cry when you let the kites go, because then they won't fly."

Atamarie and her little students decorated the kites with feathers and mussel shells. A *tohunga* explained the designs they painted in red and black. Atamarie overcame her disgust and mixed clay with horribly stinky shark oil to produce dye as tradition dictated. Finally, everyone braided strings out of flax—*aho tukutuku*. And at the very end, every kite had to prove its ability to fly.

"It'll be a shame if these little works of art crash now," said Matariki, to whom Atamarie's colorfully painted birdman seemed too heavy.

"My kite won't crash," Atamarie declared. "It doesn't matter how heavy a flier is if it makes good enough use of lift. Just wait: one day aeroplanes as big as a house will soar through the skies."

"But won't the gods get scared?" asked little Wai.

Atamarie thought quickly. "Not if we sing the right *karakia*! So, come on, children. How does the *turu manu* go?"

> *"Taku manu, ke turua atu nei*
> *He Karipiripi, ke kaeaea . . . ,"* the children intoned.
> Fly on from me, my bird,
> dance restlessly on high,
> swoop down like the hawk upon his prey,
> fly ever higher, glorious bird,
> conquer the clouds and the waves!

One of the female singers from the *haka* group who was to travel with them to Dunedin took up the song, and though she chided herself for it, Atamarie actually had the feeling that the melody was carrying her *manu* into the sky.

Chapter 2

"I had a lot of fun teaching those children," Atamarie reflected when she and her mother sat on the train on their way to Heather and Chloe's festival. "At first, they just wanted to mess around, but then they really learned something about the laws of physics."

"And about *tikanga*." Matariki smiled. "You seem to get it at last: *nga wa o mua*—the past is the future. The songs of our ancestors connect with your teachings about flying. It doesn't have to be a contradiction."

"Mom! Could we talk about something other than the spirit of Parihaka for once?"

"Better the spirit of Parihaka than the spirit of Richard Pearse."

Atamarie had honored her mother's demand that she not mention her ex anymore, but it was hard to pass by the train station in Timaru. "I'd just like to know how he's getting on," she said. "The next train leaves in just a few hours. I could follow you on that one. And I wouldn't have to go all the way to Temuka. Really, I wouldn't even want to." Matariki looked skeptical. "I could ask in the store, casually, as if I just happened by."

Atamarie made a halfhearted move for her suitcase, but Matariki shook her head.

"What do you want to know? If he's already married Shirley? Or if he's flown after all? We would have heard about the first motorized flight in New Zealand. Whatever you could learn here would only hurt you, Atamie. Forget him."

Atamarie sank indecisively back into her seat. "And what about the past that determines the future?" she asked slyly.

"Child! Richard isn't the canoe in which your ancestors came to Aotearoa. He was just your first love. It's time to close that chapter of your life, Atamie. Be happy for Roberta instead. She seems to have finally managed to stop thinking about Kevin Drury. Violet writes that she's as good as engaged to a very nice veterinarian."

Atamarie made a face. "'As good as' doesn't count, Mom. I was 'as good as.'"

***

Heather and Chloe put the Maori artists and dancers up in a hotel, but Kevin insisted Matariki and Atamarie stay with him. Matariki was a few years older than Kevin and Patrick, but they'd always been close. Maori traditions had also strongly shaped the boys' worldview. All three had looked upon the Ngai Tahu as their extended family. The fact that Matariki was technically a half sister had never been a consideration. Thus, it hadn't occurred to Kevin to prepare Doortje before they met Matariki and Atamarie at the train station.

While Kevin rushed forward to hug his sister, Doortje froze, stunned at the woman's dark complexion and her thick, black hair, which she wore shamelessly loose. Like the other women from Parihaka, she wore reform-style clothing, woven traditionally in the tribal colors, but adapted to Western conceptions of length and propriety. She was a beautiful woman and assuredly not white.

"I—I didn't know," Doortje stammered, but Matariki did not take notice.

"You must be Dorothea," she said warmly. "Kevin wrote me your real name, but I don't trust myself not to butcher it until I hear how it's pronounced." She laughed. "When I was little, they called me Martha at school. It didn't bother me, but I wanted to make sure no one would call my daughter, Atamarie, Mary."

Matariki wanted to hug Doortje as she had Kevin, but she sensed her resistance and thought better of it. Perhaps hugging was frowned upon in South Africa.

Atamarie offered her hand amiably, even though she could decipher Doortje's abrasive behavior. Roberta was a loyal letter writer, and the odd woman's prejudices had been a frequent subject.

Doortje felt less aversion toward Atamarie than Matariki. One could hardly detect the native blood in her husband's niece. Yet, she was puzzling in other ways. Atamarie distinctly resembled Kathleen Burton—she had the same hair color and aristocratic features. During the ride to their apartment, Doortje brooded on how that could be possible. She knew that Sean Coltrane was a son of Michael and Kathleen. Matariki must have been a misstep of Lizzie's. But how was it that Atamarie resembled the reverend's wife? Was Sean the father? She wouldn't have expected such behavior from the distinguished lawyer.

Now, though, Doortje had more-pressing problems than this confounding family tree. In Transvaal, no one would have asked her to share a table with non-white relations. No one would ever have admitted to the shame of having any. During the ride, she was monosyllabic, and she rebuked Kevin when Matariki and Atamarie withdrew into the guest room to freshen up before they all went out to dinner with Lizzie and Michael.

"You could at least have warned me."

"You knew very well that Matariki was coming from Parihaka. With the Maori artists. What did you think she was doing there?"

"You said she was a teacher," Doortje said. "So, naturally, I thought—"

"That she was bringing the poor natives a bit of civilization?" mocked Kevin. "Doortje, you've heard the history of Parihaka. Do you really believe they need *pakeha* to teach them to read and write?"

"But you said Matariki's husband served in Parliament."

Kevin threw his hands up. "Kupe Parekura Turei is a well-known attorney and serves in Parliament. Maori won the right to do so some years ago. You would know that if you showed just a little interest in the country you now live in. But you're as ignorant as ever. Do me a favor and at least behave in my sister's presence. Matariki is a very intelligent and lovable woman. If you could set aside your pigheadedness for one minute, you'd like her." With that, he left the room, slamming the door behind him.

Doortje balled her fists in powerless rage. Kevin's outburst felt unfair and hurtful. She really was trying. She wore the customary clothing, even though she could hardly breathe in that awful corset, she was studying manners, and she read novels in order to be able to converse at social events. Recently, she had even started accompanying her husband to Reverend Burton's Sunday sermons, which often seemed blasphemous to her. She preferred the women's group, and she was slowly adapting to the Anglican notion of charity. Kevin couldn't ask more from her. He couldn't!

Doortje rarely wished so much that she could cry, but she managed only a dry sob.

***

Mere moments after his outburst, Kevin regretted it. Of course, it was awful that Doortje had rejected Matariki, but he should have prepared her. And lately, she truly was trying to plant her feet in Dunedin. No, his agitation had other causes. Juliet was the same seductress she had always been. Only, the relationship was no game now. Kevin knew exactly what he was risking when he gave in to her over and over. Patrick would never forgive his betrayal, and he would probably lose Doortje too. However, he could not manage to resist Juliet when she lay in wait in his practice, drew him into the garden during the late hours at parties, or when she once ambushed him in the stables. Juliet was walking a thin line between seduction and extortion—when Kevin desperately tried to say no, she threatened to reveal their affair.

"I'm leaving that little brother of yours one way or another, dearest," she had said the last time. "Life up there in Otago is unbearable. The only thing keeping me here is you. In that regard, you're almost doing Patrick a favor, Kevin, my Saint Kevin." She laughed throatily. "My sweet Kevin who goes to war to free the slaves and takes in fallen women."

"I don't know what you're talking about," he objected. "Doortje's honor is beyond any doubt. She was never a 'fallen woman.'"

Juliet grinned, and Kevin knew she saw the fear in his eyes. Juliet Drury seemed to have a sharp eye for scandal. Every day, she saw Kevin's features in the face of her daughter—but Abe, ostensibly his son, did not resemble him in the slightest.

"Who's talking about Doortje," she whispered in his ear. "I'm speaking of myself, Saint Kevin, without a doubt a fallen woman whom you lift up again and again. And now I urgently need your blessed love."

Kevin told himself that he had to protect Doortje from a possible revelation—then lost himself in Juliet's charms. Later, he loathed himself for it. It couldn't go on like this, but even in good faith he did not know how to end it.

Now, in any case, he needed some fresh air—or at least distance from Doortje. He could work on a few files in his practice. He would never have admitted that some small part of him wondered whether Juliet might be there waiting.

***

Matariki heard choked sobs coming from the Drurys' bedroom as she made her way toward the bath—just as she had heard the door slamming. She did not want to get involved in a marital spat, especially as Atamarie had just indignantly explained Doortje's rudeness to her.

"Robbie says they still kept slaves there until the war, and some surely still do. The blacks are totally dependent on them and aren't even allowed to go to school, and—"

Matariki had raised her hand. "I've heard that as well," she said calmly. "All whites were like that once. Just think of the difficulties in Parihaka—and how we handled them."

"Plowing and building fences?" scoffed Atamarie.

"Over time, it improved the situation," Matariki said cautiously.

At the time, Parihaka's resistance against the government's land seizure had not done much. Nevertheless, since then, Sean Coltrane and Kupe Turei had secured reparations for the Maori, and others were also fighting dogged legal battles for Maori rights. Everywhere, Maori men and women showed the *pakeha* that they were in no way inferior.

Besides, sharing a handkerchief took less effort than building fences, Matariki now thought, throwing her bathing plans to the wind. Her new sister-in-law needed encouragement, whatever her dreadful misconceptions. Determined, Matariki knocked on the door to Doortje's room and stepped in at once when she heard no reply. The young woman sat on the edge of her bed, doubled over but with dry eyes.

"Is there anything I can do?" asked Matariki softly. "Kevin can sometimes be short-tempered, I know. It's the Irish temperament, my mother always says. He gets that from our father. Now, calm yourself a bit, then tell me what's bothering you." She smiled at Doortje and sat next to her.

Doortje bolted to her feet. To sit next to a colored person . . . She nervously glanced at the mirror.

"I look terrible," she whispered. "People will be able to tell."

"What will they be able to tell? That you were upset? If you wash your face, do your hair up nice, and smile, nobody will notice anything."

"But I can't always smile," Doortje whimpered. "I can't always act as if—"

"Oh, my dear," she said, relieved that the woman's distress had a less abominable source, "I understand. *Pakeha* society can be merciless. Always keep your posture; always be perfect—these corsets alone! You look ravishing, by the way.

That's one of Kathleen's dresses, isn't it? Today, though, it's just family. You don't need to torture yourself on our account. Atamarie and I won't be wearing corsets, and I can guarantee Lizzie won't either. And you're beautiful even without fishbones, Doortje. My father's crazy about you, you know."

"Michael Drury isn't even your father."

Matariki leaned back slowly. "Ah, the fight wasn't about your manners after all," she said, more coolly but still at ease. "Atamarie was right. You didn't know that I'm Maori."

Doortje made another choked sob. It sounded almost ghostly. Matariki wondered how she did not simply break out in tears, but Doortje kept an iron mastery of herself.

"But you're not even that," she whispered. "You're a half-breed. Colored. Like that—that Juliet. And that's worse than black because you carry the mark of Cain on your face."

Matariki laughed, tossing her long hair. "Well, until now, everyone has always told me how good I looked. What's more, I'm a chieftain's daughter. I used to be very proud of that. A real princess."

"But a colored woman can't be—in Africa no one wants them, not even the Kaffirs."

"Poor things," said Matariki. "Rejected everywhere. It must be terrible for such people in your country. No wonder they think of it as a mark of Cain. But here, it's completely different. Maori tribes happily take in all children. And once, when there were hardly any *pakeha* here or back in Polynesia, where the Maori originally came from, it was an honor for a woman to give birth to a mixed child. As we say, 'Every *iwi* has its own *tikanga*.' You could translate it as 'Every tribe has its own customs,' or 'Every tribe has its own truth.'"

Doortje shook her head passionately. "There's only one truth, the divine Truth. And the Bible says only we were chosen."

She was astonished when Matariki laughed. "Forgive me, but I've heard that one before. In the Bible, it meant the Israelites. So, the Jews."

"The Jews? The Jews are more like the English. God doesn't like them at all. But the Voortrekker, they're the Israelites. Because both peoples were driven out and had to fight through hostile regions to get to the promised land."

Matariki rubbed her forehead. "The Israelites of the Bible are the ancestors of the Jews of today. Look it up. And their promised land was later taken away from them by invaders. Just like yours, Doortje. And ours. According to the teaching of a certain Te Ua Haumene, you see, the Maori are the chosen people. My birth father used to preach that—and so, he sent many people to die. Just like your Boer leaders did."

"I'm the daughter of Adrianus van Stout," Doortje said bitingly, "one of these 'Boer leaders' as you so contemptuously put it. In my country, it's an honor—"

"So, you're something like a princess too." Matariki smiled. "It's not always easy, is it? People have expectations for you. I, for one, was happier to simply be the daughter of Michael Drury. He's no hero—without my mother, he would have been lost in this country. But he's a good man. Just like Kevin."

Doortje glared at her. "You mean, I should just forget everything? My people and my beliefs?"

"In any case, you should leave it to the gods to decide whom they like and whom they don't. Or, believe Reverend Burton, who says God loves us all. The Maori lead a sort of peaceful coexistence with the gods and don't really hold them responsible for the problems of the here and now. Pick something. There's no proof for any of it. But now, it's time we freshened up." She stood up, went to the little washing table in Doortje's room, wet a washcloth, and placed it in the younger woman's hand. "Princess Matariki says, 'The court ceremonial requires the washing of the face with cold water and the fixing of hair.' Or do you still not want to go eat with Atamarie and me? Then we can say you had a headache. Besides, Maori princesses aren't permitted to fraternize with common tribe members anyway." Matariki raised her nose in the air and looked haughtily down at Doortje in jest. "On the North Island, you'd be damned if my shadow but fell on you. Though I'd be prepared to carry out a cleansing ceremony with you afterward. Then it wouldn't be so bad."

Matariki was dismayed when Doortje did not laugh. Rather, her fingers cramped around the washcloth, and her body seemed to shake.

"For your people, damnation can be taken away?" she asked, her voice quavering.

At that moment, it became clear to Matariki that dinner with Michael and Lizzie would have to wait. She got up, marched into the hall, and locked the apartment door. Let Kevin knock once he had cooled off. She heard Atamarie singing to herself in the bath—her spoiled daughter seemed to be enjoying her return to civilization. All the better.

Matariki returned to the bedroom and sat back down on the bed. Doortje was distractedly running the washcloth over her face.

"So, and now, just between us princesses: Why do you think your God has damned you?"

***

The women were to remain undisturbed a long time because Kevin, too, forgot about dinner with his parents. While Doortje poured out her heart to his sister, one floor below, he was satisfying Juliet Drury.

Chapter 3

"I'm sorry, Rosie, but you're imagining it. There isn't a thing wrong with this horse. Don't be hysterical."

Vincent was sorry for his harsh words as soon as he had spoken them. There was no reason to take out his bad mood on Rosie, even if she'd just had him examine her horse for the fourth time in three days.

Rosie pressed her lips together tightly. "I'm not hysterical, Dr. Taylor. Trotting Diamond has something. She was shaking again earlier. And this morning she looked, well, she looked at me as if she had a fever."

Vincent pointed his flashlight once more at Diamond's eyes and checked the pupil reaction. Completely normal.

"Did she?"

"No," Rosie confessed. "And she ran really well. Though she was a little wild during training. She broke into a gallop twice. She never does that. And afterward, she shook, and I got the feeling she was dizzy."

Vincent smiled. "I think both you and your horse have a case of nerves. Totally understandable. The Auckland Cup is a big deal. And the voyage by ship, an unaccustomed racetrack—that can get to your stomach. Take a look at Lord Barrington's horses." Vincent had just treated the second one in three days for colic. "Your Trotting Diamond just has weak nerves."

"She's never had weak nerves before," Rosie declared, "and her heart isn't racing because she's afraid of your stethoscope either, as you said last time. Trotting Diamond's not afraid of anything."

This business was starting to get on Vincent's nerves, but he could not dismiss Rosie's argument out of hand. Trotting Diamond was usually calmness itself. She trusted Rosie entirely and had dutifully boarded the ferry first. She had not found her new box at the racetrack in Ellerslie any more frightening than the somewhat different track. She had been eating well from the beginning and looked unperturbed during Vincent's examinations.

"Then maybe you're the one with weak nerves, Rosie," Vincent concluded. "And it's carrying over to Trotting Diamond. That does happen. It also explains why she's always better when I arrive. You calm down because the veterinarian's here, so Diamond calms down too. She will run wonderfully tomorrow, believe me."

Although Rosie did not seem completely satisfied, she let him go.

"I'm still going to sleep by her."

Vincent nodded. "By all means, as long as I don't have to. I'm taking the train to Auckland to look around the city. You should, too. You've never traveled so far before, have you?"

Rosie didn't answer, just thanked the veterinarian again and said good-bye. As a child, she had traveled from Wales to London and from London to New Zealand, then to the West Coast and again back to the fjord lands. Really, she had only liked it in the stables where everything was safe, warm, and orderly. She most certainly would not give up this security just to look at a harbor or some buildings.

On his way from the stables, Vincent thought morosely of how he had dreamed of seeing Auckland with Roberta. There were so many romantic places and secluded beaches. Roberta, however, had not come to see him in Christchurch since that Juliet woman had returned to Dunedin. Vincent did not understand the connection, but something was clearly amiss. Even Kevin's letters had become strange and evasive. He mostly just listed events and festivities he attended with Doortje. From Roberta's letters, too, it was evident the woman was assimilating with great success. Even the society section of the *Otago Daily Times* had repeatedly mentioned Kevin's beautiful wife. He ought to have been happy, but when his letters mentioned Doortje at all, it was only to complain about her bad relationship with his brother, Patrick, and his wife.

Vincent was inclined to put two and two together. Was Kevin cheating on Doortje with the femme fatale? Vincent hoped not. He recalled his own failed marriage only too well. Divorce was terribly unpleasant, and he saw no chance of Kevin being happy with a woman like Juliet. His own wife had been similar: stunning, scintillating, droll, but unstable and unfaithful. Vincent had learned his lesson. Now, he only dreamed of a woman like Roberta. Kind, patient, and absolutely loyal—even to a childhood crush on a man she'd never so much as kissed. But what could she possibly hope for with Kevin?

Now Vincent was determined to force a decision. Roberta would come to Christchurch for the New Zealand Trotting Cup. Then, Vincent would ask for her hand.

If only Roberta would say yes and finally leave her childish dream behind.

***

Rosie's next visitor at the stables was Bulldog. The transportation entrepreneur was deeply disappointed when Rosie declined to go out with him that evening.

"Don't you think that Trotting Diamond might like a bit of alone time before tomorrow's race, Miss Paisley?" he suggested. "She is in very good company here."

Indeed, Trotting Diamond got along well with her stablemate, a bay gelding she knew from Barrington's racing stable.

"I have to look after Triangle too," Rosie replied seriously. "He had colic before. And his trainer doesn't even take care of him. I don't want to tattle, but I've been thinking about telling his lordship. Finney only does the bare minimum."

Finney, a short, haggard Irishman, had been hired after Rosie, shaking with nervousness, had asked Lord Barrington to release her from her job as caretaker. After Trotting Diamond and Spirit's Dream had both run successfully in harness races, three more horse owners had overcome their objection to hiring a female trainer. She could live well off the money, and Bulldog had even suggested renting his own stables in Addington. But so far, Rosie was undecided, and his lordship hesitant.

"If you stay here, Rosie, no harm can come to you or the horses. The stable master is reliable, and the security arrangements are good," Barrington had said. "But if you're off on your own—"

Bulldog would have gladly taken over the role of Rosie's protector, but for that, the relationship between them would have to deepen. Rosie was cautious, however. And besides, both Lord Barrington and Chloe thought Bulldog too guileless in his dealings with people like Joseph Fence and the other trainers. Bulldog could only laugh at that. He had gotten the best of much harder blokes.

And, just as tenaciously as he had fought his way through London, mastered steerage on the ship to New Zealand, and built up his transportation enterprise, he now wooed Rosie Paisley.

"I admire your dedication to the horses, but you have to eat something, Miss Paisley," he argued. "Wait a minute; I have an idea. I'll fetch us fish-and-chips from the nearest pub, and we'll have a picnic right here in the stables!"

Rosie nodded—she really was hungry. Bulldog returned with a feast, as well as a beer for each of them. Rosie was in quite high spirits when Finney stopped by late that evening. The Irishman smirked at the two of them after glancing briefly at the horses, and then made a comment about alcohol in the stables.

"We stableboys ought to try that sometime. But our grand trainer 'Ross' seems to be able to do as 'he' pleases."

Bulldog wanted to reply, but Rosie put a finger to her lips as the surly man stomped off. "No, he's right. Maybe you should go now, Bulldog." She smiled. "Did you know I always still think of you that way? I can't bring myself to say Mr. Tibbs."

"You could call me Tom. But of course, I answer to Bulldog as well. Only, then you can't say Mister. And I could call you Rosie?"

Bulldog inducted her into the ritual of toasting, drinking to their new familiarity. He only kissed her on the cheek, though, after she warmly consented. After that, Rosie rolled herself up contentedly in her sleeping bag.

"Now, it really does need to be quiet here," she said. "Trotting Diamond needs her sleep before the big race."

Bulldog smiled and retreated to a storage space on the other side of the stable. There, he spread out a blanket in the straw for himself.

She peered over nervously at him.

"We can go to sleep, Rosie, but I can't leave you alone here," he declared. "The stable grounds are too big, too many blokes running around."

Indeed, Finney reappeared hardly an hour later.

"The man doesn't seem so neglectful if you ask me," said Bulldog when Finney woke them by coming by a third time. "Just the opposite. Maybe he should stop fussing over poor Triangle every five minutes and let the animal sleep."

"But he's not," Rosie answered. "He barely glances at Triangle. He can't see anything in the dark."

That was true. Finney had not even made the effort of bringing a lamp. Probably he was only reluctantly fulfilling a task assigned by the stable master.

***

In the morning, both Trotting Diamond and Triangle were in good health, and Bulldog stole Rosie away for a hearty breakfast in the racetrack's café. Afterward, she met Vincent in the stables. Lord Barrington was likewise inspecting his horses. Rosie exercised Diamond lightly, as it was almost time for the race. Vincent watched from the edge of the track while Lord Barrington withdrew to the elegant owner's box. Harness races did not interest him nearly as much as normal races at a gallop, but he was not going to let the Auckland Trotting Cup pass him by. Bulldog let himself be talked into going along for a glass of champagne during the first race. However, just before the final race, he returned to Rosie. She had already changed into her racing outfit, and he helped her harness Diamond.

To his surprise, Rosie was a mess. "She has that look again," she explained, pointing to Trotting Diamond who pranced with unusual nervousness toward the sulky. "Don't you think her eyes have gone funny?"

Bulldog looked skeptically at the mare. "She has beautiful eyes," he declared. "Just like yours. It's just the excitement."

"And she's shaking a bit." Rosie wound the lines carefully around the sulky's poles.

"She's nervous, Rosie," Bulldog soothed her. "She'll get past it as soon as she's on the track. Or should I call Dr. Taylor again? I saw him earlier."

Rosie cringed. Dr. Taylor had called her hysterical just the day before. If she dragged him to the stables for another imagined malady—

"No, you're right, it must be the excitement. Are you going to accompany us to the paddock?"

Rosie swung up into her seat, and Bulldog walked alongside Trotting Diamond to the starting line. They were both surprised when the mare pulled reluctantly and trotted in place instead of waiting well-manneredly until the starting gate was cleared. Moreover, she was coughing. Bulldog saw Rosie struggling with herself once again.

"If she caught a cold—"

"Just let her trot this mile and a half, and then Dr. Taylor can take another look."

It would have been too late to call the veterinarian anyway. The bell sounded, and the race began.

***

For this race, Bulldog joined Vincent in the grandstand. True, it was loud and crowded there, but he didn't feel comfortable in the aristocratic owner's box.

"I completely forgot to bet on her," Bulldog muttered as Trotting Diamond pressed straight into the middle of the pack.

Rosie had her trot the first half mile very loosely. But Trotting Diamond pulled on the reins, wanting to rush forward. For the first time that Vincent had seen the mare race, she seemed to run the risk of galloping. She also coughed again, but then seemed to overflow with energy as Rosie let her go on the final stretch. Trotting Diamond pressed ahead of all the horses from Fence's racing stables before also passing the stallion Joe was riding himself. Ultimately, only one horse remained ahead of her—Rebel Boy, an elegant black horse from Auckland.

An infernal noise now dominated the stands. Bulldog roared along, rooting for Rosie and Trotting Diamond. Vincent held his ears closed, laughing happily—he had no doubt Trotting Diamond would pull past Rebel Boy. But then something happened. Diamond shied slightly from Rebel Boy's sulky but did not stop trotting. Rosie could easily have closed the gap, but she did not move to do so. Instead, she kept her horse behind Rebel Boy—and did not speed up when Joe Fence brought his horse level with Trotting Diamond or even when he passed her by a nose.

"The winner is Rebel Boy, followed by Sundawner, and Dancing Rose's Trotting Diamond!"

Vincent and Bulldog were already running down the stairs to the finish line. Rosie stood next to her horse, stroking Trotting Diamond and crying.

"Whatever's the matter, Rosie?" Vincent asked. "You did marvelously. But why did you let them leave you behind? She could easily have won this."

Rosie shook her head. Next to her, Joe Fence was triumphantly accepting the ribbon for second place. But when he saw the veterinarian, his face clouded over.

"Come, come, little Rosie, you don't mean to contest the outcome, do you? Crying about it. Such a woman."

Rosie paid him no mind. She soothed Diamond, who now shied from the man trying to place the third-place wreath around her neck.

"She couldn't see," Rosie told Vincent in tears. "She was startled by the other sulky. It was as if something blinded her, but there wasn't anything there. And suddenly I had the feeling she was going to stumble. So, I thought it best to go slowly."

"We didn't see anything like that," Bulldog said. "Take a look. She didn't even work up a sweat."

Trotting Diamond's skin was hot but dry. The mare drank thirstily when Rosie held water out, but most of it ran right back out of her mouth.

"Look, Dr. Taylor!" Rosie called to the veterinarian, but the horses were already lining up for the lap of honor, and she could hardly hold Diamond back.

"I'll take a look in a moment, Rosie," Vincent assured her.

"That really was strange," Bulldog mused. "As if she were choking on something."

After the lap of honor, Diamond seemed calmer. Rosie washed her and took her to the stables, where she drank normally.

Vincent set aside his stethoscope. "Right as rain, Rosie. Her heartbeat is markedly faster, but that's no wonder after the race."

"Could it be something she ate that didn't agree with her?" Bulldog asked helplessly.

Vincent and Rosie shook their heads.

"If she had eaten something bad, she would have colic," they said in unison.

Bulldog squinted anxiously. "I just mean, well, maybe poison?"

***

"But if someone had poisoned the horse, it would be dead," Lord Barrington observed later.

He had sought out Rosie in the stables to congratulate her on third place—but in contrast to Vincent and Bulldog, he had also noticed the mare's odd swaying after she had shied from Rebel Boy's sulky. The view from the owner's box was much better.

"Maybe the devil didn't know how much to give her," Bulldog mused.

"Nonsense, Mr. Tibbs. These trainers know every trick in the book. They wouldn't make such a rookie mistake."

"Maybe they didn't want to kill her?" Rosie offered. "Just prevent her from winning."

"Now, that amount of poison wouldn't be easy to calculate," Lord Barrington declared categorically. "Though, I've never encountered something like it. What does our vet say?"

"Your vet can only repeat that I don't see any evidence. It's true that Diamond was uncharacteristically keyed up. But you'd expect poisoning to weaken a horse. It would be counterproductive for a competitor to make it want to go faster."

"Not if it starts galloping," Rosie noted.

His lordship arched his eyebrows. "Come now, you can't seriously believe someone would try to make your horse misbehave in hopes it would be disqualified? Besides, you did manage to control it. If you hadn't gotten scared when Diamond shied, she would have gone on trotting to victory."

Rosie opened the stall door and snuggled against Diamond.

"Exactly, it didn't quite work," she said softly. "So, he'll give her more of whatever it is next time. We need to keep a closer eye on her, Bulldog. But how?"

Chapter 4

The Drury family reunion was ill-fated. Lizzie, at least, was already thinking as much when she and Michael were still sharing the table in the hotel restaurant a half hour past the agreed-upon time with no one but an anxious Patrick, his eyes fixed on the clock. He apologized repeatedly for Juliet's delay, although she was the last person Lizzie was missing.

Their relationship had not improved since her daughter-in-law's return to Elizabeth Station, and Patrick's attempts to mediate only increased the tension. He was torn between his work and Juliet's constant need for attention, and his attempts at finding some sort of occupation for his wife were doomed. Juliet did not want to plant a rose garden or breed lapdogs. She could ride but was not enthusiastic about it. The elegant Thoroughbred Patrick had purchased for her only caused further aggravation: Lizzie was scandalized by the price, and Michael, who would have liked to ride the mare himself, disliked her almost equally expensive sidesaddle. Ultimately, Juliet asked to lodge the horse in Dunedin. Patrick seized the opportunity to at least get it out of his parents' sight and found an expensive boarding stable. In truth, Juliet used the horse for little but her rendezvous with Kevin.

In turn, her piano had finally been moved to Otago. Patrick thought Juliet could keep it in the gold miner's cabin, but she moaned that it was too far, and playing without an audience was no fun for her. The suggestion that she teach piano to a few of Haikina's students unleashed a fit of rage.

As time went on, Patrick could not deny that Juliet lived only for their weekends in Dunedin. These excursions were a rather long journey and an additional financial burden: when the Drurys spent time in Dunedin, they slept at the Leviathan Hotel.

"She'll be here any minute, I'm sure," Patrick declared for the umpteenth time.

Michael ordered wine for the wait. That would relax Lizzie, at least—though not too much, he hoped. In the meantime, Lizzie offered Nandi a seat. She had just come down to order some milk from the Leviathan's kitchen for May. Lizzie's and Patrick's eyes lit up at the sight of her.

"Mrs. Juliet Drury will complain," Nandi refused anxiously. "And Mrs. Doortje Drury—"

Lizzie poured the young woman a glass of wine. "I see neither hide nor hair of them at the moment. Come, dear, sit and tell us what nice things you and May did today. I'm going to guess that Juliet didn't pay any attention to the girl?"

Nandi looked down, reluctant to speak against her mistress, but unwilling to lie. Worse than Juliet's lack of maternal care were her trysts with Kevin. Why else would she need such an eternity of beautifying before visiting her brother-in-law? And a bath drawn right afterward? Nandi fervently hoped no one ever asked her about it.

"Oh, May saw many ships today. Mr. Patrick Drury drove us to the harbor and bought us fish-and-chips. We could eat them with our fingers."

Nandi beamed as if Patrick had treated her to a prix fixe meal at a four-star luxury hotel. Patrick returned the smile, proud that her English was now almost perfect. She had devoured all the children's books and novels in the Drury household, then the Bible, and more recently, even books about viniculture. Nandi seemed to find the subject fascinating and gladly helped in the vineyard when Juliet allowed her to do so. Now, very seriously and with a great deal of interest, she tasted the white wine Lizzie had poured.

"Nandi!" came a shrill voice from the entryway.

She leaped to her feet.

"I must go help Mrs. Juliet Drury freshen up."

Juliet waved to the table and gestured that she would be right back. Lizzie wondered why she did not join them at once. This was not a formal dinner, after all, and Juliet's afternoon dresses were more daring than most of the evening gowns worn in Dunedin.

"What's taking her so long?" Lizzie asked as she drank her second glass of wine. "And where are the others? Was Matariki's train delayed?"

For the time being, nothing remained for Lizzie and Michael but forced conversation with Patrick. When she did finally join them, Juliet was in top form. She entertained the group for the next quarter hour with harmless gossip about people she had ostensibly met in town and talked breezily about the latest concerts and soirees.

And then, Michael, Doortje, and their guests from Parihaka arrived at last. When Matariki hugged her parents, it seemed she never wanted to let go.

"Maori don't do that, by the way," she told Doortje, who listened with great interest. "We exchange *hongi*." She briefly demonstrated how Maori first touched foreheads and then gently pressed their noses together. "That goes back to the god Tane, who first breathed life into mankind. When we exchange *hongi* during a greeting ceremony, we're taking the visitor into our family."

Juliet laughed. "Such an archaic ritual. It could practically come from your backward country, don't you think, Dorothy? Although it does make it easy to get close to someone." She winked at Michael.

Matariki frowned. She had heard Juliet's story in broad strokes. Where Atamarie, Kathleen, and Violet had noted the strange jump from older brother to younger, Lizzie's letters had instead provided vivid depictions of domestic misery. Now, Matariki saw her fears confirmed: little May unquestionably bore Kevin's likeness—and Juliet only had eyes for her former lover.

Apparently, both of her brothers were raising other men's children. Juliet, however, seemed not to have made peace with her situation. The woman relentlessly humiliated Doortje and flirted with Kevin—and she was undeniably beautiful. No wonder Doortje had reacted with downright panic when she and Matariki had hardly had any time left to beautify themselves. Their heart-to-heart had been interrupted when, an hour after he'd gone, Kevin began pounding furiously on the apartment door. He'd refused to so much as look at Doortje, instead shutting himself in the bathroom. Now, Matariki wondered how her brother had spent the missing hour.

"Oh, the *hongi* also serves a very practical purpose," she now told Juliet. "We exchange them equally with our enemies—that way, we get to know their figure, their form, their scent, their way of thinking. The closer people are, the better they can fight one another. Would you like to try, Juliet? I'd love to get to know you. It is Juliet, isn't it?" Matariki smiled sarcastically.

Once again, Patrick looked mortified. But now, at least, they could order their food, which would give them something to do. He handed May, who had been sitting on his lap playing with teaspoons, to Nandi. The woman stood like a shadow behind Juliet. If anything here was archaic, Matariki thought, it was that.

Juliet jokingly declined the *hongi* and assured Matariki that she was dying to get to know her husband's sister.

"Not everyone has such exotic relatives," she said, letting her gaze wander suggestively to Lizzie.

Matariki cheerfully noted that Lizzie did not blush. Doortje did, though. Would seeing racism in her rival help her confront her own? Matariki was beginning to enjoy this dinner. It had been a long time since she had crossed swords with another woman, but one never unlearned the verbal fighting lessons of Otago Girls' High School.

"That's where you're wrong, Juliet," she replied warmly. "You're our exotic relative. I count myself among the natives. But now, let me have a look at my niece." She smiled at Nandi and turned to three-year-old May, who immediately stretched her little arms out toward her. "Since, so far, my nephew's been kept from me."

She turned to Doortje and Kevin with a playfully punitive look—and registered that the latter was glaring at Juliet. Interesting. Kevin seemed to feel responsible for Juliet's behavior, whereas Patrick was merely embarrassed.

"That's true." Lizzie took the opportunity to change the subject. "Kevin, Doortje, where are you hiding my Abe?"

Doortje looked at the massive grandfather clock against the dining room wall.

"Paika must be bringing him back to our house," she said, looking guilty. "We left so late. Really, we should already almost be back."

Kevin grimaced. "I hadn't even thought of that. How could you be so careless, Doortje?"

She recoiled from the rebuke as if he had struck her.

"Paika?" repeated Atamarie. "Don't tell me you have a Maori nanny."

Doortje met the young woman's eyes nervously. "Paika is the Dunloes' maid. She watches Abe sometimes. Today is actually her 'day off,'" Doortje overenunciated the foreign term, "and she wanted to go to a picnic on the beach. Kevin thought Abe could go with her."

"Of course, how nice," Matariki reassured her. "She'll look after him like her own. That's the custom among the tribes. And I don't think the delay's such a serious matter. The Dunloes live right around the corner. If Paika needs to, she'll bring him here."

Doortje looked relieved, and Lizzie ecstatic to cuddle both babies at once, but Kevin seemed to tense up anew. Matariki wondered at it. Why did he not wish for Paika to bring little Abe to the hotel?

Soon, their food arrived, and it was exceptional. Lizzie saw how easily Doortje now practiced her table manners and that she even drank two glasses of wine. Kevin was astounded too. He regretted having left Doortje alone with his sister. Something had happened between the two women.

Juliet likewise noticed that Doortje seemed different. It was as if a weight had been lifted from her. And although there was certainly tension between her and Kevin, if Juliet was not careful, this new Doortje could stand in her way.

Finally, coffee and cognac were served—and the waiter addressed Kevin and Doortje. "Dr. and Mrs. Drury, your nanny is waiting at reception with your son."

Doortje leaped up at once. Atamarie did the same.

"I'll come along. I want to see my little cousin."

Atamarie had been bored for hours. In principle, she liked spending time with her grandparents and uncles, but Juliet and Doortje were something else entirely. The conversation had remained formal, and in any case, Atamarie would have preferred to spend the evening with Roberta. She was going to meet her for lunch the next day to finally exchange news.

Matariki saw to her amazement that Kevin wanted to hold Atamarie back, while Doortje did not raise any objections. The two women rushed to the reception desk and returned a few minutes later. Atamarie held little Abe, who resembled her so strongly that they were like two peas in a pod.

Matariki nearly dropped her fork. Doortje had told her about the rape, as well as the death of her tormentor. But she had not mentioned his name.

"Kevin?" Matariki tried to get ahold of herself. "Kevin, can you come with me for a second? There's something I need to discuss with you."

***

Juliet watched as Kevin left the table with his older sister. *He looks like a whipped dog,* she thought.

Matariki hurriedly asked the front desk for the use of a room. "Even if you don't normally rent by the hour."

The receptionist smiled maliciously. "Of course not, but you don't mean to—?"

Matariki snorted. "Just give me Waimarama Te Kanawi's key. The Maori artist, you know who I mean. I'm sure she's still out. Tribal business, you understand?" She grabbed the key and pushed Kevin ahead of her.

"Now, let's hear the truth, Kevin Drury. Don't deny it. Abe is the son of Colin Coltrane. Does Doortje know?"

Matariki spotted an open bottle of wine—Waimarama and her friends must have toasted their safe arrival. She emptied the rest into a glass and tossed it back.

"Well, uh, she knows his name was Coltrane, but she doesn't know—"

"That the bastard was also Atamarie's father? And Kathleen's son? Does Kathleen know, at least?"

Kevin narrowed his eyes defiantly. "The family resemblance can hardly be missed. At least for anyone who knew Atamarie—and surely Colin too—as a baby. Somehow, Mother hasn't noticed anything."

"That's just a matter of time. People aren't so critical of their own grandchildren. Dunedin society, though—Kevin, that metallic shimmer in his hair? And once his facial features are more defined? Tongues will be wagging soon. You're throwing Doortje to the wolves."

"People will just think it runs in our family. Atamarie is Abe's cousin, after all."

Matariki huffed scornfully. "Some people may think that. But Doortje's not stupid. Maybe she hasn't quite figured out who here is related to whom. But in five or six years? You have to talk to her, Kevin. When the poor thing finds out that she's friends with her rapist's mother and his sister is painting her portrait and her sister-in-law has a child by him too—and when, by the way, were you planning on informing Kathleen, Heather, and Atamarie about the demise of their son, brother, and birth father?"

Kevin cowered under the verbal fire. "Heavens, Riki, they haven't heard anything from him in years."

Matariki groaned. "So? Don't you think Kathleen, at least, would like to have some certainty? Whatever became of him, she was his mother. She has a right to grieve."

Kevin held his tongue and stared at the floor. Matariki gave the empty wine bottle a regretful look, then turned to the little washbasin in one corner of the room and cleaned the glass. Then she heaved a sad sigh and resumed her attack.

"And what exactly is between you and that Juliet, Kevin? She looks at you as if she were the hunter and you the prey in her sights, while Patrick's a deer already bleeding out. Are you sleeping with her?"

Kevin did not answer, just buried his face in his hands.

"I'm so disappointed in you, Kevin. It's time to decide. Do you want Juliet or Doortje?"

Kevin raised his head.

"I don't want to hurt Doortje," he whispered. "I don't know how much of her I really have. But I don't want to lose any of what I do."

***

Juliet noticed that Matariki and Kevin's sudden disappearance registered with confusion. Lizzie and Michael tried to distract from the embarrassment by playing with Abe. Patrick excused himself to help Nandi put May to bed.

Juliet sipped her cognac. How delicious it all was. That Matariki, who had been so in control, had slipped into panic when she saw her nephew instead of being charmed by his resemblance to her daughter. Whereas Doortje had looked only browbeaten. She seemed baffled over what she had done wrong this time in this world of pitfalls where she found herself stranded.

Juliet took another drink. She had long suspected that there were secrets surrounding Kevin's marriage to Doortje. No doubt it would serve her purposes to uncover them.

Chapter 5

The only person the army had informed of Colin Coltrane's presumed death was Joe Fence. When the war was finally over, missing soldiers' effects had been sorted, and Joe's address had been found on some unsent letters.

After Eric Fence's death, Colin had wanted to keep young Joe as his stableboy, but Violet had sought an apprenticeship for Joe with a reputable trainer. Joe planned to use his position to spy for Colin, but Coltrane's own stable was soon liquidated, and Colin disappeared to escape the bookies. Later, during the restless years before he rejoined the army, he would secretly pop up in Invercargill, and Joe would place bets for him, helping him through some dire financial straits. Now, Joe honestly mourned his loss. Colin Coltrane had been something like a second father to him.

The young man had grown up in the shadow of the racetrack, had observed how horses were bought and sold, how they were trained, and, most importantly, how winners were made. It had not bothered his father, Eric, or Colin when Joe sat in on their carousals and absorbed every word that came out of their mouths. He heard vilifications of his mother, as well as of Chloe Coltrane, who at the time was desperately trying to keep her husband's stud farm solvent. Cheating and dirty business had to be organized behind Chloe's back. A promising plan often fell flat because she caught on and protested. Colin and Eric would then curse all the women in the world—Joe quickly learned to despise the opposite sex.

And then, Chloe cheated on Colin and left him, while Rosie, whom everyone thought feebleminded, caused Eric's death. So, Joe kept his distance from women; the occasional visit to a prostitute was enough. Really, he preferred other pleasures. Gambling, for example. Joe was a crafty poker player and shone at blackjack. But above all, he loved betting on horses—especially when the race was fixed. The thrill came not when the bell sounded and the race began, but from the intricate machinations ahead of time. You had to know whom to confide in, who was open to taking bribes, which horse was suited to which sort of cheating, and which races came into question.

All of that gave Joe a feeling of unlimited power. He was free; he was a master of circumstance; he determined the future. The apprentices in his stable worshipped him like a god—and no wonder, for he could either advance their careers or end them. They hung on his every word when he gave them tips at the beginning of a race, and they feted him lavishly when they'd managed to improve their meager salary by means of a well-placed bet. To a certain degree, that went for the horses' owners, too, who heavily supplemented the trainer's income. They knew their horses were in good hands with Joe. Nearly every one of them won now and again—and if one did not, he'd find a sucker who'd overpay for it.

Business had been booming—until he'd foisted a chronically unreliable jade on that novice, Tom Tibbs. Spirit's Dream was fast, no question, but his tendency to slip into galloping made him an unreliable candidate even for fixed races. Then Tibbs had given him to Rosie to train, and suddenly the stallion trotted—right past Fence's horses. Tibbs was raking in victories, and the previous owner was complaining. Recently, that man, too, had turned to Rosie, and there was nothing Joe could do about it. He had already made repeated complaints to the Jockey Club about her sex, but with no success. Lord Barrington took "Ross Paisley" under his wing, and there was no bylaw that explicitly banned women. It was just that no one had dreamed some hussy could make her way in the traditionally male domain. Furthermore, Rosie was proving so successful that the club thought it less embarrassing to let her continue as—on paper, at least—a man.

The news of Coltrane's likely demise strengthened Joe's determination to go after Rosie with everything he had. It was bad enough she had gone unpunished after sending his father to his death. But to show Joe up on the racetrack? If he wanted to maintain his leading position as a trainer, he needed to win the upcoming New Zealand Trotting Cup. So, he rented new stable facilities right next to the racetrack. Presentation was everything. Colin Coltrane had taught him that.

And Joe had long held on to a piece of Colin's estate no one knew about: when the stud farm had been dissolved, the boy had saved the colorful, flashy sign that had hung above the stables: "Coltrane Station—Stud and Training Stables."

It had not been easy to hold on to the massive object over the years. For ages, he had stashed it between his bed frame and mattress, then later in a barn. But now, its time had come once again. A painter was hired to freshen up the colors and replace "Coltrane" with "Fence." Joe beamed when he secured it over the entrance to his new stables.

Rosie, on the other hand, paled when she saw it. Chloe Coltrane had always hated the flamboyant sign. When Bulldog asked what was wrong, Rosie haltingly told him a bit about the sign's history.

But Bulldog was unconcerned. "I think it's really rather handsome," he said, earning a withering look from Rosie. "All that red and gold. It speaks to you. But I'll have a much nicer sign made for you if you want. You just need to think of a good name."

Rosie declined. The last thing she wanted was to draw too much attention to herself and her horses. Besides, she had been a bit of a mess since the Auckland Cup. Although Trotting Diamond's mysterious illness had not flared back up since their return, the elegant mare had been transferred to the stables of Bulldog's freight company and had quickly become the darling of the two- and four-legged crew. The stable hands treated her like a princess, the drivers stroked her clumsily and promised to bet on her, and the stallions among the giants that pulled Bulldog's wagons whinnied and blubbered in love when she pranced past. Trotting Diamond seemed well pleased. However, the mare's new lodgings meant that Rosie was forced to constantly commute between Christchurch and Addington. Bulldog's house and freight stables lay two miles away from the racetrack.

Bulldog would gladly have spared her the trouble and offered to rent stables in Addington where all the horses trained by "Ross" Paisley could be lodged. But Rosie was hesitant. In the weeks since Auckland, she seemed to be hounded by bad luck. Spirit's Dream had somehow injured his leg in his stall and now labored under a torn ligament. Another horse she trained, which had always held a trot before, had suddenly broken into a gallop in the last race and gone hopelessly out of control. Rosie could not explain it. And yet another got sick with colic just before an important race and could not start. Rosie could hardly open a new race stable with nothing but invalids and losers.

The squarely built freight baron had been begging Rosie for weeks to go out with him, but she was too shy for restaurants and hotels. And since she thought walks rather silly—she got plenty of exercise with the horses—Bulldog could only court her in the stables. Since the night before the races in Auckland, she no longer shied away from being alone with him. So, Bulldog strained to make picnicking together a ritual. His employees observed good-naturedly how he had a table set up and meals delivered from restaurants to wine and dine Rosie—with Diamond playing chaperone.

"But I won't play waiter," laughed the stable master, a patient, older man. "At most, a groomsman. Just take care you don't have to set the bed up in the stables too."

Still, he gladly pocketed the couple pounds with which Bulldog bought privacy. The stable master had an apartment next door and boasted that at night he could hear every cough his four-legged charges made. And as much as Bulldog otherwise welcomed that, he did not want anyone eavesdropping on his rendezvous with Rosie.

***

Two days after the first qualification races for the New Zealand Trotting Cup, however, it was not Rosie but Violet Coltrane who first appeared at Bulldog's. He was in the process of preparing one of his legendary picnics for two. Bulldog recognized Rosie's elegant older sister at once.

"Violet! You haven't changed a bit! Oh, pardon me, no, I must say 'Mrs. Coltrane' now."

Violet smiled. "Mr. Tibbs, I'm happy to see you again—or I hope, at least, that our reunion proves a happy one. You've done well for yourself in our new country. You didn't stay a gold miner long?"

Bulldog grinned. "I think I understand what you're asking, Mrs. Coltrane. Here's the whole picture: I spent half a year in the goldfields, paid a few pounds for a mule, and since then, I've put every penny into my freight company. Now, I've got branches in Auckland and Wellington, Blenheim, Queenstown, and Christchurch. I'm well off, Mrs. Coltrane, so not to worry, Rosie's in—oh God, I can't believe it. I mean, if I understand the seriousness of your popping in here aright, then Rosie's really hinted—oh God, and here I was thinking she might not know what I was after."

"Mr. Tibbs," Violet snapped, "my sister is not feebleminded. I've spent half my life trying to make people see that. But if you really are interested in her—"

Bulldog raised his hands. "Oh, Rosie's clever," he declared. "The cleverest woman I've ever known. She just knows horses better than people. A fabulous trainer and driver. Recently, she drove a cold-blooded team just for fun—and I tell you, Mrs. Coltrane, I'd send her straight off with a four-in-hand to Otago." Pride shone in his eyes.

"Ah," Violet said. "Then maybe I should sit."

Bulldog pulled a chair out for her at the handsomely set table. "I do have a house, Mrs. Coltrane. This is just on account of Rosie, because she doesn't like to go out. But she likes to eat, Rosie does. God, even as a kid she was always hungry. I liked her even back then, you know?"

"Of course, I remember. And that's precisely what makes the matter dubious to me."

"Dub—?" Bulldog frowned.

"It seems strange to me to the point of being unsettling," Violet explained. "By the way, we don't need to rush. Rosie's still out at the racetrack, showing Trotting Diamond and all the facilities to my husband."

Bulldog looked relieved. "I was starting to get worried. She's usually never late. She's got her very regular routines, Rosie does, very orderly."

Violet knew that Rosie clung to routines. Change frightened her.

"Listen, Rosie was a little girl back then. You can't have fallen in love with a little girl and then with the woman she has become twenty-five years later."

Bulldog looked confused. "Why not? Though I grant you, little Rosie wasn't as dear to me as grown Rosie is." He sat down as well. "Not in the way a woman's dear to a man. Back then, she reminded me of my little sister who died in London. And now, I don't even remember London well. Just my sister's sweet smile. She needed to be looked after, only, I was too young. Then, she was suddenly gone. The bobbies said a customer stabbed her, and then I was alone. But now I've found Rosie again. I can look after Rosie. And I'd like to do it, Mrs. Coltrane, if you'll let me."

To her astonishment, Violet saw tears in the eyes of the square-jawed man.

"You were never married before?"

Bulldog shook his head. "No. Moved around too much—had a girl here and there. You know how it was here. There weren't many women, especially not any who'd look at a little nothing from London. Now, it'd be different. But I don't want one who has that knowing look, d'you understand? One of them hoity-toity girls who'd look down on me. I'm sure they're aright, but I'd be scared of them."

Violet laughed. "Well, Rosie gets scared easily too."

"I know. I know she does, Mrs. Coltrane. But she doesn't need to be scared anymore. I'll be very careful with her, I swear." He held a paw out to Violet and waited with an innocent look in his eye until she hesitantly shook his hand. Then a huge smile broke across his puppy-dog face. "You know what, Mrs. Coltrane? I'll send someone to the pub now and tell them to bring some extra food for you and your husband. And we can all break bread together and pretend we're in one of your nice restaurants. Rosie'd like that."

Violet smiled. "We'd be honored, Mr. Tibbs."

"Call me Bulldog. Rosie always does. Ah, look now, here come Rosie and Trotting Diamond and your husband."

"Call me Violet. And this is Sean," Violet said as Sean, a little green around the gills, stepped from the sulky. He had crammed himself in behind Rosie.

Rosie's whole face shone. "She ran a new record," she said gleefully, "despite the extra weight."

Apparently, she'd had the horse trot from the racetrack all the way to Bulldog's stables.

"She went monstrously fast," confirmed Sean, "and she takes turns rather sharply. Apparently, I get a little motion sick."

Bulldog grinned. "Well, to be a racer, you've got to be a real man's man—like our Rosie. Wait a moment, Sean; I've got a beer for you. Fix you right up. Rosie, get Diamond settled for the night. I've invited Violet and Sean to join us for a real fine meal right here, like we're in a restaurant."

"But not the kind where you can get your forks confused, right?"

Bulldog shook his head. "Nonsense, Rosie, you know me. Violet, Sean, I hope you like fish-and-chips."

Chapter 6

Juliet did not need more than a few days to uncover Atamarie's ancestry. In fact, the truth offered itself up on her next visit to the Gold Mine Boutique. Although Patrick always groaned at the price, Juliet would not be denied. And she really did need a dress for the fast-approaching race weekend in Christchurch. And another for the post-race parties. It was bad enough she was being forced to attend the *L'art au féminin* events in her old things. Juliet slipped into a changing room with a dream in dark-red chiffon while Atamarie turned in front of a mirror out in the store. Juliet wondered where the little Maori got the money for these dresses—which, moreover, she hardly seemed to appreciate.

"It's gorgeous, but this corset—I'll hardly be able to eat anything," she was complaining.

Juliet peeked around the curtain. The young woman exemplified the fashionable S-bend body shape in a delicate-green velvet dress.

"Now, don't be like that," said Kathleen. "I hardly needed to tighten it around that slender waist. You're going to make me jealous."

Claire Dunloe laughed. "There! Now you know how we all felt when you were her age, Kathleen Burton. Atamarie looks more like you every year. I was almost startled just now when she came out of the dressing room. In the wide dresses and with her hair long, you don't notice it as much. But now—I still recall how we drank tea in the White Hart in Christchurch and everyone stared at you."

"You're exaggerating," Kathleen said.

"I think I look like my mom," Atamarie declared.

Juliet stepped out of the changing room. One look in the mirror convinced her that she still effortlessly surpassed little Atamarie. But Claire was right: there was a clear resemblance between Atamarie and Kathleen.

"So, do you want the dress, Atamie?" Kathleen asked. "Come on, you can't go to concerts in outmoded fashion. You have a duty to the Gold Mine."

"To advertise? Well, Mom won't wear a corset. She said so."

"She looks Maori, so people don't expect it of her. But you'd stand out. Come with me. I'll make the adjustments around the hips. Then you can take the dress home with you. Pardon me for a moment, Mrs. Drury. You look bewitching."

Kathleen disappeared with Atamarie into the back room, and Juliet turned sourly toward Claire.

"Who decides which ladies get to advertise for you in free clothing? Is there a beauty contest I don't know about?"

"You'd be the first we'd call on if we really needed advertisements," Claire flattered. "But like all the better sort in Dunedin, you're happy to pay for the honor of wearing our dresses, aren't you?"

"And the girl?"

"Kathleen's granddaughter," Claire explained.

"Her granddaughter?" Juliet marveled. "But I thought Matariki's husband was Maori?"

And Claire Dunloe guilelessly told Juliet about Matariki and then Chloe's entanglement with Kathleen's son Colin.

"And whatever happened to this Colin Coltrane?" Juliet asked casually.

"Kathleen hasn't heard from him in an eternity. My husband's theory is that he joined some army. He used to be a soldier, after all. Probably he's long since dead."

Juliet continued trying on clothes, ultimately choosing one evening dress and two afternoon dresses. She left the shop highly satisfied. Now she had quite a precise idea of where Colin Coltrane had been two years prior. She could hardly wait to confront Kevin.

***

"Please, Juliet, you have no idea how it was."

Kevin had first reacted with shock, then grown angry, and finally resorted to pleading, which more than suited Juliet. She liked to see her lovers prostrate themselves a bit.

"What am I not understanding?" she asked, and ran her fingers sensuously across his neck, down to his collarbone, and along his chest. She gently forced him back into the pillow. Patrick had gone to a meeting with old friends from the Ministry of Agriculture, and Juliet had summoned Kevin to her hotel room. Kevin felt terrible about making love to her in his brother's bed. On the other hand, it was much more comfortable than his office floor. "Do I not understand that your little Boer did it with Colin Coltrane?" Juliet's finger described tiny, gentle circles on his skin. "It's not hard to imagine. I've never met Heather's brother, but when I look at his children—he must be rather good-looking." Kevin opened his mouth but managed to keep himself from correcting her. Juliet already knew too much; she did not need to learn of Colin's death too. "And seems also to have had some charm. The women here all seemed to have fallen for him. Matariki, Chloe—"

"Juliet, you've got the completely wrong idea."

Kevin attempted to get up, but Juliet held him back. "Oh, I've got the right idea," she cooed. "The only thing I don't understand is why you gave the child your name. Why you have to drag that goose around and act as if you loved her."

"You don't understand anything. And I don't intend to explain because it's none of your business. We need to talk seriously. Not about me and Doortje, but about you and me. This has to stop, Juliet. You're a remarkable woman, but it can't go on. It's time to accept that you're married to Patrick, and I'm married to Doortje."

"But she doesn't make you happy." Her hands wandered lower. "Kevin, your Doortje is and remains a South African goose. Maybe she used to be a fascinating battle-ax. You must have fallen in love with her for some reason, I suppose. But here, she's just a farm girl—cute, but boring. Don't try to deny it."

"She's my wife."

Kevin shifted beneath Juliet's skilled fingers.

"But that can be rectified," whispered Juliet. "Come, Kevin, we've both made mistakes. Let's correct them. You'll send your Doortje back into the wilderness where she belongs, and I'll separate from Patrick. It'll be a little scandal, of course, when we announce that May's yours. But in the end, everyone will agree that we're made for each other. Patrick stepped in because you were gone. Very noble. But now, now, nature needs to take its course."

She bent over him and let her lips follow her hands.

There would be no more talk of ending their relationship, at least not that day. And Juliet still had many ideas for how to employ her knowledge about Colin Coltrane.

***

Matariki Parekura Turei possessed the glorious ability not to let the ugliness and prejudice of her environment get to her. She had been that way even as a child: while Lizzie and Michael worried immensely about how their daughter would handle the arrogance of the little sheep baronesses in Otago Girls' High School, Matariki breezed through all the hostility and teasing. When her birth father kidnapped her to the North Island, she did not let the fanaticism of the Hauhau movement impress her any more than the anti-Maori hatred in the town of Hamilton where she ended up stranded. After she had been kept prisoner there for a year by a Scottish couple, fanatical adherents to the Church of Scotland, she tried to hate all *pakeha*, but that quickly became too much of a strain. She embraced the spirit of Parihaka less for spiritual reasons and more because she felt comfortable in the Maori model village, and because the pragmatic pacifism of the leader, Te Whiti, appealed to her.

However, Matariki knew when a battle had been lost. When she sensed she was being threatened with jail, she fled Parihaka. Later, she worked with various women's and Maori organizations to fight for the right to vote, and here, too, her resilience proved invaluable. Matariki was committed to suffrage, but the fanaticism of some members of the Temperance Union influenced her not at all—she liked to have a glass of wine at hand while drafting and sending dozens of petitions to stubborn, mean-spirited, or stupid politicians. Matariki never lost patience and remained persistent. That also helped with her work as a teacher after she had returned to Parihaka. With never-flagging enthusiasm, Matariki introduced the Maori children to both their culture and the culture of the *pakeha*. Even though she had never attended a college like Roberta and no one taught her pedagogy or technique or disciplining, Matariki was a born teacher.

All of these qualities made her a godsend for Doortje. She had been able to overcome technical social problems with relative ease thanks to Kathleen's book of manners. But Doortje still struggled with Dunedin society's cattiness, innuendos, and unwritten rules. Observation did not help here either, particularly as the people's actions constantly diverged from their stated views.

"None of them even says a word to Nandi," she explained to Matariki. "Everyone treats her like a Kaffir, no different than back home. But if you call her stupid or uncivilized, then they all get angry."

"But Nandi isn't stupid or uncivilized at all," Matariki told her. "According to Patrick, she's now read more books than probably half of these so-called ladies. It's called hypocrisy, Doortje, or sanctimoniousness. People pretend to be open-minded, but they think and act completely differently. Don't think we Maori don't know what that's like! Officially, we have the same rights as *pakeha* now. We vote and sit in Parliament. However, Kupe's up in arms against a new law meant to take away our right to deal with our own land. Or, when it comes to women, the politicians fall all over themselves to praise us, but behind our backs, they're convinced we don't have any brains."

"But it is the case that God made Eve from man's rib." Doortje was sometimes overstrained by Matariki's constant changing of the subject. "While Adam received the divine breath."

"The Maori say the exact opposite. Take a look at the old people who are still tattooed. Women only have *moko* around their mouths to show that the gods gave them the breath of life. We should ask Nandi sometime how the Zulu see it."

"But—" Doortje broke off, recalling her sister-in-law's earlier lectures, and then tried a shy smile. "I know, I know, there's no proof for any of it."

Matariki smiled, then turned to Kevin's bookshelf. "This time there is, Doortje. Wait a moment, I'm sure Kevin has *The Origin of Species*. It could be he keeps it down in his practice, but really that would be too risky."

"The book would be risky?" Doortje asked.

Matariki pulled a row of books out and found the little volume behind. "I knew it. And here you have it: even my little brother is a hypocrite. He's convinced by Darwin, but he doesn't display the book. Reverend Burton is much braver on that point. This, in any case, might be the truth, Doortje. At least, Mr. Darwin presents a lot of very convincing evidence. God did not make mankind out of a lump of clay. All life developed slowly. Give it a read. But not just the table of contents. Most people who get outraged about it haven't even read it, you see. But now, let's head to Heather's to take a look at this exhibition. Do you really want me to lace you up first? I hate corsets."

Doortje hated them, too, but she did not want to be gossiped about. So, she dutifully forced herself into one with Matariki's help, even if she was uncomfortable showing herself half-naked to her sister-in-law.

"We never did this back home," she admitted. "Saw one another naked, I mean. Children do, of course. But for grown women, it's indecent. The Kaffirs do it, of course, like apes."

Matariki patiently explained to her that in this, too, Maori women had no compunction, and furthermore, that apes did not enter into the equation. They could not take off or put on their fur, after all.

"I don't think there were ever such *tapu* in warmer countries. There, no one wore enough clothing to totally cover their bodies anyway."

"*Tapu*? What does that mean?" asked Doortje.

Matariki began another lecture.

***

Doortje found Matariki's explanations peculiar, but they did help her understand her new world—and sometimes helped her gain new perspective on her old one. Doortje did not like that, but it was as if her reason were defying her. She still resisted things she could not comprehend, but Matariki did not simply prescribe doing things this way or like Kathleen's book of manners. Matariki explained. During their visit to the big opening at the main exhibition, for example, her sister-in-law elucidated the artists' colorful, large-format paintings in Heather's gallery and showed her that, with the pictures painted in the pointillism style, one had to keep distance from the canvas to properly register the image. Doortje observed with concern that the landscapes did not properly resemble their models in nature.

"Photography exists now, Doortje. You can't get more similar than that. So, paintings no longer need to depict reality. You can portray it however you see it."

"But everyone sees the world the same."

Matariki indicated Juliet, who was flirting with Jimmy Dunloe while exerting herself to reduce Heather and Chloe's champagne reserve. "Doortje, do you really believe you see that lady with the same eyes as Jimmy?"

Every day Doortje attended the festival's exhibitions and concerts, she learned more. She read Darwin and was outraged by his theories, but her roused intellect could not completely deny the theory of evolution. Doortje came from a farm; she understood animal breeding. There were now dozens of subjects about which she could have talked with Kevin, and she no longer embarrassed him in society. On the contrary, Doortje was slowly gaining a reputation similar to Matariki's—her comments sometimes seemed strange, but they were always well-reasoned. Her English was less and less stiff, and social graces had become second nature. That gave her space to develop charm. She imitated Matariki's easygoing, self-assured demeanor.

"You're allowed to be different, Doortje," Matariki encouraged her, "and you're allowed to say what you think. Just don't proclaim it as the absolute truth."

Kevin should have been proud of his wife. He could even have been jealous when she chatted with other men. Gentlemen now fell over one another to sit next to her at dinner. Yet Kevin did not even seem to notice the changes. Their relationship remained tense. He did not touch her at night. He was obviously avoiding Matariki.

"He doesn't like it when I talk to you," Doortje observed. "Maybe we shouldn't spend so much time together."

"He's not in charge of whom you spend time with," Matariki replied. "Anyway, it's not what you think."

She stopped herself, but Doortje was already looking at her questioningly. Of course, Matariki could not tell her that Kevin simply had a guilty conscience. He had probably still not ended things with Juliet, and the secrets surrounding the business with Colin were weighing on his heart. Matariki had made him promise to tell Doortje the truth as soon as possible. But she had not given him a deadline.

Now, she regretted that.

Chapter 7

"They're just so lovely." Roberta praised Atamarie's *manu* while helping her arrange them for the Maori art exhibition in Reverend Burton's community room. "And what happened to the man who showed you how to build them?"

"No one needed to show me! When I see something like that, I can build it myself. As for Rawiri, he's wandered into the sciences. You won't believe it, but he's sitting—or was sitting, at least—at the feet of the Wright brothers."

"Well, there can't have been much room for him in that little flier," she teased her friend. "Are you mad that he helped, hmm, the competition?"

"I imagine they would have managed without him. And Richard wouldn't have either way."

"So, you don't care about Rawiri at all now?" Roberta asked. "Or Richard?"

"Well . . ." There was no point lying to Roberta. "I think he could have at least sent a, um, postcard from his honeymoon, don't you?"

"You're saying he married that Shirley girl?"

Roberta was obligingly arranging the carefully knotted *aho tukutuku*, the laces of the kites.

"I'd be surprised if he didn't. Anyway, enough about that. What do you think, should I really try singing at the exhibition? The women say it'd be nice if we sang *karakia*. To show that *manu aute* are not just kites but represent a connection to the gods. I don't know. The gods and I aren't exactly familiar with each other."

"Won't the singers be there?" Roberta asked. "I'm sure they could take that over."

"No, that wouldn't work. Waimarama just explained it to me earlier. They could join in, apparently, but the kite-building *tohunga* has to start and sing the most significant parts. And actually, you also have to let a kite fly when you do. But here?"

"Maybe on the roof?" Roberta asked.

Atamarie laughed. "Are we going to make all of Dunedin society climb up there with us? I can see Juliet climbing in her corset now. And Patrick and Kevin fighting over who gets to hold the ladder for her."

"You're so mean. Kevin would hold the ladder for Doortje, of course. Although Juliet's certainly doing all she can."

"To seduce him, you mean? It's screamingly obvious. And I have to say, he doesn't seem like much of a rock himself. More like a blade of grass."

"He would never, Atamarie! Just because such loose morals prevail in Parihaka, you can't project them on Kevin." Roberta turned away.

Atamarie made a face. "Adultery doesn't prevail in Parihaka. When two people there seal a marriage, they stick to it. Kevin, on the other hand, I'm sorry, Robbie, but just because your dreams haven't come true, that doesn't mean he's not betraying Doortje."

Roberta's voice grew thick. "It's not true that I'm still trying for Kevin. I—"

Atamarie took a deep breath and moved one of the kites to the side to let another shine more. Then she turned back to her friend. "You're hoping for the exact same thing as Juliet. Don't bother arguing, Robbie; it's all over your letters. At exactly the moment when it became clear that Kevin and Doortje were having difficulties, you stopped mentioning your veterinarian. Instead, it's Kevin, Kevin, Kevin. Kevin's doing this, Doortje's neglecting that, Juliet's trying that. What ever happened to Vincent? Should he still be getting his hopes up, or are you going to idolize Kevin until his silver anniversary? With Doortje or with Juliet, but definitely not with you?"

Roberta dropped into a chair. "I don't know. Vincent is—he's so nice. He'd be a wonderful husband and father. But he's also—"

"A bit boring?" Atamarie said. "You feel adventure is missing? But Robbie, Kevin doesn't lead an exciting life either. The only thing that was ever exciting about Kevin were his stories about women. And it's not particularly adventurous to be cheated on." Atamarie wiped her eyes. Then she sat down beside her friend. "I wish I knew if he married Shirley," she said quietly. "If he didn't—"

Roberta gave her a sad smile. "Then you'd try again? Until, say, the twenty-fifth anniversary of the Wright brothers' flight? We're both pretty crazy, Atamie. Give me a hug."

***

The opening of the Maori exhibition that evening found surprising resonance, even though Caversham lay nowhere near the center of town. Other exhibitions were taking place in more attractive venues than a church community room. Chloe and Heather had been thinking economically, however.

"We need to sell artwork, Matariki, otherwise the numbers won't work. All the venues and artist lodgings we've rented cost a pile of money—the entrance fees to the concerts don't cover it. And so far, there are just too few people interested in buying Maori art. People like to look at it—and that's good news, of course. But they don't assume that these pieces are a good investment."

"They could just buy the works because they're beautiful," Matariki had objected.

In Parihaka, they sold many textiles, paintings, and jade carvings to visitors. But those were considered souvenirs more than art.

Tonight, however, Dunedin society's great interest surprised the artists and gallery owners. The usual crowd did, in fact, make its way to Caversham, marveled at the colorful paintings, and stared with fascination at the tiny faces of the *hei-tiki*—figurines of gods that could be worn as amulets or displayed.

Atamarie's *manu* found special acclaim among the men.

"Do they really fly?" asked Jimmy Dunloe, touching the birdman decorated with feathers. "The kites I flew as a child were lighter and had a tail."

Atamarie smiled. "Only if you sing while you fly them," she replied. "With them, one could carry messages not only to the gods, but also to various tribes living farther away. A kite like this can be seen across great distances. Thus, the painted symbols or decorations are part of the message." She told the gathering crowd of Pa Maungaraki's conquest with the help of a glider kite. "Long before the Wright brothers," she added, earning applause. "And now, I'm also supposed to sing some *karakia*. However, I can't sing particularly well, and I'm not a *tohunga* either—I can only build kites. Others know far more about the gods."

"Maybe you should give Reverend Burton the text," Jimmy Dunloe said with a smirk.

Peter Burton shook his finger at him.

But Atamarie ignored the interjection. In her high-pitched voice, she intoned the simplest prayer to the gods she knew, and paused, dumbstruck, when a deep voice joined her:

> *"Taku manu, ke turua atu nei*
> *He Karipiripi, ke kaeaea . . ."*
> Fly ever higher, glorious bird,
> conquer the clouds and the waves,
> fly to the stars,
> dive into the clouds
> like a warrior into battle!

Atamarie sought the singer in the crowd and caught sight of Rawiri's gentle face, transported by the song. As they finished together, he beamed at Atamarie.

Atamarie cleared her throat and pointed to the young man. "I—I'll hand things over to a real *tohunga*. This is Rawiri. What I know about *manu*, he taught me."

She stepped aside so that no one would notice how much the sight of Rawiri unsettled her. He had changed during his time in the United States. Not only did he wear his hair shorter, but he also looked more grown up, stronger, and more self-assured. And, of course, he had a share in the Wright brothers' glory. Atamarie felt a tiny flare of envy as Rawiri now explained her kites to the visitors.

"Sometimes, the spiritual meaning and practical use coincide," he said. "When we used the kites to decide on settlements, for example. You could practically survey the land with them—but they also asked the gods to bless it. But I'll stop talking now. The *manu* are impatient. I hear them whispering behind my back."

The listeners laughed, but Rawiri was quite serious. "Birds want to fly," he told the crowd gently. "Atamarie, which should we set free?"

"This one," called Jimmy Dunloe, still not convinced that the heavy bird-man could climb into the air.

Atamarie shook her head. "Better the *manu whara*. There's hardly any wind here."

The church did have a very pretty, if somewhat overgrown, garden, but it was surrounded by a high wall. Not ideal for flying kites.

"It will only work on the roof," Rawiri agreed placidly. "From the church bell tower would be best."

Reverend Burton cleared his throat. It was Kathleen, however, who intervened.

"Don't you dare," she declared in a half-jesting tone. "What do you think the bishop would say to us about your making contact with your spirits from our bell tower?"

"More like the ancestors," said Atamarie, "if we take the *manu whara*. It's shaped like a canoe, you see, which—"

"Ancestors, spirits, whichever, they'll stay out of our church," Kathleen replied. "Peter, forbid it."

Peter Burton smiled. "I think God is pretty flexible on the point, and a prayer's a prayer whether it flies to heaven upon a kite's string or directly from our hearts. But my wife's right. The bishop might see things differently. He's particularly indignant about the word 'ancestors.'"

A few parishioners laughed. Peter Burton's career had thoroughly stalled because of his unconventional sermons. He made no secret of being a Darwinist and saw it as completely compatible with his spiritual office. The horrified bishop was always on the lookout for complaints from the more sanctimonious parishioners.

"Then we'll just use the roof," Rawiri whispered to Atamarie. The two realized with amazement that no one was paying attention to them anymore. Instead, they were excitedly discussing Peter Burton's position and that of his bishop. "Come on."

Rawiri and Atamarie took the *manu whara* and the birdman with them. The wind was scarcely sufficient for the birdman, but Atamarie felt her honor impugned by Dunloe's doubt. Now, she followed Rawiri up to the roof, hungry for adventure and invigorated by the surprise reunion. Fortunately, she had chosen one of her most comfortable dresses for the opening and not the captivating torture device from the Gold Mine.

"You're not afraid of heights, are you?" Rawiri asked as he helped her up.

Atamarie stuck her nose in the air. "I'll bet I've already flown higher than you."

Rawiri laughed. "I believe that. But even so, be careful not to slip in those shoes."

A short time later, Roberta, who had been watching Atamarie and Rawiri's breakneck climb with concern from the garden, called out to the exhibition visitors. Awestruck, they funneled into the garden and listened to Atamarie and Rawiri sing as their two kites danced in the evening sky.

"Did you sing *karakia* for the Wright brothers?" Atamarie asked Rawiri when they finished.

"No. They don't appreciate such things. And it was too loud at Kitty Hawk anyway. It was a show, Atamarie, not worship."

Atamarie wondered whether it had been worship for Richard Pearse. Of course, that was the wrong word. Still, she remembered her first flight in Tawhaki. It had been spiritual, somehow. She wanted to make a joke about that, but Rawiri looked at her.

"Did you sing *karakia* for Richard Pearse?" he asked.

Atamarie furrowed her brow. "How did you know—?"

"That you flew? I saw it in your eyes. Besides, you just told me."

"Do you make a note of everything I blabber about?" she asked evasively.

"Every word of yours becomes a song in my heart," Rawiri said, but then came back to Richard Pearse. "And that he flew, well, that's what he told Wilbur and Orville."

"He what?" Atamarie almost fell off the roof. Rawiri held out his hand to secure her. "Richard wrote letters to the Wright brothers?"

Rawiri nodded. "They didn't take him that seriously, though. It was a strange correspondence too. Sometimes he would write constantly; sometimes nothing for months. Sometimes he exchanged scientific observations; sometimes he seemed confused. The time it took letters to get back and forth made it all much harder, of course. At any rate, Wilbur and Orville thought he was a crackpot. But they've been in contact for years. These people all know one another."

"He never told me about that," Atamarie muttered. "He really—he really wrote them that he had flown?"

"At some point, he wrote that it didn't work, that he hadn't flown, that God didn't want men to fly. There was something about crashing in a hedge."

Atamarie sighed. "That cursed hedge. But if he wrote the Wright brothers about his flier and his attempt, then they must have realized that he had either flown or was about to. And then they staged their flight. Heavens, Rawiri, how could he be so stupid?"

Atamarie calculated with lightning speed. It added up. The Wright brothers had forced their first flight right after Richard had given up. They thought he was a crackpot, but they also knew he had flown, and they did not want to run the risk of not being first.

"You did sing for him," Rawiri said, "but the spirits did not hear you."

"Probably you can only sing for yourself," she murmured. "Will you sing with me again?"

Rawiri began the song to the gods, and Atamarie joined in. The Maori singers down in the garden took up the song, and in the twilight, an almost ethereal duet between heaven and earth unspooled.

***

"It's beautiful," Doortje whispered as the kites danced and the *tohunga* sang. She felt shyly for Kevin's hand.

She did not know if that was proper, but lately she had sometimes longed for his touch, another thing she would never have admitted to herself a few months before. But why should she not desire Kevin? He was her husband. Kevin did not reject her either, squeezing her hand tenderly.

This gesture did not escape Juliet. And it filled her with rage.

Chapter 8

"They were holding hands," Roberta reported the next day to Atamarie. "While you two were singing up there. Doortje has completely changed. Your mother—"

"My mother invited Rawiri to the Matariki celebration," Atamarie answered distractedly, "with our tribe at Elizabeth Station. Since we're both here for once, we're going to celebrate with the Ngai Tahu. And he agreed. He's going to make kites with the tribe's children beforehand; he promised. Maybe we'll do that together."

"Atamarie, are you even listening to me? I was talking about Kevin and Doortje."

"It's nice that they're finally happy," Atamarie said. "Or would you prefer he picked Juliet? I already told you, Robbie; it won't be you."

"And what about you and Rawiri?" Roberta asked.

Atamarie shrugged. "He's nice. When I'm with him, it's lovely. And he loves me. But did I tell you that Richard apparently wrote letters to Wilbur and Orville Wright?"

Roberta groaned.

***

Over the next few days, Atamarie and Rawiri grew closer. After his arrival in Wellington, he had learned that she was on the South Island, and he made his way straight there. Atamarie, who until then had only seen Rawiri in the context of Parihaka, was pleasantly surprised. Furthermore, Rawiri was now educated, he had seen more of the world than Atamarie, and he knew how to tell interesting stories about it. Rawiri spoke of monstrously high buildings in New York. He described the Brooklyn Bridge, considered the longest suspension bridge in the world, and talked about spectacular feats in railroad engineering, of automobiles, and of plans for giant oceangoing steamships.

"And flying, of course. It's going to develop rapidly now." He smiled. "Whether we sing or not."

Atamarie told him about her recent exams, her uncertain plans for the future, and her last trip to Richard's farm. She did not want to lay out the whole story, but she was dying to compare Richard's aeroplane with the Wrights'. Rawiri did her the favor of describing their machine in painstaking detail.

"Professor Dobbins would also be interested in hearing about it," she said. "If you travel back through Christchurch, you should offer to give a lecture to his class."

Rawiri looked at her incredulously. "You really believe I could? In front of all those learned people? I always had the feeling I was just some stupid Maori hick to you, who thought he could fly by jumping toward the sea, singing."

"It's no worse than silently crashing into a hedge," she said. "Besides—Richard never finished college either. Still, he built his aeroplane. And it flew better than the Wrights'."

A shadow crossed Rawiri's face. "Again and again, you come back to Richard. Do you still love him, Atamarie? You know that I—I don't want to pressure you, Atamarie. But I thought maybe we'd both go to Christchurch. You said yourself that the professor offered you a position at the institute. And I could study at Canterbury College—engineering. I'd like to build aeroplanes myself, teach a motor to sing. Have you ever considered that, Atamie? That they're singing, whispering to the spirits?"

Atamarie smiled. She had often listened to the sound of the Otto motor. For her, too, it was like music when it ran smoothly. But whispering?

"You think someday there'll be motors that whisper?" she asked.

"Why not? They shouldn't drown out the wind, and they can't be so loud that people can't hear themselves think."

Atamarie's eyes flashed. "If you could reduce the vibrations—"

Rawiri touched her arm. "Forget the motor for now. I have to know if there's still something between you and Richard Pearse. Are you going to go away again to be with him? And come back when he doesn't want you anymore? I might be your second choice, Atamarie, but you're going to have to make a choice."

Atamarie leaned against the young man. The two had walked to the beach to fly Atamarie's kites. Rawiri insisted that they could not be locked up in a museum, and Atamarie was beginning to feel that he was right. The other Maori pieces seemed to lose some of their luster in the community room, far from their *marae* and *wharenui*, from their wearers' throats and the walls of the meeting-houses. But the *manu* could fly away. Now they smelled of the sea; the wind had tousled their decorative feathers. It gave them a different expression. The birdman seemed to tell of adventures in the air, the hawk looked fierce, and the canoe held its peace about the secrets of the ancestors.

Now, the *manu* lay next to Atamarie and Rawiri in the sand while the two drank beer and gazed out to sea.

"I don't know if I have a choice, Rawiri," she said. "I could love you. Maybe I already do. But sometimes I feel as if there were an *aho tukutuku* between me and Richard. Flax doesn't tear so easily."

"Roberta says he's probably married," Rawiri said, and looked at Atamarie questioningly. "Doesn't that break the line?"

Atamarie shrugged helplessly. "I can still feel it, Rawiri. I can't help it. It's stronger than I am."

"In other words, he just needs to pull the line in," Rawiri observed bitterly, and sought her gaze.

Atamarie looked away. "Give me time," she murmured. "Just give me time."

***

Roberta had come decidedly too early. Half an hour before the agreed-upon time, she was standing in front of the house on lower Stuart Street to attend a concert with Atamarie and Matariki—and Kevin and Doortje, of course. Still, she told herself that this was a coincidence. Just as it had only been on a whim that she had opted for a half-hour stroll to the city center instead of a ride in Sean and Violet's coach. But the air was lovely that day, and Kevin would surely still be in his office while Doortje, Atamarie, and Matariki changed for the concert. Maybe he would have left the door to his practice ajar. Roberta would then be able to peek inside and maybe chat with him a bit. But only if chance dictated, of course. Roberta would never have planned something like that.

Still, she was disappointed when she found the door closed. Was he already upstairs? But then she heard concerning noises from inside. A sharp cry—but she could have imagined that—and moaning. Kevin must have a patient, maybe an emergency. But his nursing assistant had surely gone home. Roberta could step in. In South Africa, she had occasionally helped out in the hospital. Uncertain, she slipped into the waiting room and saw the closed office door. Should she knock? The moaning could clearly be heard here—but somehow, somehow it did not sound pained.

Curious, Roberta tiptoed closer to the door. A woman's laughter. And a man's voice. Kevin's voice.

"No, Juliet. No, no, really, you little beast, you're a devil."

"Totally wrong, you know I'm an angel. I'm going to ride you until you admit it."

Roberta's first impulse was to turn and flee. But there she remained, spellbound.

"Juliet, really, I don't want to anymore."

"Kevin, dearest, you don't speak for your little fellow here. He just doesn't want to come out of me, you see."

"Little fellow? Are you trying to insult me?"

Giggling. "Oh, forgive me, naturally, I was speaking of your mighty member. You're a stallion, dearest. Is that better?"

"Much better. But you really shouldn't. And I need to go upstairs. This concert—"

"Should I sing for you? Let my body sing for you. Our duet is better than anything you'll hear on the stage. Come, my stallion, now it's your turn to ride."

"We can't do that." Kevin's voice sounded pained, but Roberta wondered why, if he meant any of it, he did not simply get up and go.

What she was hearing was repugnant, a far cry from the nights with Kevin she had dreamed of. Roberta had imagined tenderness and lovers' oaths—and blissful, shared silence after the climax, itself like a sunrise or a shower of shooting stars. But this, if it was this lust and absurdity that he wanted, the last thing Roberta wanted in that moment was to be in Juliet's place.

She spun around hastily—and startled herself to death when a Victorian monstrosity of a vase fell and smashed on the floor.

Kevin threw open the office door before Roberta had quite reached the exit. He was naked, a towel thrown hastily around his waist.

"Roberta?" His eyes reflected his fright, but also relief. Thank God it was only Roberta. "What, uh, are you doing here? I was just freshening up. The three ladies are up in the—" Kevin smiled apologetically, begging her understanding.

That was when Roberta realized that he took her for a clueless child. Just as he always had, no matter how hard she had worked in South Africa. Kevin might have found her useful, but he did not take her seriously. She felt a rising cold within her.

"Don't bother lying, Kevin. I heard everything. Tell Juliet she can come out. I could help lace her up. She does want to look presentable when she faces Doortje, doesn't she?"

Kevin's face fell. "Roberta, please, don't tell anyone. I know we shouldn't see each other. I want to end it."

"Then why don't you?" she asked contemptuously.

"Please, Roberta, I love Doortje. But I can't. I—"

From the office came guffawing.

Every word here was wasted. Roberta ran out and slammed the door behind her.

"Roberta," Kevin yelled after her.

She ran down the stairs. Under no circumstances could she face the other women now. Atamarie would instantly see that something was wrong. And she could not tell her friend that she had wasted years of love and respect on a cheater who held Doortje's hand one day and the next did disgusting things with Juliet Drury. And who still talked of love.

***

Roberta took a cab to her parents' house. Violet and Sean would worry when she did not appear at the concert, but she could tell them later that she suddenly felt ill. She'd blame it on the corset, which Violet had already scolded her for wearing. And tomorrow, she would take the train to Christchurch a few days early. Her family was going to see Rosie and Diamond, who had qualified for the New Zealand Trotting Cup. More than anything, Roberta wanted to see Vincent again. Roberta longed for his warm, understanding smile and his gentle eyes—eyes that recognized someone like Juliet at a glance.

Roberta had finally had enough of unrequited love. Not to mention the wrong man.

Chapter 9

The next morning, things no longer seemed so simple.

It surprised Violet that her daughter felt sick one day and wanted to set out on a journey the next, supposedly to visit a friend from school.

"Did something happen, Roberta? You look pale."

"Nothing happened. I was just, um, tired. But now I feel better. I can travel, Mom. Don't worry." Roberta carefully laid skirts and blouses in her suitcase. "I'll leave the corset at home too."

Violet observed her with a frown. "Something happened. But if you don't want to tell me—it's nothing really bad, is it, Robbie? Does it have something to do with a man?"

Violet had been raped at a young age, and the associated fear still stuck in her bones. No matter how often she told herself that Roberta was quite safe in Dunedin, she hated it when her daughter went out alone.

"Nothing happened to me, Mom. All it was, was that something—I—"

"Saw something, Roberta? Did a man approach you improperly? There are those who take pleasure in, well, exposing, um, themselves to women. It's called—" Violet thumbed through the dictionary in her head.

Roberta laughed. "Mom, I did not see anything of the sort! I'm fine, really. I just want to go to Christchurch a couple days early. I'm sure Rosie will be happy."

"And the young man you got to know in South Africa? Is this about him? Roberta, I really don't approve of you—without accompaniment. We don't even know him."

Roberta looked at her mother indulgently. "You'll get to know him this weekend. Now, enough, Mom. I'm fine. I've traveled alone to Christchurch before. No one's going to gobble me up, least of all Vincent Taylor."

But Violet did not give up so quickly. "What's he going to say when you come two days early, Roberta? It'll look like you're throwing yourself at him."

"I'm going to visit my friend first!" she repeated the lie. "She, uh, she has a problem, you see. She wrote me about it, and I think she really needs support. She's a teacher, but she got involved with a man, and now she's—"

"Pregnant?" Violet took the bait. "Oh, the poor thing. But it does urgently need to be done away with, this nonsense of celibacy for female educators. A male teacher can marry at any time, but a woman's supposed to live like a nun. Robbie, send your friend to the Women's Christian Temperance Union. Perhaps they'll find some work for her. Taking care of children for poor families."

Roberta acted as if she were listening attentively to Violet's various offers of help for her nonexistent friend. She hated to lie to her mother, but she simply had to get out of town.

***

In the end, Violet personally hailed her daughter a cab and sent her off to the train—but as Roberta sat happy within, doubts about what she was doing began to stir. Her mother was right. Even in Addington, they would find it strange when she showed up two days early. And she could not simply run to Vincent, apologize for her distance these last weeks, and offer to marry him. The best thing really would have been to wait for the weekend and to greet Vincent so warmly that he took courage and asked again. Then she could accept the proposal and blame her fickleness on not wanting to give up her profession. It was just a question of whether he would believe her. After all, he clearly suspected her infatuation with Kevin. Later, perhaps, they could talk about it—the last thing Roberta wanted was to keep a secret from her husband. Now, however, was no time for such confessions. Vincent shouldn't assume he was her second choice.

But what was she going to do with two unplanned days in Christchurch? Brood alone in a hotel room?

The perfect solution came to her when the conductor announced Timaru as the next stop. What if she got out and looked into a few things? Now that she knew the truth about Kevin, maybe she could learn the truth about Richard for Atamarie.

Ready for action, Roberta pulled her bag down from the rack. Maybe she would even get to lay eyes on the fantastic Richard Pearse at last. She only knew him from Atamarie's descriptions—he might look very different to an outsider.

She took a room in the nearest proper inn and asked directions to the rental stables.

"I'd like to get to Temuka," she explained to the innkeeper. "How long is the ride?"

"Two hours if you hurry," the woman replied. "I used to have a young woman stay here frequently who had an acquaintance there. She told me she once made it in just over an hour. But Miss Turei rode like the devil himself."

Roberta smiled. Things were going better than she had hoped.

In the rental stables, she asked for a calm horse and a chaise, then made her way along the largely unpaved road to Temuka. The sheep pastures and plains had a cheerless effect on Roberta, but that may have had to do with the weather. It was raining buckets, and although she had chosen a two-wheeled chaise with a roof, Roberta's clothing was slowly getting wet. She sighed with relief when she reached Temuka, a typical village with neat wooden houses, a school, and a church. She hailed an approaching rider and inquired about the way to Richard's farm.

A while later, the infamous broom hedge came into view. Roberta had to smile. Atamarie had described all of it so vividly.

The farm, however, was a surprise. Atamarie had told her that it was somewhat run-down, the yard full of farming equipment. Yet this house was newly painted—lovingly, the shutters snow white and the porch in blue. A rocking chair stood on it, and everything had a homey quality. Two well-nourished horses stood in the pasture. The yard was impeccably ordered. The farming equipment, lined up neatly by the barn, was neither old nor rusted.

As the carriage approached the yard, a curtain moved behind a window. A moment later, the door opened, and a woman stepped out. She looked middle aged and motherly beneath her wide-brimmed hat.

Was that Shirley?

"Hello," the woman greeted her cheerfully. "What can I do for you? Go on and hitch the horse in front of the barn; come in out of the rain."

Roberta climbed shyly out of the carriage. The rain soaked through her light shawl at once.

"I'm actually looking for Richard and Shirley Pearse," she said. "This, this is the Pearse farm, isn't it?"

"No, I'm sorry, young lady. You've come too late. This used to be Richard Pearse's farm, but my husband and I bought it five months ago. Mr. Pearse offered us a good price. A nice young man, if a little distracted." She smiled indulgently. "But come in anyway; I just made coffee. I'm happy for the company. I'm Emma Baker, by the way." She held out her hand.

Roberta took it and followed her hostess into the house.

"Why did he sell it? Mr. Pearse, I mean," Roberta asked as a cup of coffee and a plate of cookies were placed in front of her. Mrs. Baker even heated up the oven so she could dry her shawl. "Forgive me, I didn't really know him. But my friend knew him quite well, and she said that he didn't feel he could leave. Particularly not once he married."

"He got married?" Mrs. Baker took a cookie. "Well, I don't know anything about that. He just told us he was moving to Milton."

"Milton?"

Roberta almost choked on her coffee. Milton lay only thirty miles from Dunedin, an easy train ride. Yet Pearse had never turned up looking for Atamarie.

"He bought a new farm there. Sheep breeding, I think. Said he didn't like it here anymore. People were always talking about him, which must have been awful. It's understandable he wanted to get away."

"He was a flier," Roberta explained. "He flew earlier than the Wright brothers."

"Yeah, we still have that strange flying machine in the barn. Mr. Pearse did not want to take it, but neither did he want to give it to his father who wanted to scrap it. My Rob thinks it might as well stay here. It doesn't eat our bread, after all. And who knows, maybe it'll still be worth something." She laughed. "Now, the neighbors think we're a little strange. But it'll all work out. It takes a bit of time in the country before people warm up."

"Well, if you bake these cookies for the next parish bazaar, everyone will love you."

Mrs. Baker laughed. "Or hate me. We come from Sussex, and I used to win all the baking competitions at the fair. It doesn't necessarily make you popular. But that reminds me—if you want to know more about Mr. Pearse, ask at the

Hansleys', the second farm down the way. They know the older Pearses well, the ones who don't much like us. Digory Pearse claims we took advantage of his son when we bought the farm. But it's not true. Given the condition the house was in, he couldn't in good conscience have asked for more."

"The Hansleys? Didn't Richard mean to marry their daughter Shirley?" asked Roberta, standing up to take her leave.

"I'm afraid I don't know, sweetheart. But it was really nice that you happened by. Really, everyone's so nice here in New Zealand. Except for our neighbors, but that'll work out."

Roberta left her to her optimism, unhitched her horse, and rode past the Petersons' farm to the Hansleys'. A big farm, considerably more extensive than the Bakers', but just as well kept. Her reception, however, was not half as cordial.

"What do you want?" A tall blonde woman shot into the yard as soon as Roberta's horse had trotted to the hitching post. "You're not wanted here. You—"

Roberta looked out from under the roof of her chaise, and the woman drew up short.

"Oh, pardon me. I confused you with someone else. I only saw the horse, but of course, it's a rental carriage. Please, forgive my impoliteness. I thought you were an impertinent little Maori—"

"You thought I was Atamarie Turei," Roberta said. "What do you have against her? She's a friend of mine."

"Your friend? But you're white—well, it's none of my business. The past is past anyway. Back then, we thought she'd addled young Pearse's brain, and Digory and Sarah still do. But he didn't need some Maori slut for that. He was addled enough on his own. He broke our Shirley's heart." The woman sniffed.

"Atamarie said they'd gotten married."

"They were supposed to! Sarah Pearse and I have always wanted to get those two married, since they were little. Especially seeing as Shirley's so patient. Dick really does need a tolerant woman. But he just wasn't interested. We were giving up, thinking he didn't care for girls at all. But then he hauled that Maori here, and Sarah made an about-face."

"Sarah's Richard's mother?"

Roberta was having some difficulty following, but at least Mrs. Hansley was talking her head off, even if she did not invite her guest inside despite the rain.

"Surely. And first, she thinks the slut'll do Dick good. She messed everything up, the slattern thing. The boys here were strutting around like roosters in love, but she just wanted to tinker on that flying nonsense with Richard. And Sarah'd thought she'd put other thoughts in his head. But everything was a mess. Well, and then he finally sent the Maori girl away. We tried again with him and Shirley, but the slut kept showing back up. Then it seemed like she was gone for good. He was real amenable for a while, working on the farm. But then he got ornery again, like he always does. His madness comes and goes. But Shirley stuck with him. My girl has a heart of gold. Until he up and left her behind. Now, he's got a farm in Louden's Gully, somewhere in Otago. And we married Shirley off to a fellow in Westport. She cried her eyes out, the dear, to leave Temuka."

Roberta thanked Mrs. Hansley and rode back toward town. She wanted out of the rain, and she needed to think. Should she tell Atamarie about her discoveries, or was it better to keep Richard's story to herself?

Chapter 10

Roberta rode back to Timaru, spent the next day there, and boarded the train to Christchurch the following morning. She disembarked in a suburb so she could change to the train on which her family would be traveling. That would calm her mother and make her story believable. While Violet did immediately ask about her pregnant friend, Roberta was ready. She claimed the young teacher had lost the baby.

"A blessing in this case," said Violet, and squeezed her hand.

Roberta sighed with relief.

Heather and Chloe were anxious about the race, but in high spirits. Their women's art festival had been a triumph. They had sold a great deal of artwork.

"We could have sold Atamarie's kites thrice over, but she couldn't part with them. Her new boyfriend was of the opinion that she would thereby be handing over part of her soul, and that the souls of the kites would suffer if they just hung in people's living rooms instead of flying. I guess we'll just have to live with that." Heather leaned back with a laugh.

Sean seemed in a festive mood, but Violet looked anxious. She was happy for Rosie, of course, but she hated racetracks, thought the morality of gambling more than questionable, and dreaded encountering her son. During her last visit with Rosie, she had seen Joe, but the reunion had been short, the atmosphere tense. The new, flashy sign in front of Joe's stables had reminded Violet of bad times, just as it had Rosie. Furthermore, the resemblance between her son and her deceased husband, which had already been apparent in Joe's childhood, now positively repulsed her. Joe Fence had looked down on his mother all his life and hated her in the end.

Sean put his arm around his wife. "You did what you could for the boy, even if he sees things differently. But you had to keep him away from Colin. It was precisely the right decision to send him to apprentice with that other trainer."

"But what good did it do?" Violet asked unhappily. "He looks like Eric and deals with horses like Colin."

"Fence met his maker a few years too late," said Sean. "Joe had been shaped by him too strongly to change. But that's not your fault, Violet. Don't beat yourself up."

"I was a bad mother to him," Violent said, even though Roberta constantly assured her it wasn't true. She had almost died giving birth to the boy and felt enormous guilt that she had never been able to love him.

"We'll invite him to the family dinner regardless," she now declared, making Sean hang his head in frustration.

At the train station, Rosie and Tom Tibbs were waiting, but to Roberta's disappointment, Vincent had not come.

"The vet sends his regrets," Tibbs explained with a grin. "It involves a surprise, Miss Fence."

Rosie nodded eagerly. "Yeah, it might be coming today, and I've already—"

"Rosie, shh, it's supposed to be a surprise! If you tell her now where you're, uh, going to put it—"

Roberta looked at him. "Is it a wedding present for Rosie? Mom says you've asked her, Mr. Tibbs. Did you really? I still can hardly believe it."

Rosie grabbed Chloe and Heather's bags. "No, this present's for you, Robbie. Your—"

"Rosie," Bulldog interrupted his excited fiancée again with an affectionate smile, "you're going to spoil everything for the vet. It'd be better if you told them when you're going to marry me."

"After the race," Rosie said. "Well, now, if we lose, or not until spring or at Christmas—in any case, after the New Zealand Cup. Because I need to look after Trotting Diamond first. Bulldog doesn't want to move into the stables."

Violet was horrified. "You don't mean to tell me you're sleeping in the stables, Rosie."

"It's not what you think, Mrs., uh, Violet." During their fish-and-chips feast, Violet and Sean had offered to be on familiar terms with their future brother-in-law, but Bulldog still found it difficult to treat such genteel people as his equals. Although, as Rosie kept reminding him, as a racehorse owner—and a well-off one, considering the fortune he had quietly amassed—he himself counted among the better sort. "My stable master offered her his apartment next to the stables. Otherwise, she can't sleep for concern about Diamond. But just until this race. Afterward, we'll have to work out something new. You're still planning on moving into my house or at least back to your room at his lordship's if nothing happens this time, right?"

"So, there haven't been any more incidents?" Chloe asked. "That mysterious shaking and the nervousness?"

Bulldog shook his head.

"Yes, there were," Rosie contradicted him. "One time, she had those shiny eyes during training. I rode anyway, and she was a little jittery, but otherwise—"

"Doc Taylor examined her after, and she was fine," said Bulldog. "Watch out, Rosie, or you'll drive yourself crazy. Everything's going to go smooth tomorrow."

But Rosie was not convinced, and she absolutely refused to leave Trotting Diamond alone to take part in the family dinner at the White Hart Hotel. She received support from Chloe, who also had no interest in any dinner that involved Joe Fence.

"I haven't had fish-and-chips in forever," Chloe declared. "What about you, Heather? The pub across from Bulldog Freight has recently become famous for them." She winked at Tibbs and Rosie. "Care to invite us to dinner in your stables, and tomorrow we'll celebrate your win with pomp and ceremony at the White Hart?"

***

Roberta wasn't too enthusiastic about dinner with her brother herself. Fortunately, Vincent appeared shortly after their arrival at the White Hart, apologized a thousand times for his delay, and gladly accepted their invitation to dinner. He seemed somewhat beleaguered. Apparently, he had been rushing about quite a bit, trying to pull off his surprise, and it had not worked out in the end.

Roberta seized the opportunity. The sight of this absolutely reliable man worrying himself over a little delay made her heart beat faster—and made her sure of her decision. It was so simple and natural to love Vincent Taylor—why had she made things so hard for herself?

"Give me something else," she declared. "Whatever made this exciting surprise so complicated, it can't be too hard to buy a couple of rings. I'll still act completely surprised."

***

While Bulldog, Rosie, Chloe, and Heather had a wonderful time in the stables, dinner with the Coltranes and Fences passed in a strangely divided atmosphere. Vincent Taylor radiated happiness, and Violet hardly recognized her glowing daughter. Until a few days ago, Roberta had still sometimes seemed immature, but now Violet recognized a woman finally at peace with herself. Her questioning of her future son-in-law proved mild, and Sean Coltrane also left Vincent unscathed. The two men were immediately simpatico and spoke about politics and South Africa. Joe had nothing to contribute there, so Roberta and Violet struggled to make conversation with him.

"You have your own racing stables now," Roberta noted, and tried to put something like admiration into her voice.

Joe, who looked out of place in his checkered suit and newsboy cap, nodded. "I've had it for a while. But just got a new one since the racing clubs got put together. It's bigger and brings in more. I'd gladly take you for a ride. You, too, Mother."

"Yes, of course. I'd love to take a look at what you've built for yourself."

"And you've got a horse in the qualification races tomorrow?" Roberta folded her napkin delicately.

Joe ran his hand over his mouth. "Three," he said proudly. "I drive the best myself. My apprentices take the others. If all goes well, we'll take places one to three."

Roberta furrowed her brow. "What about Rosie? Do you think she doesn't stand a chance?"

"A lady with a pony?" He laughed.

Vincent Taylor interrupted his conversation with Sean. "Well now, Fence, that lady and pony have placed ahead of you more than once. Rosie stands a good chance, Roberta. Joe does, too, of course. Hopefully, the best trainer will win." He scrutinized Joe as he spoke.

Fence met his gaze innocently. "You said it, Doc. Now, where can I get a beer around here?"

***

The bustle around the races began early the next morning. The horses had to be fed, groomed to a shine, and warmed up. In addition to all of that, Trotting Diamond was being moved. The qualification race was one of the most important that day and would not take place until the afternoon, but Rosie wanted to present two of the other horses she had trained in races for younger horses. Diamond was to spend the time until the race in her old stables near the track—and Rosie had already appointed Bulldog to keep watch over her.

"We'll be there too," Chloe said, taking off her hat and, despite her elegant dress, grooming Trotting Diamond a little more. "Oh, I loved harness racing," she sighed. "If only Colin hadn't been such a scoundrel."

"Just don't tell me I need to buy you a stud farm to make you happy," Heather teased.

Chloe smiled at her. "A racing stable. We'll only race mares: *La vitesse au féminin.*"

The two of them giggled. Rosie looked on uncomprehendingly.

"Just keep a close watch on her," she admonished her guards as she drove the first of the young horses onto the track.

Bulldog placed himself dutifully next to Diamond's stall while Heather and Chloe quickly defected. The owner's box lured them away with its canapés and champagne. Their breakfast in the stables had been rather spartan.

Rosie steered her first horse, a handsome bay mare, sovereignly around the track, and the early spectators clapped when she crossed the finish line third.

The race day looked to be promising. Fortunately, even the weather was playing along. It did not matter to the owners in their box, of course, and part of the new grandstand for spectators was covered, but to the horses and their drivers, it was preferable not to race in the rain.

Violet, Sean, and Roberta were in no great hurry to get to the track. They treated themselves to a hearty breakfast in the hotel, and Roberta was happy about the good impression Vincent had made on her parents.

"I just don't like that you'll be ending up at another one of these racetracks," Violet said. "Raising children in this environment—"

Sean stopped her. "Violet, dear, there's a difference between working as a veterinarian at a racetrack and as a trainer. Vincent might take the children with him sometimes, but I'm sure he won't be leading them into gambling, let alone cheating. He's more likely to put them off the racing business. Especially as he seemed very concerned about the animals and not to care much for Joe."

"Who does care for Joe?" Roberta asked.

"Roberta," scolded Violet, "he's still your brother. And he, well, he's certainly made something of himself here. Maybe we should show him a bit more respect. We—"

"You're a very good mother," Roberta and Sean intoned at the same time, and laughed.

When they arrived at the track, Violet and Sean were happy to let Chloe lead them into the owner's box, but Roberta went to the stables to look for Vincent. However, a stableboy turned her away.

"You have to understand. We can't just let everybody into the stables today. Things are already confused enough without strangers coming and getting the horses even more excited." He smiled disarmingly. "But why don't you sit there on the little grandstand? We keep that for the trainers and the like. I'll tell the veterinarian you're here. If he's got a moment, he'll come look for you. Sound good?"

Roberta nodded. In truth, she was quite happy to have a seat. She had once again sacrificed comfort for fashion and was wearing a corset and a very elegant velvet outfit in a dark lilac shade with a matching hat. It looked good, but rather limited her movement and was anything but suited to a visit to the stables. So, Roberta waited, and waved quickly to Rosie, who was driving in her second race. This time, a black stallion was pulling the sulky. Just before the starting signal, Bulldog appeared in the grandstand next to Roberta.

"Just real quick, Rosie mustn't see me. I'm supposed to stay with Diamond, you know. But I had to see how Dream's running. He's my horse, you see. Handsome fellow, ain't he? And a sort of good-luck charm. If I hadn't bought him, I'd never've found Rosie again. He's named Spirit's Dream. And Rosie knew his father before. She thinks he's got promise. But he's been limping a long time now. It's a wonder he can even run. Rosie didn't want him to at first, but the veterinarian says she can go ahead and race him. And I have to see it."

Rosie and Dream did not disappoint their most ardent admirer. The black stallion was in the best of spirits and ran the race of his life. He crossed the finish line a whole horse's length ahead of a horse from Joe's stables.

Bulldog screamed and cheered like a little boy but then recalled his other duties.

"Oh man, I have to get back to the stables. If Rosie catches me here, she'll be mad. And I have to pretend I didn't know about his win. Don't squeal on me, Roberta."

Roberta watched him go with a smile and raised her arms in victory as Rosie trotted past her for the lap of honor. She could not resist waving to Joe, too, who looked chagrined. He waved gruffly. Dream's victory was no doubt a slap in the face. But the most important race of the day still lay ahead.

Vincent turned up around midday and once again apologized verbosely.

"This was supposed to be our weekend together, Robbie. I was so looking forward to it. But today nearly every horse scheduled to race seems to have gotten a minor injury. Joe alone has called me three times, and Rosie just had to show me Dream's trot once more right before the race, as if she could not see for herself whether he limped. But tomorrow I'll have time for you for sure, and before that, hopefully—"

"Doc? Fence is asking for you again. Colic." The stableboy made a regretful face. "Sorry, Doc."

Vincent sighed. "Well, then I'd better hurry. I want to see the qualifying race no matter what. Save me a seat, Robbie."

He kissed her quickly, at which the stableboy grinned cheerfully and went on his way.

***

"Something's not right, Bulldog. She's got that look in her eye again."

Rosie had harnessed Trotting Diamond, which had not been easy. The mare was nervous, unhappy to part from her stable mates, and she seemed to fidget as Rosie led her in front of the sulky.

Bulldog looked at Diamond probingly. "But she's not sweating. It's not colic or anything like that. I'm sure she's just excited again."

Indeed, the mare's body was hot but dry. Even her mouth seemed to be dry.

"Maybe she needs something to drink." Bulldog ran to fetch a bucket, and Diamond did, in fact, drink greedily. "See, she's in such a hurry, it's running out of her mouth," he said. "That was the problem."

"But she had water in her stall," said Rosie, glancing at the bucket in the stall. "Though I suppose it could be dirty. When did you last change it?"

Bulldog gave her a pained look. "Am I supposed to haul water or not take my eyes off this treasure? Doesn't matter, she's had a drink. Now, she can run." He stroked Trotting Diamond's broad forehead. "Good luck, cutie. And even more luck, my cutier." He wanted to kiss Rosie, but she pushed him away nervously.

"Tom, I know I'm being crazy. But if you can find the veterinarian—it would just be better if he took another look at her. So we don't take any chances. We—"

Resigned, Bulldog nodded. "I'll look for him. But if I can't find him, don't wait here, Rosie. Run the race, and this time, don't hold the horse back."

"But what if someone poisoned her?" Rosie reached for the reins uncertainly.

"Dear Lord, we haven't taken our eyes off her for more than three minutes. Go on and take her out. I'll look for the vet. Good luck, Rosie."

Rosie nodded. Diamond pranced as she began to trot. The mare did not seem to feel weak, at least.

Chapter 11

Vincent did not join Roberta in the stands until the horses were already assuming their starting positions.

"Phew, just in time. A false alarm. Which is new coming from Fence; usually he likes to scrimp on the veterinarian. And it isn't that easy to misdiagnose colic. In any case, the horse was in tip-top shape. Is Rosie at the starting line?"

At that very moment, Bulldog hastened to the stands.

"There you are, Doc. But you weren't here the whole time, were you? Harry"—he gestured to the stableboy at the entrance—"said you were seeing to some colic?"

Vincent nodded. "Just got here. What's the matter?"

Bulldog raised his hands apologetically. "The usual: Trotting Diamond's nervous, has strangely shiny eyes, feels hot to the touch."

"But doesn't have a fever," Vincent continued. "I'm sorry, Tom. I'd love to comfort Rosie, but—"

"Shiny eyes?" Roberta asked, smiling. "Is she using belladonna drops? I was just reading about how ladies used to put them in their eyes to look impassioned."

Bulldog laughed, but Vincent grew serious. "God in heaven, atropine. Belladonna extract. Everything fits: the hot, dry skin, the shaking, and the apparent swaying. Did she have trouble swallowing, Tibbs?"

"She was thirsty. And the water ran out of her mouth a bit. She—"

Vincent leaped to his feet. "A low dose, otherwise she'd be dead. Come on, Tibbs, quick, we have to stop the race. If she falls over in the middle of the race—"

Vincent and Bulldog hurried down the grandstand, Roberta following.

"But we watched her all day," Bulldog objected. "We—"

"Who was watching her during your horse's race?" asked Roberta. "Was she alone?"

Bulldog shook his head. "Of course not. One of his lordship's stable hands. That Finney fellow. I asked him to keep an eye on her."

Vincent stopped a moment. "That sleazy fellow he hired to replace Rosie? The one Rosie always said was a lousy worker?"

Bulldog shrugged. "I never noticed. Really, he was rather active, even at night."

Vincent slapped his forehead. "Listen, Tibbs. Go down now and try to stop the race. And I'll see about the stable hand. We have to know how much he gave her."

"You really think she might die?" Bulldog looked desperately at the track. The horses were already beginning to trot. It would not be easy to stop now.

"Get going," Vincent insisted. "Until I know how much she received, I can't say. But there's grave danger. So, go already."

Bulldog ran toward the race directors, but then seemed to change his mind and took a different way. Vincent and Roberta charged into the stables.

Indeed, Finney was there, working with Barrington's racehorses. None of them were harness racers, though, making it all the stranger that the fellow was fooling about there.

Roberta was startled when Vincent seized the man by the jacket, spun him around, and punched him in the face.

"I hereby apologize if I've got the wrong man," he said curtly, "but if I've got the right one, take that for preamble. What did you give the mare and how much?"

"What mare? And how—"

Vincent struck him a second blow. "Maybe you'd also like to tell us who's paying you. But first: What and how much?"

Vincent held the man fast, so he could strike again if he did not talk. Roberta looked at him, stunned. Had she really thought just the day before that he was a bit weak?

"I—I don't know, five drops. I don't know what's in it. Some tonic." The stable hand wheezed the words from his bloody lips.

"Tonic. Of course. Where are the drops? And don't you dare run away." Vincent let the man go, and he stumbled into a grooming box.

"No tricks." Vincent followed him, pressing protectively in front of Roberta. "If you come at me with a weapon—"

The man raised his hands anxiously. "Hey, I surrender. Don't have any weapons. Just the dropper with the bottle there." He pointed to a shelf behind them.

"Bring it to me, Roberta." Vincent fixed his eyes mercilessly on his victim. "Does it say anything?"

"Atropine," Roberta read.

Vincent clenched his jaw. "Did you always give her five drops?"

The man shook his head. "Usually three. But this time, Mr. Fence said—"

Vincent gave him a closing uppercut. "Get lost. Really you ought to be locked up, but I have more important things to do. So, get going. But if I find out you've lied—"

Vincent rushed out of the stable. Roberta ran after him, wheezing.

"Will she die of it?" she asked.

"Hopefully not. But she needs to rest. The strain on her circulatory system from running—damn it, I should have figured this out earlier. Fence is a gaming man. He didn't want to kill her, just to make her show poorly. And he chose the perfect means. In small doses, it makes animals euphoric. That explains her tempestuousness. And it affects vision—her shying in Auckland. Oh God, what's that?"

During the races, a roar always came from the stands. Vincent and Roberta had not paid it any mind. But now, it sounded like a collective scream or an expression of amazement.

"Something's happened."

Roberta ran behind Vincent as fast as her corset allowed. She swore to herself never to wear one again.

A terrible accident was not spread out before them when they finally reached the track. The field was even then rushing onward. The horses were coming around the curve and toward the finish line. The first lap had been run.

"Well, no one seems to have fallen," Vincent panted, looking at the horses.

But Roberta was looking in the opposite direction. "Vincent, there."

Bulldog was climbing the barrier in front of the stands and was about to throw himself in the path of the horses.

"He's trying to stop them."

Vincent ran in Bulldog's direction. "Tibbs, Tibbs, are you mad? They'll never stop."

Vincent roared his warning, but neither could Bulldog hear him, nor could he reach Bulldog in time to pull him away. A few men in the audience were already trying that, but the freight entrepreneur was strong as a bear and flung them off like annoying insects.

Roberta could not watch—if he threw himself in the horses' path, he would be run over without a doubt. But then Bulldog suddenly stopped and looked at the lawn in the center of the track. Rosie was steering her mare at a walking pace across it, though she did speed up, alarmed, when she saw her fiancé climbing over the barriers. The track was not divided within. Rosie and her horse must have left it unimpeded at some point between the starting line and the second curve.

Bulldog looked as if he wanted to run across the track to her, but then he came to his senses and leaned heavily against the barrier until the field thundered past. Only then did he storm toward Rosie and Trotting Diamond, laughing and crying at the same time.

Vincent and Roberta followed.

"You're not mad, are you?" Rosie asked her fiancé anxiously, although she should really have been able to tell from his exuberant embrace that he felt anything but anger. "Trotting Diamond, she was running fast, but something wasn't quite right. Doc?"

Vincent had already taken out his stethoscope and was listening to the mare's heart. Diamond seemed to sway a bit.

"It's all right, Rosie. You did the smartest thing you could have. Now, let's unharness, take her to the stable, and give her some charcoal. Don't cry, Rosie. She won't die. She'll recover. But it's—"

"Who was it?" Bulldog asked through clenched teeth. "Who was the swine? When I get my hands on him—"

Vincent pointed at the field of horses, which had begun trotting again.

"If you hurry, you'll catch him right when he's getting his prize. Don't hold back. But don't kill him just yet either. It was Joe Fence."

***

"So, what's going to happen to him?" Rosie could not stop crying.

Three hours after the race, Trotting Diamond's condition had improved markedly. The dose hadn't been terribly high. Theoretically, she could have run her race and maybe even have won. But she could just as easily have swayed, stumbled, and pulled Rosie and the sulky down with her. That was dangerous enough when only one horse was involved. But in such a big qualifying race, other horses would most likely have run into the crashed equipage. Fence had been risking the lives of numerous people and animals.

"Happen to whom?" asked Vincent. "Tibbs or Fence? Tibbs they'll probably let out of his cell soon. Sean Coltrane's already taken his case, and there's no fear of him running riot any further. But Fence'll have to carry that busted jaw of his around for a few weeks. His nose took a beating, too, didn't it? Regardless, he won't be enjoying his victory today."

"And he'll be going to jail, won't he?" asked Roberta.

She had accompanied Vincent and Rosie into the stables and had missed Bulldog's appearance during the award ceremony. According to Heather and Chloe, however, it had been ferocious. The powerful freight entrepreneur had taught Fence a lesson in front of all of the spectators, the race management, and the other drivers.

"Well, Bulldog's more likely to face punishment," Chloe observed realistically. "It'll be hard to prove anything against Joe. You shouldn't have let that stableboy get away. Couldn't you have tied him up with your garters, Robbie?"

"It seemed more important to us to save the horse," Vincent said. "But I sent little Harry out to check all the pubs around here. With a little luck, the bloke's not gone yet but washing his wounds out with whiskey first." He laughed grimly. "If Fence denies it, there won't be a case to prosecute against him. Here on the racetrack, however, he won't have a leg to stand on anymore. The trainers and drivers will believe me—and they ought to be quite furious. The bastard didn't just risk Rosie's life, after all, but theirs too."

"So, they're going to lock up Bulldog and not Joe?" Rosie asked. "But that's not fair."

"In the face of this realization, maybe you've finally had enough of racing?"

Violet's energetic voice came from the entrance to the stables, and Rosie threw herself sobbing into her older sister's arms. Her concern for Trotting Diamond had already been significant, but if Bulldog ended up in prison on top of it . . .

Violet gently stroked her hair, and Sean, arriving close behind her, shook his head.

"Now, don't scare her, Violet," he said. "Tom Tibbs is already out of police custody, Rosie. He's waiting for you 'at home,' he said. He was a bit too worked up to come here with us." It had taken three strong men to pull Bulldog off Joe, and the police had not treated him especially gently during his arrest. "He wanted you to take Diamond to his stables when she's doing better. He's also expecting Roberta and Vincent—something to do with a surprise. It arrived earlier." Sean winked at Vincent. "Oh yes, and in case anyone's hungry—Tom's ordering fish-and-chips again."

Everyone exchanged looks when Rosie entrusted Vincent and the stable master with the task of taking Diamond to Bulldog's stables—she wanted to look after her fiancé first.

"Chloe and I will meet you all there," Heather said. "We're happy to have fish-and-chips again, but this time let's wash it down with champagne. I'll never get used to beer in this life. I'm sure the White Hart will sell us a couple bottles."

***

Sean held Violet back when she started to follow Roberta and Vincent into Bulldog's stables. "Now, let them enjoy their surprise alone," he said. "The whole thing's flowing into the next engagement. With all these joyful events, you won't need to look for reasons to drink champagne with us."

Violet was about to begin a lecture about how the discovery of Joe's cheating was anything but joyful. In her heart, she felt she'd lost her son again that day—and for good.

But Sean, who sensed her sorrow, put his arm around her. "Now, now, forget the past. You saved your sister, you saved your daughter—and most of all, you saved yourself. You couldn't save Joe, but you gave him every chance in the world. And that one will land on his feet. He'll probably just go to the North Island and start all over."

***

The cold-blooded horses and cobs in Bulldog's stables greeted their Trotting Diamond with loud, deep whinnying as Vincent led the mare inside. But beneath all that, Roberta picked up a high, soft blubbering. Amazed, she followed the familiar sound while Vincent gave the stable master feeding instructions for Diamond—and did not believe her eyes when she recognized the white Basuto pony in the farthest stall. Lucie recognized Roberta and whinnied at her, just as she had in South Africa.

"Vincent, is this the surprise? But how can it—you fetched my horse?" Incredulous, she stroked Lucie's soft nostrils.

Vincent beamed as he approached her. "I wanted to make a big to-do about the surprise, at least tie a ribbon around her neck, but you already found each other. Do you like it?"

"Oh, I do. But how did that work? Bringing a horse all the way from Africa—that must have been expensive."

Vincent smiled. "I just put a few connections to work. She traveled here with the cavalry regiment from Christchurch."

Roberta leaned against her boyfriend. "I never said so, but I was worried about her. I wondered what had become of her back there."

Vincent pulled her close. "See, you do like horses. And I thought, if you had a living one, you'd finally part from this one here."

He pointed to her handbag, and Roberta blushed. She still hadn't been able to part from the stuffed horse Kevin had won for her years before. Now, it was dangling from her leather bag. She had finally decided to throw it away before the journey, but then she could not bring herself to do so.

"It's a lucky charm," she whispered.

Vincent looked stern. "It was a fetish, dearest. Don't deny it. I know where you got it. Kevin told me."

Roberta thought she would die of embarrassment.

"Kevin knew?"

"Everyone knew, Robbie. But I thought, with a little patience . . . You'll have to tell me sometime what made you finally change your mind. So, will you throw it away now?"

Roberta shook her head. "No. It doesn't deserve that. Maybe I just misinterpreted it. Because, in the end, it did bring me luck, didn't it?"

She raised her face to Vincent's, and he saw the light in her eyes when he kissed her.

And as he did, Lucie the pony chewed on the little leather band with which Roberta had attached the stuffed horse to her bag, until it ripped.

Chapter 12

"And what's going to become of your brother and Rosie's funny fiancé?" Atamarie inquired. She was sorry not to have accompanied her friend to Christchurch after all, and especially loved hearing how Roberta's kindly veterinarian had gone berserk when they'd discovered Joe's cheating. "Which one's going to jail?"

"Neither," Roberta said, happily playing with her engagement ring. "Harry, the stableboy who was on the trail of this Finney character, really did find him. And naturally, he squealed on his employer to both Lord Barrington and the police. He hadn't made just Trotting Diamond sick, but all the horses Rosie was training. It was simple—they were all in his lordship's stables. Joe even admitted it. But he played it off as a prank. He swears he didn't want to hurt any person or animal, just ruin Rosie's reputation as a trainer. In the end, he hoped he'd be able to buy Trotting Diamond and get the other horses back to train. There's a lot of money in it, you know."

"But he's not going to jail?"

"Chloe and Rosie withdrew the complaint," Roberta reported, "and in return, Joe's going to forego pressing charges against Bulldog for the beating. He would have been in more trouble than Joe, otherwise. In principle, once Joe's recovered, he can keep his stables—if anyone's stupid enough to entrust him with horses. Vincent says people at the racetrack are claiming he plans to emigrate to Australia."

"The farther, the better! Now the field's clear for Rosie."

Roberta shook her head. "Rosie's career as a trainer is over. In that sense, Joe achieved his goal. After the scandal, she can't pretend to be 'Ross Paisley' anymore. It was in the papers that 'he' is a she. It was an open secret before, but now it's been raining complaints from other racing clubs. Rosie gave up her license. She doesn't want to race anymore, anyway. The climate at the track is too rough for someone who truly loves horses. Instead, Rosie's driving four-in-hands pulled by cold-bloodeds. Mr. Tibbs is joking he's finally got the fastest delivery service in New Zealand."

"Well, the main thing is everybody's happy." Atamarie leaned back and lifted her face to the wan winter sun. It was not raining for once, and the two women had found seats in the garden of the little café near the cathedral. "Are you going to come with us to visit the Ngai Tahu?"

Roberta shivered. "For Matariki? To sit around outside, staring at the sky and freezing while you flirt with Rawiri?"

"Kevin and Doortje are coming," Atamarie said slyly. Even a week before, this revelation would have caused Roberta an immediate reconsideration. Now, however, she only looked annoyed. "And Patrick and Juliet."

Roberta had not yet told her friend what she'd seen. "Doortje should keep an eye on Kevin," she began cautiously.

But even as she was formulating her words, Rawiri entered the garden.

"Here you two are," he called, and touched his forehead and nose lightly to Atamarie's. A *hongi*, although there really was no call for a formal greeting here. But Rawiri shied away from a kiss. Until Atamarie had made her decision, he would not impose. "Why are you two sitting out here in the cold?"

"We're practicing for Matariki," Roberta joked. "Atamarie wants to take me along, but I don't want to go."

"It really is very uplifting," Rawiri enthused. "At least when it's a clear night. All the singing and dancing, the kites—don't you have any greetings to send the gods in the heavens? Special wishes?"

"There's nothing more for me to wish for," Roberta said, holding out her engagement ring to him.

Rawiri smiled. "We should all be so lucky. Atamie, Professor Dobbins has written to me. He really would like me to give a presentation on the Wright brothers. And to organize a seminar on Maori kite building, if you can imagine. Moreover, he'd be happy to take me on next semester as a student. So, if you wanted . . ."

Atamarie's face clouded over. She, too, had received mail from Dobbins. He was again offering her a job as a research assistant, which was very generous.

Her applications for other advertised positions had proven that female engineers were not exactly in demand.

"I wrote"—Rawiri pulled his jacket tighter around himself as if trying to hide in it—"I also wrote that I wouldn't have anything against working with Richard Pearse."

Both women sat up, alarmed.

"You did what?" asked Atamarie.

Rawiri lowered his gaze. "Well, I thought he might present on his flier and his attempts at flight, and I'd present the Wrights'. Something like a comparison."

"That's, that's very magnanimous of you," she murmured.

"Well, I wasn't the one who flew, after all."

"But you'd be giving him a forum." Atamarie was becoming visibly excited. "He could introduce his work at last, get a little recognition. What did Dobbins have to say about it?"

Rawiri looked at her sadly. "He liked the idea, but he couldn't reach Pearse. I'm sorry, Atamarie. I thought—I wanted to help you decide. But the gods play an unfair game. I'll have to keep fighting a ghost."

Roberta inhaled sharply. She liked Rawiri immensely—but she, too, had seen the light in Atamarie's eyes at the thought of seeing Richard again.

"The ghost," she said, "lives in Louden's Gully, near Milton. About thirty miles from here, Atamie. You could take the train tomorrow."

***

Atamarie and Rawiri forgot the cold as Roberta reported on her detour to Temuka. Rawiri listened with feigned calm, Atamarie with growing excitement.

"He didn't marry Shirley?" she asked. "He—he up and left there?"

Roberta nodded.

"For you, it seems," Rawiri said. "Why else would he move to Otago?"

"For me?" Atamarie leaped up, her eyes seeming to spray sparks. "But if he wanted to come for me, then he could have gotten out when the train stopped here. If he wanted to come for me, why did he buy another farm in another godforsaken dump? Louden's Gully—do you know that area? It's all hills. If you took off in an aeroplane, you'd fly down one hill and into the next. You can't fly there. So, if he wanted to come for me, if he wanted me—" Atamarie turned away, fighting back tears.

Roberta looked at her friend. "Do you want him, Atamarie, or do you want to fly?"

Atamarie lowered her head. "I don't know, Robbie. I don't know. But I think if he wanted me—"

Rawiri stood. "Think about it, Atamie," he said softly. "If you want to try again, then just go tomorrow. Talk with him; convince him to do the presentation." He looked at Roberta, then back at Atamarie. "But don't ask yourself if you want him or to fly. That's the wrong question. You do want to fly, and you can fly. If he gives up on his dreams, that's his business. Don't give yours up for him."

***

Atamarie thought harder than she ever had in her life. She caught a ride out to Elizabeth Station with Patrick and Juliet, who were traveling home after another weekend in town—and had an enervating journey while Juliet pouted about how much she hated going back to the farm. Patrick spent the first few hours trying to console her, but then gave up and got into an animated conversation with Nandi. She had become deeply engrossed in viniculture and asked Patrick countless questions. She expressed herself in perfect English and seemed quite happy—but she kept an anxious eye on Juliet.

Atamarie could imagine why. Juliet was horribly moody and surely took it out on her maid. Atamarie wondered what Roberta had wanted to say about Kevin before Rawiri arrived.

When they finally reached Elizabeth Station, Lizzie and Michael were delighted to see her—and Michael offered to lend her a horse the next day.

"Louden's Gully is half a day's ride," he informed her. "The roads are paved and good for riding. Back then, it was also gold-mining territory, you see. But do you really want that man? Sorry, Atamie, but if you ask me, you're chasing him."

"Some men you have to chase a bit," Lizzie teased her husband. "If I hadn't followed you to Gabriel's Gully back then, you'd still be digging in vain for gold."

Michael laughed. "No, dearest, I'd've returned to making whiskey long ago. Besides, you didn't need some friend to tell you where I was. You knew where to find me. I wasn't ducking you."

Atamarie looked at her step-grandfather, horrified. "You think he's running away from me?"

"I don't know, sweetheart. I don't know him at all, of course. Maybe he's running away from something else. But look at it from a farmer's perspective: it's the same if I work a farm in the plains or in Otago. Your young man just wanted a change of scenery. And not to hear or see anything from his past. For whatever reason."

Atamarie added this to the subjects she needed to think about and withdrew to the waterfall. Rawiri, she thought, would probably ask the spirits. Had his generous offer of inviting Richard to a shared presentation at Canterbury College perhaps been providential?

Atamarie smiled. But why not?

***

The next morning, she rode into the mountains. She quietly sang the traditional songs as she went in search of a raupo bush, and asked the gods reverently for permission before cutting a few leaves. Atamarie did not make a big kite, but she put a lot of effort into the frame of manuka wood and carefully calculated the wingspan of the birdman. The *manu* should not only be capable of flight but also beautiful. Without quite knowing why, Atamarie intoned the old prayers and songs while she cut the pieces and bound them together. But that night, when she lay beside the fire in her sleeping bag, looking up at the stars, she let her thoughts wander. *Taku* and *toku*—the past and its importance. How often had she traveled to Richard, how often had she comforted him, encouraged him, helped him? And how often had he done those things for her? They had shared passion, and it had been lovely. He had touched her heart. But what about her soul?

Atamarie considered how he would fit into her *pepeha*, her description of her life, if she had to give one. Could the past be the future for him? What anchored him in the present? Atamarie could not discern any *maunga*, any mountain, in the real or figurative sense, that held Richard back or kept him grounded. Just a broom hedge—the symbol of his failure.

She wavered between laughing and crying when, after three days of work and just before Matariki, she let the kite fly. It somehow resembled Richard. Birdman—the Maori had called him that. A being between heaven and earth—perhaps worthy of admiration, but nothing that could find its place in the here and now.

Atamarie followed with her eyes. She held it on a single *aho tukutuku*. Not she, but the gods should steer it. At first, the wind seemed gentle and pleasant. The birdman rose quickly as Atamarie sang. But then she fell silent and waited. The kite swayed. It pulled at its line. Atamarie held it fast. Then, a gust of wind seized it. The *manu* shot to the side. Atamarie tugged on the rope, but she knew that she could not stop the crash. It was hard to let go. The kite seemed to stabilize briefly as she let the line slide between her fingers. It rose steeply into the sky, but then it faltered. Atamarie saw it fall and disappear somewhere in the brush. It was not a broom hedge. But in her people's beliefs, the spirits dwelled in every stream and bush. Their judgment had been passed.

Atamarie did not look for her kite.

Nor did she ride to Louden's Gully.

The Return of the Stars

Lawrence,
South Island
1904

Chapter 1

Kevin Drury had never been so ashamed as that evening when Roberta Fence stumbled into his office. Roberta, of all people, the girl who had idolized him her whole life. He did not want to imagine what she thought of him now. Kevin hated himself for cheating on Doortje. Especially as there was no longer any excuse for it, if there ever had been. Doortje was thawing, she was finding her way in her new world, and she seemed ready to love Kevin. Or to admit that she loved him already.

Juliet, on the other hand—Kevin had known even before fleeing to South Africa that there was no love between them. They could have ended the affair without any trouble if Juliet hadn't been fixated on the idea that she could exchange Patrick for Kevin like a pair of shoes. And Kevin kept playing into her hands. But now, he swore to himself, that was over. Since Roberta had caught the two of them, he had successfully avoided Juliet. Their next encounter would take place at Elizabeth Station. Matariki was to be another family reunion. Lizzie wanted finally to have all three of her children back in the farmhouse, even though it would be bursting at the seams. There would be no opportunity for Juliet to catch him alone—at least not for more than a few minutes. No longer than necessary to tell her that it was over for good.

Kevin was brooding about that while he steered his carriage toward Lawrence. He sat on the box, while Matariki and Doortje chatted behind him and played with Abe. Matariki loved the little boy. He did not remind her of Colin. She had long ago finished with that story. And for Doortje, it was a blessing she had never seen the man before his face was deformed.

Doortje, at any rate, seemed to have overcome the trauma of Abraham's conception and not to hold it against the child. She was a good mother, or at least what her people understood a good mother to be. Matariki was just then trying to loosen her ironclad principles about a child's upbringing.

"Oh, come now, he's not going to become a coward just because you pick him up and comfort him when he cries. Maori children are constantly being cuddled and carried around, no one beats or frightens them, and still, the boys grow up to be brave warriors and the girls powerful leaders. Did you know we have women chieftains? Once, there were many more. The English were a bad influence on that. They simply did not take the women *ariki* seriously. So, few were elected. Maori tribes think practically. However, I can still show you war clubs and other weapons made for our women. We can fight just like your people, even though we're affectionate with our children."

Kevin smiled at his sister's efforts, which were slowly having an effect. Doortje had not said a word in opposition to celebrating the heathenish New Year festival with the Ngai Tahu. On the contrary, she seemed excited about it. And she had even gotten along with Lizzie at their last family get-together. If she did not turn up her nose at Haikina and the other Ngai Tahu this time, she would surely get a second chance on Elizabeth Station.

Kevin was determined not to mess this up. He would end his relationship with Juliet and then speak to Doortje about the Coltrane matter. He caught himself whistling a cheery tune as Silver handled the hills between Lawrence and Elizabeth Station with his accustomed verve. The future was bright. He would finally put his life in order.

***

A weight was lifted from Matariki's heart when Atamarie met them at Elizabeth Station. She had spoken with Roberta and Rawiri after her daughter's precipitous departure from Dunedin, and she'd shared their fears: another attempt with Richard, disappointment, and further tears and doubt. But at last, her daughter seemed to see things clearly. Atamarie greeted her happily, was looking forward to the festival, and asked when Rawiri would arrive. Now, Matariki could only hope that he had not changed his mind and returned to Parihaka instead of participating in the festival here as planned.

There had been a skirmish about where to lodge Juliet's maid. Normally, Nandi slept in Matariki's old room, but since Atamarie and her mother were visiting, Juliet wanted to put Nandi in the barn or the hallway outside their rooms. Lizzie had been incensed.

"Under no circumstances is it acceptable that she sleeps outside your door like a dog, Juliet. And the barn? Poor thing would freeze to death. Not to mention the baby—unless you're offering to take May for once?"

Lizzie had fetched a children's bed from the attic and shoehorned it into the little room. And when Atamarie came back from the mountains, she unrolled her sleeping bag on the floor next to the two beds. Nandi was shocked at the prospect of sleeping in a bed while a white girl lay on the floor.

"I'm not white," Atamarie assured her. "I'm Maori. And what does skin color have to do with a bed? Possession is nine-tenths of the law, and this is usually your room."

The three women got along brilliantly, and little May was spoiled by all.

Doortje demonstrated her newly learned diplomacy by not even addressing the subject, but perhaps the icy stares coming from Juliet's direction already gave her enough to manage. Lizzie had put Kevin, Doortje, and Abe in Kevin's childhood room, and Juliet took umbrage at that. While living on Elizabeth Station, she had claimed Kevin's old room as her personal "dressing room" and tended to sleep there as well. She "visited" Patrick in his room or reluctantly let him into hers. She had long since disabused him of his dream of falling asleep in her arms.

"We all need to squeeze in for a few days, Juliet," Lizzie said, "but a family reunion like this is worth it. I don't want to hear another word on the subject."

But Juliet was determined to ruin everyone's mood with her pouting and her occasional caustic remarks about the size of Elizabeth Station. A manor house that offered only four bedrooms was unthinkable to the plantation owner's daughter.

"We should be thinking about building additions, or, better yet, building anew," she declared.

Michael and Lizzie bore it with composure. They, too, had grown accustomed to Juliet's moods.

"I simply cherish the thought that someday she's going to run away again," Lizzie confided in Matariki. "She is wretchedly unhappy here and means to make us unhappy as well. I guarantee she's only waiting for a suitable opportunity. When the right man appears, she'll disappear again."

Matariki wasn't so optimistic. The looks Juliet still gave Kevin suggested she'd already set her sights on the "right man."

***

Indeed, on the evening of his arrival, Juliet did not let Kevin out of her sight. Intoxicated at being together again and also from Lizzie's wine, the family members all talked over one another. Atamarie talked about Roberta's engagement and her adventures in Christchurch, Matariki about the successful art festival, and Patrick about a curious encounter with a sheep baron in the hills who was interested in Michael's flock. Matariki drew Doortje into the conversation, asking about the last book she had read—and Nandi provoked a minor scandal by eagerly joining in. She had also devoured *The Last Days of Pompeii* and now offered her opinions. Doortje looked stern but did not rebuke her, whereas Juliet reprimanded her sharply.

"Servants hold their tongues while their betters speak, Nandi. Those, you see, are the fundamental principles of a civilized household. Isn't that how it is in South Africa, Dorothy?"

Doortje opened her mouth but then closed it. In South Africa, she had thought Nandi too stupid to join in, and besides, she would never have learned to read. Nor would they have been discussing a novel, but at most the Bible, on which no differing opinions were tolerated.

"I'd be careful, Juliet," Matariki replied instead. "The book depicts quite nicely how masters are sometimes forced to rely on the kindness of servants. If Nydia hadn't led Glaucus and Ione to the port, they would have died in the volcano's eruption. Atamie, do tell Juliet a bit about volcanic activity in New Zealand."

The others laughed. Only Nandi stared at the ground. "I wouldn't let you die in a rain of ashes, Mr. Drury," she said quietly and very seriously to Patrick while Atamarie described the last eruption of Ruapehu. "Nor little May."

Patrick smiled at her. "I know, Nandi. And I certainly don't think it's right that the slave kills herself at the end of the book. Mr. Bulwer-Lytton should have found some way of making her happy."

***

"Should I help you unlace?" Kevin asked Doortje when he later entered the small room they were sharing. "You looked beautiful tonight, but you really don't need to wear a corset here. Mother doesn't, and Matariki and Atamie certainly don't."

Doortje allowed him to open her light-blue dress printed with flowers. It was an afternoon dress, but still too formal for a family dinner. Matariki had told her the same, but Doortje did not want Juliet to outshine her. That evening, Juliet had been wearing her dark-red dress. A clear signal to Kevin. To the others, just another appearance in a dress that was far too provocative. Doortje's dress was not that. It had a rather high neckline and emphasized her natural beauty with its friendly colors.

"You like how it looks?" Doortje asked uncertainly. "You like how I look?"

Kevin smiled. She had never asked that before. He dared to kiss her shoulder when the dress slid over it. Doortje flinched but did not pull away.

"I always like how you look, but in this dress especially. Although you'd look even better without any dress."

Kevin continued kissing her neck and shoulders. Before, she had always pulled away immediately. Though she was available to her husband at night if he desired, she awaited him in a modest nightgown under the sheets. Now, the light had not even been put out.

"Do you like that?" he asked her gently between kisses.

Doortje turned to face him shyly. "I don't know," she admitted. "But I've—in the Bible, it says—"

Kevin sighed.

"No, it's not what you think," Doortje said. "I've read the Song of Solomon, the Song of Songs."

Kevin grinned. "Well, I don't know it by heart, but if I recall, isn't there talk of two breasts like baby goats?"

He pulled her dress all the way off, loosened her corset, and let his lips wander from the neckline down to her breasts.

"Like twin deer," Doortje whispered, and felt her breathing quicken with his caresses. "And it's—it's in the Dutch Bible too."

"Why shouldn't it be? It is the most beautiful Bible, isn't it, my dear? At least that's what you're always saying. When we get back to Dunedin, I'll look for the passage and learn it by heart, I promise."

Doortje pressed her body against his. "No, you'd pronounce it all wrong anyway. Like 'Mejuffrouw van Stout.'"

Kevin picked her up and carried her to bed. "Mevrouw Drury. That's right, isn't it?"

Doortje nodded. "Just right," she said happily.

***

Juliet saw at first glance that something had changed. There was a new intimacy between Kevin and Doortje when they came to breakfast. They laughed together, their eyes shone—and Matariki, who likewise noticed, looked like the cat that got the cream. Juliet fumed.

"What's on the docket for today?" she asked the group with feigned cheer as she bit into her honeyed toast.

Juliet was again wildly overdressed. Doortje was wearing a loose dress from Parihaka, a present from Matariki.

"Well, we are going up to the village," Matariki replied. "I want to visit my friends, and Atamarie is apparently dying to learn more about kite making, even though I thought she knew everything. Still, she wants to check whether a particular *tohunga* has arrived."

"Mom," Atamarie moaned.

"And you wanted to show me the village," Doortje said. "The carvings on the houses and—"

Matariki nodded proudly. She did not mention how Doortje had previously lived for weeks on Elizabeth Station without paying her neighbors a single visit.

"You'll see, it's very different from the kraals in South Africa," Kevin said. "A completely different building style, and not really comparable to the huts in Polynesia, right, Riki?"

"I've never been to the islands where the Maori originally came from," Matariki said, "but I know it's much warmer there than here. So, people would have built airier huts, perhaps more like your people's, Nandi. Wouldn't you like to join us? I'm sure Juliet can look after her daughter herself for once. It wouldn't be a bad thing, Juliet. Otherwise, it'll be embarrassing later when May doesn't recognize you at parties."

Juliet looked daggers at her sister-in-law. But she also saw her chance. Kevin would surely accompany the women. And Patrick had work to do on the farm.

"Actually, I'll come too," she declared. Lizzie almost dropped her coffee cup in surprise. "If it doesn't bother all of you, of course. I've always been interested in carvings." She smiled sarcastically. "Statues of the Greek gods, for example, or *David*." She let her gaze wander over Kevin's body.

"That's statuary," Atamarie corrected her through a mouthful of food. "Sculptors chip away at marble. Maori generally carve wood. Or pounamu jade."

"But primary sex characteristics are also found on our *tiki*," Matariki noted drily. "So, Juliet will no doubt get her money's worth."

To her surprise, Nandi suppressed a chortle. Doortje and Lizzie did not know where to start with the innuendo. Matariki, however, wondered whether Nandi was taking a page from Violet and had begun to read dictionaries.

***

Lizzie remained at home with the children while Kevin accompanied the women up to the village. It was drizzling, and Matariki and Atamarie threw angry looks at Juliet, who made her way slowly in that ludicrous outfit and had her maid shield her from the rain with an umbrella, while Nandi and the rest of the group slowly froze in their wet wraps and shawls. Only Doortje did not seem to notice the cold. She radiated from the inside out.

Juliet shoved herself next to Kevin while the women chatted.

"We need to talk," she whispered.

"Yes, we do," he agreed. "Maybe we'll get a chance in the village. It'll be quick."

Juliet smiled.

After a while, the village came into view. It was enclosed with a low fence, surrounded by pens. The Ngai Tahu bred sheep, too, and theirs did not come much behind Michael's in quality.

"Construction on the South Island is less elaborate than on the North Island," Matariki began. "The region is colder and less fertile. That's why the tribes wander so often, so they can hunt and fish elsewhere. It's also less populated. Tribes encountered one another rarely, and there were hardly any military confrontations. But this tribe here is rich, due to its animal husbandry, so there's no shortage of food. At most, people go wandering for pleasure or to acquire knowledge, and then, not with the whole tribe. So, this *iwi* has become settled and has built some very beautiful buildings."

Only a few people were out in the rain, but news of the visit spread quickly. It did not take long for the women to find themselves surrounded by the villagers. Matariki, Atamarie, and Kevin exchanged *hongi* with half the village. The villagers marveled at Nandi. Many, particularly older people, had never seen a black person. They admired Nandi's skin and laughed at Juliet's corseted figure.

"Just what do you *pakeha* like about such skinny women?" asked the chieftain.

Kevin laughed. "Men don't set the fashion. The ladies decide it among themselves. But believe me, *ariki*, it's fun to open a laced-up present at night."

Atamarie had eyes for only a gentle-eyed, slender young man thronged by a horde of children.

"Come on, Rawiri, we have to finish our kites. Otherwise, Matariki will come, and we won't be able to send greetings to the spirits."

"You're also a *tohunga* for *manu*?" asked a little girl skeptically.

Rawiri put his finger to his mouth. "She's much more than that," he whispered, as if revealing a secret. "Atamarie can fly. But come along now. Let's keep working on the kites. Are you coming, Atamarie?"

Atamarie crossed to him, and placed her nose and forehead against his face as he bent down to her. Then she opened her lips.

Rawiri proved that he had also mastered kissing in the *pakeha* fashion.

Chapter 2

Juliet seized the first opportunity to pull Kevin into one of the empty lodges. The rain had stopped, and the villagers were pursuing their occupations outside. Most of the men set out to hunt and fish. Ample meat was needed for the imminent festivities. The village women had claimed Matariki, Doortje, and Nandi. Haikina and the others wanted to hear about Parihaka—and the elders bombarded Nandi with questions about her homeland.

Kevin looked around to see if the coast was clear before he followed Juliet into the richly decorated building.

"Oh, how good it is to finally be alone," she sighed. "Being cooped up on that farm makes me sick. We should also give up the apartment in Dunedin. A proper town house, Kevin, with servants' quarters in the basement and guest rooms . . ."

Juliet went toward him and moved to put her arms around his neck. Kevin pushed her away.

"Juliet, please. I don't want to anymore."

Juliet scoffed. "You're repeating yourself."

Kevin took a deep breath. "I'm sorry, Juliet, but I'm very serious this time. I'm never again going to—"

"Don't worry. You don't have to do a thing."

Juliet lowered herself in front of him, thrust her hands under his shirt, and undid his pants.

"Juliet!" Kevin tried to pull away and almost knocked over a statue of a god as he did. But she had already bared his sex and was beginning to rub herself on him. "Juliet, really. It's over. You—"

"It's over when I say it is."

Kevin was in danger of losing himself again, but then pulled himself together and grabbed her by the shoulders to push her away. Neither he nor Juliet heard the door.

"Kevin." Doortje and Matariki stood in the doorway of the meetinghouse. Matariki turned away. Doortje, however, stared openly.

"Kevin, what—what are you doing?"

Juliet laughed as she slowly stood up. "What does it look like, little Dorothy?"

Doortje struggled for words. Her eyes were wide, and she felt lamed, empty, and cold. Juliet straightened her dress and brushed back her hair while Kevin desperately tried to close his pants as discreetly as possible.

"You really ought to know how it goes," Juliet purred, "as a married woman. And before that, you weren't exactly a blank slate. Or have you forgotten Colin? Dear Colin Coltrane. Before you, he made sweet Chloe a happy woman, before that, the charming Matariki. Did you never tell her about that, Matariki? About the father of your daughter?"

Doortje began to tremble. "That's not true. With him, I never—no one here knows about—about that. I—"

Juliet had hit the mark and now turned the knife.

"And good Kathleen, the pastor's wife? Does she not know you've made her a grandmother? But she must, Dorothy. Your son is her spitting image."

The meetinghouse began to spin before Doortje's eyes. She saw Colin Coltrane's face again before her, his broken, scarred face bent over her in mad, evil lust. It was nothing like Kathleen's or Atamarie's. But their hair, that metallic blond like Abraham's—Doortje had noticed that. And now Juliet was saying that everybody knew. Everybody knew her shame. What was worse, Juliet clearly assumed she had given herself freely to that monster.

Doortje let out a strangled cry. She gave Kevin a look of horror. Then she spun around and fled.

Kevin looked into Juliet's smug face. In a fit of desperate rage, he slapped her across it.

"Kevin," Matariki shouted, and rushed to restrain him. "Leave her. It's too late for that. You need to catch Doortje. You—we—need to explain everything to her. Heavens, how could you be so stupid?"

The rain had set in again, and the village women had returned to their houses or gone into the cooking lodges. It was time to prepare lunch. The men were not yet back from the hunt. And Doortje was nowhere to be seen.

Kevin and Matariki ran through the whole village to look for traces and witnesses, but they found neither. Atamarie and Nandi were squatting in a cooking lodge where the women were listening to Nandi describe dishes from her homeland.

Atamarie did not understand Matariki's panic. "She can't have gone far," she said. "She's probably bawling it out somewhere. I'm sure she'll come back. God, Kevin should be so ashamed."

Matariki left her clueless daughter and ran back to Kevin. But he had made no further progress. The ground in the village was packed firm, and so many people walked around the meetinghouse that Doortje's tracks could not be discerned. At least, not by Kevin, who was no great tracker—and moreover, completely hysterical.

"Riki, if she hurts herself—" Tears welled in his eyes.

Matariki put an arm around him. "Now, stay calm. Nothing will have happened so quickly. Do you think she's capable? As religious as she is?"

Kevin saw Johanna's pale face before him, her long, wet hair, after they had pulled her from the river. The other van Stout sister had been just as religious but not able to live with her shame. Doortje had managed once, but would she succeed a second time?

He nodded.

Matariki looked around. She herself would have known exactly where to find a lake or a cliff. Doortje, by contrast, must have run blindly into the woods.

"We need good trackers," she said. "Hemi and Rewi and Tamati."

The hunters would surely be returning soon. During the rain, both birds and rabbits hid themselves. Until then, there was little to be done.

Matariki went back into the meetinghouse to confront Juliet. It would not do any good, but she needed to vent her anger and helplessness.

Juliet, however, had also disappeared.

***

It took an hour for the hunters to return, but then they found Doortje's trail quickly. The young woman had gone straight through the woods in the direction of the mountains. She must have avoided the trails. She had run at first, but then the underbrush and the incline slowed her down. Kevin climbed doggedly behind the hunters. He knew precisely where this ascent ended. By chance, Doortje had run up a mountain that, on the other side, abruptly dropped down to a valley. The view was breathtaking, and the Maori considered the place *tapu*—sacred. They went there to meditate and to unite their souls with the landscape.

Kevin had been to this overlook only once, together with Patrick as a boy. The two of them had read about the spectacular climbing of mighty mountains and had been planning to lower themselves down the precipice on a rope to prepare for Everest. Hainga, the area's wisewoman, had stopped the boys before they fell to their deaths. They were immediately in double trouble—with Michael and Lizzie for their stupidity and with their Maori friends for violating the sacred cliff.

"Her trail ends here," Hemi declared when, after they had done a roughly one-hour climb, the forest cleared, revealing a view of the gorge.

Despite the rain, the vista was impressive. Far below them meandered a stream, and beyond that, a valley stretched out toward forested hills. On the horizon, they could just make out the snow-covered southern mountains.

"She could have run off to the left or right," another hunter said, "but I can't find any further trace of her." The ground was rocky, but worn smooth by countless *tohunga* and their adepts who had come here. "Perhaps she simply went back along the trail."

Doortje had fought her way through the forest, but there was also a well-trod path back to the village. She would have to have seen it.

"That seems likely in this weather. She must be completely soaked by now."

The man followed the path for some distance, looking in vain for further tracks. Hemi and Kevin peered down the cliff.

"What was she wearing?" Hemi suddenly asked. His voice sounded strained.

"A dress woven in Matariki's tribal colors." Kevin could still picture his wife and the way she had beamed at him at breakfast. They had finally managed to find their way to each other. Everything had finally been good. And now this. And it was all his fault. "And a wool shawl over that. Lizzie's wool shawl, the old blue one."

She had looked so beautiful as she had wrapped herself almost from head to toe in the long shawl.

"In the Orient, women hide their hair from everyone but their chosen husband," he had said. "It's an honor to me that you now uncover your head for me even in public."

Now, he thought guiltily of her response.

"You didn't like my bonnet before."

That evening, he had wanted to tell her how much he had liked her bonnet. How it had excited him when she hid her hair beneath it, the way it—

"The shawl is there below," Hemi said.

Kevin felt the words like a knife wound.

"Just the shawl?"

"I can't tell. But look for yourself. There, where the rock juts out. Do you see? She could—"

Kevin began to tremble. She could be lying beneath the shawl. Or her body could be hidden by the rock.

"Is it possible to climb down here?" he asked quietly.

"It would be *tapu*," Hemi said hesitantly, "but we could do it in this case, of course. Only, we'd need rope, hooks. It wouldn't do any good if we also fell to our deaths, Kevin." Hemi laid his hand on his friend's arm.

Kevin wanted to contradict him. He wanted to say that Doortje was worth any risk in the world, that he would rather die than—but he pulled himself together. If she had jumped or fallen from here, she could no longer be alive. Climbing down would only serve to provide certainty and to recover her corpse.

"Then," Kevin said hoarsely, "let's fetch ropes. And hooks and whatever else we need." He was thinking of a stretcher.

Hemi nodded. "The others can go. I'll stay here with you."

Kevin slowly sat down on the promontory as the men went. Hemi sat down beside him.

"It's my fault," Kevin whispered.

Hemi was silent. Nothing could change Kevin's mind or comfort him now. He could only stay with him and do what his ancestors had done there since time immemorial—become one with the world and the sky, the mountain and the valley, the past and the future.

Perhaps Kevin's wife had also succeeded in that, although her *maunga* must have lain far away, in that strange land with its heat, its giant animals, and its combative people. Hemi tried to sense her soul. Perhaps he would even succeed in drawing Kevin into his connection with the land and the world and the gods behind the sky.

***

Hours passed, and Kevin could not make peace with their forced inaction. He stood up repeatedly and looked down at the blue shawl. The weather cleared, and a sharp wind picked up, which dried the material and inflated it. Could Doortje still be alive? Was she moving beneath the shawl? Again and again, he asked himself where the rescue expedition could be.

There was no cordage long enough in the Maori village. However, the news of Doortje's disappearance had made it to Elizabeth Station. Michael and Patrick gathered together what they could find in the barns and stables. Michael also offered horses, which would make the climb much quicker, of course—and both Hainga and the *ariki* were generous enough not to mention the unavoidable damage to their sacred place. Haikina encouraged them to consider going around the cliff, and Patrick did indeed know a way into the valley.

"It would take at least a day, though," he said. "Though I wouldn't reject it out of hand. As sad as it is, if she really did fall down there, then no one can help her anymore. We have all the time in the world."

"And the animals?" Nandi had been crying despairingly since she'd heard. "By then, the wild animals will eat her. They'll drag her away. Please, please, Mr. Drury."

Patrick wanted to reply that there were no wild animals there big enough to drag off a human corpse. But the expression on Nandi's face touched him.

Patrick did not know what had happened at the meetinghouse—he had only heard about a fight and about Doortje and Juliet's disappearance. He could clear up Juliet's location, at least. She had returned to Elizabeth Station and was now barricading herself in their room. Patrick felt vaguely guilty, but he could not worry about her now, and he did not want to either. In the past weeks, Juliet had responded to all of his attempts at intimacy with a fit of rage. Who knew what he would have to listen to this time, what Doortje—or Kevin or Matariki or whoever—had done to vex her.

"I promise we'll do everything we can for her, Nandi," he assured her. "But you should head back to the farm and check on Juliet." Something flashed in Nandi's eyes. A brand-new spark of anger or defiance. Her face remained unchanged, but Patrick understood. "I know, Nandi. She's difficult." He sighed. "But she, some things aren't easy for her either. With some patience—"

Nandi wanted to scream. "She is—she has . . ." But then she held her tongue. He should not hear it from her.

At this point, half the village could guess what had played out in the meetinghouse. Matariki had not been especially discreet. She had told Haikina and Hainga what she had seen to emphasize the urgency of the rescue and to justify the breaking of the *tapu*. No one had needed to tell Nandi. She knew Juliet.

"I will go, Mr. Drury," Nandi said. "But you bring Mrs. Doortje Drury home."

***

Before the men could get all the climbing material set up, twilight filled the sky. Michael and Hemi gently made it clear to Kevin that the rescue would have to be put off until the next day.

"We won't be able to get down at night, and you wouldn't see anything down there anyway. What's more, there are clouds coming in again. We won't even have moon- or starlight. But we'll all stay up here, and tomorrow, we'll climb down at first light."

***

"It might suffice to lower a big mirror down there," Atamarie observed. She had made her way up to the cliff with Rawiri and made camp with him a short distance from the others. "Then we could see under the rock. Maybe lower a hook to move the shawl in case she's underneath. Climbing down from here seems too dangerous."

Rawiri smiled. "Would you not be afraid to fly down?"

"Less than climbing. But we'd need a glider. And by the time we'd built one, the men would have climbed down or ridden around. I, for one, don't think she's there—at least not under the shawl. Just take a look at the angle. Nothing heavier than a shawl blown by the wind could have that angle of descent. Has no one thought of throwing a rock over to test it?"

Rawiri brushed the hair out of her face. She was lying in his arms for the first time, and despite the tragedy, he felt unendingly happy.

"Atamie, leave it to the gods," he said softly. "No one here wants to hear about mirrors or angles of descent. Kevin most certainly doesn't. He has to see with his own eyes. It has to become real to him. Only then can he get on with his life. Which will be hard enough."

Atamarie snuggled against him. "But if I asked, you'd build a kite for me so I could fly down there? I love you, Rawiri."

Rawiri kissed her. "Of course I'd do that for you," he whispered, "but first, let's go to Christchurch. I'm grateful to the gods that the Canterbury Plains are rather flat."

Chapter 3

Lizzie passed a hellish night. She would gladly have traded the warmth of her house for a place beside her husband and sons. Lizzie had lived among the Ngai Tahu and been inducted into many of their mysteries. She knew the cliff well, and the thought of climbing down it sent a shudder up her spine. She not only worried about Doortje, but also for Michael, Kevin, and Patrick. She would have ridden up there to keep them from doing anything stupid, but she was still watching the children. She had taken May to bed with her that night. Juliet never cared for the little girl, and Nandi was not only shaken to her core by the loss of Doortje but also had her hands full with Juliet's vile mood. After a while, Lizzie could take no more of it and intervened.

"Nandi is off-duty now, Juliet. Every workday has its end. Lie down and go to bed, and tomorrow I'll hear what caused all this mess. I know you well enough to be certain you're not completely innocent in this. So, think it over and leave Nandi in peace."

Juliet did keep quiet after that, but Nandi cried until late at night, which confused Lizzie. It must be a strange relationship these Boers had to the natives. Doortje had not seen Nandi's humanity, yet she had insisted on not leaving her alone in South Africa because she felt responsible. And Nandi had run from Doortje, but now she mourned her like family.

When it was finally quiet in the house, Lizzie drank a glass of wine to help her sleep. She almost felt guilty about not mourning, but she did not really believe that Doortje could be dead. At first, the woman's stubbornness and bigotry had driven Lizzie into a burning rage—but even then, she had impressed her in a certain way. Lizzie did not like to admit it, but she sometimes thought Doortje resembled her a little. Lizzie would not have made it to where she was if she had not been fiercely determined and true to herself. She had experienced a hard and tumultuous life. Lizzie knew what it meant to go hungry and to be demeaned. Yet she had never thought of giving up, and she could not imagine that of Doortje either.

Lizzie's imagining of the events in the meetinghouse came quite close to reality. Doortje was used to Juliet's teasing and meanness. To drive her so far that Kevin was afraid of suicide, something more must have happened than an argument.

Lizzie brooded half the night until she fell into an uneasy sleep. She awoke again at dawn. The men would now surely be making themselves ready for the descent, and Lizzie thanked God that it was not raining. She stayed in bed awhile, reflecting. Then, she got up. She could no longer stand it in the house. Lizzie threw on a housedress and a shawl and went up to the waterfall. Her *maunga*. Even though she was a devout Anglican on the outside and treasured Reverend Burton, she met her gods here.

The curled-up form that had sought protection from the night's cold in the shadow of a rock, however, had nothing divine about it. In the still-wan light of the new day, Lizzie recognized Doortje's blonde hair. The young woman was cowering, leaning against the rock, her face pressed against her knee, and her arms wrapped around her. Her thin dress was soaked, dirty, and torn. No wonder—she must have wandered through the woods for hours.

"Doortje." Lizzie ran to her daughter-in-law. "My God, child, why didn't you come into the house? Kevin thinks you're dead. The men are looking for you below the cliff. You were there, weren't you? Heavens, Doortje, you're frozen solid."

At once concerned, angry, and relieved, Lizzie wrapped her own shawl around her. Doortje squinted into the sunlight, and her bereft gaze touched Lizzie.

"I lost your shawl," she murmured. "At the cliff. I wanted—I'm sorry."

Not saying any more, she curled up again. Lizzie could only think of a wounded animal. She squatted beside her daughter-in-law and took her gently in her arms.

"What happened, Doortje? What exactly happened?"

At first, Doortje seemed to want to give in to the embrace, but then she jerked back.

"Colin Coltrane," she blurted out. "You knew it too?"

Lizzie saw despair in Doortje's eyes and the helpless wish to be able to trust her mother-in-law, at least.

"Knew what, dear? What am I supposed to have known?" The rock on which they were sitting was still damp and cold. It was not comfortable there. "It'd be better if we went inside to talk."

Doortje shook her head. "Not while she's there. I never want to see her again. She knew, but she—it was all completely different."

"Juliet. You don't want to go into the house while Juliet's there? I can well understand that. But what did she know, Doortje? And who's Colin Coltrane to you?"

"So, you do know him?" Doortje whispered. "Then it's true what she said. About Matariki."

"I don't know what secret knowledge we're talking about here, but yes, I knew Colin Coltrane. He seduced Matariki and then Chloe after her, although Matariki got lucky. He left her a beautiful daughter, but he almost destroyed Chloe's life. He's a cheater and a bastard, Doortje—no matter what somebody might have said to you about him. Although, I shouldn't really presume to pass judgment on him. I—" She stopped, but then something in her told her that she owed this young woman a sign of confidence. She was prepared to share the darkest secret of her life with her. "I destroyed his life," she said, "by killing his father. No one else knows that, Doortje, just Michael, Reverend Burton, and me. It was self-defense. I don't have anything to blame myself for. But it's my fault that Colin grew up without a father. Even though Kathleen did everything she could for him. She was a good mother to all of her children. She—"

"It's true that Kathleen . . . ?"

Doortje's voice was flat. She had liked Kathleen, trusted her, but that woman, too, had betrayed her. Kathleen, whom she had taken for a friend, was the mother of her tormentor. And she also had to know about Abraham's parentage.

Lizzie put her arm around her shivering daughter-in-law. Now, the sun had risen, and Lizzie hoped that it would soon grow a bit warmer. Otherwise,

Doortje would catch her death in her wet clothes. But for now, there was nothing she could do about it. Lizzie stroked Doortje's shoulder gently and began to tell her the story. Of Kathleen and Michael's youthful love, of their son together, Sean, and their separation. She told of Kathleen's desperate attempt to give her son an honorable name by marrying the horse trader Ian Coltrane, and how she'd had two more children by him, Colin and Heather.

"But Colin took after his father, and when Kathleen finally fled from Ian, Colin didn't want to go with her. He remained with Ian and became a scoundrel just like him. And when I killed Ian—"

"You really killed his father?" Doortje asked in disbelief.

Lizzie nodded. "In self-defense," she repeated. "He wanted—" She had to force herself to keep talking. Ian Coltrane had intended to rape and murder her. It had been because of the gold source beneath the waterfall, over which Elizabeth Station now stood watch. "He wanted to kill me," she said. "Out of cruelty and avarice. I beat him to death with a Maori war club."

Doortje shivered, but no longer from the cold. "Colin," she whispered, "he put his hands on me. And my sister. My sister is dead. And I, I survived, but I was pregnant. And Abe, Abe isn't Kevin's child, and they think, they think I was unfaithful to Kevin." She swallowed.

Lizzie pulled Doortje closer to her and rocked her like a child. "Oh God, I should have noticed. Abe has that strange hair color—and he does resemble Atamarie. I must have been blind. But I swear, Doortje, I didn't know anything."

"I didn't either," Doortje cried. "I would never have come here if I'd known everyone would see this shame."

Lizzie shook her head. "Well, I didn't notice until now, and Michael hasn't either. I suppose people only recognize it if they knew Colin or Atamarie as a baby. Michael and I first saw her when she was a little girl. Riki was living in Wellington back then. So, surely not 'everyone' knows. In fact, I'll bet it's just Kathleen and Matariki—perhaps Claire Dunloe too. How Juliet figured it out, I can't imagine. Maybe she's also guessing more than she knows." Lizzie considered. Then her face hardened. "Or do you think Kevin—"

"No. No, he can't be that stupid. He'd be putting himself at her mercy."

Lizzie laughed. "Because of the paternity? Well, you know—"

Doortje shook her head more violently. "No, because of the—the murder. I took my revenge, Lizzie." Doortje breathed in sharply. "I killed Colin Coltrane. With a knife."

Lizzie listened to the story, stunned. Doortje told her about Colin's death, about Kevin's involvement, about Roberta's plan to make the corpse disappear.

"And Kevin offered to marry me. I needed a father for my baby."

"Kevin must love you very much," Lizzie said simply when her daughter-in-law had finished. "And no, I don't think he told Juliet any of that. He—"

"Why was he talking with Juliet at all? If he loves me, why then is he cheating on me with her?"

Lizzie sighed. Sometimes Doortje really did remind her of a clueless girl in the Land of Oz.

"Doortje, my Michael is just like your Kevin; they're good people at heart. Captivating men, charming, vivacious. But Michael always needed a woman to watch after him. Kathleen was too young to do so back in Ireland. And it took me half my life to understand that. But without me, Michael would be like a leaf in the wind, and it's similar with Kevin. In a certain way, Juliet understood that—she has mastery over him, but she's not good for him. Luckily, he knows that, even if he let himself be seduced again. He's run away from her before."

Lizzie took Doortje's cold, trembling hand between hers. She knew she was further destroying Doortje's world by telling her about May, but only ruthless honesty would do here. Otherwise, Kevin's child would just be Juliet's next weapon against Doortje. To Lizzie's surprise, Doortje received this revelation almost with amusement.

"Kevin's not Abe's father, and Patrick isn't May's. And I always thought those strange society novels were too far-fetched. But you are Kevin's mother, right?"

Lizzie smiled. "I swear," she said. "And as far as secrets go, Kathleen can keep quiet, and so can Matariki. And I bet both spoke to Kevin as soon as they noted the resemblance between Abe and Atamarie. Kevin won't have told them about Colin's death, but no doubt he'll have told them how Abe was conceived. You'll have to live with the fact that a few of your friends know about it; accept that there's no cause for shame. And no one, Doortje, will think you capable of cheating on your husband."

Doortje wiped her eyes. "I think now I can live with just about anything," she said, "except Juliet. You think I should forgive Kevin, but that can only happen when she, when she—well, how, how can I get rid of her?"

Lizzie smiled. "We won't need war clubs or kitchen knives. There are much easier ways to rid oneself of people like Juliet. We can take advantage of the early hour. I'm going to teach you how to pan for gold, Doortje Drury. And by doing so, I'm taking you definitively and irrevocably into our family. Because, this secret, only the real Drurys and Ngai Tahu know."

***

Juliet did not get up until Lizzie and Doortje came back into the house. Doortje was hesitant to face Juliet, but Lizzie insisted.

"We're going to do this together, Doortje. Maybe I should have done it a long time ago, but I didn't want to cause Patrick this hurt. We're about to break his heart. There's no other way. But don't make me do it alone."

Doortje looked at her, and in her eyes she saw again the toughness of her upbringing. "Hearts don't break that easily," she said gruffly, and Lizzie sighed but did not respond.

The two women found Juliet at the breakfast table. Nandi was puttering about the stove, making pancakes and looking devastated. But then she saw Doortje. She let out a cry and dropped the pan. Hot grease splashed across the room and onto Juliet's dressing gown.

"*Baas*! Mevrouw Drury!"

Nandi stammered the words in Afrikaans and fell crying to the ground. Doortje helped her up and embraced her like a sister.

"Didn't Lizzie forbid you saying *baas*?" she murmured, embarrassed.

Lizzie smiled. Then she turned to Juliet, who had begun cursing Nandi for ruining her dressing gown. Lizzie raised her hand curtly. Her gesture was as commanding as her expression.

"You will not speak to her that way, Juliet," she said calmly. "In fact, we've had enough, Doortje and I and Nandi. And Kevin—I think I'm speaking for him as well. Perhaps Patrick won't admit it right away, but I think nothing better could happen to him than for you to get lost. So, let's keep this short. How much?"

Doortje looked on, stunned, and Juliet sized up her mother-in-law with an irritated smile.

"Why should I go? I'm Patrick's wife, have you two forgotten that already? And May's mother. I have every right in the world to be here."

Lizzie nodded. "How much?"

Juliet brushed her hair back. "How much what?" she asked sanctimoniously.

"Money, Juliet," Lizzie replied. "You do know something about that. Granted, until now, you've been paid to come instead of to go. But now we're doing things differently. So, how much?"

"You think I can be bought, Lizzie?" Juliet leaned back.

Lizzie groaned. "We did want to make this short. I really have other things to do. But fine, let's speak in complete sentences. How much money do you want to disappear today?"

"Whither?" asked Juliet.

Lizzie rubbed her forehead. "To America. Or Europe. The Fiji Islands. But away from New Zealand. Immediately."

Juliet snorted. "I don't think it'll be possible to go that quickly. Or do you just mean to buy me a ship too?"

"If I have to. But I'm warning you: it wouldn't be seaworthy. So, how much?"

Juliet crossed her arms and contemplated her approach to the negotiations. She had to set the price very high.

Finally, she smiled. "Ten thousand pounds."

Lizzie's countenance did not change. "All right, then. Go pack. You should be out of the house by midday. You can take the chaise with the covering so you don't get wet if it rains again."

Juliet's jaw dropped. "You mean to—you're going to pay ten thousand pounds? But how?"

"Drive the chaise to Dunedin and lodge the horse in the rental stables. After that, take the train to Christchurch and get a room at the White Hart. Within three days, tomorrow if at all possible, an attorney will call on you. You'll sign your consent to divorce Patrick as well as give up all rights to your daughter."

"There was no talk of May until now," Juliet objected. "If I'm giving up my rights to her, then I want—five thousand pounds more."

There was only contempt left in Lizzie's face. "Interesting to hear what she's worth to you. So, you will give up expressly in writing all rights to your daughter. In exchange, the attorney will hand you fifteen thousand pounds in cash. And then you'll be gone on the next ship."

Juliet smiled. "And if I don't go?"

Lizzie's face became hard. "There are men in this country," she said, "who would get rid of you for far less than fifteen thousand pounds. Don't make it come to that." She turned away. "Come, Doortje, we'll go up to the Maori village and then to the cliff. Nandi can help Juliet pack. We'll take the little ones with us. Maybe we can still stop the men from this madness about climbing down. Even though, of course, I'd love to get my shawl back. It's a nice shawl, and one shouldn't waste money." She smiled conspiratorially at Doortje.

Doortje thought of the gold she and Lizzie had panned for that morning. Undoubtedly, one could buy a great many shawls with it.

Or freedom from Juliet Drury.

Chapter 4

The women in the village fell all over themselves with joy and surprise when Lizzie appeared with the children and Doortje. Matariki hugged her, laughing and crying.

"Kevin told me everything, Doortje. Do you remember how I went off with him the first time I saw Abraham? I knew at once. Kathleen, too, saw it at first glance, but she only knows about the paternity, not Colin's death. She doesn't need to either. And you have to believe me: I tried to make Kevin tell you. I almost did it myself—anything would have been better than what just happened. But he didn't want to hurt you, Doortje, and he knew that he was doing it anyway. That damned Juliet—"

"Is history," Lizzie said calmly. "You really should have told me, Riki. I didn't know anything. But now, let's all go up to the cliff and see if we can stop the men."

Matariki looked uneasy. "They planned to climb down at first light." She checked the position of the sun with a glance. "In fact, they should be back soon. Oh, look, there's Haraki."

Haraki, a wiry, ten-year-old boy, came bolting into the village square. "News," he shouted, "I have news from the men. Kevin's *wahine* did not fall from the cliff. But Kevin—"

Doortje did not understand a word of the boy's speech, delivered in rapid Maori, but she couldn't mistake Matariki's and Lizzie's faces.

"What's going on? What happened?"

Haikina stepped in to translate. "Kevin fell. He was in a great hurry to get down and seems to have misjudged the end of the descent. I don't know how seriously injured he is, but he won't be coming back up the cliff by his own strength. They'll have to rescue him somehow. We should make our way there with Hainga."

Hainga, the wisewoman, was also the tribe's healer.

"He's not going to die, is he?" whispered Doortje. "He can't, he can't now."

Matariki quickly asked Haraki more questions, which he answered at length. Doortje was desperate for a translation, but Matariki shook her head.

"The boy doesn't know much more," she explained quickly. "Just that Kevin was still moving—they could see that from above—and that he still seemed able to speak. Hemi is down there with him. The others are now attempting a rescue using a stretcher they luckily took with them."

"He might fall again when they try to rescue him with the stretcher," Doortje whispered.

"He won't," Matariki assured her sister-in-law. "Atamarie and Rawiri are up there, and they're engineers. Atamarie will calculate every detail before she lets down a rope. Don't you worry, Doortje. If he's alive, they'll bring him up."

"He can't be dead. Not him too. And it would be my fault—"

"I heard the same thing from Kevin yesterday," Matariki responded, "and you're not dead. So, don't lose your courage just yet. Let's go and see what really happened."

***

The women hurried through the forest, but they did not need to go all the way to the cliff. Halfway there, the men were already coming toward them.

A chill ran through Doortje when she heard the voices and footfalls. That had gone faster than expected—there couldn't have been enough time to rescue someone seriously wounded using an improvised stretcher. So, either the injury was not so bad, or—one didn't need to be that careful while hauling a corpse up a cliff.

Lizzie and Matariki were nursing the same thoughts, but they calmed down when they were close enough to overhear scraps of conversation. Hemi and a few others were heatedly discussing where Doortje might be. They would hardly have been doing that if there had been another death. Doortje, however, only saw the stretcher. Something lay on it, covered in Lizzie's shawl.

"Kevin!" Doortje rushed to the stretcher. "Kevin."

She flung the shawl aside—and stared at the huge pile of cordage the men hadn't taken the time to wind up. Uncomprehending, she looked around, but she did not see Kevin among the men.

"Doortje! Oh my God, Doortje!"

Kevin's voice came from above—and Doortje only then noticed the two horses Michael was leading back from the cliff. Kevin was sitting in the saddle of one, looking rather battered. His face was covered in scratches. He carried one arm in a sling. Doortje ran to the horse and clutched Kevin's leg.

"You're alive, Kevin, you're—"

"I wasn't in any danger," Kevin said, and the men around him broke into laughter.

"He fell about thirty feet into a thornbush and broke or sprained the leg you're currently hanging on," Atamarie explained. "Otherwise he'd be screaming, you see, instead of making such stupid comments. These hedges really soften a blow."

But Kevin and Doortje weren't listening. Only with some effort could Michael prevent Kevin from dismounting to embrace Doortje. He bent over to her as much as possible, touching her hair and face in disbelief.

"I was so afraid for you," he whispered, "when we saw the shawl down below. And it would have been my fault."

"I shouldn't have run away," Doortje murmured. "And you wouldn't have climbed down. Now, it was nearly my fault that—"

"Can you two discuss this later?" asked Matariki. "Perhaps in the village where it's dry?" It was just beginning to rain again.

Lizzie gave Doortje her shawl. "Here, you have it again, but next time, lose it somewhere that's easier to get to. Michael, we'll take Kevin straight home."

Kevin looked doubtfully from her to Doortje.

"Mother, maybe it would be better if we drove straight back to Dunedin. Or stayed with the Ngai Tahu until Hainga's checked my leg. But I wouldn't want Doortje and Juliet—"

Patrick stepped forward and cleared his throat. "So, what exactly happened between you and my wife?"

Doortje sought Kevin's gaze. He looked at her pleadingly, and Doortje struggled with herself. Patrick, too, had been deceived. Did he not deserve to know? But then he might hate Kevin his whole life.

"Nothing," said Doortje. "Nothing. We, we just had a fight. She was horribly mean to me."

Patrick nodded seriously. "I'll see to it that doesn't happen again, Doortje. Believe me, I'm really going to do something. It can't go on like this. She can't—"

Doortje wanted to say something, but Lizzie shook her head almost imperceptibly. Patrick would learn soon enough that Juliet was gone.

***

It was evening when the family returned to Elizabeth Station. The women in the village had cooked for the members of the rescue expedition after their extensive cleansing rituals. After all, a *tapu* had been broken. The priests and priestesses of the tribe had to ask the gods for forgiveness and pacify them. Hainga was occupied with that for hours, leaving the care of Kevin's injuries to Lizzie and Doortje, who proved astoundingly skillful.

"There aren't any doctors among us," she explained. "We women do everything ourselves—and it's not true what the English say, that all our patients die." She gave Kevin a stern look. He returned it lovingly.

"You are quite remarkable," he said gently.

The sumptuous meal transitioned into a festival. Musicians played, whiskey and beer were passed, and every single expedition participant described his experience at the cliff. The tribe sat up late into the night, awaiting Matariki, but the stars did not yet appear.

***

Lizzie was exhausted when they finally got home. She and Doortje had taken turns carrying Abe all day. Kevin rode, but he was already doing so well that he could hold little May in the saddle in front of him. After the long day, even the sociable toddler was fussy. On the ride home, she finally fell asleep. Kevin carefully handed her down to Patrick when they arrived at Elizabeth Station.

"I'll put her straight to bed. Although Nandi's sure to be asleep."

While Michael helped Kevin from the horse—since his foot had been bound, he could walk on crutches—Lizzie nervously followed her younger son into the house. He knocked cautiously on Nandi's door.

"That's strange," he said when she didn't answer. "She normally sleeps so lightly."

Lizzie calmly opened the door to the room. She was surprised to find it empty except for Matariki's and Atamarie's things.

"I think she's gone, Patrick. I'm so sorry."

Patrick looked at her in horror. "She's gone? She ran away? Nandi is—? Juliet." Patrick handed his daughter to Lizzie and rushed to the other bedroom. "Juliet, you beast, what have you done? What did you do to her?"

Michael was just entering with Kevin, Doortje, and little Abe. In the village, Lizzie had told him about Juliet's coerced departure. In broad outlines, anyway. She did not want to mention the money right away. Michael had not broached it either but had immediately thought of Nandi.

"But what about Nandi?" he had asked. "Is she taking her?"

Lizzie had furrowed her brow. "No, why should she? Nandi helped her pack. She wouldn't want to go with that woman."

Michael had rolled his eyes in his characteristic manner. "Lizzie, Nandi's still not used to being asked if she wants to go somewhere. Doortje dragged her here from South Africa. Then Patrick wooed her away. But Juliet's kept her in holy terror ever since. To her, she's not much more than a slave."

Lizzie felt like crying. It had been a terrible mistake to leave Nandi with Juliet. But heavens, she could not think of everything. And now Nandi had disappeared with her mistress, and Patrick . . .

"Juliet is gone too," he declared. "She's—what's gotten into her?"

Lizzie breathed deeply. "I sent her away, Patrick," she said softly. "I'm sorry, but she could not stay here. She knew that herself. She—"

Patrick did not even seem to be listening. He had left Juliet's room again and returned to Nandi's. He tore open the wardrobe doors helplessly.

"She wouldn't just leave me. And what about May? She, she loved her. Even if not, I thought that maybe—I thought we'd have time."

Lizzie shook her head. She did not know how often she would have to repeat it. "Juliet didn't love you," she said patiently, "and she never much noticed May. She—"

Patrick glared at her. "Who's talking about Juliet?" he asked icily. "Don't bother, Mother. I've known all of that for a long time. But Nandi, I never thought that she would leave May alone."

"Just May?" Michael asked. His face broke into a wide grin.

"Don't you start now," Lizzie scolded him. "This is more complicated than I thought. But maybe it's better. We have to go to Dunedin tomorrow, Michael, to speak with Sean. I can't push this through with a lawyer we don't know. But it looks as if, aside from a divorce contract and a child, we're also going to have to buy a slave."

***

"Come on now."

Night was falling again over Elizabeth Station, and if the Drurys wanted to wait with their Maori friends for the appearance of the Pleiades, it was time to set out. Atamarie and Matariki had already put on their festive clothing, and Doortje was again wearing one of the Parihaka dresses. She simply radiated happiness, and Kevin did likewise, even though he still looked rather battered after his adventure the day before. Lizzie and Michael were not yet back from Dunedin, but they would surely join the festival as soon as they made it home. Patrick had barricaded himself in his bedroom with May. Matariki and her daughter had been trying to talk him out of there for half an hour.

"Moping about isn't going to help anything," Matariki insisted.

"And May definitely wants to see the kites," Atamarie added.

She herself was in the best of spirits—in fact, she had only come back to the farm to change. She had been spending blissful nights with Rawiri in his tent, though she'd rejected his proposal that they use the festival to sleep together in the communal lodge and thus seal their marriage.

"I'm too much of a *pakeha* for that," she'd told him. "I picture a wedding in a church, in a dress from the Gold Mine Boutique."

She laughed when Rawiri gave her a blank look.

"After the wedding, you two could sleep a night in the communal lodge," Matariki had suggested, "to pay homage to tradition. Perhaps in Parihaka."

Atamarie nodded. "Sleeping would work. But I don't need any witnesses to the rest. And for the moment, sleeping would be more like wasted time."

She had winked at Rawiri and then immediately disappeared with him back to the tent. The two of them seemed perfectly happy—their kites would only be taking the gods messages of gratitude into the sky.

Patrick, however, now shook his head at all his sister's and niece's urgings.

"I'm not in a celebratory mood, Atamie. At least not in company. But you're right that staying in here won't do any good. May and I are going to wait for the stars at the waterfall. Alone." To make it clear that the conversation was over, he got up, picked up May, and went to the door. "And if I do decide to send the gods a message, I don't think they'll want to hear what I have to say."

She and Matariki followed him outside.

"Should I lend you a *manu* with a direct line to the celestial complaints office?" Atamarie offered. "I do have one here, a birdman. It's richly decorated, a very fine messenger. Maybe it'll touch some goddess's heart, and she'll bring Juliet back to you."

Patrick spun on her angrily. "Who's talking about Juliet? You, none of you know anything!"

The women ran after him down the trail. This path led to the pond, not to the waterfall, but Patrick did not seem to care.

"This is about Nandi, right?" asked Matariki. "I wondered the whole time if there wasn't something special there. But I wouldn't give up hope, Patrick. Mother mentioned something about that. Maybe they're bringing Nandi back."

Patrick exhaled sharply and walked as fast as he could with a wriggly three-year-old in his arms.

"No," he said. "I won't tolerate it. I understand that Mother instigated Juliet's disappearance. And that's disgraceful enough. But now to 'buy' Nandi back from her? That's, that would be—"

Patrick drew up short. In front of them lay the pond fed by their waterfall. And at the water's edge kneeled a woman with curly hair cascading down her back.

May made a squealing sound. "Nandi!" she called, and stretched her little arms toward her. "Daddy, I need Nandi."

The little girl insisted on being let down and then ran as fast as she could to the young woman, who had just stood up. She beamed at Patrick and bent down to embrace his daughter. Nandi was not wearing shoes, and her dress was dirty. Patrick stared at her, speechless.

"Mr. Drury, I, I was allowed to run away, wasn't I?"

Patrick raised his arms helplessly. "You can go wherever you want, Nandi," he whispered, and stepped closer to her. "You know that. But I, well, I was so sad when I saw that you'd gone." He reached both hands out to her, and the girl took them, trembling.

"I didn't run away from you," she said. "I've run back to you."

Tears filled Patrick's eyes. "But where did you run from? And why are you so—? But that's not important. Come, you must be hungry. Did you come on foot? From where?"

"From Dunedin. Mrs. Drury wanted me to go with her. To Christchurch and then to America. But I don't want to go there. And I've been thinking a long time about what Mrs. Doortje Drury always read me from the Bible, that I should be a good servant. But also, what you said, that I'm free. And what Mrs. Violet Coltrane says about women and the unions. And then, then I—how do you say?—flew Mrs. Drury?"

"Fled," Patrick said happily.

"I fled, yes. I was supposed to buy her something to eat before the train left, but I ran away. With the money. But I still have it here, Mr. Drury. I didn't want to steal."

Nandi smiled shyly at Patrick.

Atamarie, however, was concerned by something else. "You came the whole way on foot? From Dunedin? Is that possible?"

Nandi nodded. "My people are good walkers," she declared proudly. "But I am so tired now. Is it all right if I sleep awhile?"

"Let's go home, Nandi," May said again, and then, surprising everyone, "I love you, Mommy."

"Looks like this one's already made her choice," Atamarie laughed.

"Smart girl," said Matariki. "We should leave you three in peace."

"Yes," said Atamarie. "And you and I should go to the village. It's getting dark, and Rawiri's waiting for me."

"Look." Matariki pointed at the sky. The first stars were showing in the firmament, and the brightest among them were the eyes of the god Tawhirimatea—the bright star Whanui with its six radiant daughter stars in tow.

"Ka puta Matariki ka rere Whanui
Ko te tena o te tau e!"

Matariki greeted the constellation for which she was named with the old song. Atamarie joined in, and they both hugged Patrick, Nandi, and little May, who cheerfully sang along.

***

"Happy New Year!"

Up in the village, people were also laughing, dancing, and embracing one another. Rawiri and his students were sending the first kites into the air. The children began singing the *karakia* to steer them and to greet the stars. The old people cried and mourned as they did every year.

"Why are they crying?" Doortje asked her husband as Atamarie had once asked her mother. "I thought Matariki was a happy festival."

Kevin nodded. "Matariki marks the changing of the years. An ending and a beginning. Matariki rises up, and the eyes of the god rest on us after he has been gone a long time. The tribal elders are now telling him what's happened during that time. One last time, they mourn the dead of the previous year and lament the bad things that have happened to the tribe. But with that, the sorrow is then sealed. The dead go to the ancestors and become part of the past. After tonight, they won't be thought of with tears or anger. They become part of memory and so also determine the future."

"A beautiful custom," Doortje said hesitantly. "Do you think—do you think this Maori god would listen to me too?"

Kevin kissed her. "Of course. Just go to the elders. Sing with them, tell them about your family, about all you lost, about your country, and they'll understand you. The people and the stars."

"And if I cry?" Doortje asked, choked up.

"Then you cry, Doortje. Like the others. It's good to cry today. The future begins tomorrow."

Kevin put his arm around her and led her to the group of elders. Hainga drew Doortje into the circle of sorrow and old songs.

***

Doortje Drury cried that night for the first time since she was a little girl. With a flood of tears, she conjured once more her dead, named her parents and siblings, and mourned her lost home and country.

But Kevin held her in his arms as she did, and during the night, the wind dried her tears. In the morning, the songs of children woke her. Atamarie and Rawiri sent their kites and dreams up to the gods. And the colorful *manu* carried the sorrow away.

Afterword

The South Island of New Zealand was home to a pioneer who took off in his motorized flier *before* the Wright brothers?

I, too, stopped short when I learned where the Richard Pearse Airport in Timaru got its name. It really is true: Richard Pearse was without a doubt one of the world's first pilots of a motorized flier, and many signs point to him floating over Waitohi months before the Wright brothers' flight, only to crash into a broom hedge. It was not much different for Wilbur and Orville. Their first flights ended similarly, but less thornily, in sand dunes. However, the date of the first flight is under dispute because Pearse never invited members of the press or experts, and he did not otherwise document his test flights. Yet there was no shortage of accidental witnesses such as neighbors and family members.

There are still television and radio interviews with these witnesses on the internet. That apparently none of them can remember whether Pearse first took off in the first months of 1903 or not until 1904 is often explained as the "simple mentality of country people," who didn't pay close attention to things like dates. That does not seem credible to me—a farmer seeing an aeroplane floating above his fields for the first time is going to remember whether those fields were harvested. And even if they don't recall an exact date, there are personal time references that enable later investigation. Why no one dug deeper remains unexplored, and so Richard Pearse remains in the second or third row of flight pioneers. What's more, he really is supposed to have corresponded with the Wright brothers—whether before or after his and/or their flight and to what extent could not be determined. The details given on that point in my book are fictive. His activity as an assistant at Canterbury College and his participation in the Taranaki expedition are also invented, along with the love story with Atamarie and Shirley, of course. In reality, Pearse remained unmarried his whole life and had no known relationships with women.

However, most of the information in this novel about Pearse's life, his history, and his family background corresponds to the truth. For a few details, such as the horsepower of the motor he used, I found differing information in various sources. Instead of trying to verify them, I simply adopted what seemed most suitable to me. I'm not an expert on flight, and, despite my efforts to learn the basics, aerospace engineers may find mistakes, for which I apologize.

I only intentionally falsified Pearse's story once: the real inventor did not move from his old farm near Christchurch to a new one in Otago until 1911. His reasons for the move may have been similar to those depicted in the book, but there are extensive blank spots in the documented course of his life, as well as further strange inconsistencies, such as his claim that he had not really flown. All of this was the reason for my massive speculation regarding Richard Pearse's mental and emotional state: the man whom Atamarie gets to know in this novel suffers from a manic-depressive disorder, an illness still unknown at the beginning of the twentieth century and a condition instead described as melancholy. For me, such a disorder would explain much about the course of the real Pearse's life, perhaps even motivating his family and neighbors to protect the unstable man from publicity. Nevertheless, this assumption naturally remains fictive. The only truly solid indication of mental illness is found at the end of Pearse's life. He was admitted with severe paranoia to a psychiatric clinic in Christchurch in 1951 and died there two years later.

***

In contrast to Richard Pearse, Professor Dobbins, the dean of the Canterbury College of Engineering, is a largely fictional personage. He was inspired by the real-life Professor Dobson, who counted among the founders of Canterbury's engineering department. However, I could not find out whether, alongside his other work in Christchurch—the city owes to him, among other things, its municipal water lines—he still taught at the university during those years. The college's course requirements are authentic, and although it is rather unlikely that a girl would have graduated from the program so early, it would theoretically have been possible. The colleges in New Zealand were ahead of the rest of the world in opening themselves, often at their very founding, to female students.

***

The Egmont National Park around Mount Taranaki was, in fact, established in 1900, but I thought up the expedition to survey it.

All the information about the Maori art of making kites comes from authentic sources. The artistically decorated *manu* still belong to their living culture to this day. The reports of early flights by people on kites, however, are entirely legendary, which is why I refrained from having Atamarie and Rawiri take to the air.

***

New Zealand's involvement in the Boer War and the story of the Rough Riders as presented are largely historically correct, as are the conditions of the concentration camps. Moreover, this term was first used in connection with the camps in South Africa. Though the Karenstad camp is fictional, it is heavily based on the Kroonstad camp.

In the book, the town of Wepener is located "on the border of Basutoland." It still lies there today, but Basutoland is now called Lesotho. Basuto ponies have kept their name, however. They remain robust riding- and workhorses with a height at the withers of 14.2 hands or 56.8 inches, and they often run wild in the Maloti and Drakensberg Mountains.

***

As for the history of harness racing in New Zealand, the races mentioned actually did take place, and the New Zealand Trotting Cup was run for the first time in November 1904.

Acknowledgments

As always, many people worked together to make this book happen, from my wonderful agent, Bastian Schlück, to my no less extraordinary editor, Melanie Blank-Schröder, and exceptional copyeditor, Margit von Cossart. Without Margit, I would have gotten hopelessly tangled up and lost once again in my books' thicket of time. Dates and compass points are not my thing. Thanks to my English language translator, Dustin Lovett, and AmazonCrossing editor, Elizabeth DeNoma, as well as developmental editor Anna Rosenwong.

Many thanks to my test readers as well and this time to my parents and friends in Mojácar who for weeks had to live with a certain absentmindedness on my part. A special thanks to my landladies, Joan and Anna Puzcas, who can now even read my books since they now appear in Spanish as well. Without you all, nothing would work, neither reading tours nor sinking for months into foreign cultures.

And, of course, many, many thanks to all the people who help bring this book to readers, from the marketing department and sales and distribution at Bastei Lübbe to the booksellers. Certainly, readers themselves have the greatest share in the success of Sarah Lark. Recently I enjoyed getting to know many of them personally.

Sarah Lark

About the Author

Photo © 2011 Gonzalo Perez

Born in Germany and now a resident of Spain, Sarah Lark is a horse aficionado and former travel guide who has experienced many of the world's most beautiful landscapes on horseback. Through her adventures, she has developed an intimate relationship with the places she's visited and the characters who live there. In her writing, Lark introduces readers to a New Zealand full of magic, beauty, and charm. Her ability to weave romance with history and to explore all the dark and triumphal corners of the human condition has made her a bestselling author worldwide.

About the Translator

Photo © 2011 Sanna Stegmaier

D. W. Lovett is a graduate of the University of Illinois at Urbana–Champaign, from which he received a degree in comparative literature and German as well as a certificate from the university's Center for Translation Studies. He has spent the last few years living in Europe. He has brought numerous titles by Sarah Lark into English, including the In the Land of the Long White Cloud saga, as well as *Toward the Sea of Freedom* and *Beneath the Kauri Tree.*